MEETING IN CRISIS AND DESIRE, TWO CULTURES CLASH, HEARTS DIVIDE . . . AND A NATION IS BORN.

ADAM VINCENT—An officer and a gentleman stripped of his rank by a woman's selfish treachery, he chose a new identity as a common soldier . . . and a destiny of passion and glory.

LADY KITTY BROOME—Her marriage to journalist Johnny Broome could be destroyed by her pampered past. Her steamy affair with a rich rancher could cost Johnny his life.

CAPTAIN MARCUS FISHER—A coward and a blackguard, he'd show his true colors in a moment of heart-stopping danger . . . but live to seek revenge on his rival, Adam Vincent.

KERI—A beautiful Maori, she offered a dark, sensual love to a valiant British officer . . . but a night of rapture could lead to a morrow of tears.

TE UA—A savage priest, he struck terror into the hearts of settlers and soldiers alike as his followers killed in blood lust and vengeance.

Other books in THE AUSTRALIANS series
by William Stuart Long

THE EMPIRE BUILDERS

VOLUME IX OF THE AUSTRALIANS

William Stuart Long

A DELL BOOK

 Created by the producers of
**The Kent Family Chronicles,
Wagons West,** and **Stagecoach.**

Book Creations Inc., Canaan, NY · Lyle Kenyon Engel, Founder

Published by
Dell Publishing Co., Inc.
1 Dag Hammarskjold Plaza
New York, New York   10017

Dell ® TM 681510, Dell Publishing Co., Inc.

ISBN: 0-440-12304-6

Printed in the United States of America

July 1987

10 9 8 7 6 5 4 3 2 1

WFH

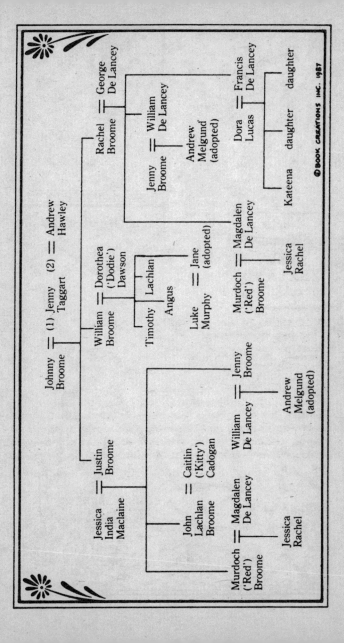

© BOOK CREATIONS INC. 1987

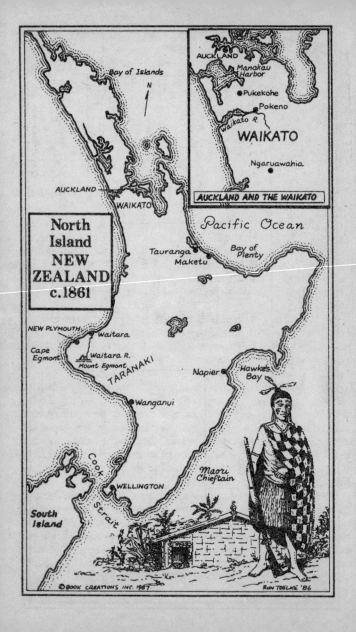

Bay of Islands

N

AUCKLAND
Manukau
Harbor

• Pukekohe

Pokeno

Waikato R.

WAIKATO

• Ngaruawahia

AUCKLAND AND THE WAIKATO

AUCKLAND

WAIKATO

Pacific Ocean

Tauranga
Maketu

Bay of
Plenty

**North
Island
NEW
ZEALAND
c.1861**

NEW PLYMOUTH
• Waitara
Cape
Egmont
Waitara R.
Mount Egmont
TARANAKI

Napier

Hawkes
Bay

• Wanganui

*Maori
Chieftain*

Cook

• WELLINGTON

Strait

South
Island

©BOOK CREATIONS INC. 1987

RON TOELKE '86

Prologue

HER MAJESTY'S STEAM-SCREW frigate *Kestrel* arrived in Port Jackson to relieve H.M.S. *Galah* on New Year's Day, 1859. The *Galah*'s commander, Red Broome—newly promoted to post rank for his services in India during the Sepoy Mutiny—swore aloud as he watched the new arrival come to anchor in Watson's Bay, for she was two weeks ahead of her anticipated appearance on the station.

His own ship had completed her refit only ten days previously, and with the damage she had sustained on her passage from Calcutta now repaired, he was unhappily aware that he would have to sail for England to pay off as soon as he had handed over his responsibilities on the station to the *Kestrel*'s commander.

Nevertheless, it would be inhospitable in the extreme were he not to make his successor welcome. A dinner party at his house would best fill the bill, Red decided, after the formalities were completed. His wife, Magdalen, was a skilled hostess; she would be as distressed as he was by the *Kestrel*'s unexpected early arrival, but in spite of that, he knew he could depend on her to make the meal a memorable one, since it would be his farewell, as much as his relief's welcome to the colony.

He had cause, however, to regret his impulsive decision during the ensuing days as he prepared for departure. The *Kestrel*'s captain, Commander Rupert Harland, proved to be a small, bombastic man, considerably older than Red himself and several years senior in service, his lack of promotion the result of the findings of a court of inquiry, which had held him to blame for the death of a midshipman serving under his command in the West Indies.

The boy had been the youngest son of the Second Sea Lord, and because of that, Harland confided sourly within half an hour of meeting Red for the first time, Their Lordships had kept him on half pay for the past five years. His appointment to the *Kestrel* had come only after the death of the vengeful old admiral, and the last station he had wanted was the one he had been ordered to take up.

"A damned convict colony!" he asserted belligerently. "And for two years, God forgive them, for I cannot!" He eyed Red's tanned, good-looking face with sour displeasure, mentally calculating the years between them and clearly finding the difference in their ranks a cause of resentment that he took no pains to hide. "Damme, I had my lieutenant's commission when you were still a newly joined mid! Served under the late Admiral Stirling, didn't you?"

"I did, yes—the *Success* was my first ship. But—"

"And you were born out here, I was told?" Harland made it sound like an accusation, and Red stiffened.

"Yes, that is so. I—"

"Then no doubt you'll find it a wrench to leave. Devil take it, I'd give my eyeteeth to exchange with you, Captain Broome! I've a wife and family in Dorset, and after skimping and saving on half pay for five long years, I cannot afford to bring them out here."

And he, Red thought as he listened with restraint to the tirade, would gladly have given more than his eyeteeth to make the exchange, had that been possible.

His instinctive dislike of his successor came to a head within two days of making his acquaintance. Claus Van Buren—now one of Sydney's most valued merchant traders—brought his beautiful American-built clipper *Dolphin* into port when Red was with Harland in the commodore's official residence, overlooking the harbor. Harland had watched the schooner with admiring eyes—despite the fact that his command was powered by auxiliary steam, at heart he was a sailing-ship man, which was a point in his favor—and, on his expressing interest in the superbly designed vessel, Red offered to arrange a visit of inspection for him.

Having known Claus since boyhood, it did not occur to Red to mention the shipowner's mixed ancestry; Sydney society had long since accepted him for what he was, and in any event Claus's dark skin was evidence enough of his native Javanese blood, his aristocratic Dutch name proof of his breeding.

The visit to the *Dolphin* went well initially, for Rupert Harland's interest was genuine, his knowledge of clipper design remarkably comprehensive, and his manner toward Claus, if a trifle condescending, polite. Claus's pretty American wife, Mercy, and their two young sons were on board, and when the lengthy inspection was at last completed, Mercy came on deck to issue an invitation to the visitors to take refreshments in the great cabin.

Entering and observing the beautiful paneling and luxurious fittings of the cabin, the hand-carved dining table and chairs, the silver, cut glass, and exquisite bone china on the sideboard, Commander Harland was visibly impressed. His manner changed, the hint of condescension vanished. He bowed respectfully over Mercy's hand and confessed his readiness to take a cup of Peking tea, and as she poured it he continued the discussion he had been engaged in with Claus concerning the *Dolphin*'s rig and cargo-carrying capacity.

"I'm surprised you did not have her ship-rigged. If you want speed—and I presume you do, if you engage in the wool trade—I should have thought you—" He broke off, startled, his jaw dropping in shocked astonishment. "Who in the world—"

The curtain covering the cabin doorway had parted, and the young Maori chief Te Tamihana came in, with the easy familiarity of long custom, to accept a teacup from Mercy Van Buren and take his seat at the table.

Red, aware of the chieftain's friendship with Claus, and having been previously introduced, greeted the young Maori by name, but Harland continued to stare at him as if he were an apparition from another world. With his heavily tattooed face and lithe, copper-colored body, which was naked save for the woven flax kilt draped about his waist, Te Tamihana's appearance as he solemnly sipped tea was, perhaps, understandably startling to a newcomer from England. Even so, Red was unprepared for his brother officer's reaction.

Harland leaped to his feet, his teacup falling from his hand, as he exclaimed furiously, "In God's name, Broome, you may have gone native, but I have not! I was prepared to stretch a point where Captain Van Buren was concerned, but I cannot be expected to sit at table with a damned aboriginal savage. That is asking too much, sir, damme it is!"

Te Tamihana eyed him in mild surprise and then, carefully setting down his own cup, observed in faultless English, "If you will forgive me, Claus, I will go on deck with the boys. We were, as it happens, in the middle of a most entertaining game, in which I was hard put to hold my own. Excuse me, please, Mrs. Van Buren."

No one spoke until the curtain had swung back behind him, and then Claus, with a warning shake of the head in Red's direction, said coldly, "The young man you have just insulted, Commander Harland, is not an Australian aboriginal. He is, in fact, a Maori—one of the most influential chiefs in New Zealand's Bay of Islands, and an honored friend of mine—like yourself, a guest on board my vessel. He—" Harland attempted to interrupt him, but Claus would have none of it. "Hear me out, Commander. I spend a great deal of my time in New Zealand, where I have extensive trading interests—more important by far than my interest in the wool trade these days. These interests are based and, indeed, are largely dependent on the friendly relations I have built up over the years with the Maori tribes. In all my dealings with them I regard them as equals, and I respect their culture, their standards, and their honesty. Sentiments which they reciprocate, sir."

Rupert Harland recovered himself. Very red of face, he retorted with a sneer, "That, for one of your color, is understandable, Captain Van Buren. Like calls to like, does it not? Unlike ourselves, the Dutch, I believe, tend to intermarry with their subject native peoples, and clearly you—"

Angrily, Red attempted to restrain him, but once again Claus shook his head. "Permit me to explain the current state of affairs in New Zealand to this gentleman, Red, if you please. If he is to replace you on the Australasian station, it is important that he *should* understand."

"Then carry on," Red invited, tight-lipped.

"Certainly." Claus turned to face Harland, his dark eyes cold but devoid of anger. He waited until Mercy, meeting his gaze, excused herself and slipped away, and then he observed quietly, "I must tell you, sir, that there could well be war in New Zealand in the imminent future, more serious than the conflict of twelve years ago. Settlement has increased tenfold, and everywhere on the North Island it is expanding with alarming rapidity—and I do mean alarming, because the settlers are bringing trouble on themselves. Too many of them are greedy and dishonest, and they pay scant heed to the Maoris' just rights and grievances. They cheat and dispossess them of their land, lull them with false promises, and fail even to make fair reparation for the vast acreages they have seized."

"New Zealand is a British colony," Harland blustered. "The

settlers have a right to land, under the treaty signed by the Maori chiefs."

"True," Claus conceded, with another warning glance at Red. "But the Maoris were there many years before the first white man set foot on New Zealand soil. And, sir, the Maori people cannot be dealt with as the aborigines of Tasmania were—they cannot be banished to some barren island to die of disease and neglect. There are too many of them. They are a proud, strong, and warlike people—they will fight for what is theirs. And, sir, the settlers are in no state to join battle with them—they are mostly farmers and merchant traders, like myself. Or missionaries. If the Maori tribes are provoked into war, and if the tribes unite under an elected king, as they seem likely to do, it will take a great many of your Royal Navy's ships and Her Majesty's fighting regiments to prevent a bloodbath. I ask you to remember that, Commander Harland."

Claus again looked across at Red and added regretfully, "I'm distressed to learn that you have been ordered to England, Red. I had hoped, I am bound to tell you, that you and Her Majesty's ship *Galah* would have been permitted to remain on this station, in order to pour oil on troubled waters."

His tone throughout had been conciliatory, but Rupert Harland was in no mood to respond to conciliation. He picked up his cap, jammed it wrathfully onto his head, and prepared to depart, glaring at Red when he remained seated and made no move to follow him.

"In my view," the *Kestrel*'s commander said spitefully, "the only way to deal with recalcitrant native populations is by force. It is all most of them understand. And if it's left to me, Van Buren, and your Maori friends engage in plotting and rebellion, my ship's guns will not be silent. There may be a bloodbath, as you predict—but it will be Maori blood that is spilled, not British. I give you good day, sir."

He stormed out of the cabin, and Red said apologetically, "The devil take the fellow! I'm sorry I brought him aboard, Claus—deeply sorry."

"Let him go," Claus responded. "Stay with us for dinner, Red. You could not possibly have known how he was going to react. Besides," he added, smiling, "if you stay, you can at least pour some oil on Te Tamihana's troubled waters . . . and believe me, my friend, it is necessary. That young man is inclined to support the King Movement, and who can blame him?"

Red frowned. "You think that this King Movement is a serious threat to peace, then?"

"Well . . ." Claus hesitated. "It would have been, if the great Hongi Hika had still been alive. No doubt your father has told you about him—I believe he met Hongi once."

"Yes—yes, he did, when he was first lieutenant of the *Kangaroo.*" Red's frown lifted. "I understand it was quite an encounter, the way my father tells it. He admired Hongi."

"So did the Maoris. Hongi led by right of conquest—no tribe dared to oppose him. He armed his warriors with muskets when the rest had only spears and tomahawks, and on his return from a visit to the English court, he appeared in a suit of armor the King had presented to him. His prestige was immense."

"Is there no chief of Hongi's stature now?" Red questioned.

Claus shook his head. "No, there is not. The two great tribes—the Ngapuhi in the land north of Auckland and the Waikato to the south—have a long history of feuds, with scores of ancient wrongs still to be avenged. Neither was willing to bow to a king chosen by the other." Claus spoke thoughtfully. "The Ngapuhi did agree to meet a deputation from the Waikato some time ago, but then announced that they would remain loyal to the Queen of England—mainly, I think, out of respect for the late governor, Sir George Grey. The Maoris always trusted him, believing he was more on their side than that of the settlers. They're not so sure of his successor, Sir Thomas Gore-Browne." Claus's broad shoulders rose in a shrug. "In any case, the result is growing ill feeling, which could lead to bloodshed. And the southern tribes *did* elect their own king."

"Did they, now? Is that good news or bad?"

"In truth I do not know, Red," Claus confessed. "The man they chose—Potatau, he's called—is a famous old warrior, held in almost universal esteem. But he *is* an old man, and his fighting days are over, so I personally doubt whether it lies in his power to unite all the Maoris against us—or even whether he wants to. Unfortunately, his son Tawhiao, who is likely to succeed him, is a young hothead, who could make trouble, given the chance."

Claus was silent for a moment or two, lost in his own thoughts, and then he said, brightening, "I suppose you've heard that your brother-in-law, the gallant Colonel De Lancey, has decided to settle in New Zealand, instead of remaining here?"

"Yes," Red confirmed. "He told me."

Will De Lancey had gone initially to the Illawarra district south of Sydney, seeking suitable land and determined, after his harrowing experiences in India during the Sepoy Mutiny, to turn his sword into a plowshare, as he wryly put it. But his friend Henry Osborne, owner of the Mount Marshall property, had died during his absence, and the price of good land in the fertile Illawarra had risen to almost prohibitive heights.

"I've come too late to acquire land as the squatters did," William had said regretfully. "Henry, I'm sure, would have sold me some of his at a reasonable price, but, alas, he is no longer with us, and on a soldier's pay I could not possibly afford what is presently being asked. And besides, Mount Marshall holds too many memories of my darling Jenny—we spent part of our honeymoon there, you know, and when I went back I found I could not drive them from my mind. New Zealand offers better opportunities, and . . . well, we should be making a completely fresh start, the boy and I."

Claus, as if reading Red's thoughts, offered, smiling, "I ran into the colonel in town, after we made port, Red, and he's booked passage to Auckland with me for himself and the youngster he had with him—what is his name?"

"Andrew Melgund," Red supplied. "He was orphaned in the mutiny—both his parents were massacred at Cawnpore. And Jenny, my poor little sister Jenny, who also died there, saved the boy's life."

"He struck me as a fine boy," Claus observed.

"He is indeed," Red agreed. "In fact, I think he's been the means of saving Will's sanity." He added soberly, "I hope, for Will's sake, that peace will prevail in New Zealand, Claus. After the Crimea and the Sepoy Mutiny, Will has had his fill of war. When do you sail?"

"In about ten days' time. We're living on board and not opening the house for so short a stay—Mercy and my boys are coming with me, as always." There was warmth in his voice. "I'm a fortunate man, Red. I live the life at sea that I love, and my wife and family share it with me. In that respect, I'm a good deal better off than you are. For all your exalted rank in Her Majesty's Navy, you will not be permitted to take Magdalen and your little daughter with you, will you, when you sail for England?"

"Sadly, no," Red answered. "Their Lordships of the Admiralty have withdrawn that privilege from us. I shall have to book them passage in a commercial vessel."

"I have a wool clipper—the *Dragonfly*—sailing next month," Claus offered. "She's a ship of seven hundred tons burden, and I could give them passage. But of course Magdalen may prefer to make the voyage by steamer, although I can promise that my *Dragonfly* will make a fast passage. And," he added, his smile widening, "I could quote you privileged rates."

"I'll speak to Magdalen about it—I'm sure she will jump at the offer." Red returned his friend's smile, the earlier unpleasantness with Commander Harland almost forgotten. "My grateful thanks, Claus. You are a good friend."

When the dinner party to welcome the *Kestrel*'s new commander and to bid farewell to his predecessor on the Sydney station took place two days later, at Justin Broome's Elizabeth Bay house, the atmosphere—Red noted with dismay when he arrived—was unusually tense. Not surprisingly, it was Rupert Harland who proved to be the cause of the trouble.

The *Kestrel*'s commander, while admitting he was the only stranger in what was largely a family gathering, had made not the smallest effort to respond to the friendly overtures he was offered. His manner was aloof almost to the point of rudeness, as if he were intent on emphasizing his superiority to the members of a colonial society who, he clearly supposed, had sprung from a discreditable convict ancestry and, as such, could not expect to merit the courtesy he would normally have displayed.

Magdalen, who had taken over the kitchen of the Elizabeth Bay house from an early hour and given much thought to the dishes that were served, was at first worried and then affronted by the newly arrived commander's failure to do justice to the excellent fare. As course followed course and Rupert Harland picked disdainfully at the contents of his plate, Red observed his wife's increasing embarrassment, and his anger rose. Devil take the fellow, he thought wrathfully, hard put to it to contain himself and regretting the impulsive invitation he had issued on first acquaintance with his successor. This was a gross and ill-mannered abuse of hospitality, it— He caught his father's eye and saw, to his astonishment, that Justin Broome was amused rather than offended by Harland's behavior.

As the ladies rose to take coffee in the withdrawing room, his father, having held the door for them, paused by Red's side. "Don't worry, Red," he said in a low voice. "I've met his kind

before. Indeed, I once served under one of his kidney—Captain
John Jeffrey, of His late Majesty's ship *Kangaroo*. The officer who,
you may recall, fell foul of the famous Hongi Hika in New Zealand
some years ago. I must have told you the story." He smiled. "Mr.
Harland will learn because we shall teach him, rest assured of
that." Moving back to his own seat at the head of the table, Justin
Broome raised his voice. "Magdalen gave us a memorable dinner,
Red. Now, my dear boy, be seated and we'll take a glass of port
and drink to your safe return to English shores!"

The toast was duly proposed and drunk, and as cigars and pipes
were lit and the port decanter circulated, a brief silence fell, and
Red heard his father say, "Ah, Commander Harland, I've been
thinking . . . I fancy that I made the acquaintance of a relative of
yours. It was quite a long time ago—indeed, it must be well over
twenty years, soon after the first settlers moved from Holdfast Bay
to what is now the city of Adelaide, in South Australia. You have
not been out here before yourself, have you?"

Rupert Harland's fleshy face was, to Red's surprise, suffused
with angry color. For a moment, it seemed as if he were about to
choke with indignation, but he recovered himself and said in a
hoarse voice, "No—no, sir, I have not. I—er—I'm not sure to
whom you are referring."

"Are you not?" His father, Red observed, appeared in no way
put out. In a conversational tone, he gave a brief description of the
difficulties that had faced Adelaide's early settlers, who had been ill
prepared for the conditions they were called upon to endure—the
lack of labor, of adequate shelter and food, in addition to the prolonged disagreement between the governor, Captain Hindmarsh,
and the surveyor general, Colonel Light, as to the final site for the
town.

"Those unfortunate people were close to starvation," Justin
Broome went on, sagely nodding his white head and avoiding Harland's suddenly pleading gaze. "They had money, most of them,
but money could not buy them what they so desperately needed.
Until—" His tone changed, and now, Red saw, he was looking at
the *Kestrel's* discomfited commander with alert and searching blue
eyes. "Until the arrival of one of H.M.'s sloops of war—the *Ringdove,* if my memory serves me aright. Her purser supplied them
with most of the stores from his ship, at considerable personal
profit it was said . . . and scarcely with Their Lordships' approval." Again he paused, and Harland's face drained of its hith-

erto hectic color. "I remember the matter . . ." His father had the attention of the whole table now, Red realized, and no one spoke as he went on, "because I was a member of the board of inquiry that subsequently sat, here in Sydney, to look into it. The purser's name, Commander Harland, was the same as your own, to the best of my recollection."

"Mine is not an uncommon name, sir." Harland was on his feet, prepared to bluster. "I know nothing of the—the affair, I—and now, if you will be so good as to excuse me, sir, I will take my leave. I—er—that is, I thank you for your hospitality, Captain Broome."

"Be so good as to see the commander out, John," Justin requested. There was a gleam of satisfaction in his eyes, Red saw, as his younger brother rose to comply with their father's courteously voiced command.

Justin Broome waited until Johnny returned and then, smiling broadly, answered Judge De Lancey's explosive "Good God, what was all that about, Justin?"

"A little ploy devised by the commodore and myself, George, because he too has had about all he could stomach of Harland's arrogance." Justin resumed his seat. "To be truthful, I'd forgotten all about the *Ringdove* affair, but the commodore chanced to recall that he was also a member of the board of inquiry—he was first lieutenant of the old *Buffalo* at the time. And the purser *was* our Harland's father. We checked the records, so he can deny it all he likes—the proof is there. Needless to add, Harland senior did not continue in the service, and Their Lordships did not award him with a pension."

Judge De Lancey laughed, with genuine amusement.

"I see. But what prompted you to—ah—to air the matter here this evening?"

Justin paused to light a fresh cigar. "Oh, I had no intention of doing so initially," he confessed. "We had intended to bring it up privately, in the commodore's office, to serve as a warning to the fellow to mind his manners. But this is Red's farewell, and when Harland deliberately set out to cast a damper on a party we'd all taken a good deal of trouble over, I . . . well, decided that it was an appropriate moment. I trust you will all agree that it was?"

There was a murmur of assent, and Red said gravely, "Thank you, Father. The commodore has not been alone in finding Harland's attitude a mite hard to stomach."

His father gestured to the port decanter. "Fill your glasses, my friends," he invited, "and I will give you another toast before we join the ladies." They did so, and Justin Broome raised his glass. "To my son-in-law Will De Lancey and to my son John and his wife, who will shortly be leaving us for New Zealand—John is to undertake a report for his newspaper on the land claim problem there. God speed them on their way and, of His mercy, bring them all safely home to us one day!"

They drank the toast, Red taken momentarily by surprise at the news of his brother's impending departure, and as they left the table together, Johnny told him apologetically, "It's only just been decided, Red—this afternoon, in fact. We're going with Will and the boy in the *Dolphin.*" He reddened and added, in a low voice, referring to his wife, "Kit's not happy here, so I thought—no, dammit, I hope that a change of scene may prove beneficial to her and to our marriage. Unlike you, I don't seem to be great shakes as a husband, alas!"

Red eyed him with affectionate concern, but Johnny clapped him on the shoulder and managed a wry smile.

"Don't worry your head about it, Brother. It will work out in time, I don't doubt. But it's going to be quite a considerable breakup of the family, isn't it? I'm not so happy about that."

And neither, Red thought glumly, was he. But that was life; nothing lasted forever, and separations were inevitable. He strode purposefully to his wife's side, seated himself on the arm of her chair, and put his arm lightly about her slim waist.

"Commander Harland left rather abruptly, Red," she stated uneasily.

"Yes, my love," Red agreed. "Thanks to Father, he is liable to be less obnoxious in future." His arm tightened about her. "Magdalen, I love you! And it's breaking my heart to have to leave you— you know that, don't you?"

"Yes," she answered softly. "I know that, Red. But I'll follow you. I—I want to be with you always, to the end of my days, my dearest."

They both looked across, as if by common consent, to where Johnny stood, grim-faced and alone. Kitty Broome, seemingly unaware of her husband's presence, was talking animatedly to Judge De Lancey, and Magdalen whispered softly, "We are fortunate, Red. Never forget that, will you?"

Red bent to kiss her gently. "No," he said. "I'll not forget."

Chapter I

AFTER A LARGELY uneventful passage, accomplished in sixty-nine days, the *Galah* came to anchor at Spithead. Within twenty-four hours of paying off and taking regretful leave of his ship's company, Red Broome received a summons to serve as a member of a court-martial, convened on board the battleship *Copenhagen,* flagship of the vice admiral of the Channel Fleet.

The summons came as a surprise, but at least it was a means of putting off the evil hour when he would be relegated to half pay, plus an indefinite—and, until Magdalen could join him, lonely—wait for fresh employment. Red accepted the summons philosophically, supposing that, as the court was to examine and pass judgment on the loss of a small sloop of war off the Irish coast, the charges would be purely formal and the matter swiftly dealt with. The loss of any Royal Navy ship, whether in war or peace, required that her commander stand trial; but usually—unless cowardice or negligence was proved—the verdict resulted in acquittal, or at worst a reprimand or loss of seniority.

This case, however, as he learned when he reported on board the *Copenhagen,* had more serious implications. The sloop *Lancer,* of sixteen guns and under sail, had been driven ashore in a gale, with a fire raging on board, and she had gone down with the loss of her captain and all but five of her complement. The officer on trial was her first lieutenant, and Red heard, with some consternation, that his name was Adam Colpoys Vincent.

The honorable Adam Vincent, a younger son of the Earl of Cheviot—Major General the Earl of Cheviot, who had been one of the Duke of Wellington's staff at Waterloo. Red frowned as memory stirred. Young Vincent had been an acting lieutenant with the

Shannon's naval brigade, which had served so gallantly in Sir Colin Campbell's relief of Lucknow during the mutiny, less than two years ago. He himself had been attached to the brigade, and he remembered Adam Vincent well as a cheerful, courageous young officer, who had been awarded the Victoria Cross as a midshipman, while serving under Captain William Peel—the *Shannon*'s commander—in the Crimea.

He and Edward Daniel had both won V.C.'s, and . . . Red's frown deepened. He recalled the moving ceremony at which, in front of a full-dress parade of the *Shannon*'s brigade, on their way back to Calcutta, Captain Marten—Peel's successor in command —had belatedly presented the two young men with their decorations . . . the small bronze crosses, which represented the highest award for gallantry a grateful nation could bestow on its military heroes.

But now one of the same youthful heroes was to stand trial on no less than three serious charges. With the other eleven members of the court, Red was sworn in and, taking his seat to the president's right, listened to the charges being read by the judge advocate, his incredulity growing as their significance slowly sank in.

Shorn of the legal jargon in which they were couched, the charges amounted to a damning indictment of the young officer's conduct. Adam Vincent was accused of being in a state of intoxication when—the *Lancer*'s captain being ill and, in consequence, confined to his cabin—command of the brig-sloop had devolved on him during a severe storm off the southwest coast of Ireland, in the vicinity of Bantry Bay and the Dursey Head light.

Although the sloop was apparently being driven onto a lee shore by gale-force winds, evidence to the effect that Vincent had failed to shorten sail in time to prevent this would, the judge advocate stated, be brought before the court. More damning still, it seemed that Lieutenant Vincent, when informed that fire had broken out in the after part of the ship, not only had failed to act with promptitude in dealing with this additional hazard, but had prematurely ordered the ship to be abandoned. As a result of his premature order, the boats in which the ship's company had attempted to reach the shore had been swamped and capsized, with the loss of one hundred eleven lives, including that of the *Lancer*'s ailing captain, Commander John Omerod.

The final charge, although less serious, astounded Red, for it conflicted completely with the impression he had formed of Adam

Vincent's character during their association in India, when serving
in the naval brigade. Vincent, he recalled, had been a reliable and
competent officer, with a healthy respect for naval discipline. The
late Captain Peel, who had known him longer than anyone else,
had held the young acting-lieutenant in high esteem. In one of the
last dispatches he had sent to the Admiralty before his tragic
death, the *Shannon*'s captain had recommended him, with several
others, for well-merited advancement.

"Indeed," William Peel had said, "if it were not for the fact that
he has already been awarded a Victoria Cross, young Vincent
would have been among those whose names I have put forward for
the decoration. He does not know what fear is, and he earned the
honor twice over at the Shah Nujeef."

High praise, and yet . . . Red listened in frank bewilderment
as, in a flat, unemotional voice, the judge advocate read from the
paper in his hand.

"You are further charged that, from five o'clock in the evening
until midnight on the tenth day of March of this year, when held
under arrest pending your trial by this court, you did absent yourself from the quarters assigned to you on board this ship, and from
the custody of the officer appointed to act as your escort, namely
Lieutenant Fleming."

The judge advocate paused, his face set in stern lines beneath the
bell-bottomed wig that was the badge of his office. Then, looking
across the courtroom to where the accused officer was seated, he
invited him to make his plea in answer to the charges.

Adam Vincent responded by rising to his feet. Red had not had a
clear view of him until now, and he was shocked by what he saw.
Flanked by his counsel, a portly man in wig and gown, the young
lieutenant looked nervous and ill at ease, his face deathly pale and
his handsome, fair head bowed. Remembering him as an easygo-
ing, athletic young giant, whom little had ever seemed to deter,
Red was startled by the change in him. His reply to the judge
advocate's formal question was inaudible, but before he could be
asked to repeat it, the bewigged barrister at his side stated firmly,
"The plea is not guilty, sir."

Vincent held his ground. Recovering some of his lost composure,
he drew himself up. "I beg the court's indulgence, sir," he requested, in a louder voice. "I wish, if you will permit me, to conduct my own defense, sir."

The president—the *Copenhagen*'s captain—eyed him with raised brows. "You are entitled to the advice of an attorney, Mr. Vincent," he pointed out. "And as I understand that learned counsel, in the person of Sir David Murchison, has been retained to advise you, I confess I do not comprehend the reason for your request. Do you not wish to avail yourself of Sir David Murchison's services?"

Adam Vincent inclined his head. "Precisely, sir. I do not require legal advice, sir. I did not ask for it."

The president's brows rose higher. "You would be well advised to think again, Mr. Vincent," he stated patiently. "You are facing very grave charges, and you are not, I venture to suggest, fully conversant with the law in relation to those charges. In order properly to conduct your defense, and in fairness to yourself, you will need advice. You—"

"I beg your pardon, sir," Vincent put in, his voice strained, "but Sir David Murchison—that is, learned counsel, sir—we do not see eye to eye in the matter of my defense. I wish to conduct my own case, if you please, sir. To—to question the witnesses on matters with which I am conversant."

The president glanced, frowning now, at the judge advocate, who offered, not unkindly, "Do you mean that you are desirous of questioning the witnesses, Mr. Vincent? If so, then perhaps I should explain that you are permitted to do so, when you have heard the evidence to which they will testify before the court. Or you may have an officer of your own choosing put questions to them on your behalf, if you do not wish learned counsel to do this. But as the president of the court has told you, the charges against you are exceedingly grave, and it will be in your own best interests if you avail yourself of Sir David Murchison's expert advice."

"Thank you, sir," Adam Vincent acknowledged. "But with respect, sir, I beg the court to allow me to conduct my own defense as—as I see fit, sir."

The president gave vent to a faintly impatient sigh. The portly barrister, Sir David Murchison, said with asperity, "Then, gentlemen, I will withdraw from the case." He bowed stiffly to the court and crossed to the two rows of hard-backed chairs reserved for members of the general public. Barely half of these were filled, Red saw, and most of the occupants—judging by the notebooks resting on their knees—were journalists . . . representatives, probably, of local newspapers. But, seated at the end of the back row, a well-dressed, distinguished-looking gentleman of unmistakably military bearing caught and held his gaze. He was white-haired and was, perhaps, in his middle or late fifties, and when the discomfited barrister paused at his side, to engage in a brief, whispered exchange, Red identified the older man as, in all probability, Adam Vincent's father, the Earl of Cheviot.

Evidently, he thought, the Earl had engaged a leading Queen's counsel to defend his son, without first obtaining the boy's permission, and the look of annoyance on his patrician face seemed to lend credence to this supposition. Two or three of the journalists turned in their seats, as if they too had recognized him, and their pencils moved busily as Sir David Murchison, with another stiff bow, gathered his robe about him and left the courtroom, the marine sentry coming to attention as the door swung shut behind the portly barrister.

There was another gentleman of military appearance seated among the reporters in the front row, Red noticed as his gaze ranged round the small gathering. A few years younger than Lord Cheviot, he was equally well dressed, but he looked less well preserved, his face deeply lined beneath its faint coating of tan, his hair and the heavy cavalry mustache he wore thickly flecked with white . . . a man who had recently recovered from a serious illness, Red decided, wondering, at the same time, what his relationship to young Vincent might be. A friend, perhaps, or an army officer with whom he had made acquaintance in India. The dearth of reporters suggested that the case was not of much interest to the press, but it was possible that when the Earl of Cheviot's presence became known, the London dailies would scent the makings of a scandal and send their best men hurrying to Portsmouth, to pick up what they could.

The president had been conferring with the judge advocate, and the members of the court—all strangers to Red—were talking in low voices among themselves; but silence fell when the judge advocate returned to his place. The president, raising his voice, announced that the accused officer's request would be granted.

"You may conduct your own defense, Mr. Vincent," he said coldly. "Although I must again advise you that it will not be in your best interests to do so." When Vincent remained obstinately silent, the *Copenhagen*'s captain shrugged his epauletted shoulders and, turning to the prosecuting officer, invited him to open his case.

The prosecutor—a commander, wearing the neatly trimmed

beard now permitted in the Royal Navy—after a brief preamble
addressed to the court, called his first witness.

The witness was sworn and gave his name as Amos Cantwell,
third lieutenant of the ill-fated sloop of war *Lancer*.

He was clearly nervous, and as he replied to the prosecuting
officer's questions in a low, strained voice, he glanced repeatedly
toward the officer he was required to give evidence against, as if
mutely pleading for his forgiveness. Vincent responded with a sin-
gularly warm smile and a nod of the head, and, seemingly encouraged by this, Cantwell became more confident, and his replies, if
still almost monosyllabic, were less hesitant.

Skillfully, the bearded prosecutor elicited confirmation of the
events set out in the first two charges. The storm had been building
all day; by evening, the wind had become southwesterly and risen
to gale force. Cantwell gave details of the *Lancer*'s position; he
described how she had battled against mountainous seas, with a
strong set to leeward. Captain Omerod had been taken ill very
suddenly, the lieutenant testified. He himself had had the last dog
watch, and at one bell—six-thirty—Lieutenant Vincent had informed him of the captain's indisposition. The ship, in his own
view, had been carrying too much canvas for the prevailing conditions—he supplied brief details, and Red listened with a bewilderment shared by the other members of the court, all of them aware
that prudence would have dictated an order to shorten sail.

"You received no such order, Mr. Cantwell?" the prosecuting
officer demanded.

Cantwell shook his head. Reluctantly, in reply to a series of
questions, he admitted that both he and the officer he had relieved
at the end of the first dog watch, the *Lancer*'s second lieutenant,
had requested permission to take in sail.

"The first lieutenant said that the captain had refused permission, sir. He went below, after I made my request, sir, to speak to
Captain Omerod. Then, when he returned to the deck, sir, he informed me that the captain had been taken ill and that he was in
command. It was then he gave the order to take in sail."

"Lieutenant Vincent gave the order?"

"Yes, sir, he did." Amos Cantwell hesitated, stealing another
anxious glance at Vincent. Receiving another nod, he went on.
"The topmen were—well, they were scared, sir. We were carrying a
number of raw hands, and going aloft in such a wind was bound to

be risky. Mr. Vincent swore at them, sir, and said he'd show them how."

"And did he?"

"Oh, yes, sir. He kicked off his seaboots, and he and the captain of the maintop, Petty Officer Kay, went up together. The other men followed them." Once launched on his description, Cantwell recounted events with eagerness, displaying considerable admiration for Vincent's conduct.

The bearded prosecutor brought him abruptly back to earth. "At the time, Mr. Cantwell, was the first lieutenant completely sober?"

"Sober, sir?"

"Yes, sober, Mr. Cantwell. You said in your deposition that he appeared to be unsteady and that you caught the whiff of spirits on his breath. You said you thought he had taken a drink with the captain, did you not?"

"Well, yes, sir," Cantwell conceded unhappily. "It was a very rough night, cold and—well, I'd have taken a drink, sir, if I'd been offered one. Mr. Vincent ordered a tot of rum for the topmen, after they came back on deck. He said they deserved it, sir. And he had a tot himself—he was soaked to the skin, sir, and freezing cold. They all were. And one man—a new rating, Ordinary Seaman Bowman, who's one of the witnesses, sir—he slipped from the main shrouds, when he was about eight feet from the deck. Luckily for him, he landed on a heap of canvas, sir, and wasn't badly hurt. His shoulder was dislocated, and the first lieutenant ordered him a double tot and then put it back for him, sir. His shoulder, I mean, and—"

The prosecutor cut him short. "Yes, yes, we shall hear from Ordinary Seaman Bowman in due course. What I am trying to ascertain and what this court wants to know is Lieutenant Vincent's state of sobriety when he came on deck, after visiting Captain Omerod in his cabin. Was he in fact drunk, Mr. Cantwell?"

"I—I can't say, sir." Cantwell reddened.

"You must say. You are on oath, Mr. Cantwell."

Again the young officer looked across at Vincent uncertainly, and once again he was given a reassuring nod.

"I . . . sir, I supposed that he had taken a drink with the captain. But he wasn't drunk, sir. He knew what he was about, and the ship was pitching heavily. None of us were able to move steadily on deck, sir."

"Very well, Mr. Cantwell," the prosecutor acknowledged. "I will leave it to the court to judge. Let us go on to the circumstances in which your ship was abandoned."

"That was much later, sir," Cantwell supplied, clearly pleased to be asked no more questions concerning Vincent's sobriety. "After the fire, sir." With reasonable fluency, he described how, having gone below at the end of his watch, leaving Vincent in command of the first watch, he had been roused from sleep by shouts of alarm and the pipe summoning the watch below to turn up.

"We all turned up, sir. It was six bells of the middle watch and Mr. Rayburn had the deck, but the first lieutenant was there too. He said that a fire had broken out below. He didn't say where, sir, but Mr. Rayburn told me it was in the captain's cabin. Mr. Vincent called for hoses to be rigged, and he went below with a fire party. I stayed on deck, sir. I could see we were dangerously close to the shore—the Dursey Head light was clearly visible." In graphic detail, Amos Cantwell described the frantic efforts the *Lancer*'s crew had made to claw her off the rocky shore. "Mr. Vincent had ordered the forecourse set, but wind and tide were too strong, sir. We had two good men on the wheel, and I went to help them, but she wouldn't answer to her helm. Mr. Rayburn told me that they'd been fighting a losing battle for half the night, and the fire was just about the last straw. Then the first lieutenant came back on deck, sir. He said he would try to bring her about and clear the Dursey Head. . . ." Cantwell talked on, needing no prompting now, and Red imagined himself in a similar predicament, certain in his own mind that he would have done exactly what Adam Vincent had done, given the circumstances in which the *Lancer*'s unfortunate first lieutenant had found himself.

"We were bringing her head round, sir—or I thought we were," Cantwell said hoarsely. "But then she shipped a ton or two of water and was thrown on her beam ends. She seemed to hang there for—oh, for an age, sir, and then she righted herself. And then—" He broke off, his young face suddenly draining of color. "Mr. Vincent sent me below, to take charge of the fire party. I saw the captain come on deck—Mr. Lee and a seaman were assisting him, and he looked very ill, sir, barely able to stand. I—that is, I'd only just found the fire party when the order was given to—to abandon ship."

"Who gave the order, Mr. Cantwell?" the president asked sharply.

Cantwell turned to face him. "I don't know, sir."

"What do you mean, you don't know?"

"I only heard it repeated, sir. I ordered the fire party to obey it, and they didn't waste any time. They went on deck at once, sir."

"But you did not?" the president pursued, after consulting a sheaf of papers on the table in front of him. "Why not, Mr. Cantwell?"

Cantwell stiffened. "I stayed to make certain that no one was left below, sir. The cook had been badly scalded earlier on, and I knew he was in the sick bay. And there was Ordinary Seaman Bowman —he has been sent there, after his fall from the shrouds, and he'd been given a dose of laudanum. I thought that probably they wouldn't have heard the order, you see, sir."

"And hadn't they?" the president demanded, frowning.

"No, sir," Cantwell answered. "And neither had our passenger, Lieutenant Lane of the Royal Marines, sir. I found him in his cabin —he said he'd been asleep all through the storm, sir. And . . . I ran into the first lieutenant in the sick bay. He had come on the same errand as myself, you see, sir."

"I see." The president nodded to the prosecutor, who concluded the questioning with a crisp invitation to the witness to describe what had next occurred.

Cantwell's young face seemed suddenly to age.

"I helped Mr. Vincent to take the two men from the sick bay on deck, sir. Lieutenant Lane had gone ahead of us, and he—sir, I heard him cry out, 'They've gone down, the lot of them! The boats have been swamped!' And when I reached the deck I—I saw that he was right. It was hard to pick out with such a sea running, but I saw the whaler turn right over, spilling her crew into the water. There were heads bobbing about, but . . . they didn't last long, and there was nothing we could do to help them, sir. There was only one boat left on board the ship—the gig, sir, but the sea had stove it in. We—we just had to watch them drown."

"You have our sympathy, Mr. Cantwell," the president said, with gruff kindness. "It must have been a terrible sight."

"Yes, sir, it was," Amos Cantwell confirmed bleakly. He shivered and, after another glance at Lieutenant Vincent, added in a whisper, "I—I wish I could forget it, sir." He braced himself and, sensing that his ordeal was almost over, spoke in a louder tone.

"The ship was driven ashore about—oh, about two hours later, sir, and the people in the lighthouse had seen our plight, and they helped us swim ashore. Even so, sir, I was nearly swept away. The first lieutenant, Mr. Vincent, saved my life—he held on to me, and then he went back for Bowman, who couldn't swim. He—Mr. Vincent shouldn't be on trial, sir. He—"

"That," the president interrupted sternly, "is not for you to judge, Lieutenant Cantwell." He sighed audibly and then addressed the accused officer. "Do you wish to cross-examine this witness, Mr. Vincent?"

Vincent rose. "No, sir, thank you. Mr. Cantwell has given his evidence admirably. I question nothing he has said, sir."

The president glanced inquiringly to either side of him. "Gentlemen? Have you any questions to put to Mr. Cantwell?"

Only one member of the court—a thin-faced, elderly commander—availed himself of the invitation. For almost ten minutes he tried aggressively to browbeat Amos Cantwell into admitting that the *Lancer*'s first lieutenant had been drunk. He failed in this endeavor, but Vincent looked flushed and angry when, at last, the commander abandoned his questioning and allowed the witness to be dismissed.

The next witness, however, had the commander smiling in unconcealed satisfaction. He was in Royal Marine uniform, a short, stout individual with iron-gray hair and the faint suggestion of a Cockney accent—a long-serving ranker, Red decided, whose career had suffered from lack of education.

Giving his name as Thomas Arthur Lane and his rank as lieutenant, he bore out, in substance, much of young Cantwell's evidence, while admitting that he had slept throughout the worst part of the storm.

"Seein' I was a passenger, sir, with no duties to perform, and as it was certain sure we was in for a rough night, I got me head down in me cabin. But Captain Omerod's cabin wasn't far away—in earshot, if anyone there raised his voice. And they did, sir—him an' the first lieutenant. At it hammer an' tongs, they were, the pair of them."

"Do you mean, sir," the prosecutor asked, "that you heard the captain and the first lieutenant engaged in some sort of altercation?"

"It was more than an altercation, sir—more like a quarrel," the marine officer asserted with conviction. "I couldn't hear what was

being said, you understand, but I didn't have to, not in order to
know that they were far from being in agreement. Shouting at
Lieutenant Vincent, the captain was, calling him names, as nearly
as I could judge. I did catch a word or two, but not enough to say
what they were quarreling about." Becoming conscious of the rapt
interest of the entire courtroom in his testimony, Lane paused, his
thin lips curving into a mirthless smile. "I did hear Mr. Vincent
say that the ship would be in trouble if they didn't shorten sail.
And the captain told him to be damned. 'I'll take in sail when it's
necessary,' he said."

"Did you hear any more?" the prosecuting officer prompted.

Lane shook his head. "No, sir, because they stopped. I heard the
first lieutenant leave the captain's cabin, and I went to try to intercept him, intending to ask him what was going on. But he just
brushed past me without giving me an answer."

"Did you—think carefully, Mr. Lane—did you form any opinion as to Mr. Vincent's state of sobriety?"

"He was drunk, sir," the marine officer answered without hesitation. "Stumbling and staggering, and he was reeking of liquor.
Besides that, his speech was slurred."

The president intervened. "I thought you said that Mr. Vincent
did not speak to you when you endeavored to accost him?"

Lane smiled again, passing his tongue over his lips. "I said he
didn't give me any answer, sir, and he didn't—not to my question,
sir. But he spoke to me. 'The captain has been ill,' he said. 'I'm
taking command.' He went on deck, staggering, like I told you,
and I went back to my cabin and turned in."

"You turned in, Mr. Lane?" the president exclaimed. "You
turned in and went to sleep?"

"Yes, sir, I did. And I slept until the young officer, Lieutenant
Cantwell, wakened me and said I'd best get on deck, as the order
had been given to abandon ship."

Once again, Red saw the president's brows rise.

"You were able to sleep, in spite of knowing that Mr. Vincent,
who, according to your—er—observation, was drunk, had taken
over command of the ship? Were you not alarmed?"

"No use me getting alarmed, was it, sir?" Lane defended ag-
grievedly. "I'm not a deck officer. There was nothing I could do
about it. And I heard the pipe, I heard the order to the seamen to
go aloft and take in sail. I thought we'd be getting out of trouble,

and—well, I was tired, sir, so I got me head down. Next thing I knew was Lieutenant Cantwell yelling at me to go on deck."

The rest of Lieutenant Lane's evidence corroborated that of Amos Cantwell, although he gave the story of their rescue somewhat sourly and offered no praise where Vincent's part in it was concerned. Questioned concerning the accused officer's state of sobriety at the time, he conceded, still sourly, that "he was sober enough by then. He'd had time, hadn't he?"

Vincent, to Red's surprise, when invited as before to cross-examine the witness, declined to do so; and of the members of the court, only the thin-faced, elderly commander—whose name, his immediate neighbor told him, was Sigsworth—attempted to delve into the nature of the disagreement between the *Lancer*'s captain and her first lieutenant. All he was able to persuade Lane to admit to was his personal opinion, which the judge advocate ruled to be inadmissible.

"But you are quite certain, are you not, Mr. Lane," Commander Sigsworth persisted, "that Lieutenant Vincent *was* in a state of insobriety, when you accosted him outside the captain's cabin?"

"I'm as certain as I can be of anything, sir," Lane asserted. "Lieutenant Vincent was drunk. Not incapable, but he had difficulty in keeping his feet, sir. And like I said, his speech was slurred —I could hardly understand him—and he reeked of liquor, almost as if he'd spilt the stuff over him."

He was permitted to stand down, and the court was adjourned for luncheon, which—in the admiral's absence—was served in the spacious day cabin. At the table, Red was formally made welcome by the court-martial president and flag captain, whose name, he learned, was Duckworth.

"Captain Broome has just returned from the Australasian station, gentlemen," Duckworth announced. "Indeed, his frigate, the *Galah,* paid off only yesterday, and he might be forgiven for wondering why his well-earned shore leave has had to be postponed, in order that he serve on this court-martial. The reason, my dear fellow, was an unexpected shortage of post captains, due to half the Fleet being at sea with the rear admiral, on a visit of friendship to our allies, the Portuguese." He smiled pleasantly, introducing the other members of the court by name, on learning that Red was not acquainted with them. "You have been away a long time, it would seem."

"Almost four years, sir," Red supplied.

"Were you not with the *Shannon* naval brigade in the recent mutiny in Bengal?" one of his fellow captains asked.

"I was attached to the brigade, sir, yes," Red replied. He helped himself from a dish offered by a smartly uniformed mess steward, hoping that he would not be questioned concerning his previous acquaintance with Adam Vincent. But the inevitable question came—predictably from Commander Sigsworth—and he inclined his head in assent. "I served with Lieutenant Vincent throughout the campaign, Commander, and his conduct was exemplary. That is not only my opinion, I might add—the late Captain Peel recommended him most highly for promotion. I—well, I was both surprised and distressed to find him on trial, I must confess, particularly with such grave charges being brought against him."

He would have said more but thought better of it, lest his impartiality be held in doubt, and Captain Duckworth, sensing his embarrassment, put in quickly, "It is distressing for all of us, Captain Broome, to have to sit in judgment on an officer who seemed destined to make an outstanding career in the service—and one, furthermore, who was awarded the Victoria Cross for his gallantry in the Crimea. But . . ." He shrugged resignedly, turning to reply to a remark from Sigsworth that Red did not hear.

By common consent, the conversation shifted to other topics, and it was not until, the meal over, the officers were preparing to return to the courtroom that Red found Commander Sigsworth at his elbow.

"You've been out of the country, Captain Broome," the older man said, lowering his voice, "so you will not have been privy to the scandal involving Lieutenant Vincent. But . . . gossip has been rife, sir, coupling Vincent with the wife of his late commander, John Omerod. She's a very beautiful woman, Caroline Omerod."

Red stiffened, reluctant to hear more, but Sigsworth grasped his arm, holding him back. "You expressed surprise and, I think, distress to find Vincent facing such charges as those we heard leveled against him this morning. But surely, Captain Broome, you do not need me to tell you that a man's whole character can change when he becomes infatuated with a beautiful woman?"

"No, of course I don't," Red began. "But are you implying that Vincent—"

"John Omerod had requested that Vincent should be replaced as first lieutenant of the *Lancer*," Commander Sigsworth put in, "only a few days before she sailed. I fancy he had found out that he had been cuckolded. Certainly there was bad blood between them, and they made no secret of it, when previously they had been the closest of friends. Indeed, the last time I encountered them, poor old John was drinking very heavily, and they almost came to blows, when Vincent attempted to take him back to his ship. Neither of them was sober, and I had to intervene, in order to prevent an ugly public confrontation, which would have harmed both their careers."

"Was Omerod a friend of yours?" Red asked, an edge to his voice.

"A friend, but not an intimate one. We'd served together as mids a good few years ago and then in this ship, before John was given command of the *Lancer,* eighteen months ago. He wasn't the kind of fellow I take to, but . . . I was sorry for him. And with reason."

"With reason on Adam Vincent's account?" Red suggested.

"Certainly," Commander Sigsworth returned with emphasis. "I believe in loyalty, particularly in loyalty between an officer and his captain. But Vincent wasn't loyal—anything but." He lowered his voice to a sibilant whisper and added, his tone faintly malicious, "Caroline Omerod had a son, who was the apple of John Omerod's eye. Only about a couple of months old—a beautiful, golden-haired child the poor fellow doted on. But John was dark, almost Spanish-looking, with a swarthy complexion . . . and you know what Vincent looks like. A damned Nordic hero! Draw your own conclusions, Captain Broome. I fear John did."

"Gentlemen!" The president's summons cut Sigsworth's confidences short, but Red was uneasy as he followed the other officers back into the courtroom. *Could* a man's whole character change, he asked himself, as a result of an infatuation with a beautiful woman? His own brother Johnny was perhaps proof that it was possible; his marriage to Kitty Cadogan was far from happy, and Johnny had undoubtedly changed, in half a hundred different ways. But had Adam Vincent also changed?

He took his seat, glancing across at Vincent as the young lieutenant was escorted into court by the officer assigned to guard him, with a drawn sword. A second officer was with them—the lieutenant who was entrusted with the role of prisoner's friend, whom Vincent had ignored through the first part of his trial. Both appeared to be urging some course on him, but the accused officer firmly shook his head. He seated himself, his escort sheathed his sword, and, with a shrug, the defending officer subsided into the chair beside him, a resigned expression on his face.

Vincent, Red thought, was still obstinately determined to conduct his own case, whatever it might cost him. And it might well cost him dear, for the remaining witnesses—the *Lancer*'s cook and the rating who had been injured in the fall from the rigging—were able to say little to refute Lieutenant Lane's undoubtedly damaging testimony.

The cook had been in the sick bay and had seen and heard nothing until Vincent had come below to tell him that the ship was to be abandoned; and thereafter his recollection of the events bore out, almost exactly, young Cantwell's account. In a well-intentioned attempt to aid the accused officer, the cook gave him credit for having saved his life; but pressed by the prosecutor, he finally admitted that, when he had encountered Vincent earlier in the passageway outside the captain's cabin, the first lieutenant had given the appearance of being drunk.

After a whispered and obviously heated exchange with the defending officer, Vincent reluctantly rose to cross-examine the witness on this point but succeeded only in making the man's statement seem more damaging.

"I'm sorry, sir," the cook said, with genuine contrition, "but I'm on oath, an' I got to tell what I seen, ain't I, sir? An' what I heard. And I *did* hear the captain yellin' at you an' you yellin' back, sir."

"Yes, of course you had to, Loomis," Vincent assured him. He sat down, tight-lipped and white of face, avoiding the defending officer's reproachful gaze.

The final witness, a young ordinary seaman who gave his name as Alfred Bowman, was clearly frightened and overawed by the presence of so many senior officers, but the prosecutor dealt with him kindly, and the youngster's nervousness vanished. He was able, however, to add little to what Lieutenant Cantwell had stated.

"I was scared, sir," he admitted. "By the storm, like. It was me first time at sea, and it was real bad, sir, with the ship heeling over an' pitchin' something cruel. Some o' the older men, they was scared too. They reckoned we was carryin' too much sail, an' they was grumblin' about it. But when the order *did* come to take in sail an' I knew I'd have to go aloft, I . . . well, I hung back, sir. I feared me last hour had come, that I'd get up an' never get back to the deck again. An' I wasn't the only one. The cap'n o' the main-top—Kay, sir—he was swearin' at us, but we just went on hangin' back. An' then the first lieutenant, Mr. Vincent, he told us we was a bunch o' useless layabouts. 'I'll show you how,' he says. 'An' if I can do it, you can. Come on,' he says. ' 'Cos if you don't she's goin' down an' we'll be lost!' Him an' the petty officer went shinnin' up the shrouds, sir, an' we went after 'em, 'cos we didn't want them puttin' us to shame, you see, sir."

"Quite so, lad," the prosecutor encouraged. "Go on."

Bowman continued his narrative, his young voice harsh with strain as he described his fall, the excruciating pain his dislocated shoulder had caused him, and the swift, competent manner in which Vincent had dealt with it.

"He gave me a double tot, sir" the young seaman added, smiling, "an' sent me below to the sick bay, where they give me somethin' else. I slept, sir, till Lieutenant Vincent an' Mr. Cantwell roused me, 'cos we was to abandon the ship, sir."

The bearded prosecutor took him briefly through the circumstances of his rescue; yet for all the boy was compelled to curtail his account, his admiration for the *Lancer*'s first lieutenant was in every word he spoke.

"He saved me life, sir. But for Lieutenant Vincent I'd not be here, sir, an' that's the gospel truth. I can't swim, sir, an' wiv' me arm—I'd have gone under for certain sure if he hadn't hung on to me."

In its way, it was a moving tribute to Adam Vincent's courage and devotion to duty, Red reflected; nevertheless, neither the prosecuting officer nor Commander Sigsworth was content to allow Ordinary Seaman Bowman's evidence to rest there. Under a spate of sharp, probing questions, the boy admitted that Vincent's recklessness in leading the topmen aloft could have been because he had been drinking before coming on deck; that his language had been more forceful than normal; and that his breath had reeked of spirits when he had bent over, in order to restore the dislocated bone to its socket.

Vincent refused the invitation to cross-examine the witness. The evidence relating to the third charge—that of absenting himself without leave, when held in arrest—was given by his escorting officer, Lieutenant Fleming, briefly and with studied lack of bias. It was not questioned, and on the prosecuting officer's announcement that this completed the case, the president declared the court closed.

"We shall resume at nine-thirty tomorrow morning to hear evidence for the defense," he said, and added, a trifle caustically, "I trust that you will reconsider your decision to conduct your own case, Mr. Vincent. Undoubtedly it will be in your best interests if you seek informed legal advice in the preparation of your defense. I am given to understand that, although he has left the ship, Sir David Murchison has remained in Portsmouth town and is willing to be called in consultation, should you wish to avail yourself of his assistance."

Adam Vincent bowed in acknowledgment but, not entirely to Red's surprise, said nothing. He left the court with his escorting officer, and the lieutenant appointed as his defending officer approached the still-seated members of the court.

"Forgive me, sir," he said unhappily, addressing the president. "I think I ought to tell you that Mr. Vincent says he will not see Sir David Murchison."

"Won't see him, eh? Well, it's his decision—I cannot compel him to change his mind, Mr. Mitchell. And you, I feel sure, have done your best."

"Indeed I have, sir," Lieutenant Mitchell confirmed. "And I'll go on trying, but he—he seems quite adamant, sir. And his father's here—Lord Cheviot. Mr. Vincent refused to see him too, sir."

"Devil take the boy!" The president's tone was regretful rather than censorious. "He would have made such a fine career—a Victoria Cross, a glowing record." He caught Red's eye and sighed. "You knew him well in India, of course, Captain Broome. And thought very highly of him, didn't you?"

"I did, sir, very highly indeed." Red hesitated, his conscience dictating the offer he was about to make—an offer that might be considered highly irregular, since he was a member of the court convened to sit in judgment on Adam Vincent. "With your permission, sir, I'd be more than willing to try to reason with Mr. Vincent. Though I'm not sure—"

Vincent's defending officer put in, with a bitterness he did not attempt to conceal, "It would do no good, sir. Adam won't listen to anyone. And he told me that whoever asked to see him, I was to say no."

"Then that is your answer, Captain Broome," the *Copenhagen*'s captain decided. "And perhaps it's just as well, in the circum-

stances, since you're a member of the court. But you shall have the
opportunity to speak up for the obstinate young idiot, when we
discuss our findings." He laid a friendly hand on Red's arm. "Join
me for a glass of Madeira before dinner, my dear fellow, and you
can tell *me* anything I don't know about Mr. Vincent—in confidence, of course. Because frankly, unless he can offer a very telling
defense indeed, it's likely to be the end of his career in the service."
He turned to Mitchell and said decisively, "But the boy should see
his father. Find Lord Cheviot, Mr. Mitchell, if you please, and say
I'd like to have a word with him."

Chapter II

REACHING HIS CABIN—one of a dozen in the after part of the *Copenhagen*'s lower gun deck—Adam Vincent stripped off his tight-fitting full dress coat and empty sword belt and flung himself down on the lower berth, releasing his breath in a long, pent-up sigh.

Lieutenant Robert Fleming, his official escort, returned his own sword to its scabbard and came to stand, arms akimbo, looking down at him, an expression of mingled exasperation and bewilderment on his homely face.

"Have you gone completely out of your mind, Adam?" he demanded. "Not content with sending one of the leading Q.C.'s in the country packing, you've as good as scuppered your chances by refusing to cross-examine any of the witnesses! In heaven's name, why?" His heated words met with no response, and he went on, in a more placatory tone, "Poor young Cantwell did his best for you. And that pathetic little apology for a seaman, Bowman, was ready to lie down and die for you, if you'd given him half a chance. But you didn't, did you? And you let that sour old swine Lane blackguard you without so much as a challenge! To claim that you were reeking of spirits—damn it, man, why did you let him get away with that? And he said it twice!"

"Well, it happened to be true," Adam Vincent returned glumly.

"True? You mean you *were* drunk?"

"No, I was not drunk. But I *was* reeking of spirits when I barged into him in the passageway." Adam hesitated, eyeing his companion uncertainly, the need to unburden himself to someone becoming suddenly overwhelming. He had kept silent for so long, kept his own counsel, resisting the overtures of friendship and sympathy

Rob Fleming had been so generously offering since the arrest and their enforced intimacy. Finally, coming to a decision, he said tensely, "Will you swear to keep it to yourself, Rob, if I tell you what happened?"

"Yes, of course I will. You have my word." Fleming unbuckled his sword belt and came to seat himself on the end of the narrow bunk. "You've clammed up like the proverbial oyster all the time I've been acting as your escort. Even when you ran out on me, you wouldn't tell me why, would you?"

"I couldn't. I still can't."

"All right, that's over and finished now. It might be a help if you talk about things, Adam. And it won't go any further . . . you can rely on me, I promise you. For God's sake, I don't want to stand by and watch you wreck your career, without at least trying to help." Fleming spoke earnestly, and Adam warmed to him. No one could help, he had long since recognized; his naval career had been in jeopardy from the moment he had first set eyes on Caroline Omerod, and there was nothing he could do now to save himself.

"Carry on, then," Rob Fleming prompted. "Tell me why you were reeking with spirits, as Lane testified, but yet you weren't drunk."

"Well, John Omerod had just thrown most of a decanter of brandy over me, and as you know, brandy stinks to high heaven. That's why I reeked of the stuff."

"Good God!" Fleming was visibly taken aback, but he recovered himself quickly. "You'll state that in your defense, I presume? Tomorrow, when you have the chance to answer the charges?"

"No." Adam's denial was emphatic. "I can't."

"Why not, for the Lord's sweet sake?"

"For one reason, because it would be my word against John's— and John is dead. There were no witnesses, apart from Lane. And he wasn't exaggerating when he said he heard us going at it hammer and tongs. We had a blazing, ghastly row—I can't tell you what it was about, because it was personal and I'm not proud of it. And I provoked him. I . . . oh, the devil, I *had* to! He hadn't been on deck for twenty-four hours, he didn't know the sort of weather we'd run into, and he refused to give me permission to take in sail. Archie Rayburn had tried to get his permission as well, and we—our ship was heading for disaster! You heard Amos Cantwell's evidence, so I needn't spell it out. Amos was not exaggerating, either. Damn it, Rob, we had tops'ls and courses on her!"

Adam went into details, his voice flat and devoid of expression while, against his will, the scene with John Omerod flashed vividly and sickeningly into his mind, as real as ever, despite his efforts to obliterate it from his memory.

John Omerod had come on board, after spending the night ashore with Caroline. He had been morose and ill-tempered, and—save when it was necessary and in the presence of others—Adam had been at pains to avoid him as the sloop butted her way down-Channel before a fresh easterly breeze. But then, following a savage burst of rage over a comparatively trivial matter, the captain had publicly bawled out Archibald Rayburn and the whole of the afternoon watch and retired to his cabin. He had not been seen on deck for twenty-four hours after that, yet Adam had known—because Rayburn had told him—that John Omerod was drinking himself into a paralytic state, quite oblivious of the fact that the *Lancer* had run into a force-ten gale, in dangerous proximity to the Irish coast.

He had had to go below, Adam recalled wearily, when Rayburn had failed to persuade their captain to see reason, but . . . he had not anticipated the reception Omerod had accorded him. The captain had been beside himself, crazed with bitterness, flinging accusations at him, not all of which were true. Adam had guessed, to his dismay, that Caroline had told her husband that she was leaving him, that their marriage was at an end and that she intended to take the child with her.

Adam drew in his breath sharply as the memories came flooding back and he heard John Omerod's voice, as if it were coming from beside him.

"You miserable, treacherous young swine! You betrayed my friendship by stealing my wife! Not content with that, you foisted your bastard on me, let me believe he was my son! But Caroline's told me the truth at last—I forced her to tell me, damn your soul! Do you think I care if this blasted ship goes down? I've nothing to live for anymore, and I hope to God you go down with her. . . ."

It had gone on and on; he had tried to shut his ears to it, sought vainly to deny that the boy was his or that he had ever asked Caroline to break up their marriage, but John had shouted him down. "I'll take in sail when *I* decide it's necessary, Mr. Vincent—and the devil take you for the vile lecher that you are!"

Rob Fleming's voice broke into his thoughts, and, realizing that he must have fallen silent, Adam said hoarsely, "What did you say?"

"I said that you *must* refute the charge of drunkenness when you go back to the court tomorrow, Adam," Fleming told him vehemently. "It's your only hope! Even if you have to admit that it was Omerod who had been drinking himself under the table, you've got to say so. For the Lord's sake, man, it was his fault the *Lancer* went down, not yours."

"I was responsible, Rob," Adam reminded him. "I'd taken command, and I'm on trial for losing her. And besides—" He broke off, reluctant—despite Rob's promise—to tell him the whole, appalling truth. But Fleming persisted, warning him of the consequences and urging him to try to save his career.

"They'll throw you out of the service, Adam. They'll have no option, if you're proved guilty. Over a hundred officers and men lost their lives, don't forget."

"As if I could forget," Adam retorted, with harsh bitterness. "Dear heaven, don't you think they're on my conscience and always will be, as long as I live?"

"I'm sorry—that was tactless," Fleming apologized. "But even so, Adam, you've got to think of yourself. At least try to convince the court that you weren't drunk, and that by relieving Omerod of the command you did all in your power to save the ship and those lives. It can't hurt Omerod now. Adam—" Rob Fleming caught at Adam's arm, forcing him to meet his gaze. "You'll be on oath—tell them the truth!"

It was no use arguing, Adam thought, suddenly weary of the whole sorry business. He had brought it on himself—or he and Caroline had, between them—and he neither hoped nor wanted to escape blame for what had happened.

"If I do tell the truth, Rob," he answered, his voice not steady, "I should have to admit that I took over command by laying my captain out and locking him in his cabin. Which, I fear, could lay me open to a charge of mutiny."

"Oh, my God! Did you really do that?" His admission had taken the wind out of Rob Fleming's sails. The younger man regarded him in shocked disbelief; but eventually, seemingly realizing that what he had said was indeed the truth, Rob got to his feet.

"I can understand why you did not want Sir David Murchison to advise you," he managed at last. "But Lane didn't hear anything —he would have testified to it, if he had. Did anyone else know?"

"I told Archie Rayburn. And John Omerod's steward—I had to warn him. He knew John had been drinking, of course . . . he couldn't fail to. But—" Adam sighed. "He was a good man, with fifteen years' service and a leading rate. Symons, his name was, poor devil. I gave him the key and posted him in the passageway, outside the cabin."

Rob frowned, digesting this information. "Did Symons let the captain out, then, when the fire started?"

"Yes," Adam confirmed shortly. He was on dangerous ground now, he was aware, and he lapsed into a repressive silence, calculated to discourage further questions. Neither the prosecuting officer nor any member of the court had, as yet, sought to ascertain the cause of the fire or demanded to know precisely where and how it had been started, but . . . His lips tightened. Undoubtedly they would, if he were to give evidence on oath. He glanced at Rob Fleming, wondering whether he had said too much and thus enabled him to draw his own conclusions. But if he had, Rob was keeping his own counsel, and Adam breathed a relieved sigh.

Symons had reported the fire, but he had done so discreetly, being the kind of man he was . . . *had been,* God rest his loyal soul!

"The captain must have knocked over his table lamp, sir," he had told Adam in the passageway, "and the fire had taken quite a hold before I smelled the smoke. He's taken no harm, the captain hasn't, and I shifted him into Lieutenant Rayburn's cabin, where he's sleeping as peaceful as you please. But we'll need a fire party quick and lively, sir, if we're to stop it spreading."

There had been no way to tell whether John Omerod, finding himself locked in, might have flung the lamp down deliberately, but Symons's eyes had held more than a hint of doubt, and Adam was conscious of a sick sensation in the pit of his stomach as he recalled how his captain had erupted in fury, when he had told him that he was taking over the command. The poor fellow could hardly stand, though, and his resistance had been short-lived, settled by a clenched fist to the jaw.

Which, beyond any shadow of doubt, amounted to an act of mutiny on his part . . . Adam glanced again at Rob Fleming, who said explosively, breaking the silence, "Lord, Adam, you were every kind of a fool to take over command in the—the way you did!"

"Yes," Adam conceded, again taking the wind from Rob's sails.

"I know that only too well. But at the time I—well, I could not see any other way of doing it." And, he thought wretchedly, with John Omerod fighting mad, there *had* been no other way. "I had to relieve the ship of the canvas she was carrying. As it turned out, I was too late."

But it had been a near run thing, he knew, memory returning. They had come within an ace of saving the little sloop from her tragic fate. Granted another hour—even another half hour—it might have been possible, but John Omerod had come on deck and given the order to abandon her. He was the captain, and his order had been obeyed without question by the ship's company. Deprived of her crew, the *Lancer* was doomed, and the boats, hastily lowered into the seething, storm-wracked sea, had foundered, one after another, shattered and swamped by the mountainous breakers.

"I was too late," Adam repeated, more to himself than to Rob. "And a hundred and eleven men lost their lives. Can't you see why I've no defense to offer?"

A loud knocking on the cabin door saved Rob from the necessity of a reply. He went to open it, and Lieutenant Mitchell, who had been appointed as defending officer, made his appearance. Closing the door behind him, he said, without preamble, "Vincent, it's your father, Lord Cheviot. He insists on seeing you."

Adam could feel the color draining from his cheeks. The last person in the world he wanted to see was his straitlaced martinet of a father, and he started to say so, but Mitchell cut him short.

"His lordship will not take no for an answer. I'm sorry—I tried to explain, but he says he's leaving Portsmouth tomorrow morning. He told me to tell you that he will not be in court tomorrow, and it's important that he sees you before he goes."

Adam was on his feet instantly, reaching for his discarded frock coat, his fingers clumsy in their haste, as he fumbled with buttons and buckled his sword belt hurriedly about his waist, absurdly conscious of the fact that, as naval custom decreed, he had yielded up his sword at the beginning of his trial. It now lay across the table in the courtroom, and when the time came for the court's findings to be announced, the position of the sword would signal the outcome. If he were found guilty, the blade tip would be pointing toward him. . . . Adam drew a quick, uneven breath as he heard heavy footsteps approaching the door of his cabin.

The youngest of four sons, he had since his earliest boyhood gone in awe of his formidable, aloof father. Alexander Forbes Vincent, ninth Earl of Cheviot, retired major general and colonel of his regiment, the Scots Fusilier Guards, had a distinguished military record, dating from the Peninsular campaign and Waterloo, when he was a young ensign, to the Sikh wars in India, when he served as one of Sir Hugh Gough's brigade commanders and subsequently Sir Walter Gilbert's chief of staff in the Punjab.

Despite his prolonged absences from the family's ancestral estate of Newton Hall, in the Border country, when military duties took him abroad, their father had always exerted an influence that encompassed them all, Adam reflected grimly. His two elder sisters had dutifully married Guards officers, and his brothers had followed in their father's footsteps and entered the regiments he had chosen for them.

His eldest brother—also named Alexander but known to them by his courtesy title of Newton—had fulfilled all his father's hopes and expectations. Newton was a major in the Scots Guards, had fought with distinction in the Crimea, and, having married his commanding officer's daughter, was now the proud father of a growing family of his own. Adrian was in the North British Dragoons—the Greys—and had served in the cavalry division under the Earl of Lucan, and Richard had just purchased a captaincy in the Royal Scots.

Only he had broken with family tradition and chosen to enter the Royal Navy. Adam fastened the last, recalcitrant brass button on his immaculate blue coat and instinctively squared his shoulders, in expectation of what was to come. The medals pinned to his chest glinted in the light from the lantern above his head; when he had first worn them on a visit home, Adam recalled, on his return from India, his father had expressed pride in his achievements. But now? Rob Fleming flashed him an anxious glance, clearly not understanding what a visit from his father, in these circumstances, might portend, and Adam smiled back at him thinly, as Mitchell opened the cabin door and stood aside.

The Earl thanked him brusquely and, ducking his white head, entered the cabin. He was in civilian dress, but despite the sober black frock coat, the stiff, erect figure was unmistakably that of a soldier, his manner imperious, as it always was, and his voice commanding.

He offered no greeting but, addressing Fleming, requested him, in the same brusque tone, to leave the cabin.

"I wish to be alone with my son, if you please. I will call you when I have done. This will not take long." He waited until the door had closed and then said, with icy disapproval, "I have been given to understand, by the officer who brought me here—your defending officer, I believe—that you have refused to avail yourself of Sir David Murchison's counsel, when you endeavor to answer the charges against you tomorrow morning."

Adam passed his tongue over lips that had gone dry. Avoiding his father's coldly searching gaze, he said with what firmness he could muster, "That is so, sir. I—I'm sorry."

"You're sorry! Why, you young scapegrace, you should be sorry. I had done my best for you. I had engaged the most eminent barrister in London to defend you, and—even though you chose to insult Sir David publicly this morning—I had persuaded him to delay his return to London, in the hope that you would think better of it. Now I'm told you haven't, and that you've refused to let Lieutenant Mitchell act in the capacity for which he was appointed. Is that also true?"

Still Adam could not bring himself to face the condemnation he knew was blazing in his father's eyes.

"Yes, sir," he managed huskily, head still averted. "It is true, sir."

"Then I can draw only one conclusion, boy—that you are guilty of the charges on which you have been arraigned. You were drunk, and you lost your ship and most of her officers and men in consequence."

The accusation struck Adam with the force of a physical blow, but somehow he contrived to gather his scattered wits. "I was responsible for the loss of the ship, sir, but I was not drunk. I beg you to believe that. Only I—there is no way that I can prove it. It would be futile to try."

"Certainly, if it merely proved you were incompetent," his father countered disdainfully. "And what of the third charge? *Did* you absent yourself without leave, when you were under arrest, awaiting trial?"

"Yes, I did, Father. But it was a—an urgent personal matter. I cannot tell you what it was, I—"

"The devil take you, boy!" His father's interruption was angry. "I've heard rumors since your case opened. It's said that you were involved with your late commanding officer's wife. Mrs.—what the devil is her name? Omerod, Mrs. Omerod. Is *that* true? Were you involved with her?"

Adam faced him, suddenly as angry as he. "Who told you that, sir?"

"It's of no consequence who told me. It is common gossip, I understand. Was this woman, was Mrs. Omerod the 'urgent personal matter' that caused you to break your arrest?" Adam remained silent, his lips tight, and his father said, with biting contempt, "So you have ruined your career and dragged my family name in the dust on account of a woman! Well, perhaps I should have expected no more of you, Adam. You will be cashiered, you know—thrown out of the navy in disgrace! Well, I do not intend to witness it. I shall leave for home first thing tomorrow morning."

Still Adam could find no words to answer him, and his father spread his hands in a helpless gesture. They were old hands, Adam noticed suddenly, blue-veined and wrinkled . . . and his father's face was that of an old and unhappy man, etched with deep lines that he had never observed before. Had he done this to the proud old soldier who had sired him, he asked himself, conscious of shame. There had, it was true, been little affection between them; his father's affection had always been showered on Newton and the girls—if affection was the right word. Pride, perhaps, was more fitting—he had always been intensely proud of Newton, anxious to advance him, to gratify his eldest son's ambitions, since they matched his own. And when Adrian and Richard had been commissioned they, too, had become the objects of their father's pride.

In his own case, it had been different, Adam recalled, stirred by the memory of pain inflicted on him when he had been too young to sense the reason for it. His mother had died in giving him birth; that, undoubtedly, had been the root cause, but it had been years before he had realized it. And his insistence on entering the navy had incensed his father, although it had sprung initially from a longing to leave home and escape from his father's clutches—a boy could join the navy at a much earlier age than he could expect to be granted a commission in the army, and he had been twelve when he had been accepted for the Royal Naval College. To him, service at sea had represented freedom.

But even so . . . He found his tongue at last and said, with deeply felt contrition, "Father, I am truly sorry. I—I wish there was something I could say, I—"

His father brushed his stammered words aside.

"There is nothing you can say, Adam." He drew himself up, tall and unbending, the bewhiskered jaw sternly set. "Even if you are not cashiered, I shall cease to regard you as a son of mine, and you will no longer be permitted to set foot in my house. If, as I fully anticipate, you *are* cashiered, my advice to you is that you seek to redeem yourself in one of the colonies. Australia, perhaps. If you decide to take my advice, I will arrange for my lawyers to provide you with funds with which to make a start there. No—" The general held up his hand as Adam attempted to speak. "I will hear no more. And I will say no more, save—" The cold blue eyes rested for a moment on the bronze symbol of valor pinned to Adam's coat, and he added, with stark bitterness, "Your Victoria Cross will be forfeited, if you are cashiered. No woman is worth what this— this Mrs. Omerod has cost you."

He turned to the door and went out without a backward glance, and Adam stood as if turned to stone. Caroline, he thought dully . . . dear God, she was not to blame. It was not her fault or his that they had fallen in love. Neither of them had intended it; neither of them had been prepared for the tide of passion that had engulfed them, sweeping all other considerations, all other loyalties aside. Least of all had they intended to betray John Omerod. They . . .

Lieutenant Mitchell came in, Rob Fleming hovering uneasily at his back.

"Was it bad, Vincent?" the defending officer asked sympathetically. Receiving Adam's barely perceptible nod, he sighed. "I'm sorry I brought your father here, but there wasn't any way I could prevent him from coming—he had tackled Captain Duckworth over my head. It was as much as my life was worth to refuse. But —there *is* one man I think you might like to see. He's a member of the court, and—"

"Oh, for the Lord's sake, Mitchell," Adam protested with a weary flash of temper, "I don't want to see anyone! I have had as much as I can stomach for one day."

"You need not see this officer," Mitchell assured him soothingly. "In fact it probably wouldn't be ethical if you did. But he knows you—he served with you in the *Shannon*'s brigade in India, and you may have cause to be glad he *is* a member of the court, because he seems to have a good opinion of you. His name's Broome, Captain Broome, and he's just brought the *Galah* frigate back from Australia."

Red Broome, Adam thought—and for all the despair his father's visit had caused him, his flagging spirits lifted. Broome was the best of fellows, a good officer and a staunch friend, who never lost his head in the most trying circumstances. He had come up-country to Cawnpore with the volunteers that James Vaughan, the *Shannon*'s first lieutenant, had raised from ships anchored in the Hooghly at Calcutta, and had proved a tower of strength in the brigade's subsequent operations. Adam smiled.

"Thanks for giving me that piece of good news," he said to Mitchell. "I can only hope that Captain Broome will see fit to speak up for me, when the court deliberates its findings. His may be a lone voice, but—" He shrugged resignedly. "It might help."

"You're still set on conducting your own case tomorrow?" Mitchell asked. He sighed when Adam inclined his head in assent. "I could help, you know. At least let me take you through your evidence, Vincent."

"I shall not be giving evidence on oath," Adam returned with finality. "There are reasons why I cannot. No reflection on you, please understand that. My reasons are personal, and—" He thought then of Caroline, and as a vision of her lovely, serene face filled his mind, his resolution hardened. "My father has only reinforced them."

He held rigidly to his decision when the court reassembled next day, rejecting advice from both the president and the judge advocate and making, in the end, a plea in mitigation, which did not require him to take the oath. This, he sensed at once, was not well received; members of the court attempted to question him, but he fended off their questions in a low, strained voice, which, he became increasingly aware, failed to carry conviction. But he persisted, and only once did a question come close to penetrating his defenses.

It came unexpectedly from Red Broome.

"Who," he asked, in a deceptively quiet tone, "Mr. Vincent, who gave the order to abandon ship? You or Captain Omerod?"

Flustered, Adam could feel the awkward, unhappy color leaping to his cheeks. He attempted to prevaricate, but the president intervened to insist that he must answer.

"I will rephrase it, sir," Broome said. "Did *you* give the order, Mr. Vincent?"

Adam was compelled to shake his head, and Red Broome said crisply, "Then if you did not, your captain must have done?"

He had given Caroline his word, Adam reminded himself, suddenly assailed by panic. Within half an hour of receiving her tear-stained note from the unsuspecting Fleming, he had broken his arrest and gone ashore to keep the rendezvous for which she had pleaded, giving no thought to the consequences, either to her or to himself, and still less to poor Rob Fleming.

She had been in widow's weeds, her face heavily veiled, and she had wept, unable to contain her bitter grief, blaming herself for her husband's tragic death. And—Adam faced his questioner, reading pity and comprehension in his eyes. But he could not respond to Broome's attempt to help him; he had promised Caroline that John Omerod's record should be untarnished.

He drew himself up and said firmly, "Sir, the captain was seriously ill, and I had assumed the command. It was my responsibility, sir. I had his steward and Midshipman Lee carry Captain Omerod on deck."

Red Broome was frowning, he saw, the comprehension gone from his eyes. He did not continue his questioning, but the president did, compelling Adam to admit that the order to abandon the *Lancer* had been premature, the chances of any boat reaching the shore very poor in such a sea.

It was the end for him, Adam recognized. The court was cleared and he went out, with Rob Fleming at his side and Mitchell following him, both of them grim-faced and silent, yet their thoughts as plain as if they had shouted them aloud. They talked of anything save the trial as they waited, Rob doing his best to offer consolation, but Mitchell, although he tried to conceal it, convinced that Adam had brought disaster on himself.

The time dragged past; the court's deliberations were taking longer than either of his companions had expected, Adam thought, attempting vainly to hide his impatience. After an hour had gone by in desultory conversation to which he contributed very little, Mitchell said, with a mirthless smile, "Captain Broome must be putting up a fight for you, Adam." He hesitated and then plunged in, "For my own peace of mind—it won't go any further—*did* you give the order to abandon ship?"

It was Rob who answered him, with an indignant "Of course he did not, David! And—" He broke off when Adam warned him fiercely to hold his tongue. "I'm sorry, Adam. But we're both on your side, you know."

"Yes," Adam acknowledged flatly, ashamed of his outburst. "And I thank you, but—it's done, isn't it? There's no going back."

He lapsed into moody silence, and for all three of them, the summons to return to the courtroom came almost as a relief.

As he resumed his accustomed place, Adam's gaze went to his sword, lying on the baize-covered table, and he saw, as he had anticipated and feared, that the blade was pointing toward him. He squared his shoulders, bracing himself for the blow to fall, yet for all his efforts to concentrate on what the president was saying, he consciously heard only a few, disjointed words.

The court had found him guilty on all charges . . . he was to be cashiered from Her Majesty's service and was never to hold commissioned rank again in the Royal Navy . . . his name was to be erased from the roll of those gallant officers and men who had been awarded the Victoria Cross, and the decoration was forfeited, together with the campaign medals to which he had been entitled.

Numbly, he heard the president express his deep regret that so courageous an officer, with a promising career in front of him, should be lost to the naval service as a direct consequence of his addiction to alcohol. There was mention of the sad loss of life, but Adam, standing stiffly to attention, his heart turned to stone, took little of it in. He unpinned the medals from his coat, and someone —he had no idea who—took them from him. The members of the court filed out, and Rob Fleming touched his arm.

"I'm to see you ashore, Adam," he whispered awkwardly. "There's a boat standing by, and I'll have your gear sent to the Keppel's Head, when you've changed, if that's convenient. I . . . oh, God, I'm sorry. I—I don't know what to say."

"Then don't say anything, Rob," Adam bade him. "I'll change, and you can put me on the beach."

Feeling as if he had lived through a nightmare, Adam led the way blindly to the cabin he had occupied and started to divest himself of the uniform he would never wear again.

Chapter III

TWO O'CLOCK WAS striking from a nearby church tower when Adam, in civilian dress, stepped ashore at the sally port, the landing place for boats from the fleet anchorage. He took a constrained leave of Rob Fleming, offered his thanks but did not wait to watch the *Copenhagen*'s boat pull away, aware that, from the sternsheets, both Rob and the boat's midshipman were staring after him.

He ascended the stone steps briskly—those same steps that Nelson had used on his way to H.M.S. *Victory* and Trafalgar—experiencing a pang as he did so, with the realization that, in future, they would be barred to him.

Captain Broome had sent a note, before leaving the flagship, inviting him to dine in private that evening in town, but although he had thrust the note into his pocket, Adam knew that he could not accept the invitation. It was best to make a clean break; he would try to see Caroline, then—

A voice, crisp and authoritative, called him by name. Adam came to a halt, to see that a tall, well-dressed gentleman, whom he did not at first recognize, had descended from a closed carriage drawn up on the far side of the sally-port bridge. The stranger was, like his father, of unmistakably military bearing, but he had a gaunt, cadaverous face and walked with a pronounced limp—a man not in robust health, yet one who had not lost the habit of command. He did not look like a journalist, but . . . Adam frowned, recalling that he had observed this same man in court, seated in the row of chairs occupied mainly by the press. Instinctively he made to avoid an encounter, mumbling an apology, but the stranger called out to him to wait.

Drawing level, the man said quietly, "Mr. Vincent, I can understand your reluctance to hold converse with one who is unknown to you, after the ordeal you have endured so recently. I was in court throughout your trial."

"I am at a loss to imagine of what interest my trial could have been to you, sir," Adam countered stiffly.

"Oh, it was of interest," the tall stranger assured him. He gestured to the waiting carriage with the gold-headed cane he carried. "If you will join me, I should like to speak to you, and I will, of course, drive you to wherever is your destination. What I have to say to you is of some importance, and part, at least, may well be to your advantage."

Adam held his ground, still perplexed and reluctant to accede to the unexpected invitation. "Forgive me, sir," he began, "but you have the advantage of me. That is—"

The stranger smiled. "Mr. Vincent, permit me to introduce myself. I am Caroline Omerod's father. My name is Mason, Clive Mason, late of the East India Company's Political Service and now invalided, with the rank of major."

Caroline's *father?* Adam stared incredulously into the pale, high-boned face, seeking a likeness and finding a hint of it in the dark, expressive eyes and the engaging smile. Caroline, he recalled, had mentioned her father on several occasions. She had said that he and her mother had survived the long siege of Lucknow and—yes, that her father had been severely wounded and had taken retirement. Numbly he let Major Mason lead him to the carriage and usher him into its dark interior. The coachman whipped up his horses, and the heavy vehicle moved away from the curb.

"I was one of those your naval brigade helped to bring out of Lucknow," Mason volunteered. "So was my dear wife. I came out on a stretcher, so that I never personally made your acquaintance, Mr. Vincent. But I know the debt we of the garrison owed you and the other brave men under Sir Colin Campbell's command." He sighed and then went on gravely, "I also know the perhaps much greater debt my daughter owes you."

"Sir, I—" Flushed and ill at ease, Adam attempted to deny it, but the older man motioned him to silence.

"Listen, I beg you. Caroline has told me everything. She is heartbroken by the turn events have taken and by the sacrifice you have made—that is why I have been present throughout your trial. Frankly, I did not believe her when she confided to me what you intended to do, but . . . I have seen and heard you carry out your intention. I am aware of what it has cost you to keep the promise you made to her." With an abrupt change of tone, Major Mason added harshly, "It was, of course, my son-in-law—your commander, John Omerod—who was intoxicated and incapable, wasn't it? No—" he interrupted as Adam again attempted to protest. "Hear me out, Vincent. I know what was between you and Caroline—she has told me."

Had she, Adam wondered dully—had she told her father everything? Had she told him about the boy, and . . . dear God, had she told him about their last meeting and the recriminations she had heaped on his head, when he had been driven to confess how John Omerod's last hours were spent?

"It was your doing, Adam . . . you drove him over the edge. Your doing and mine, because we betrayed him. Is our son to grow up with a stigma always adhering to the name he must bear?"

She had wept, Adam remembered, bitter, distraught, and ready to reject him until he had given her the promise she had wanted. He stifled a sigh, making an effort to listen to what her father was saying to him.

"My daughter," Major Mason stated, his tone one that brooked no argument, "will not see or communicate with you again, Vincent. She has asked me to tell you that. She feels and feels very strongly that this is the price she must pay for her—well, let us call it infidelity, shall we? I hesitate to use a stronger word."

"But, sir—" Sick with dismay, Adam was moved to voice his dissent. "We were in love with each other. We—that is I am still deeply in love with Caroline. Believe me, sir, I—"

It was as if he had not spoken. Ignoring his protest, Mason said sternly, "Caroline and her child—my grandson—will leave for my residence this afternoon. You have made a very considerable sacrifice, Mr. Vincent, as a result of which Caroline's late husband is left with his honor intact, Caroline has his pension, and you yourself have nothing. They have even ordered that your Victoria Cross be forfeit, haven't they? You have paid and paid very dearly for your misconduct, and as I told you earlier, my daughter *is* in your debt, and I should like, if I can, to make reparation to you."

There was a brief silence, and then, with another quick change of tone, Major Mason observed, "I have interests in New Zealand, Mr. Vincent. I own land near Wellington, purchased through the New Zealand Company. I should be willing to make the deeds over to you, on the condition that you will go out there as soon as you can book a passage—and I will defray the cost of your passage. Are you willing to accept my offer?"

Like his own father, Adam thought bitterly, Caroline's father was also seeking to dispatch him to the colonies . . . even to pay his fare. He reddened and shook his head. "I thank you, no, sir. But I should like to see Caroline . . . to hear from her own lips that she wishes to have no more to do with me. Sir, I—"

"That is impossible," Mason said with finality. "But she entrusted me with a note for you. Perhaps you had better read it."

The note was brief—a mere two lines—and Adam's heart sank as he read it: *"Adam,"* it stated, *"I have decided that it will be best for both of us if we do not meet again. I am going to my parents' house with the boy."* The signature was simply "Caroline."

"I have assured my daughter that her wishes will be respected," Major Mason said. "You will not be admitted if you attempt to call on her, and we shall, in any case, be leaving here this afternoon."

Could it really be happening, Adam wondered; could it be true? Had Caroline's love been a transient emotion, to be discarded and forgotten, after all they had been to each other? He looked up to meet her father's gaze and read into it the same finality as his words—and Caroline's note—had expressed. Grasping at the last shreds of his composure, he managed somehow to contain himself and speak with dignity.

"Then there's no more to be said, sir, is there? Save to ask you to convey my respects to your daughter and—and assure her that I will bow to her wishes. I . . . if you please, sir, be so good as to set me down here."

"Very well." Major Mason did not attempt to detain him, but offered his hand and added, with evident sincerity, "I am sorry that I had to bring you such unwelcome tidings, my dear young man. And I am also sorry that you feel you must refuse my offer of the land in New Zealand. But, if you should change your mind—" He took a calling card from his pocket and scribbled a few words on it, in pencil. "This is the address of my man of affairs. Contact him if, on reflection, you are willing to reconsider the offer. Needless to say, I hope you will."

Adam took both the card and the offered hand, keeping a firm rein on his temper. The carriage drew up to the curb, and Caroline's father leaned across to open the door and permit him to alight. They had been driving along the waterfront, in the opposite direction from the lodgings Caroline had occupied when her hus-

band was alive, and the carriage, Adam saw, was turning around.
Major Mason, it seemed, was going to pick up his daughter. He
would take her away from Portsmouth, to wherever he and his
wife were living—take the child too, and . . . Adam started to
walk blindly away, numb with despair, realizing suddenly that he
was alone, with no purpose in life and no plans for the future. Until
this moment, he had planned to seek employment—any employment that would enable him to keep a wife and child—and, in the
fullness of time, when the period of her mourning came to an end,
to seek out Caroline and ask her to wed him. But now . . . Shoulders hunched, Adam moved on, his throat tight.

A little knot of men, crowding the pavement, blocked his way.
He was about to skirt them by stepping into the road when a
handwritten poster, displayed prominently outside the door of a
public house, the Bedford-in-Chase, caught his eye. This was, he
knew, a popular rendezvous for the commanders of newly commissioned ships to recruit their crews; but today, it appeared, the army
had occupied it for the same purpose, for the poster proclaimed

RECRUITING FOR SERVICE IN AUSTRALIA!
HER MAJESTY'S 40TH REGIMENT OF FOOT
DRAFT LEAVING SOON—INQUIRE WITHIN.
SERVE YOUR COUNTRY AND SEE THE WORLD.

Struck by the uncanny coincidence, Adam halted and read the
poster again, and the men on the pavement eyed him with curiosity, evidently taking him for an officer. One of them said, jerking
his head to the rear of the little group, "Yer carriage is waitin', sir
—not thinkin' o' enlistin', was yer?"

Enlisting in the army had been the last thing he had considered,
but . . . The carriage *had* stopped, as his informant had said, fifty
or sixty yards down the road, and Caroline's father was alighting
from it, Adam saw, leaning on his cane and watching him with as
much interest as were the would-be recruits gathered about the
door of the Bedford-in-Chase. The devil take it, he told himself
recklessly, what had he to lose? Major Mason wanted him to exile
himself in New Zealand, and his own father had suggested Australia as his future destination. And . . . Caroline, it seemed, never
wanted to set eyes on him again. He was accustomed to a service
life; perhaps that was all he was suited for, all he knew. Perhaps—

A scarlet-uniformed recruiting sergeant opened the inn door—a stout, fine-looking man, with medals for the Afghan and Gwalior campaigns pinned to his tunic.

"Come in, my lucky lads!" he exclaimed, holding the door wide. "You'll not take a better step in your young lives, and you'll not find a better regiment than the Excellers in the whole o' the British Army—or a better station than Australia! Sign on today and you'll be boarding the troopship in a few weeks' time, for a voyage halfway round the world, with adventure at the end of it. *And* good pay and conditions, with the chance to serve your country. Right, who's first, eh?"

The others hung back. Adam glanced to where Major Mason was standing and then stepped forward, his mind made up.

After a brief but searching inspection, the old sergeant nodded and led the way inside, motioning him to follow.

"It takes all sorts," he observed philosophically. "Creditors pressing you, are they?"

It was, Adam reflected cynically, as good an excuse as any that he could devise on the spur of the moment.

"You could say that, Sergeant," he answered quietly. "Certainly I want to get away from England."

"Then you've come to the right place," the sergeant told him, frowning as he again subjected Adam to a careful scrutiny. "Well, you look fit enough—you'll have no trouble passing the doctor. Not on the run from Her Majesty's Navy, are you?"

"No, Sergeant," Adam assured him. "I'm not."

The old sergeant grunted. "All right, you lads," he said, raising his voice as the other men came crowding in. "Into line there! That's the style . . . two and two."

A trifle sheepishly, the man who had sought to mock him took his place at Adam's side.

"Name of Burnaby," he offered. "Tom Burnaby. An' I'm sorry if I spoke out of turn."

He would have to assume a name that was not his own, Adam realized, in sudden panic—his father would take it very much amiss if he used the family surname. The recruiting sergeant seated himself at a table beside a gray-haired clerk and reached for a quill.

"Now, then," he invited, "your full name, *if* you please."

After a moment's hesitation, Adam answered him.

"Shannon, sir—Adam Shannon."

The sergeant's pen spluttered as he filled in the name.

* * *

Caroline had a visitor, with whom she was drinking tea, when Major Mason returned to her lodgings in Melville Road. For no reason that he could have explained, Clive Mason was more than a little shocked when the visitor rose, bowing in response to his hostess's introduction, and he recognized him as the lieutenant of marines, Thomas Lane, one of the witnesses at Vincent's court-martial.

"Mr. Lane," Caroline told him, with a hint of asperity, "came to tell me the result of Adam Vincent's trial, Papa. And as you had not seen fit to do so, I was grateful to him." She expressed no regrets but, turning her smile with bewitching charm on the elderly marine officer, offered him her hand.

"He has to leave now, haven't you, Mr. Lane? And we, too, must shortly be on our way, if we are to reach Hamble before dark."

Lane accepted his dismissal, and when he had gone, Caroline turned to her father.

"Adam was sentenced to be cashiered?"

"Yes, that was the court's decision. The only one, in the circumstances, since the boy offered no defense, but—" Mason frowned. "For all that, a harsh one. He kept his promise to you to the letter, Caroline."

"I was sure he would. Poor Adam!" Caroline gestured to the tea tray on the table in front of her. "Tea, Papa? It's still quite hot."

He shook his head, again faintly shocked by his daughter's attitude but reluctant to judge her. "No, thank you. As you told Lieutenant Lane, if we're to reach home before dark, we should be on our way. Is the baby ready? I take it your luggage went this morning, in the wagonette?"

Caroline gathered her shawl about her. "Yes, the luggage went hours ago. And little Jon has been ready since lunchtime—that half-witted nurse kept him from his afternoon sleep, although I told her that you would probably be late. So I expect he will wail most of the way. He's a difficult child, heaven knows!" She paused, eyeing her father speculatively. "Did you talk to Adam Vincent?"

"Yes, I talked to him."

"And you gave him my note?"

"Yes, of course."

"Did he—that is, did he accept it? Does he understand that I cannot see him again, Papa? Because I cannot, I—oh, God, if I had never met him, John might be alive today!"

For a moment, her father did not reply. He had told Adam Vincent that she was heartbroken, but . . . He studied his daughter's lovely, untroubled face and wondered what she really felt—if, indeed, she felt anything at all—for the unhappy young man who had been her lover and who, it seemed not improbable, had fathered her child.

Finally he answered her question, his voice flat and carefully controlled. "He understood, my dear. You made your feelings plain enough."

"I had to, Papa," Caroline defended. "Adam wanted me to *marry* him, if you please, when my mourning for poor John was over! I could not possibly marry him, could I, when his career is in ruins? What will he do, now that he's no longer a serving naval officer? He's not trained for anything else. He's been in the navy since he was twelve years old!"

Adam Vincent, her father thought, had enlisted in the 40th Foot, as a common soldier. The man who had signed on with him—a decent young fellow named Burnaby—had confirmed it; and for the cost of a paltry five sovereigns, Mason had extracted a promise from him to report regularly on Vincent's progress. Whatever Caroline felt—or did not feel—Vincent was on *his* conscience, and there was still the land in New Zealand. Perhaps, after a taste of life in the ranks, the poor young devil would change his mind about accepting the deeds. It should not present much difficulty to arrange to buy him out of the regiment; there were still some strings he could pull, and . . . Mason looked again at his daughter. He would not tell her what Vincent had done, he decided; she would undoubtedly pour scorn on the young man's choice of a new career.

He shrugged noncommittally and changed the subject, taking his fob watch from his waistcoat pocket.

"Shall we make a move, then, my dear? The carriage is at the door, and as you know, your dear mama is not in the best of health. She will worry and upset herself if we are late arriving home. Call your nursemaid and have her bring the child down."

Caroline smiled. "Gladly, Papa. I shall be thankful to leave this place." She took a key from her reticule and gave it to him. "Be so good as to hand this over to the landlord, will you please? He's been waiting in the kitchen since I don't know when—anxious to find new tenants, I suppose. And—" She hesitated, looking up at her father with dark, expressive eyes. "I'm afraid I owe him some rent. Only a few pounds, but if you could be very kind and settle with him, I . . . I'd be very grateful."

Clive Mason accepted the key. The arrears of rent amounted to considerably more than his daughter had implied, but he paid what the lodging house keeper asked, and the man thanked him profusely and, eager to show his appreciation, bustled about, carrying various pieces of baggage out to the waiting carriage.

The nursemaid, a slim, pretty girl, came downstairs with the baby, whom she had well muffled up for the journey. Major Mason studied the small face, half hidden beneath a thick woolen shawl, and found it was hard to detect any telling likeness in so young a child. Little Jon certainly had his mother's cast of countenance, her finely chiseled nose and small, rosebud mouth; but his eyes were blue, and such wisps of hair as had escaped from his knitted bonnet were undoubtedly fair. Contrary to his mother's disparaging forecast, the little fellow was sleeping peacefully, and Mason warmed to him. Young Jonathan Clive Omerod might well come to bless his parentage when he grew to man's estate, and indeed—

"We are ready and waiting, Papa," Caroline reminded him impatiently, disrupting his thoughts. "And I do believe it's starting to rain."

"Very well, my dear." Her father gave her his arm, and with the nursemaid preceding them, they hurried out to the carriage, where the baby—still sleeping—was transferred to a wicker cot, and the nursemaid, unbidden, climbed onto the box beside the coachman.

Alone with her father in the interior of the well-padded carriage, Caroline became more talkative, asking about the friends her parents had made since their return from India and the social life in Hamble, where they had now made their home.

"We do not go out a lot these days," Clive Mason confessed. "Your mother's health—and, come to that, my own—restricts us a good deal. But we entertain. The house is large and beautifully situated, overlooking the river, and we've been fortunate in finding a staff of excellent servants. I think you will be happy with us, my dear. In fact, I feel sure you will. True, there are not many young people in the village; but one of our friends, Sir Christopher Forsyth, who was in the Indian Political Service with me, has a large family of about your age. His eldest son, Leonard, is a frequent visitor. He's second-in-command of the Seventieth Regiment, stationed at their depot in Canterbury, and he seems to get plenty of leave. There are two—no, three daughters, one of whom is married. We'll ask them over to meet you. The married daughter has young children, I believe."

Caroline listened, displaying little enthusiasm. After a while, she asked unexpectedly, taking him by surprise, "Papa, when you spoke to him this morning, did Adam Vincent tell you what he intended to do, now that the navy has dispensed with his services?"

Why should she not be told, her father asked himself, reluctantly revising his earlier decision, which had been made when she had shown so little interest in the fate of the young man she had once professed to love. He said gruffly, "He did not confide in me, but as it chanced, I saw what he did. He enlisted in the Fortieth Foot—a regiment which is currently serving in Australia. They were recruiting in town."

Caroline turned in her seat to stare at him in wide-eyed astonishment. "Adam *enlisted?* In the ranks, do you mean—as a common soldier?"

"Yes, as a common soldier, Caroline. He could do nothing else. Commissions are not granted to cashiered officers, you know."

"Yes, I know that. But to enlist in the army . . . and go out to Australia, of all places! I can't believe it."

"It is the truth, my dear." Relenting in the face of her evident concern, Clive Mason reached for his daughter's hand. "I was able to make contact with a young fellow who enlisted with him, in the same regiment. In return for a small payment, he has promised to keep me informed of Adam Vincent's doings. I thought, in the circumstances, that you would want to know how he was faring."

Again his daughter surprised him. Her slim shoulders rose in an indifferent shrug, and she said, with biting emphasis, "Well, you may wish to know what happens to him, Papa, but *I* do not! Adam has put himself beyond the pale, as far as I'm concerned. He must have—oh, goodness, he must have gone out of his mind to do such a thing! I—please understand, Papa, I do not wish to hear his name mentioned again. Certainly not whilst I'm living in Hamble with you and Mama."

She lapsed into a repressive silence, defying her father to break it, as the carriage bowled swiftly along, eating up the miles, rain lashing against the windows and the light starting to fade.

After a while, the baby wakened and emitted a plaintive cry. Caroline bent forward and scooped him into her arms. She did not,

as Clive Mason had expected she would, whisper endearments in
order to soothe him or give him the breast. Instead she held him
up, stripping off bonnet and shawl with rough, impatient hands.

"Look at him, Papa!" she urged. "He's your grandson. Jonathan
Clive Omerod, and no one shall call him anything else. He's not a
bastard, whatever you may think or—or whatever Adam Vincent
may have claimed. I'm your only child, and little Jon is your heir.
Take him, Papa—please take him!"

She *was* his only child, Mason told himself. She was his beloved
daughter, his beautiful Caroline, whom he had adored during her
early years in India but whom, because the climate had necessitated it, he had been compelled to send to England to school when
she had reached her tenth year. He had missed her growing up,
had taken leave only twice during those formative years, and, on
the second occasion, had returned only in time to give her away at
her wedding to John Omerod. And the Sepoy Mutiny had kept
him imprisoned in Lucknow so that, when her marriage had
started to go wrong, neither he nor her mother had been there to
help and counsel her.

He took the baby from her and, for the first time, held him close.
Little Jon looked up at him with wide, innocent blue eyes and then,
soothed by the swaying of the carriage, closed them again and
drifted back to sleep.

Across the child's downy head, Caroline smiled at him. "Thank
you, dearest Papa," she said softly. "Thank you!"

Chapter IV

ADAM HAD COMPLETED the initial three-week recruit training course, held at the Chatham depot of the 31st Regiment, before the officer who was to command the 40th's draft made his appearance.

He had met with few difficulties until then. The instructors, drawn from both regiments, were veteran NCOs who, if demanding a high standard, were patient with the less able of the recruits and more than ready to encourage those displaying ability and keenness. From the outset, his naval training and the experience of serving with the *Shannon*'s brigade on land in India stood him in good stead. The *Shannon*'s seamen had drilled like infantry, marched for long distances carrying heavy packs, and the rifle contingent in which he had served had been issued with the Enfields, which had replaced the old Brown Bess muskets. Training as an infantryman thus presented no problems, but Adam found it less easy to accustom himself to the close contact of barracks life, the rigid discipline and lack of freedom—more marked than in even the tautest of naval ships of war—and, most trying of all, the monotonous, badly cooked food.

There were times when he deeply regretted the impulse that had led him to enlist in the ranks; times when the uncouth company of some of his fellow recruits and the endless menial chores he was called upon to perform irked him almost beyond endurance. But by the end of the third week, he had contrived to adjust to his changed circumstances and even to take pride in the standard of competence he had achieved.

The fifty men who composed the draft for Australia had treated him, at first, with suspicious resentment. They had nicknamed him the Toff and resisted all Adam's attempts to establish friendly relations with them. But after a while, when they found that he was willing to share his skills and knowledge with any who asked, their resentment had vanished, giving place to respect. Young Burnaby had been the first to seek his aid. A cheerful, happy-go-lucky lad, possessed of some education, he was clumsy and inept, constantly in trouble for his poor performances on the drill square and shooting range, for losing his kit, failing to clean his rifle to the army's exacting standard, and being late on parade. With the aid of Adam's painstaking tuition, his improvement was soon evident, and it had not been long before a number of other recruits had followed his example—some a trifle sheepishly, but not many now held aloof from him, although his nickname had stuck.

His platoon sergeant, a fine old soldier named Doran, was quick to appreciate his merits. Doran had fought in every action in the Sutlej campaign and in the trenches in the Crimea, earning the Sardinian *al valore* decoration and a Meritorious Service Medal for heroism in the final attack on the Russian redan and the capture of Sebastopol. He had been badly wounded but, anxious to continue his service, had transferred from the 31st to the 40th Regiment in the hope that, in faraway Australia, his physical infirmities would escape official notice. A widower, the old sergeant occupied a small, curtained-off section of the barrackroom, where he brewed tea in the evenings and relaxed with a foul-smelling clay pipe in the company of some of his cronies, talking nostalgically of half-forgotten battles and old comrades, whose battlefield graves bore witness to their sacrifice and the regiment's glory.

It was held to be an honor to be invited into Doran's inner sanctum, and Adam was at once pleased and surprised when the invitation was extended to him at the end of a day on the ranges. He went in and was waved hospitably to a sagging, chintz-covered armchair by the stove.

"Smoke, if you want to," Doran greeted him. "And I take it you won't refuse a cup o' tea?"

The tea was strong and bitter, the air blue with tobacco smoke, but Adam lit his own pipe and sipped cautiously at the tea. Sergeant Doran came to the point without preamble. "You're good, Shannon—you're very good. But to my mind, you're just a mite *too* good. D'you understand me?"

"I'm not sure I do, Sergeant," Adam evaded.

"I think you do, lad. You're no raw recruit, are you? You've served Her Majesty before, *and* on the field o' battle, if I'm any judge. That's true, ain't it?"

"Yes, it's true. But—" Adam reddened. "That is—"

Doran waved him to silence with his pipestem.

"I'm not one to pry nor tell no tales, but I like to know whatever there is to know about my men. Were you an officer?"

It was no use attempting to deny it. Adam nodded, his color deepening. "Yes, in the navy, Sergeant Doran."

Doran's leathery face wore an oddly satisfied smile. "That's what I figured, and I reckon you didn't quit willingly. Cashiered, were you?"

"Yes. For the loss of my ship. I was held to have been drunk on duty."

Once again Doran's blackened pipestem described an admonitory circle. "All right, you needn't say no more. Far as I'm concerned you're number eight-five-six Private Shannon and you've not touched a drop o' liquor since you've been here at the depot, so I'll presume you've learned your lesson. Keep that up and you'll make a good soldier. Fact, I'm going to recommend that you're made up to corporal when you're through here—you've earned a step up, and you know how to handle men. There's just one thing, though—" He paused, eyeing Adam speculatively from beneath beetling gray brows. "I'd not want what I'm going to tell you to go no further."

"It won't, Sergeant," Adam assured him.

Doran helped himself to another brimming mug of tea. "The draft commander's due back from leave tomorrow—Captain Marcus Fisher," he said, frowning. "Young feller, he is—not above twenty-two. Come to us from the cavalry, the Fifteenth Hussars— no war service. His pa's a rich City o' London merchant—bought young Mr. Fisher his captaincy."

The sergeant lowered his voice. "I've not had all that much to do with the young gentleman, but let's say he's not the officer *I'd* have chosen to command the draft. You'd be wise to watch your step with him, Shannon, because he'll spot you for what you are as soon as he claps eyes on you. And he don't like gentlemen rankers —I know that for a fact. He gave one decent youngster we had in Fermoy a hard time, for no better reason, seemingly, than because his uncle was master of a foxhunt." He shrugged and reached for the teapot. "Like another cup, would you, before you turn in?"

Adam thanked him and declined. He was not unduly worried by

what the old sergeant had told him. The depot officers, including the commandant, had treated him no differently from the other recruits, whatever they might know or speculate concerning his past. The court-martial findings had been reported in the local newspapers but given no prominence, and he had no reason to suppose that the newly arrived draft commander was likely to single him out—provided that, as Doran had advised, he watched his step.

The following morning, the recruits were ordered to parade for Captain Fisher's inspection, and they did so eagerly, proud of their soldierly bearing and immaculate uniforms. It was, however, to prove a lengthy ordeal, for which they had not been prepared.

Fisher was revealed as a small, dapper young man, with ginger whiskers framing his face and a cavalry mustache, retained from his previous regiment, together with a pronounced lisp, which, in the past, Adam had come to associate with the officers of certain fashionable cavalry regiments. His commands, delivered in this manner, were not always audible to the marching men, who inevitably fell into confusion, and the drill movements and formations that had been practiced so assiduously had to be repeated.

The midday cookhouse bugle was ignored. Captain Fisher stood, tapping his highly polished boots impatiently with his cane, and the men, sweating under full packs, marched up and down in front of him, the sun beating down on them and the dust raised by their plodding feet wafted, in choking clouds, into their faces.

"They are a slovenly, idle lot, Sar'nt Doran!" he complained loudly. "For the Lord's sake, they will have to do better than this before I'm satisfied! You'll have to take them for extra drill every morning from now on—I'll see the depot commandant to arrange it. God's truth, man, we are due to embark for Sydney in ten days time, and you are the senior NCO! I'd expected a higher standard from you, I must confess." He took out his pocket watch, affecting to study it in surprise. "Good heavens, is that the time? All right, Sar'nt—dismiss them. I'll be ready for kit inspection at two o'clock. *Punctually* at two o'clock, mind."

Sergeant Doran, it was evident, was fuming, but he came smartly to attention and saluted before bawling the order to dismiss the parade.

Kit inspection, Adam knew, had been anticipated for the following day, giving the men all evening to prepare for it; now they would have to devote their dinner hour to the cleaning and scouring, the polishing and setting out of every item of kit they possessed, in the meticulous order that army regulations demanded.

With the aid of hastily summoned volunteers from the depot staff and their own instructors, it was done, but, predictably, the result fell short of Captain Fisher's expectations. With his cane, the draft's commanding officer flicked at neatly rolled blankets and greatcoats, at folded tunics and piles of socks and underwear, leaving a disordered mess in his wake and the recruits in a state of shocked dismay as they watched their painstaking efforts demolished and saw their sergeant publicly humiliated.

"This won't do, Sar'nt Doran!" the young officer drawled. "It simply will not do. This barrackroom is filthy, and half your men's kit is missing. And look at this rifle!"

Adam's bed was at the end of the long row, and it was his rifle Fisher chose to examine. Breaking it open, he held it to the light from a nearby window and squinted contemptuously down the gleaming interior of the rifled barrel.

"Filthy!" he stated. "Thick with oil! Put this man on a charge, Sar'nt Doran. If there's one thing I will not tolerate it's a dirty rifle. Don't you realize, man," he added, addressing Adam, "this is the weapon you are required to fight with? When you go into action, your life and the lives of your comrades will depend on it!"

Intercepting a warning glance from Doran, Adam stood woodenly at attention, saying nothing. Fisher threw the rifle back at him. "Well," he demanded, "what have you to say for yourself? Speak up, man—I'm listening!"

"I've nothing to say, sir," Adam responded.

"Haven't you, now? Good Gad, Sar'nt Doran, where in the world did you find this dumbcluck?"

"He's a good man, sir," Doran defended. "The best in the draft. I'm recommending him for a stripe, sir."

Captain Fisher made an elaborate show of astonishment. *"This* fellow? A man who doesn't know how to clean his rifle? Or, come to that, how to prepare his kit for inspection?" The cane descended, scattering a pile of gray army shirts and sending Adam's mess kit and water bottle after them. "You're wanting to promote *him* corporal?"

"Yes, sir," Sergeant Doran confirmed obstinately. "Like I told you, he's a good man, sir."

"Well, you amaze me!" Fisher exclaimed. His pale, slate-blue eyes held an odd gleam as he studied Adam in silence for a long moment. Then he said, frowning, "There's something about you . . . demmed if I know what it is, though. What's your name, man?"

"Shannon, sir." Adam met the young captain's baleful gaze without flinching.

"Shannon, eh? Is that not the name of a naval ship—one of Her Majesty's steam frigates, if I'm not mistaken? And—yes, by George, of an Irish river! I thought it sounded familiar. Is it really your name, my man? Or—" Fisher smiled unpleasantly. "Is it just a name you picked, to avoid using your own? You're not a deserter from the Royal Navy, are you, Private Shannon?"

"No, sir, I am not." Despite the flagrant attempt to goad him, Adam managed to speak without heat, mindful of Sergeant Doran's warning. He resisted Fisher's effort to outstare him, his expression carefully blank, and received a nod of approval from the old sergeant as the draft commander finally passed on, to complete his inspection on the opposite side of the room. His querulous, lisping voice continued to express displeasure at what he found, and it came as no surprise when, following his departure, Sergeant Doran announced that the kit inspection was to be repeated next day.

"And reveille for you is to be an hour early, my lads," Doran said flatly. "You'll muster on the square for arms drill every morning this week."

The men grumbled bitterly among themselves, but by the end of the week their passing-out parade was held and the salute taken by the depot commandant, whose praise went some way to compensate for their own officer's strictures. They were granted embarkation leave—the first leave they had had since their enlistment—and Adam found himself promoted to the rank of corporal in depot orders.

It was a small enough achievement, but it pleased him mightily, and the men of his platoon, led by Tom Burnaby, surrounded him in a gleeful crowd to insist that it was cause for celebration.

"We got to wet them stripes, Shannon," Burnaby told him, grinning. "An' seein' they've given us just twelve-hour passes, the only ones that can go home are the lucky sods that live round here. *My* folks live in bloomin' Leeds! But we've got our pay, and we don't have to be back in barracks till midnight. Come on, will you? There's over a dozen of us ready an' willing to shout you a beer, in return for what you done for us, an' the King's Arms is just down the road!"

Adam yielded to their insistence. They marched out of the depot gates together, brave in their scarlet tunics and crested forage caps, happily exchanging banter with the corporal of the guard who inspected their passes, and laughing in good-humored derision when he warned them to be back by midnight in a state of sobriety.

"We ain't bin let out o' barracks for a month, Corporal," one of the youngsters retorted, "an' our tongues is hanging out. You'll let us back in, won't you, even if we're a bit merry? After all, we're going foreign in a couple o' days, an' the Lord only knows when we'll see England again!"

"If it's left to me," the guard commander answered, "I know 'ow to turn a blind eye, lad. But there's some as don't, so watch it, will you?"

It was a convivial if slightly rowdy evening, and despite his initial misgivings, Adam entered into the spirit of the gathering and enjoyed himself. He had forced himself, during the strenuous weeks of training, not to think of Caroline, but he thought of her as he stood in the cosy taproom of the King's Arms and found, to his own surprise, that the pain engendered by her loss was no longer acute. It was there, of course; he had loved her so deeply and passionately that losing her still hurt him, but . . . he had become resigned to the fact that she had rejected him, and it was with a feeling of relief that he contemplated his imminent departure to the other side of the world and the prospect of a new life, in which Caroline would have no part.

He drank as sparingly as he could, restricting himself to cider, determined that he would shepherd his little party back to the barracks well before their passes expired. The recruits, with no such inhibitions, downed their beers and engaged in some spirited horseplay; but the landlord was tolerant, as they did no damage, and when the time came for them to leave, they obeyed Adam's summons without argument—although with noisy ribaldry, their voices raised in song.

They laughed and joked as they made their way through the darkened streets, all of them in a state of happy insobriety, but Adam managed to silence them as they approached the barrack gates, and, recalling the guard commander's promise to turn a blind eye, he was not unduly concerned. There had been quite a few occasions during his naval service when he had turned a blind

eye to seamen returning from a run ashore in a much worse state
than that of these young soldiers, and it did not occur to him to
wonder whether any of the depot officers held different views.

To his dismay, however, Captain Marcus Fisher seemingly did,
for as they reached the gate, he emerged from the guardroom to
stand there, tapping his boot with his cane, the guard commander
at his side, holding a raised lantern and looking woodenly to his
front, as if to absolve himself from responsibility for the officer's
presence.

"Ah, *Corporal* Shannon, is it not?" Fisher greeted, with thinly
disguised sarcasm. "Devil take you, man—is this the way you exercise your new authority? You and these recruits are drunk and
disorderly—disgustingly drunk! I could hear you coming from half
a mile away! You're a disgrace to your uniform and to the regiment, the whole miserable bunch of you! What have you to say for
yourself, eh?"

Adam stood at attention, saying nothing, and the men, sensing
that he was in trouble, made an attempt to form up behind him.
Unhappily, two of them were unable to keep their feet, and
Burnaby, who had been supported by one of his comrades, lost his
precarious balance as he tried to reach Adam's side and fell igno-
miniously flat on his face. He jumped up, hiccuping loudly and
plastered with mud, to confront Fisher defiantly.

"I'm drunk, sir, but Shannon ain't. An' none of us is disorderly.
Why—"

Fisher's glance froze him. "When I want your opinion, my man,
I will ask for it. All right, be off with you to your barrackroom. I'll
deal with you in the morning, when you've had time to sober up.
Not you, Corporal Shannon—I've decided to place you on a
charge. Lock him up in the guardroom," he bade the guard commander. "Go on—jump to it!"

"What's the charge, sir?" the NCO asked, his voice carefully
expressionless.

"Charge? Good God, you should know that—you're an old soldier. Drunk on duty. No, conduct prejudicial to good order and
military discipline—that'll serve. I'll have him up before the commandant tomorrow."

He turned on his heel and strode off into the darkness, still
tapping his boot with his cane. The sound of his footsteps slowly
receded, and the corporal of the guard clapped a not unfriendly
hand on Adam's shoulder.

"Come on, lad," he said gruffly. "You heard the officer—into the guardroom with you. We're brewing up, and I'll see you get a cupper. I'll have to lock you up, but you won't be too uncomfortable. There's a camp bed and plenty o' blankets." He studied Adam's face curiously. "You look sober enough to me. Got it in for you, has he—Fisher, I mean?"

"He appears to have," Adam conceded reluctantly. "But don't ask me why. I don't know any reason."

The corporal ushered him into the stone-built guardroom, gesturing to a barred space at its far end. Followed by the eyes of the men of the guard, Adam crossed to the padlocked gate and, ducking his head, stepped through it, to hear it click shut behind him.

The corporal lingered, his key in his hand. He said, lowering his voice, "I don't know the rights or wrongs of it, Shannon, but whilst we was waiting for you and your lads to report back to barracks, the captain let slip that he reckoned you'd bin an officer. A naval officer, he seemed to think. He wasn't sure, mind, but he said he was going to find out before you left here." He waited, clearly expecting confirmation or denial, but Adam gave him neither, his thoughts in chaos. It should not be too difficult for Fisher to find out the truth, he knew, but . . . time was short. The draft was due to embark for Sydney in two days.

He passed an anxious night, sleeping fitfully. Old Sergeant Doran appeared just before the guard changed, and seating himself on Adam's truckle bed in the barred lockup, he announced gravely, "Fisher'll have you off the draft if he presses his charges, Shannon. But I had a word with him, an' he agreed he would drop the charges, provided that you'll be willing to accept *his* punishment, once we embark."

Adam eyed the sergeant uncertainly. The mere thought of missing the draft and being compelled to remain in England filled him with dismay. "What sort of punishment do you suppose he has in mind, Sergeant Doran?"

Doran shrugged. "Your guess is as good as mine. But I reckon he'll reduce you to the ranks for sure, and that's not liable to be too great a hardship, is it, now?"

"No—no, it's not." Adam sighed. "But before heaven, I don't want to be taken off the draft! That's the very last thing I want."

Doran nodded his satisfaction. "That's what I reckoned you'd say, because—" His faded blue eyes held a fugitive gleam of anticipation as he laid a folded newspaper on the bed. "Because, if this paper's to be believed, we could well be going on active service, soon after we land in Sydney! They say there'll be war in New Zealand, between the settlers an' them Maoris. There's a couple o' Queen's ships on the way to Auckland, an' the governor's asked for troops from Australia. Them settlers is organizing theirselves into militia, but they won't be able to fight a war without properly trained regiments, will they? And our regiment's the present garrison in Australia. It'll be the first to go, Shannon."

Adam's heart lifted. "Do you really think so, Sergeant?"

"Aye," Doran asserted. He gestured to the newspaper and rose. "Read that, lad, and you won't have no doubts." He grinned. "I've had me fill o' peacetime soldiering. Well—shall I tell Captain Fisher that you'll accept his punishment?"

What, Adam asked himself, could Fisher do, when all was taken into account? He inclined his head. "Yes, if you will, Sergeant Doran. And thank you."

When Doran had gone, he settled down to read the newspaper report from Auckland. The headlines read, WAR CLOUDS OVER NEW ZEALAND.

The governor, Colonel Thomas Gore-Browne, has requested that imperial troops should be sent to aid in quelling a Maori rebellion in the Taranaki area, where settlers have been attacked and driven from their farms.

The trouble apparently arose because a Maori chief refused to permit the sale of land urgently required for settlement, after negotiations had been concluded with the native owner of the disputed land, one Te Teira.

The Maori tribes' recent decision to elect a king is causing grave concern in the colony, raising fears that tribes who for many years have engaged in fierce internecine battles may unite to wage war against the colonists.

The newly elected king is said to be a famous old warrior by the odd name of Potatau, although other influential chiefs are believed behind what has become known here as the King Movement.

We understand that, in response to the governor's request, troops will be sent here from Australia as soon as possible, and that a Royal Navy frigate, H.M.S. *Niger,* is under orders to proceed here.

The guard commander interrupted Adam's reading. "Seems it's your lucky day, Shannon," he announced cheerfully. "The charges have been withdrawn, an' I've got the order to release you." He unlocked the door and waved to Adam to follow him. "Your draft's to embark aboard the transport *Pomona* first thing tomorrow morning, so on your way, lad. And good luck to you."

Adam smiled his relief and hastened to obey him.

The *Pomona* was lying in the river at Gravesend. She was an old transport, built twenty years earlier as a convict carrier, but during the Crimean War she had been converted to auxiliary steam-screw and rigged as a bark for use as a horse transport. She had just completed coaling when the 40th's draft embarked, and her decks bore a liberal coating of coal dust, as did the weary, sweating seamen working to batten down hatches and prepare for sea.

The soldiers were directed to cramped quarters on the orlop deck, where it quickly became evident to them that their bunk bays had seen much service as stalls for horses; they were clean but decidedly spartan, ill lit and airless. Adam, accustomed to a cabin of his own on the gun deck of the *Lancer,* looked about him with a disgust he found hard to disguise and, envying the *Pomona*'s crew their hammocks on the mess deck above, was further dismayed to learn that, across the passageway, a hundred and thirty convicts were accommodated.

"I thought transportation to Australia ceased years ago," he confided to Sergeant Doran. "Has that changed?"

The sergeant shrugged, and a number of the crew, overhearing Adam's question, replied to it with a dry grin.

"They're still taking convicts in Western Australia, matey— that's where this lot are goin'. We put 'em ashore in Perth, see? An' you lads'll be responsible for guardin' 'em during our passage." His grin widened. "But they won't give you no trouble. Chosen for good conduct, they are, an' promised land grants in the colony when they've served their time. And there's no women, more's the pity—but I guess that makes for a quiet life!"

But there were to be women among the passengers, Adam learned—free emigrants, bound for Melbourne and Sydney, with their husbands and families, whose accommodation was only fractionally better than that of the soldiers, and a handful traveling first class, who would occupy upper-deck cabins and take their meals with the ship's officers in the commodious cuddy in the stern.

The emigrants embarked next morning, when the decks had been hosed down and the last water lighter had cast off and made for the shore. There were some thirty of them, all told, twenty being children. They were soberly dressed, respectable folk, carrying heavy hessian sacks containing the provisions they would require for the voyage and the pots and pans with which they would cook them. Most had trunks in addition, which were winched up and lined up on deck, for their owners to claim them, and at Adam's suggestion the soldiers went to assist in taking baggage below, which won them grateful thanks and ready smiles, particularly from the women.

Finally, a tender came out, laden with yet more trunks and the half-dozen privileged holders of first-class tickets, who were received courteously by the ship's master. Four were elderly married couples, the other two a mother and daughter with whom, it seemed, Captain Marcus Fisher was already acquainted, for when they had bowed in response to the master's greeting, Fisher stepped forward to hail them by name and offer the elder of the two his arm.

"Mrs. Carmichael—Miss Emily! How delightful to see you again. Permit me to escort you below. Which is your baggage? This?" He indicated two leather trunks, surrounded by hatboxes and packing cases and a number of smaller packages and cases, which two seamen had just taken from the baggage net and stacked neatly in front of him.

The daughter, who looked about seventeen or eighteen, gave vent to a little gasp. "Oh, not *all* those, Captain Fisher! Just the two trunks and the hatboxes and Mama's reticule. But you cannot possibly carry them—the trunks are very heavy."

She was a pretty girl, Adam observed, her fair hair worn in ringlets about her small, piquant face, and her eyes of a deep blue, wide-set and beguilingly innocent. She was well dressed but not elegantly so, with a fur tippet and a cloak of dark brown velvet topped by a bonnet laced tightly beneath her chin. Without conscious thought and forgetful of his present role, he smiled at her, only to be swiftly brought to earth by Captain Fisher.

"Don't worry, Miss Emily—my fellows can shift the trunks. Here you—what's your name? Shannon, isn't it? Don't stand there grinning like an ape—make yourself useful. Bring these trunks to the cabin flat. Jump to it, man!"

Burnaby, who was standing nearby, moved to help him, but Adam waved him away. He lifted one of the trunks and, balancing it on his shoulder, picked up the other and said politely, "If you would care to show me where you want these stowed, Miss Carmichael, I'll be happy to shift them for you."

The girl looked surprised for a moment—clearly she had not expected a common soldier to speak in so educated an accent—but, recovering herself, she gave Adam a grateful smile and led the way below. "I'm not sure which are our cabins, Mr. . . . Shannon, isn't it? But I suppose there will be someone to tell us."

Her supposition, in the form of a white-jacketed steward, proved correct, and Adam followed her into a spacious single-berth cabin on the starboard side and set down both trunks.

"Which is your mother's, Miss Carmichael? I'll take it to her cabin, if you wish."

Emily Carmichael shook her head. "No, leave them both here, if you please. Mama is not very strong, you see, so I shall unpack for her." Her blue eyes studied his face with a bewilderment that did not escape Adam's notice, but he forestalled the question he sensed she was about to ask, hearing Fisher's voice coming from the passageway.

"I'll see the heavy baggage stowed in the hold," he offered. "If that's all, Miss Carmichael."

"I . . . oh, yes, thank you very much. Our boxes are all marked —I did them myself. We're bringing some of our household treasures out to Sydney—china and glass, that sort of thing. And paintings, for my father." She smiled. "He's already out there, you see—he's a High Court judge—and I'm so excited at the prospect of seeing him again. But—" Her small face clouded. "It will be quite a long time before I do, I suppose. I mean, it's a very long voyage—over two months, I believe. I've never been on a long voyage before, and I'm a bit frightened, to tell you the truth, Mr. Shannon, in case we run into bad weather before I've got my sea legs. But I don't suppose that worries you, does it? I mean, you will have been on long voyages before?"

Adam answered without thought. "Oh, yes—to China and India. But don't worry your head about bad weather. The Channel's usually like a millpond at this time of year." He was enlarging on this when Fisher entered, to eye him with a disapproving scowl, and he broke off, coming rigidly to attention. "I'll see to your packing cases, miss," he said hastily, and made to leave the cabin.

Emily Carmichael, with misplaced gratitude, took a shilling from her pocket and sought to place it in his hand, repeating her thanks, and Fisher barked furiously, "No need for that, Miss Emily! My men are here to make themselves useful, don't you see? I don't intend to permit any idleness during our passage. All right, Shannon, get on with it! There's a whole pile of baggage waiting to be stowed. And don't forget you're still on a charge, which I've yet to deal with."

It was an unpleasant reminder, and Adam reddened. As he left the cabin he heard Emily Carmichael say, "He seems such a well-spoken young man, Mr. Fisher, and he's been most helpful—" and Fisher's contemptuous "Don't you believe it, Miss Emily. Shannon is a drunken rogue and, if I'm any judge, a deserter from the navy into the bargain. Furthermore, he's on a serious charge."

Adam did not wait to hear more. In a barely controlled rage, he went back on deck to assist with the baggage stowing and learned, when the task was completed, that he had been rostered for sentry duty during the convicts' exercise period. Fisher's second-in-command, a young ensign named Edwards, having passed on the order, eyed him speculatively.

"What have you done to fall from the captain's graces, Corporal Shannon? Captain Fisher's, that is. He told me you're on a serious charge and I'm to bring you up before him tomorrow morning."

"You had better ask Captain Fisher, sir," Adam returned, with bitterness. "I think he wants to reduce me to the ranks."

The *Pomona* weighed anchor the following morning. In the bustle of departure, Captain Fisher spent his time on deck, in close attendance on Emily Carmichael and her mother, the charge seemingly forgotten, and Adam, on Sergeant Doran's advice, kept well out of his way. The old transport proceeded downriver under her engines and, emerging into the North Sea, ran into an unseasonable gale, which sent the temperature plummeting. An icy northeasterly wind began to whip viciously across the open deck, sending the passengers—including Fisher—posthaste below. The wind persisted, growing in force, and the *Pomona* revealed herself as unweatherly, rolling unpleasantly as she battled her way southward under storm canvas. Then, as they entered the Dover Strait, the storm died as suddenly as it had arisen, and bright sunlight welcomed first the convicts and then the passengers back to their respective parts of the deck.

Adam was again on duty, supervising the convicts as they exercised on the railed-in square on the fo'c'sle, when the orderly sergeant—a grizzled veteran like Doran—summoned him to report forthwith to Captain Fisher.

"Looks like you're in for it, if you're not careful, Shannon," he warned, with gruff sympathy. "The captain's in a real bad mood. Been seasick, his poor devil of a servant says, and cursing ever since he ventured out o' his nice warm cabin 'bout an hour ago. He's put four men on a charge, apart from you—but you're first. Take my advice, lad, an' don't try to argue with him. The worst he can do is take your stripes off you, an' that won't break your heart, will it, now?"

It would not, Adam thought, trying to curb his resentment. He had encountered officers of Fisher's type before—although, mercifully, very few of them, and only one in the service he still thought of as his own, the Royal Navy. They were usually men who were uncertain of themselves and who sought to sustain their authority by bullying and harassing their subordinates, in the belief that by instilling fear, they could gain respect. The army system, which permitted the purchase of commissions, also allowed promotion to those who could afford to buy their steps in rank when, on merit, they were unlikely to be given advancement, as . . . Adam's mouth tightened. As in Marcus Fisher's case.

But the orderly sergeant's advice was good, he told himself, and he would be wise to follow it, whatever charges the draft commander might bring against him. He followed the gray-haired NCO in silence and, still in silence, listened to the accusation that his conduct, when he returned from embarkation leave, had been prejudicial to good order and military discipline.

"You are not denying it?" Fisher demanded aggressively.

For a moment, in memory, Adam was back in the courtroom on board the *Copenhagen,* when he had been compelled to offer no denial of the much more serious charges leveled against him there. He remembered listening to the court-martial president's strictures, seeing the point of his own sword turned toward him, and hearing the words that had ended his naval career. . . . He drew in his breath sharply. What could this little jumped-up army captain do? What punishment could he impose that would compare with the punishment he had already suffered?

"No, sir," he managed, his voice devoid of expression. "If that is your view of my conduct, sir."

"My *view?*" Fisher flung at him. "It is the army's view. You were drunk and disorderly, and—an NCO—you permitted the recruits, of whom you were in charge, to return to barracks in a drunken and disorderly state. *That* is conduct prejudicial to good order and military discipline, Corporal Shannon, according to Queen's Regulations. And Queen's Regulations lay down what punishment I am required to mete out to you. You agreed, did you not, to accept my punishment, if I permitted you to remain with this draft?"

It went against the grain to signify his agreement, but this had been the condition Doran had wrung from the draft commander, and Adam, his voice still flat and expressionless, answered, "Yes, sir."

Marcus Fisher looked disappointed, as if he had expected defiance and, meeting with none, had failed in his objective. He took a different tack.

"You still expect me to believe that you are not a deserter from the Royal Navy?"

"I am not, sir." Adam's gorge rose, but he controlled himself, more determined than ever not to be provoked.

"And yet," Fisher pursued, with a thin smile, "I'm given to understand that you confided to one of our passengers, Miss Carmichael, that you had previously made voyages to China and—yes, to India. Do you then claim to have made these voyages as a merchant seaman? Or a merchant *officer?*"

It cost an effort to reply without heat, but Adam managed, somehow, to do so. "I made no such claim, sir."

"Then you were boasting—trying to impress Miss Carmichael? Or are you suggesting that the young lady misunderstood you?"

"Perhaps she did, yes."

"Ah!" Marcus Fisher was triumphant, convinced that he had wrung the admission he wanted, at long last, from the man standing stiffly in front of him. "Then you have never previously made voyages to the Far East?"

"I did not say that, sir." Resentment finally wore down Adam's precarious self-control. "Permit me to tell you, Captain Fisher, that whether I have or have not is none of your business. I am neither a deserter nor a liar, and I take exception to your questions and your accusations . . . sir!"

"You take exception, do you? As your commanding officer, I

have a perfect right to question you, since I have strong reason to believe that you are a fugitive from justice, if not a deserter, and that you enlisted under a false name. Do you deny *that*, Corporal Shannon?"

Adam was white with rage, his whole body shaking as he sought vainly to suppress an insane desire to smash his fist into the pale, bewhiskered face of his tormentor. He took a pace forward, hands clenched at his sides, ignoring the old orderly sergeant's attempt to restrain him. A moment later, realizing the dangerous folly of his action, he stepped back and came to attention. But he was too late; Fisher's triumph was complete.

"Attempting to strike a superior officer is a serious crime, Shannon—and that's what you did, was it not, in front of witnesses?" Fisher gestured to the sergeant and to his clerk, who was listening openmouthed to what was being said, and went on, with a satisfaction he did not try to hide, "Add *that* to conduct prejudicial and insubordination, and I'm entitled to have you flogged!" He turned to the clerk. "The sentence is that this man shall receive two dozen lashes and be reduced to the ranks—note it down. Private Shannon, whatever his regimental number is, found guilty as charged. The sentence to be carried out tomorrow morning. Sar'nt Jamison, place him under arrest, and see to it that arrangements for punishment are made. I'll speak to the ship's master. All right—dismiss!"

Sergeant Jamison grasped Adam's arm firmly. "Hold your tongue, Shannon," he hissed, in sibilant warning, his mouth close to Adam's ear. "You'll only make things worse if you answer him back." Raising his voice, he snapped, "About turn! Quick march!"

Adam obeyed automatically, a sick sensation in the pit of his stomach. He had seen men flogged before; as a young midshipman, he had served under a sadistic captain, who had resorted to the lash for even trivial breaches of discipline, but . . . He swallowed hard, his mouth suddenly dry. Since then, the barbaric punishment that could scar a man for life had been curtailed—Captain Peel had not believed in it, and even John Omerod, who had prided himself on being a taut hand, had seldom found flogging necessary. While it had not been officially discontinued, Adam recalled, no ship's captain in the navy was permitted to order more than a dozen lashes for any offense; more than that required a trial by court-martial of the offender. Yet Fisher, the devil take him, had ordered two dozen!

Unable to speak, he looked at Jamison, and the sergeant said gravely, "There's nothing to be done, lad. You should have held your tongue. He's within his rights—he can swear blind that you threatened to strike him."

"But I didn't strike him!"

"You did the next best thing, Shannon. Truth to tell, *I* thought you were going to hit him."

And, Adam told himself wretchedly, he had come within an ace of doing so. . . . He shivered, and Jamison offered consolingly, "I've had the lash in my time. You get over it, lad."

Still grasping Adam's arm, he led the way below.

Emily Carmichael awoke very early the following morning and, donning a shawl over her dress, made her way up to the poop deck, anxious for a breath of fresh air after being confined for so long to her cabin.

Her fears concerning her sea legs—or the lack of them—had not materialized, but her mother had felt unwell during the mercifully brief North Sea storm, and Emily had stayed below to look after her. Her mother's frail health had been a source of anxiety for some months now. Alice Carmichael had never been robust, and the family physician had diagnosed a weak and failing heart, which, on the long voyage to Australia, he had warned, would require care.

"But it will do her good; the sea air will certainly be beneficial," he had added. "Just so long as she does not overdo things, Emily. It will be up to you to ensure that she rests as much as possible."

Her mother was sleeping peacefully now, and the weather had improved—indeed, Emily thought as she emerged onto the open deck and looked about her, the sea was like the proverbial millpond that the handsome young soldier, Corporal Shannon, had forecast, and the sun was rising in a cloudless sky, with a promise of a fine, warm day to come. It might be possible to persuade her mother to come on deck—well wrapped up, of course—in order to inhale the beneficial sea air Dr. Lowndes had spoken of. The poop deck was reserved for the cabin passengers; being in the stern part of the ship and elevated, it afforded a splendid view of the *Pomona*'s length. Leaning against the rail, she could see the master, Captain Clifford, on the quarterdeck, talking to one of his officers; the helmsman was standing nearby at the wheel, and some seamen were busy at work, removing a grating from one of the cargo hatches and lashing it in an upright position to the gangway.

A soldier was with them—Emily glimpsed his scarlet jacket—a sergeant, from the stripes on his arm, and as she watched, more soldiers emerged from one of the forward hatchways. They marched onto the quarterdeck, headed by a drummer, his instrument slung from his shoulders, and in response to shouted commands formed three sides of a square about the raised grating.

They were engaged in some military maneuver, Emily decided, at a loss as to what its purpose might be. The soldiers were armed; they stood at ease, seemingly waiting, their rifles at arm's length, the butts grounded. She stayed where she was, unnoticed and alone on the poop deck, curious but not alarmed. The ship's surgeon—a stout, bearded man, who had visited her mother conscientiously and who had seemed pleasant and kindly—was next to make his appearance. Dr. Farrar—that was his name, she reminded herself —Dr. Farrar went up to the master, and although she could not hear what either of them said, Emily formed the opinion that both were unwilling participants in whatever the soldiers were about to do.

Then Captain Fisher and the young ensign who was his second-in-command strode across the deck to join them, and what was evidently an altercation took place, all four officers speaking in loud voices. Emily caught a word or two, but beyond registering the fact that Captain Clifford and the doctor were raising objections and Captain Fisher was overriding them, she was still at a loss to understand what their differences of opinion signified.

She did not like Captain Fisher, she reflected, although he had gone out of his way, admittedly, to put himself on friendly terms, particularly with her mother. They had met, by chance, before boarding the *Pomona*, in the office of the ship's owners, and he had been very helpful over the cargo space her mother had wanted for the furniture they were bringing out with them to Sydney. Her mother had been grateful, but . . . Emily frowned, recalling the captain's treatment of the well-spoken young soldier, Corporal Shannon, who had carried their trunks down to the cabin. He had spoken to poor Shannon as if the young man were an inferior being, unworthy even of consideration—or the shilling she had tried to give him—and had asserted that he was a deserter and— yes, a drunken rogue, who was facing a serious charge. He—

There was a stir on the deck below. Two soldiers marched a man into the center of the square, and Emily gasped with sudden horror when she saw that the man was the one who had been in her thoughts. It was Shannon, clad only in trousers and a shirt—a prisoner, with his hands pinioned—and as she watched, his shirt was stripped from him, and his guards brought him to stand facing Captain Fisher.

It was then that she understood the purpose of the soldiers' parade and the presence of the ship's surgeon, and, numb with dismay, she gripped the rail in front of her. They were going to *flog* poor Shannon! One of the soldiers was carrying a red bag and, as she watched, took out a whip—a terrible-looking instrument of torture, with several knotted thongs attached to the handle. The dreaded cat-o'-nine-tails, which she had heard of but never seen . . . Sickened, Emily watched the soldier pass his fingers through the knotted tails to free them, and then slash the empty air with an ominous crack.

Captain Fisher had been saying something in stentorian tones, but she took in little of his announcement, her fear and horror growing. She felt as if she were paralyzed, unable to move, her grip on the rail in front of her all that held her upright. The hatchway leading to the deck below was a scant ten yards from her, but she dared not attempt to reach it, lest she fall. It was very early in the morning, none of the other cabin passengers were about, and— Emily felt waves of nausea sweep over her as the drum rolled, and, immediately after it, she heard the sickening sound of the knotted lashes descending on human flesh.

Poor Shannon did not cry out. Again and again, her eyes tightly closed, she heard the sound repeated and a disembodied voice calling the number of lashes that had been administered.

"Five! Six! Seven! Eight!" It went on, but Emily could bear no more. With a strangled sob, she relinquished her grip on the rail and stumbled blindly across to the hatchway, both hands held out in front of her in a vain attempt to locate the steps that led below.

One of the passengers, an elderly gentleman to whom Emily had spoken briefly on the first night of the voyage, saved her from what might have been a dangerous fall. He caught her as he stood half-way from the top of the hatchway, and, having assisted her to the deck below, put a protective arm about her waist and led her to her cabin.

Pausing there, he said gently, "These things happen, I'm afraid, my dear young lady, when troops are involved. There has to be discipline. But it was most unfortunate that you should witness it

—that was never intended, I'm sure. Lie down, won't you? I will tell the cabin steward to bring you a glass of brandy."

Emily flung herself down on her bunk and, her face buried in the pillow, lay sobbing uncontrollably, her heart close to breaking.

Her mother, in the cabin next door, slept on, undisturbed.

Chapter V

PETER RYAN WAS seething with futile anger as he mounted his horse and started back toward his farmhouse, driving what was left of his small herd of in-calf heifers before him. Maoris of Chief Te Kawana's tribe had raided during the night and set on four of his best animals, butchered them, stolen the meat, and left the carcasses for him to find, without troubling to conceal them.

He was saddened, as well as angry, for his milch cattle were his livelihood, and after all the work he had put in over the past three years, the little farm he had fashioned from virgin land had just begun to show a profit and repay his efforts. Neighbors now bought breeding stock from him, paid stud fees for his fine red Devon bulls, and patronized his small dairy—his wife's venture, as well as his—and some of them even sought his advice on feeding for better milk yields.

Peter Ryan had come out to New Zealand from Devon, with his wife, Deborah, their four young children, and a dream in his heart. It had been a dream of a better life, as a landowner instead of a tenant farmer, and it had seemed to be within reach of fulfillment only a few short months ago. But then had come the trouble over the land at the mouth of the Waitara River—six hundred acres of fertile land, ripe for settlement—which the supposed owner, a minor chief named Te Teira, had agreed to sell on fair terms to the government. With more and more would-be settlers pouring into the township of New Plymouth, hungry for land, the purchase had been agreed and all had appeared in order.

But then—Peter scowled, yelling impatiently at a recalcitrant heifer, which was attempting to wander off on its own—then, without so much as a by-your-leave, Te Teira's tribal head, a fellow called Wiremu Kingi, had stepped in and forbidden the sale, and there had been hell to pay. Surveyors sent out to parcel the land into lots had been attacked by Kingi's warriors, their posts and markers torn up, and the wretched men themselves driven to panic-stricken flight.

The trouble had spread like wildfire, taking in settlements like his own that had previously had no trouble from the local Maoris. Indeed, he and his family had always been on good terms with them, Peter reflected bitterly. He had acquired a working knowledge of their language, traded with them, given them hospitality and received it in turn, and generally prided himself on understanding their culture and their aspirations. But then the so-called King Movement had taken root—only with some of the east coast tribes initially; the powerful Taranaki had too many old scores to settle with their erstwhile enemies to give their support. Certainly they had not concurred with the choice of the old warrior Potatau as the Maori king. But his election had led to the formation of the Maori Land League, and—Peter passed a hand over his sweat-soaked brow—there was now concerted opposition to the sale of land to European settlers, and even established settlements, like those in this area, were now being attacked and raided every other night.

So far, no white settlers had been killed—the Maoris had stopped short of that, contenting themselves with the theft of stock and the burning of crops—but it would come, he had no doubt, for the tribes were becoming more rebellious with every day that passed. There were rumors that the commander of the small military garrison in New Plymouth, the nearest town, had declared martial law after the harassing of the government surveyors, and it was believed that he had asked for a naval vessel to be sent from Auckland. But out here in the bush there was little evidence that, in the event of a serious attack, help would be forthcoming.

Peter's hand closed over the shotgun he carried strapped to his saddle. It was an old weapon, which he had bought when he first took possession of his land, and he had intended it for nothing more lethal than the shooting of game for the pot. But he kept it with him constantly now, and Deborah had a pistol, which he had tried—albeit not very successfully—to teach her to use. He expelled his breath in a weary sigh.

The farmstead was now in sight, and despite his anxiety, Peter was conscious of a feeling of pride as he looked at the little cluster of buildings, nestling in the slight hollow in the distance. They had grown in number over the years, all built with his own hands, latterly with the aid of his two sons. Neighbors had helped too, of course, as he, in his turn, had helped them. The ground had had to be cleared of its thick covering of fern and timber; then the first primitive shelter had been erected, to replace the hired tents and enable his family to join him; then had come sheds for the stock, a byre for the milkers, a fenced-in fold yard, a granary, and a well.

Now the house was commodious—still timber-framed, with a shingle roof, but white-painted and with a veranda encircling it, front and rear, and inside Deborah and the two girls, Letty and May, had worked tirelessly to give it the comforts of home. Peter found himself smiling, his anger suddenly evaporating. He whistled to his two cattle dogs and, trotting ahead, opened the gate into the fold yard. Aided by the dogs, he drove the heifers inside. The yard meant close quarters, and the heifers would have to be fed hay, but he dared not turn them out on the grass again, with the Maoris seemingly bent on molesting them.

He dismounted and, his horse's rein over his arm, started to walk across to the stable, only to come to a startled halt when his elder son, David, came to meet him at a run.

"Glad you're back, Dad," the boy exclaimed breathlessly. He was tall for his fifteen years, a well-built lad, who had done a man's work for almost half his young life, his father reflected with pride. But he looked worried, his mouth tightly pursed, as if he were trying to keep his emotions in check.

"Is anything wrong, Davie?" Peter asked sharply.

"Yes, I reckon there is. A party of soldiers came by, and the officer says the Maoris are working themselves up to open warfare. Against *us*, Dad—the settlers! He advised Mum to leave, with the girls, even if you don't want to quit. He said they'd come back, after they've been to some of the other farms, and give all who want to leave an escort to New Plymouth. But you won't quit, Dad, will you?"

Peter evaded the question. "What did your mother tell them? Did *she* say she wanted to go to New Plymouth?"

The boy shook his fair, tousled head. "She told the officer she couldn't decide till she'd spoken to you. Dad, we can't just walk out of the place, can we? Abandon the stock, the house, everything! It'd be such a waste!"

A waste of all the years of struggle, Peter thought, his throat tight. The Maoris would simply slaughter his herd, as they had slaughtered the heifers during the night. They would loot the house, maybe even set it on fire, and make off with the furniture, the contents of the granary—everything. He would return to devastation—*if* he was able to return, and the good Lord only knew when that would be. Deborah ought to go to where she would be safe—Deborah and the girls, certainly, and perhaps Davie and Harry, if the Maoris really did mean business.

Who else would go, he wondered—which of his neighbors? As if he had spoken the question aloud, Davie answered it.

"The soldiers were going on to Colonel De Lancey's place, they said, Dad. They seemed to think that the colonel would go back with them to town, and Andy too. *I* shouldn't have thought a man like the colonel would run away, though, would you?"

"He has less to lose than we have," Peter said dismissively, still concerned with his own problems. "He's not been out here long enough to stock his farm. And if there's going to be a war, they probably need him to organize the militia. He's been a regular, and he'd be worth his weight in gold to them, no doubt of that."

The boy Andy—De Lancey's adopted son—had almost died out in India, he recalled, during the Sepoy Mutiny. The colonel would not want to risk any sort of repetition, in Andy's case.

"They'll be coming back here, will they, Davie?" he asked.

"That's what the officer told Mum, when he advised her to leave with Letty and May," Davie confirmed. He eyed his father anxiously. "But we'll stay, won't we—you and me? I can handle a rifle, Dad, you know I can."

"We'll have to see what your mother thinks," Peter returned. "But she'll have to go. I daren't let her stay here. Put my horse away, will you please, while I talk to her."

"All right," Davie agreed. "But if you stay, I'm staying."

The safety and well-being of his family were of more importance than his possessions, Peter thought as he made for the house. Debbie would not like leaving him. She would argue, would try to persuade him to let her stay, or, if he would not agree to that, would beg him to leave with her, but . . . He pushed open the door, to be greeted with the appetizing smell of cooking ham. The devil take King Potatau and the infernal Maori Land League, Wiremu Kingi and the rest of them! Life had been good, until all this business started. He called to his wife.

Deborah, slim and pretty despite the sprinkling of gray in her hair, carried in a plate of ham and eggs and set them on the table, at his place. Her eyes avoided his, and Peter knew that she had been preparing her case, waiting to put it to him, as soon as he came in.

She said flatly, "Davie told you the soldiers called here?"

"Yes." Peter sat down and started to eat, letting his wife's argument fall on deaf ears. As he had anticipated, she argued fiercely and at some length, but he waited until she had done and, pushing away his now empty plate, shook his head emphatically.

"It's no use, Debbie love. You'll have to go, with the girls and Harry. I'm not risking your lives."

"And you intend to stay—with Davie?" she countered coldly.

"I must. I'm not sure about Davie. Perhaps he should go. He—"

"You mean you'll stay here by yourself? Is that what you've decided?"

"They killed four of the heifers in the long paddock, Deb—left the carcasses for me to find," Peter said. "By way of a warning, I suppose. They're out for trouble."

"Yes, but—"

"I can't just walk out and let them do their worst. I've put too much into this place for that. Deb, I *have* to try to stop them."

"Alone, Peter? How could you stop them by yourself?"

How could he indeed, Peter wondered. But he returned obstinately, "At least I wouldn't make it easy for the devils. And I might be able to reason with them. After all, we've had no trouble for all the while we've been here. If I leave, they'll just be able to walk in and—"

"And kill you," his wife said accusingly. "Oh, Peter, don't you see—we're a family. You're my husband—you're the children's father! Without you, we should be lost."

"We'll be lost if the blasted Maori destroy this place and the stock, Deb. Why—"

Deborah cut him short. "We built up what we have from nothing, and we can do it again, if we have to. But not without you, Peter. And we could drive some of the dairy herd with us, perhaps."

"The soldiers won't wait for a slow-moving herd," Peter pointed out wearily. "And there'll be nowhere for them in the town. They would have to be slaughtered for meat. Deb, if I stay, I may be able to save them."

Out of the corner of his eye, he glimpsed two bright, golden heads, peering out from behind the cookhouse door—his daughters, he realized, listening to every word, and his heart contracted. They were so young and vulnerable—Letty barely ten and May still almost a baby, who had just celebrated her sixth birthday. God in heaven, he could not risk their precious lives!

Peter gulped down the cup of scalding tea Deborah had poured for him and rose to his feet. "There's no more to be said, wife," he stated decisively. "Off you go and pack up what you can. Only essentials, mind. I'll hitch a couple of horses to the dray. The soldiers will be back before we know it, and we'll have to be ready for them."

Deborah's eyes were full of tears, but to his relief she ceased to dispute his decision. Calling the two little girls to her, she went in frozen-faced silence to make preparations for their departure.

Outside, Peter opened the front of the big barn, in which his carts and other farm implements were kept, and leaving his shotgun propped against the entrance, he moved the dray to the center of the shed. Contrary to his normal practice, he looked around carefully as he walked across to the stable to fetch two of his workhorses, and seeing nothing out of the ordinary, he took a harness from the tack room and went brisky to work preparing the two animals for their task. This done, he led them to the barn and hitched them to the dray. In normal circumstances, he would have taken the dray to the front of the farmhouse, to facilitate loading, but prompted by an instinct for caution, he left it where it was and called out to Davie to find his brother and carry the gear Deborah had packed across to the barn.

The two boys had made their second, laden journey when Peter felt the hair pricking at the back of his scalp. A gully ran a winding course round the west side of the farm buildings, with a small stream—the source of his water supply—at its foot. Behind it, the ground rose steeply in a mass of interlacing, breast-high fern and brush that he had never bothered to clear, since the hill was useless for grazing and too exposed for any other practical purpose.

But now . . . He put a hand up to shade his eyes, straining into the distance. Was it his imagination, or . . . was a section of the fern *moving*? The prickling increased, and his heart lurched . . . God in heaven, it *was* moving—slowly, cautiously, but undoubtedly coming nearer!

Peter waited to see no more. He grabbed his gun and yelled to the startled Davie.

"Drop what you're carrying! Run and fetch your mother and the girls! Get them out here fast, Davie—whatever they're doing. There's no time to be lost." To Harry, who was staring at him in wide-eyed mystification, he added hoarsely, "Your mother's pistol, Hal—where does she usually keep it?"

"In—in the cookhouse, Dad. She—"

"Then go and get it, boy—quick as you know how!"

Both boys ran off obediently, and Peter found himself praying as he watched them go. Deb could be obstinate, he knew. She would cling to such possessions as she could, delaying until she had packed everything neatly and going back for some article she had forgotten. She— He glimpsed a dark body emerging momentarily from concealment and then vanishing again. He raised the gun to his shoulder, but after a moment lowered it, recognizing that the range was too long. If it was a *tana muru*—a party bent only on robbery—all might yet be well. He had plenty of ammunition; he could hold them off, from the comparative safety of the angle of the barn, while his family made their escape in the dray. He would tell Davie to head for Colonel De Lancey's property, in the hope that they would make contact with the soldiers, and—

The sound of voices—Deborah's shrilly protesting—brought his head round. Thanks be to God, they were coming at last, the two girls running, with Hal urging them on, and Davie with his mother, both of them bent under the weight of bundles wrapped in sackcloth.

Rather than run the risk of further argument, Peter grabbed both bundles and flung them into the dray. The two little girls were lifted, more gently, and deposited beside the bundles, and Davie and Hal clambered up, Davie taking the whip and reins at a nod from his father. Deborah, after a shocked glance at his face, swallowed her protests and climbed onto the box beside her elder son. Peter took the pistol from Hal and thrust in into her hand.

"Use this, if you have to, Deb," he bade her. "If you make for De Lancey's place, you should catch up with the soldiers. You understand, Davie lad? Don't stop for anyone else."

"What about you?" his wife asked, in a stricken voice, catching his urgency. "Peter, we need you. We—"

"I'll ride after you, my love," Peter promised, aware that he would have but a slim chance of doing so. "Go *on*, Davie, for pity's sake! Give 'em the whip! You'll make it if you go now, boy!"

Davie did as he had been bidden. With an anguished look at his

father, he brought the long cattle whip down on the horses' rumps
as hard as he could. The dray lurched out of the barn, Hal and the
two little girls flung onto their backs among the sacks and bundles
and Deborah clinging to her seat with both hands, the pistol falling
from her nerveless grasp.

But it was too late to attempt to retrieve it now. The raiders,
Peter saw, were splashing across the stream—a party of about a
score, their naked, copper-colored bodies oiled and daubed in red
ocher, their phallic belts girt tightly about their waists. All were
armed with muskets of some kind, and most of them also carried
tomahawks or spears. Scorning concealment now, since the departing dray indicated to them that the element of surprise was lost,
they came running swiftly across the intervening distance with
cries like the baying of a pack of savage dogs.

One or two shots rang out, but the range was still overlong, and
Peter took up the position he had planned, grimly waiting for them
to come nearer, his shotgun at his shoulder.

"A, a, te riri!" He heard the chant and knew what the words
implied—*riri,* in the Maori language, meant war. The people with
whom until now he had lived in peace intended to make war.
They— Suddenly, to his horror, he saw the dray change direction
—or attempt to do so—leaving the hard-baked cart track to head
for the trees that bordered it, and he realized with a sinking heart
that the raiding party he had seen crossing the stream was not the
only one.

Half a dozen warriors, who had apparently been crouching unseen in the drainage ditch beyond the house, came to their feet, and
Peter recognized the chief's young son, Te Mawae, among them.
He was a year or so older than Davie and had been the boy's
friend, his companion on hunting expeditions, and a not infrequent
visitor to the farmhouse. But now the young Maori raised a hand,
and his companions' guns spoke. A fusillade of shots met the swaying dray, both horses went down as if poleaxed, and the dray
crashed onto its side. Deborah and Davie were flung from the box
—Peter could not see what had happened to Hal and the two little
girls. God willing, they were under or behind the dray.

Throwing caution to the wind, he started to run toward the site
of the ambush, loosing off both barrels of his gun as he ran. For all
the haste with which he had aimed, the spreading shot found their
mark, and one of the Maoris staggered and dropped to his knees.
Peter was still fifty yards from them when, sick with dismay, he

saw Davie stumble to his feet and start to move toward Te Mawae, both hands outheld as if, even in this extremity, he could not believe that his friend would want to do him harm.

Te Mawae shrieked a warning in his own language, his tattooed face contorted, his lips drawn back in a ferocious snarl, and then—before Peter could reach them—he brought his tomahawk down on Davie's unprotected head with such strength that he cleaved the boy's skull in two.

Peter was sobbing with mingled grief and fury, but somehow, his fingers shaking, he managed to reload his shotgun. He fired from the hip—there was no time to raise the weapon to his shoulder, no time consciously to take aim, but at that range he could not miss. He hit the chief's son with both barrels, and Te Mawae fell with a strangled cry across the body of his onetime friend. Peter moved to reload, but then the other warriors were upon him and he was fighting a vain battle for his life, aware of pain such as he had never endured before. He fell and they were on him with their clubs and axes, hacking him mercilessly to death.

From beneath the overturned dray, one of the little girls was crying out pitifully, but Peter did not hear her, and two of the warriors, putting their shoulders to it, turned the dray right over, silencing the cries. Then they picked up the body of their young chief and, bearing it between them, made off into the scrub, their wounded comrade limping after them.

The small procession of refugees and laden wagons, with its escort of six men of the Queen's 65th Regiment and a dozen troopers of the Taranaki Mounted Volunteers, was more than half a mile from Ryan's farm when the sound of gunfire reached them.

William De Lancey, riding beside the leading wagon, exchanged a glance with Ensign Villars Butler of the 65th, and both men put spurs to their horses, followed an instant later by the volunteer troopers.

"I'll take the point," William shouted. He waved to the troopers to spread out as, with practiced efficiency, the scarlet-clad men of the 65th formed up round the wagons, their Enfields at the ready. This was the second alarm they had met with, but judging by the volume of the firing, it was likely to be the more serious. Why, William thought with exasperation, why the devil had not Ryan sent his family out with the escort, after the warning he had received? They were all the same, these settlers, clinging obstinately to their stock and their undefended farmhouses, despite increasing raids and oft-repeated warnings that the local tribes were preparing to make war and the whole area was about to erupt in flames!

Peter Ryan was a fine man, an excellent cattle breeder and a devoted family man, but . . . William increased his speed, praying that they would be in time. Ryan had young children—two pretty, flaxen-haired little girls, and his elder son—what was his name? David, Davie, that was it—Davie was only three years older than his own boy, Andrew, whom he had left behind him in the wagon.

"Over there, sir!" Ensign Butler yelled. He waved an excited hand in the direction of the farm buildings, and William saw with dismay that smoke was rising from the farmhouse roof. The devils had set poor Ryan's place alight, and ten to one they had slipped away into the forest as soon as they had done so. The tribe in this area, William knew, was renowned for its bravery and tenacity in battle but not, alas, for its compassion when victorious, according to the long-established settlers he had talked to recently. And their *pa*—their fortified village—five or six miles away, was said to be virtually impregnable.

William clenched his jaw and galloped on. He saw the upturned dray a few minutes later. Of the Maoris there was neither sight nor sound, and he flung himself from his horse, sick with apprehension. Peter Ryan's headless body—despite the lack of a head, it could only be his—lay spread-eagled on the ground in a pool of blood, and a few feet from it lay his son Davie, hideously mutilated.

With the aid of Butler and two of the volunteer troopers, William managed to lift the shattered dray, to recoil in horror at what was revealed. Mrs. Ryan and two of the children had been crushed beneath it; she was dead, and so, William ascertained from a swift examination, were the two poor little girls. At least it had been mercifully quick for them; Mrs. Ryan appeared to have broken her neck, and the little girls had both been shot—it was to be hoped before they had seen their father and brother done to death. But— There was a faint movement beneath a pile of sacking-wrapped bundles, and one of the troopers, exclaiming under his breath, moved them aside to disclose a small, terrified boy of perhaps ten or eleven cowering there, his face deathly pale and wet with tears.

"You're safe, son, you're safe," the trooper told him, lifting the frail little body in gentle arms and holding him close. "What's your name, eh?"

"H-Harry. My dad calls m-me Hal. I'm Hal Ryan."

"There, Hal lad," his rescuer asserted. "You ain't too badly hurt, I reckon." His eyes met William's over the little boy's bent head. "I'll take him back to the escort, sir. It's better if he don't stay here."

William nodded agreement. "Take him to my wagon—he knows my lad. Are you sure he's not hurt?"

"He don't seem to be, Colonel. I'll know better when I get him back." Holding Hal's face pressed firmly against his shoulder, the trooper looped his horse's rein over his arm and set off on foot.

Ensign Butler, very white about the gills, went with him, ostensibly to order the convoy of evacuated settlers and his own men to proceed to the scene of the disaster, and William, after covering the bodies, took the rest of the troopers to attempt to save some, at least, of Peter Ryan's farm buildings. But the raiders had done their work well; the fire had taken a strong hold, and despite strenuous efforts, they contrived to save only the cow byre and the stables, releasing such occupants as they found in each—three horses and an old house cow. The rest of the stock had gone, either taken back to the *pa,* William decided, or—which seemed more likely—simply driven out and set loose, when the raiders had heard the troopers' approach.

By the time the wagons came up it was midday. Young Butler had recovered from his shock; he was in official command, and aware that it would be unwise to linger, even with so strong an escort, he was anxious to proceed, in order to reach New Plymouth before darkness fell. William, to whom he looked for approval, did not question his decision. The sole survivor of the Maori attack, the little boy Hal, was in the wagon with Andy Melgund and sleeping, according to Andy, although his white, pinched face and bloodless lips spoke more of shock than health-giving sleep.

The bodies of his family were loaded onto the righted dray, and with fresh horses put in harness, the journey was resumed. A subtle change had come over the settlers, William observed. Initially they had all complained quite bitterly when it had been suggested that they seek safety in New Plymouth. Most of them had been reluctant to leave, and it had taken all his and Ensign Butler's urging to obtain their agreement. Now, however, with the ghastly evidence of Maori enmity before them in all its savagery, they

ceased to question the wisdom of retreat. There were five families
in the convoy, all newcomers like himself, William knew, with
comparatively little to lose, and the Ryans' tragic end had left
them stunned.

" 'Twas as well we let you persuade us to quit, Colonel De
Lancey," one of the men volunteered, riding up to William's side.
"I didn't want to, but . . . dear God, them bloody savages have
shown they're out to drive us off our land! But we'll be back, when
the soldiers have shown 'em that they can't get away with murder-
ing white folk. Mr. Butler says they've sent for the rest of his
regiment from Auckland, and he reckons a Royal Navy ship's on
the way as well, bringing the governor himself. If I were a few
years younger, I'd join the volunteers—I reckon most of us'll have
to, don't you, sir?"

William inclined his head in regretful assent. *He* would have to,
he knew. Officers with experience of active warfare were at a pre-
mium, and the volunteers would need to be trained; certainly one
imperial regiment and a single naval frigate would not suffice to
quell a full-scale Maori rebellion. But it was ironic, he reflected,
that he had come to New Zealand seeking the opportunity to turn
his sword into a plowshare and to find peace, after so many years
of war. Ironic and disturbing. And there was Andy to be considered; the poor little fellow had nearly died at other savage hands
back in India during the Sepoy Mutiny, and like young Hal Ryan
he had seen his whole family brutally murdered. Andy had begun
to live again, during the six months they had spent establishing
their farm; he had learned to laugh and to enjoy himself, but
now—

As if William had spoken his thoughts aloud, the gray-bearded
settler observed shrewdly, "They'll need you, sir—a colonel who
rode in the Light Brigade charge at Balaclava—nothing's more
certain. And you've the boy to think of, haven't you, sir? And now
there's the poor little chap we're bringing along with us, with all
his folks wiped out."

"Yes," William confirmed. "I was thinking about them, Mr.—
your name's Finch, isn't it?"

"Aye, that's right, Colonel—I'm Bert Finch. And maybe I can
help. New Plymouth's not much of a place, as you know—not yet,
anyways, and right now it's overflowing with new immigrants
waiting to take up land on the Waitara River. It's going to be a job
finding a roof over our heads, but if you need a place for the boys,

well . . . the wife's sister, Ellie Mordaunt—she was a school-teacher back at home—she's started a little school in town. A boy's school, it is, and she's got premises in Hodgson Street." He described these in careful detail, smiling as he added, "The house is just weatherboard, of course, like all the rest. Nothing fancy, but it's roomy. 'Deed, the wife and I are depending on Ellie to put us up, until we can get back to the farm. And she'd take both those boys, sir, I'm certain sure she would, for a reasonable charge. Would you like me to ask her?"

It would be a wrench, parting from Andy, but the boy was only twelve, and clearly it would be impossible to take him along on a military campaign, should this be the eventual outcome, as seemed very probable. William knew he would be in honor bound to volunteer his services. Governor Gore-Browne would expect all the new settlers, as well as the old, to defend their land and avenge their dead, if they were physically capable of bearing arms. And he undoubtedly was, despite his empty right sleeve.

Dusk was falling when the weary convoy entered the sprawling township of New Plymouth. Leaving Andy Melgund and Hal Ryan in the temporary care of Mr. Finch and his wife, William accompanied Ensign Butler to the headquarters of the 65th Regiment, to report the day's tragic events.

For William, the first days in New Plymouth passed in a rush. Andy and the Ryan boy had been taken in by the motherly Miss Mordaunt, and he himself had been offered temporary lodgings in the home of the 65th's second-in-command. The town itself, William thought, was typical of New Zealand's frontier outposts, with its muddy, rutted streets, its scattered, ill-sited stores, hotels, and dwelling houses, and the tent city already springing up to accommodate the steady stream of new arrivals. Its small, efficient port and sheltered harbor were the reason for the town's existence and rapid growth. Immigrant ships came directly here now, crowded with would-be settlers, laden with their household goods and imported stock, each family filled with the hope of a better life than that they had known before.

True, some of the settlers—particularly in the early days—had been of undesirable character. Ex-convicts and escapers from Australia; men who had failed to make their fortunes in the Victoria or New South Wales gold diggings; rascally sea traders and the rough crews of whaling ships—all had come, and most had played a part in alienating the native Maoris. They *had* abused the Maoris' trust, cheated them of their land, robbed and killed them . . . and some of the missionaries had not been blameless in this regard, either. But under Governor Grey, when the first Maori war had ended fourteen years ago, most of the tribes' grievances had been alleviated and their rights protected—indeed, William recalled, he had heard quite a number of the white inhabitants complain that Grey favored the Maoris much more than themselves. Although . . . William frowned, remembering something else he had been told. It had been Governor Gore-Browne who repealed the law forbidding the sale of arms and gunpowder to the Maoris, three years earlier, and in those three years the tribes had expended close on £50,000 for the purchase of weapons with which, once again, to wage war on the settlers. . . .

A few days after the raid on the Ryan farm, the governor himself arrived from Auckland, with the remaining companies of the 65th Regiment and their commanding officer, Colonel Gold, on board the steamer *Airedale*. Within an hour of their arrival, the Royal Navy steam-screw corvette H.M.S. *Niger* also dropped anchor in the roadstead. Close on the heels of the soldiers, a detachment of seamen, with their band playing, marched across the Huatoki Bridge and through the town, dragging a twelve-pounder ship's gun behind them, and the townsfolk thronged the rutted high street and cheered them to the echo.

The governor called a conference, at which the senior naval and military officers were present, along with town officials and those serving with the various hastily formed volunteer units, William among them. He had taken both Andy and little Hal Ryan to watch the 65th and the *Niger*s march in, and had left them with the capable Miss Mordaunt, having to turn a deaf ear to Andy's protests. But the boy had, to his relief, taken Hal under wing—more out of pity, it appeared, than because they had much in common.

The conference, owing to the number of those in attendance and their vastly differing views and interests, lasted a long time and achieved very little.

William had met the governor before; Colonel Gore-Browne and his handsome, vivacious wife had entertained him when he had first arrived in the colony, and he was aware of the governor's distinguished military record. As a major, Gore-Browne had commanded the 41st Regiment in Afghanistan and had served with great gallantry, and a colonelcy and the successive governorships of Saint Helena and New Zealand had been his reward. He had relieved Sir George Grey when Grey had been appointed governor of the Cape five years ago.

He was in his early fifties, slim and soldierly in appearance, with a heavy mustache and whiskers, now prematurely white, and a brisk, incisive manner. Addressing the gathering, he spoke at some length—and, predictably, with some aggression—of his abortive efforts to persuade Chief Wiremu Kingi to see reason, where the sale of the Waitara land was concerned.

"The title to these blocks is indisputably Te Teira's, gentlemen," the governor stated. "Wiremu Kingi has no right to forbid the sale, and I have issued a proclamation to this effect, in the Maori language. However, when I endeavored to enter into peaceful negotiations with Kingi, he insulted me by turning his back on me and walking out!"

The governor composed himself with visible effort.

"Much as I regret this, gentlemen, I am compelled to tell you that we must take strong military action against the Taranaki tribes, for we cannot permit them to murder and harass our settlers with impunity and drive them from the land that is rightfully theirs. The Maori believe in what they call *utu*—revenge—and the ghastly slaughter of the Ryan family cannot go unpunished."

A loud, angry murmur of assent greeted his last words.

"I have requested more imperial troops to be sent here, as a matter of urgency," the governor went on. "And I have asked for naval ships also. But in the meantime, we have Colonal Gold's regiment, the Sixty-fifth, five hundred strong, and Captain Cracroft will furnish fifty seamen and marines from Her Majesty's ship *Niger,* with one of her guns. That, with what aid your volunteers can give, will be sufficient force, in my view, to administer a sharp and decisive lesson to these rebellious tribes. Colonel Gold, gentlemen, will outline his plan of action to you now. I trust that you will all, whether military or civilian volunteer, accord him your full support."

Colonel Charles Gold, who next rose to speak, was much less impressive. A big, florid-faced man with a loud voice, he appeared to take a great deal for granted and made his plans as if—as in the Crimea—his enemy would be awaiting him in static battle lines, from which they could be driven by cannon and mortar fire, followed by a spirited bayonet charge.

Gold's regiment had arrived in the colony when the first war with the Maoris was over, William knew, and it had, at most, engaged in a few skirmishes; yet surely, after some thirteen years of garrison duty, the man must have seen a Maori *pa* and heard, from others, of the manner in which the skillful, battle-hardened tribes made war? Artillery fire had little effect on the formidable stockades they constructed, with their rows of massive palisades, their well-sited trenches and loopholed walls; and frontal assault, with the bayonet, had long since been abandoned by wise commanders, as both too costly in lives and too unlikely to result in victory. Even when a frontal charge succeeded, experienced officers asserted, the Maoris simply slipped away by a hidden exit and built another *pa* from which to defy the *pakeha* soldiers.

William curbed an impulse to interrupt the red-faced colonel's bombastic speech, but when Gold referred slightingly to the volunteer units, it was the governor who cut him short.

"I fancy that you will find our volunteers well versed in bushcraft, Charles," Gore-Browne admonished. "They know the country and are at home in the forests, and most of them are excellent marksmen. And the Mounted Volunteers can ride, I assure you."

"I don't doubt that, sir," Colonel Gold returned, with a hint of asperity. "But they lack training and are not subject to military discipline, as my men and Captain Cracroft's are. As to their officers—" He gestured disparagingly in the direction of the Mounted Volunteers' elderly commandant. "Captain Brown is, I understand, an engineer. Intending no disrespect to you, sir, but have you ever commanded cavalry in the field?"

Thus challenged, Brown reddened furiously and shook his head. "No, sir, I have not. But my adjutant, Captain Stapp, won his commission in the Crimea, and a number of my officers and NCOs fought at Ruapekapeka—the Bat's Nest—under Colonel Despard's command in 'forty-six. You need have no fears concerning their discipline or their fighting capabilities, Colonel Gold, I give you my word. And besides—" As if suddenly remembering that William had offered to join the volunteers, he turned to him in embarrassed appeal. "Colonel William De Lancey had to evacuate his property in the Taranaki area a few days ago, sir, and the colonel has offered his services to assist in the training of our Mounted Volunteers, for as long as we may require him."

The governor smiled. "You could ask no better, Captain Brown. Thank you, De Lancey." He added, for the benefit of the assembled company, "Colonel De Lancey has the distinction of having

ridden in the Light Cavalry Brigade's immortal charge at
Balaclava, gentlemen, when serving with the Eleventh Hussars. He
subsequently held a cavalry command in India, under Sir Colin
Campbell, and is the holder of Her Majesty's highest award for
gallantry, the Victoria Cross."

There were murmurs of surprised approval, and Captain
Brown's gaunt, bewhiskered face wore a delighted smile. Brown
had not even inquired into his qualifications, William recalled with
amusement, when accepting the offer of his services, and Colonel
Gold's discomfiture clearly pleased him mightily.

But Gold swiftly recovered himself. He bowed with icy dignity
in William's direction and then turned, with the air of a man engaging in more serious business, to confront the *Niger*'s commander.

"We can, I trust, count on your support, Captain Cracroft?"

"Certainly, Colonel," Peter Cracroft promised readily. "As His
Excellency has mentioned, I can furnish you with fifty seamen and
marines, plus a twelve-pounder gun. And a rocket tube, if you
want it. Just say the word. My bluejackets are spoiling for a fight!"

"That will suffice, sir," Gold answered. To the governor, he
added pointedly, "Your Excellency may rest assured that these
rebellious natives will be taught a lesson that they will not soon
forget."

As the meeting broke up and the room emptied, Gold summoned William to his side and, in a deliberately offensive tone,
inquired, "Your lieutenant colonel's commission is, I presume, an
East India Company's commission, is it not, De Lancey?"

"Yes," William conceded, without heat. "That is so, sir."

"Then your rank in Her Majesty's forces—your highest rank—
was what? That of captain?"

"I was granted the brevet of major in the Eleventh Hussars,
when I returned from the Crimea, sir."

"Ah, the infamous Lord Cardigan's regiment, of course." Satisfied that he outranked William, Gold dropped what little pretense
of civility he had shown before. "You hold no commission from the
New Zealand government, so I cannot give you a command in the
coming punitive operation," he stated bluntly. "But these farmers
who are playing at being cavalry seem to think highly of you, so
. . ." He stared a challenge at William. "Until I can find some

time to see about obtaining a commission for you, you may, I suppose, attach yourself to them unofficially. But your role will be limited to that of observer. Is that understood?"

Shaking with fury, William replied, "Perfectly."

Chapter VI

JOHNNY BROOME STOOD in the bow of the longboat and scanned the New Plymouth shoreline as the sweating sailors of the *Airedale* put their backs into the oars and rowed him in. It was the *Airedale*'s third trip ferrying supplies and imperial troops down the coast from Auckland, and Johnny's newspaper had used all its considerable influence to gain him passage aboard.

Even to a stranger, it was easy to see why Taranaki Province was so coveted by the impatient settlers, and why feelings ran so high over the fact that a few thousand Maori—who, it was said, could not possibly use a tenth part of the property to which they held confusing and conflicting titles—were blocking the sale of two million acres of some of the best land in New Zealand. Approached from the ocean, the town's situation presented a charming aspect, rising gradually from a sparkling beach toward a rich green Eden of fields, orchards, and virgin bush that climbed gradually toward the majestic, symmetrical cone of Mount Egmont in the distance.

"Careful, Mr. Broome," the coxswain called to him from the stern. "If you fall overboard, the cap'n will have our hides."

Johnny sat down sheepishly and continued his examination of the curving shore. There was no doubt that New Plymouth had grown explosively. At least four or five hundred houses and buildings, some of them substantial, were sprawled across the landscape, jumbled in the foreground and peeping out from amid the trees farther inland. The crown of one prominent hill was totally covered with an unprepossessing complex, which he took to be the immigration barracks, and he could see several churches and chapels.

"It's getting a bit crowded, isn't it, sir?" the coxswain offered. "I

don't know where they're going to put the Royal Artillery detachment we've brought them."

And that was true enough, Johnny thought, surveying the settlement. Until the hostilities had broken out, enough land had been
purchased to expand the district into a strip of about twenty miles
along the seashore and extending approximately seven miles into
the interior. But now the settlers were abandoning their little
homesteads in the open country and bunching themselves in town,
and the imperial troops that were pouring into the Taranaki were
overburdening the provincial capital still further. More than five
thousand people, Johnny had been given to understand by his editor, were now jammed into a space whose housing and drainage
were adequate for a quarter of that number. As the longboat drew
closer to shore, he could see the tent city and makeshift hovels and,
beyond them, the hasty line of trenches and redoubts behind which
the inhabitants had compressed themselves.

"Unhealthy it is, sir," the coxswain said gruffly. "Before all this
started, there was hardly a funeral in a twelvemonth. But on our
last two trips here, while we lay at anchor, hardly a day passed
without one."

The sailors shipped oars and splashed through the light surf to
beach the boat, and Johnny vaulted to the sand. "Thank you,
lads," he said, waving back, and set off along the beach toward the
center of greatest military activity, in search of someone who could
direct him to the 65th Regiment's command post.

He caught up with two men who seemed to know where they
were going—a stocky naval officer and a tall fellow in the rude
flannel shirt of a settler and an old pair of cavalryman's trousers—
and was about to hail them when he saw the latter's empty sleeve
and cried, as he drew abreast, "Will? Will De Lancey?"

William turned around and, a smile creasing his face, exclaimed
with pleasure, "Johnny, my dear fellow! What brings you here? Or
is that a foolish question—presumably you've come to report on
our preparations for war?"

Johnny nodded gravely. "It is causing much anxiety in Auckland, Will—my editor's taking a very serious view of it, as well he
might with the governor down here to oversee matters. I came in
the *Airedale,* with a detachment of the Royal Artillery."

"You've missed the governor, I'm afraid," William informed
him. "He sailed back to Auckland several days ago, leaving Colonel Gold, I'm sorry to say, unhampered by his presence. Where's

Lady Kitty? You won't have brought her with you on a troopship?"

"She is remaining in Auckland," Johnny answered, and stopped himself from saying more. He turned to the naval officer with a questioning smile.

William hastened to introduce them. "This is Captain Cracroft, commanding Her Majesty's ship *Niger*. My brother-in-law, John Broome . . . Johnny and his wife took passage with me a year ago aboard Claus Van Buren's *Dolphin*, and we haven't managed to see each other since."

"I know the *Dolphin*," Cracroft responded, a smile creasing his square, bearded face. "A splendid vessel. Captain Van Buren has been kept pretty busy of late ferrying military supplies here under government contract, but he's anxious to return to his trading post at Rangirata. If you intend to stay here a week or two, Mr. Broome, you'll probably be able to book passage back to Auckland with him."

"I'm not sure how long I'll be here," Johnny replied. "That may depend on the Maoris. Will the *Niger* be staying in these waters, Captain?"

"For as long as we're wanted," Cracroft returned. He gave a snort of disgust. "But Colonel Gold has not been overeager to make use of my tars. He wants only my twelve-pounder and the marine gunners, and the rocket tube detail. He views us simply as his portable artillery. I'm on my way now to see if he'll relent and allow my lads a share of the action in today's operation."

"Colonel Gold is a glory hunter," William asserted, with unaccustomed bitterness. "He relegates the Mounted Volunteers to a supporting role as well, and sends us into the bush to do his dirty work, while he masses his imperial troops in formal ranks in a style of warfare that has been obsolete since Waterloo."

"Yes, he understands nothing about bush warfare," Cracroft amplified. "During our last action, before the governor departed, Gold tramped all over the landscape destroying abandoned *pas* . . . abandoned because the Maoris simply left them when they heard him crashing through the bush and set up shop elsewhere. When Gold finally found an occupied *pa* whose inhabitants seemed willing to give him a fight, he drew all his troops up in front and bombarded the place for two days. Then, when he finally made up his mind to an assault, he found the *pa* deserted. The Maoris had stolen away during the first night. And Gold went triumphantly back to the governor and announced, 'Well, we taught them a lesson.' "

"This entire Taranaki war is a tragic error," William affirmed. "It's based on one misunderstanding after another. First Governor Gore-Browne alienated the tribes by refusing to see the spokesman they sent to Auckland to ask for a small loan for a flour mill—a loan the former governor, Grey, would have granted without question—and *then* he went on to exacerbate the situation by repealing Grey's ordinance against selling arms and gunpowder to the natives! Then came the Waitara land purchase dispute. Wiremu Kingi at first tried peaceful means to prevent the land from being occupied. He picked the oldest and most repulsive women in the tribe and sent them out to follow the surveyors about, hugging and kissing them. The poor surveyors had to take to their heels!"

Johnny laughed uproariously. "Hardly an act of war."

"Colonel Gold, I fear, has no sense of humor. He occupied the plot with an armed force, and when Kingi sent men out at night to pull up the survey pegs, Gold bombarded the *pa* with artillery. And so now we have war. The other Waitara tribes are rallying to Kingi's support, and New Plymouth is virtually under siege. The homesteaders—including myself—have had to abandon their property, except for a few diehards who continue to hold out."

"You've come in the nick of time to get a story, Broome," Cracroft put in. "There's a fortified *pa* at Waireka, a few miles south of here, and Gold's marching on it today to teach the natives another lesson."

"We're on our way to the briefing now," William invited. "Why don't you sit in?"

"Will Colonel Gold object?" Johnny queried.

Captain Cracroft gave a short bark. "He'll hardly notice you're there, dressed as you are." He eyed Johnny's rough tweed jacket and heavy boots. "No offense, Broome, but Colonel Gold doesn't pay a great deal of attention to colonials."

"He'll pay attention to my stories, if one half of what you said is true—that I promise you," Johnny countered unsmilingly.

The briefing took place in the large unpainted building the Town Board had been using for its hall. The room was crowded with officers of the 65th, naval personnel, and representatives of the Mounted Volunteers and their infantry counterparts, the Rifle Volunteers. Town officials were also present. Johnny found a place and settled back to listen to the proceedings.

"All the remaining outlying settlers must be brought into town without delay," Colonel Gold stated, pacing back and forth in front of a large map. Turning to Captain Brown, he added deprecatingly, "That will be a task for the Mounted Volunteers, Captain Brown, and one, I trust, they will not find beyond their capabilities?"

"Certainly not, sir," Brown asserted indignantly.

"Good! Then you will move inland, parallel to the shore, to Waireka, with Captain Atkinson's Rifle Volunteers in support, gather in the settlers, and join the main body of my troops on the Omata road, traveling across country to rendezvous with them here." His finger jabbed at the map in front of him. "But no heroics, if you please—the settlers are to be your sole concern. That goes for your Rifle Volunteers as well, Captain Atkinson. Is that understood?"

Atkinson, an impressive-looking man with a bushy beard, said tightly, "It is."

"I want there to be no mistake about that," Gold persisted. "My second-in-command, Colonel Murray, will deal with any native opposition, and if you run into trouble, you are to call on him for help."

"If there are any mistakes, they will not be made by the Rifle Volunteers," Atkinson retorted hotly.

There was a stir in the room at Atkinson's forthright reply. A settler sitting behind Johnny nudged him and said, not without a hint of pride in his voice, "That's our Harry, right enough! Gives as good as 'e gets. If 'e decides to go into politics when this war is over, 'e'll go far, mark my words. We'll 'ave 'im as premier one of these days."

Colonel Gold spent a moment or two trying to stare the Volunteer officer down. "Very well, then," he said finally, and turned to Colonel Murray.

"The main body, consisting of the Light Company of the Sixty-fifth and the gunnery contingent from the *Niger,* will proceed under Colonel Murray along the main road, going south toward Waireka Hill. The Royal Artillery detachment that arrived this morning aboard the *Airedale* has not, I'm afraid, finished unloading, but I am confident we shall not need them. The twelve-pounder and the Congreve rocket tube will be sufficient to soften the enemy up for an assault by the Sixty-fifth."

Captain Cracroft stood up to protest. "You're not leaving my bluejackets out of it again, Colonel? I can give you sixty lads with cutlasses to storm those palisades, and they'll be over them like monkeys before the Maoris know what's happening."

"That is not the way to take a fortified position," Gold said coldly. "I appreciate your enthusiasm, Captain Cracroft, and"—he hesitated for the barest instant—"and the climbing abilities of sailors, but I am sure you will admit that the science of military strategy, as it applies to land warfare, is not the strong point of the Royal Navy. You must leave that to the professionals. In any case, these maneuvers should not take long. I shall expect the operation to be completed and the troops back here before dusk."

Cracroft sat down with a disgruntled expression. Beside Johnny, William De Lancey whispered in amazement, "Before dusk? How the deuce does he imagine he can wrap up this operation by sundown? For God's sake, the morning's half gone already!"

Gold could not have heard the comment, but it was easy for him to glean, from the whispers that were going around the room, the fact that he was being criticized. He fixed William with a bulging eye and said, with choleric satisfaction, "As for you, *Colonel* De Lancey, I have written to the War Branch in Auckland regarding your lack of a commission, but as yet have received no reply. So you are again cast for the role of observer."

William held his tongue, but at the conclusion of the meeting, as the regimental and militia officers hurried out to carry on their duties, he took Johnny by the arm and said, "Come on. I suppose you'd better meet him."

Gold had just finished irascibly shaking off some of the New Plymouth civilians, and as William and Johnny approached he looked at them peevishly and said, "De Lancey, who is this gentleman?"

"May I introduce my brother-in-law, John Broome," William said. "He arrived this morning on the *Airedale*. He has come to New Plymouth on behalf of the Auckland *Star.*"

Gold reacted with swift fury. "A journalist? By God, this is too much!" To Johnny he rasped, "Are you aware, sir, that New Plymouth is under martial law?"

"I had heard that," Johnny confessed. "I was hoping to have a firsthand look at today's action, if I could tag along as an observer —" He resisted the impulse to add "Like Colonel De Lancey."

William interposed quickly, "Mr. Broome's name is well known to the public in Auckland; we shall wish to show him every courtesy. As we have done for the editor of the *Taranaki News,* who was also present at this meeting."

"The *Taranaki News* has been made well aware of the requirement of censorship," Gold growled. He again turned his dudgeon on Johnny. "I ought to have you arrested, sir! By God, I've a mind to!"

Johnny restrained his anger. "There is no censorship in Auckland," he said coolly, "and if I am not allowed to accompany the Sixty-fifth, it is my intention to ride with the Mounted Volunteers."

"You will do no such thing!" Gold stormed. "You will remain in New Plymouth—under guard, if necessary—and Captain Brown will be given orders to that effect. Do I make myself clear?"

"Exceedingly so," Johnny replied, and turned on his heel and left before his temper could get the better of him.

William caught up with him outside a few minutes later. "I calmed Gold down somewhat," he told Johnny, "but you'd best keep out of his way. I'll be your eyes and ears, and in the meantime you can wander around town and pick up what you can here. You'll find plenty of people willing to talk about Colonel Gold, I assure you."

"The man must be insane," Johnny fumed, "to split up his forces like that—send the Volunteers overland, while the troops travel the main road where their progress may be observed from behind any tree. An enemy would be hard put to divide them, and here Gold's gone and done their work for them."

"Colonel Gold does not regard the Volunteers as part of his forces," William said resignedly, "but rather as a cross he has to bear. Granted, most of them are not properly trained or equipped —they're lacking in discipline and, for the most part, are armed with old Brown Bess muskets and muzzle-loading Enfields. Still—" William shrugged. "They are eager enough. The displaced settlers and those who are waiting for land to be allocated have joined up to a man. They've got all the pluck in the world, and quite a few of them are good bushmen and excellent shots. *And* they understand the terrain, as Gold does not."

"And if they run into trouble?" Johnny asked.

"I pray that they will not. But the Maoris aren't fools, whatever Gold may think of them. Somehow, I don't think they'll wait behind their palisades for the Sixty-fifth to attack them. However, we shall see." William repeated his shrug. "As a mere observer, I'm not permitted to offer an opinion, Johnny."

Johnny frowned. "Good God, Will, don't they know who you are, what you've done?"

"It has been mentioned," William conceded. He unhitched his horse and swung up into the saddle. "I had better find Brown and Atkinson, or they'll leave without me."

Johnny watched him ride off, a tall, straight figure with a carbine holstered near his left leg, where it could be braced and fired one-handed. He saw Atkinson's blue-shirted riflemen, about fifty strong, open their ranks to let him through, and then William was riding with Captain Brown and Brown's adjutant, Stapp, to lead the way across the overland route.

Johnny turned his head to follow the progress of the 65th. Lieutenant Colonel George Murray seemed to be having some trouble getting his column formed up. The *Niger*'s marines wrestled with a ton of gun and carriage and another ton of powder, canister, and shot, while the rocket crew, their awkward weapon dismantled and shouldered, fell in behind the redcoats. At last all was in readiness, and the infantry marched smartly off, to the shrill accompaniment of regimental pipes, while the townspeople lined the road to watch.

In a few minutes they were out of sight round a bend. Johnny lingered, mingling with the townspeople to hear their comments, and then, catching sight of Colonel Gold coming in his direction, took William's advice to keep out of his way, and left to seek the views of his colleague on the *Taranaki News*.

A glint of metal on a hilltop caught William's attention, and when, surveying the spot with his eyes shaded against the noon sun, he saw movement, he leaned over in the saddle and touched Captain Brown's arm.

"They're watching our progress from the hills," he informed the Volunteer officer. "They've been following us all morning."

Captain Stapp, the adjutant, swore under his breath. "What the devil are they waiting for?" he exploded. "There must be enough of them up there by now to outnumber us, and we can't move very freely with the horses through this tangle."

"They can see the Sixty-fifth on the coastal road from up there too," William surmised. "They're waiting until our separation from Colonel Murray is to their liking."

Talk ceased as the horses scrambled up the steep side of a ravine, and William clung on to stay in the saddle. It was the second difficult ravine the Volunteers had crossed this morning; the land between Mount Egmont and the shore was riven by deep gulleys that carried off the floods. The enmeshing bush was intimidating to those used to the tamer landscapes of Europe, and the British military had decided long before Colonel Gold that bush fighting was to be avoided at all costs, and was best left to the Maoris and the settlers.

As the horsemen attained the top of the ridge, followed by the sweating riflemen, William saw the glint of brown bodies trickling through the gorges, passing under the green foliage from cover to cover and at last coming to rest in concealment. The ravines looked innocent again, but everybody who had seen that secret inundation knew what it meant.

"They've taken possession of the gullies," Brown cried in frustration. "Ahead and behind. We're cut off."

As if to emphasize the seriousness of their position, a shot rang out and a Volunteer cried out in surprise as a bullet creased him. "Take cover!" William shouted, forgetting that he had no authority, and the mounted contingent slid off their horses and led them to less exposed positions, while Atkinson's men spread out and disposed themselves behind trees and bracken. In a very few minutes the air was thick with flying bullets and shot, and two more men had been wounded, despite the dense cover.

Harry Atkinson slithered through the underbrush and came to the spot where William lay concealed with Brown. "I've told my lads to be frugal with their shots and not to fire unless they have a target," he said grimly. "We were issued only thirty rounds a man." His voice was bitter. "We weren't supposed to do any fighting, you see. Colonel Murray was supposed to see to our protection."

"Murray will hear the shooting," Brown said confidently. "He can't be more than a couple of miles away. All we have to do is hang on until he sends a relief force."

But an hour and more passed, and there was no sign of a sally by Colonel Murray. William watched as the Volunteers fought on alone, and he was impressed by their courage and daring. Atkinson was a natural leader of men, and, exposing himself to danger as he moved from position to position, he saw to it that his recruits made their few shots count.

"Where is Murray?" Captain Stapp groaned.

"I think," William said, rising to his feet, "that I had better go fetch him."

"Colonel De Lancey, you cannot!" Captain Brown exclaimed. "You'll be riding into a hail of fire, and—" He broke off with a glance at William's pinned sleeve. "It's a job for someone younger and more fit."

But William was already in the saddle, gathering up the reins. "I'm the most easily spared," he asserted with black humor. "I'm only an observer." He gave the spurs to his animal and, lying low along his horse's neck, crashed out of the underbrush down the slope. It was a temptation to proceed directly down the ridge toward the beach, but that would have made him too prominent a target, and one to be picked off at leisure. It was better to depend on speed and surprise. The horse plunged straight into the ravine, whinnying with fear, while William hung on with all his might. Then he was in among the startled warriors, close enough to see the expressions on their tattooed and painted faces. He rode deliberately through one group, scattering them, and wishing for his right arm so that he might lay about him with a saber. Then, turning his steed, he was racing along the bottom of the ravine, splashing through the thin rivulet there, toward the sea, while disorganized fire came from behind him.

Having attained the beach, more than a mile away, he galloped across the packed sands until, on the coastal road ahead, he saw the long splash of crimson that marked Murray's column. They were marching along in a marvelously disciplined manner, but they hadn't made much progress. He cantered along beside the line of tramping soldiers toiling under their heavy packs until he found Murray. In a few terse words, he explained the situation, and said urgently, "The Volunteers are effectively pinned down, Colonel. They can't move until those ravines are cleared out . . . and if that is not done, when they run out of ammunition, there will be a slaughter."

Murray, to his credit, responded promptly. He summoned a subaltern and ordered, "Lieutenant Urquhart, you will take thirty men and go to the aid of the Volunteers. You will provide cover and enable them to retire."

"They don't want to retire, Colonel," William said, puzzled over Murray's choice of words. "They only need some relief. When you begin your attack on the *pa* at Waireka, the sound of the firing will provide the diversion needed to draw off the hill parties. Then we can cut across the remaining terrain and join you, as Colonel Gold ordered."

Colonel Murray seemed not to have heard him. He turned to frown at the rocket-tube party from the *Niger*. They had set down their burden and were coming toward William with drawn cutlasses. "Here, you, men! What are you up to?" Murray barked at them.

Their officer, a boyish-faced lieutenant, grinned and said, "We thought we'd go along for the fight, sir."

"Get back to your weapon at once," Murray growled. "This is a military operation, not a schoolboy game, and you are under my orders. I shall have words with Captain Cracroft about this, and if your men desert their post again, I shall recommend a rope's end for them."

Chagrined, the young naval officer collected his men and led them back, amid protests, to shoulder the components of the Congreve launching mechanism once more.

William guided Urquhart and his redcoats to a vantage point between the first two gullies, having to argue the lieutenant out of his intention to take an easy route along the ridge, which would have left them silhouetted against the skyline and made them tempting targets. At the first hint of ragged firing, Urquhart, to William's amazement, formed the men up and had them fire a volley from a kneeling position, as if they were facing an enemy in formal ranks. The bullets flew into the forest toward unseen targets, but the maneuver, repeated several times, seemed to work. The Maoris retreated from the ravines and maintained a desultory siege from farther away, no doubt biding their time.

William made it back to the Volunteers' position with only a few stray bullets to dodge, and reported to Captain Brown.

"What, retreat?" Captain Brown remonstrated. "That can't be. You must have misunderstood him. We have only to hold these fellows off for an hour or two, until they hear the twelve-pounder and the rocket tube battering at the outer fence of their precious *pa*. Then they'll leave quickly enough to defend their village, and we'll be able to get our wounded out of here while the rest of us join the main fight."

He paused to listen to the uneven firing from the hilltops. Harry Atkinson, mildly profligate of his remaining ammunition now that Urquhart had arrived, allowed his men to get off one answering round apiece.

"What do you think, Colonel De Lancey?" Stapp put in. "It shouldn't take much more than an hour or two, should it?"

"The Waireka Hill *pa* was in plain sight from the spot where I left Colonel Murray," William replied. "An hour's march should bring them to it."

But the afternoon wore on without the expected sound of cannon shot and small arms fire. The irregular sniping from the hills continued, and another Volunteer was hit, this time fatally. Captain Atkinson swore, and demanded, "When is Murray going to *move*? Daylight's almost gone." At that juncture, a messenger arrived from Lieutenant Urquhart's position, to inquire when the Volunteers were going to retire. Atkinson looked at the man's scarlet regalia with distaste and said gruffly, "Tell Lieutenant Urquhart that we cannot move our wounded under fire, and that we are still waiting for his commanding officer to provide a diversion."

By that time, the Maori besiegers had worked up their courage for an attack. They swarmed over the ridges, firing their blunderbusses and old muzzle-loaders, screaming their war cries. The riflemen and Urquhart's party beat them off, at the cost of another man wounded. William remarked to Brown, "That must have pretty well depleted our ammunition. If they rush us again, we'll have to depend on Urquhart to hold them off."

At that point, the white-haired Captain Stapp, pausing at William's side as he made a round of the perimeter, dropped a handful of cartridges at the elbow of the Volunteer beside him.

"A brave young fellow named Pitcairn rode right through the rebels' position to bring us three haversacks of these from New Plymouth, Colonel De Lancey," he said. "He's one of ours, but he dislocated his shoulder this morning and we had to leave him behind. Gold may not think highly of us, but when we've lads like Pitcairn in our ranks, we're a force to be reckoned with, ain't we?" He scowled, peering into the fading light as a fresh fusillade of shots heralded another attack in the making. "We've got enough ammunition to repel one, maybe two more assaults. It's almost sunset. What's holding bloody Murray up? He's going to have to storm the *pa* by moonlight now."

William lifted his head. Across the green ridges, a bugle call could be heard. His spirits rose momentarily, then fell with a crash as he realized, with dismay and shocked disbelief, that the bugler was sounding the "Retire."

"What the bloody hell!" Stapp exclaimed beside him.

The thirty men of Lieutenant Urquhart's party, farther down the slope, bestirred themselves. A sergeant was rushing among them, bawling orders. The men formed into a column, while Urquhart, a stiff red-coated figure in the medium distance, stood with folded arms.

"I'd better find out," William said, and slid down the slope through the bracken, while a Maori, somewhere across the way, took a halfhearted potshot at him.

Urquhart looked genuinely distressed, but he was adamant. "I cannot disobey the call to retire, Colonel De Lancey," he insisted. "My orders are explicit."

"But what can Murray have in mind?" William protested. "He knows we have wounded here. He can't just abandon them."

"Colonel Gold's orders were for Colonel Murray to bring his troops back to town before dark," the young man said coolly, as if he were discussing an abstract problem in tactics.

"But he hasn't even attacked the *pa* yet! That, I understood, was the point of this whole exercise. If you leave us alone out here, without even a feint by Colonel Murray to draw the Maoris off, they'll pounce on us the moment you're gone."

The "Retire" sounded again from the coastal road. Urquhart's mouth compressed into a tight line. "I'm very sorry, Colonel" was all he would say, and he turned on his heel as his men, rifles shouldered, marched off as best they could in the clutter of brush across the ravine.

Willam, sick with anger, pulled himself by roots and branches back to the Volunteers' position. Brown and Stapp helped him up the last few feet. "He's left us here to die," Brown said with a smoldering anger that matched William's own, "but by God, we'll give them a fight before we go!"

Stapp looked out across the darkening greenery. "They're not waiting long," he said. "Here they come."

Dusk had fallen, but outside the dusty windows of the *Taranaki News* Johnny Broome could see people hurrying through the streets. "What's going on out there?" queried the *News*'s proprietor, a sparrowlike man named Fenwick, looking up from the still-wet proof sheets he had been showing to Johnny.

"We'd better find out," Johnny suggested, rising to his feet and snatching up his coat. He stepped out into the rutted track that passed for New Plymouth's main street, with the little editor at his heels, and stopped a heavyset colonist who was hastening past. "Where's everybody headed to?" he inquired.

"Our boys are back," the man flung over his shoulder, and ran to catch up to his friends.

Johnny and Fenwick followed the crowd to the head of the street, past a cattle pen and some ramshackle farm buildings, to where it turned into the main road on the other side of the trenches and barricades. In the deepening dusk, a double column of marching men could be seen, and the heavy tramp of feet and the jingle of accoutrements was borne on the evening air. Some of the settlers had brought torches, which together with a bright half-moon lit up the scene. Women predominated in the crowd that lined the road, many of them with babies and small children, and Johnny could plainly read the anxiety in their faces as they waited for a first glimpse of sons and husbands.

But as the whole column drew into view, it was starkly apparent that it consisted only of officers and men of the 65th, followed by a small party of marines dragging a naval gun and five bluejackets shouldering a long tube, like pallbearers at a funeral.

"They've come back without them!" an agitated man near Johnny exclaimed. "By God, they left them out there somewhere!" The crowd was becoming excited, and there were angry shouts at the redcoats as they marched past.

A distraught woman with a toddler clinging to her rushed out into the road and clutched at the arm of Colonel Murray. "My husband!" she wailed at him. "Where's my husband?"

Colonel Murray shook her off. "My good woman, I don't know," he said irritably, and strode on.

Fenwick darted off to question some officer he knew, but the man only shook his head and would not talk to him. "We'll have to apply to Colonel Gold for information," the *News*'s proprietor told Johnny. "Are you coming with me?"

"Just a minute," Johnny said. When the party of sailors from the *Niger* hove into sight, looking disgruntled, Johnny fell into step beside them and asked, "Where are the Volunteers?"

The sailors growled among themselves, and one of them spat and said, "They're in trouble out there, and Colonel Murray just left them. He sent a relief party to them this afternoon to help them out, but when it started to get dark, he just blew retreat and brought the sojers back."

Johnny could hardly believe his ears. "What about the *pa?* Did you take it?"

"Didn't even try," another sailor said in disgust. "He just turned around and came back when it started to get dark."

"We wanted to go help the Volunteers," a third sailor put in. "Asked 'im again, nice-like. But 'e wouldn't let us."

One of the officers with Murray looked back and saw Johnny talking to the sailors and, at a word from the colonel, came hurrying back. "You men, go along there," he barked at the bluejackets and, turning to Johnny, said, "Oh, it's you, is it, Mr. Broome? Colonel Gold has warned you. You had better be on your way before you get into trouble."

People were milling around, not knowing what to do. Johnny heard angry mutterings on every side. He shouldered his way through the crowd toward the defensive perimeter while Fenwick ran after him, trying to catch up.

"Where are you going, Broome?" Fenwick cried.

"The *Niger*'s lying off the beach not far down the coast. I'm going to fetch Captain Cracroft."

"Colonel Gold forbade you to leave town," Fenwick warned him. "You'll be put under arrest."

"Words cannot express my opinion of Colonel Gold," Johnny retorted, "and when I return to Auckland, it is *he* who had better look out for *me!*"

"You may be heading into a hornet's nest," the little man cautioned. "The countryside between here and Waireka must be infested with roving war parties who are feeling their oats now that Murray has turned back without doing them any damage."

"It can't be helped. Somebody's got to do it. Can you help me find a horse?"

Fenwick wrung his hands. "Colonel Gold will have my hide, and close me down entirely, if he finds out I've helped you, but . . ." He drew himself up resolutely. "Wait here, Broome. No, you'd better get out of sight in case someone wants to carry tales back to Colonel Gold. Wait over there behind that shed."

He returned scarcely fifteen minutes later, leading a big chestnut, fully saddled and bridled. "I don't know why I'm doing this," he fussed. He thrust a revolver and a bag of cartridges into Johnny's hands. "Here, you'd better have these."

Johnny thanked him and, with the revolver in his pocket, gave spurs to the horse and rattled across the thick planks spanning the ditch that was meant to sever the main road. The townspeople still hovering about by the roadside knew very well what he was about, and they sent a cheer after him; there could be only one reason for a horseman to gallop into the hostile night.

He followed the road for a mile, the moon bright enough to cast a shadow before him, and then, some instinct warning him as a burnt-down homestead loomed into view, he left the main thoroughfare and cut behind the corner of a paddock. His foresight was rewarded as a war party that had been lying in wait for travelers rose out of the blackened ruins to shout futile challenges after him and to pepper the air with a shot from a blunderbuss. Johnny's blood ran cold at the thought of raiders so close to New Plymouth, and he reflected wrathfully that, with the Maori tribes made bold by Colonel Gold's failure not only to take the Waireka *pa* but even to launch an assault upon it, New Plymouth itself was now in danger of being overrun.

There were no more incidents, and Johnny forced the pace of the chestnut until, a quarter-mile farther on along the beach, he saw the *Niger* lying at anchor, its spars bare and its smokestack sticking up from the deck between foremast and mainmast. Captain Cracroft would not have failed to post a good watch in these waters, where Maori canoes could slide right up to an unwary vessel and take it over, and Johnny dismounted and waved his arms to attract the lookout's attention. In a remarkably short interval a gig was lowered and sent ashore to fetch him. Captain Cracroft was waiting on deck for him, and, wasting no time, Johnny poured out the whole sorry tale to him.

Cracroft listened without interrupting, chewing on his cigar, and when Johnny had finished, he growled, "What does that infernal man think he's playing at, to set out with half an army and return before dark without even attempting to engage the enemy? What must the Maoris think of us?"

"They're out all over the countryside," Johnny informed him, and related the incident of his narrow escape at the burnt-out farmhouse.

Cracroft removed his cigar and said reflectively, "You're right— all the hotbloods will have gone out looking for easy pickings, like the Volunteers trapped out there somewhere, leaving their *pa* badly defended. . . ."

Johnny nodded. "I'm afraid so. The Volunteers are finished unless something is done."

"We can't go marching all over kingdom come in the middle of the night looking for them," Cracroft said firmly, "or we're liable to end up like Murray, returning home without having accomplished anything. But the Waireka *pa* is sitting up there in plain sight, not a half hour's brisk march away."

Johnny followed Cracroft's steely gaze to the fortified village on the hilltop poking up above the rolling bush country, its matchstick palisades gleaming silver in the moonlight. "An attack on the *pa* would relieve the Volunteers just as surely by drawing off their attackers," he agreed. "But, Captain, you're without your twelve-pounder and your rocket tube!"

"We won't need them," Peter Cracroft declared. He raised his voice to the sailors and officers who were crowding closer than naval discipline should have allowed. "What about it, lads? Shall we show Her Majesty's regiment what the Royal Navy can do with a few cutlasses and marlinspikes?"

An answering roar went up from the crew, and in short order grinning bluejackets were piling into the ship's boats and rowing ashore. Johnny left his horse with the detail left behind to guard the boats, and set off with the sailors. There were about sixty of them, young and in high spirits, and as they climbed the hill, they met a startled Maori war party, numbering about a dozen, who were setting out in the direction of the ravines a couple of miles away, from which gunfire could still be heard. With a blood-curdling yell, the sailors ran at them, waving their cutlasses. The Maoris took to their heels, and the *Niger*'s bluejackets chased them all the way back to the stockade.

"Ten pounds for the man who pulls down the flag!" shouted Cracroft.

It was the only battle order he gave. The bluejackets, their appetite for a fight whetted by the brief uphill chase, swarmed over the top, heedless of the few disorganized shots that came from loopholes. Their momentum caught the Maori defenders by surprise. Johnny ran with the pack, the borrowed revolver in his hand. The first man over was a coxswain named Bill Odgers, and Johnny saw him heading for the flagpole, hacking with his cutlass all around him.

A couple of sailors gave Johnny a boost over the barricade, and Johnny found himself down among the rifle pits, with Maori warriors jabbing at his legs with hatchets. He shot one, scrambled out of the way of another while a bluejacket sliced at the man with his blade, and joined the rush to the flagpole. Odgers had gotten there first and was shinnying up the pole like a monkey, as Cracroft had described his sailors, while his compatriots chased the surviving Maori inhabitants out into the bush.

The scuffle was over in minutes. Some fifty dead or wounded Maoris lay about on the ground or in the rifle pits—mostly those who had been killed in the first shock of the assault, or who hadn't gotten out of the way fast enough. The entire population of the *pa* was out there somewhere, fleeing through the bush. Of the *Niger*'s men, not one had been killed, although there were a few nasty leg wounds.

Odgers, grinning like an ape, came over to Captain Cracroft and offered him the Maori flag. "Good work, lad," Cracroft approved. "I'll see that you're recommended for the Victoria Cross for this piece of work."

"If you don't mind, Cap'n, I'd rather have the ten pounds," Odgers said boldly. Captain Cracroft laughed, clapped him on the back, and dug into his pocket.

"Well, Captain," Johnny observed a little while later as they stood on the inner rampart of the *pa,* looking out across the moon-drenched landscape, "it seems you've done in a quarter hour what all the Queen's men could not do all day."

"What they had not the stomach to do," Cracroft said with a scowl. He puffed on his cigar and listened to the sounds of the night. The firing from the distant ravines had stopped. "It seems that the Volunteers are no longer under attack. Either that, or . . ."

"Or they've been overwhelmed and gone under," Johnny finished for him. "I'll be wanting to get back to New Plymouth now and see if they straggle in."

"Ah, yes, your brother-in-law, Colonel De Lancey," Cracroft supplied understandingly. He waved the glowing tip of his cigar at the forest growth beyond. "What's that?"

In the brake below, a score of Maori warriors armed with shot-guns and spears trotted into a clearing and looked up at the walls of the *pa.* Seeing the ramparts occupied by bluejackets, and the flagpole bare, they turned tail and disappeared into the bush.

"There's your answer, Broome," the captain said. "The noise we made here drew them off. They'll build another *pa* somewhere, and we'll have to go through all this again, but Waireka Hill is ours."

"The Battle of Waireka," Johnny said, savoring the sound of the words. "I'll write it up in Auckland, where Colonel Gold's writ of censorship doesn't extend. Your coxswain, Bill Odgers, is going to be famous."

"A good lad," Cracroft rumbled. "They're all good lads."

Johnny was back in New Plymouth in time to see the Mounted Volunteers and the Rifle Volunteers come marching in by the light of the moon. As late as it was, the townspeople were there to greet them. Wives ran to embrace their husbands in joyful reunion, mothers wept glad tears over their sons, children pushed forward to be picked up by their fathers, and there was handshaking all around from the men who had been left behind. Johnny hung around until he saw Will De Lancey come through the barriers, leading a horse with a wounded man slung across its back, then slipped off to Will's tent to wait for him.

William arrived an hour later, hollow-eyed with fatigue, to find Johnny sitting on his cot. "It's good to see you alive, Will," Johnny said with understated emotion.

"I'm lucky to be here," William asserted. "We were down to our last few rounds. We couldn't have beaten off another attack. But then we heard shots and yells coming from Waireka Hill—the wind was blowing in our direction—and it sounded like a bloody riot. The Maoris who were warming up for another onslaught against us heard it too, and there was a lot of excited jabber, and then they all went rushing off. I wonder what it was all about."

"As it happens, I can tell you," Johnny volunteered with a grin. Gleefully he filled William in on Cracroft's unorthodox victory. "The bluejackets scaled the stockade like a pack of schoolboys off on a prank," he finished. "Cracroft is recommending Bill Odgers for the V.C., and, by God, he earned it twice over! The warriors who had joined in the attack on the Volunteers came tearing back to find their *pa* occupied. They fled into the bush, and we had neither sight nor sound of them after that."

"Cracroft is a splendid fellow," William agreed. "Gold can hardly reprimand him for succeeding where he failed."

"There will be questions asked in Auckland," Johnny promised. "I shall see to that."

"There will be questions asked here as well," William asserted grimly. "The good people of New Plymouth are incensed. I went with a delegation of them to have it out with Gold, but his servant informed us that he had retired and could not be disturbed."

"What cheek!" Johnny exclaimed.

"I shall pursue the matter, you may be sure," William vowed. "I am still a civilian. To hell with my damned commission! I'll get it with Gold's recommendation or without!"

"What possessed Murray to withdraw when he did? He didn't even wait to evacuate the wounded, and he could not have failed to realize the position the Volunteers were in."

William gave vent to a weary yawn. "God knows, Johnny . . . I certainly don't. According to Lieutenant Urquhart, he was simply obeying Colonel Gold's orders, which were to return to town before dusk. But I confess I'm bushed. I don't know about you. I shall sleep on it, and perhaps by tomorrow I shall be able to ask Gold for an explanation without losing my temper."

The following morning, however, a corporal of the 65th delivered a letter to the tent, addressed to "Captain William De Lancey." It proved to be from Colonel Gold, and William read it with hardly contained fury.

The contents were brief and coldly formal. Gold stated that official confirmation had come through from the War Branch in Auckland that William had been granted a commission in the rank of captain in the Taranaki Militia. "On my recommendation," the note added pointedly.

"On receipt of this order," the note continued, "you will proceed on outpost duty to the Bell Blockhouse, Waitara, commanded by Captain James Barton, of Her Majesty's 65th Regiment." William, his bile rising, digested the rest of his instructions. He was to leave immediately, taking a hundred and fifty men of the Rifle Volunteers and a twelve-pounder howitzer, with the Royal Artillery detachment that had arrived with Johnny aboard the *Airedale,* and relieve one of the 65th's companies that was presently stationed in the blockhouse. His second-in-command was to be Lieutenant Henry Morrison, as communications officer.

In silence, he passed the order to Johnny Broome, who, awake now, was sitting up on the spare cot that William had borrowed for him. Johnny read it, his eyebrows rising higher with every line, and swore softly.

"He's getting rid of you, Will. Posting you to the Waitara where you won't be in his way. And managed to get you reduced in rank, in the bargain, to keep you under his thumb. What are you going to do about it?"

"I'll go where I'm posted, of course," William said. He calmly finished shaving, rinsed the lather from his face, and dumped the basin of water outside the tent flap.

"Well, he hasn't muzzled *me!*" Johnny fumed. "Gold is nothing short of a disaster, and Murray's not much better. If the governor had stayed here, I fancy he would have hauled them both before a court-martial!"

"It seems probable," William agreed.

Johnny got out of the cot and began pulling on his clothes. "I'd better get back to Auckland right away," he said resolutely. "Before Gold finds some excuse to have me detained. I'll not wait to sail back with the *Airedale*. I'm going down to the harbor to find any ship that will take me." He stuck his neck outside the tent flap and looked at the curving bay. "Hello, what's this? Come take a look, Will."

William joined him and saw a three-master, its sails furled, riding off the beach, its slender, graceful lines instantly recognizable.

"The *Dolphin!*" he exclaimed. "She must have dropped anchor last night."

"Delivering supplies to New Plymouth," Johnny amplified. "It won't take more than a day to unload her. I'll go see Claus right now. What a stroke of luck!"

"Give Claus and Mercy my best, won't you?" William requested. "I'm sorry I won't have time to go down to the beach with you." He started to pack his few possessions; he would have to draw the Volunteers' uniform issue—a blue serge tunic and forage cap—now that he was no longer officially classed as an observer. "I'll have to see Harry Atkinson about rounding up a hundred fifty of his Rifles in a hurry, but first I'm going to squeeze in a good-bye to Andy."

Johnny shook hands with him. "Kitty will be surprised to see me back so soon," he said, with a trace of hesitation in his words. "And pleased, I hope. She doesn't greatly like being left in Auckland on her own. To be truthful, Will, she isn't enamored of New Zealand, and she talks constantly of paying a visit to her brother Pat, who's established himself on a sheep station in Victoria. It's not far from my uncle's place at Bundilly." He grinned ruefully. "At least this will give me a chance to forestall it. I'm afraid if I let her go I'd never get her back. She and Patrick are twins, you know, and this is the first time they've been parted."

William offered no comment. Johnny's marriage to the beautiful

Lady Kitty Cadogan was, he was aware, a fragile one, and there had been gossip concerning it before they had left Sydney.

"Rest assured, Will," Johnny said in parting, "that once I am in Auckland I shall not rest until I see Colonel Gold replaced—as he is bound to be. I can only hope that the next commander who is sent out from Australia will be an improvement."

William found Andy and the little boy Hal at breakfast with their fellow pupils in the big, warm kitchen of Ellie Mordaunt's school in Hodgson Street. Mrs. Mordaunt, without asking whether or not he wanted it, served him with the same ample fare the boys were enjoying, and, as he ate, William broke the news of his departure as gently as he could.

To his relief, Andy took it philosophically; it was Hal who burst into unhappy tears.

"You'll come back as soon as you can, won't you, Uncle Will?" Andy said. His small brown hand clung for a moment to William's, and then, when William assured him that he would, he resumed his meal. To Hal the boy explained patiently, "Uncle Will is an officer in the army, you see, Hal—a colonel. He *has* to fight the Maoris if they rebel and attack the settlers, so as to make it safe to farm and breed stock. But as soon as it's safe, we'll go back to our farm, won't we, Uncle Will? And Hal will come with us."

"That is it precisely, Andy," William confirmed, his throat tight. "And while I'm gone, you do the best you know at school, both of you. Learn everything you can, and do what Mrs. Mordaunt tells you, understand? I'll be counting on the two of you, and I'll expect a cracking good report on you when I get back."

"You'll have it, Uncle Will," Andy promised earnestly. "Won't he, Hal?"

But Hal continued to cry and did not cease until William took him into his arms and hugged him, as he had hugged Andy.

"Can I have you as my uncle Will, too, Colonel De Lancey?" the little boy asked, looking up with red-rimmed eyes into William's face.

The poor little devil, William thought pityingly, but before he could think of a suitably cheerful reply, Hal said anxiously, "You won't let the Maoris kill you, like they killed my folks, will you?"

"Don't be silly, Hal," Andy put in stoutly. "Of course he won't! Uncle Will is a *real* soldier—the Maoris won't get the better of him."

It was to be hoped he was right, William told himself wryly as, after thanking Mrs. Mordaunt for his excellent breakfast, he took reluctant leave of his two adopted nephews.

Walking back to the military camp, he paused to look out across the harbor. A trim little gig, whose strakes were of polished mahogany, was being rowed by four sailors out to the *Dolphin*. The big, red-bearded man in the stern was Johnny. William watched its progress for a few minutes, then, conscious that Gold's orders left him little time, strode on down the rutted street to his war.

Chapter VII

IT WAS NOT until six weeks after his first delivery of military supplies to New Plymouth that Claus Van Buren was able to return to his trading post at Rangirata. In the interim, government contracts had kept the *Dolphin* profitably employed, and on his last call at Auckland he had seen heartening evidence of Australia's answer to Governor Gore-Browne's plea for reinforcements.

The steamers *City of Sydney, City of Hobart,* and *Wonga-Wonga* had brought an advanced force of four companies of the 40th Regiment and two of the 12th, and coming to anchor in the harbor, as the *Dolphin* was leaving it, were the Royal Navy steam corvettes *Pelorus* and *Cordelia,* and the pride of the Australian navy, the *Victoria.*

"They will put down the insurrection, I do not doubt," Claus observed to his wife, Mercy. "Provided, that is to say, it is confined to the Taranaki tribes. My fear is that the Waikato will decide to forget old enmities and make common cause against the *pakehas.* That could start a full-scale war, with disastrous consequences for the settlers."

There had been a rumor, Johnny Broome had told him, that the chief of the Ngatimaniapoto, Rewi, was contemplating such an alliance, and that only the old king, Potatau, had restrained him from leading a war party to join Wiremu Kingi in Waitara, but . . . Claus would not repeat it to Mercy, or tell her of his fears. It was his intention to load the *Dolphin* with a cargo destined for the Sydney market, and once back in Australia, to insist that Mercy and their two boys stay there in safety, until the situation in New Zealand should improve.

Mercy had always accompanied him on his trading voyages—

indeed, she was more at home on board ship than on land—and she would, he was only too well aware, raise strong objections if he decreed that she must remain ashore, when he sailed back here in the *Dolphin* without her. The fact that she was two months pregnant would alter nothing; she had suffered two previous miscarriages, but both had occurred when, at his behest, she had been in their luxurious house in Sydney's Bridge Street. And as for the boys . . . Claus sighed to himself.

Joseph and Nathan were twins, now almost six years old, and it was time for them to commence their education—Mercy could scarcely dispute *that.* And if they were sent to school in Sydney, their mother's place was there with them. He would insist on it; he—

"It looks quite peaceful," Mercy said, breaking into his thoughts. She pointed with a small brown hand to the wharf and the line of warehouses and loading bays behind it, which constituted the trading post Claus had established, after coming south from Kororareka in the Bay of Islands, which had been his first post. Kororareka had never recovered from the massacre that had taken place there, fifteen years before, when Hone Heke and Kawati had razed the settlement to the ground, cut down the British flag, and driven the surviving townsfolk to seek refuge in Auckland. True, most of them had returned; but the town had stagnated, haunted by the ghosts of those who had died there, soldier and civilian, sailor and Maori warrior alike. And the once busy whaling station had been abandoned. The town, though it was now called Russell, had never managed, like the mythical phoenix, to rise from its ashes, despite its natural beauty and the fact that those who had despoiled it—Heke and Kawati—were both now dead.

Or, as Maori folklore had it, Rohe, the ferrywoman of the dead, had taken them in her canoe and ferried them away from *Ao Tea Roa,* the Long White Cloud, which was the Maori name for New Zealand . . . Claus shook his head sadly, remembering. The great Hone Heke had perished of consumption in 1850, old Kawati of measles three years later—ironically both diseases brought by the *pakeha* invaders. And Kawati's son had rejected the King Movement and declared loyalty to the British Queen.

"The canoes are coming, Claus!" Once again Mercy's voice interrupted his train of thought, and Claus put his glass to his eye as the *Dolphin,* under shortened sail, glided majestically into her accustomed anchorage. He shouted the order to let go her anchor and added, as Simon Yates, his mate, acknowledged the order, "I see your brother's coming out to us, Simon. And isn't that Te Anga's son, young Korriko, with him?"

Simon's keen eyes had already identified the occupants of the leading canoe, and he nodded as, propelled by half a dozen strong and skillful paddlers, the graceful craft came rapidly nearer. Both Yates brothers had been in Claus's employ since their return from the Australian goldfields and the death of their parents at the mission station in Rangihowa five years ago. Robert, the elder, was in charge of the trading post, and Simon, having served his apprenticeship at sea in several Van Buren vessels, had finally achieved what he had confessed was his ambition—the first mate's berth aboard the *Dolphin*.

Claus smiled to himself. When—*if*—he decided to retire, or when Mercy persuaded him to do so, Simon should have command of the beautiful clipper schooner, he had promised. They were both fine young men, reliable and honest, and Robert was on excellent terms with the local Maori tribes, speaking their language even more fluently than Claus himself, and boasting a beautiful Waikato wife, whom he had recently wed, the daughter of Chief Te Anga.

The canoe came alongside, and Robert, tall and deeply tanned, came on board with Korriko, his fifteen-year-old brother-in-law, who had a stone-headed club—a warrior's *mere*—at the waist of his flaxen kilt and a mantle of dog-skin draped about his shoulders. Greetings were warmly exchanged, Mercy and the twins included in the welcome, and then, when Korriko had agreed, with only a slight loss of dignity, to accompany the two little boys on a tour of the ship, Robert said gravely, "Te Anga asks that you speak with him as a matter of urgency, Captain Van Buren."

He spoke quietly, but Claus, sensing an underlying note of anxiety, was instantly alert. "A matter of urgency, Rob? Has there been trouble?"

"As far as the post is concerned, none, sir. But it's simmering beneath the surface. The old king, Potatau, died a few weeks ago—of influenza, poor old man. He was holding back the Waikato tribes, trying to keep the peace, but Rewi Maniapoto defied him, and there's a strong rumor that Rewi intends to lead a war party to join forces with Wiremu Kingi. Indeed, sir, I heard they were assembling canoes on the Mokau River. If they are, it could be very serious, I'm afraid."

It could indeed, Claus thought, with the British troops stretched out dangerously thin and the newly arrived reinforcements from Australia still in Auckland, awaiting transport to New Plymouth. He frowned, recalling that Johnny Broome had told him that William De Lancey had been sent with a company of volunteers to one of the danger spots—the Bell Blockhouse at the mouth of the Waitara River.

He asked a number of questions, to which Robert Yates replied as informatively as he could, and then the younger man volunteered, "Potatau had been succeeded by his son, Tawhiao, sir. He does not wield the authority the old chief did. He's very young, not much more than a boy, and they say he's a hothead, easily swayed by the older chiefs. I—well, I reckon that's why Te Anga wants to see you."

"I see." Claus instinctively glanced skyward. It was not yet noon —time enough to make the three-mile journey to Te Anga's *pa,* confer with the chief, and return to the *Dolphin* before nightfall. "Do you think I should go now, at once?"

Robert's reply was emphatic. "I do, Captain Van Buren. I'll come with you, of course, and Korriko too. You can leave Simon in charge of the ship, can't you?"

"Yes, of course I can—he's perfectly capable. We need not start loading until tomorrow. I take it you'll have a sizable consignment of timber ready for me?"

"Yes," Robert confirmed. "You can see it when we go ashore." He went into brief details, and Claus nodded his approval. He took his leave of Mercy and the boys, and, not wanting to alarm her, said only that he was going ashore and would be back on board before dark. She made a plea for the boys to go with him, but Claus contrived to ignore it, and ten minutes later he and Robert embarked in the canoe with Korriko and were set ashore on the timber wharf.

The short journey through the bush to Te Anga's *pa* was made on foot at a leisurely pace. The country round about was flat and heavily timbered, with a small, fast-flowing stream running through it and a flax swamp bordering one side of the well-used track. The *pa* was an extensive one, built on rising ground and surrounded by the tribe's crop fields of *kumara*—sweet potato— and grain, well-tended and ripening in the sun, with lines of drying fish hanging from poles close to the outer palisade.

The *pa* itself, encompassing the village, was curtained by a double palisade close on twenty feet high, constructed of timber and with a deep ditch between, the whole flanked by gullies full of entangled bracken and thickly growing brambles. Inside, gun pits, redoubts, ditches, and traverses afforded protection for the defenders, and Te Anga had caused shelters to be dug below ground, in case cannon were brought to bear—as they frequently were—in attempts to breach the palisades. Each shelter, as nearly as Claus could judge from cursory inspection, could hold at least fifty men, and men were at work putting the finishing touches to their stronghold by caulking the gaps in the palisading with green flax, the purpose of which was to prevent enemy bullets from penetrating the apertures.

Despite all these warlike preparations, the life of the village was being conducted much as usual, the women crouched beside their cooking pots, and the children—of whom there were many of all ages—larking happily together as children will. Korriko dispatched a warrior to summon his father and led the visitors to the meetinghouse—the *marae*—a lofty edifice, with space to hold all the men of the village. Entrance was through an intricately carved and latticed door, decorated by *tikis* sculpted from greenstone, each one having a different expression and a disproportionately large phallus. The walls of the building were adorned with elaborate wood carvings, most on the same theme as the *tikis* but much larger, the figures with their tongues stuck out symbolically and, like the male organs, dramatically enlarged.

Two young women served refreshments, which included pannikins of rum, then vanished, and Te Anga made his appearance. He was strikingly good-looking; in the prime of his manhood, he bore elaborate tattooing on his face and lips and was draped in a brilliant scarlet cloak of *kaka* parrot feathers, his black hair oiled and dressed into a knotted roll winged by white-tipped plumes and held in place by a bone comb.

His greeting was restrained, lacking its accustomed warmth, and Claus, sensing this, was instantly on his guard.

"Captain Van Buren, I have asked you to come here in order that I may warn you," the chief said. "You will have seen the preparations we have made to defend ourselves against attack. They are necessary, for everywhere there is talk of war against the *pakehas*. Already my uncle, Rewi Maniapoto, has answered Wiremu Kingi's call to arms. His warriors have danced their *haka* on the bank of the Mokau River and have launched their canoes."

"I have heard that this is so, Te Anga," Claus confirmed cautiously. "But why is it necessary? Do the Waikato now make common cause with those they once conquered and enslaved?"

Te Anga eyed him reproachfully. "How can you ask if it is necessary, when the governor, the one we call Gory-Browne"—he smiled briefly at his own attempt at humor—"when this cold, arrogant man refuses to give even our chiefs audience when they would speak with him, but instead sends underling clerks to lie and prevaricate? And who permits *pakeha* settlers to come in their thousands to occupy land to which they have no rights. And who, furthermore, Captain Van Buren"—all trace of amusement had gone from his voice—"who summons more ships of war and redcoat regiments to aid him in driving us by force from what is ours! The Maori people *must* unite; they must make common cause with those who in the past were enemies, for the *pakeha* newcomers are the enemies now." He appealed to Robert. "*You,* the husband of my daughter, you understand, do you not?"

"Yes," Robert admitted, without hesitation. "I understand. Yet I cannot countenance war."

Te Anga shook his head sadly. "You have the heart of a *pakeha,* Robert Yates, but like Captain Van Buren you are good and honest, worthy of trust. It is not with men of your kind that we make war. It is the governor who betrays us, he who makes the first moves to break the peace."

And, Claus reflected grimly, there was truth in the claim. Gore-Browne *was* pursuing an aggressive policy; the purchase of the Waitara land had been at best hurried, at worst illegal, and his sending for troops and warships to enforce his claim to government ownership could be seen in only one way, in Maori eyes. There were close on thirty thousand *pakeha* settlers in the colony now, the majority concentrated on the North Island, and in the first eight years of Grey's governorship, three million acres of land had been acquired, at a cost of some £36,000—and considerable bloodshed.

"Many years ago," Te Anga said, "when the great warrior chief of the Ngapuhi, Hongi Hika, waited to pass to what your missionaries call the next life, he spoke his last words to his people. 'Be brave and strong in your country's cause,' he bade them. 'Let not the land of your ancestors pass into the hands of the *pakeha!*'" An odd little smile played about his lips, but his dark eyes gleamed as he added, in his own tongue, *"Me mate te tangata me mate mo te whenua*—the death of a warrior is to die for his country, Captain

Van Buren! Our people believe that, with all their hearts. And the council of the late King Potatau cannot prevent lawlessness and rebellion, and young Tawhiao has no control of the young and ignorant. They talk down their elders and indulge in feasting and dreams of battle. My young warriors are in a like state, and I cannot find it in my heart to rebuke them."

"War will rob the Maori people of their best and finest warriors, Te Anga," Claus asserted. "And it will be a war they cannot win."

"Me mate te tangata me mate mo te whenua," the chief reminded him. "What have the *pakeha* done for us since their coming? They bring disease. Six years ago, did not the sickness they call measles take the lives of four thousand of our people? Many brave warriors died thus, without honor. And what of the treaty, the treaty our chiefs signed at Waitangi, when the sea captain Governor Hobson promised us justice, if we accepted the sovereignty of Queen Victoria? Forty-five chiefs signed the treaty, persuaded to do so by that treacherous friend of the *pakehas,* Waaka Nene. But they signed for themselves only, not for the Maori people, Captain Van Buren; and others, under the influence of the missionaries, were said also to have signed during the ensuing months. What were we promised? Do you recall the terms of the Treaty of Waitangi?"

The treaty, Claus recalled, had been monstrously deceptive. The Maoris had been promised the Queen's royal protection and the rights and privileges of British subjects, among other things. . . .

Te Anga went on, his tone bitter as he recited from memory, " 'The lands, forests, fisheries and food-places of the Maori people should remain inviolate, but the right of preemptive purchase of their lands should rest with the Crown.' We believed, as one of our great chiefs stated, 'The shadow of the land belongs to Queen Victoria, but the substance remains with us.' But it has not been so. Those *pakehas* who had taken land wrongly were deprived of it, only to be permitted to buy it once more, at prices as low as ten pennies for an acre! Our hunting grounds are gone, our fisheries lost to us, and when we demand justice, the governor tells us we are rebels and sends his redcoats to bring us to submission! We are proud people, Captain Van Buren. We will fight for what is ours, and we will stem the tide of *pakeha* settlers or go to our deaths trying!"

Claus was silent, unable to find words with which to counter the chief's claims, for in his heart he was in sympathy with Te Anga.

Governor Gore-Browne was a soldier; he viewed the Maori raids on the settlers' farms, the theft of their stock, the destruction of their crops—and, of course, their deaths at the raiders' hands—as rebellion, for which there could be only one solution, and that a military one.

Te Anga eyed him searchingly, sensing his unease.

"Kahukura—our god of war, who is symbolized by the rainbow—calls to us, and my young men hear his call. They demand *utu*—revenge—and our priests, our *tohungas,* say that the time has come. Captain Van Buren, we know you as a good man, an honest trader and a friend . . . a *pakeha* Maori; and Robert also. But if there is war—and there will be—you will have to choose which side you will support."

Drawing his feathered cloak about him, Te Anga rose to his feet, indicating that the meeting was at an end. He strode out, and Claus grasped Robert's arm as they prepared to follow him.

"It is more serious than I had supposed, Rob," he admitted anxiously. "If the Waikato tribes join the Taranaki, there will be hell to pay. And if Rewi Maniapoto is already on his way to give support to Wiremu Kingi, then it's just a question of time, isn't it?"

"I fear it is, sir," Robert agreed unhappily. He added, as they left the *pa* and started their descent to the tree-shaded track, "I don't know about you, Captain Van Buren, but I have to confess that my loyalties are in question. If Te Anga asked it of me, I should give him my support. And if that renders me unfit to continue as manager of your trading post, then—" He shrugged resignedly. "Then so be it."

"We will do nothing hastily, Rob," Claus answered. "But rest assured that I understand how you feel. You have a wife to consider now, and so have I. A wife and sons. I shall take Mercy and the boys back to Sydney and leave them there—I'd already decided to do so. For myself . . . damn it, I don't know."

He was reminded of the scene with Commander Harland, over a year ago, when Red Broome had brought the newly arrived captain of the *Kestrel* to inspect the *Dolphin* as she lay at anchor in Sydney Cove. The young chief Te Tamihana had been on passage with him, and Harland had, in his ignorance, supposed the young man to be an Australian aborigine and insulted him. And . . . Claus still remembered what Harland had replied, when he himself had sought to turn the insult aside by stating that he regarded the Maoris as equals and respected their culture and their standards.

Harland had sneered and said, *"That, for one of your color, is understandable. Like calls to like, does it not?"*

Well, perhaps it did. Perhaps, as the son of a Javanese mother, he was closer to Te Anga's people and Tamihana's than to those they called *pakehas*—strangers. Fortunately, Captain Harland had been ordered to China not long after Red Broome had left Sydney to go to England. At least the *Kestrel* was not one of the ships of war soon to set their bluejackets and their guns ashore at New Plymouth in order to deal with what Harland—devil take the man! —had called the "recalcitrant native populations."

Darkness was falling as they came in sight of the trading post, but the wharf was ablaze with light—torchlights, fashioned from *kauri* branches—and swarming with dark bodies. And, as she lay offshore at anchor, the *Dolphin* was surrounded by war canoes, several alongside and empty.

"Oh, God!" Robert exclaimed, his voice taut with anger. "It's a raid! They're plundering the warehouse!"

He set off at a run, and Claus, his heart pounding, followed him, cursing himself for a fool for not having foreseen the possibility of a raid. Had not Te Anga admitted that his young warriors were spoiling for a fight? If they plundered the warehouse, that would be of no account; but if they seized possession of the *Dolphin,* with Mercy and the boys on board, then . . . He drew in his breath in agonized fear, not daring to visualize what might be the outcome.

"Are you armed, Rob?" he called out, but guessed the answer before Robert's headshake confirmed his fears. It had not seemed to him politic to carry a weapon when making a friendly call at Te Anga's *pa,* and Robert seemingly had felt the same way.

The raiding party numbered about fifty, apart from those in the canoes. They were all young, all armed with muskets or tomahawks, and without exception appeared to be in a state of intoxication, the casks of rum they had stolen from the warehouse lying about on the wooden floor of the loading bay, no doubt empty of their contents. No hindrance was offered when Claus and Robert broke into the midst of the crowd, but before either of them had a chance to remonstrate, several torches were flung at the roof of the timber store, and it caught fire moments later.

"I'm going to look for Paoa," Robert gasped, referring to his wife, "and I'll get a rifle."

He vanished into the swirling smoke, making for the small, tree-screened dwelling house that was his home, and Claus, understanding his anxiety, did not attempt to detain him. He recognized Korriko among the yelling mob of young warriors and thrust a way to his side, but the boy stared through him, his young, only recently tattooed face blank and shuttered. One of his companions, a year or so older, started to drag him away, expressing his contempt in the time-honored Maori fashion with an extended tongue, and Korriko muttered an insulting *"Pakeha!"* before collapsing a few yards away in a limp heap, overcome by the liquor he had imbibed.

Shocked by this totally unexpected show of animosity, Claus attempted to reason with a group who were barring his way to the wharf, but they turned deaf ears to his appeal, and then, to his relief, Robert returned to join him, a hunting rifle slung from his shoulder and a pistol in his hand.

"She's gone—Paoa's gone," he rasped, handing Claus the pistol. "One of our people told me she went out to the ship. But—" He swore despairingly as another storehouse erupted in flames, to exultant shouts from the mob. "God, they've gone mad! What did we ever do to them?"

Claus gestured to the darkened silhouette of the *Dolphin* and said urgently, "Come on, Rob, we'll go out to the ship. We don't want them running amuck there, with the women on board."

There were several oared boats tied up at the end of the wharf, and the young warriors, faced by the pistol and rifle, melted away, no longer disputing Claus's passage. And the boats, Claus saw thankfully, were undamaged. He flung himself into the gig in which he had come ashore, and as Robert cast off and jumped in beside him, he took up the oars and started to pull with the strength of desperation, sending the light craft skimming across the water toward the anchorage.

The scene on the *Dolphin*'s deck sent his heart plummeting. There were perhaps a dozen young warriors clustered about the rails, all armed and, in contrast to their fellows on the wharf, sober and ominously silent, as if they had been waiting for his arrival. The ship was in darkness, but as he hauled himself aboard, Claus saw the bodies of two of his seamen spread-eagled on the deck, and even in the fitful light of the moon it was evident that they were dead. Old Ben Knowles, his sailmaker, was one, and the other, although he lay face down, appeared to be a lad named Farquhar, a digger who had signed on as a deckhand in Geelong, only a few months before.

Of Mercy and the boys, of Paoa and Simon Yates and the rest of his crew, there was no sign. Sickened and angry, Claus controlled himself with an effort of will and faced the circle of young Maori warriors who clustered menacingly about Robert and himself.

"What are you doing aboard my ship? Where are my people?" He spoke in the Maori tongue, his tone deliberately brusque and authoritative, and looking from one to the other, he demanded curtly, "Which of you is the leader of this *tana muru?* Is Chief Te Anga aware of what you have done?"

The man who stepped forward—older than the rest and heavily tattooed and ochered—eyed him uncertainly for a moment, clearly taken aback; but then, recovering himself, he retorted defiantly, "I am Hori Kaka, an *ariki* of the tribe of Te Anga, and I lead this war party. There will be war—we shall drive all the *pakehas* from our land. We have destroyed your warehouse, Cap'in Van Buren, as you see!" He gestured with his musket toward the glowing fires on shore. "When that is gone and your trade goods become ashes, you will go whence you came, and we shall see you no more! We have not set fire to your ship, as we could have done, so that you may have the means to leave. But before you go, there are goods that we need."

"First tell me where are my people," Claus challenged. "You have killed two of my seamen, wantonly and without cause! I have come to you for many years in friendship, Hori Kaka. I have traded with you and trusted your tribe. Where is my wife? Where are my sons? And where is Paoa, the daughter of Te Anga?"

Sullenly the Maori jerked his oiled, dark head to the stern hatchway. "Your sailors are below—my warriors guard them, Cap'in. As to your wife and sons—them I have sent ashore, also the daughter of Te Anga. They—"

Robert broke in furiously, "Have you harmed them? By all I hold sacred, Hori Kaka, I will kill you if you have done them harm!"

"They are safe, Yates," Hori Kaka retorted with scorn. "We do not make war on women and children. But they will not be sent back to the ship unless Cap'in Van Buren yields up to us what we require. You have muskets and powder locked away in your arms chest, Cap'in—this we know, but we cannot find the arms chest key."

He had the key on his person, Claus thought; indeed, he always kept it on him these days, in case of trouble. The arms chest was heavy and metal-bound; clearly the raiders had tried unsuccessfully to break it open and were now resorting to coercion, in order to obtain possession of its contents. Had Te Anga authorized the raid? he wondered. Had the chief deliberately summoned him to the *pa* and kept him talking, so as to allow his young warriors time to launch their raid? But his daughter, Paoa, Robert's wife, was apparently also being held hostage. Surely Te Anga would not have countenanced *that?*

Claus listened with half an ear to Hori·Kaka's list of demands, his anxiety growing; but aware that he must show no weakness, he managed to maintain a dignified silence and an air of indifference, which, after a while, roused the young warrior's wrath.

"You say no word!" Hori Kaka accused. "You waste time, Cap'in. Will you give us what we ask, that we may send back your wife and sons unharmed?"

He had claimed that his people did not make war on women and children, Claus thought bitterly; but in the New Plymouth settlements, the Taranaki had slain the settlers' wives and children with ruthless savagery, together with their husbands and fathers. They—

"Give us *waipooro,*" his tormentor shouted suddenly. "You have casks of spirit on board, locked away, like the weapons and the powder. My brothers on shore have taken all they want from Yates's warehouse, but here, on board this fine ship, we have nothing!"

Claus exchanged a swift, warning glance with Robert, enjoining him to keep a guard on his tongue, then handed Hori Kaka the key of the *Dolphin's* liquor store.

"Let them have what they want, Rob," he said. "Go with them, and let them help themselves to all the liquor they can hold. And—" As Robert took the key, he added in a whisper, "Find out where they are holding our crew."

Robert nodded his understanding. Hori Kaka relieved him of his rifle, jerking it roughly from his grasp, and they went below together, Robert offering no resistance.

Claus was thankful he had the pistol, tucked in his belt, under his jacket. The young warriors had not searched him, and he took heart from the feel of the weapon against his ribs. It was an American Colt, a six-shot weapon, long out of use and probably rusty, and he could only pray that it would fire, should he be compelled to resort to force. But the raiders, evidently satisfied that he offered no threat, went below on the heels of their leader, leaving a single black-browed youth to stand guard over him.

Claus waited tensely, interpreting the sounds from below and glancing occasionally at the blazing ruin of his trading post, conscious of mingled anger and disappointment as he recalled what Te Anga had said, only a few short hours ago.

"You are good and honest . . . it is not with your kind that we make war. . . ." Devil take him, had not Te Anga asked which side he would choose, if there should be war? And had he himself not felt deep sympathy with the Maori cause, over the years, when government promises had been broken and too many rapacious settlers had robbed and cheated them of the land and the hunting grounds they had inherited from their ancestors? Claus closed his eyes and found himself praying silently that Mercy and their precious boys were not in danger. If they had been taken to the *pa*, Te Anga would surely see to it that they came to no harm; but if some of Hori Kaka's volatile young men had taken them off into the bush, there was no knowing what might happen—even if Paoa were with them.

A hubbub of voices reached him from below, Maori and *pakeha*, suggesting that Robert, having given Hori Kaka the spirits he had demanded, had also contrived to make his presence known to the imprisoned crew. Their voices were coming from the fo'c'sle, evidence that the men had been confined in their own quarters. . . . under guard, certainly, but not under lock and key, as they would have been had the raiding party herded them into one of the holds.

Claus's spirits lifted. He must play for time, attempt to make them bargain for the key of the arms chest for as long as Hori Kaka's patience would allow, in the hope that, like their comrades on the wharf ashore, his young men would drink themselves into stupefied carelessness and give Robert and himself a chance to free the *Dolphin*'s crew. He glanced reluctantly at the two bodies lying on the deck and suppressed a shiver of apprehension. If his ploy failed and the raiders instead ran amuck, he might well lose not only his crew but the *Dolphin* herself, for had not Hori Kaka implied that it would have been all too easy to set fire to her?

Robert returned to the deck, an expression of grim satisfaction on his tanned face. He confirmed Claus's guess as to the whereabouts of the crew.

"They're not tied up, Captain Van Buren, and Simon's with them. He saw me, but I couldn't get near enough to speak with him. All the same, I'm sure they'll be ready to break out whenever you say the word. There are five or six warriors guarding them, all armed with muskets. But when I broke out the rum casks, they were all onto them like bees going for honey. Even Hori Kaka was gulping the stuff down. And the arms chest was still secure—I saw it. It has resisted all their efforts to hack it open."

"Thank heaven for that!" Claus answered, with genuine relief. "We shall just have to be patient, Rob, and choose the right moment. I have the Colt, and if it's necessary I'll use it—for old Ben Knowles's sake!"

Their chance came sooner than either of them had expected. After less than an hour, most of the young Maoris were incapably drunk, and Hori Kaka's demands that Claus yield up the key to the arms chest had deteriorated into maudlin pleas, made, the raiders' leader assured him, to one he knew to be a friend.

"You are not like the bad *pakehas* Queen Wiktoria sends here, Cap'in. You are a good man. You are—" He hiccuped loudly. "You are *pakeha* Maori. You want your wife and sons back on board—I send them. Only you give up key of arms chest that we may possess ourselves of good weapons to meet those of the red garments, the *pakeha* redcoats, who will be sent against us. Cap'in, if I do not have these, my *mana* will be lost in the eyes of my people—I cannot lead them, if I lose my prestige."

"You have not only stolen my wife and sons, you have killed two of my sailors and imprisoned the rest," Claus reminded him sternly. "And you have destroyed my warehouse. That is not the action of a friend, Hori Kaka. I ask you again—does Te Anga know of this night's work?"

The Maori shook his dark head, and for the first time fear dawned in his eyes. "No, Cap'in. The plan was Korriko's and mine. Te Anga does not know."

"Then he will be angered, will he not?"

"Not if we bring him your guns. Cap'in, we will make good your loss. We will build a new warehouse and fill it with flax and timber, all that you want. Give us the guns, Cap'in, that is all I ask. Guns and the powder you have locked in your hold. Your wife and sons will be set free, your sailors also, if you give me the guns."

"Come below," Claus invited. His eyes flashed a warning to Robert, and the younger man moved swiftly to his side. Between them, they lifted Hori Kaka off his feet, and as Robert grabbed the man's musket, Claus thrust the muzzle of the Colt hard against his ribs. "Now," he said, in a voice that brooked no refusal, "we will go below, and you will tell your warriors to free my sailors."

For a moment it seemed as if the raiders' leader would show fight; but realizing that he was alone, he capitulated and, without struggling, let them take him below. The guards, bemused by the rum they had drunk, obeyed his order to stand aside, and the *Dolphin*'s men came stumbling out, Simon Yates with them, a bloodstained kerchief about his head bearing mute witness to the resistance he had offered when the raiding party had come on board.

The young Maoris—most of them little more than boys, Claus realized—were swiftly disarmed. They gathered on the fo'c'sle in a shamefaced, dispirited little group, their earlier arrogance deserting them. He sternly ordered them back into their canoes, and they tumbled into them, to beat a humiliating retreat, wielding their paddles with little semblance of their accustomed skill.

Only their leader remained, his head bowed, his *mana*—the prestige so precious to a Maori—lost with the completeness of his defeat. For all the anger he felt, Claus found it in his heart to pity the young *ariki,* and he said, not ungently, "I will give you a good rifle for yourself, Hori Kaka, when my wife and sons and the wife of Robert Yates are returned to this ship unharmed. We will go and fetch them now, and you will take us to them, is that understood?"

But even before Hori Kaka could answer him, Robert shouted exultantly, "Sir, they are coming back—Te Anga is bringing them! Look, sir, they're on their way!"

Claus followed the direction of his pointing finger and, sick with relief, saw that a single canoe had put off from the shore. It was manned by a score of paddlers—a large, ornately carved craft, unmistakably that of a chief—and seated in the stern was Te Anga himself, Mercy at his side, with the two little boys clasped in her arms, and Paoa crouching close by.

Claus felt a surge of happiness sweep over him as Mercy stepped onto the deck. His little sons ran to him, and he dropped to his knees, holding out his arms to them—but his gaze was on his wife's calm, untroubled face.

"You suffered no harm, love? They did not hurt you?" The words were wrung from him, despite her calm, but her headshake gave him all the answer he needed.

Te Anga faced him with dignified contrition.

"Your wife was brought to me as a hostage, Captain Van Buren,

after you departed from my *pa*. The evil young man who skulks in
the shadows behind you, Hori Kaka, sent her to me, with my
daughter and your sons. Until then, I knew nothing of all this, and
I did not know that my own son, Korriko, had involved himself in
this most regrettable affair. But I have come in person to restore
your wife to you and to offer you, in all sincerity, my regrets for
what was done to your family and for the damage my young warriors have caused to your property ashore. I have learned also that
two of your sailors were killed."

"Yes, that is so, Te Anga," Claus confirmed. He pointed to the
bodies. "They were good men; they did not deserve to meet their
deaths at the hands of your warriors."

"We will make reparation," Te Anga promised. "As far as we
are able. My young warriors shall rebuild your warehouse with
their own hands, and they shall make good the loss of your trade
goods. As to my son and Hori Kaka—" He paused, turning his
gaze on the unhappy Hori Kaka, who shrank back, wide-eyed with
alarm. "Their lives are forfeit, and it will be for you to decide
whether they are to live or to die, Captain Van Buren. If you wish
them to live, then you may take them as slaves to work on board
your ship, in place of the two men they have killed. If you wish to
take their lives in *utu,* then—"

Claus cut him short. "You are an honorable man, Te Anga, and
you offer an honorable solution. I will accept all you have offered,
and I will take your son and Hori Kaka as members of my ship's
company. I will take them for two years, and then I shall bring
them back to you."

The chief permitted himself a hint of a smile.

"It shall be so, Captain. I will send Te Korriko to you. And at
first light tomorrow, I will order the rebuilding of your trading
post." He looked at Robert, and his smile widened. "Husband of
my daughter, will you stay with us here, even if there is war between our people?"

Robert, with Paoa's small hand in his, replied without hesitation, "I will stay here, Father of my wife, even if there is war."

"Heiahai korero tia ae," Te Anga observed. "Comment is needless. I give you farewell, Captain Van Buren—*eh no ho!* For you
will sail soon, will you not?"

"I will sail with the dawn, Te Anga," Claus assured him. "But I
shall return."

Only he would return without Mercy and their small sons, he

thought, his resolution hardening. For as long as there was war in the Land of the Long White Cloud, their lives were too precious to him to be put in jeopardy.

He watched Te Anga descend to the great double canoe, his hand raised in parting salute. Then, clasping his wife's swelling waist, he kissed her gently, and with the boys scampering happily ahead, they made their way aft to the great cabin.

On shore, the fires flickered and died, and the darkness hid the devastation they had left in their wake.

Chapter VIII

THE POMONA LEFT Hobart in brilliant sunshine, and two days out, in the Tasman Sea, there was scarcely a cloud in the blue arc of sky. With only a faint breeze to speed her on her way, she was proceeding under her engines at a steady eight knots, expecting within a few hours to sight the coast of mainland Australia.

Seated beside her mother on the poop deck, Emily Carmichael reflected thankfully that their long voyage was almost over. It had been, all things considered, a trying voyage, although the kindly old master, Captain Clifford, and his officers and crew had done all in their power to ensure the comfort and well-being of the passengers.

But there was no denying that the *Pomona* was old and unweatherly, and the storms they had met with during the passage had not contributed to the enjoyment of any, from the emigrant families between decks to the convicts crowded within the dark, airless confines of the orlop. And the soldiers had fared little better. . . . Emily sighed. The convicts had been set ashore at Fremantle, Western Australia, and some of the soldiers had moved into their quarters, in preference to their own—Adam Shannon among them.

Emily cast an anxious glance at her mother. Alice Carmichael's health had benefited little from the sea air by which their family doctor had set such store. All too frequently the inclement weather had rendered the open deck untenable for the passengers, and gale-force winds—both before and after calling at the Cape—coupled with extreme cold in what Adam Shannon had told her was forty-six degrees of south latitude, and a storm in the Great Australian Bight, had necessitated virtual imprisonment in her cabin for the poor sufferer, often for days on end.

But at least, Emily told herself wryly, dancing attendance on her invalid mother had spared her from having to endure Marcus Fisher's company and his increasingly unwelcome attempts to pay court to her. She did not like Marcus Fisher, and her sentiments were, she knew, shared by the *Pomona*'s officers, her other passengers, and the unfortunate soldiers under his command. She had formed her opinion of him after inadvertently witnessing the barbaric punishment he had inflicted on Adam Shannon, and . . . She flushed guiltily as she saw the soldiers muster for the daily inspection on the fo'c'sle and recognized Adam, when he fell in, as marker, in the front rank.

Captain Fisher did not know of the clandestine friendship that had grown up between her and the man he had flogged that morning, and, Emily thought, if it killed her, she would never allow him to discover her secret. Moved by pity and greatly daring, she had obtained the ship's surgeon's permission to visit Adam Shannon in the sick bay, and had found him, as she had initially suspected, to be a gentleman. More of a gentleman, certainly, than Captain Marcus Fisher.

Dr. Farrar had kept his patient in the sick bay for almost two weeks, refusing to permit him to return to duty, despite Marcus Fisher's demands. With the doctor's connivance—nay, his encouragement, for he, too, had been moved by pity—she had made her visits to the sick bay a daily occurrence.

"The poor young fellow needs womanly sympathy," Dr. Farrar had told her. "I don't know his story, Miss Carmichael, but I can hazard a pretty shrewd guess that he comes of good family and has met with some traumatic misfortune. It might do him good to speak of it, and perhaps you might be able to persuade him to do so. Captain Fisher insists that he is a deserter from the Royal Navy, but this I take leave to doubt."

She had not succeeded in her efforts to persuade Adam to confide in her, Emily thought regretfully, but he had told her part of his story—the bare facts that he had been a commissioned officer, a lieutenant, in the navy, and had been tried by court-martial for the loss of his ship, and sentenced to be cashiered. No more than that. He had not told her his real name or the circumstances that had led to his trial, yet . . . she had sensed that he had found some solace in telling her even as little as he had. Their friendship had grown from those visits to the sick bay, and after Dr. Farrar had finally and with reluctance discharged him, Adam had found ways of seeing her, often very briefly, and always—for his sake and hers, Emily knew—always discreetly. Her mother had no inkling of the social *gaffe* her daughter, a first-class cabin passenger, was committing in even making contact with a common soldier; still less did she imagine that, on one occasion, her daughter had joined the soldiers and the seamen on the fo'c'sle when they had held an impromptu concert, singing and dancing to the music of fiddles and a kettledrum.

She smiled, remembering how lighthearted she had felt and how carefully Adam had guarded her from any prying eyes on the quarterdeck or poop and, equally carefully, from any attempt on the part of the other men to take liberties with her. And she had enjoyed herself, listening to the sea chanties the sailors had sung and watching them demonstrate the dancing of the hornpipe, with folded arms and tapping heels as the old ship—finding, that night, a favorable wind—had glided ghostlike over the still, dark waters of the Indian Ocean.

There had not been very many nights like that, but she remembered every one, and looking back now, Emily realized it had been Adam's presence, his company, that had made them memorable. Not that he had paid court to her. His attitude had been unfailingly correct; he had addressed her always as "Miss Carmichael," and even on the few occasions when they had been alone together, he had never overstepped the bounds of propriety. She—color rose to her cheeks at the thought, but it was true—she had more than once wished that he had paid less heed to the present difference in their social positions, for he attracted her strongly. Indeed, if the truth were known, she—

A hand fell on her shoulder, and a voice that had become all too familiar greeted her by name.

"Ah, Miss Emily! I trust this fine morning finds your lady mother improved in health and yourself, as always, blooming?"

It was Marcus Fisher, smiling down at her ingratiatingly, and Emily recoiled. She had supposed him to be engaged in his troop inspection on the fo'c'sle, but seemingly he had left that task to Ensign Edwards this morning, for he was in undress uniform and bareheaded, while the soldiers were standing rigidly to attention, the sergeants passing up and down between their ranks.

Annoyed that his sudden appearance had caught her unprepared, Emily reddened, and to her relief her mother answered the young captain's overeffusive inquiry.

"I am feeling very much better, thank you, Captain Fisher," Alice Carmichael said politely. "Although, I confess, I shall be thankful when we reach Sydney. It has seemed a very long voyage to one unaccustomed to the sea, but my daughter has been wonderfully good to me. Indeed"—she clasped Emily's hand warmly—"I do not know what I should have done without her."

"Miss Emily's devotion to you is wholly admirable, Mrs. Carmichael," Marcus Fisher affirmed. He drew up a chair and seated himself, uninvited, at Emily's side. "It is my hope, ma'am, that our acquaintance may continue after we disembark. Although, from the talk in Hobart Town, it appears not improbable that my stay in Sydney will be brief. Four companies of my regiment have been sent to New Zealand to aid in quelling a Maori rebellion there. I shall undoubtedly have to follow, with my draft, if the rebellion continues or if it should develop into a full-scale war."

If he had expected sympathy from either her mother or herself, he did not receive it, Emily thought, pleased. She herself said nothing, but her mother, with a beaming smile, observed quietly, "That will offer you the chance of military glory, won't it, Captain Fisher? Like all ambitious young officers, that is what you seek, I feel sure."

A trifle nonplussed, Marcus Fisher agreed that, of course, all he had ever wanted was the opportunity to serve his country.

"My men will acquit themselves well, Mrs. Carmichael," he added, with more enthusiasm. "So often on a long voyage they become slack, and discipline suffers. But I have made sure that they have been kept up to the mark. If this voyage has done nothing else, it has shown them that I will tolerate no slackness."

It had indeed, Emily reflected without humor. Adam Shannon had not been the only soldier to suffer a flogging, and she knew, from the little he had seen fit to tell her, that Captain Fisher was universally despised and hated by his men. Certainly Fisher's claim to have kept them up to the mark was no exaggeration. No matter what the weather, they had been drilled daily on the fo'c'sle, constantly subjected to kit inspections, and when their commander could devise no military exercises for them, they had been ordered to assist in the working of the ship, allocated to regular watches, which left them little time for leisure. Adam, she knew, had been detailed to toil in the engine room with the stokers when the engines were in use, and all the men had had to assist in coaling, when the *Pomona*'s bunkers had been replenished at the Cape, at Fremantle, and again at Hobart.

"I do not doubt, Captain Fisher," she heard her mother say, with a faint hint of sarcasm in her soft, pleasant voice, "that your commanding officer will be gratified when he learns how conscientiously you have carried out your duties." The sarcasm was lost on Marcus Fisher, who beamed with pleasure at what he took to be a compliment, and Alice Carmichael leaned forward to touch Emily's arm. "I am afraid, dear child, that the sun has gone in. Let us go below, shall we? Now that we are so nearly at the end of our passage, I do not want to risk catching a chill."

The sun had, in fact, only disappeared briefly behind a small cloud, but grateful for her mother's intervention, Emily rose at once to her feet.

"Of course, Mama," she echoed eagerly. "Take my arm, won't you? It *is* becoming a trifle chilly."

In the privacy of her cabin, Mrs. Carmichael turned to her daughter with a quizzical smile.

"Emily dear," she admonished, with mock severity, "did you have to make it quite so evident to poor Captain Fisher that his attentions were unwelcome?"

"I would not treat anyone else like that, Mama," Emily protested. "But I find Captain Fisher—oh, I find him an odious person!"

"He is not the most likable of young men," her mother conceded. "A braggart and one who is full of self-esteem. Oh, don't worry, child, I am not reproaching you. Indeed, I am relieved that your response to Captain Fisher's advances was so discouraging. But whilst I have spent most of my days lying here, I have observed that you have frequently come below with your eyes like stars and a blush on your cheek, and I . . . well, I wondered, Emily."

Emily's blush was betrayal, but she attempted to hide her confusion, hastily turning her back and crossing to the porthole to look out at the blue-gray expanse of water, which was all that was to be seen. In a muffled voice, she asked defensively, "What did you wonder, Mama?"

Alice Carmichael sighed. "I wondered whether, in the absence of my chaperonage, you had permitted yourself to become enamored of one of our fellow passengers—or a member of the crew. Captain Fisher appeared to be the most likely, since he was always somewhere about, paying you extravagant compliments, when I was able to bear you company on deck or in the saloon. I freely confess, dearest Emily, that I am thankful to see with my own eyes that you have *not* responded to his advances."

"I would never respond to them, Mama," Emily declared, "if he were the last man on earth! Truly, I cannot stand him."

"But there is some young man on board who has taken your fancy, isn't there?" her mother persisted. "Come, child, I know you too well to be deceived. Is it Captain Fisher's second-in-command, young Ensign Edwards?"

Emily did not turn round, contenting herself with an emphatic headshake. "No, Mama. Alan Edwards is very pleasant, but—oh, he is just a boy. I talk to him at meals and on deck sometimes, but that's all." And Marcus Fisher, she thought, made sure that it *was* all the contact Ensign Edwards had with her; the boy was sent to attend to some duty or other if he ventured to say more than two words to her. But . . . She flashed an uncertain glance at her mother's face, seeking to guess, from the expression it bore, how much—or how little—was suspected concerning her feelings. She had always been close to her mother, and there was a deep bond of affection between them. Emily was the youngest of the family, the only girl and the possessor of no less than four elder brothers, all now making their way in the world, and the two eldest, Tom and Harry, already practicing barristers, as their father had been, and both married. Alec was employed by a City stockbroker, and Duncan—her senior by just a year—was a cadet at Addiscombe. He—

"Well?" Alice Carmichael prompted gently. "Is there a young man, Emily?"

She could not tell her mother the whole truth, Emily thought, seized by sudden panic. Her mother came of a generation that subscribed to rigid class barriers, and Adam Shannon—whatever he had been before their meeting on board the *Pomona*—was now serving in the ranks of Her Majesty's 40th Regiment and probably, at this moment, was on his way to the ship's nether regions to spend the next four hours shoveling coal, stripped to the waist and covered in black dust.

Anxious to spare her mother anxiety and herself from a lecture on propriety, she sought to evade the question.

"There's no one in particular, Mama. I'm—well, I've enjoyed our passage, apart from the storms, of course. The other passengers are exceedingly kind and friendly, especially old Mr. Cassell and his wife and Major and Mrs. Ashe. Mr. Cassell was telling me about the early days in New South Wales—he went out as a sheep farmer, twenty years ago. It's a shame that you've been too unwell to get to know them properly, because they are such pleasant company. I've learnt a lot about Australia from all of them. Now"— she sought to change the subject—"do you feel up to taking luncheon in the cuddy, Mama? Or shall I ask the steward to serve you here?"

Her tactic succeeded. Mrs. Carmichael considered the question and finally shook her head to the suggestion of joining their fellow passengers for luncheon.

"I don't think I'm *quite* up to that yet, Emily," she admitted. "Ask the steward, if you will, please. Tell him I want only a very light luncheon. Some broth, perhaps, and a few fingers of toast. If the weather continues like this, I might sit on deck again during the afternoon. I'm sure the sea air does me good."

The steward, however, dashed her hopes. "The glass is falling, ma'am, and the wind's veering westerly," he said, setting down the tray Mrs. Carmichael had asked for. "Bin a real bad passage for storms, this has, an' no mistake. And I reckon we're in for another before we make port in Sydney. You bide here, ma'am, because it won't be long before it hits us."

Emily and her mother exchanged dismayed glances.

"Oh, dear!" Mrs. Carmichael exclaimed, unable to hide her disappointment. "It was such a beautiful morning. I thought all our troubles were over."

"That's the way of it in these parts," the steward told her glumly. "One minute there's no wind to speak of, an' the next it's blowing a gale." He tucked his napkin under his arm and looked inquiringly at Emily. "Would you like me to serve your luncheon in the cabin, miss? It'll be no trouble."

Emily hesitated. She had prided herself on having become a good sailor during the long voyage, but . . . perhaps she would be as well not to tempt providence by taking her meal in the saloon, which was stuffy and airless, and made the more so by smoke from Major Ashe's pipe and old Mr. Cassell's cigars, when inclement weather drove them down from the deck.

"Thank you, Simmonds," she answered, accepting the old steward's advice. "If it really is no trouble, I'll have my lunch in the cabin."

"Very wise, if I may say so, miss," Simmonds approved. "I'll be along with your tray right away."

He was as good as his word, but Emily had scarcely sampled her first course when the ship started to pitch violently, its ancient timbers ominously creaking as the wind rose, whipping the hitherto calm sea to sudden fury. Robbed of every vestige of appetite by the *Pomona*'s unpleasant motion, she put her tray aside and, having made sure that her mother was warmly tucked up in her cot, sought the sanctuary of her own bed, pulling the blankets about her and closing her eyes.

Lying thus, she felt better and her nausea gradually eased, and after a while she drifted into a light, uneasy sleep.

Adam was in the engine room when the storm struck. Stripped to the waist, his sweating torso begrimed with coal dust, he shoveled coal into the *Pomona*'s seemingly insatiable furnace, working to a practiced rhythm with the stokers of the watch. They toiled in semidarkness, and sounds from the deck came faintly and were difficult to interpret, but he sensed, from the constant jangling of the engine room telegraph as much as from the heaving of the boards beneath his feet, that the old ship was, as always, making heavy weather of her attempt to ride out the storm.

The master was demanding more of her worn engines than they could be expected to deliver, and Adam, without surprise, heard the chief engineer, Angus Macpherson, cursing furiously when yet another shrill signal rang impatiently in his ears.

"Damn it to hell, Mr. Clifford! I'm doin' the best I can, but I cannot do the impossible. We've a head o' steam on her now that she's not fit to take. Do you want to blow us to kingdom come, for God's sake? What's the gauge readin', Geordie? I'll take my oath 'tis way over the danger mark, and—"

The ship lurched violently, and he was flung off his feet, his language lurid in the extreme as he picked himself up. Beside him, the man with whom Adam was working was hurled against the half-open door of the furnace, and both his hands were badly burned before Adam was able to grasp him about the waist and drag him back, where he collapsed in a whimpering heap, his face contorted with pain.

"Take the poor laddie to the surgeon, Shannon," the chief ordered. Grabbing a handful of oily cotton waste, he thrust it in

Adam's direction. "Cover his hands wi' this. Geordie, I'm wantin' a reading o' the gauge. Jump to it, man!"

He was never to get his reading, for the next moment, with a rending crash, the ship struck some unseen, unyielding obstacle. She recoiled and struck again, to the hideous sound of tearing metal, and was flung into a heavy list to starboard as a mighty cascade of water came flooding into the engine room. The water rose rapidly, and Adam, halfway up the catwalk with the injured stoker, looked back in horror at the pandemonium he had left behind him.

Chief Macpherson bawled a warning to his men to abandon the engine room, and they struggled desperately to obey him, but the list was so great and the water rising so fast that already it was lapping about their knees. The overhead lamps on the starboard side flickered to extinction, adding to the confusion, and a shattered steam pipe sprayed a scalding jet into the faces of two men who had been slow to react to the disaster.

"Cut along to the sick bay on your own, Mason," Adam hissed urgently to the man he was aiding. "I'm going back to try to help the others."

He did not wait for the injured stoker's reply but slithered down to the base of the ladder, reaching for a lamp that was still burning to act as a beacon to the men who were trying to make their escape from the dark floodwater. Shouting to them at the pitch of his lungs to make for the light, he waited as five of them clambered to safety unaided; then he grabbed two others and hauled them up beside him as the chief himself came splashing out of the darkness, up to his waist in water, to grasp Adam's hand and, breathing hard, lever his stout body onto the submerged rungs of the catwalk ladder.

"All my men are out," he managed. "Good work, Shannon." He paused to look back, as Adam had done, shaking his white head in stunned disbelief as the last glow from the furnace was extinguished, leaving only a blackness and hissing steam in its wake. "She's done for, I fear, poor old girl," he added bitterly. "Must have run onto a reef. There's a damned great hole in her hull, starboard side, ten, twelve feet long, I reckon. Maybe she'll settle on the reef, if that's what she struck, and not go down before we're able to get the boats away. Give me a hand, laddie. I must get topside and find out what the captain's aimin' to do."

On deck, however, when they reached it, chaos reigned. The

young second mate, Nicholas Archer, with whom Adam had recently struck up a tentative friendship, confronted them, white-faced and clearly stupefied with shock. Cupping his hand round his mouth, in order to make himself heard above the savage howling of the wind, he stammered, "The—the captain's gone—him and Mr. Dixon. W-when we grounded on—on a reef, she went down by the head, Mr. Macpherson. The—sea was breaking over her and—God, sir, it was terrible! W-when she struck the second time, she was flung broadside onto—to the sea, and . . . sir, a wave that must have been th-thirty or forty foot high came crashing down from astern. They didn't have a chance, the captain and the first mate, sir. It carried them away and two of—of the hands with them. They—they just disappeared. I—I tried to lower a b-boat, but it was hopeless, sir. They'd gone."

Adam's heart plummeted as he listened. Although it was still early afternoon, the sky was as black as night, the old ship held in a viselike grip on what appeared to be the edge of an extensive reef. They were broadside to the wind, as young Archer had said, and being driven remorselessly farther onto the coral shelf by the pounding waves. Her list to starboard was not as acute as he had feared, but unless wind and sea abated, she would inevitably break up. Already the fo'c'sle was awash, and as far as he could make out in the spray-lashed dimness, her foremast had gone by the board.

In memory, he was suddenly back on the *Lancer*'s deck, recalling in all its horror the scene he had witnessed then—the boats, lowered in the teeth of a gale-force wind, being swamped almost as soon as they reached the water. But the *Lancer* had stayed afloat, whereas this ship almost certainly would break up and founder, so that the boats *had* to be lowered, the women and children loaded into them at once, if any of them were to survive. As a passenger-carrying vessel, the *Pomona* was equipped with an adequate number of boats, and it should be possible to lower them from the starboard side, with the ship's bulk making a lee, and the water probably shallow on the surface of the reef.

But . . . Adam looked about him, shocked to see that young Archer had done nothing to muster the passengers from below. A few of the emigrants had come up from the lower deck and were huddled in a terrified group at the head of the forward hatchway, fearing to venture beyond it, lest, in the absence of lifelines, they were to share the master's fate. Then he caught sight of Marcus Fisher, with half a dozen oilskin-clad soldiers—men of the afterguard—and saw that Fisher, at least, had not lost his head, for they were working on the falls of the master's gig, preparing to lower it, with Fisher balanced in the stern, armed with a boathook, with which he was trying to fend the small vessel clear of the ship's side.

Without conscious thought, Adam took action, seizing the speaking trumpet from Nicholas Archer's nerveless hand and shouting through it the orders that had to be given. The men of the draft, led by Sergeant Doran, lined up in disciplined order, and they obeyed him without question; Chief Macpherson led a party of seamen and took charge of the lowering of the boats; lifelines were rigged, and with their aid the women and children, brought from below, were able to gain the deck and cross to the starboard side, to be assisted by the soldiers into the boats, as each was hoisted out and manned.

Predictably, the gig was first into the water, the men who had been lowering it standing back without a word of dissent, the places they might have taken given to emigrant families and the boat's crew. But, Adam saw with stunned surprise, Fisher had remained in it, after guiding it down with his deftly wielded boathook; and it was he who took the tiller and shouted to the seamen to pull away.

Sergeant Doran saw this too and, his mouth close to Adam's ear, spat the one word, "Bastard!"

Adam shrugged and said nothing. Ensign Edwards, whom he had sent to aid the cabin passengers, came on deck with his party, and Adam saw with relief that little Emily Carmichael and her mother were with them, Mrs. Carmichael well wrapped in blankets. Both held back, shaking their heads to his indication that there were places in the next boat that Macpherson was swaying out, and instead the two elderly couples, whose names Adam did not know, permitted themselves to be lifted into it by the soldiers.

"Go with them, Chief," Adam urged. "You can make sure the boats keep together." The stout old chief started to argue and then thought better of it.

"You seem to be in command, Mr. Shannon," he shouted back hoarsely. "And since you seem to know what you're about—aye, aye, sir!" With unexpected agility for one of his bulk, he swung himself into the boat, an odd little smile playing about his bearded lips as he bawled the order to the oarsmen to "Give way together!"

All the women from the emigrants' quarters, with their shivering, sobbing children, had gone now, and their boats, Adam saw with heartfelt thankfulness, were afloat, pulling away from the ship but keeping to what shelter it provided from the wind. But the old vessel would not last for much longer, he knew, with the waves pounding at her worn timbers and the sharp fangs of the coral on which her hull rested tearing and ripping her to pieces. She was heavily waterlogged, her buoyancy gone and her fo'c'sle half submerged and obscured by a curtain of spray.

The longboat remained to be lowered, and as Edwards and Sergeant Doran took charge of a mixed party of seamen and soldiers and started to move it into position, Adam sent Archer to the charthouse.

"We're going to need navigating instruments, Nick—" He listed them, having to shout and repeat himself, as the young mate, still deeply shocked, stared at him uncomprehendingly. "And any charts you can lay your hands on. Pull yourself together, lad! You know what we'll need. Get them, will you, fast as you can? We haven't got much longer."

Archer, his young face white and strained, nodded and went stumbling aft, clinging to one of the lifelines; yet even as he did so, the deck canted steeply beneath his feet and he almost fell. The old ship shuddered from stem to stern, and with an ominous crash of mangled timbers, she was hurled farther onto the reef. She settled sluggishly and sank slowly into deeper water, and Adam guessed that, by now, not only the engine room but also the crew's mess deck and probably the cabin flat were completely flooded. There was no time to be lost. All too soon the sea would invade the upper deck, and the *Pomona* would go down, leaving scarcely a sign of her presence, save the stark outline of her teetering mainmast and, perhaps, her smokestack showing above the white-capped waves as they broke over her.

Above his head, the wind screeched and howled eerily in the rigging, sounding, to Adam's ears, as if some monstrous musician were plucking at the shrouds and stays to draw from them a melancholy dirge with which to mourn the old ship's impending doom. But at least, he told himself fiercely, the mourning would be for the ship alone; apart from her master and those who had been swept overboard with him, all her passengers and crew had taken or were about to take to the boats, with a reasonable chance of survival.

Nicholas Archer came staggering back from the charthouse, and

Adam relieved him of a sextant and some rolled charts and waved him to take his place in the longboat. Edwards and Doran were lifting Mrs. Carmichael into it, he saw, and, his conscience troubling him, he went to where little Emily Carmichael was standing. Until this moment, he had been intent only on organizing the evacuation of the other passengers, conscious of the responsibilities he had taken upon himself for their safety, and he had given neither attention nor thought to the girl who had befriended him. But when he reached her side, he saw that she was calm and unafraid—able, even, to smile at him when he spoke her name.

The longboat was virtually level with the deck now, so swiftly was the *Pomona* sinking. Choosing his moment carefully, when the boat rose on the crest of a wave, Adam picked Emily up in his arms, entrusting her with the cased sextant, and lowered her into the waiting arms of two soldiers in the longboat's stern. Edwards and then Doran, on his nod, jumped in after her, and he followed them, landing with a painful jar as the boat descended into a wave trough.

"She's g-going!" Archer yelled. "Out oars and pull, for the Lord's sake!"

The men at the oars needed no second bidding. The sturdy longboat drew away, pitching violently, but the *Pomona* stayed afloat, wallowing in the trough of a mountainous swell, yet seemingly reluctant, even in her extremity, to give the storm best and meet her end.

Adam picked himself up and took the tiller. In the storm-wracked darkness, he could see only one other boat, which he thought was Macpherson's, but his hail elicited responses from two others, and he shouted to them to close up. The first to do so was the gig, with Marcus Fisher crouching in the sternsheets and the other occupants frantically bailing. For all their efforts, the gig was waterlogged, and Fisher shouted that it was in imminent danger of sinking.

"You'll have to take us off, Shannon," he added, a high-pitched note of fear in his voice. "Our bottom boards are stove in. It's all we can do to keep afloat."

There were emigrant women and children in the gig, Adam re-called—eight or ten of them, at least, in addition to Fisher himself, and . . . He tried to count the heads. Four—no, five seamen at the oars. The longboat was not quite loaded to capacity, but fifteen or sixteen more might well jeopardize any chance of survival for them all. He raised the speaking trumpet to his lips.

"Come alongside. We'll take the women and children, and we'll take your boat in tow."

He did not know whether Fisher had heard him, but the gig came looming out of the darkness, gunwales awash, and obviously badly damaged. Without the deadweight of the emigrant families, it was possible that the damaged craft could be kept afloat; and with the coming of daylight and if the wind abated, perhaps repairs might be effected. All the boats held some provisions—he had seen to that—and if they managed to stay together . . . Once again Marcus Fisher's concern for his own skin took Adam by surprise. This time, however, he contrived to disguise it by clambering from the gig with a child in his arms, and the others in his vicinity, with instinctive concern for his blanket-wrapped burden, made room for him.

The other passengers in the gig—four adult women and four small children—were transferred to the longboat without mishap, and young Nicholas Archer, balancing precariously on a thwart, managed to attach a towrope to the gig's bow. Then, unbidden, he joined the five seamen in their waterlogged craft and let the towrope pay out.

It was a long, anxious night, but when dawn broke at last, Adam was relieved to see that all the *Pomona*'s other boats, including the gig, were still afloat, separated by a gray waste of tossing water, but all five clearly in sight. From the gig, Archer shouted the information, between his two cupped hands, that they had managed to plug the holes in her bottom and had been able to cease bailing.

"We can take some of your people, if it would help, Mr. Shannon," he offered. "We'll come alongside."

The transfer was made, Burnaby and Ensign Edwards among the four volunteers who responded to Adam's call, but Captain Fisher pointedly ignored him, meeting his questioning gaze as if it were unworthy of notice.

Adam unrolled one of the charts that Archer had salvaged, and while the two boats were alongside, he attempted, with the young mate's aid, to ascertain their position. They had drifted during the hours of darkness; of the *Pomona* and the reef on which she had grounded there was now no sign, but Nicholas Archer was able to confirm that an island called Gabo—situated southeast of Cape

Howe—had been sighted and recorded in the log when he had come off watch, to be relieved by the ill-fated first mate.

Until the sun again became visible, it was impossible to take a sight, but Adam decided to set course northwestward by compass, in order to close the Australian coast and, if they were lucky, the coastal shipping route, where a passing vessel might be expected to see and answer a signal of distress.

Toward noon, the wind moderated a little but continued to blow from the west, so that they made little progress, and already some of the emigrant women and children were giving Adam cause for anxiety. The women were stoical enough and did not complain, but several of the smaller children were suffering from cold and exposure, and their pitiful crying became a strain on all the boat's occupants. The heavy, ceaseless pitching and rolling of the boat in the still-angry sea added to the general distress, and for the men at the oars—even with frequent relief on an hourly roster—it was a severe test of strength and stamina.

Adam was most anxious on Mrs. Carmichael's behalf, aware of her frail health and the heart condition that had compelled her to spend most of the earlier part of the *Pomona*'s passage in the confinement of her cabin; but like the emigrant women, she uttered no word of complaint. Emily, seated beside her on the bottom boards, pillowed her mother's head on her lap and smiled bravely, when Adam sought reassurance.

"My mother is bearing up wonderfully well, Mr. Shannon. Do not concern yourself on our account. There are others much worse off than we are."

The *Pomona*'s surgeon was in Chief Macpherson's boat, Adam recalled. So long as all the boats kept together, his services could be called upon, should Mrs. Carmichael require them.

He glanced at Fisher, frowning. The draft commander lay, like Mrs. Carmichael, on the bottom boards, his eyes closed, speaking to no one. Since transferring to the longboat, he had been silent, taking no part in the discussion Adam had had with Archer, uncharacteristically offering no advice, and ignoring the call for volunteers to relieve the men at the oars.

Sergeant Doran, following the direction of Adam's gaze, shrugged disgustedly. "Scared out o' his wits," he said. "An' sufferin' from what they call *mal de mer*. We'd have been in a right pickle if we'd had to depend on *him*, I can tell you." He eyed

Adam with an approving smile. "We was lucky to have you, an' no mistake, *Mr.* Shannon! I reckon we owe our lives to you."

"We're not out of the woods yet," Adam cautioned.

"No, maybe we ain't. But at least we've got a chance, haven't we? An' that's thanks to you." The old sergeant's smile widened. "You told me once that you was an officer in Her Majesty's Navy —before we left England, remember? An' I said I wouldn't pry."

"Yes," Adam agreed, reddening. "I remember that, Sergeant Doran."

"*He* did plenty o' pryin'," Doran asserted, jerking his head at the recumbent form of Marcus Fisher. "Tried to make me tell him what I knew about you. Oh, I didn't, of course, but I reckon some-one did, because he'd got you figured out, Shannon. He told Sar'nt Jones you was court-martialed an' cashiered for drunkenness an' the loss o' your ship."

"And so I was," Adam rasped, suddenly angry. "I told you that."

"Aye, I ain't forgotten. But watch that bastard, Mr. Shannon. Because he'll have it in for you more'n ever if the good Lord sees fit to preserve us. He won't give you no credit for what you've done, an' you know how it is—he's an officer, and you ain't anymore, so it's him they'll believe."

It probably would be, Adam thought, with newfound indiffer-ence. He thrust the problem of Marcus Fisher from his mind and went to take his turn at an oar.

Darkness fell and with it the spirits of those in the boat. The small rations of rum and ship's biscuit were doled out, and merci-fully all the children lapsed into apathetic silence and were rocked to sleep in their mothers' arms. It was Emily Carmichael who, sensing the melancholy atmosphere, asked Adam to lead them in prayer and then started to sing, in a small, pure voice, her choice of a hymn they all knew an inspiration. Virtually everyone joined in the singing, hesitantly at first, but finally they roared the words.

"Eternal Father, strong to save,
Whose arm doth bind the restless wave,
Who bidd'st the mighty ocean deep,
Its own appointed limits keep:
O, hear us when we cry to Thee
For those in peril on the sea!"

Even Mrs. Carmichael roused herself, and as the sound carried across to those in the other boats, their voices, too, could be heard faintly above the roar of the wind.

It was a hymn they had sung each Sunday during the passage—the poor old master's choice, Adam recalled. He leaned forward and touched Emily's arm.

"Well done, Miss Carmichael!" he said, with sincerity. "That was just what we needed. Can you give us more?"

She smiled. "Oh, yes, if you want me to, Mr. Shannon. I used to teach in Sunday school at home, so I have quite a repertoire. Perhaps 'Fight the Good Fight' would lift our spirits."

She started to sing, and listening to her brave, sweet voice, Adam was oddly moved. Would Caroline, he wondered, have reacted to disaster as this quiet, composed little girl had done? Somehow he doubted it, recalling the demands Caroline had made on him, her possessiveness, her preoccupation, always, with her own comfort and well-being. Yet it was Caroline who still held him in thrall, blinding him to all other women, she who had only to crook her finger to bring him running to her side, no matter what the cost. And, God forgive him, the cost had been high. . . .

The long night passed, as the previous day had done, with little relief from the storm; but with the coming of daylight, the wind backed to the south and some of its fury abated, a strong swell succeeding the buffeting whitecaps. Not long after Adam had issued the morning rations, a watery sun came to shed a faint radiance across the gray vault of sky, and by noon Adam was able to take a sight and make an estimate of their position. He again consulted with Nicholas Archer, and their hopes rose with the realization that the Australian coast was now probably less than twenty miles distant.

Using the speaking trumpet, Adam was able to pass on these tidings to the other boats. All save the gig carried sails, and to give the oarsmen a much needed rest, it was agreed that the masts should be stepped and the gig again taken in tow. As on the previous night, the boats had become scattered, but none had been lost, and Adam breathed a prayer of thankfulness when Chief Macpherson's boat, the largest of the six and the one carrying the greatest load, hoisted its dingy mainsail and headed their small procession with an unexpected turn of speed.

But hopes were dashed when, by the time darkness again fell, there was no sign of land. As a precaution, Adam ordered the sails taken in, and it was then, to his shocked surprise, that Marcus Fisher came wrathfully to dispute the order.

"What the devil do you think you're doing, Shannon?" he demanded. "We were making good progress at long last, and now you're proposing to slow us down! This blasted boat won't get us anywhere near land if we have to depend on the oars."

"We have to keep company with the other boats," Adam answered shortly. "I have the only navigating instruments and the charts. Under sail, in darkness, we could well lose contact, and—"

"There'll be a moon, won't there?"

"Yes, but not a full moon. I know what I'm doing, Captain Fisher."

"And so you should, Shannon, so you should. But—" Fisher sneered. "Shannon's not your real name, is it? Perhaps, in the future, you should use your real name, which is Vincent, I believe. Adam Colpoys Vincent, onetime lieutenant, Royal Navy, sentenced to be cashiered as the officer responsible for the loss of Her Majesty's ship *Lancer*, due to . . . what, Mr. Vincent? Drunkenness, wasn't it, allied to incompetence, which resulted in the loss of the *Lancer*'s commander and all but five or six of her crew? The survivors, of course, included yourself. Well, do you deny that what I've just said is true?"

Adam shrugged. "You may believe what you like, Captain Fisher. But give me credit for being an experienced navigator. I—"

Fisher cut him short. "You lost the *Lancer*, with appalling loss of life. I was unwell, but I have now recovered, and for the safety of all concerned, I shall relieve you of command, since I do not trust your competence. I am a commissioned officer, Vincent, and you are a private soldier serving under my command. If you question my orders, I'll place you under arrest, and you can expect to be brought before a court-martial when we reach Sydney."

"On what conceivable charge?" Adam asked, tight-lipped.

"Insubordination, failure to obey an order from a superior officer . . . oh, I'd see you thrown out of the regiment, don't worry. A dishonorable discharge—is that what you want?" Adam shook his head, so angry that he was momentarily bereft of words. Others in the boat had heard their exchange, he realized, for all Fisher had spoken quietly. Sergeant Doran and . . . yes, Emily Carmichael also must have sensed the gist of it, for she was sitting up, a worried frown creasing her brow.

Fisher's tone was cold as he snapped, "Very well, then. Hand over the navigating instruments to me, Private Shannon, and the charts."

"Can you use a sextant, sir?" Adam demanded equally coldly. "Or plot a course from the stars?"

"No—but Archer can. Call the gig to come alongside. You can transfer to it, and Archer can take your place. And," Fisher added, with emphasis, "we shall continue under sail. For the sake of the women and children, we can afford no unnecessary delay. There'll be shipping near the coast. We'll stand a better chance of being picked up than we shall out here in the middle of nowhere, that's for sure. Well, what are you waiting for? You have the loud hailer —call the gig alongside!"

Doran started to voice a protest, in which several others joined, but Adam waved them to silence. He said quietly, to Doran, "Mr. Archer is a qualified navigator. He's competent to take over—and we can't be far from the coast."

The old sergeant raised his eyes to heaven and lapsed into a resentful silence, as Adam hailed the gig. The transfer was made, Archer's bewildered objections peremptorily cut short, and Fisher took the tiller.

"All right," he ordered sharply. "Get that sail hoisted again." He raised the speaking trumpet to his lips and repeated the order to the other boats. Then—the movement so carefully masked that Adam did not at once realize what had been done—he cast off the gig's towrope. The longboat's sail filled, and in a matter of minutes it had vanished into darkness. The other boats, vague shapes in the distance, followed suit, passing the gig without seeing it.

Ensign Edwards, who was at the gig's tiller, turned to Adam in shocked astonishment.

"They've left us, for God's sake! Shouldn't we hail them?"

"We're safer where we are," Adam told him calmly. "If they strike the shipping route, in this murk, without lights, they could be run down by a steamer. I fancy Chief Macpherson will realize the danger and change Fisher's mind before they've gone very far. We'll probably sight them again in daylight."

"Yes, but—" Edwards's indignation boiled over. "Why the devil did you let Fisher take over? He's no seaman and you are, according to him. He told me—" Edwards hesitated and then lowered his voice. "He said you had been a lieutenant in the navy and that you were cashiered. I think he found out from one of the passengers, or it may have been from Dr. Farrar. I—that is, I presume it's true?"

"Yes, it's true," Adam answered. He shrugged resignedly. "But I'll thank you not to talk about it. As to why I let Captain Fisher take over, I had no choice. He is my superior officer, as he was at pains to remind me. And Archer's with him in the longboat. He can navigate, and—"

"Archer is a useless young idiot, Shannon! He went to pieces when we struck the reef! For the Lord's sake, you saw him! He didn't spare a thought for anyone else. Not even for Miss Carmichael. All he worried about was his own skin. If it hadn't been for you, half of us wouldn't have made it this far. You knew exactly what had to be done. Thank God you did!"

"I can't take credit for that," Adam denied. "I was at sea since I was fourteen years old. And, alas, my last ship went down in the Irish Sea with the loss of a hundred and eleven lives, Mr. Edwards. I couldn't let anything like that happen again, could I? Even—" He broke off, a sudden note of excitement in his voice. "For the love of heaven, look! Astern of us and to port—a ship's lights! Do you see them?"

"God, yes, I do!" Edwards exclaimed. "But she's a long way away, isn't she? Will she see us?"

"She's not so far away that she won't see a rocket, if she's keeping a proper lookout," Adam told him.

Excitement spread through the boat, and some of the men started to cheer as, perhaps a bare half mile ahead of them, a rocket went up, spiraling into the night sky in a shower of sparks. It was followed by a second and then a third, and by their eerie, spreading light it was possible to discern a cluster of boats, all rising and falling on the slight swell within a few yards of each other. Adam counted five and breathed a relieved sigh. Chief Macpherson's advice had clearly been given and followed, since none of the boats had sail set.

The ship they had sighted came nearer, revealing herself as a steamer of considerable size. She changed course in evidence of the alertness of her lookouts, and a signal lamp woke to flickering life from her towering upper deck as she reduced speed. Cheers from all the boats hailed her, and Adam had no need to bid the gig's crew put their backs into their rowing. Within less than an hour, all the *Pomona*'s survivors had been made welcome on board the Peninsular and Orient mail steamer *Salsette,* bound for Sydney. Wrapped in blankets, Mrs. Carmichael was carried to the sick bay, smiling happily and assuring her rescuers that she was none the worse for her ordeal. Emily went with her mother, and as the 40th's draft mustered on the *Salsette*'s fo'c'sle for the roll call Fisher had ordered, Adam saw her raise her hand to wave in shy farewell.

It was Marcus Fisher who responded to it; he who, when the draft was sent to the crew's mess deck for a meal, shook hands warmly with the *Salsette*'s white-uniformed master and permitted himself to be escorted with some ceremony to the first-class passenger's dining saloon, talking animatedly.

Sergeant Doran paused at Adam's side and, as he had done just before the *Pomona* went down, spat the single word, "Bastard!"

Chapter IX

THE MORNING HERALD published a graphic account of the loss of the *Pomona* and the safe arrival in Sydney of her surviving passengers and crew.

Judge Carmichael read it aloud to his wife and daughter as they took their luncheon together in the large, pleasantly situated house he had purchased from his predecessor. Overlooking Hyde Park and conveniently near the law courts and the Church of Saint James, the house had been designed in the '30s by the talented architect John Verge, and both Emily and her mother had instantly felt at home in its cool, high-ceiling rooms, exclaiming with delight at the beautiful Australian cedar paneling with which the reception rooms and hall were lined.

Indeed, Emily reflected thankfully, her mother seemed to have taken a fresh lease on life since disembarking from the *Salsette*. Even the loss of the furniture and household treasures, which had gone down with the *Pomona,* no longer distressed her, for their new home was elegantly furnished, and her husband had made light of the loss, assuring her that all he had wanted and prayed for had been the safe arrival of the two who were most dear to him in all the world.

Emily smiled, studying her father's face as he read from his newspaper, conscious of the deep fondness she had always felt for him. He had been so worried, so concerned for them, especially on her mother's account; but now she had to make an effort to listen to the somewhat overdramatized description of the *Pomona*'s last hours, and found herself wondering from whom the newspaper had obtained such lurid details.

With shocked astonishment, she listened as her father read on:

"Hero of the disaster was undoubtedly the gallant young captain in command of the draft of Her Majesty's Fortieth Regiment, who, by good fortune, was among the passengers. With a modesty that does him great credit, Captain Marcus Fisher assured our reporter that he did no more than his duty. 'My men behaved in exemplary fashion,' he stated. 'In the best traditions of the regiment, they obeyed my order that the women and children must be first into the boats. Not a man attempted to leave the *Pomona*'s deck and seek his own safety until all the emigrant families had been assisted into the lifeboats, although the sea was pounding the ship to destruction and the deck was awash.' "

Emily stifled an exclamation, and her father paused, looking at her inquiringly over the top of his rimless spectacles. "Did you wish to comment, my dear?" he asked.

"Yes, indeed, Papa," she declared indignantly. "Because it's simply not true! None of it is! Captain Fisher wasn't a hero—just the reverse. The man who saved us and then navigated the boats with the survivors was one of the soldiers. His name is Adam Shannon, and—"

"He is mentioned here, Emily," the judge put in. He looked at the papers. "Fisher goes on to tell the *Herald* reporter that 'the boats, six in all, were kept on course for the shipping lanes by the second mate, Nicholas Archer, who had the presence of mind to save the master's navigating instruments before the *Pomona* went down, and one of my men, Private Shannon, who had previously served in the Royal Navy.' He gives your soldier credit, doesn't he?"

"Not the credit he deserves," Emily insisted. She glanced across the table at her mother. "It's true, isn't it, Mama? We owe our lives to Mr. Shannon."

"I believe we do, Gerald," Alice Carmichael confirmed. She spread her thin, blue-veined hands in a gesture expressive of regret. "I was not in a position to observe what went on, because, to be honest, I was paralyzed with fear, and I—my heart was playing up, you see. But Mr. Shannon *did* take full charge of the loading of the boats, and it was he who made sure that they all kept together after we left the ship. He made a great point of that—I remember his saying that he had the only navigating instruments, and so it was terribly important that they all maintained contact. Especially at night—he said that, didn't he, Emily?"

"Yes," Emily said with conviction. She turned again to her father and gave him a detailed account of everything she remembered of their ordeal, ending with an openly derisive description of Marcus Fisher's conduct. "He wasn't even there when Mr. Edwards helped Mama and me on deck—he was already in one of the boats! And later, when he transferred to ours, he just lay in the bottom with his eyes closed, insisting he was ill. And what does it say in the newspaper about Mr. Shannon, Papa?"

Her father obligingly repeated the last paragraph. " '. . . one of my men, Private Shannon, who had previously served in the Royal Navy.' Do you also question that statement, Emily my dear?"

"Yes, most certainly I do," Emily exclaimed. "Mr. Shannon was an officer, a lieutenant in the Royal Navy, Papa!"

"Hmm," her father murmured, assuming what Emily, as a child, had called his judicial look. "Then what, pray tell me, is he doing serving in the Fortieth's rank and file?"

Emily flushed, realizing that she did not know enough about Adam Shannon's previous career to be able to offer a convincing defense or even, come to that, an explanation of his present circumstances. "I only know the little he told me, Papa," she confessed.

"And that was?"

"He was court-martialed for the loss of his ship and sentenced to be cashiered." Emily hesitated, reddening. "But I *do* know what he did when our ship struck the reef. The captain, poor Captain Clifford, and the first officer, Mr. Lowe, were washed overboard, as I told you, Papa, and Mr. Shannon took command. I—" Indignation got the better of her, and she added reproachfully, "Why did the newspaper reporter not ask us what happened, Mama and me? Instead of taking Marcus Fisher's account and—and publishing it?"

"Ah, that is my fault, I'm afraid," her father conceded. "The *Herald* man wanted to interview you both, but I refused him permission. For your mama's sake, my dear—I felt it would place too great a strain on her, after all she had gone through." He gestured to the paper. "There is quite a lot more in here that you haven't heard. A Major Ashe and a station owner named . . . where is it? Ah, yes, a Mr. Cassell and his wife gave their accounts. None of them appears to contradict anything Captain Fisher said. And the chief engineer and the surgeon are quoted only as paying tribute to the *Pomona's* unfortunate master, I think." He again consulted the paper, his white brows gathered in a frown as he turned to the second page. "No, I'm wrong, my child. Mr. John Macpherson, the engineer, does praise your paragon. I'll read you what he said. 'Much is owed to Private Shannon, of Her Majesty's Fortieth Foot, whose previous service in the Royal Navy stood us all in good stead when it became necessary to abandon the ship. It was largely thanks to him and to the exemplary discipline of his comrades in the regiment that only four lives were lost in this disaster.' Does that satisfy you?"

It would have to, Emily thought resentfully, since the paper had printed the story as it had, and most of the inhabitants of Sydney Town would, by this time, have read and believed it. "Did Dr. Farrar not say anything?" she questioned.

"No more than I've told you, Emily. See for yourself." Her father passed the newspaper to her. "The good doctor gave his interview from a hospital bed. It would seem he suffered from exposure and collapsed after they brought him ashore."

Emily heard her mother exclaim in distress.

"Oh, dear, I *am* sorry to hear that! Dr. Farrar is such a kind person, and he took excellent care of me during the voyage. Nothing was ever too much trouble for him. I do hope he's not seriously ill, because he's not a young man, is he, Emily? We must visit him whilst he is in the hospital."

"It says here that he is making a good recovery, Mama," Emily volunteered. Dear old Dr. Farrar, she thought, had been more than kind to Adam Shannon, as well as to her mother and, indeed, to any of the passengers who had called upon his medical services during the voyage. And he had *not* held Marcus Fisher in high esteem.

Judge Carmichael glanced at the mantel clock and rose to his feet. "I must go, my dear," he said to his wife, pausing beside her chair to kiss her lightly on the cheek. "I'm due back in court at two-thirty. Don't overdo it while I'm gone, will you? And Emily—"

"Yes, Papa?" Emily put down the paper and rose too.

"About this soldier, Private Shannon. If you and your dear mother owe your lives to him, as you insist you do, then it is incumbent on me to do what I can to repay him, I think."

"Oh, Papa, *would* you?" Emily's resentment faded, and she clasped his arm affectionately and walked with him to the entrance hall. "Would you really?"

"Of course, child," her father assured her. "You and your mama are very precious to me, you know. If it lies in my power to help this young man, I will most gladly do so. Especially if—" He looked down at her with keen, searching gray eyes. "If he means something to you, as I suspect he does. Your mama told me that she thought someone on board the *Pomona* had greatly taken your fancy, but she did not know who had done so. Was it Shannon?"

Emily felt the swift, betraying color rise unbidden to suffuse her cheeks. "I do . . . think very highly of him, Papa. Not that there is anything between us. He has always treated me with respect and never—never presumed on our acquaintance, because of what he now is. But he is a gentleman and of good family, I am sure. And he has received the—oh, the most cruel treatment at Captain Fisher's hands. He—"

Her father cut her short. "Leave the matter in my hands, Emily. I will have a note delivered to the barracks, inviting him here. And I will certainly see what can be done for him to improve his lot. Perhaps I could assist him to buy himself out of the army and find civilian employment in this colony, or something of that kind. But I really must go, my dear child. It won't do for Her Majesty's justice to appear late in court."

To Emily's joy, her father was as good as his word. Two evenings later, Adam Shannon presented himself at the front door of her new home, immaculate in his walking-out uniform, and her father greeted him with all the warmth she could have desired.

"Mr. Shannon, I am delighted to meet you, since I understand from my wife and daughter that it is largely thanks to you that they survived the *Pomona* disaster and have been restored to me, here in Sydney, in good health and excellent spirits."

Adam reddened and attempted to parry the judge's praise, but the older man would have none of it.

"Nonsense, my dear young man; I know that Emily does not exaggerate. And, lest you ask, I have read the report in the *Morning Herald*, which—" Emily met her father's gaze and saw that he was smiling broadly. "Which both my womenfolk hotly deny has any truth in it."

"I assure you, sir—" Adam began, but again the judge cut him short.

"Did the *Herald* reporter interview you, Mr. Shannon? Or any of the rank and file of your regiment?"

"Not to my knowledge, sir. But it's of no matter, so far as I'm concerned."

"Is it not? You surprise me, Mr. Shannon."

"Sir, we are embarking for New Zealand at the end of the week," Adam countered. "The Twelfth are embarking four companies, and our draft is to go with them, under the command of their Major Hutchins. Our forces have met with serious setbacks in the Waitara region, near New Plymouth, I understand—although that is not official, so you will not have seen it in the papers yet."

Emily recoiled, a hand to her mouth, but Adam studiously avoided her gaze as he added, "My regiment has suffered heavy casualties, if the word reaching us is accurate, sir."

"And you can't wait to get into the thick of it?" the judge suggested dryly.

Again Adam reddened. "It's not that, sir, believe me. But I joined the army to fight. I—Miss Emily has no doubt told you that a naval court-martial sentenced me to be cashiered. I'm anxious to wipe out the stigma of that, you see, sir, and I think it's the only way I can do so."

"There are other ways, Mr. Shannon. For a young man of your caliber, there are many better ways than fighting a war with the rank and file. The infantry private soldier is popularly believed to be cannon fodder, as I'm sure you well know."

"I've been in action before, sir," Adam argued. "In India, during the Sepoy Mutiny."

A manservant interrupted with the announcement that dinner was served, and throughout the meal the judge steered the conversation into general channels. Despite the easy ebb and flow of talk, Emily felt tense and strained, and she left her parents to entertain their guest, herself contributing little, fearing to reveal the regret she felt at Adam Shannon's imminent departure from Sydney.

Her mother, sensing her mood and the reason for it, offered consolingly as they left the two men to their port and cigars, "Your father will spare no effort to persuade Mr. Shannon to change his mind, Emily dearest. He *likes* the young man—that was evident in the way he was talking to him during dinner. And it does not surprise me, because he is a fine young man and obviously of good breeding. It is a shame to see the way he has been treated, particularly by Captain Fisher."

"Yes, it is!" Emily exclaimed with heat. She assisted her mother to seat herself in an armchair and poured coffee for them both from the tray that had been placed in readiness for them. Balancing herself on the arm of her mother's chair, she volunteered with restrained bitterness, "Captain Fisher had poor Mr. Shannon *flogged*, Mama, only a few days after we sailed. I never told you because I feared it would upset you, but I—I *saw* it! It was very early in the morning, and I'd come up to the poop deck for a breath of air, when none of the other passengers were about. It was a terrible sight. Adam Shannon was lashed unmercifully until his poor back was a—a bloody pulp, and Captain Fisher just stood by, counting the lashes, with an unpleasant smirk on his face. I—that was when I took a dislike to him."

"Oh, my poor child!" Her mother regarded her with shocked pity. "That was a dreadful sight for you to witness. I'm glad you did not tell me at the time, because if you had, I should have found it difficult even to be civil to Captain Fisher." She sipped her coffee and then said, with an understanding smile, "I suppose as a result of what you saw you became friendly with Mr. Shannon?"

"Well, yes. I asked Dr. Farmer's permission to visit him in the sick bay, you see, and we—oh, we talked a lot while he was there. I realized that he wasn't just a common soldier, but I—" Emily breathed a frustrated sigh. "It was impossible for me to really be on friendly terms with him, because I was afraid of getting him into fresh trouble with Marcus Fisher. There were so few occasions when I could even see him without taking a risk, once he returned to his duty. There's no privacy on board ship, is there?"

"No," her mother confirmed, and Emily sensed that she was relieved as she questioned, "Then there is no serious attachment between the two of you? Mr. Shannon made no advances to you?"

Emily shook her head regretfully. "Nothing like that, Mama, I assure you."

"Perhaps that is as well, child."

"But, Mama—"

"Emily dear," her mother chided gently, "you are very young, and you have all the time in the world before you commit yourself to a serious attachment. Take that time—you would be foolish not to. Leave it to Papa to do what he can to assist Mr. Shannon. I'm sure he will know what is best to be done."

When her father and Adam Shannon joined them in the withdrawing room some ten minutes later, however, it was evident to Emily that no agreement had been reached between the two men. Her father—unusually for him—looked perplexed and even a trifle put out, and Adam, after expressing his thanks for the hospitality he had received, excused himself on the plea that his leave pass expired at eleven o'clock.

Emily accompanied him to the entrance hall.

"Are you going to the war in New Zealand?" she asked, and her heart sank when he inclined his head.

"I cannot back out now, Miss Carmichael. My regiment's in the thick of it, as I told your father, and—well, I suppose I have something to prove, something I must live down for my own peace of mind." He relaxed a little and smiled at her. "It is good of you to be concerned for me. Your father was very generous—he offered to assist me with funds to buy myself out and to find me employment here in Sydney. But I couldn't accept his offer, for the reasons I've given. You . . . please try to understand."

Emily felt tears stinging her eyes, but she forced herself to echo his smile. "We owe you a great deal, Mama and I. I'd hoped—we both hoped that you would allow us to repay you, Mr. Shannon."

He hesitated, eyeing her uncertainly, and then impulsively reached for her hand and bore it to his lips.

"You gave me more than you will ever know, Emily," he told her softly. "And God willing, I shall not be gone forever. When I can come to you with—with honor, I promise you I'll be here. But if that is not to be, then you would do best to forget me, I think. Or at all events, just to remember me kindly as one who greatly valued your friendship."

"I shan't forget you, Adam," Emily whispered, unable any longer to stem her tears. "I shall never forget you. And I shall pray for your safety."

Adam released her hand. He crammed on his cap and became the stiff soldier again, reerecting the barrier between them.

"Good-bye, Miss Carmichael," he said, and was gone, the door into the street swinging shut behind him.

Emily waited, dabbing at her tear-filled eyes with the back of her hand and fighting desperately for composure. When she rejoined her parents, she was dry-eyed and quietly resolute, meeting their anxiously searching glances with a brave little smile.

"That is a fine young man," her father asserted, smothering a sigh. "And he resisted all my offers of aid. I did my best, believe me, Emily my dear, but he would not hear of deserting his regiment when it is going to war. For which I respect him. He would not divulge his real name or any details concerning the charges brought against him at his court-martial, save to say that he was found guilty on several counts, including the loss of his ship. But he did inadvertently let slip a clue to his identity." Her father put his arm about Emily's waist and drew her onto his knee, as he had been wont to do when she was a child, holding her in an affectionate embrace. "He said that he had served in India with the *Shannon*'s naval brigade—hence the name he chose to adopt, of course. I shall find out who he is, Emily. I have friends at the Admiralty and in the Judge Advocate's department. Rest assured, dearest child, I intend to do all I can for him, however long it takes."

Emily's arms went round his neck, and she hugged him. Then, to her dismay, the tears returned, and with a muffled sob she excused herself and fled to the privacy of her bedroom.

Husband and wife exchanged concerned glances.

"She will get over it, Gerald," Mrs. Carmichael said. "She *is* only a child, and it was her first experience of love. She never looked at a young man before we boarded the ship to come here."

"I'm sure you are right, my dear. All the same, I'll have a word with Will Hutchins before his regiment leaves, and ask him, as a favor to me, to keep an eye on young Shannon. Now"—he rose and held out his hand to her—"you must be tired, Alice my love. Let us go up, shall we? Tomorrow is another day."

Alice Carmichael took the offered hand, and, more slowly than Emily had done, they ascended the stairs together.

The next day, the Sydney papers carried lengthy accounts of what appeared to have been a military disaster in New Zealand. Judge Carmichael, in his robing room at the Supreme Court, read the *Herald*'s account, which began under a banner headline that proclaimed, DEFEAT FOR OUR FORCES IN NEW ZEALAND.

Under the command of Major Thomas L.K. Nelson, of Her Majesty's 40th Regiment of Foot, a force of 350 men of that regiment, augmented by 60 seamen and marines of H.M.S. *Pelorus,* led by their captain, the Hon. Fredrick Beauchamp-Seymour, R.N., advanced from the Waitara camp to attack a double *pa* known as Puketakauere on June 27.

The *pa,* held by the rebel Maori chief Wiremu Kingi, was well constructed, according to reports from our special correspondent, and stood on a ridge flanked by deep gullies full of brambles and thick, entangled bracken, dropping away to a swamp close to the Waitara River. The position was strongly defended, and a preliminary bombardment by two 24-pounder howitzers had less effect than anticipated.

At 7 a.m. the attack went forward, divided into three columns, the center led in person by Major Nelson, and the others attacking on the flanks. All three were met by a devastating fire from concealed rifle pits, which inflicted many casualties. Captain Beauchamp-Seymour's seamen and marines carried the first trenchworks, but then, meeting point-blank fire from the Maori defenders, they were driven back, the Maoris falling upon them with tomahawks as they retreated, the brave captain being among the wounded.

Major Nelson's frontal attack fared no better, and they, too, were compelled to retreat, losing over 60 of their number. But it was the two flanking columns that suffered the most, being attacked by large numbers of the rebels as they struggled to make their way through the gullies and swamps. So ferocious were the attacks that many wounded had to be abandoned there, to meet their deaths at the hands of the Ngatimaniapoto tribesmen, who descended on them out of the bush.

Reinforcements, under Colonel Gold, commanding officer of the 65th Regiment, were believed to be on the way from New Plymouth, but this column advanced only as far as the flooded Waiongana River, where, finding a crossing impossible, the colonel ordered a return to New Plymouth.

A call was made to the Volunteer Rifles manning a nearby outpost, and a mounted party under Colonel William De Lancey—at present serving as a captain in the Taranaki militia—rode out to the scene of the disastrous attack and succeeded in bringing a number of wounded to safety. Colonel De Lancey, well known in Sydney and a holder of the Victoria Cross, was slightly wounded in the action.

More regiments are being sent to New Zealand with all possible dispatch, and Major General Thomas Pratt, general officer commanding in Australia, will soon embark from here for New Plymouth, together with four companies of the 12th Regiment, under Major William Hutchins, and the recently arrived draft of the 40th, who survived the wreck of the S.S. *Pomona* and will join the main body of the regiment already serving in the theater of war.

The judge was frowning as he laid down the newspaper. It would be as well, he decided, to keep the news it contained from little Emily, if possible. Undoubtedly the poor child had lost her heart to Adam Shannon, and as much as he himself had liked—yes, and admired—that young man, there could be no future in it for Emily, and he would have to try to offer her some distraction. With Sydney virtually drained of the normal garrison troops, there would be no personable young officers whom he could invite to the house, but . . . there was his own profession, which had no lack of personable young barristers.

David Milne, for example, his legal clerk, or Nigel Bartholomew, who had put up so spirited a defense of the fellow accused of robbery under arms a week or so ago, and whose father had been elected to the Assembly. Perhaps, if his wife felt up to it, they would give a dinner party. At all costs, Emily must not be allowed to brood.

On July 17, the troops bound for New Zealand marched through the streets of Sydney, with a band playing and enthusiastic crowds cheering them all the way to the waiting transport steamer.

Emily, although her father did not know it, was among the cheering throng who followed in the wake of the marching soldiers right up to the point of embarkation. Long after most of the crowd had dispersed, she stood watching, her eyes half blinded by tears, as a tug took the transport in tow and eased her away from the wharf.

Chapter X

ON THE MORNING of September 26, 1861, Red Broome brought his new command, the steam-screw frigate *Cossack,* into Auckland's Manukau Harbor. On board was His Excellency Sir George Grey, returning to New Zealand for his second term as governor, and as the signal guns boomed their customary salute, Red saw that his distinguished passenger's deep-set blue eyes were bright with pleasure.

But there was something more there, as the governor caught sight of the cheering throng gathered on the Queen Street wharf to bid him welcome. Among the crowd was a large group of Maoris, the chiefs in ceremonial cloaks, and their cheers, at times, drowned those of the settlers as they pressed forward eagerly, unable to hide their delight. The governor, Red saw, was moved momentarily to tears, as if this were the homecoming for which he had longed yet had not been sure he would receive. Then, shamed by his display of emotion, he drew himself up, and the tears swiftly vanished.

During the five-week-long passage from the Cape, Red had come to know and admire the austere and brilliant man into whose hands the troubled colony's future had once again been entrusted. That Grey was also a sick and embittered man he had realized, from the moment the governor had stepped on board the *Cossack* at Cape Town, a pale, gauntly handsome figure, leaning on the arm of one of his aides. It had been common gossip among those of his staff who had accompanied him that the acrimonious breakdown of his marriage had affected him profoundly, but his bitterness, Red had sensed, stemmed from another cause.

Pacing the quarterdeck in Red's company during the night watches, he had talked, never easily but always honestly, his judgment of himself at times harsh, at other times bordering on arrogance—or what might have been taken as arrogance, had it not been for the fact that he believed passionately in his own judgment and the causes for which he had fought for most of his life.

Sir George's governorship of the Cape had not been an unmitigated success. Although the colonists had hailed him as the best governor Great Britain had ever sent to South Africa, the reforms he had advocated and the measures he had taken to implement them had found no favor with the British Colonial Office. He had repeatedly crossed swords with British officialdom, aroused the implacable hostility of the Colonial Secretary, defied the Admiralty and the Horse Guards and, it transpired, made countless enemies in the British House of Commons.

On his own admission, only a change of government had saved him from ignominious and permanent recall. The new Colonial Secretary had reappointed him as governor of New Zealand when it had become evident that the Maoris of the Taranaki tribes would never make peace with Colonel Gore-Browne, whose high-handed attempts to crush their resistance had invoked such deep-seated mistrust.

"I, too, shall meet with mistrust, Captain Broome," the governor had said, more than once, toward the end of their passage. "The settlers will expect me to suspend the constitution and continue the war, which I have no intention of doing. And, when I fail to do so, they will accuse me of favoring the Maoris' cause at the expense of theirs. I want to see justice done to both factions, and I want also to make peace—but not peace at any price, you understand. It must be a lasting peace, and that will not be easy to achieve, for I shall be serving two masters—the British Parliament and the New Zealand Assembly. And their solutions to the problems are utterly and completely incompatible!"

From his vantage point at the rear of the small procession that escorted the governor ashore, Red watched as his former passenger accepted the greetings of Colonel Gore-Browne, Bishop Selwyn, Henry Sewell, and other leading personages and prominent members of the Assembly. Among them, stiff as a ramrod in his bemedaled scarlet uniform, was Major General Cameron, now commanding the imperial troops in New Zealand. A formidable officer in appearance and by reputation, Cameron greeted Sir George Grey with an impeccable salute but, significantly, did not smile, despite the governor's cordial acknowledgment of the greeting.

The military band struck up, and with former governor Gore-Browne and General Cameron seated on either side of him, Sir George Grey—after pausing deliberately to address a few words in their own language to the group of Maori chiefs and their retainers —permitted himself to be driven in an open carriage to Government House. As the cheers died away, Red heard a familiar voice calling to him by name, and turning, he found himself confronted by the tall figure of his brother Johnny, clad, to his surprise, in the blue serge uniform and peaked forage cap of a colonial volunteer.

"My dear fellow, it's good to see you!" Red embraced his brother warmly and then stood back, to study him with puzzled eyes. "I had supposed you to be reporting on the war, not taking an active part in it, for God's sake!" He was tempted to inquire whether Johnny's wife approved of his transition, but thought better of it and, instead, gestured to the ship at his back and took his brother's arm. "Come on board and take a drink with me. I'm anxious to hear all your news."

"And I yours," Johnny assured him. "Is Magdalen with you?"

Red shook his head. "Their Lordships would not permit me to give her passage. She and the children—we have a small son now, born in England while I languished on half pay—they came out in the P and O mail steamer *Salsette,* ahead of me. All being well, they should be in Sydney already, and I'm eager to join them. The boy's name is Andrew Justin, and he's a fine little fellow." Red smiled and led the way to the *Cossack*'s gangway, returning the salutes of the men on duty at its head. Reaching his day cabin, he waved Johnny to a seat, poured two glasses of Cape brandy, and lifted his own in salute.

"Your very good health, brother John! Tell me—how is the lovely Lady Kitty?"

Johnny moodily quaffed the contents of his glass.

"She is very well, but—alas, she does not like New Zealand overmuch. And my joining the colonial forces has displeased her greatly, I'm afraid," he added, answering Red's unvoiced question. "She talks incessantly of going back to Sydney. Her brother's there —you remember Pat, don't you? Well, he wearied of farming, persuaded Luke Murphy to take over his sheep run in Victoria, and has hied himself back to Sydney with all possible speed. I have no idea what he plans to do there. But Luke, good fellow that he is, has certainly fallen on his feet. You heard, I suppose, that he married Uncle Will's little adopted daughter, Jane?"

"No." Red shook his head, leaning across to refill his brother's glass. "No, I hadn't heard that. But I'm glad, for both their sakes. The girl is deaf and dumb, isn't she?"

"Yes, but a charming little creature in spite of it."

Red refilled his own glass and leaned back in his chair, a thoughtful frown creasing his brow. "Do you think your wife *will* go back to Sydney?"

Johnny shrugged. "I honestly don't know, Red. I don't want her to, but . . . well, you know Kitty. She is a law unto herself, and I know she misses Pat. They're twins and they've never been apart—not until she married me, that is. What she really dislikes is being left here alone, which is understandable, of course. And since I joined the militia, I have to go where I'm sent."

"Why *did* you join the militia, Johnny?" Red asked. "Your reports on the war in the Taranaki were first-rate. I even read extracts from them in the English papers, under your name."

Johnny frowned. "The ghastly defeat Major Nelson suffered when he attacked Wiremu Kingi's *pa* at Puketakauere last June made me decide that I couldn't just be an onlooker. You read about that, I imagine?" Red nodded, and he went on. "Nelson's one of the bravest fellows I ever met, but he made a hideous mistake trying to attack with the bayonet. And that incompetent bastard Colonel Gold let him down by turning back, instead of bringing up reinforcements, as he had promised he would. And it wasn't the first time, either." Bitterly, Johnny described the manner in which the 65th's veteran commander had abandoned the Volunteers at Waireka by ordering the withdrawal of his regiment at sunset, when—heavily outnumbered—the militia were fighting for their lives. "At Puketakauere the naval commander, Beauchamp-Seymour of the *Pelorus*—a truly remarkable fellow, who wears a monocle and whose sailors call him the Swell of the Ocean—was very severely wounded. In fact, the poor fellow nearly died, but his seamen carried him back to camp. You know him, I expect?"

"I've met him," Red confirmed.

"Will De Lancey was also wounded," Johnny said. "Only slightly, I'm glad to say. He came to our aid from the Bell Block with fifty of the Volunteers, after Gold turned back with his entire column and two guns, when he might have saved the day. It's said that the men of his regiment hissed him, when he gave the order to retire."

"And has he been permitted to continue in command?" Red exclaimed. "I should have thought—"

"So did everyone concerned," Johnny asserted disgustedly. "There was a military court of inquiry a few weeks ago, but its findings were hushed up. Gold's gone, seemingly without a stain on his character! General Pratt saw to that. Now *he* has done a most excellent job. Feelings between the army and the settlers were running very high when he arrived from Sydney in July of last year, and the casualties were alarming. The weather was appalling too, so the general couldn't make a decisive move until the middle of September—almost exactly a year ago, in fact, Red. I was with the force as a reporter, and Governor Gore-Browne was urging him to avenge Puketakauere. Well, he did, but in his own fashion. No more disastrous frontal attacks with the bayonet for General Pratt."

Johnny again drained his glass and broke off as Red refilled it.

"What do you mean by 'his fashion'?" Red asked curiously. "The reports I've seen suggested that General Pratt was succeeding where others failed, but the last newspaper I saw was a three-week-old copy of the *Times* in Cape Town."

Johnny was smiling now. "Thomas Pratt—soon to be *Sir* Thomas, I'm led to believe, with a damned well-earned K.C.B.— was determined to cut down the casualty rate. And he did it by sapping up to the *pas*—digging well-protected saps, right up to the palisades, building redoubts, and siting his guns in them. He took three major *pas* in less than a month, Red, at the cost of five casualties! The Maoris simply couldn't understand what was going on—they kept on urging us to come out and fight! In November, when the general returned to New Plymouth, with a bloodless victory under his belt, word came that the Waikato were crossing the river in force. They occupied a disused *pa* eight miles from the town, but General Pratt didn't wait for them to restore its defenses. He advanced right away, and on that occasion he didn't take time to sap. The Waikato weren't ready, and he attacked them from three sides. He routed them and lost only four killed and fifteen wounded, most of those in the hand-to-hand fighting." Johnny's smile widened. "It was then, Red, that I decided I could not stay out of the battle, whatever Kitty thought about it. I'd been thinking about it ever since Puketakauere, and the general offered to get me a commission. I'm an acting captain, believe it or not, and I've been in all the actions we've fought against the Waikato. I've sapped at Wiremu Kingi's *pas* at Matarikoriko, Hiurangi, and Te Arei with the Sixty-fifth and the Fortieth and the Twelfth. I've heard the British soldiers grouse and grumble at the sweat they've had to expend digging their trenches and redoubts, but I've seen how effective the general's tactics are. I've seen many good men die, in spite of Pratt's efforts to preserve their lives, but he's done wonders, and I reckon that peace will be concluded before we're much older. Unfortunately, Wiremu Kingi's not ready to put out a white flag just yet. They say he's left Taranaki, vowing to support the King Movement." Johnny shrugged in resignation. "Our late governor made it too plain that he was out to destroy the Kingites, I fear. The rebel Maoris call him Angry Belly and don't trust him an inch. Hence the Colonial Office, in its wisdom, has sent Sir George Grey back here to replace him."

"A good move, surely, Johnny?" Red suggested.

"You probably know the answer to that better than I do, since you brought him out; but . . . yes, on the whole, I'd say it was a good move. The Maoris hold him in very high esteem, and the friendlies, like old Chief Waaka Nene, trust him implicitly. On the other hand—" Johnny repeated his shrug. "The majority of the settlers and many of the politicians are not sure that Grey will put *their* interests first. He could meet with considerable opposition, Red. We shall just have to wait and see what will happen, I suppose."

Offered another glass of brandy, Johnny declined. He took out his pocket watch and swore softly. "Lord, how the time flies! Kitty expects me for lunch, and this is the first leave I've had for close on six months. Red, I shall have to go, but . . . dine with us this evening, will you? I'll pick you up at about seven-thirty, if that suits you. And you know, of course, that you will be more than welcome to take up residence with us, should you feel so inclined. You are staying here, I take it?"

"No, alas, I'm not," Red answered, conscious of a momentary regret. "My orders are to proceed to Australia, giving passage to any who require it—mainly wounded and disabled soldiers and seamen, I believe. Or possibly His Excellency Colonel Gore-Browne. I shall have to report to the commodore and ascertain from him whether or not my orders have been changed."

"Commodore Loring?" Johnny's tone was faintly derisive.

"You'll find him at the anchorage, on board the *Iris*. Apart from a short sojourn in Wellington, he's been here, officially consulting with Governor Gore-Browne as to tactics, but . . . well, not to put too fine a point on it, Red, Auckland gossip has it that he and H.E.'s lady wife have been conducting a passionate affair behind the old gentleman's back. Mrs. Gore-Browne is thirty years younger than her husband and possessed of much charm. And Loring's a dashing sort of fellow, Crimean veteran and all that. But keep that little tidbit under your hat, won't you?"

Johnny rose, setting down his empty glass. He glanced again at his watch and sighed. "Loring's to be relieved as commodore, we are led to believe, with Beauchamp-Seymour acting until his relief arrives. Anyway, there's talk of several of the naval ships leaving, once peace is concluded. But you'll probably find out what's in the wind in that quarter before I do."

"Yes, doubtless I shall," Red agreed. "My respects to your Lady Kitty, John. I look forward to seeing her."

He accompanied his brother to the gangway, and they parted on the understanding that he would dine with Johnny and his wife that evening. His attempt to make contact with Commodore Loring, however, was unsuccessful, the commodore being ashore at Government House. But early in the afternoon, a signal from the steam-screw corvette *Pelorus* informed him that Captain Beauchamp-Seymour was on his way to call on him.

A smartly manned boat, its crew in striped white jumpers and beribboned straw hats, came alongside, and Red received the acting commodore with the appropriate ceremony. As the bo'sun's mates' twittering calls faded into silence, Beauchamp-Seymour fixed his monocle firmly in his eye and returned the side party's salute, before offering Red an affable greeting.

Fredrick Beauchamp Paget Seymour was a handsome man of forty, who came of an aristocratic family with a record of distinguished service in both the navy and the army. Red had met him briefly when Seymour had been serving as flag lieutenant to his uncle, Rear Admiral Sir George Seymour, in the eighty-gun line-of-battle ship *Collingwood* on the Pacific station, and as they descended to the day cabin, Seymour surprised him by recalling their meeting.

"We missed each other in India—you were attached to poor Peel's naval brigade, weren't you?" Seymour went on, "I, for my sins, was dispatched to Burma just as the mutiny broke out in the

Bengal Presidency. We had to occupy a filthy, crumbling fort up the Irrawaddy, at Meaday, for almost three months, and half my men went down with dysentery! Frankly, Broome, despite the casualties we've suffered since being posted here, I infinitely prefer New Zealand. The Maori are pretty ferocious foes, but they are incredibly brave and astonishingly chivalrous in battle. I shall be sorry to leave."

Red, pouring drinks, turned to look at him in mute question, and Captain Seymour inclined his well-groomed head. "Yes, we're to sail for Australia as soon as peace is signed—the whole squadron, apart from the *Victorious*. Mind, I do not expect peace to be concluded immediately. We'll be here for a while yet, but the naval brigade has been disbanded, and our men have returned to their ships."

"Do you have any fresh orders for me, sir?" Red asked.

Seymour shook his head. "No, none. You're to proceed to Sydney, aren't you? Well, you are free to sail whenever it suits." Seymour smiled. "Doubtless you will have heard the reason for Their Lordships' anxiety to base the squadron at Sydney?"

"No, sir," Red admitted.

The acting commodore's smile widened. "My dear fellow, they fear the outbreak of war with the northern states of America!"

"Good God!" Red stared at him incredulously. Though he was well aware that relations between Washington and London had been steadily deteriorating, owing to the British government's support for the cause of the southern states, Red had never envisioned the possibility of open hostilities. "Do they really consider that seriously?"

"It would seem they do, Broome. Furthermore, they appear to suppose that a naval attack on Port Jackson is a possibility! So you will be responsible for warding it off, should it come, because, as I told you, my squadron must stay here until peace in the Taranaki is concluded." Seymour screwed his monocle back on, after wiping it carefully with a silk kerchief, then accepted a cigar from Red and, leaning back in his chair, started to talk at some length about the recent campaign in the Taranaki area. As Johnny had done, he paid tribute to the courage and skill of the Maori warriors, describing the formidable *pas* they built and defended with such tenacity.

"I don't know whether anyone has told you of the disaster we suffered at Puketakauere, Broome," he went on, a pensive frown

drawing his brows together. "It was an eye-opener to me, I can tell
you. . . ."

Red, although he had seen the *Herald*'s lengthy account of the
battle, did not interrupt, and Seymour, after giving a colorful description of the action in which he had been wounded—indeed,
almost killed, according to Johnny—went on without a pause to
relate his part in other battles. He supplied details of each with
infectious enthusiasm, and then said thoughtfully, "Certain events
and certain individuals remain in the mind, you know. My ship's
company, of course—Lord, I was proud of them! But there was
one incident in particular that has haunted me ever since, because
I'm as sure as I can be of anything that I recognized the fellow in
question. Heroes come in all guises, and we had quite a few among
our own bluejackets—but the particular fellow I'm talking about
was a soldier of the Fortieth, a Private Shannon. I think he's been
made up to sergeant since, but . . . devil take it, Broome, I could
swear I knew him in India! Only he was in our service then—a
lieutenant—and his name wasn't Shannon."

Red's interest quickened, but he said nothing, and Captain Seymour went on, an odd note in his deep, pleasant voice. "It was at
Te Arei, by repute the most impregnable of the Maori *pas*. It stood
on a steep rise, the Waitara River, with clifflike banks, protecting
the position to the right and left. Between our saphead and the *pa*
itself there was a mile of level ground, with enemy rifle pits, covered over and quite invisible, some of them sited at the edge of
dense bush, so thick with undergrowth that we had to hack our
way through it. General Pratt sent in the Fortieth and two companies of the Sixty-fifth in extended order to take a small, fern-cov-
ered hill that commanded the whole line of Maori rifle pits. They
were ordered to dig in, when they had gained the hill, and occupy
it, preparatory to constructing a redoubt on its summit."

Seymour sighed and, as if anticipating Red's question, said
dryly, "The general knew there would be some casualties, but the
position being what it was, he had no choice, really. And casualties
there were, including the Sixty-fifth's commander, Captain
Strange, and two of his subalterns, who were shot down almost at
once. But I saw the fellow I'm talking about, Shannon, take command. He led them and they took the hill in splendid style, and
once there they outflanked the rifle pits, so the general's objective
was achieved. During the night, Shannon brought in five of the
wounded, alone, carrying them on his back and braving a heavy

fire from the palisades of the *pa*. Then he went back to the hill and stayed there. In the morning all the rifle pits were abandoned, and we brought a gun up to the hill. It was a truly incredible effort. Shannon, in my opinion, ought to get the V.C." He frowned, in evident perplexity. "I talked to him a couple of days later, but when I said I intended to recommend him for the Cross, he pleaded with me not to do so! I tried to question him, in the hope of finding out who he was and where I'd met him before, but . . . he evaded all my questions and denied ever having set eyes on me in his life! But I don't easily forget a face, and I'd swear I met him before."

Vincent, Red thought—could it possibly be young Lieutenant Adam Vincent, on whose court-martial he had served? On the face of it, the idea was wildly improbable, but Vincent had served in the *Shannon*'s naval brigade during the Sepoy Mutiny in India, so that the name he had assumed—if, indeed, the name *was* an assumed one—left room for speculation, even if it did not afford proof.

On the point of confiding his thoughts to Captain Seymour, Red hesitated. It seemed evident, from what his fellow captain had said, that Vincent—if indeed it *was* Vincent—had strong personal reasons for not wishing to be identified. He had refused to permit Captain Seymour to recommend him for a Victoria Cross, fearing, no doubt, that were the recommendation to go forward, it would lead to the disclosure of his real name and his record. The trial, the sentence of the court-martial, the fact that he had been cashiered . . . good Lord, the poor young devil would not want any of it to be known! He had chosen to enlist in the army, to seek anonymity in the ranks of the 40th Regiment; he—

Seymour rose reluctantly to his feet. "I must go and make my number with the new governor, Broome," he said. "Indeed, I was on my way to Government House when I decided to pay a call on you. And I fear I've let my tongue run away with me, yarning over old battles and no doubt boring you unforgivably. I crave your indulgence, my dear fellow."

"It has been of great interest, sir," Red assured him truthfully, rising at once.

"It's been good to go into action again." Captain Seymour settled his monocle carefully in his eye and donned his hat. "We shall meet again in Sydney, if and when the peace here is agreed and I'm permitted to depart. In the meantime, Captain Broome"—his smile was almost boyish—"the defense of Port Jackson will become *your* responsibility, should Their Lordships' extraordinary fears be realized and the Americans launch a seaborne attack on the colony!"

He was still chuckling at the absurd notion when he took his departure.

Johnny arrived at the wharf, as promised, in a gig, drawn by a pair of handsomely matched bay horses, but it was evident, when Red joined him, that he was embarrassed and annoyed.

"My wife, I regret to have to tell you," he announced with restraint, "will not be at home to receive you, Red. When I went back to our lodgings, I found a note from her in which she informed me that she had accepted an invitation to dine with William Fox, our ex-premier! Her escort, it seems, is a wealthy settler from Ireland by the name of O'Hara, who is a member of the Assembly. He has taken her out to view his property, prior to dining with his friend Fox. Apparently—" Johnny's subdued annoyance suddenly came to the surface, and he added wrathfully, "The infernal fellow breeds blood horses, and Kitty's been dying to take a look at them, and she'll buy one given half a chance, though God knows where she'll keep it! But it leaves me with no alternative, Red, I'm afraid—I'll have to take you to the Auckland militia mess for a meal."

Red, seeking to spare his brother's feelings, did not demur, and, indeed, he spent a pleasant enough evening in the company of Johnny's fellow officers, although their talk was—as Captain Seymour's had been—almost exclusively of the war, with few of them holding out any real hope of a permanent peace.

It was with oddly mixed emotions that, the following day, he received formal permission to proceed to Sydney, taking on board some fifteen wounded men of the 12th and 40th regiments, whose injuries rendered most of them unfit for active service.

But, Red reflected as the pilot disembarked and he set course for Australia, Magdalen and his children would be awaiting his return, and, God willing—whatever the militia officers feared—Sir George Grey would contrive to act as peacemaker between the settlers and the Maoris. As to the supposed threat of attack from America, he found himself sharing Captain Beauchamp-Seymour's skepticism, as he dispensed with the *Cossack*'s engines and ordered the topmen aloft to make sail.

Chapter XI

MOUNTED ON ONE of her host's spirited young thoroughbreds, Kitty Broome gave herself up to the sheer pleasure the occasion offered. Since her arrival in Auckland over a year ago, the only riding she had done had been decorous promenades on hired hacks, within the boundaries of the town, and it was with a joyous sense of newfound freedom that she gave her mount his head and galloped at breakneck speed across the lush green turf surrounding Sean O'Hara's farmhouse.

The farm, which he called Killaloe, was situated seven miles south of Auckland. The homestead was unpretentious—a single-story dwelling house built of native timber, with a spacious veranda encircling three sides of it—but inside it was furnished with excellent taste, and Sean O'Hara employed an elderly Irish couple, who kept the place in immaculate order and cooked for him when he was in residence.

By New Zealand settler standards, he was a wealthy man, the owner also of a town house. His wealth, as he had confided with disarming modesty, stemmed from a lucky strike in the Victoria goldfields, near Ballarat.

"I hadn't two pennies to rub together when I stepped ashore from the leaking old tub that brought me out from Cork, with over a hundred others," he had said, in his lilting Irish voice, smiling as he said it. "And every last one of us sure in his heart that he'd only to get himself to the diggings and his fortune would be made! Only it wasn't like that, when we reached Ballarat. You needed tools and a tent, and there was food to buy and the cost of the license to find, with everything costing four times what it should. I had to hire myself out for grub and a small wage for over six months before I'd

scraped together enough to work a claim of my own. But then my
luck changed, and I did make my fortune, Lady Kitty. And faith, I
cannot think of a better way to spend it than the way I've chosen,
can you?"

Indeed, Kitty reflected, turning to look at him as he drew level
with her, she could not. Sean O'Hara had established the finest
bloodstock stud in the colony—if not the only one, come to that.
He had imported two stallions, with Arab blood, purchased from
one of the famous Rowe brothers of Melbourne, and his brood-
mares had come from other Victoria Turf Club breeders. He also
had three new fillies, which he particularly prized, from Ireland,
chosen and shipped out to him by his father.

By the arbitrary standards of colonial society, Sean barely
passed muster, despite his wealth. He came, on his own frank admission, of a poor Tipperary farming family, the youngest of six
sons, and his father had bred horses as a sideline, selling them in
the Cashel market to the hunting gentry or hawking them round
the big houses, with what his son jestingly described as "a fine line
of patter."

Studying his tanned, smiling face now, Kitty sought to analyze
what there was about him that was so attractive, for undoubtedly,
she was compelled to admit, he *did* attract her, despite the differences in their upbringing and social standing.

He was darkly handsome and possessed more than his fair share
of Irish charm—a charm that had won him influential friends and
his election, quite recently, to the Assembly, which ensured that he
was received in viceregal circles. Indeed, Kitty recalled, she had
first made his acquaintance at one of the staid and somewhat
dreary dinner parties given periodically by Governor Gore-Browne
and his wife. The fact that Sean was Irish had drawn them together
initially, and on further acquaintance she had found that they had
much in common.

A love of horses and for Ireland, to begin with . . . memories
of the land that had given them birth, which were hard to share
with anyone else—even with Johnny, she thought guiltily, for Ireland was a closed book to the man she had married. And she had
been lonely. Johnny had been caught up in the war, first reporting
it for his paper from New Plymouth and then—Kitty frowned,
conscious of a deep and abiding resentment—then deciding, without consulting her, to enlist in the Volunteers, which had meant

that his absences had become even more protracted and less predictable.

Auckland society possessed little appeal for her. The officers' wives held themselves determinedly aloof from those of the settlers and the civilian officials. The naval officers—with the sole exception of Captain Cracroft of the *Niger,* who had defied the Admiralty by bringing his wife out with him as a passenger—came alone, and so contributed little to the social scene, their ships and their sailors being engaged, like the army, in fighting the war. And the governor's lady—the *late* governor's lady—with whom she might have formed a friendly alliance, had been too taken up with her beau, the naval commodore, to have time for feminine company.

If her brother Patrick had been there, as he had always been in the past, she would have been content and looked for no other companionship. But Patrick had *not* been there, and in her loneliness she had turned to Sean O'Hara—innocently enough up till now, grateful for his escort to functions that a lone woman could not properly attend.

Only perhaps, without really intending to, she had let things go too far. Meeting Sean's gaze and reading the challenge in his dark, expressive eyes, Kitty felt a flood of warm color suffuse her cheeks. Sean wanted her; he was already making demands, presuming a little more each time they met and ensuring that their meetings were frequent. At recent dinner or luncheon parties, the touch of his hand on her arm had become more possessive, and when they had waltzed together to the music of one of the military bands, she had been conscious of his desire and tempted to respond to it.

But Johnny had come on leave then, and her conscience had held her back. Johnny was her husband, Kitty reminded herself unhappily. She owed him her loyalty, for all he appeared to think the war more important than their marriage, and . . . she ought not to have come out here with Sean today, however much she had wanted to visit his stud and ride his horses. And to have agreed that he should escort her to dine with Mr. Fox and his family this evening, when properly her husband should have done so, was . . . God forgive her, it was a betrayal of her marriage vows, no matter how unwillingly she had made them.

She remembered the odd little ceremony in the smoke-filled cuddy of the mail steamer *Gloria,* when she had married Johnny Broome—a ceremony that had been hurriedly performed, just before they had disembarked in Hobson's Bay, on their way to Melbourne. Recalling her own reluctance, Kitty stifled a sigh, wishing that she could forget it. But she could not forget; it was stamped indelibly on her mind, and Father O'Flynn's words came back to her: *"Forsaking all other, cleave thee only unto him . . ."*

"You're so beautiful, Kitty," she heard Sean say. "The most beautiful woman I ever set eyes on in my life, I swear you are! And seated on that chestnut, before heaven, you are a sight to gladden a man's heart, for you ride him like a dream. You must have the horse for your own, whatever your husband says. He's made for you, so he is."

"He is truly a lovely creature," Kitty agreed. "But I cannot take him, Sean. I—"

"But I *want* you to have him," Sean insisted eagerly. "We'll bring him back with us this evening. We can lead him behind the gig, and I'll arrange with the livery stable to keep him for you, so that you can ride him whenever you wish." He leaned forward to pat her mount's gleaming chestnut neck, and then let his hand rest for a moment on Kitty's bridle hand. "The creature's name is Gold Dust of Killaloe, and his breeding is almost as impeccable as yours, Kitty. You *must* allow me the pleasure of giving him to you. You—"

"You know I can't, Sean," Kitty protested. "It would set people talking. Even if I bought him, the gossips would read something into it. And Johnny would be upset."

"Faith, they're talking already," Sean told her, with angry frankness. "And to hell with it if they are! I'm proud to have my name linked with yours. And if your husband is upset, hasn't he brought it on himself by leaving you alone for months on end? He doesn't deserve you, Kitty." His hand tightened about hers. "For the Lord's sweet sake, do you not know the way I feel about you? Do you not know that I am madly in love with you and that I'd give everything I have, including my immortal soul, to have you for my own and be with you for the rest of my days?"

His voice was low, the passionate longing in it alarming in its naked intensity, and Kitty's conscience plagued her anew, for her instinctive response was far from that of a respectably married woman, whose husband had only recently returned from the war.

Oh, God, she thought wretchedly, I have led him on, I have let him believe what he wants to believe. I have behaved as if I were free, but I am not free. I have a husband who loves me, and I have no right to seek Sean's company or take his love. . . . She caught her breath on a sob. Desperate for a distraction, she waved a trembling hand toward a low hill half a mile ahead of them. It had not been cleared; the ubiquitous fern grew thickly on its lower slopes, and the summit was heavily timbered. The ground between was swampy, and neither this nor the hill invited a wild gallop on a valuable horse.

In spite of it, Kitty called out a reckless challenge. "I'll race you to the hill, Sean. To the top, if you wish!"

She did not wait for his rejection of her challenge but kneed the chestnut forward and, bent low over his neck, made for the hill, swiftly gathering speed. Sean hesitated and then, perforce, followed her, maintaining a much steadier pace and shouting out a warning to her to have a care.

From behind the concealment of the tall ferns, half a dozen tattooed brown faces peered out, curiously at first and then, as the two mounted figures came nearer, with apprehension. The six were young warriors from the upper Waikato, who had entered the town of Auckland earlier in the day to witness the arrival of Sir George Grey. Now on their way back to their tribe, to report on what they had seen and heard, they were anxious to avoid discovery, and the sight of the two horsemen galloping straight for their hiding place unnerved them.

From where they watched, crouched by a stream at which they had paused to drink, the fact that one of the riders was a woman was not immediately apparent, and Sean O'Hara's shout, although addressed to Kitty, was misunderstood.

The young warriors were a long way from their home, and their spying mission had been fraught with danger—magnified, in their estimation, by their present isolation and by the unfriendly reception they had met with in the town from those of their race who had welcomed the old governor's return. Panic seized them.

"They come to attack us!" one of the young men exclaimed excitedly. "It is an ambush—the *pakehas* will bring men of the soldier tribe to kill us!"

"Then let us defend ourselves! Did not Chief Rewi Maniapoto say 'Kill the *pakehas*'?" One of his companions raised the musket he carried and, taking careful aim, pulled the trigger.

The ball struck Kitty's speeding horse in the chest; the poor animal emitted a shrill squeal of agony and crashed to the ground, flinging Kitty out of the saddle, to collapse motionless beside the thrashing body. A fusillade of shots followed the first, but Sean ignored them. He put spurs into his own horse's sides and, jerking to a halt when he drew level with the still-struggling chestnut, flung himself down at Kitty's side, frantically calling her name.

He was unarmed; there had been no trouble from the Maori tribes in the immediate vicinity of Auckland for months, and an attack was the last thing he had expected. Three or four more musket balls passed harmlessly over his head, and then, to his stunned relief, there was silence. Had the attackers gone? He waited, hearing no sound, holding Kitty in his arms, his own broad back interposed between her and the clump of ferns from where the shots had come.

She stirred and opened her eyes, looking up at him in bemused uncertainty, and he whispered to her to lie still.

"I think they've gone," Sean said at last. "Oh, my God, Kitty darling, are you hurt badly?"

Gently he laid her down, taking off his jacket to make a pillow for her head. She was deathly pale, her breathing strained and rapid, and when he sought to move her right arm, he saw her gasp with pain. A broken collarbone—if that was the worst she had suffered, he thought, then she had been fortunate indeed. With infinite care, he searched for other injuries but, apart from bruises, could find none. The arm would have to be strapped to her side before he could attempt to move her, he knew, and he started to fashion a bandage from the torn tail of his shirt.

"Sean—" Her voice was a faint whisper of sound, but Sean heard it with joy.

"I'm here, my little love," he told her reassuringly. "How do you feel?"

But Kitty's concern was not for herself. "My—my horse, Sean— Gold Dust. Is he—is he all right?"

But Gold Dust of Killaloe had given up the struggle for life, Sean saw. The poor, beautiful young animal lay still now, in a steadily spreading pool of its own blood.

"He's not suffering now, Kitty," he answered evasively, and was thankful that—since he lacked the means to put an end to the young horse's suffering—Gold Dust had ended it unaided. "We must fix this arm of yours and then get you to the house. Leave it to me, my love, and just lie still. The Maoris have gone."

Very competently, he applied the torn linen of his shirt, bandaging the injured arm to Kitty's side, with her forearm suspended in a sling made from her folded kerchief and his own belt.

"How does that feel, Kitty?" he asked anxiously, and was rewarded by her quick, grateful smile.

"It scarcely pains me at all," Kitty assured him. "No doctor could have done better."

Sean echoed her smile. "I'm a man of many parts, my dearest. Believe it or not, I worked my passage to Melbourne as assistant ship's surgeon, on the strength of having served a brief apprenticeship with an old physician named Callahan in the town of Cashel. Now—" He got to his feet. "I must catch my horse, and then we'll get you back to the house."

His own horse, frightened by the shooting, was cropping grass only a short distance away, and Sean had no difficulty in recapturing it. With strong arms, he lifted Kitty into the saddle, but as he did so, she caught sight of the dead chestnut, and he felt her shudder.

"They killed the poor creature—those Maoris killed him! *Why,* Sean? Why did they attack us? And what were they doing here?"

"The Lord only knows, Kitty. As far as I could tell, there weren't very many of them—five or six at the most. They were probably hiding in the fern and thought that we'd discovered them." Sean eased his tall body into the saddle behind her and, holding her protectively against him, turned his horse's head toward the distant homestead. "Are you all right? We'll take it very slowly, so as not to jerk your arm."

"I'm all right. But I—Sean, I shan't be able to dine with the Foxes, I—"

"Of course you will not, my poor love," Sean asserted tenderly. "As soon as we've put you to bed, I'll send one of my men to town to summon a proper doctor and inform William Fox that you have suffered an accident. What you need now is to rest in comfort and have that collarbone properly set. A good night's sleep, Kitty, and—"

"But I cannot stay overnight in your house, Sean," Kitty protested. "Just imagine the scandal it would cause! And Johnny, my husband—oh, goodness, what would he think? I *must* go back! I can't possibly stay here."

Sean stiffened. "You would be well chaperoned. The woman who cooks for me, Bridie Riordan, is of impeccable virtue—indeed, she is something of a dragon. She can sit with you. Faith, Kitty, you are in no state to face the drive back to Auckland, on my honor you're not! In any case," he added, with a hint of sullenness, "if you are so concerned about your husband, I can send a note to him, too, and he can come out here to take care of you and drive you back to Auckland himself, tomorrow, if that's your wish."

"Oh, Sean!" Kitty, conscious of having hurt him, was instantly contrite. She had only a confused memory of the Maori attack and, indeed, had not seen any of the men; but Sean, she realized, must have taken a considerable risk to come to her aid as swiftly as he had. She attempted to turn her head to look back at him, but the movement sent a savage ripple of pain coursing through her injured arm, and she bit her lip to stifle the cry that threatened to escape her.

His arm tightened about her waist, and he laid his cheek, for a moment, on hers.

"It is you I'm thinking of," he reminded her. "You had a nasty fall, Kitty, and a shock into the bargain, quite apart from the broken collarbone. You could have been killed, you know, and I—before God, my love, I feared you were! It made my heart stop, you—you mean so much to me, darling."

The sound of galloping hooves saved Kitty the necessity of a reply. Two of Sean's workers came pounding up to them, calling out in anxious inquiry.

"We heard shots, Mr. O'Hara, and we came as quick as we could. Are you hurt, sir?"

"No, but her ladyship is," Sean answered brusquely. He told them, in a few angry words, what had happened. "They killed Gold Dust, Ben. He's lying up there, below the hill."

"Maoris?" the man he had addressed as Ben asked.

"Yes. A band of about five or six, armed with muskets."

Ben swore. "Would you like us to go hunt for the swine, Mr. O'Hara?"

Sean shook his head. "They'll be miles away by now—you would be wasting your time. But what you can do, if you will, is ride ahead of us to the house. Tell Bridie her ladyship's been injured and ask her to have a bed prepared for her and some tea. And then I'll want one of you to ride to Auckland for me. We're going to need the doctor and . . ."

His voice trailed away into silence as Kitty slumped against him, a dark mist closing about her, clouding her senses. She had no recollection of the rest of their ride or of her arrival at the house, but it seemed to her only a few minutes later that she was lying, propped up on pillows, in a warm and comfortable bed, with a gray-haired, buxom woman gently sponging her face.

"Dere now, my lady," Bridie Riordan urged her solicitously, "just you lie dere quietly, and when you're able to take it, I've a pot o' tea made. Ben Davis has gone for a doctor, and he'll be here before long. T'at was a terrible bad fall you had, and you'll be powerful sore for a day or two, I don't doubt, for you must have come down very hard. Could you fancy a cup o' tea now or not?"

"I think I could fancy it very much," Kitty answered, suddenly conscious that her mouth was dry and her body seemingly on fire. Someone—the kindly Irishwoman, she supposed—had undressed her and clothed her in a thick flannel nightgown. It was a voluminous garment, several sizes too large for her, and felt rough to the touch.

But the tea was delicious, and it banished her thirst, and after a while she drifted into sleep and did not waken until a tall, bearded man, who gave his name as Dr. Mason, approached her bedside and requested permission to examine her.

His examination was thorough. He replaced Sean's makeshift bandage with a firmer one, deftly clicking the fractured collarbone into place with skillful fingers and once more applying a sling, as Bridie Riordan held her in a sitting position, the woman's plump, rosy face the picture of concern.

"You are badly bruised, Lady Kitty," the doctor told her. "But the collarbone should heal very nicely, and you will be able to return to Auckland in a couple of days, if you have to . . . though I'd prefer it if you were to rest quietly here for a little longer. Now I will give you a sleeping draft, which will ensure that you pass a comfortable night, and you can, of course, send for me again if you need me. Otherwise, dear lady, come to my rooms when you return to Auckland, so that I may assess your progress."

He silenced Kitty's halfhearted protests, stood over her sternly as she drank the sleeping draft he had prepared, and took his leave, with the advice that she was to worry about nothing until she felt stronger.

Kitty slept deeply, and it was not until noon the next day that she wakened, feeling so much better that she was able to enjoy the light but excellent luncheon Bridie Riordan brought to her on a tray. Sean came in while she was eating, expressing his pleasure and relief at the extent of her recovery.

"Mr. Fox will inform the military of the Maori attack on us," he added. "And I suppose they will send out search parties to hunt for them, although in my view I'm sure it was an isolated incident and the miscreants will long since have made their escape. And he—Mr. Fox—sent his condolences to you and hopes that you will soon be yourself again. But you must rest, Kitty, as the doctor advised. You must not even think of returning to Auckland for at least a couple days. You're comfortable here, aren't you? And Bridie is looking after you well?"

"Oh, yes," Kitty assured him. "But I'm worried about Johnny. Your man *did* tell him what had happened and why I'm still here, didn't he?"

To her dismay, Sean shook his head. "No, Kitty, I'm sorry, he did not . . . or rather, he could not. The house was empty when Ben called there, and he could get no answer to his knocking. He tried, he told me, for about ten minutes."

"He could have left a note, surely?"

"Aye, he could, had I written one. Unfortunately I omitted to do so. And Ben can't read or write. I'm truly sorry, Kitty—it was an oversight on my part." Sean came to reach for her hand, but Kitty eluded him.

"Then I must go back—now, at once, Sean!" Her tone brooked no argument. "Heaven knows what Johnny will be thinking!"

"I'll ride into town," Sean offered contritely. "This is my fault, Kitty. Let me put things right."

"No, you will only make the situation worse. I must go myself. Please, will you lend me your gig? I want to leave right way, Sean."

"You're not well enough," he objected. "And the doctor said—"

Kitty cut him short. "I'm well enough. Please don't try to stop me. I *have* to go!"

Sean gave in. Reddening, he turned to the door.

"At least allow me to drive you, Kitty."

With a vision of her husband's reaction, if she presented herself at their door accompanied by the man he suspected of being her paramour, Kitty shook her head, her refusal vehement.

"No, *no!* Couldn't your man drive me—what's his name, Ben?"

Recognizing the futility of further argument, Sean answered stiffly, "Very well, if that's what you want, Kitty. I'll tell Ben to make ready, and I trust you will permit me to accompany you on horseback. I have to see Mr. Fox personally and give him details of the attack, and it's more than likely that I'll be required to see His

Excellency also, in due course. But do not worry about appearances, I beg you. We can part company before we reach the town."

"Thank you, Sean," Kitty acknowledged. Realizing that she had hurt his feelings by her insistence on returning without him, she sought to make amends by adding her thanks for the care he had taken of her. But still stiff and affronted, Sean brushed her thanks aside.

"We can leave in half an hour. I will send Bridie to assist you to dress, and she can also accompany you in the gig. That will reassure your husband, I hope."

The drive to Auckland was accomplished without incident. Kitty experienced some discomfort from the jolting of the gig, but it was a warm and pleasant afternoon, and in other circumstances she would even have enjoyed it. True to his promise, Sean took leave of her on the outskirts of the town and cantered ahead, neither waving nor looking back . . . evidence, she knew, that he still harbored some resentment on account of the haste of her departure. But it was Johnny's feelings that were now her main concern, she told herself and sighed, wishing, a trifle belatedly, that she had never accepted the invitation to visit Killaloe.

She directed Ben to the house, pressed a sovereign into Bridie Riordan's hand, and, rejecting the kindly woman's offer to assist her, went in alone, anxiously calling Johnny's name. There was no answer until the young settler's daughter she employed as a maid came running from the kitchen, exclaiming in alarm at the sight of the sling her mistress was wearing.

"Oh, ma'am, did you hurt yourself?"

"I had a fall from a horse," Kitty told her evasively. "Elspeth, where is the master?"

"He's not here, ma'am," the girl began. "He took all his gear and—"

"Took all his gear?" Kitty interrupted. "What do you mean, for goodness' sake?"

The girl reddened. "He left a note for you, ma'am. I'll fetch it. And there are some letters that came in the mail. I—" She hesitated and then added awkwardly, "I think the master's gone back to the war. He rode out with some of the soldiers, ma'am. But he said I was to see you had his note, just as soon as you came back. And the letters. He said you'd be pleased to see one of them. Sit down, ma'am, won't you, and I'll fetch them for you. And I'll bring you some tea."

Kitty, really worried now, sank into an armchair. Johnny's leave had barely begun, she told herself. He had been back from New Plymouth for less than a week and had assured her that they would have at least another ten days together; yet now . . . now, if the maid were to be believed, he had gone back to the war, and the only reason for his having done so was—*must be*—that, not having learned of her injury or the Maori attack, he had jumped to the conclusion that she and Sean O'Hara had spent the previous night together. In—her throat was tight—in amorous dalliance. He—

The maid Elspeth returned and nervously put a little pile of letters into Kitty's hand.

"I'll ask cook to make you tea, m'lady," the girl said, but Kitty scarcely heard her. The note from Johnny was on top of the pile— a mere scrap of paper, torn from a notebook and folded, but lacking an envelope—and her heart sank as she unfolded it and saw how brief it was.

"Kitty" it began, without the customary endearment. "Since it seems evident that my presence here is unwelcome to you, I have volunteered to escort a party of surveyors to Drury, where it is proposed to extend an existing road into Waikato country later in the year."

"I cannot tell you when I am likely to return."

The note was signed simply "Johnny." He had scribbled a postscript: "I called for mail before leaving. There is a letter for you from your brother Patrick, which I am sure you will be pleased to have. If he wishes you to join him in Sydney, I would raise no objection."

Rereading the short, uncompromising missive, Kitty felt tears well in her eyes. Johnny *had* misunderstood the reason for her absence—that was abundantly clear—and it was most unfortunate that Sean's messenger had been unable to elicit a reply to his knocking when he had called at the house. Johnny, she could only suppose, had given Elspeth and the cook the evening off, or else they had gone early to bed and had not heard Ben's summons. And Johnny himself must have dined elsewhere, without troubling to contact Premier Fox, in order to ascertain that she was dining there. If only he had done so, he would have learned the truth; but instead, thinking the worst, he had seized the first opportunity that offered to absent himself from Auckland . . . and from her.

Kitty blinked back her tears, as Elspeth set a tea tray beside her and slipped silently away, evidently aware of her mistress's state of mind and sensing that she was best left alone. Perhaps, Kitty thought bitterly, both she and Mrs. Dickens, the cook, had read Johnny's carelessly folded note and knew why he had written it. Summoning the remnants of her shattered dignity, she opened Patrick's letter, determined to give no outward sign of her distress.

"If he wishes you to join him in Sydney," Johnny's postscript had said, *"I would raise no objection."* Well, if Patrick wanted her, she reflected rebelliously, she would take the first passage available and go to him, since there seemed little point in remaining here.

Patrick's letter was considerably longer than Johnny's had been. It began, unsensationally enough, with news of mutual friends in Sydney, and contained no hint of regret over his having left the farm near Urquhart Falls, in Victoria.

. . . I do not honestly think that I was cut out to run sheep, but Luke Murphy has farming in his blood. So he has taken over—officially as manager, but I've promised him a partnership if all goes well, as I am confident it will. Luke and his bride—Mr. and Mrs. William Broome's adopted daughter, the beautiful little deaf and dumb girl—are happily settled in, and I haven't a worry in the world on their account.

Here in Sydney, all that most people talk about is the war in New Zealand, and there has recently been a move to enlist volunteers to join the N.Z. militia. I've felt rather at a loose end, and I confess I miss you more than you would ever believe, Kit. So I decided to take the first opportunity to join you . . .

Kitty drew in her breath in shocked dismay. Surely, she told herself, surely Pat was not about to embroil himself in the war with the Maoris? Her heart sinking, she read on:

. . . and, in consequence, you may expect to see me before very long—unless, of course, peace should result from the reappointment of Sir George Grey as governor.

The authorities here are organizing the recruitment of what are loosely termed "military settlers," and the inducement offered includes a grant of land in New Zealand to all who volunteer for military service in the colony. I have put my name down as a volunteer, and I think I shall be offered a commission if I can contrive to pull a few strings and bring the required influence to bear.

So Pat *was* about to embroil himself in the war, Kitty thought wretchedly—partly because he felt at a loose end in Sydney, and partly because he missed her as much, seemingly, as she missed him. With unhappy tears blurring the words, she read to the end of the letter.

It may be quite a while before I am able to arrange matters —a couple of months, probably, before passages to Auckland are available. But if the New Zealand government succeeds in making peace with the rebel Maoris, then volunteers from Australia will not be needed. In which case, sister mine, I will take passage in one of Claus Van Buren's trading ships and at least pay you a visit. Unless, of course, you can bring yourself to part from your husband for a few months and instead *you* visit me.

The irony of the final sentence roused Kitty's resentment. If only her brother knew, she told herself, how easy it would be now to "bring herself to part from her husband" and return to Australia! Johnny had not waited for an explanation of her absence; he had given her no chance to explain, but had simply gone away to some place called Drury and, on his own admission, could not tell her when he was likely to return. And he had virtually given her his permission to join Pat in Sydney—

The street doorbell rang, interrupting her thoughts, but before she could tell Elspeth that she did not wish to receive visitors, she heard voices in the hall—one a man's deep, pleasant voice that sounded familiar—and a moment later the maid opened the door into the sitting room and announced that the unexpected caller was Colonel De Lancey.

"And two boys, m'lady," she added. "I'll bring some fresh tea."

William De Lancey came in, the two unnamed boys at his heels. He was in uniform, and he looked, Kitty saw, tanned and fit, if a trifle thinner than he had been when they had first traveled to New Zealand together. She recognized the elder boy as Andrew Melgund, William's adopted son, and greeted him with pleasure. The younger boy was small and dark-haired, and he eyed her shyly as William introduced him as Harry Ryan.

"My family grows, Kitty. I now have two sons, instead of only one." Noticing her sling, he broke off to ask with concern whether she was in pain. "We heard about your brush with a party of Maori troublemakers—Mr. Fox reported it to the general. I'm on General Cameron's staff now, so . . . I got to hear of it as soon as he did. I trust you were not too greatly alarmed by the attack?"

"It was frightening when it happened," Kitty confessed. "But it was soon over. They fired a few shots and then made off into the bush. Unhappily, they shot and killed the horse I was riding, and I came down rather painfully." She gave a brief account of the attack, and conscious of the boy Harry's wide, dark eyes on her face—eyes that suddenly filled with tears—she deliberately made light of the incident. The little boy said nothing, however, and when Elspeth came in with a tray of tea and cakes, the tears vanished, and both boys, in obedience to William's suggestion, took their cups and plates out onto the veranda, leaving him alone with Kitty.

"Harry, poor little devil, lost his whole family in a raid on their farm in the Taranaki," William said. "So he and Andy have much in common." He took the chair opposite Kitty's and accepted the cup of tea she poured for him. "I spoke to Johnny earlier," he went on, "which is the reason for my call, Kitty. You know he has gone on escort duty to Drury? He told you?"

"Yes," Kitty confirmed flatly. "He—he left a note to tell me. I did not get back here until after he had gone, you see—only about an hour ago, in fact. I . . ." She looked up into William's face, searching it anxiously, and then forced herself to ask, "Will, did he—did Johnny know about the attack at Sean O'Hara's stud?"

William shook his head. "No, my dear. Fox and O'Hara have only just reported it to the general—in detail, that is. Mr. Fox explained that he did not want to cause an unnecessary scare in the town, so he waited until he had heard O'Hara's firsthand account, and then they both saw the general. Johnny was on his way before noon." He smiled, sensing Kitty's need for reassurance and added quickly, "I'm sure he would not have volunteered to command the escort if he had realized that you were injured, Kitty."

"But he—Johnny *volunteered?*" Kitty persisted.

"Yes. An officer named Baines of the Mounted Volunteers was to have escorted the party, but he was taken ill. Johnny offered to take his place, very much on the spur of the moment, I believe. And—" William hesitated, eyeing her with concern. "Perhaps I should explain, Kitty. When I talked to Johnny, just before the escort set off, he said that you very much want to go to Sydney for a spell. Your brother's there, isn't he?"

Kitty nodded abstractedly, her mind still seeking a reason for the precipitate decision her husband had made—a spur of the moment decision, William had called it, but even so . . . She bit her lip, aware that it was trembling.

"Yes," she agreed. "Patrick is in Sydney. But . . ."

"I told you that I have been appointed to General Cameron's staff," William put in. "I knew him in the Crimea, and he's a hard taskmaster, so it will mean that I shall be very fully occupied, with little time to spend with my two boys. Up till now they have been at a little boarding establishment in New Plymouth, and I'd hoped that, once things were cleared up in the Taranaki, I should be able to see more of them—perhaps even return to my farm. It was burnt to the ground by the rebel Maoris and what little stock we had carried off, so it would be a mammoth task, rebuilding and restocking, as you may imagine."

William set down his teacup. "But this staff appointment has precluded my return for the foreseeable future, Kitty—and the boys' future has to be considered, in the light of my new commitment. I came to the conclusion that the best thing I can do, for the boys' sake, is to send them to Sydney. My sister Magdalen—your sister-in-law—has promised to take care of them and enter them both in the Grammar School, which has an excellent reputation."

He paused again, eyeing Kitty speculatively, and she made an effort to concentrate on what he was saying. It seemed to have no relevance to Johnny's absence, but . . .

"Yes?" she offered.

William's smile returned. "You're wondering what on earth all this has to do with you," he suggested.

"Well, yes, I confess I am, Will."

"I booked passages to Sydney in Claus Van Buren's *Dolphin,* for myself and the boys," William said. "She's due here within the next week or so, but—" He shrugged in resignation. "I'd arranged to take leave so that I could go with the boys, but now General Cameron says I cannot be spared. I mentioned this to Johnny, and he said he thought that *you* might be willing to avail yourself of the passage. You know Claus, of course, and you know the *Dolphin,* so I thought I would ask you, in case the idea appeals to you. Johnny's likely to be away for a couple of months, at the very least. It will mean taking responsibility for Andy and Harry, but they are good youngsters and will do as they're told. And if you want a change from Auckland and the war, then—"

Goodness, Kitty thought, she wanted a change from Auckland and the war, wanted it more than William could possibly know, and . . . she wanted to escape from the temptation Sean O'Hara offered, in Johnny's self-imposed absence, when it would be all too easy to yield, marriage vows or no. And there was Pat; she might be in time to persuade her twin not to volunteer for military service in New Zealand. His letter had implied that it would be two months or more before he was likely to leave Sydney, and if Governor Grey succeeded in making peace with the Maoris, the need for Australian volunteers would cease to exist.

And besides, had not Johnny told her that he would raise no objection if she were to join Pat in Sydney? Had he not told Will De Lancey, only this morning, that she might be willing to avail herself of the passage he had booked in the *Dolphin*?

William was looking at her questioningly, clearly expecting an answer, and Kitty faced him, her eyes suddenly bright and eager.

"I'll be only too delighted to accompany the boys to Sydney, Will," she said. "Johnny was right—I *do* want to go back to Sydney for a while. And I'm so glad you booked the passage with Claus Van Buren, because I shall be with friends. I—I can't thank you enough for giving me the opportunity."

"And I can't thank *you* enough for saying that you will take it," William assured her warmly. "It is a weight off my mind, believe me. The boys could have gone alone, but I wouldn't want them to; and with you I know they'll be in good hands." He rose and stood, smiling down at her, adding softly, "Johnny will come back to you, Kitty, never fear," and Kitty wondered fleetingly whether he had heard the gossip concerning her and Sean O'Hara or whether, perhaps, Johnny had hinted at it, when they had talked earlier that day.

But William did not enlarge on what had probably been a chance remark; instead he moved toward the door that led to the veranda.

"I'll break the good news to the boys," he told her. "They will be overjoyed."

Neither appeared to be as pleased as he had claimed they would be; evidently, Kitty thought, the prospect of parting from William was not one they relished. But Andy Melgund, polite as always, assured her with almost adult gravity that he would welcome her company on the passage.

"It will be almost like it was when we came out here, won't it, Lady Kitty? The *Dolphin* and Captain Van Buren and his crew. It's just rather a pity that Uncle Will and Mr. Broome won't be with us, isn't it?"

It was, Kitty reflected wryly. It was a thousand pities, but . . . She smiled from the tall young Andy to his smaller friend and promised softly, "I'll do my best to make up for their absence, Andy. And we shan't be leaving here forever, you know. We shall all be back."

"Yes, ma'am," Andy echoed dutifully. But his eyes were on William's face, and they were suddenly full of tears. . . .

Chapter XII

" 'TIS CAPTAIN BROOME, ma'am—your honor!" the Irish maid, Biddy, exclaimed excitedly. She stood aside, beaming her delight, and Red strode past her into the room.

Magdalen was instantly on her feet.

"Oh, Red—we saw your ship come in, but we had no idea that you would be able to come ashore so soon!" She went into her husband's arms, and Red embraced her warmly before turning to his father with hand outstretched.

"It's good to see you, Father! And in sound health, I trust?"

"I confess to feeling my age, Red," Justin Broome responded. "And age, alas, does not come alone! But your wife has been looking after me with exemplary skill and patience ever since her return." He smiled from one to the other of them. The smile lit his face, but for all that, Red noticed with a pang that his father had indeed aged during his absence. In less than three years, the tan had faded from his cheeks, and the maze of lines that crisscrossed his face had become deeper and more apparent. Even his broad shoulders were more stooped, as if standing upright took greater effort now than it had in the past.

And Magdalen, he saw, was concerned for him, coming to take his arm and gently but firmly guiding him back to the chair he had occupied by the window, looking out over Elizabeth Bay.

It was not until the end of the busy day—and a rapturous welcome from his five-year-old daughter, Jessica, and a less enthusiastic one from his baby son—that, in the privacy of their bedroom, Red learned the truth from Magdalen concerning his father's state of health.

Clasped in his arms, her dark head resting lightly on his shoulder, she confessed that Justin Broome was causing his family and friends some anxiety.

"He suffered a slight stroke, Red, about a month before I returned here. Oh, he makes light of it—you know how he hates to be ill—but if you watch him closely, you'll notice that his right side is partially paralyzed. He uses his *left* hand to write with, though he makes a great effort to hide the fact; and his movements are much slower now."

"I thought he had slowed down," Red conceded. "But I didn't imagine it was anything more than what he himself called it— feeling his age."

"It's more than that, I'm afraid, darling." Magdalen sighed. "My father and mother were the ones who told me about the stroke—*he* has never mentioned it, of course! But he did ask me to move in here, with the children, on the plea that this is too large a house for one person. And he admitted that he was lonely, so I was only too pleased to accept the invitation, because Cove Cottage is too small for us now, alas. And your father loves having his grandchildren for company—he's most attached to Jessie, and she to him. He calls little Andrew Rufus, and—" Magdalen smiled. "I'm afraid that name is going to stick, Red. The boy refuses to answer to anything else!"

"Well, it's not a bad name, my love—Rufus the Red. I observed that he's grown a fine crop of the Broome red hair." Red's fingers played gently with his wife's dark head. "But otherwise I think he takes after you. And Jessie certainly does, for which I'm duly grateful. Tell me—what is this dinner party my father mentioned? Tomorrow evening, isn't it?"

"Yes, it's tomorrow."

"I had supposed that, in view of Father's somewhat precarious health, you would not be entertaining very much. I mean—"

"I know what you mean, Red." Magdalen's tone was rueful. "But your father likes to entertain, and I've not been able to stop him. To be honest, I haven't tried. He enjoys seeing and talking to his friends, and I believe it does him good. He and my parents see quite a lot of each other, as they always have, and we have a new High Court judge now, with whom my father has formed a warm friendship. His name is Carmichael—Gerald Carmichael—and he has a most charming wife and daughter. By coincidence, I met Mrs. Carmichael and Emily on the voyage out." Magdalen propped herself up on one elbow, looking down at him gravely. "You will meet them tomorrow evening."

"Were they fellow passengers of yours in the *Salsette?*" Red asked.

Magdalen shook her head. "No, it was more dramatic than that. They were pasengers on board a ship called the *Pomona.* She was an old ship, and I don't suppose you will have heard this, but—she went down in a storm in the Tasman Sea. It was a very bad storm, but we were fortunate—the *Salsette* was in port at Hobart when it struck, so we missed the worst of it. But we picked up the survivors from the *Pomona,* who were in open boats—six or seven oared boats there were. Mrs. Carmichael and her daughter were among them. Poor Mrs. Carmichael is far from strong, and I shared my cabin with her, after she was discharged from the sick bay. And we put little Emily in with Jessie and Andrew. They were both wonderfully brave, and they never ceased singing the praises of the soldiers who, they both said, saved their lives. They were men of the Fortieth Regiment . . . poor fellows, they are now in New Zealand, fighting the Maoris."

"Indeed they are," Red confirmed. "In the thick of it, from what I heard in Auckland." He frowned. "And likewise, as I told Father at lunch, my brother John. But I hope peace is likely to be concluded before long. There have been a lot of casualties. I brought some of them back with me, to recuperate here or take their discharge, if they are unfit for further service. Poor devils—quite a few were no more than boys! Let's hope our government permits them to settle here on free land grants. Tell me, my love, did any of the *Pomona's* people go down with her?"

"The captain did, and . . . the first mate, I think. I don't remember, but there was a long report in the *Herald.*" Magdalen's brow puckered. "I kept it. I can find it for you, if you want to read it, Red. The *Herald* made out that the hero of the occasion was the young captain who was in command of the Fortieth's draft, Captain Fisher. But Mrs. Carmichael and her daughter told me that wasn't true. Emily insists it was one of the soldiers who saved them —I forgot his name. But I *can* find the report for you if—"

"Darling, it will do in the morning," Red asserted. He drew her down beside him, his lips seeking hers. "I've been away from you for a long time, wife—*too* damned long! And I have missed you, by heaven I have!"

"And I've missed you, Red," Magdalen whispered softly. She

went into his embrace eagerly and happily, and as he held her close, feeling the familiar response of his body to hers in all its joyous recognition, he found himself thinking fleetingly and with pity of his brother Johnny. But then the thought faded, and, his lips on hers, he murmured exultantly, "I love you, darling! I'll love you as long as I live!"

During breakfast, which he took alone with Magdalen, and which his father took in bed, Red glanced through the *Herald*'s report of the sinking of the *Pomona*.

He had seen and known many more tragic disasters at sea during the course of his naval service, and the account, embellished somewhat extravagantly by the journalist who had compiled it, held only cursory interest for him. Indeed, he thought, the old transport had fared much better than many of her kind, since most of her passengers and crew had survived—thanks, if the reporter was to be believed, in no small measure to the exemplary discipline of the military draft she had been carrying and, in particular, to the draft commander, Captain Marcus Fisher.

He said, folding the newspaper cutting and returning it to his wife, "Well, according to this, my dear, your friends the Carmichaels are doing Captain Fisher an injustice. He certainly appears to have kept a cool head and to have done all and more than could be expected of one who was not a seaman."

Magdalen refilled his coffee cup. "Ask Emily Carmichael yourself this evening, Red. I was not on board the unfortunate ship, so I don't know. But I did meet Captain Fisher, very briefly, at Government House before the Fortieth sailed for New Zealand. I cannot say I took to him, although we scarcely exchanged half a dozen words. He struck me as a boastful young man and one who considered himself socially superior to mere colonials. I could be wrong, of course—my judgment is based on a very brief acquaintance. I—" She broke off, seeing Red glancing at the clock on the mantelshelf. "Oh, Red, do you have to go?"

"I'm afraid I must, my love," Red answered regretfully. "I have to report to the governor, and then I shall have to see the dockyard about some necessary work on my ship. What is he like, His new Excellency? I gather you've met him."

"Oh, yes," Magdalen confirmed. "He's scarcely new to us—he's been here since the end of March." She smiled. "Sir John Young, baronet, privy councillor, king's counsel, knight grand cross of order of Saint Michael and Saint George. He is a lawyer and a politician, not a soldier, and he was chief secretary for Ireland in the Aberdeen ministry. He—" Noticing her husband's blank look, she paused, her smile widening. "Have you heard enough, dearest?"

"More than enough, my love," Red assured her dryly. "For a simple sailor!"

"Actually, I think you will like His Excellency, Red, although you may find that he is a trifle pedantic, as lawyers often are."

"I stand forewarned, dearest." Red bent to kiss her. "I will be back in plenty of time for your dinner party."

He spent a busy but not unproductive day finding, as Magdalen had predicted, that he liked the governor, who received him courteously, listened with interest to what he had to report on the current situation in Auckland, and—obviously well informed—offered a number of shrewd and even farsighted comments.

"I have the greatest admiration for Sir George Grey," the governor said, when finally the interview came to an end and he rose to signify Red's dismissal. "He is, without exception, one of our most able administrators, Captain Broome. But I confess I do not envy him his task. Mine is, by comparison, easy, since I have only to reconcile the big landowners—those who, I understand, are called 'squatters'—with their poorer but no less worthy brethren. Well, Captain Broome—" Sir John Young held out his hand. "I will not detain you any longer. Thank you for your comprehensive report —it has been very useful. I shall be happy if you would dine here— you and your wife, of course, whose acquaintance I have made and much enjoyed. One day next week—I'll see that you are sent an invitation. I have to welcome my new military secretary, who has just arrived with his wife and family—Colonel Leonard Forsyth of the Seventieth. Perhaps you know him?"

Red shook his head. "No, sir, I don't recall the name. His regiment's in New Zealand, as you will know. But—"

"The Horse Guards or whatever the military hierarchy call themselves," the governor said, without enthusiasm, "appear to think that, since I am a civilian, I require a military adviser, so they've sent Forsyth out from England to act in that capacity." Walking with Red to the door of the office, he came suddenly to a halt and added, with more than a hint of asperity, "Probably they share the prevailing notion, held by the Admiralty, that Australia is likely to be attacked by the United States! I confess, Captain

Broome, that I have never heard anything so absurd. But . . ." He
expelled his breath in exasperation. "What do *you* think?"

Taken by surprise, Red hesitated. Beauchamp-Seymour had
mentioned Their Lordships' warning, but he, too, had dismissed it
as absurd.

"I heard the—the possibility mentioned, sir," he answered.
"Mail takes a long time to reach us here, I'm fully aware. Even so,
in my view, sir, such an attack, by a nation with whom we are not
at war, is a very remote possibility indeed."

"Good," the governor said. "Well, perhaps this Colonel Forsyth
will be able to shed some light on the matter. He's due this morning to report to me. In the meantime, I trust your frigate will be in
readiness to defend Sydney Harbor, should we both prove wrong."
He acknowledged Red's salute, smiled thinly, and returned to his
office.

After lunching on board the *Cossack* and a lengthy visit to the
dockyard with his first lieutenant, Red returned to his father's
house in Elizabeth Bay in time, to Magdalen's evident pleasure, to
spend an hour with their two children in the room—once Jenny's
—that had been converted to a nursery.

At eight, the dinner guests started to arrive, and he was happily
occupied in greeting and exchanging news with relatives and old
friends, his father at his side, affable and smiling, giving little sign
of the stroke Magdalen had said that he had suffered.

Introduced to Judge Carmichael and his wife and daughter, Red
took an instant liking to all three, although Emily, a slim, pretty
girl with a charming smile, held shyly aloof, listening attentively to
the conversation but contributing little to it. The young man whose
arm she took to go into dinner fared no better. He was a barrister,
it appeared, and Red noticed with amusement that Emily was at
pains to keep him at arm's length, replying with downcast eyes and
discouraging lack of interest to his attempts to entertain her.

Magdalen, seemingly with deliberate intent, had placed the girl
on Red's left, and when the young barrister turned in despair to his
other neighbor, Red leaned toward her.

"You are not enjoying yourself, Miss Carmichael," he accused,
with feigned severity.

Emily's small face flooded with color. "I—I am, Captain
Broome," she defended. "Truly I am. This is a beautiful house, and
Mrs. Broome, your wife, has been most kind and gracious to me. I
always like coming here."

"Perhaps the company is too old for you," Red suggested. "With the exception of—" He paused, smiling. "I didn't catch his name."

"Nigel Bartholomew, you mean?" she replied, lowering her voice.

"Yes, that's who I mean."

"He is very young," Emily qualified, her color deepening. "And all he is interested in is the law, his work in the courts."

"That is surely understandable, isn't it?"

"Well, yes," she was forced to concede. "I suppose it is. But I—I find it tedious." Her smile returned. "We get enough of such talk from my father."

She was responding, Red thought; she was not shy of him, at all events. He waited until the next course had been served, and then, remembering what Magdalen had told him, asked quietly, "You met my wife on board the *Salsette,* I believe? After you were wrecked in the Tasman Sea, in the vicinity of Cape Howe, wasn't it?"

"It was on a reef off Gabo Island, Captain Broome. The *Pomona* —our ship—went down in less than an hour."

"I read the report in the *Morning Herald,*" Red began, "but—"

"That report wasn't true!" Emily Carmichael exclaimed. Suddenly she lost her shyness and spoke with crisp authority, giving him a vivid account of the *Pomona*'s last hour, describing how the seas pounded her to destruction, driving her farther and farther onto the reef.

"I was very frightened," she admitted, and shivered, as if the memory still haunted her. "My mother is delicate; she has a weak heart, you see, and I was so worried, wondering what would become of us and whether poor Mama would be able to stand the strain. Even to gain the deck and then cross it, with the sea washing over it, might, I feared, be too much for her. But I need not have feared, because Mr. Shannon had taken charge, after the poor captain and the first mate were washed overboard and drowned. *He* saved all our lives. He sent soldiers below to help us reach the deck, and when we got there, he was supervising the lowering of the boats and making sure that all the women and children were safely loaded into them. Adam Shannon was the hero, Captain Broome, not Captain Fisher, although he tried to take the credit. And in that report in the newspaper, he—"

"Did you say *Adam* Shannon?" Red put in, recalling what Captain Seymour had told him of Shannon's gallantry in the attack on the Maori *pa* at Te Arei. Good Lord, he thought, this was surely the confirmation of his earlier suspicions concerning Shannon's real identity—it had to be! "Was he serving in the ranks of the Fortieth, Miss Carmichael? Serving as a private soldier?"

"Yes," Emily Carmichael confirmed, without hesitation. "But he was in the navy, he was an officer, Captain Broome. He told me that he was court-martialed and cashiered, but that was all he told me. I never knew his real name, you see. I—that is, I don't think he wanted anyone to know. In fact I am sure he didn't." She sighed and, encouraged by Red's evident interest, went on to describe the ordeal the *Pomona*'s survivors had endured in the open boats, before being picked up by the *Salsette*.

"Adam Shannon kept the boats together, and he made sure that we reached what he called the shipping route. He undertook the navigation, not Mr. Archer or Captain Fisher. Marcus Fisher just lay on the bottom boards and did nothing." Her tone was indignant, and Red warmed to her as he listened, for her words carried conviction. Others at the table were listening too, young Bartholomew with an expression of stunned surprise on his face. Emily, it seemed, had never previously spoken to him of the sinking of the *Pomona*.

Her father, however, had heard her story before. When she fell silent, the judge observed quietly, "My daughter feels very strongly that justice was not done to the soldier who once adorned your service, Captain Broome. Having met him, I believe that she is right. He struck me as an exceptionally fine young man, but he rejected my attempt to help and reward him. I offered to assist him to buy himself out of the regiment and to find employment here in Sydney, but he would not hear of it. He went with his regiment to New Zealand and, I suppose, has been in the thick of the fighting since they landed. But you will not have come across him, I imagine?"

Red hesitated, conscious of Emily Carmichael's eyes fixed pleadingly on his face, and finally he shook his head.

"No, sir, not personally. But I heard of him from Captain Seymour of the *Pelorus*, by chance. The captain had occasion to commend him for gallantry in an action in which his seamen and the Fortieth Regiment took part." He did not enlarge on his brief statement; time enough, he decided, to tell Emily without the whole table hearing his disclosure. Clearly, the pretty child cared a great deal for the young soldier she knew as Adam Shannon, and, equally clearly, her attachment to him had caused her father some concern.

Magdalen, as always swift to sense his unspoken thoughts, caught his eye, smiled, and gave the signal for the ladies to rise. They followed her from the room, and Red started the port decanter circulating and offered the guests cigars. The conversation became general, his father and Magdalen's talking animatedly about the current political scene, and Judge Carmichael, his cigar lit, moved to occupy the chair next to Red's. He said, lowering his voice, "Reverting to your conversation with my daughter, Captain Broome, concerning the young soldier who calls himself Adam Shannon—"

"Yes, sir?" Red acknowledged politely.

"I formed the impression," the judge suggested, "that you are aware of his real identity. Is that so?" Red hesitated, and Carmichael went on, "I have—er—set wheels in motion to find out the truth about him, Captain Broome, through legal contacts at home. But you know how long the mails take. As yet I have had no answer to my inquiries, but I do not doubt that an answer will be forthcoming. You would be betraying no confidences if you gave me that answer now."

Red met the older man's shrewd gaze and inclined his head. "Yes, Judge, your impression was correct. I do know, with reasonable certainty, who the young man is. I served with him in India, under the command of the late Captain Peel, in the *Shannon*'s naval brigade during the mutiny. And I was a member of the naval court-martial that sentenced him to be cashiered, on the evidence put before it. He offered no defense, so that no other verdict was possible. Nevertheless, I regretted having to concur with it."

"Ah!" The judge's heavy brows rose. "Then you do indeed have the answers I was seeking, Captain Broome." He glanced round the table, but the other guests were talking among themselves, paying Red and him no attention, and he asked, "Would you care to tell me about the trial and the charges, very briefly? What you tell me will, I promise you, go no further, if you do not wish it to. My motive for this request is, as you have probably guessed, a personal one. My daughter Emily lost her heart to the young man in question, and nothing I can do or say has the smallest effect on her. But for my own peace of mind, I should like to be assured that —er—Shannon is worthy of her."

It was an honest plea, Red knew, and as concisely as he could, he detailed the trial and the evidence the court had heard. The judge occasionally interposed a question, but for the most part he listened in silence, a frown of concentration drawing his brows together, his port glass untouched and his cigar disintegrating in the ashtray beside him.

"I doubt whether a civil court would have imposed so severe a sentence, on that evidence," he observed thoughtfully, when Red came to the end of his recital. "But you are, are you not, of the opinion that Adam Shannon was shielding someone else, to whom blame for the loss of the ship should rightly have been attributed? That is so, isn't it?"

"Yes, I am sure he was," Red asserted.

"His captain? It could be no one else."

"I think so. But Adam took command. Technically the responsibility was his, sir, and he accepted it." Again Red hesitated. Judge Carmichael had asked for the truth; for his daughter's sake, he was entitled to know the truth, but . . . Recalling the rumor one of the members of the court had disclosed to him, Red found himself of two minds. The commander—Sigsworth, that had been his name—had said that gossip had been rife, coupling Adam Vincent with the wife of his captain, John Omerod. *Had* it been only gossip, or had Omerod's wife been the reason for Vincent's refusal to defend himself? He had no means of knowing, Red decided, and therefore it would be doing Vincent an injustice were he to mention the rumor to Emily Carmichael's father.

To his relief, he heard his own father say, "Shall we join the ladies?" and saw him rise to his feet.

Carmichael put a detaining hand on his arm.

"You have not told me Adam Shannon's real name, Captain Broome," the judge reminded him.

"I . . . then in strict confidence, sir, it is Vincent—the Honorable Adam Colpoys Vincent. He is a younger son of the Earl of Cheviot."

"Good heavens!" The judge's astonishment was mirrored in his face. "General Lord Cheviot, of course. No wonder the young man is reluctant to reveal his name! I can imagine Lord Cheviot's reaction to his being cashiered."

"You know him, sir?" Red questioned.

The judge fell into step beside him. "Indeed I do—we are members of the same London club. And I also know Sir David Murchi-

son, the Q.C. who was retained to defend the unfortunate boy.
Well, well, you have surprised me, Captain Broome." At the open
door of the drawing room, he halted and again laid his hand on
Red's arm. "I'd be very greatly obliged to you if you would refrain
from telling Emily what you have told me, Captain. I think it's best
if she does not know, in the circumstances, because clearly nothing
can come of it where she is concerned—nothing. However—" He
paused, frowning. "I will try to see if I can help young Vincent. I
have some influence in judicial circles, and possibly a new trial
might be arranged." He added his thanks, and Red followed him
into the drawing room.

There was, he thought, perhaps a very slim chance of a fresh
trial, if Judge Carmichael used his influence; but it *was* extremely
thin, since the Admiralty had confirmed the verdict of the court-
martial. And probably Adam Vincent would not want it—good
Lord, hadn't he begged Captain Seymour not to bring his gallantry
at Te Arei to public notice, lest it lead to recognition and unwelcome notoriety?

Magdalen, he saw, when he followed Judge Carmichael into the
drawing room, had Emily seated beside her, and the two were
talking animatedly, as if they were old friends.

A second tray of coffee was brought in, and Magdalen rose and
crossed the room to serve it. His father took her place on the sofa
and engaged Emily in conversation, and Red went to join his wife,
relieved that the girl had been given no opportunity to question
him.

With the heavy silver coffeepot poised, Magdalen said softly,
"Little Emily Carmichael asked me whether you had known the
soldier to whom, she is quite sure, she and her mother owe their
lives. I tried to tell her that it was unlikely, but . . . *did* you know
him, Red?"

"Yes," Red answered. "It so happens that I did, my love—and I
have just told Emily's father all I know about him and been
pledged to secrecy, where Emily is concerned. *He* wants her to
forget him, and I daresay, for her sake, he's right . . . so I had
better avoid the poor little girl, I think. Give me some coffee to
pass round, will you? That will serve as an excuse for my churlish-
ness."

The evening ended pleasantly, with Magdalen giving an attractive rendering of some favorite songs, the others singing the chorus
refrains, and Emily—shyly and after some persuasion—offering

two pieces from *Don Giovanni,* sung in a small, sweet voice of unexpected purity.

As they were making their adieux, Rachel De Lancey mentioned the recent arrival of the governor's new military adviser and his family.

"Colonel and Mrs. Forsyth, Justin," she told her brother. "They have taken the house the Dawsons used to have, in Pitt Street. They came from England, I understand, in the new Dunbar Indiaman, which arrived about a week ago. I can't recall its name, but—"

"The *Duncan Dunbar,*" Justin supplied. "Their latest and finest clipper ship, built only four years ago."

"Yes," Rachel agreed. "I called on the Forsyths, and I think you should, Justin—or anyway Magdalen and Red should. They seem pleasant enough. He is a good deal older than his wife and struck me as something of a martinet. She is about twenty-five or -six and very pretty indeed, and they have two children—a little boy of about two and a baby, born during the passage out, she told me. Her name is Caroline, and from what she said in the course of conversation, I gather that she was a widow and this is her second marriage."

"You seem to have learned all about them, Aunt Rachel," Red said, amused.

"Well, they are newcomers," his aunt defended. "And she talked very freely, despite our short acquaintance. Curiously enough, Red, she asked me about the soldier you and Judge Carmichael were discussing during dinner . . . what was his name?"

"Shannon," Red supplied. "Adam Shannon, who is serving in the ranks of the Fortieth Regiment in New Zealand."

Rachel De Lancey shook her head. "That was not the name Mrs. Forsyth mentioned. It began with a *V.* Venner, Victor . . . no, it was Vincent. I'm almost sure it was Vincent. Well, never mind; it's of no matter if it isn't the same man. Good night, Red dear, and we have much enjoyed seeing you again." She raised her small, lined, but still attractive face for his kiss and then followed her husband to their carriage. Reaching it, she paused to call back, "Francis and Dora will be coming in a week or two, from their farm in the Hunter Valley, and I know they will want to see you. You must both dine with us, Red, and your father too, of course."

"Thank you, Aunt Rachel," Red responded. "If I'm still here, we should be delighted to see them."

The carriage moved away, and Magdalen said, taking Red's arm, "Dora is with child again, and they are overjoyed and hoping for a son. After three daughters, they deserve one, don't you think? At least Claus and Mercy were fortunate enough to have a daughter, which they were both longing for." She paused, watching Justin Broome as he walked with the Carmichaels to their carriage. "Your father stood up to our dinner party splendidly, didn't he, darling? I think he enjoyed it. He likes Judge Carmichael, I know."

"I liked him too," Red returned. "And little Emily. I didn't have much chance to speak to her mother."

"Oh, she is a sweet person," Magdalen assured him. "And her health has greatly improved since she arrived here. How strange, though, Red, that Mrs. Forsyth should have asked Mama about the soldier Emily is so interested in—the one she insists saved the lives of the *Pomona*'s passengers, including her own. And yet by a different name."

"By his real name, my love," Red told her. "Which is passing strange."

"I will do as Mama suggested," Magdalen promised, "and call on her." She hesitated, looking up at him thoughtfully. "I was going to say that I would try to solve the mystery, but . . . it's no mystery to you, is it? You know all about Mr.—I suppose I had better call him Vincent, not Shannon, hadn't I?"

"It would be a kindness if you did not, dearest," Red cautioned. "The poor young devil has gone to great lengths to conceal his real identity, and with reason. But you are right—I *do* know just about all there is to know about him. And—" He sighed. "As it happens, I was a member of the court-martial that sentenced him to be thrown out of the service."

"Oh, Red!" Magdalen exclaimed, with instinctive sympathy. "How wretched for you! That was when you got back to England and paid off the *Galah*, wasn't it? Before I arrived there?"

"Yes, that's so," Red confirmed. "They found themselves short of a post captain, so I was hauled in without knowing who was being tried or on what charges." His mouth tightened as he remembered going on board the *Copenhagen* and learning, for the first time and to his dismay, that Adam Vincent was the accused officer and that he was to be examined concerning the loss of the *Lancer* and all but five of her complement.

He gave Magdalen the briefest of details, and added, "I have no idea where Mrs. Forsyth fits into the story of poor young Vincent's downfall, my love, so it might be as well if you keep a guard on your tongue when you meet her."

"Do not worry, Red, I will," his wife promised. "But what a small world it is! Who would have supposed that so many people, all involved in some way with that unfortunate officer, should be together in Sydney, on the other side of the world!"

"Who indeed?" Red echoed. He tucked his wife's arm under his and led her toward where his father was waiting, by the front door, for them to join him. "Let's call it a day, shall we? And see that my dear father takes a nightcap and retires to his bed." He smiled down at her. "It's good to be home and with you again, dearest Magdalen. And that was a most excellent meal."

Magdalen's fingers tightened about his, and although she said nothing, she, too, was smiling.

Chapter XIII

CAROLINE FORSYTH PUT her baby daughter from her and, quickly covering her breast, handed the child to the nursemaid.

"Take her away, Milly," she ordered petulantly. "And Jon too. And try to keep them quiet, for goodness' sake! My head is splitting."

"Very good, ma'am," the girl responded dutifully. She had come out from England with her mistress and had learned that the best, if not the only, way to avoid Caroline's sudden outbursts of anger was to give the appearance of docile obedience. The children, of whom Milly was very fond, were both left largely in her care. Only when it was necessary to suckle the baby did her mother hold her in her arms, and even then she displayed few signs of affection for the frail, pretty little infant, who had been delivered—two months prematurely—when the *Duncan Dunbar* had been beating her way across the Great Australian Bight.

And as for Jon, who was an adorable little boy, if somewhat boisterous . . . Milly reached for his chubby hand and started to lead him away. You would not think, the girl reflected sadly, that any mother worthy of the name would regard her firstborn with an indifference that bordered on dislike. Yet that was how Caroline Forsyth *did* regard him, and Jon, for all his tender years, was aware of it and reacted accordingly. In his mother's company he was rude and disobedient, as well as noisy, whereas in the nursery alone with her . . . Milly smiled down at her charge. Alone with her, little Jon was an angel. He looked angelic, too, with his dazzling blue eyes and golden, softly curling hair, and even his stern martinet of a stepfather was not immune to his blandishments.

Milly looked back, hoping that her mistress would at least bid her son farewell, but . . . She bit her lip, her smile fading. Mrs. Forsyth had picked up the newspaper she had been reading earlier and was now deeply engaged in devouring its contents, to the exclusion, it seemed, of all and everyone else.

"Come along, darling," the nursemaid urged little Jon. "We'll pop your sister back into her cot to sleep, and you and me will play out in the garden for a while."

Jon shrieked with delight at this prospect and ran eagerly to the door ahead of her, oblivious of the fact that his mother had clapped both hands to her ears to dull the sound of his merriment.

Left alone, Caroline lowered her hands and let the crumpled pages of the newspaper fall from her lap. Her head was throbbing unmercifully, and she sighed in exasperation and closed her eyes. Why, she asked herself bitterly, had she been encumbered with a child who was unable to keep still for an instant and could not move without emitting the most penetrating shrieks? Or, come to that, with an infant daughter whose fretful crying and failure to gain weight was, for some reason she could not understand, attributed to *her* blame by her husband? Caroline lay back on the chaise longue, still keeping her eyes closed.

Leonard, she thought miserably, had changed a great deal since their marriage. At Hamble, in her parents' large, well-appointed house, when he had come courting her, he had seemed everything she had ever wanted in a husband—everything, indeed, that John Omerod had *not* been. Tall, handsome in a rugged way, articulate and extremely well read, considerate—oh, yes, above all Leonard had been considerate, ready to gratify her every whim, a strong, masterful man to whom she could look up but who was also gentle and protective, ready to worship and indulge her.

Professionally he was impeccably well qualified; he had served with the 80th Regiment in the Burma War in 1852 and in the suppression of the Sepoy Mutiny in India six years later, emerging from both with distinction and without a scratch, to be gazetted to a majority in the 70th and made a brevet lieutenant colonel very soon after taking command of the regimental depot in Canterbury. And he was a bachelor. . . . Caroline suppressed a weary sigh. She had been naive, of course. Or perhaps she had expected Leonard to give her the adoration John had given her, save for the last few months, when jealousy had overwhelmed him and he had started to drink to excess.

But, very soon after their honeymoon, Leonard had become a

different person. He had become demanding, expecting to be waited on and obeyed. Her headaches and the physical weaknesses, which had always evoked John's sympathy, he had brushed aside, insisting that they existed only in her imagination and could easily be overcome if she exerted herself, adhered to a sensible diet, and took more exercise.

Before he had been posted to Sydney, he had been a veritable slave driver, making her ride with him daily, follow the hunt, walk for miles in the country in every kind of weather, and entertain his brother officers and their wives to elaborate meals, which, he had told her curtly, if their cook could not produce, she herself must prepare.

It had been almost an answer to prayer when she had found herself pregnant, since that, at least, put an end to the horseback riding and hunting, if not to the walks or the endless dinner parties and buffet luncheons that, her husband asserted, his position as commanding officer of the depot demanded.

And now, heaven help her, he had brought her to Australia, to this large, rather dilapidated house, with its overgrown garden and ugly furniture and its staff of improperly trained and uncouth servants, who addressed her as "missus" instead of ma'am and who seemed incapable of understanding the orders she gave them, still less of carrying them out.

Caroline felt tears aching in her throat. Why, oh, why had she allowed Leonard Forsyth to deceive her? Why had she given up her parents' loving care and beautiful home, in order to marry so insensitive a man and let him drag her halfway round the world, to a country she had never wanted to visit, peopled by the descendants of convicts and petty officials, who gave themselves airs they would never have dared to exhibit in England?

True, there were a few who might merit the title of gentlefolk; but they *were* only a few, and— Shrill cries and gales of laughter, coming from the garden, broke into Caroline's thoughts. Irritably, she again clapped both hands over her ears, aware that Leonard must have returned from his call on the governor, since some of the laughter was almost certainly his. His devotion to Jon—who was *her* son, not his—was another source of resentment where she was concerned. Leonard doted on the little boy and spent every minute of his spare time playing with him, with Milly's foolish encouragement and giggling enthusiasm.

On the voyage out he had done so, and . . . Caroline felt futile

anger well up inside her. The voyage, in a splendid new clipper
ship of almost a thousand tons, might have been very enjoyable,
had it not been for her pregnancy and the manner in which her
husband had gone out of his way to prevent her from making
friends with their fellow passengers or even from mixing with
them. Even after the premature delivery of their daughter—named
Naomi after *his* mother—Leonard had seen to it that she established no intimacy with anyone, save himself, and the awful walks
had been resumed, ostensibly for the good of her health, round and
round the *Duncan Dunbar*'s holystoned deck, until she had contrived to faint and the ship's surgeon had mercifully intervened on
her behalf and forbidden all strenuous exercise for the rest of the
passage.

The laughter sounded again, and Leonard's deep voice reached
her faintly.

"Go on, Jon—run, laddie, run! You'll never grow into a big,
strong chap like me unless you take plenty of exercise, you know.
Fine, that's the ticket! Well done, boy, very well done!"

He was trying to turn the boy into a replica of himself, Caroline
thought resentfully. And Milly was as bad, never scolding him or
attempting to teach him good manners. She was a trifle better than
the new Australian servants, but that, alas, was not saying much
for her.

One of them—the so-called butler—brought in the tea tray she
had ordered, set it down beside her so roughly that he set the
teacups clinking, and announced, in the insolent fashion they all
adopted, "Tea, missus, like you was askin'. I put a cup on for the
colonel."

Caroline inclined her head in acknowledgment but did not thank
him, and the man eyed her expectantly for a moment and then
departed, deliberately slamming the door behind him. Pouring herself a cup, Caroline observed that the tray cloth was grubby and
creased and the silver teapot dull and unpolished. And Leonard
would be in, disturbing her peace, such as it was, and in all probability demanding that she take a walk with him to the Domain to
listen to a military band concert there—on foot, like the common
people, when the gentry went in carriages or on horseback! She
could plead a headache, or course, but her husband would still
insist that the cure for headaches was exercise in the fresh air, and
he would undoubtedly insist on taking little Jon with them . . .
and the boy would be permitted to run wild and mix, to his heart's

content, with the rough, badly dressed convicts' children who thronged the park every evening.

Sipping her tea, Caroline found herself thinking of Adam Vincent. What a pity it was, all things considered, that Adam had thrown up his naval career to such little purpose. It had, in the end, done John's memory scant good; too many people had known of his drinking, and the clacking tongues had torn his reputation to shreds, after the verdict of the court-martial had been announced. She had not stayed in Portsmouth, it was true, and had not heard the talk, but several acquaintances had told her what was being said, and for quite a long time her father—her own *father!*— had reproached her for what she had done, as if she could have prevented Adam from falling in love with her. Or, come to that, from sacrificing himself in a vain bid to hide the truth.

It was a pity, and she was sorry that things had turned out as they had, because there was no doubt that Adam Vincent would have made her a better husband than Leonard ever could. But . . . Caroline refilled her cup, pleased that Leonard had not yet joined her. She could not have married Adam, she reflected, after he had been cashiered and disgraced—it would have been out of the question. And, in any case, he had made it impossible by enlisting in the army as a common soldier, probably on a stupid impulse for which she had certainly *not* been responsible.

It was a strange coincidence, though, that Adam should have come out to Australia and that she herself should have done so, just over a year later. That was something she could not possibly have foreseen. Not that he was in Sydney now; the 40th had been sent to New Zealand, like Leonard's regiment, and both were fighting the Maori rebels and looked like they would continue to do so for considerable time to come.

Her father, for some reason best known to himself, had arranged to obtain news of Adam. He had bribed a soldier in the same regiment to send him reports, and these had come in the form of three brief, ill-spelled letters, which had not made happy reading. . . . Caroline's small, perfectly shaped mouth tightened involuntarily. Her father had insisted that she should read the letters, and when he knew that she was about to accompany Leonard to Sydney, he had warned her with what, for him, was tantamount to an ultimatum, that she must make no attempt to see or communicate with Adam.

"That unhappy young man has chosen his way of life," he had

reminded her. "Leave him free to work out his destiny for himself, Caroline. You cost him more than any man could be expected to pay, but he paid the price, for your sake and because he loved you. Ask no more of him. You are Leonard's wife now and have your own life to live with him. Let that be the end of the matter."

Caroline put down her cup, her hand not quite steady as she recalled her father's words and the stern expression on his face as he had spoken them. She had not intended to disobey him, but by chance she had read a report in a newspaper picked up at the Cape, in which the loss of a ship called the *Pomona* was described at some length. One of the letters from Adam's fellow soldier had mentioned that the draft of the 40th Regiment was to take passage in that vessel; she had remembered the name and known that Adam had been on board. The newspaper report had stated that, with the exception of the *Pomona*'s master and first mate, all the passengers and crew had been picked up and taken to Sydney . . . Adam, presumably, among them.

Curiosity, rather than a desire to go against her father's wishes, had prompted her to question Mrs. De Lancey, when that charming, friendly woman had called on her—the first Sydney resident to do so. Thoughtlessly, though, she had used Adam's real name and so, of course, had learned nothing beyond the fact that all the soldiers had survived the wreck and had gone, shortly afterward, with the Sydney detachment of the 40th to New Zealand.

"The Fortieth suffered a number of casualties after they landed in New Plymouth," Mrs. De Lancey had told her and, as an afterthought, had volunteered the information that the *Sydney Morning Herald* would have the casualty lists on file. "And Mrs. Carmichael—Judge Carmichael's wife and daughter were passengers on board the *Pomona*. I feel sure that they would be able to give you news of your friend Mr. Vincent, Mrs. Forsyth, since they must have known him."

A judge's wife and daughter would have had no social contact with a rank-and-file soldier, Caroline told herself, and since that was what Adam now was, it would be a waste of breath to ask them. In any event, the draft commander had been the hero of the *Pomona* disaster, according to the newspaper report, and Adam had received only a brief mention, in his assumed name—which, for some inexplicable reason, she kept forgetting. Bannon—no, Shannon, that was it. Private Adam Shannon of Her Majesty's 40th Regiment of Foot. She—

With strident, excited cries, her son erupted into the room and flung himself onto the couch beside her. His hands and face were plastered with mud and dust, his white sailor suit was torn and filthy, and his cheeks were pink from his exertions, but regardless of the disapproval in his mother's gaze, he flung his thin little arms round her neck and hugged her.

"Cricket!" he burst out. "Papa teached me to play *cricket*, Mama! Oh, it was fun!"

"And the boy's quite a dab hand with a bat," Leonard affirmed, advancing into the room in his shirtsleeves, his jacket over his arm.

"Papa *taught* me, Jon, not teached," Caroline corrected. "And you are simply filthy! Off you go, at once, and tell Milly to give you a tub and put you into clean clothes. Then you can come in here and tell me about it."

Crestfallen, the little boy descended from the couch and obediently ran off in search of Milly. Leonard frowned and said reproachfully, "You might sometimes encourage him, Caroline, instead of always putting him down. He's a fine little fellow, and, damme, he is your son! Is that tea still hot?"

"I think it is," Caroline answered indifferently. She poured him a cup of the lukewarm brew and added sullenly, "I have a dreadful headache, and Jon always makes so much noise."

"Headache, have you?" Leonard made a grimace when he tasted the tea and put his cup back on the tray. "This is undrinkable—all but stone cold." He crossed the room and hauled impatiently on the bell rope. "Bring some fresh tea, Larkin," he instructed the butler, when he came in answer to the clanging summons. "And something cold for Master Jon—milk, if there's nothing else."

"There's barley water, Colonel—aye, an' some cider. They're coolish, I reckon. Which will I bring?"

"Barley water," Leonard snapped. "But I'll have a glass of cider, instead of the tea. Don't be all night drawing it, will you?"

"No, Colonel, 'course I won't." Larkin shuffled out, taking no offense at the peremptory tone, and Leonard sighed.

"God, they're all pretty awful, aren't they? Willing enough, I suppose, but—it's a pity I haven't a batman from the regiment. He'd smarten our staff up." He returned to Caroline's side and settled his long, well-muscled body into an armchair, eyeing her from beneath scowling, fair brows. "These darned headaches of yours—you spend far too much time indoors, you know. All right, so it's hot in the daytime; but the early mornings and evenings are cool, and there's usually a fine breeze. We'll take a stroll to the Domain, Caroline, and listen to the band. Go and get yourself ready, will you? We'll take Jon with us."

Inwardly rebellious, Caroline knew better than to argue with him. She rose reluctantly from the couch, a hand pressed against her aching head. The stroll to the Domain would, she knew, be one of the brisk walks her husband delighted in, with Jon and herself having almost to run in order to keep up with him. But at least, apart from having to suckle the baby, she had spent a restful afternoon, and perhaps the Domain would be cool, if it was not too crowded.

The Domain, when they entered it, half an hour later, was indeed cool, a vista of well-tended grass and colorful flower beds, but as Caroline had glumly anticipated, it was thronged with people, and all the seats surrounding the bandstand were occupied. Children played in small groups, scampering eagerly across the grass and making their own entertainment, while their elders listened to the band or paraded slowly along the graveled pathways, greeting and pausing to talk with friends and acquaintances, the women shading their faces from the sun beneath parasols of every hue in the spectrum. These, combined with the variegated shades of their dresses, formed bright patches of color in the evening sunlight, set against the more sober browns and blacks of their escorts' coats and jackets.

Leonard, observing a group of scarlet-clad officers on the far side of the bandstand, excused himself and strode across to join them, and Caroline, with Jon clinging unwillingly to her hand, was left to her own devices. Unlike her husband, who appeared to have made a wide circle of acquaintances since their arrival, she knew no one. Even their fellow passengers from the *Duncan Dunbar* were virtually strangers to her, to be nodded to or smiled at vaguely, when she recognized them, but not to be engaged in conversation or accompanied on their leisurely strolls.

Jon, however, had no such inhibitions. To him, other children playing acted as a magnet to steel filings, and, growing restless, he tugged at his mother's hand, begging her to set him free.

"Cricket, Mama!" he exclaimed excitedly. "Papa teached—taught me to play cricket. And they're playing over there, see? Please let me go. I'll come back, I promise, when you call me."

Anything was better than to have a sulky little boy whom she had to drag after her, and Caroline let him go, although the noisy band of hatless young cricketers was quite evidently not of the class she would have chosen for her son's companions. His going left her alone, and, looking about her for an unoccupied park bench on which to take refuge, she saw a carriage draw up on the roadway a short distance from where she was standing. To her pleased surprise, she recognized Judge De Lancey's wife alighting from it. There was another lady with her—a frail-looking elderly lady, over whose bonneted gray head Mrs. De Lancey solicitously held a parasol—and a slender, pretty girl of perhaps eighteen.

The three advanced together to the vacant park bench Caroline herself had just then observed, and she hesitated, uncertain whether to claim acquaintance and join them or to continue on her way alone. Her dilemma was solved by Mrs. De Lancey, who, after a swift, puzzled glance, smiled warmly and called to her by name.

"Mrs. Forsyth! How delightful to see you. You remember me, don't you—Rachel De Lancey?"

"Yes, indeed I do." Relieved, Caroline echoed her smile and stepped lightly across the neatly cropped grass to the bench, accepting Mrs. De Lancey's small, gloved hand as it was extended in greeting.

"This is Mrs. Forsyth, Alice dear. I think I told you that she and her husband, Colonel Forsyth, are recent arrivals here. Mrs. Carmichael, Mrs. Forsyth, and her daughter Emily. Now, let us all sit down, shall we? We are rather a long way from the band, but at least we have a seat and can talk without having to do so above the music."

They seated themselves, Caroline finding herself between the frail Mrs. Carmichael and her pretty daughter. She was glad of their company but not particularly interested in the Carmichaels, until she heard Rachel De Lancey say, "I was hoping for an opportunity to introduce you to each other, you know. You were asking about a young man named Adam Vincent, were you not, Mrs. Forsyth?"

Startled, Caroline turned to stare at her, as she went on, "Who, you thought, was on board the *Pomona* when she was wrecked in the Tasman Sea? Well, Mrs. Carmichael and Emily were passengers in the unfortunate ship, so I am sure that they can tell you about your young friend. Did you not say that he was an officer in the Fortieth?"

It took a moment for Caroline to gather her scattered wits.

Adam, she thought—goodness, these two had traveled out here in the same ship as Adam! But of course he was not an officer, and he had enlisted in another name . . . Shannon. She must remember Shannon. And—how stupid of her! Mrs. De Lancey had *told* her about the Carmichaels, had said that they had been passengers in the *Pomona!* She ought to have remembered that and been prepared when she met them, instead of which . . . Conscious of the color rushing to her cheeks, she made an effort to recover her composure.

"There was no officer named Vincent with the Fortieth Regiment's draft, Mrs. Forsyth," Emily Carmichael said, with quiet conviction. "Captain Fisher—Marcus Fisher—was in command, and there was a young ensign called Alan Edwards. They were the only officers who took passage in the *Pomona."*

She looked almost pleadingly at Caroline, as if she wanted to say more, but in her mother's presence and that of Mrs. De Lancey she was reluctant to do so.

Confused, Caroline met her gaze blankly, affecting not to understand, and it was then that Jon came unexpectedly to her rescue. The boys in whose game of cricket he had so eagerly taken part were all older and a great deal more practiced than he, but tiring of their own efforts, they had let him take the bat. It was a heavy, roughly made bat, too cumbersome for Jon's short, untutored arms, and the bowler sent down a fast, accurate delivery, at which the boy aimed wildly and missed. The ball struck him hard between nose and chin, and his wails of pain echoing across the intervening distance brought Caroline instantly to her feet.

"Oh, dear, it's my son!" she exclaimed. "I must go to him—he's been hurt."

"I'll come with you," Emily volunteered. Together they ran across to the improvised cricket field, Caroline fearful that Leonard might hear the little boy's wails and blame her for her lack of attention. But there was no sign of her husband, and she quickly gathered the sobbing child in her arms, soothing his cries with the promise that he should be given a stick of the licorice he loved if he stopped crying.

"A—a whole stick, Mama?"

"Yes, a whole stick, Jon—as soon as we get home."

He was only superficially hurt, Caroline realized, but already his upper lip was swelling, and his small nose was pouring blood. Emily, with swift ingenuity, dipped her handkerchief in the water from a small drinking fountain, and between them they managed to stanch the bleeding and wipe the child's face clean. The lads who had been playing with him crowded round, offering excuses and condolences almost in the same breath.

"We didn't mean to hurt him, ma'am. But he told us he could bat, see, and he couldn't."

"We let him play, even if he is small. Took pity on the little chap, like, 'cos he kept asking us to let him."

"He'll be all right—you will, won't you, kid? 'Twasn't Toby's fault. You shoulda guarded wiv your bat."

Caroline impatiently shooed them away.

"There's no real harm done. Off you go, all of you. I don't blame you; it was not your fault."

They scampered off thankfully, and Caroline put Jon down, firmly grasping his hand. There was still no sign of Leonard, and she said, turning to Emily, "Thank you for your help, Miss Carmichael. I—I think I had better take Jon back to the house. He will need a raw steak on his lip, to bring out the bruising. Would you be kind enough to explain to your mother and Mrs. De Lancey for me?"

"You aren't going to walk, are you?" Emily questioned. "I'm sure Mrs. De Lancey would let us drive him home in the carriage. You live in Pitt Street, don't you? Wait, please, Mrs. Forsyth, and I'll ask. It won't take a minute."

She was back moments later, with Mrs. De Lancey's willing assent. Jon was lifted into the rear of the waiting carriage, and Caroline held him on her knee as Emily climbed in beside her.

"Poor little fellow," the girl said pityingly. "Does your face still hurt?"

"A bit," Jon admitted stoically. "Only a bit." He snuggled down against his mother's breast, a thumb in his mouth—a habit from his babyhood—enjoying, Caroline reflected guiltily, the affection she could so seldom bring herself to show him, as the coachman whipped up his horses and the carriage gathered speed.

Emily broke the little silence that had fallen between them. In an oddly aggressive tone, she asked suddenly, "Mrs. Forsyth, it *was* Adam Shannon you wanted to know about, wasn't it?"

"Yes," Caroline answered guardedly. "It was."

"But you called him Vincent, didn't you?"

"Yes, of course I did! Vincent was his real name." Caroline paused, wondering how much the girl knew, how much Adam had told her. Probably very little, she decided, since it was evident that he had not told her his real name.

"Then you knew him, Mrs. Forsyth—you knew him when he was a lieutenant in the Royal Navy?" Emily persisted. Receiving Caroline's nod of assent, she went on, her voice suddenly fraught with emotion. "I owe him my life, you see—we all do, all the passengers who were on board the *Pomona* when she was wrecked. There was a terrible storm, and the ship went aground on a reef off Gabo Island, in the Tasman Sea. I don't suppose you will have heard about it, but—"

"As it happens I read a report of it in the Cape Town paper," Caroline interrupted. "Which appeared to cite a captain of the Fortieth—I forget his name—as the hero, not Adam. I think Adam was mentioned, but that was all."

"That report wasn't true, Mrs. Forsyth," Emily returned forcefully. "I *know* what happened—I was there!" Her words tumbling over each other in her eagerness to convince her listener of the truth, she described the events leading up to the loss of the old steamer and Adam Vincent's part in the rescue of the surviving passengers and crew.

"If it had been left to Captain Fisher, very few of us would have been saved. It was Adam who took command, after the poor captain and Mr. Dixon, the first mate, were washed overboard and drowned. *He* knew what had to be done, and they all obeyed him —the soldiers, the seamen, everyone. He saw to it that the women and children reached the boats, Mrs. Forsyth, and he kept all the boats together until we were picked up by the *Salsette,* more than forty-eight hours later. Truly we do all owe our lives to Adam— Adam Vincent. He was the hero, not Marcus Fisher, but he was given no credit for what he did. Marcus Fisher stole that by—oh, by lying!"

She spoke with so much feeling that Caroline experienced a sudden surge of jealousy. This little chit of a girl imagined herself in love with Adam, she thought contemptuously . . . this child! As if a man like Adam would have the smallest interest in her. True, she was pretty enough, but an innocent of . . . what? Barely eighteen, with no experience of life or of men, whereas Adam Vincent . . . Memory stirred, and for an instant the Sydney street vanished and she was back in the lodgings at Portsmouth, waiting for Adam to come to her, to hold her in his arms and to make love to her. She—

Jon, who had dozed off, wakened and began to sob as the carriage entered Pitt Street and slowed down. Caroline silenced him abruptly and set him down on the seat between Emily and herself, irritated by the interruption.

"Stop whimpering, for goodness' sake!" she bade him. "I won't give you any licorice if you make a fuss, Jon. And Papa will be cross with you."

Emily looked down into the little boy's bruised and swollen face and ventured diffidently, "Perhaps he is in pain, Mrs. Forsyth. I'll hold him, shall I?"

For no reason that Caroline could have explained, the girl's simpering compassion, as she lifted Jon onto her lap and kissed his tear-wet cheek, angered her beyond endurance.

She said, with calculated cruelty, "You want to know about Adam Vincent, don't you? Well, I will tell you. He was in love with *me* . . . he wanted me to leave my first husband and run away with him! Do you understand, Emily—Adam Vincent *loved* me! And as to his court-martial, I can tell you about that, too. He was found guilty of drunkenness, and the court declared that he was responsible for the loss of H.M.S. *Lancer* and over a hundred of her officers and men—including my late husband, John Omerod, who was his captain! He was cashiered and utterly disgraced— that's why he enlisted in the Fortieth as a common soldier. And that's why he knew so exactly what had to be done when your ship was wrecked—he had lived through it all before. But saving your life will not bring my first husband back, will it? Adam Vincent has all those other lives on his conscience, as well as poor John's!"

Caroline's anger gradually subsided, but the stricken look on Emily's face evoked in her no pity. She lifted Jon roughly from the girl's lap, and as the carriage drew up outside her own house, she jumped out, ignoring her son's plaintive cries. Dragging him after her, she started to make for the front door, pausing only to call back over her shoulder, "If you'll take my advice you will do best to forget him!"

Then she was gone, the door closing behind her and cutting off Jon's wails.

Chapter XIV

RED RETURNED FROM the dockyard to his father's house to find, to his surprise, his wife entertaining Kitty Broome and two well-mannered small boys. He recognized Andrew Melgund, after a moment's hesitation, and then recalled that Magdalen had told him she had promised her brother William that she would take care of the boys and see to their education, when he was able to arrange their passage from Auckland. He had not listened with full attention to what she had said concerning the boys, but Magdalen, as always perceptive and sensing his momentary confusion, said with a quick smile, "Red dear, Andy and Harry—Harry Ryan—have arrived to stay with us. And wasn't it fortunate for them—Kitty decided to pay Sydney a visit, and she looked after them on the passage. They came in the *Dolphin* with Claus Van Buren."

He had seen the beautiful *Dolphin* clipper working into the harbor, Red remembered, and had intended to contact Claus as soon as he could, but the dockyard had held him up. They were making difficulties, in the manner of dockyards, over the replacement of the *Cossack*'s mizzen topmast, and he had been caught up in a lengthy argument, which had not improved his temper. But he forced a smile, greeted Kitty politely, and then turned to the boys.

Andy had long been a favorite of his, and—Lord, how the lad had grown! Tanned and up to his shoulder already, as sturdy and well built as any youngster half again his age. By contrast, his companion, Harry Ryan, looked thin and more than a little scared by the company in which he found himself. He was an unnaturally subdued, dark-haired little fellow, a few years younger than Andy.

"Well, now, Andy, tell me what you've been doing since I last saw you," Red invited. "It's been a long time, hasn't it?"

"Nearly three years, sir," Andy confirmed.

"Your uncle Will took land, didn't he, with a view to farming?"

Andy inclined his head. "Yes, sir, in the Taranaki, near New Plymouth. Harry's family were our neighbors, but the rebel Maoris destroyed our farms, burnt down our houses, and made off with the stock . . . and they murdered Harry's folk, before they could make their escape. We had to go to New Plymouth for safety. Uncle Will volunteered for the militia, and he put us in school at a Mrs. Mordaunt's, in the town. He was in all the fighting, sir, as you'd expect." There was pride in the boy's voice. "But then, when the new general came out—General Cameron, sir, who'd known Uncle Will in the Crimea—well, he sent for him to serve on his staff. That meant we had to go to Auckland, and Uncle Will decided to send us here, sir, and enter us for the Sydney Grammar School. He said it was important for us to have a good education, if we were to make proper careers. I—well, both of us, really, were sorry to leave, weren't we, Hal?"

Little Harry Ryan nodded his tousled head but said nothing, and Andy went on, "I want to enlist in the Volunteers, as soon as I'm old enough, and go back and fight the Maoris."

"You've never thought of the Royal Navy?" Red questioned, meeting Magdalen's gaze and suppressing a smile.

"Oh, yes, sir, I've thought of the navy," Andy admitted. "But there's talk of sending the naval ships *here,* once peace is signed with the Taranaki tribes, so that wouldn't be any use, would it? I want to fight the Maoris, sir. I want to get back at them for what they did to us."

"I had understood that Governor Grey is exerting every effort to make peace with the Maoris," Red countered.

"It will not last, sir," Andy asserted, with complete conviction. "The Waikato tribes have elected a king, you know, and one of their chiefs, called Rewi Maniapoto, who is a famous warrior, is said to be stirring them up to rebel. Oh, the governor's trying, I know, but the odds are against his succeeding. Besides, the settlers —folk like us, sir, whose land has been laid waste—we have a score to settle."

He spoke, Red thought with surprise, like an adult, and in all probability his was the voice of a great many of the North Island settlers, dispossessed of their land and their homes and determined on vengeance against those who had despoiled them and done so many of them brutally and savagely to death.

As if he had voiced that thought aloud, Harry Ryan broke his silence and confirmed Red's reasoning.

"I feel like Andy does, sir," the boy said tensely. "The Maoris murdered my ma and pa and my brother, Davie, and my sisters. I *saw* them, Captain Broome—I was there. The chief's son was my friend and Davie's friend, but he was there—he was leading them! I saw him kill Davie." As suddenly as he had spoken, Harry lapsed back into a constrained silence, his thin little face scarlet with embarrassment. Andy came instantly to his rescue.

A hand on his shoulder, he glanced anxiously at Kitty Broome and then burst out, "Lady Kitty thinks we shouldn't talk of such things, don't you, ma'am? Not here, that is, where maybe folk wouldn't understand. But Harry—well, you see, sir, Harry can't forget what happened, and neither can I. We both mean to go back and fight for what is ours, just as soon as we're old enough."

Kitty spread her slim, beautiful hands in a helpless gesture. "You see how they feel, Red. I cannot convince them that peace—a lasting peace—between settlers and Maoris would be best for the future of the colony. I couldn't even convince my husband. You know that Johnny has joined the militia, don't you?"

"Yes, I know," Red confirmed. "I saw him when I was in Auckland." He did not enlarge on his meeting with his brother but, recalling Johnny's anger when he had found Kitty gone, and their enforced dinner in the militia's mess, found himself wondering whether her presence here was the result of some misunderstanding between them. Sensing his unspoken question, Kitty said flatly, "Johnny went off to Drury with a party of surveyors. They are planning to build a military road through the forest to the Waikato River, it seems. He did not know how long he would be away, so . . . I decided to come back to Sydney for a while. To see my brother and . . . oh, to escape from the war."

As an explanation, it sounded a trifle lame, and glancing again at Magdalen, Red observed that she, too, was puzzled. But she expressed no opinion; instead she held out a hand to each of the boys and suggested brightly that they might care to see their rooms and make the acquaintance of Jessie and Andrew.

"Only we call Andrew Rufus," she added, "because he has red hair like his papa. But at least that will avoid his being confused with you, Andy. And Captain Broome senior will be getting up soon, after his afternoon rest, and he will want to meet you, I know."

Both boys went with her willingly, and when they were gone Kitty said ruefully, "I'm afraid they regard me as more of a dragon than their old schoolteacher, Mrs. Mordaunt! But I *did* have to instill some discipline during the passage—their beloved uncle Will has spoilt them terribly. But they are both good boys, Red, and I'm sure that you and Magdalen will have no trouble with them."

"Magdalen has a way with youngsters," Red assured her. "And probably a change of scene will be of benefit to both of them. The Grammar School is excellent, I'm told—and renowned for its discipline!" He helped himself to a second cup of tea, feeling a trifle awkward in her presence, the memory of Johnny's reaction to her unexpected absence still rankling.

She had changed, he decided, studying her lovely, piquant face over the rim of his cup. The easy, infectious charm for which Kitty Cadogan had been noted was no longer in evidence. She looked pale and tired, even disillusioned. Her marriage to Johnny, he was aware, was not the happy union he had hoped his brother might find, but . . . Red set down his cup. To make conversation, while avoiding the subject of Johnny, he inquired about her passage.

"You came back with Claus Van Buren in the *Dolphin*, Magdalen said."

Kitty smiled. "Yes. It was pleasant to see Claus again, and travel on board the *Dolphin* is always enjoyable. She is a beautiful ship, and her crew are so much better than those of other traders. Two of them are Maoris, believe it or not. One, named Korriko, is the son of a chief. I don't know the story behind it—no one told me— but I gathered that both young men were compelled by their chief to serve Claus, in reparation for some injury the tribe did him. But —" She laughed, with something of her old spirit. "They both seemed as happy as sandboys, and Korriko was being instructed in the skills of navigation. Claus told me he intends to return them to their tribe on his next trip, as a reward for good behavior, but I don't believe that either of them really wants to be returned."

Red smiled to himself. What Kitty had just told him about the two Maori seamen was, he thought, typical of Claus Van Buren's dealings with New Zealand's native inhabitants. He trusted and respected them, and they returned his trust in full measure, which made him what they called a *pakeha* Maori. He had not seen Claus's trading post at Rangirata, but he had heard much about it and knew that one of the Yates brothers—the elder, Robert—acted as manager and had married a daughter of the chief, Te Anga. Te

Anga had strong links of kinship with the Waikato and, in particular, with Rewi Maniapoto and Wiremu Kingi, so that his position, should the Waikato break out in rebellion, was a matter for speculation.

To his surprise, Kitty went on, "Robert Yates was with us, as well as Simon, Red."

"Robert? I thought he was managing the trading post for Claus?"

"He was," Kitty confirmed. "I'm not quite clear as to what happened, but his wife, who was a Maori girl, was recalled to the tribe by her father, the chief. And the chief advised Robert to leave Rangirata for a while. The post is being managed by a Maori."

Which did not augur well for Te Anga's adherence to peace, Red decided. And probably it was the reason why Claus intended to put his two Maori seamen ashore on his next call at the trading post.

Uncannily, as if she had read his thoughts, Kitty said, in a flat, expressionless voice, "I have tried to wean those two boys from the prospect of war, Red, but in truth, I fear that peace between settlers and Maoris is a long way off, for all the governor's efforts. He went with General Cameron, Captain Seymour, and Premier Fox to Russell, in the Bay of Islands, just before I left Auckland, and they say he reached a good understanding with the tribes there—the Ngapuhi, I think they are called. But it is the Waikato tribes everyone mistrusts, and the general opinion in Auckland was that the new road that is planned from Drury will be a red rag to a bull. And Johnny's there."

"The governor has a considerable military force now," Red pointed out. "Imperial and volunteer. And there is also the navy."

"But not for much longer, Red," Kitty said. "All the naval ships are to leave during the next few months—Captain Seymour himself told me. He's expecting to return here, to Sydney."

When Red, in his surprise, gave no reply, Kitty rose and started restlessly to pace the room. "Patrick," she said, over her shoulder, "was out of town when I arrived, so I haven't seen him yet. I sent a message, telling him that I would be here, so I hope he will call before long to pick me up."

"I can take you wherever you wish to go," Red offered, but Kitty shook her head.

"I'm sure Pat will turn up. He will be as eager to see me as I am to see him. We're twins, you know, Red, and this is the longest time we've ever been apart in our lives. Over two years! I thought he would settle down happily on the farm near your uncle's place at Bundilly, but no. He found it tedious, or so he told me in the last letter I received from him, in Auckland. He left Luke Murphy in charge of the farm and came to Sydney, and . . ." Kitty sighed deeply, sounding half anxious and half exasperated. "What do you suppose he wants to do?"

Red stared back at her in bewilderment, and she answered her own question.

"Why, volunteer for military service in New Zealand, if you please, of all the foolishness! It appears that they are recruiting men from here to go out as military settlers, and my brother told me he has put his name down to join them. That was one reason for my coming back to Sydney, Red—to stop him, if I can."

"One reason, Kitty?" Red echoed quietly. "And the other, no doubt, was Johnny?"

She halted and stood facing him, her beautiful face suddenly pale and tense. The story of her encounter with the Maori warriors was briefly and bitterly told, and she said wretchedly, "Johnny didn't wait to learn why I hadn't come back, Red. He—oh, he jumped to the wrong conclusion, made up his mind that I was having an affair with Sean O'Hara, and . . . he just went off to Drury. He did not have to go; he volunteered and simply left me a note to say he didn't know when he would be back. I—I thought it was no use my staying, and, out of the blue, really, Will De Lancey offered me the passage he had booked in the *Dolphin* and could not use, if I would take care of the boys and deliver them to Magdalen." Kitty drew in her breath sharply and added, an edge to her voice, "It was Johnny who told him I wanted to come back to Australia, Red. My husband!"

At a loss for a suitably sympathetic reply, Red was silent. It was as he had feared, he reflected regretfully—his brother's marriage, unlike his own, was the reverse of happy and secure. Johnny had been angry and put out by his wife's absence, but . . . he had reacted impulsively and, as Kitty had said, without waiting to learn the reason for her failure to return from her visit to Sean O'Hara's stud farm. Perhaps, giving Johnny the benefit of the doubt, he had cause for jealousy. Kitty was a lovely young woman; she was Irish, and so, judging by his name, was the owner of the stud farm, O'Hara. The two of them would have memories of their homeland in common—more to talk about, no doubt, than she and her husband had. But . . . There were tears in her dark eyes, Red saw. Johnny had evidently wounded her deeply, and she, too, had reacted impulsively and fled to her brother—her twin brother—in an attempt to assuage her hurt.

"I'm sorry, Kitty, truly sorry." Red got to his feet and put his arm around her bowed shoulders. "But you will go back, won't you? Back to Johnny, I mean?"

"If he wants me to go back, Red," she countered. "I cannot be sure of that, can I?"

She moved away from him and went to stand by the window, looking out across Elizabeth Bay and mopping at her tear-filled eyes. Magdalen came into the room. She glanced uncertainly from Red to the silent figure of her sister-in-law and offered, with suspicious brightness, "The boys are with your father, Red, and all three seem to be enjoying themselves, talking nineteen to the dozen. I was wondering—" She hesitated. "We dine at eight, Kitty, and I hope you will stay and eat with us. We . . ."

The sound of a carriage drawing up outside caused her to break off, and Kitty turned, her face lighting up.

"Oh, that must be my brother! That must be Pat! He will have received my message." She started toward the door and then halted and turned to apologize. "I'm forgetting my manners, Magdalen—forgive me. It's just that I haven't seen Pat for such a very long time, I—I couldn't help myself."

"Don't worry," Magdalen answered. "We understand, don't we, Red? Go and meet your brother and bring him in here for a drink when you've exchanged your greetings."

When they came into the drawing room, a few minutes later, they came hand in hand, both their good-looking young faces aglow—like two lovers, Red thought, as he stepped forward to bid Patrick welcome—and so alike that, save for their clothing, it was hard to tell them apart.

Patrick was not in uniform—that, at least, would be a relief to Kitty—and he said at once, "Oh, I'm still a civilian, Captain Broome. Apparently the rumor is that it's to be peace in New Zealand—for the time being, at any rate. We've simply been told to hold ourselves in readiness for a call-up, if we're needed, so I shall do just that. Now that Kit's here, I'm in no hurry. It was a delightful surprise to receive her note." He smiled at his sister, accepted a glass of brandy, and raised the glass in courteous toast. "Your very good health!"

They did not stay for long but took their leave and went out to Patrick's waiting curricle, as they had entered, hand in hand.

"Poor Johnny," Red said regretfully, when he returned from seeing them off. "Poor old Johnny!"

Magdalen eyed him questioningly. *"Poor* Johnny, Red? Why do you say poor Johnny?"

Red shrugged and went to put his arm round her.

"Because, my love, he has to compete with Pat Cadogan—Lord Kilclare—for his wife's regard, and I very much fear that he's fighting a losing battle."

"They are twins," Magdalen reminded him.

"True," Red conceded. He laughed. "Then I suppose I should say thanks be to God that you are not!" He bent to kiss her. "Well, perhaps we should rescue my father, darling—he's probably had his fill of those two boys by now, don't you think?"

"I doubt that," Magdalen denied. "But he may have had as much of them as is good for him." She linked her arm in Red's. "We've acquired quite a family, haven't we? And, you know, I'll never forget what Andy said, when I first introduced him to Jessie. He looked at her, with his head to one side, very seriously, and he said, 'She reminds me of my little sister Rosie, Mrs. Broome. Rosie was awfully pretty, and Jessie looks just like her now.' Poor little fellow—he still hasn't forgotten, has he?"

"No, and I don't believe he ever will—or young Harry either, come to that, poor little devil." Red held the door for her. "Building an empire costs lives. It's a pity, though, that so many of those lives are of the young and innocent, who do not even know what they died for. India, Canada, Burma, Australia, and now New Zealand—I sometimes wonder if our descendants, our grandchildren, my love, will deem it worth all the effort and all the bloodshed."

"Oh, I think they will, Red," Magdalen asserted with conviction. "Look what a few shiploads of convicts have built up here. Surely that is something to be proud of."

Red was reminded suddenly of the speech Governor Phillip had made, soon after the First Fleet had landed in Sydney, which—according to his father—his grandmother had so often quoted.

Here are fertile plains, needing only the labors of the husband-man to produce in abundance the fairest and richest fruits. Here are interminable pastures, the future home of flocks and herds innumerable. . . .

Well, that farsighted prophecy had been amply fulfilled, he thought; the fertile plains and the interminable pastures, the innumerable flocks and herds existed throughout the land of his birth, and brave explorers and settlers had pushed the frontiers farther afield than even Governor Phillip could have dreamed was possible.

He caught his wife's hand, as they stood at the foot of the staircase in the shadowed hall, and answered softly, "Yes, you're right, Magdalen. It *is* something to be proud of."

Her Majesty's corvette *Pelorus,* flying a commodore's blue pennant, steamed into Sydney Harbor early in the New Year, and Red, with alacrity and anxious for news, obeyed the signal inviting him on board.

Captain Beauchamp-Seymour, his monocle firmly in his eye, offered a greeting with his usual heartiness and, in the day cabin, poured drinks with a lavish hand, beaming the while.

"Peace would seem to be the order of the day," he said, settling himself in a chintz-covered armchair and waving Red to another. "And I must say, Broome, I have a profound admiration for Sir George Grey, who has brought it about. He won the promise of loyalty from the Ngapuhi and even talked them into accepting his notion of 'devolved government'—tribal *runangas,* to which he proposes to give considerable power. But of course the Kingites and the Waikato would have none of it. The governor, with more damned guts than I've got, is talking of going *unescorted* by canoe and on horseback to Ngaruawahia, in the heart of the King country, to endeavor to parley with King Tawhaio and Wiremu Kingi and try to convince them that the road he's building from Drury is for commercial purposes, not the prelude to war. He'll have his work cut out to make them believe *that,* I can tell you!" He talked on, giving details of the governor's peace moves and the political opposition he was meeting with in the Assembly and from the dispossessed settlers.

"I'm afraid he was not best pleased when I told him I would have to withdraw my ships." Seymour shrugged ruefully. "But Their Lordships still have this infernal bee in their bonnets concerning a threatened attack on Sydney by the Americans. I had no choice but to withdraw, Broome. They're sending out my relief as commodore in the *Orpheus*—Captain William Burnett, an old Crimea hand—but until he arrives, I'm acting. The governor has asked for more ships, and—" Seymour eyed Red guardedly. "He asked for *you.*"

"For me, sir?" Red exclaimed, startled. "And my ship?"

Seymour shook his head. "No, not the *Cossack,* I'm afraid—I must keep her here." He smiled, without amusement. "To defend Sydney! H.E. wants you in the capacity of naval adviser and, as you may know, to command the flotilla of river gunboats he's asked the home government to supply."

"Gunboats? No, I know nothing of any gunboats."

"The matter is, as they say, in hand," Seymour said vaguely. "And it's a valid request, if the Kingites do rebel. H.E.'s idea is light-draft vessels, capable of ascending rivers, well armored, under steam, of course, and mounting up to thirty-two-pounder guns. You would have a lively time with them, my friend, believe me."

"Yes, sir, I don't doubt that," Red returned without enthusiasm. He was silent, considering what the acting commodore had said, and then asked bluntly, "Am I definitely to relinquish command of my ship, sir? And being posted to New Zealand?"

Captain Seymour smiled. "My dear fellow, nothing can be done immediately. But if Governor Grey fails to make peace, then I think his request for your services must be granted. As I mentioned, I am acting commodore, and at least until Captain Burnett relieves me, I have a free hand where appointments and postings are concerned. Grey seemed very keen to have you—you evidently impressed him very favorably during the passage from the Cape. And quite honestly, Broome, that road of his will stir up hostility among the Kingites. The military are to build it, with each regiment responsible for one section, and then, when it terminates at the Waikato River, Grey plans to have redoubts built, manned by imperial troops, and defended by guns. But . . ." He rose and refilled both their glasses. "It hasn't been started yet, and there's still hope that H.E. may succeed in his efforts for peace . . . always provided he can manage to carry the politicians with him."

"But you don't think he will?" Red suggested.

"Frankly, no. They're under too much pressure from the settlers, who are agitating to be allowed to reclaim their land in the Taranaki, and by new arrivals, crying out for land anywhere. Poor Sir George appealed for more ships and hopes to get them from India or China, if Their Lordships and the home government agree. *If!* So he does need you, Broome, and those river gunboats, you know."

"It's up to you, sir," Red conceded reluctantly. "And what about command of my frigate? Have you an officer in mind?"

Seymour sipped his drink. Avoiding Red's gaze, he said cautiously, "Yes, I have one in mind—a most deserving fellow, who has long merited a command. It would be temporary, you understand, and subject to Their Lordships' approval, but—my first lieutenant, Brattiscombe. He was outstanding in our recent operations against the Maoris. Indeed, I twice had occasion to mention him in my dispatches to the Admiralty. Your *Cossack* would be in very good hands with young Brattiscombe, I can promise you. She's ready for sea, isn't she?"

"Yes, sir, she is ready for sea," Red confirmed.

"Right, fine—that's settled, then," Seymour said heartily. "If Governor Grey applies for you officially, you will go to Auckland, and Brattiscombe will assume command of your ship. He's ashore at the moment, but I'll see that he calls on you. Another drink, Broome?"

"No, thank you, sir. I'd better make tracks."

Red excused himself, his feelings decidedly mixed. But when he returned to the *Cossack*, a note from Magdalen, summoning him urgently because his father had been taken ill, put all other thoughts from his mind.

Reaching the house, he found his father in bed, the family doctor in attendance, and Magdalen, white of face but controlled, endeavoring to comfort Andy and Harry and their own little daughter, Jessie, who was in tears.

"Oh, Red!" Magdalen clung to him for a moment, as if seeking strength. "He's very ill, I'm afraid. It's another stroke, a—a very severe one, Dr. Maitland says. He's doing all he can, but—" She did not complete her sentence, but he read her fear in her eyes, and his heart sank. His father had seemed so well of late, he thought wretchedly, spending his time with the two boys when they were not at school, as if their coming had given him a fresh lease on life.

"Take Jessie up to the nursery, will you, Andy?" Magdalen asked. "Tell her a story, if you can, or read to her from one of her books."

"Yes, Aunt Magdalen," Andy responded. "You take one of her hands, Hal, and I'll take the other." He turned, as the three of them reached the door, and said, with adult gravity, "Don't worry about Jessie—we'll look after her. And we'll say a prayer, all three of us, for Grandpa Justin."

"They are such good boys," Magdalen whispered as the door closed behind them. Tears welled in her eyes and ran, unchecked, down her pale, anxious face. "And it wasn't their fault, Red. Your father had arranged the game, ready for when they came in from school. He put up the—the stumps himself, and he was looking forward to it, I know. But I'm afraid it was too much for him. They were playing on the lawn, and I was watching them from the window and—and thinking how happy they looked. Then—Andy was batting and he hit the ball right across the garden. Your father ran to—oh, to try to catch it, I suppose, and he just collapsed by the shrubbery." She bit back a sob. "He was unconscious when I reached him—"

Red held her close until she recovered her composure and went on.

"Andy had done all the right things—loosened his collar and his belt—and Harry and Jessie were trying to pillow his head. The servants came, and we carried him into the house, and I sent for Dr. Maitland. He came very quickly. Lockhart's helping him."

What more could they—could anyone—have done? Red reflected. If he had been there, he could have done no more. He crossed to the sideboard and poured a glass of brandy, putting it gently into Magdalen's hands.

"Drink that, darling," he begged her when she turned her head away. "Please—it will ease the shock."

She took a few sips and then gave him back the glass. "I—I can't, Red. I simply can't."

He did not insist. They waited, virtually in silence, he with his arm about her slim waist, for what seemed to them both a very long time. Then Dr. Maitland came in, in his shirtsleeves, his round, red face beaded with perspiration.

"You had better come to him now," he said, with gruff pity. "I fear the end is very near for your father, Red. He has suffered another stroke, and there's nothing more I can do for him, alas."

They followed him into the darkened bedroom, and Lockhart, who had been the old doctor's coxswain and had served him since they had both retired from the naval service, rose from the chair beside the bed and stood aside, yielding his seat to Magdalen.

His father was not conscious, Red saw. He lay very still, his eyes closed, his breathing barely perceptible, and Red doubted whether he was aware of their presence. He leaned forward and took one of the limp hands that lay motionless on the coverlet, holding it in his own and wishing, with all his heart, that he might somehow put off the moment of his father's dying.

As if his touch had roused him, Justin Broome opened his eyes, and a slow, warm smile spread across his face. His lips moved, and Red, leaning closer, just caught the words.

"I've been a long time . . . away from them. From your mother and Jenny, Red. It's time I went to them now."

The blue eyes closed, the hand he held slipped from his, and Red knew that his father's life had ended. Magdalen's fingers grasped his arm.

"Look, Red," she bade him softly. "How calm his face is. He is at peace."

And it was true, he realized, with wonder. The lines had gone from his father's face, as if by some miracle, and the face of a young man looked back at him, still and silent. And, as Magdalen had whispered, it was at peace.

Chapter XV

IN THE PA of Te Mata Atia, a chief of the Ngatihaua tribe, the elders gathered to hear the news brought to them by the mission-educated spy they had dispatched, two moons earlier, to report on the road the *pakeha* soldiers were building through the Hunua forest to the great Waikato River.

The spy, a well-built young man named Wiremu Tata—christened, in fact, William by his missionary mentors—had worn the blue serge uniform with the letters *V.R.* on the breast, which denoted a so-called friendly of Waaka Nene's tribe, but he had stripped it off as soon as he entered the *pa,* as if it were a badge of shame.

However, under questioning by Te Mata, a commanding figure in his ceremonial cloak of vivid *kaka* feathers, the youth conceded that his disguise had served to win the trust and confidence of the soldiers. He was, he claimed, on terms of friendship with one young soldier in particular, a beater of the drum known to him as Dickie.

"This red garment, this Dickie who beats the drum," one of the elders questioned, "he is a man or a boy?"

"A boy," Wiremu was forced to admit. To regain his prestige, he added, "No longer do the *pakeha* warriors dress in red. This color is too easily seen in the bush. Now all wear garments of dark blue, such as those I wore when I returned here and like those from the ships, who are called bluejackets."

"Do bluejackets aid in building the road?" The question came sharply from the chief, and Wiremu turned obsequiously to face him.

"No, O Great One. It is said that the ships have gone. I do not know if this is so, but I have seen no bluejackets on the road, certainly."

"And what of the road?" Te Mata pursued. "Is it a good road?"

"Indeed it is," Wiremu assured him, without hesitation. "The *pakehas* have worked all summer to make it good. They have felled trees, cleared fern, broken stone. They pack the stone and hammer it, so that even when there is rain, it takes no harm. Great guns are brought along it, drawn by beasts of burden, and—"

"Great *guns!*" Te Mata exclaimed. He looked about him, seeing his own alarm mirrored in the faces of the elders. "To what purpose, Wiremu?"

"Why, to arm the redoubt they are building at the riverbank. It is vast and very strong. Not constructed as our *pas* are, with palisades and ditches, but built also of timber and earth, with platforms for the guns and huts for the soldiers within the walls." He described the redoubt in detail, sketching its outline in the dust covering the floor of the *marae*. "They call it the Queen's Redoubt, Te Mata, after Queenie Wiktoria, and it is situated at Pokeno. Now that winter comes and the rains have begun, the *pakeha* warriors will withdraw to Otahuhu, leaving only some of their number to guard their redoubt."

"How many soldiers will they leave?" Te Mata demanded, his heavily tattooed face creased in a frown.

Wiremu had to confess that he did not know. "I have asked Drummer Dickie many times, but he could not tell me."

"A boy, Te Mata!" one of the elders put in contemptuously. "Wiremu Tata depends on a boy—a common soldier—for the information he brings us. We need one of the *pakeha* officers to put to the question, one of their commanders."

"Yes," the chief agreed, still frowning. "But Wiremu Tata has brought us much information of value. He has done well. He has brought us proof that Grey, the governor, is not to be trusted. This road is for military purposes, not to carry our produce for trade, as he sought to make us believe. If he uses the road to carry guns into our territory, is that not proof that he means to make war?" Heads were vigorously nodded in agreement, and he continued, "True, Grey is a brave man and a valiant warrior, as we all know. He journeyed to Ngaruawahia without escort by red garments, as we had asked, and that is proof of his courage . . . but not of his peaceful intentions. For did he not say, after his meeting with King Tawhiao, when Te Tamihana asked him what his intentions were

—'I shall not fight against your king with the sword, but I shall dig around him, until he falls of his own accord'? Those are not the words of a friend but rather of an enemy!"

Almost with one voice, the council shouted their approval of the chief's reasoning.

"Grey is our enemy!" one old warrior burst out angrily. "We cannot trust his word. He makes promises, he offers us these *runangas*, by means of which we are supposed to govern ourselves . . . yet at the same time he builds a military road into our territory and sends great guns along it, to threaten us!"

"It will be war," another prophesied gravely. "Sooner or later, it must be war."

"The brave Rewi Maniapoto bids us prepare to do battle," Te Mata observed as silence once again fell. "Governor Grey is more to be feared than Gore-Browne—he is quiet and cold, and he speaks our language and purports to give us justice. But he serves the Queen Wiktoria. We should never forget that. Will he give up the Waitara land to the Ngatiawa, as he told Te Tamihana he would, when hundreds of *pakehas* in New Plymouth demand that he yield it to them? Grey is a *pakeha*—it will be their voices he will hear."

There was a chorus of assent.

"Kill the *pakehas!*" One of the elders rose to his feet, his right arm raised. "Is that not the message from Rewi Maniapoto? Let us attack and destroy the redoubt the soldiers build, overlooking our river, before they have had time to install their great guns!"

A full-throated roar signified the feelings of the council. All looked toward the *tohunga,* the tribe's witch doctor, and several voices demanded that he seek for omens. The emaciated old man emptied his bag of sticks on the ground in front of him and mixed colored powders into intricate designs in the sand, studying them with half-closed eyes, his gray head on one side. He lit one of the powders, and a long blue flame rose almost to the roof of the *marae* as, in a trance, he called in a thin, high-pitched voice to Kahukura, the god of war, to make answer to his questions.

Silence fell over the assembled elders as they waited, without impatience, for their wizard to give them the verdict of the gods he had invoked—Ruhua, god of thunder and lightning, Tane, the forest god, and Whiro, god of darkness.

At last his deliberations came to an end, and the *tohunga* leaped to his feet, his scrawny arms forming a circle in front of him.

Conscious that all eyes were on him, his voice rose to a shrill crescendo as he said, "The omens are favorable—Kahukura will lead us to victory, as he led our fathers before us! The spirits augur well. Death to the *pakehas!* Perform the *haka* and go into battle like brave warriors. Remember always—the death of a warrior is to die for his country!"

He motioned the elders to the carved door of the council chamber, and when this was flung open, it was seen that sun and rain had formed a rainbow in a great arc across the sky—the symbol of Kahukura, god of war.

Te Mata drew his *mere* and held it aloft, and from behind him came a roar, *"Te riri! Te riri!* War!"

"Tonight we will feast and our warriors shall perform the *haka,"* the chief declared. "And one day soon we will march with all the tribes of the Waikato to attack the *pakehas* in their capital of Akarana, which they call Auckland. Before that, we will destroy the redoubt at Pokeno." He paused, waiting for silence, and then went on in ringing tones, "But it is needful that we should be well informed concerning its strength, the position of the great guns, and how many of the soldier-tribe are left to guard its walls. Te Motohi has said that we should take an officer captive and learn from him all that we must know. I have given this matter some thought, and I have a plan. Wiremu Tata, approach me!"

The young mission-school boy obeyed the summons, dropping to his knees before Chief Te Mata in token of submission.

"You will again don the traitor-garments in which you came," Te Mata ordered. "And you will return to Pokeno. The boy who beats the drum—this Dickie—can you lure him to the river, to where our warriors will be waiting in their canoes, in the darkness, for your coming?"

"I will try, Great Chief," Wiremu responded doubtfully. "But I—"

"You will do it, Wiremu. We shall allow you from now until the moon is but a silver sliver in the sky; then you will bring the drummer boy, and when we have seized him, you will run at all speed back to the soldiers' camp and make report to the officer who is in command. You will tell him that the drumbeater is made prisoner and is like to be killed and beg him to send a search party to save him. In this way," the chief added, addressing the elders and ignoring Wiremu's frightened glances, "in this way, my broth-

ers, we will seize an officer, who will be able to tell us all we shall
need to know before we attack the redoubt."

Nodding heads approved the plan. Old Te Motohi, who had first
mooted it, was loud in his praise.

"An officer—the commander of the soldiers—yes, that is good,
Te Mata. But can we be sure that he will come himself, if he orders
a search for the drumbeater, who is but a boy?"

Te Mata smiled at him. "The drumbeater will scream and cry
for mercy, Te Motohi. That will bring the officer." His smile widened. "Armed with his knowledge, we will seize the *pakeha pa* and
raze it to the ground! Ho, my brothers, that will be a night for
celebration! We will hurl the great guns into the river, and no
pakeha soldier shall be left alive to tell the tale! Go, Wiremu Tata,
and do as I have bidden you. There is no time to be lost!"

It was useless to plead with his chief, the boy knew, and perhaps
he could do as he had been bidden. The drummer boy trusted him;
they were friends . . . he would think of some way to lure him
into the trap. The promise of a woman, perhaps, or . . . Wiremu
Tata stumbled to his feet. The offer of food—a feast that would
make Dickie's mouth water, for was he not always hungry, always
complaining that he did not receive sufficient food to satisfy his
appetite?

It was a pity that Te Mata had not given him permission to stay
for the *haka,* which was a sight that thrilled him and set his heart
beating faster. They would light extra fires, to give added light to
the scene, and the picked warriors would prepare to dance, their
naked brown bodies daubed in red ocher, their phallic belts girded
about their waists, and their spears held aloft, as the chant began,
slowly at first, then quickening to a throbbing crescendo. The
dancers would bend each leg in turn, then leap into the air in
unison, as if held together by a single cord, and come thundering
down, beating their thighs with the palms of their hands, their
voices rising in savage chorus, their mouths open, the tongues
thrust out and downward, their eyes wide and rolling, with only
the whites displayed.

Wiremu Tata passed his tongue over his dry lips, remembering
the war dances he had witnessed and those few in which he had
taken part. To dance a *haka* with the warriors of his tribe was
infinitely more desirable than the docile hymn-singing of the mission school, the wearisome lessons he had been compelled to learn,

the ranting sermons to which he had had to listen in submissive silence—or face a beating administered by a muscular lay brother.

And, when the *haka* ended, the women and girls would be waiting. . . . Wiremu sighed deeply as he obediently clothed himself once again in the blue serge garments of shame and prepared to return to the soldiers' camp and the hated road. Not for him the rituals the warriors would follow, before going into battle, the precautions against evil sorcery, the symbolic cleansing in the river, which would render them *tapu* and under the protection of Kahukura, the god of war.

For him it was to be treachery, the betrayal of a true friend, whose death would be laid at his door. . . . He crammed on the peaked blue forage cap and watched sullenly as a group of women went out to gather *kumara* and *hinan* berries and some young men followed them, laughing and in high spirits, to trap birds and net fish for the feast that was to come. They paid him no heed, and Wiremu bewailed the day his parents had adopted the Christian faith and handed him over to the missionaries to be taught to read and letter, and to speak and understand the ugly, harsh *pakeha* language. Resentfully he shouted out a string of English obscenities, which, since the young men did not understand their meaning, occasioned no response.

The elder, Te Motohi, chancing to pass by, admonished him and bade him sharply to go on his way. Then, relenting, the old man laid a gnarled hand on Wiremu's arm and said, not unkindly, "The task you will perform is no unworthy one, Wiremu Tata. Victory for our warriors will depend on you alone. Be proud, boy, that you have been chosen to undertake it. When it is done, you may return to your tribe with honor, and your valor shall be written in the *moko* on your countenance. Remember that, and do your duty well!"

Much heartened, Wiremu saluted, and his step was almost light as he set off on his long journey back to the soldiers' camp.

It had been a long, hot summer, and the work of road building had been hard and monotonous, but with each regiment being allocated a measured number of miles to complete, friendly rivalry had helped to lighten the toil. Now the original twenty-five-mile-long road from Auckland to Drury had lengthened by a further fifteen miles, which carried it to the Waikato River, where the Queen's Redoubt had been nearly completed and its guns installed.

Three companies of Her Majesty's 70th Regiment were to occupy and defend it, the other regiments to be withdrawn to winter quarters at Otahuhu and Auckland; and with the coming of the first heavy rains, none of the departing regiments would be sorry to leave.

Adam Vincent's promotion to the rank of sergeant had greatly improved his circumstances. Like the officers, senior NCOs were not required to undertake the backbreaking work of building the road. Occasionally, however, he had done it, in the hope of keeping up morale. Once Marcus Fisher had ordered him to join a timber-felling party in the Hunua forest, expecting him to refuse, Adam knew, with the aim of placing him on a charge and depriving him of his rank. But he had raised no objection, had simply picked up an ax and set to work with the other men, and soon after that Fisher had contrived to have himself posted to Auckland, and the regiment, now bivouacked not far from the Queen's Redoubt, had not set eyes on him for over three months.

But now, alas, according to Sergeant Doran, he was back. "That bastard Fisher's with us again," Doran had said, and had spat on the ground at his feet as he made his announcement. "Back an' more of a bloody swine than he was on board the old *Pomona*! He had poor Burnaby on the mat for dirty boots, if you please . . . as if any of us can have pukka polished boots on this job! And he gave Dickens and Lumley a week's fatigues for what he was pleased to call dumb insolence! You'd best watch your step, Shannon my son, when you take the picket out tonight—Fisher's in command of it."

Indeed he would watch his step, Adam thought glumly. Fisher had never forgotten the aftermath of the loss of the *Pomona* and the part each of them had played in the rescue of the survivors, and he seldom lost an opportunity to belittle Adam or get him into trouble with his superiors. Fortunately, however, Captain Charles Shawe—a Crimean veteran and a onetime cavalry officer—was now his company commander, with Lieutenants Hobbs and Dudgeon as subalterns, all three of whom were first-rate officers and whose treatment of him left nothing to be desired.

If they had heard the rumors concerning him that Marcus Fisher had started, none of them—least of all the big, cheerful Captain Shawe—had given any sign of it. And that suited him, Adam thought; he was happy enough in his new life and was, he knew, well on his way to becoming a good soldier. He . . . The subdued murmur of voices outside his tent broke into his thoughts, and laying down the Enfield rifle he had been cleaning, he rose and opened the flap, to reveal the small figure of Drummer Dickie Smith, who came rigidly to attention. Behind him was his friend and constant companion, the Maori "friendly" Wiremu Tata, whose mission education and fluent English had led to his appointment as interpreter to the regiment.

"Well, lads?" Adam greeted them. "What can I do for you, then?" He liked them both, particularly the little drummer, who, at thirteen, was the youngest member of the 40th's band. Dickie—everyone addressed him thus—was an orphan, whose father had been killed in the Crimea. Brought up by uncaring relatives in a London slum, he had enlisted to escape from them, lying about his age. But for all his skinny little body and poor physique, the boy never shirked his duty, and during the work on the road he had toiled as hard as men twice his age.

"I brought you a letter, Sergeant," Dickie announced. "Mail's just come, an' the post corporal reckoned you'd want to have your letter right away, so I told him I'd bring it to you. 'Tis from Sydney," he added helpfully, holding out the franked envelope. "You don't get many letters, do you, Sergeant Shannon?"

In truth, he received none, Adam thought wryly, and wondered who could have written to him from Sydney Town. The writing, clear and childishly rounded, was unfamiliar, and still puzzled as to the writer, he thrust the letter, unopened, into the pocket of his blue serge trousers and invited both boys into his tent. The only hospitality he could offer was some of the lukewarm beer he had been drinking before their arrival, but he poured each of them a generous measure and motioned them to sit down while they drank it.

Dickie sipped his appreciatively. "Are you commanding the picket tonight, Sergeant?" he asked.

"I'm on it," Adam confirmed. "But Captain Fisher's commanding it, Dickie. Why?"

"You couldn't take me with you, could you?" the boy requested eagerly, ignoring the jabbing elbow of Wiremu, which sought to silence him. "Wiremu doesn't want me to ask you, but—"

Wiremu jabbed him again, his dark face curiously apprehensive. "You know the sergeant cannot take you, Dickie. It's against regulations."

And so it was, Adam knew, but to avoid wounding the boy's pride, he said evasively, "The picket's been detailed, lad. I couldn't take you if I wanted to, without your name on the roster. Captain Fisher's a stickler—he'd skin me alive if I tried."

The picket was, as a rule, a dull formality, which most of the men avoided if they could. There had been no attacks on the road gangs; some of the local Maori chiefs had raised objections and had questioned the purpose of the road, but they had simply stated their objections to the senior officers and the chief engineer, and their people had seized the opportunity to trade profitably with the soldiers, displaying no animosity toward them as far as Adam could see.

He tried to explain this to the crestfallen Dickie, and Wiremu endorsed his words, with unexpected vigor.

"I'll take you to a feast with some of my people, Dickie," the young Maori offered. "I told you I would. They'll eat well—you'll enjoy it."

Dickie finished his beer and nodded assent, though without enthusiasm. "Yes, all right, Wiremu," he said, cutting short the young Maori's description of the delights in store for them in the way of food. He got to his feet and came smartly to attention.

"We'd better go. Thank you for the beer, Sergeant Shannon."

When the two boys had gone, Adam finished cleaning his rifle and then, remembering the unopened letter, went to stretch out on his cot to read it.

The address at the head of the single sheet and the signature at its foot answered his question. It was from Emily Carmichael. . . . He found himself smiling, remembering the pretty, bright-eyed girl with whom he had formed a tentative friendship during the *Pomona*'s passage from England.

She had not written to him before; his farewell to her and his rejection of her father's well-intentioned offer to help him had, he had supposed, severed the tenuous links between them, since he had made it clear—for her sake, as much as for his own—that nothing could come of it. He was a soldier, for good or ill, and he had told the kindly old judge that he would serve his enlistment and go to war with the regiment, in the hope of living down the shame of his court-martial. Lord . . . He felt his cheeks burning. He had told Emily that he had something to prove, something to live down for his own peace of mind, and . . . poor child, her eyes had filled with tears. He had wanted to take her in his arms, to kiss the tears away and comfort her, but instead he had simply kissed her hand and beaten a shamed retreat. But now . . . now, after all this time, Emily had written to him.

Suddenly he wished that matters might have been otherwise between them. If he had stayed, if he had accepted her father's offer, how different it might have been. It would have been easy to fall in love with Emily—too easy, perhaps, and the shame would still have been there. He had *had* to go, Adam told himself; in honor, he could not have stayed. True, building a road had not enabled him to redeem himself; but in the fighting in the Taranaki, at least, he had proved himself as a soldier.

His hand shook a little as he held the letter to the fading light, but he steadied it and concentrated on the closely written lines.

Dear Adam,

I have thought about you often since you left Sydney to go to the war against the Maoris. Indeed, I have often wanted to write to you and have begun several letters which I never sent.

But recently I have met and talked with two people who knew you. The first was Captain Red Broome, who arrived here in command of the ship called the *Cossack,* from Auckland. He spoke of you highly and said that you had been commended for gallantry at some place called Te Arei.

And then I met a lady who is also a recent arrival in Sydney, with her husband, Colonel Forsyth, the military adviser to His Excellency the governor. Her Christian name is Caroline, and she has a little boy called Jon. She told me the story that you would never tell me, about the loss of H.M.S. *Lancer* and your court-martial and how her first husband, Captain Omerod, was drowned. Adam, I am sorry to say I do not like her, but if what she told me is true and you were in love with her, I thought you would wish to know that she is here in Sydney.

If you should want to get in touch with Mrs. Forsyth, write to her in care of myself, and I will see that she receives your letter.

Startled almost out of his wits, Adam read the letter again. Red Broome, of course, he remembered well—Red had been a member of the court that had tried and condemned him. But . . . *Caroline!* Caroline was in Sydney, and she had married again—married a colonel by the name of Forsyth—and the boy was with her.

Jonathan, Jon, the boy she had told him was his son, not Omerod's . . . oh, God!

For the third time, he read the last few lines of the letter. Caroline had told Emily his story—or her version of it, that was to say—and little Emily understandably was shocked and hurt, because she had learned it from Caroline and not, God forgive him, not from him. Yet, being Emily, she had offered to act as go-between if he wished to—how had she put it? If he wished to "get in touch" with Caroline. . . . In an agony of self-reproach, Adam buried his face in his hands, the letter crushed between them.

He did not want to get in touch with Caroline, he realized. He did not care if he never again set eyes on her, whether she had remarried or not. But she *had* remarried. Her new husband was an army colonel by the name of Forsyth, acting as military adviser to the governor. . . . Slowly it all sank in, and he found, to his own surprise, that what angered him most was the fact that Emily Carmichael had been hurt.

He must write to her, without delay, Adam thought. There was no time now—the letter would require a good deal of thought, and the damned picket was due to parade in—Lord, in about twenty minutes. With Fisher inspecting it, he could afford to take no chances.

He flung himself off his cot, cursing, and reached for the blue serge jacket hanging from the tent pole. At least the buttons were dulled and required no polishing. His rifle and his boots were clean, his belt and bandoliers checked and ready. He was putting on his cap when Burnaby appeared at the tent flap.

"You ready, Adam—Sergeant? That bastard Fisher's on the rampage already an' yellin' for you, an' half the picket ain't mustered yet. I reckon you'd best come right away."

"Fisher's early," Adam gritted angrily. He straightened his cap and, pausing only to pick up Emily's letter and thrust it into the breast pocket of his tunic, followed Burnaby out of the tent, the Enfield slung from his shoulder. The twenty men of the picket were lined up outside the guard tent when they reached it, and Marcus Fisher was pacing impatiently up and down in front of them, tapping his boot with the cane he always carried.

"Devil take you, *Sergeant* Shannon!" he roared as Adam approached him. "Can't you be in time and see that your men are in time? What sort of NCO are you, for God's sake? I've told you before and I'll tell you again—I will not tolerate slackness. It's up to you to maintain discipline, damn your eyes! And these men are slovenly."

"Sir!" Adam acknowledged woodenly, aware that, as usual, Fisher was trying to provoke him.

Disappointed by his response, Fisher proceeded to inspect the two lines of men, keeping them standing at attention and meticulously examining their weapons, their uniforms, and their boots. He found fault with them all, exclaiming with exaggerated displeasure at the evidence of slack discipline the whole picket displayed.

It took a long time, and when Adam saw the day picket and the troop of Volunteer Horse come in, he ventured a mild reminder that the night picket was due to relieve those whose duty was finished.

Fisher glared back at him disdainfully.

"I am not taking these men out until I am satisfied with their turnout, Sergeant. And I am far from satisfied—they are a disgrace to the regiment! Dirty rifles, filthy boots, shoddy uniforms—God, it makes me sick to see trained soldiers parading in such a state!"

"They have been building a road, sir," Adam pointed out. "Bivouacking, sleeping on the bare ground, and—"

"Spare me your excuses, Shannon!" Fisher interrupted. "They are soldiers, are they not? Every man is on a charge, d'you understand? All right—move them out, Mr. Edwards. You know what to do, don't you?"

Ensign Edwards stiffened. "Yes, I do, sir," he answered, and not waiting for Fisher to change his mind, he gave the necessary orders briskly, and the men thankfully obeyed. It was the practice of the night picket to vary the route they took, mainly on the chance of intercepting local Maoris engaged in illicit trade with the soldiers or, Adam reflected with a faint smile, soldiers, like young Dickie Smith, sneaking out to hobnob with the "friendlies" after the last post had been sounded. The men, of course, never reported either their comrades or the Maoris, and most of the officers turned a blind eye to such minor breaches of discipline, but . . . it was unlikely that Fisher would do so. Therefore it might be safer to take a roundabout route, first going to the river and the unfinished redoubt, circling its walls, and then returning to patrol the camp perimeter.

He quickened his pace to catch up with Edwards and whispered this suggestion as the men spread out in skirmishing order and the tents were swallowed up in the darkness. Young Edwards, still fuming after the protracted inspection and the treatment Fisher had meted out to the men of his platoon, nodded his understanding.

"Good idea, Shannon," he whispered back. "We'll be less likely to run into anyone by the river. And if the captain gets his feet wet, he may understand why it's a damned waste of time to polish boots out here. Lead on, by all means."

There were sentries posted in the redoubt. The picket circled it, meeting and responding to the expected challenges. At the extremity of the wall, however, there was no challenge, and where two sentries normally paced on either side of the gun emplacement overlooking the river, Adam could detect no movement. Conscious of danger, he hissed out an order to halt. The moon was new and it cast no light, and as he moved forward cautiously, his rifle at the ready, he stumbled over an obstacle—which, he realized with dismay as he picked himself up, was the body of one of the missing sentries.

The man was dead. It needed only a moment to ascertain that; then his probing fingers told him that the corpse was headless. Maoris, he thought, sickened—it was a Maori practice to take the head of a fallen enemy. Edwards joined him, exclaiming in horror when Adam told him what he had found. Of the other sentry there was no sign. They had probably thrown his body into the river or, more alarmingly, had clambered silently up the rampart and killed him where he stood.

"Go back and report to Captain Fisher, sir," Adam urged. "I'll see what we can find here. It may be an ambush."

Edwards had taken only half a dozen paces when, from the darkness ahead, a shriek of terror rent the prevailing silence, followed by the high-pitched sobs of a soul in mortal agony. A woman, Adam decided, or . . . a boy. The men about him tensed, and Burnaby exclaimed, shocked, "Oh Gawd, Adam! What are they doing? They must be torturin' some poor devil, the bloody swine!"

"Hold your tongue, lad," Adam bade him. "And listen. We don't know how many there are. We—" He bit back the words as, with startling suddenness, a figure broke cover and came staggering unsteadily toward them. Burnaby's rifle came up to his shoulder, but Adam pulled it down. Silhouetted against the swift-moving water of the river, the figure was that of a man in uniform, not a half-naked Maori warrior, and he was yelling in warning. "Friend! Friend! Don't shoot!"

"Hold your fire, lads," Adam ordered. "It's one of ours."

Fisher came striding up, with Ensign Edwards, his voice harsh as he demanded to know what was going on; but before anyone could answer him, the man who had broken cover reached the line of crouching soldiers, and Adam recognized him as Wiremu Tata, the young Maori friend of Drummer Dickie Smith. He jumped up, grasping the boy by the shoulders and holding him upright.

"You're safe, Wiremu," he told the shivering youth. "You—" Fisher thrust him roughly aside, his pistol pressed threateningly into the boy's heaving chest.

"You treacherous little swine! Trying to lead us into an ambush, are you? How many blasted Maoris are out there? Tell me, you benighted savage, or I'll blow your infernal brains out!"

Wiremu was beside himself with fear, Adam saw, and he had been savagely beaten about the head and face. He sobbed out his story, much of it almost unintelligible, as Fisher's pistol jabbed viciously at him, the jabs punctuated by threats.

There were many Maoris, a war party. They had killed two sentries and taken the boy Dickie Smith, the drummer, as hostage. He was alive, but they had said they would kill him, unless the *pakeha* officer met with them to agree on a ransom.

"Ransom?" Fisher said angrily, when this was explained to him. "Before heaven, I'm not paying a ransom for a damned drummer boy! He asked for what he got! Obviously he was out of bounds, or they wouldn't have caught him, would they?" No one contradicted him, and he added, with finality, "It's a trick, a blasted ambush, of course! I'm not risking the lives of twenty men. Mr. Edwards, the picket will withdraw at once. Pick up the sentry's body as you go. We'll call on reinforcements and drive their infernal war party out before they know what's happened to them."

"Sir—" Adam was stunned by his decision. He had always known that Marcus Fisher valued his own skin, but . . . with twenty well-armed, well-trained soldiers under his command, he could send for reinforcements and in the meantime keep the Maori war party contained. Or even parley with them . . . He started to say as much, but Fisher cut him short.

"I've given my orders, Shannon. The picket will withdraw."

"And leave that poor little devil Smith to die, sir?" Adam countered. "They'll kill him for certain if you won't parley with them.

I'll try and talk to them, if you wish—see if I can get them to release the boy."

"Are you volunteering, Sergeant?" Fisher asked. In the dim light, Adam saw that he was smiling as he added, "Then by all means do so, with my permission."

Too late, Adam knew that he had fallen into a trap of his own making. Fisher was not likely to change his mind, and it was evident, from his tone and the sudden smile, that he was pleased by the turn events had taken. But there was no doubt that young Dickie Smith was in grave danger; the Maoris would think nothing of taking his life if their demand for a parley was rejected. Remembering the sentry's headless body on which he had stumbled, Adam felt his stomach heave.

"Very good, sir," he acknowledged stiffly, controlling himself. "I'll do what I can."

Several of the men who were in earshot stirred uneasily, and Burnaby moved to Adam's side. "I'll go along with Shannon, sir," he began. "If—"

"No," Fisher rapped. "He goes by himself. Mr. Edwards, withdraw the first section. At the double, man!"

Adam had covered several yards before he realized that he was not alone. A hand grasped his arm, and Wiremu Tata whispered urgently, "To the river, Mr. Shannon. This way."

"Oh, for God's sake!" Adam halted, jerking his arm free from the boy's clutching fingers. "Go back, Wiremu. D'you want them to kill you?"

"They won't kill me, sir. I am of their tribe, the Ngatihaua. I will speak for you and for Dickie. They don't speak English."

There was logic in his reasoning, Adam recognized, and he did not argue. "All right," he said. "Then lead me to them, Wiremu, and you shall speak for me. Thank you."

With the Maori boy padding swiftly ahead, they reached the river and followed its course for perhaps five hundred yards. Dark shapes close to the bank resolved themselves into canoes; then, without warning and with scarcely a sound, half a dozen Maori warriors rose, it seemed, from the ground, and Adam found himself flat on his face, his rifle wrenched from him and a man's knees on his back, pressing him down. They pinioned his hands behind him and hauled him to his feet, ignoring Wiremu's shrill pleas, a musket butt urging him forward.

The war party had gathered beyond the canoes. In the darkness it was difficult to count them, but Adam realized that they must number at least a hundred—perhaps more. And the boy Dickie was there, bound like himself, sobbing Adam's name in tearful relief as he hobbled to meet him.

"Oh, Mr. Shannon—you came! I've bin—so scared. But you came. And Wiremu. Oh, thank God!"

One of his captors thrust him aside. The man had a torch of sizzling pine branches in his hand, and by its light he subjected Adam to a careful scrutiny, rapping a question to Wiremu in his own language, to which the young Maori nodded vigorously.

"He ask if you are officer," Wiremu whispered. "I tell him you are lieutenant. It is important."

There were several more questions. Seemingly satisfied with the answers Wiremu gave him, the inquisitor lowered the torch and gestured to the boy drummer. Two of the warriors lifted him up, slashed the cords binding his wrists, and set him free.

"They keep their word, Mr. Shannon," Wiremu said softly. "Dickie can go back to camp. They take you in his place."

So they had meant what they had said, Adam thought dazedly. As Wiremu had put it, Dickie could go back to camp; he had been a hostage, and now their roles were reversed—*he* was the hostage. Well, Marcus Fisher would not be displeased, and . . . dear God, did they intend to kill him? Was that the reason for this strange charade? They had had no compunction in killing the two wretched sentries and would probably have no more in his case, so that . . . He felt his throat tighten, as the warrior who held the pine torch approached him again. The Maori was tall, his face heavily tattooed, and he held himself proudly. He said something in his own language, and Wiremu translated.

"They will take you to the *pa* of Te Mata Atia, a chief of the Ngatihaua, Mr. Shannon. Te Heata says I am to tell you that you will not be harmed if you offer no resistance."

But he could not let them take him to any Maori *pa*, Adam thought, in sudden desperation. He could not and would not. Let them kill him, if they must, but at least he would put up a fight for his life. They should not carry him off, trussed up like an animal, shamed and humiliated, without his lifting a hand to save himself.

He found himself thinking of the letter in his pocket and of Emily Carmichael, who had written it, and for a moment a vision of her small, sweet face floated in the dark night sky above him. Then it appeared to plunge down into the river and vanish among the cluster of waiting canoes, toward which two of his captors were now urging him. His hands were, he could feel, too tightly and firmly bound for there to be a chance of breaking free, but they had not bound his legs, and their hold on him was slack.

Depending on the element of surprise, Adam let them lead him almost to the river's edge; then, turning, he managed to kick one of the warriors' legs from under him, and as the man went down with a yelp of pain, he set about the other, his booted feet striking knee and groin. He was strong and fit, and he managed to break away, running swiftly from them to hurl himself into the water among the canoes. In the darkness and confusion, he might have made good his escape had his arms not been bound; but unable to use them, he floundered helplessly in the deep water, and the Maoris were after him, plunging recklessly in between the canoes with yells of fury.

A heavy object—he had no idea what it was—descended with great force on the side of his head, and he felt himself falling into a deep and bottomless pit, choking and scarcely able to breathe as the water closed over him.

A long time later, Adam opened his eyes, to find it was daylight, with a thin rain falling. He heard the swish of paddles and men's voices—Maori voices—raised in song. Hammers were pounding in his head, and, he realized, as he attempted to move in order to shut out the light, both his legs and his arms were now tightly pinioned, and movement was impossible.

A hand touched his cheek, and he heard Wiremu say in an apprehensive whisper, "Lie still, Mr. Shannon. We take you to Chief Te Mata Atia. You will not be harmed if you will lie still."

Adam groaned softly and let his eyelids fall as the canoe in which he was lying skimmed rapidly over the river water and the cool rain dripped, like a healing balm, on his upturned face.

As he drifted again into unconsciousness, he saw—or imagined he saw—Emily's face bending over him, close to his own. Above the pulsating rhythm of the Maori warriors' deep voices, he heard her say, "Adam Vincent, I love you! Come back to me, Adam!"

It was imagination, he told himself; Emily Carmichael would say nothing of the kind to him. But . . . it was comforting, for all that, to imagine that she had.

He slept, with a smile on his lips.

Chapter XVI

MAGDALEN STOOD AMONG the crowd that had assembled to bid farewell to the Sydney contingent of military volunteers bound for New Zealand, and with a heavy heart she watched the men board Red's new command, the light-draft steamer *Mercia*.

She was an iron vessel, built in Sydney under Red's supervision, having a burden of three hundred tons, armed with two twelve-pounder guns in armored cupolas, and with a speed, Red had told her proudly, of between twelve and fourteen knots.

Magdalen found her eyes suddenly misted. She hated to see her husband go, aware that the news from Auckland was of war in the Waikato, as well as fresh outbreaks of hostility in the Taranaki area, characterized by the murder of settlers and their families and the wholesale burning of crops. But Red had been restless and ill at ease since his father's death, and when word had reached Sydney of the tragic sinking of H.M.S. *Orpheus* at the entrance to Manukau Harbor, with the loss of the new commodore, William Burnett, and over half her company, Red had warned her that he would have to go.

"Governor Grey has applied to Their Lordships for my appointment as naval adviser, and it has been approved, my love," he had told her gently. "As soon as the *Mercia* completes her sea trials, I shall have to deliver her for service in New Zealand. There's a crying need for flat-bottomed craft that can navigate the rivers in the army's support. The *Mercia* will be the first, but we should have another three before the year's end, including the *Pioneer,* which is being built here, as you know."

He had kissed her with sudden, unexpected tenderness, Magdalen remembered, and then—which was somehow typical of him—

he had listed the ships of the naval squadron that had been sent to the colony, in response to Governor Grey's urgent request for reinforcements.

"The steam frigates *Harrier, Eclipse, Miranda,* and *Falcon* are already there. We shall be able to form a naval brigade . . . and the *Esk* and the *Curaçao* are expected in a few months' time, with the new commodore, William Wiseman, from England." He had paused, as if in thought, and then added with conviction, "I think we'll see the end of the King Movement, Magdalen—if not this year, then next. Fred Seymour is going to be sorry he missed it!"

"There's Uncle Red!" Andy Melgund exclaimed excitedly. "Look, Harry—he's at the head of the gangway! Jessie, there's your dad. Can you see him?"

Recalled to her responsibilities, Magdalen picked Jessie up in her arms, and the child waved delightedly. But there was no response, and she said, as Magdalen set her down again, "He couldn't see us, could he? Not with all these people, Mama."

It was true, Magdalen thought. All of Sydney seemed to have turned out to watch the embarkation, and more were arriving with every minute that passed. She recognized Kitty coming toward her and relinquished Jessie's hand to Andy, with the injunction to have a care where he took her. Kitty was heavily veiled, and her progress through the crowd was slow. Her twin brother, Patrick, was among the volunteers now embarking in the troopship *Napier,* and clearly his departure had upset her profoundly, but . . . Magdalen sighed and prepared to greet her sister-in-law sympathetically. Even so, it took an effort; Kitty had lingered in Sydney in her brother's company overlong, in Magdalen's opinion, when her husband was risking life and limb in action against the Maori rebels. The marriage might not be all that Kitty had anticipated, but she had a duty to the man she had married, and in her lengthy absence she was clearly not fulfilling it.

But, when she came closer and Magdalen glimpsed her stricken face behind the veil, the momentary indignation she had felt evaporated, and her greeting was warm.

Kitty clasped her extended hand, nodded to the two boys and little Jessie, and then said, with flat lack of emphasis, "Well, Pat has gone, God preserve him. And I am going too, Magdalen."

Taken by surprise at this announcement, Magdalen stared at her. "Going? Do you mean back to Auckland, Kitty?"

"Why, of course. Where else could I go?"

She did not mention Johnny, and once again Magdalen was conscious of a nagging resentment and was hard put to it not to reveal her feelings. But Kitty appeared to notice nothing amiss.

"It will not be a pleasant change," she observed. "Auckland is a very dull, provincial town, whereas Sydney—oh, Pat and I have had such a wonderful time together here, Magdalen! People have been so kind and hospitable, and Pat has enjoyed his racing almost as much as I have. But all good things have to come to an end, I suppose, and if there's to be a new war in New Zealand, I'm dreading it, I must confess." She glanced at the boys. "They both look fit and happy. I'm so glad I've seen them again. I shall be able to reassure Colonel De Lancey as to their well-being. Are they doing well at school?"

Magdalen confirmed that they were. "They are such good boys, Kitty, and they've fitted into our family very easily." She added, a trifle reproachfully, "They have written to their uncle Will—Red is charged to deliver their letters in person."

"Oh, yes—Red is leaving too, isn't he? You will miss him."

Kitty's tone was light, to the point of indifference, and Magdalen stiffened involuntarily.

"Indeed I shall. You—" She had to ask, but the question, when she uttered it, sounded presumptuous. "You are going back to Johnny?"

Kitty hesitated, avoiding her gaze, and for a moment Magdalen thought she intended to evade not only the question but also its implications. Finally, almost defiantly, she returned, "Yes, if he wants me to. But I've no means of knowing whether he does. However—" Her tone changed, and she smiled. "Auckland—even Auckland—will be bearable if Pat is there. I'm leaving with Claus Van Buren in the *Dolphin*—she sails at the end of the week. And can you guess who else is taking passage with the good captain?"

Magdalen shook her head. "I've no idea."

"Why, the beautiful Mrs. Forsyth—Caroline Forsyth, with her children! It's a sudden decision, she told me. Her husband is rejoining his regiment—he's down there somewhere." Kitty waved vaguely in the direction of the ships. "He is going with the volunteers in the troopship, whatever it's called."

"The *Napier*," Magdalen supplied. She was a trifle surprised by this news. At her mother's request, she had called on the Forsyths, and had entertained them to dinner when her family's mourning for Justin Broome had ended, and she and Red had also dined at the home of the colonel and his wife. But she had not particularly liked either of them and had not attempted to carry their acquaintance further. Colonel Forsyth had struck her as a hard, somewhat unfeeling man, and for no reason that she could have explained, she had never felt at ease with Caroline. Their little boy was delightful—Jon, that was his name—a lively, intelligent little chap, on whom it was obvious the colonel doted. But the boy's mother had seemed . . . Magdalen's dark brows met in a thoughtful frown. His mother had seemed oddly cold toward the boy, as if she tolerated him but felt no real affection for him.

Indeed, Jon spent more time with Emily Carmichael than with anyone else. She had met them more than once on beach picnics and in the Domain, always together, and in fact . . . She looked up, with a welcoming smile, as she saw the object of her thoughts descending the slight slope and coming to join them. Harry and Jessie were frequent playmates of Jon's, and in contrast to her feelings concerning Caroline Forsyth, Magdalen felt a particular affection for Emily.

They exchanged greetings, Jon happily sitting down cross-legged on the grass with the boys and Jessie, their interest in the departure of the ships evaporating. Emily said wistfully, "They will be gone soon, won't they? I wish I were going with them."

"You would not wish anything of the kind if you knew Auckland," Kitty told her disparagingly. "Think yourself fortunate that you are able to stay here, Emily."

"I don't," Emily countered obstinately. But she did not explain, and Magdalen, her attention drawn once again to the squat, somewhat ungainly *Mercia,* which was moving slowly away from the quay, did not press her to do so. Red was going, she thought, her heart sinking; her husband, whom she loved, was leaving to go to war, and she did not know for how long he would be gone or whether she would see him again. A war—any war—cost lives. Men were wounded, hideously injured, and . . . She bit her lip, recalling what Captain Beauchamp-Seymour had told them of the Maori fighting, one night at dinner.

"They are courageous fighters," he had said. "Unexpectedly chivalrous at times, but in the main they are ruthless killers, sparing no one—least of all the wounded. Yet they respect courage in an enemy. On several occasions I saw them take water to a wounded man who had fought bravely, and once two of them risked our bullets in order to bring in a seaman of mine, from the

Pelorus, who had earned their admiration." And he had added, with a smile, Magdalen remembered, "Frankly, they earned *my* admiration in full measure, for they are a fine people, fighting for what they firmly believe belongs to them—their land."

The *Mercia*'s single funnel was belching smoke. She cast off the tug, and her paddle wheels began to churn. Magdalen sighed and waved her handkerchief above her head in farewell. Red would not see it; there were hundreds of others, doing the same thing, all bunched together, and some were in tears. She was close to tears herself, but for the children's sake she blinked them away, offering a silent prayer that came from the heart.

"Please God, keep him safe! Let no harm befall him. Father in heaven, I beg Thee—bring him back to me!"

Emily was excusing herself. "I promised I would take Jon back by teatime, so I'm afraid I shall have to go. But I wonder—" She was addressing Kitty, who turned to look at her in some surprise. "You are going to Auckland, aren't you, Lady Kitty?"

"Yes," Kitty confirmed. "Alas, I am. Why do you ask?"

The girl's cheeks flamed. "Would you—would you be so kind as to take a letter for me? I haven't written it yet, but—it's to a soldier of the Fortieth. I don't know where he is, but the military authorities in Auckland would direct the letter. You would only need to give it to them."

Her soldier, Magdalen thought, conscious of pity—the young man who had once been a naval officer and who had saved her life and her mother's from the wreck of the old steamer *Pomona.* Despite all her parents' efforts to distract her, the child, it seemed, had never forgotten him, although most of the eligible bachelors in Sydney had vied with each other to escort her to balls and parties, ever since her arrival. The most persistent of them, a good-looking young barrister named Bartholomew, had squired her to the races the previous week, but . . . Magdalen saw Kitty hesitate and, fearing that she might refuse Emily's request, put in quickly, "I'm sure Lady Kitty won't mind—will you, Kitty?"

Kitty shrugged. "No, of course not, if it's important to you, Emily. But Mrs. Forsyth's also going to Auckland, as surely you know. Why not ask her?"

Emily's color deepened and spread. With downcast eyes, she whispered fiercely, "I could not ask her, Lady Kitty. She's the—the last person I could ask. But if it's too much trouble, I—"

"No, no," Kitty responded impatiently. "It will be no trouble.

Give me your letter when you've written it—I'll see that it is delivered."

Emily thanked her breathlessly and, seizing little Jon's hand, vanished into the crowd, ignoring his tearful pleas to be allowed to stay a little longer to play with his friends.

"And what was all that about?" Kitty asked curiously. "You seem to know what the poor little girl was babbling about. Why on earth doesn't she want to entrust her precious letter to Caroline Forsyth, for goodness' sake?"

"I've no idea," Magdalen evaded. "But obviously she has a very strong reason. You should be flattered by her trust in you." The *Napier,* she saw, was under way, two tugs skillfully edging her from the quayside. She waved a summons to the boys and took Kitty's arm.

"Come and take tea with us, Kitty," she invited. "Don't go back to an empty house."

"Thank you," Kitty answered. She closed her eyes for a moment, crossed herself, and then, forcing a smile, fell into step at Magdalen's side. "There's nothing worse than an empty house, is there? Especially one that, only yesterday, was full of love and laughter . . . and may never be again. Pat didn't have to go, Magdalen—there were plenty without him."

"Perhaps," Magdalen suggested gently, "he thought it was his duty to go. As Red did—and Johnny, too."

Kitty was silent, and Magdalen, feeling the arm within hers tremble, guessed that she was weeping, though whether her tears were for her husband or her brother there was no way of knowing.

With Jessie and the two boys skipping happily in front of them, they made their way back to the waiting carriage, as the *Mercia* headed for the open sea, the black smoke from her funnel a smudge against the blue canopy of sunlit sky.

"This man—this *pakeha* officer you bring me, Te Heata, he is close to death!" Chief Te Mata Atia accused. "Of what use can he be to me thus? You were too violent—you did not heed my words. I ordered you to bring him here alive."

"He will not die, Te Mata," Te Heata defended. "We were compelled to subdue him, it is true. He is a brave man, and also he is very strong. Even with his arms securely bound, he fought us and attempted to escape. It was necessary to render him submissive."

Te Mata grunted skeptically. "You say he is a brave man?"

"Indeed, yes," Te Heata asserted. "He came alone, as we had demanded. There were soldiers with him, two score at least, but he came alone to negotiate for the release of the drumbeater. That is the act of a brave man, Te Mata."

"*Ai, ai,*" the chief conceded. "But I wish to question him concerning the *pakeha pa* overlooking the river, and I cannot do so if he sleeps. Summon the women, Te Heata. Bid them rouse him and dress his wounds and give him food and drink."

As if they were coming from a long way away, Adam heard the sound of the two warriors' voices, but what they said was unintelligible to him, and he let himself drift back into semiconsciousness. It eased a little the painful pounding in his head, but his limbs were stiff, the bonds that encompassed both arms and legs preventing even the smallest movement. After a while, however, the sound of voices again roused him, but this time they were soft and light—women's voices, he decided, and opened his eyes, blinking as a shaft of daylight slanted through the open doorway.

There were four women, three of them old, with gray hair and lined faces, but the fourth was young, scarcely more than a girl, with a lovely, intelligent face, the skin tanned golden brown, and two deep-set dark eyes, which were regarding him with mingled curiosity and compassion. Speaking to each other but not to him, two of the women freed him from his bonds, removed his still-damp jacket and shirt and, turning him onto his back, proceeded to rub oil into his arms and chest with skilled and gentle fingers. One of the other women examined the wound on his head and, her tongue clicking with what appeared to be disapproval, cleansed and dressed it, using pungent-smelling leaves for the purpose, while another massaged his legs until the circulation was restored.

They propped him up into a sitting position, draped a skin rug of some kind over him, and then brought him food—first a broth, which the dark-eyed girl patiently spooned into his mouth from a wooden bowl, and then some mixed-up concoction, with sweet potato as its main ingredient, that looked unappetizing but tasted extremely good. Realizing that he was hungry, Adam ate with gusto, feeding himself with his fingers, the four women standing round him in a semicircle, beaming encouragement.

They addressed the girl as Keri, he noticed, and, the bowl satisfactorily emptied, he handed it to her, echoing the smiles of the others.

"Thank you, Keri," he said, slowly and distinctly, and they all laughed aloud when, pointing to himself, he announced, "Adam."

One of the older women repeated the name.

"A-dam," and they all took it up in chorus. They were a great deal friendlier than the warriors who had abducted him, Adam thought wryly, and seemingly had no fear that he might attempt to escape, since they made no move to replace the bonds they had removed. In truth, though, he was very weak, drained of energy, and his head still ached as if there were demons inside his skull, belaboring it with hammers. The food had helped to restore him, but it had not recouped his strength, and when he tried to stand, waves of nausea swept over him, so that he was glad to lie back once more on his couch of woven mats and let the women cover him with the skin rug.

They left him then, and as they opened the door of the hut, he saw that two warriors stood guard outside, armed with muskets. Resigned to the knowledge that he had no chance of escape, Adam let his throbbing head fall back, to seek forgetfulness in sleep. What report would Captain Fisher have made concerning his absence, he wondered, and decided bitterly that the picket commander would almost certainly have given out that he was "missing, believed dead"—and in consequence no search party would have been sent to hunt for him. Even if they failed to find his body, it would be taken for granted that the Maori raiders had disposed of it in the fast-moving waters of the river. Poor young Dickie Smith would be able to add nothing to whatever Fisher chose to say; and even if he tried, no one would listen to him, if he sought to contradict an officer.

And sooner or later, when the casualty lists were published in the Sydney newspaper, Emily Carmichael would see his name and, perhaps, grieve for him a little.

Adam slept, and it was dark when he was awakened, this time by Wiremu, who shook him urgently by the shoulder. The boy had discarded his uniform, donning in its place the flax kilt of a tribesman, a tomahawk suspended from his belt.

He said excitedly, "Mr. Shannon, wake if you please, sir. Chief Te Mata Atia comes to ask you questions."

He sounded awed, and certainly the warrior who followed at his heels was an imposing figure, in kilt and mantle, the dark hair oiled and dressed into a knotted roll on the crown of his head, the heavily tattooed face proud and inscrutable. There were two others with him, older and less imposing, and standing by the carved wooden door of the hut, Adam saw, was the tall young warrior who had led the raiding party.

Wiremu whispered, "They are elders of the tribe of the Ngatihaua, Te Motohi and Te Taiapa. And Te Heata waits by the door. He it was who brought you here." He aided Adam to sit up. "They will ask the questions, and I will tell you in English what they wish to know. Please, Mr. Shannon, make answer. If you do not, the chief will bid them kill you."

His mouth dry, Adam faced his interrogators. All three voiced questions, which Wiremu translated, and he realized that what they wanted to find out pertained to the Queen's Redoubt at Pokeno—its strength, the number of guns it mounted, and how many men would be left to hold it when the main body of troops retired to the winter camp at Otahuhu. Clearly, he decided, Chief Te Mata was contemplating an attack on the redoubt, but before launching it he wished to assure himself that such a move held out at least a prospect of success. It had been for this reason that he had been abducted, Adam realized, for this reason that Te Mata had had him brought here and not killed.

"I tell them that you are officer," Wiremu said, in a low, strained voice. "Lieutenant Shannon."

Adam hesitated, his brain racing. There was nothing to be gained by denying Wiremu's claim, but there would be a great deal gained if he were able to convince the chief that the Queen's Redoubt was impregnable. And—he drew in his breath sharply—what he told Te Mata would be the more convincing if he could make it seem that the information was wrung from him, against his will. If only he did not feel so appallingly weak and, God help him, if only his head would cease its incessant throbbing!

The questions came, thick and fast, and Wiremu's voice grew even more strained and anxious as he repeated them.

"Please, Lieutenant Shannon, make answer! Chief Te Mata grows angry."

Obstinately, Adam shook his head, feeling the walls of the hut dance round him as he did so.

"Tell the chief that I cannot answer. I cannot betray my people. As—as an officer, I have my duty."

Wiremu cringed as he translated. He received a cuff for his pains, and Te Mata wrathfully waved to the warrior Te Heata, shouting out a string of commands. Te Heata and two other warriors advanced to Adam's side. He was hauled roughly from his couch and, supported by the two warriors, compelled to stand, half naked, in front of the chief. Te Heata leveled a spear and jabbed its sharpened head viciously into Adam's bare chest. The weapon drew blood, and the jabs were repeated, but somehow he retained sufficient self-control not to cry out. He must make it look good, he told himself, his stomach churning, and—the warriors were not anticipating any resistance; their grasp of his arms was slack. It would need only a swift jerk, a turn and a leap backward. . . . Almost without conscious thought, Adam translated this realization into action.

His backward leap carried him out of reach of his two surprised custodians. He sidestepped their rush to recapture him and flung himself at Te Heata, both hands out and reaching for the spear. He wrestled it free and, with the last of his ebbing strength, kicked the warrior's legs from under him. As the tall Maori went down, Adam directed the spearpoint at his throat.

It would have been easy enough to plunge it in and thus make an end to one of his enemies, but aware that to do so would almost certainly lead to his own end, Adam did not let the spearpoint fall. Instead, with a scornful gesture, he stood back and, placing the haft of the spear across his knee, broke it in two and flung the pieces from him. The two other warriors hurled themselves on him, and he went crashing to the dirt floor beneath them, the breath driven from his body.

He had gone too far, he thought, gasping for air. They would certainly kill him now, they . . . But he dimly heard the chief roar an unintelligible order, and moments later, his chest heaving, he found himself back on his couch, with Wiremu kneeling beside him.

The Maori boy was sobbing, clutching at him with trembling hands, but there was pride in his voice as he whispered, "Mr. Shannon . . . Chief Te Mata say you are indeed a brave man. He say he will spare your life if you answer his questions now. Please, Mr. Shannon, do what he wants! Te Mata will not break his word."

Adam was assisted to sit up. Someone held a wooden cup to his lips, and, able at last to get his breath, he drank thirstily.

Then the questions started again. What was the strength of the redoubt at Pokeno? How many guns did it mount and of what caliber? How many *pakeha* soldiers would be left to garrison it? What was the best approach to it?

They went on, seemingly endlessly. Adam answered them, exaggerating and lying without compunction. The redoubt was immensely strong . . . he described it in a wealth of untruthful detail and, seeing the faces about him fall, added that the guns were heavy naval guns and the dreaded twelve-pounder Armstrong guns of Her Majesty's Royal Artillery. And there would be a regiment of imperial troops, at least six hundred strong, retained to defend the stronghold.

"Could we not take it?" one of the elders asked.

"No," Adam returned firmly. "Not without heavy loss." Wiremu's dark eyes reproached him, but, recalling a word he had picked up from the boy, he added, "You would lose *mana.*" It meant prestige or honor, and he saw the men's faces reflecting disappointment when Wiremu repeated his words. *Mana,* it seemed, meant much to the Maori.

"You could lead us into the redoubt?" the chief suggested. "By secret ways, known only to the *pakeha* soldiers?"

"No," Adam answered. "There are no secret ways. Every way will be guarded."

There were a few more questions, but his interrogators, he sensed, had lost heart, now that the scheme they had devised had been shown to be impracticable. They left the hut, and a little later the women returned, to repeat their ministrations and give him food. There were now three warriors on guard outside. . . .

For the next week, he was kept in the hut, seeing only the women and, occasionally, Wiremu. The boy appeared apprehensive and ill at ease, telling him little, save that he was to be held captive and could not hope for release.

"Chief Te Mata respects you, Mr. Shannon. Te Heata wanted to kill you, but the chief forbade him. When you have recovered and are again well, you will be permitted to join with our people in their daily work. But you will be guarded."

This forecast proved to be true. At first, Adam was allowed very limited liberty, and always Heata and another warrior watched over him jealously, accompanying him wherever he went and forbidding him access to certain parts of the *pa* and to the river and the canoes. For a time, too, he was compelled to eat alone, with guards at the door of the hut, and two of the older women serving his food.

Winter set in, bringing heavy rain and a chill wind, and he became increasingly irked by his enforced inactivity, whiling away the empty hours by attempting, with occasional help from Wiremu, to learn the language of his captors. Heata, who had initially displayed intense hostility toward him, became more friendly when, using a few words that he had managed to pick up, Adam asked if he might join the men in their hunting and fishing. The chief's permission was sought and obtained; Adam was given a flax kilt and a dogskin mantle, in place of his now worn and faded uniform, and with his guards always in close attendance, the men of the tribe initiated him into their bushmen's skills.

The days passed more swiftly now, to Adam's relief, and he learned much during the ensuing weeks. The warriors taught him no secrets; he was still excluded from the defensive works of the *pa*, but he learned to move silently through the forest, to set snares and spear fish, to paddle a canoe, to make a fire without flint or tinder, and to eat food that, before his capture, would have turned his stomach.

He thought often of attempting to make his escape, but his guards never relaxed their vigilance, and the few tentative moves he made seemed always to bring Heata to his side, smiling and shaking his head.

"I would have to kill you, A-dam," the tall Maori warned. "We will not let you go." But his smile had been the smile of a friend, and he added, speaking slowly and carefully to make sure that his words were understood, "You can be *pakeha* Maori. We respect you."

The idea, with its implication of permanence, filled Adam with despair, and when Chief Te Mata referred to it, using Wiremu to make his meaning clear, his heart sank.

"The chief says," Wiremu told him eagerly, "that he will make you a warrior and give you a woman for your wife. All you must do, Mr. Shannon, is to pledge your word that you will never run back to your people. Then no guards—you will be free!"

Free, Adam thought morosely, free to wander the forest, to eat rats and eels and bright-hued birds, and—he choked on the bile that rose in his throat—free to do battle against his own kith and kin, against the men of his regiment, for, inevitably, that would come. He might be excluded from Te Mata's council and from the *haka* of the warriors, but he had learned enough of the Maori tongue now to know that the talk was of war. The tribes of the Waikato were ready to rebel. The men growled Rewi's message:

"Kill the *pakehas!*" Te Mata might not launch the attack he had planned on the Queen's Redoubt, but he was preparing for war.

Not here, since he had made no move to build up the defenses of his *pa,* but probably by journeying south, to join his warriors with those of another Waikato chief, and . . . Adam's mouth tightened as he once again rejected Te Mata's offer to make him a member of the Ngatihaua tribe. Escape, whatever the risks, he told himself, had become imperative. He *had* to get away . . . and to this end, and as a sign of his continued defiance, he donned his uniform again, and carefully trimmed the beard he had grown.

Two nights later, with Heata on guard, the girl Keri crept into his hut. Adam had been asleep; he wakened to feel a warm, soft body on the couch beside him, the girl's arms embracing him, her naked breasts pressing against his chest.

She whispered, her lips to his ear, "A-dam, it is I, Keri. Te Mata has sent me. He will give me to you as your woman—your wife, A-dam!"

In his loneliness and isolation, he was sorely tempted to take what he was being offered. Keri was beautiful, with her slim, golden-brown body and air of shy innocence, but . . . to yield to desire would be, he knew, halfway to surrender, perhaps even an end to his determination to escape. He held her close, not wanting to humiliate her, and felt his body respond to the light pressure of hers. It would be all too easy to let himself be held in thrall to her beauty, to spend his nights with her and forget that he had ever been a British soldier, who had sworn allegiance to the Queen. Or, for that matter, to forget that he had also once been an officer in his country's navy, with his honor still to prove.

And then, to his glad relief, Te Heata came to bolster up his resolution. The tall young Maori was furiously angry. He pulled Keri from the couch and flung her violently across the dirt floor, heaping abuse on her, cursing her in a low, guttural voice.

Turning to Adam, he said bitterly, "Keri is my *wahine,* A-dam! She is promised to me long since, and I have taken her freely, when we have had *tangi* and danced the *haka.* Why does she come to you? You have no right to her!"

"Chief Te Mata sent me," Keri cried tearfully, but her indignant lover ignored her.

"There are other women," he asserted aggressively. "Plenty of other women—*puhi,* even. Ask for one of them." His dark eyes searched Adam's face. "You have not touched her, have you?"

Glad that he could do so truthfully, Adam denied it, the germ of a plan for his escape taking shape, suddenly, in his mind. If he could cajole Heata into staying in the hut, taking his place on the couch with Keri, there would be only one guard to contend with, instead of two, which would offer at least a slightly better chance of getting free of the Ngatihaua village . . . perhaps, even, of stealing one of the small canoes. He shrugged and, at pains not to sound too eager, made his suggestion.

Heata was aflame with jealousy and desire; in normal circumstances, the man's native good sense and his fear of the chief would have brought a swift refusal. Now, however, he wanted to punish Keri and reestablish his relationship with her, and he hesitated, uncertainty in his eyes as they met Adam's.

"What will you do?" he demanded.

Adam repeated his shrug. He picked up his uniform jacket and slung it carelessly about his shoulders.

"I will sit at the door with Hongi," he said, naming Heata's fellow guard. "Do not feel concern, Te Heata—I shall not tell Te Mata."

Satisfied, Heata signified his agreement. He crossed the floor and, seizing Keri in powerful arms, rained half a dozen stinging blows across her face. Adam slipped outside, his heart suddenly pounding as he took in the fact that, thus far, his hurriedly devised plan had succeeded. He had no provisions, no weapon, and, he knew, very little time, but . . . he was now fit and strong; he knew how to survive in the forest; and probably a chance like this would never occur again.

Outside it was raining, the sky pitch-black, and Hongi was crouching, muffled in a blanket, finding what shelter he could beneath the eaves of the roof. His gun—an ancient, muzzle-loading musket—was lying across his knees. He displayed no surprise when Adam came to squat down beside him, but flashed his white teeth in a knowing grin, clearly aware of what his comrade's intention had been when he entered the hut.

Hospitably, he threw back the blanket, prepared to share it with the man he was ordered to guard, and Adam, hating the betrayal of the young sentry's trust, gritted his teeth and made a quick grab for the musket. It was in his hands and he raised it, bringing the butt down on Hongi's defenseless bare head before the Maori had time to cry out. He went down without a sound, and in feverish haste Adam divested him of his tomahawk and the pouch in which he carried powder and shot. That done, he donned his own jacket, then wrapped the unconscious Hongi in the blanket and propped him up against the wall of the hut.

From inside, he heard the sound of Keri's sobs and Heata's voice, still raised in anger, and then he was away, running as silently as he could toward the river. Rain and darkness aided him. He met no living soul, and even the dogs were inside, sheltering from the downpour and not, as they usually were, on the prowl.

Finding a small canoe took longer than Adam had anticipated, but he lit on one at last, slipped into it, and paddled frantically toward the far side of the river. It was swollen from days of rain, the current running swiftly, but exerting all his strength, he sent his small, expertly designed craft skimming across the torrent at a fair speed. There was no need to seek directions; the Queen's Redoubt overlooked the river, and he had only to proceed upstream to reach safety. And on such a night pursuit was unlikely, even if Heata spent less time with Keri than he might be expected to—or if Hongi recovered consciousness and gave the alarm.

He had the remaining hours of darkness, and, Adam told himself grimly, he must keep going and put as great a distance between himself and the Ngatihaua as he could during those hours, without stopping even for a moment to rest or slake his thirst.

Dawn came, gray and overcast, with the rain still pouring down, chilling and soaking him. His arms ached unmercifully, but he went on paddling steadily upstream, fighting the current with every stroke. His pursuers were bound to catch up with him, he recognized, despite the start he had had; a great war canoe, with thirty or forty men plying their paddles with practiced skill, would be bound to gain on him in the next few hours, and he would have to abandon the canoe he had stolen before the hunters caught sight of him. Pray God he would hear them first. . . .

He did hear them, at what he judged was an hour before sundown, and without hesitation he swung across to the far bank when the sound of voices was still quite faint. There was plenty of cover at the point he reached. He ran his canoe into a mass of vegetation growing at the water's edge, and satisfied that it would not be seen by any, save a searcher on foot, he took the musket and the small bag of ammunition and headed for the forest in search of concealment.

The Ngatihaua were masters of bushcraft, he knew from experience, but, Adam thought, he had learned much from them—

enough, at all events, to anticipate how they would conduct their hunt. There would be several parties of searchers, those in the canoes giving warning of their approach, as decoys, while others, on foot, would seek him silently, spreading out to cover a wide area, their sharp ears alert for any betraying sound.

It would be best, then, to remain still, until they had passed, avoiding obvious hiding places and choosing rather one from which he could retreat, should they come too close. He found what he wanted after he had run for ten minutes or so; a shallow depression in the forest floor, overgrown by fern and brambles, with a rivulet at its rear, and he wormed his way into the hollow, careful to replace the undergrowth he had disturbed.

Then he could only wait and listen, praying for darkness. He lay still—cold, wet, and infinitely weary, conscious of hunger and thirst, both rendered the more acute by the knowledge that, although the rivulet was only yards away, he dared not attempt to drink . . . and he dared not sleep, either. To keep himself awake, he thought of the court-martial and the evidence to which he had listened, the dreadful moment when he had returned to the courtroom to see that the verdict had gone against him and to await the sentence that would be imposed. He thought of Caroline, without any desire to see her again; thought of his strange meeting with her father and the offer he had made—ironically, in the circumstances —of land in New Zealand.

Events, so varied and unpredictable, coursed through his mind, dredged up from memory: the weeks as a recruit in the 40th; Fisher's persecution; embarkation with the draft for Australia; his flogging, and the visits by little Emily Carmichael when he had been in the ship's sick bay; the tense, nerve-wracking moments when the *Pomona* had gone down.

Emily, Adam thought, was enshrined in his memory now, a source of happiness in a harsh and difficult life. The fighting in the Taranaki, the bloodshed and savagery, and then the long months building and guarding the governor's military road, with finally those spent as a captive in Chief Te Mata's village, when hope had yielded to despair. . . . All that was— He stiffened. All that was until now. Now, at last, he could hope again. He could make good his escape, or die in the attempt. Emily had written to him—the letter, sodden and probably no longer legible, was in the pocket of his uniform jacket. But if he died at the hands of Te Mata's warriors, she would never know, for there would be no one to tell her

what had happened to him or where he had died. And he wanted
to see her again, one day when the war was over, and when he had,
God willing, redeemed himself—as Adam Shannon, if not as
Adam Vincent.

Somewhere, quite close at hand, he heard a faint sound: a bare
foot moving softly, cautiously . . . then a man's breathing, and
the rustle of the head-high fern. One of the hunters had come
within yards of his hiding place, while he had indulged in bitter
memories and a light-headed dream.

Adam's cold fingers closed about the stolen musket. It was too
damp to fire, and he had not loaded it, but it was still a useful
weapon, and so was the tomahawk that had been Hongi's. If the
hunter came any closer, he—

Startled, he heard a voice call his name. It was only a whisper of
sound, but he knew the voice.

"Mr. Shannon—it is I, Wiremu. Let me come with you."

Was it a trick, Adam wondered, his heart thudding . . . a ruse,
to make him reveal himself? But he had to trust someone, and
Wiremu had never behaved as an enemy.

The whisper came again. "Mr. Shannon, I am alone. I came
after you. I am wearing the *pakeha* uniform. Let us go back together."

He *was* alone, Adam realized, and . . . He raised himself
warily, parting the fern. The boy was wearing the dark blue Maori
"friendly" uniform, with the V.R. letters on the tunic; and he was
unarmed, as cold and wet as Adam himself. He held out his hand,
and Wiremu took it and slipped in to crouch down beside him.

"They hunt for you," he said. "But not near yet. The canoes are
a long way also. Soon they will all join together and make a fire
and eat. Then we will go. I will show you the way, Mr. Shannon."

Adam put an arm round the thin shoulders and hugged him.
"You are a brave man, Wiremu. When you say it is safe, we will go
together."

They left their hiding place when darkness fell, and under
Wiremu's guidance walked through the night. The boy knew the
forest well; he never hesitated, padding confidently through the
trees, a small, silent shadow in the surrounding blackness.

Daylight was breaking when Adam heard the sound of a bugle,
signaling reveille, and then, through the trees, caught sight first of
the river and then of lights flickering some distance beyond.

A startled sentry called on them to halt when they were a few yards from his post, and Adam, his heart leaping, identified himself. The sentry, gazing down suspiciously at the two strange figures, kept his rifle trained on them and summoned the guard.

"You don't look like no sergeant o' the Excellers to me," the guard commander exclaimed, eyeing Adam's beard and his sodden, threadbare tunic in shocked disbelief. "But I suppose you must be. Well, come inside, the pair o' you, and we'll give you a bite to eat before you explain yourselves to the company commander."

"Thank you, Sergeant," Adam answered. He put his arm round Wiremu and smiled down at him. "We made it, boy! By heaven, we made it!"

"Yes, Mr. Shannon," Wiremu agreed. "Of course. You see," he added earnestly, "I had to come back. I have to see the drummer, Dickie Smith, to tell him I am sorry that I lied to him." His small, dark face echoed Adam's smile. "We are two brave men, are we not, Mr. Shannon?"

"Two damned hungry men," Adam corrected. "I don't know about brave, Wiremu. Lucky, perhaps. Very lucky. And thank God we were."

Chapter XVII

MAJOR ARCHIBALD RUTHERFORD of the 70th Regiment, commanding the Queen's Redoubt, listened with considerable interest to Adam's account of his enforced sojourn in Te Mata Atia's village.

"You say they were planning an attack on us here?" he commented. "Well, damn me, we'd have made it hot for them if they had—even without the heavy guns and the Armstrongs you credited us with! All the same, Shannon, I confess I'm grateful to you, because we were still finishing off the defenses when you were abducted, and all the guns had not been mounted then. But they treated you well, it seems."

"Yes, they did, sir—by their standards very well." Adam smiled. "And they taught me how to survive in the bush, sir, and invited me to become one of their warriors—what they called a *pakeha* Maori."

Major Rutherford eyed him thoughtfully. "Did you pick up any of their language?"

"A certain amount, sir. But without the Maori boy Wiremu Tata, I'd have been lost. He was mission educated, and he speaks very good English. He guided me here. I might have made it without him, but it would have taken me longer. He's a splendid boy, sir, and I'd like to see him rewarded."

"I'll give him some money out of company funds," the major promised. He asked a few more questions and then added, "You won't be aware of what's been happening during your absence, but to put it in a nutshell, Sergeant, war with the blasted Kingites and the Waikato tribes is imminent, and fighting has already broken out again in the New Plymouth area. Some of my regiment and the 57th were involved in quite a battle there in October."

He went into details. It was the usual story, Adam thought despondently—settlers robbed and murdered, driven from their farms; small parties of troops ambushed; the Maori tribes gathering and building *pas,* calculated to test any British military advance into tribal territory.

He remembered the signs he had observed in Te Mata's village, the impression the chief had given that his people, too, would be on the move before long. He mentioned this, and Rutherford shrugged his broad, uniformed shoulders.

"Yes, Sergeant, they are preparing for armed rebellion, no doubt about it. The governor's courageous peacemaking trip into King country failed, I'm afraid . . . and he knew it had failed. He sent for more troops. The Eighteenth are already here, from England, and I understand two more imperial regiments will arrive from India and Burma very soon. We've a flotilla of naval frigates at Auckland, I'm told. So . . ." He shrugged again. "You've come back in time to see some action, haven't you? Well, I'll send you to Otahuhu, to rejoin your regiment. We have a supply convoy going back there this afternoon, and you can go with them. It's not for me to say what they're to do with you, of course, but I'll send a note to your C.O. with the suggestion that a new unit which is being formed in Auckland might find you useful. The Forest Rangers, I believe it's called. They're recruiting men who know their way in the bush."

Major Rutherford picked up a pen and wrote busily. He folded the note and gave it to Adam with a tight smile. "Better have our barber give you a short back and sides, Sergeant, and I daresay we can issue you with a fresh uniform. Frankly, with that tan of yours, I shouldn't have blamed my sentries if they had opened fire on you!"

He had half expected it himself, Adam thought wryly. But the attentions of the barber and a fresh uniform helped to restore his appearance, and at noon, accompanied by Wiremu, he took his place on one of the supply wagons, to be duly delivered to the military winter camp at Otahuhu.

The camp had grown almost out of recognition since he had last been there. Wooden huts had replaced many of the original tents, and there were canteens, a drill square, a gun park, lines of wagons and tethered horses, and everywhere signs of intense military activity, with seamen and marines mingling with the soldiers. After some searching, Adam found the 40th Regiment's orderly room. Inside was the adjutant, Lieutenant Whelan, and, to his relief and pleasure, Sergeant Doran. The old sergeant, who had been standing rigidly at attention while evidently delivering a report, turned with a look of stunned amazement on his lined, weather-beaten face, and then, forgetting—for perhaps the first time in his service life—military protocol, he shouted Adam's name and went to embrace him in a bearlike hug.

"Shannon—Adam Shannon! In God's name, lad, is it really you? We thought you were dead!"

He recovered himself a moment later, came to attention again, and apologized to Whelan.

"All right, Sergeant—I understand. It's a deuce of a shock, to me as well as to you." The adjutant looked Adam up and down, his eyes wide with disbelief. "I take it, Sergeant Shannon, it is you and not your ghost, returned to haunt us?" He continued to stare. "Captain Fisher reported you missing, presumed killed, months ago! For the Lord's sake, man, where have you been?"

As briefly as he could, Adam recounted his story. The faces of Whelan, old Doran, and the two orderly room clerks reflected their astonishment.

"I've brought the young Maori friendly, Wiremu Tata, with me, sir," he finished. "He can bear out what I've told you—he helped me to escape. I let him go off to look for his friend, young Drummer Smith, since he seemed very anxious to find him. You may recall, sir, that it was Smith the raiding party first captured. He—"

"We have Captain Fisher's report on the incident, in our files, Sergeant," the adjutant put in. He turned to one of the clerks. "Find it, will you, Soames? Dated . . . let me see . . . last May, I fancy. Or possibly June." He looked once more at Adam, an odd expression on his tanned, bewhiskered face. "Captain Fisher's report is not entirely in your favor, Sergeant Shannon."

Of course it would not be, Adam reflected resentfully. Fisher would not miss an opportunity to discredit him, even when—devil take the fellow!—he had no doubt supposed he was sending him to his death.

"I will refresh my memory," Lieutenant Whelan said. "In the meantime, perhaps I had better read Major Rutherford's *chitti.*" He did so, frowning, and then, when the clerk laid the file he had asked for in front of him, he read that also, with irritating slowness. "Well," he asserted at last, "there appear to be conflicting opinions as to your conduct, Sergeant Shannon. Captain Fisher stated that you ignored his advice when he ordered the picket to withdraw, in the face of a large Maori raiding party, and that you insisted on going to parley with them, without his permission."

"I was given his permission, sir," Adam defended.

Lieutenant Whelan sighed. "Yes, several men of the picket appeared to suppose you were. They said"—he consulted the file—"that you volunteered to negotiate the release of Drummer Smith, and that Captain Fisher permitted you to do so. Certainly your efforts resulted in the release of young Smith—there is a statement from Lieutenant Edwards to that effect. The captain's report ends thus—" He read from it: " 'Drummer Smith subsequently made his escape and rejoined the picket, which I then withdrew in order to obtain reinforcements. On our return to the area, a search failed to find the Maori raiders or the bodies of Sergeant Shannon and the Maori friendly, Wiremu Tata. I must conclude, therefore, that both these men are missing, believed killed—the sergeant's death being the result of his failure to obey my order to withdraw the picket.' "

Adam returned his gaze stonily. Sergeant Doran started to speak, but the adjutant waved him to silence.

"Mr. Edwards's view does not support this conclusion, Sergeant Shannon. He stated that you volunteered to parley with the raiders for Smith's release, were given permission to do so, and succeeded in obtaining it. The act, he says here, of a brave man, who regrettably lost his life in consequence. So—" Whelan closed the file and laid it on the table in front of him. "We are left in some doubt, aren't we? Are you insubordinate or a hero?" He smiled unexpectedly. "Major Rutherford, on the other hand, appears to have no doubt that your conduct was exemplary. He says so here, in this note. And he also suggests that you be sent to Auckland, firstly in order to give an account of the time you spent with the Maoris to General Cameron's staff. And secondly"—his smile widened—"to offer your services to a newly formed volunteer unit, the Forest Rangers, currently being recruited by a Captain Gustavus von Tempsky."

"Sir!" Adam echoed. "Sir, I—"

Whelan exchanged glances with Sergeant Doran, who hesitated and then nodded ponderously.

"Naturally, you want to stay with the regiment," Whelan went on. "But in the light of Captain Fisher's report, I cannot allow you to stay on my own authority. The colonel's in Auckland at present, Shannon, with three companies of our fellows . . . and Captain Fisher is also there. I'll send you to Auckland with B Company tomorrow, and we shall leave it to the colonel to decide what's to be done with you. I'll send this file and Major Rutherford's note with you. And—" He lowered his voice. "Look, Shannon, we all know more or less who you are now—Fisher's talked very freely about you. You're capable of better things than serving in the ranks with us, and . . . we're about to embark on a major offensive into the Waikato country. If you can obtain a transfer to a volunteer unit, they'd almost certainly give you a commission. Provided the colonel is willing to let you go, I'd take it, man! It could be your chance."

And perhaps it could, Adam thought; but he was conscious of regret. Leaving the regiment, when he had risked so much to rejoin his comrades, would be a wrench, he knew, but . . . He looked across at Doran and saw that the old sergeant was grinning and nodding at him. Doran, evidently, agreed with the adjutant, and . . . perhaps this might prove to be the chance he had wanted so much. The chance to redeem himself, to live down and, God help him, to forget the stigma of his court-martial and his father's futile anger at its outcome.

He drew himself up and saluted. "Very good, sir."

"Right, then," Whelan acknowledged. He held out his hand. "Good luck, Sergeant Shannon. Don't celebrate your return *too* enthusiastically, will you—B Company's marching out at crack of dawn tomorrow."

"Thank you, sir," Adam acknowledged.

Doran followed him out, still grinning. Out of earshot of the orderly room, he grasped Adam's arm.

"Sar'nts' mess is over to your right, lad. An' I don't know what Mr. Whelan was on about, but I'll tell you this—we're going to celebrate, that's for sure. If you've a thick head in the mornin', that's too bad. After all, 'tain't often a man comes back from the dead, is it? But I'm powerful glad you did, Shannon. Though that rotten bastard Fisher did his best ter queer your pitch, for all he thought you was killed. 'Twas lucky young Mr. Edwards spoke up for you—an' Burnaby, too, come to that. Otherwise I'd be escortin' you to the bloody guardhouse, not the sar'nts' mess, an' you'd be answerin' charges, 'stead o' celebratin'.' "

Undoubtedly, Adam thought soberly, as he had told Wiremu when they had reached the safety of the Queen's Redoubt, he had been lucky. And he would celebrate his good luck with Doran and the rest . . . to hell with having a thick head in the morning!

He considered the charges he might have faced, if Marcus Fisher had had his way—insubordination, failure to obey the orders of a superior officer, and—yes, damn it!—six months absence without leave. He would have been reduced to the ranks and . . . He tensed, as a sudden doubt assailed him.

Fisher had reported him "missing, believed killed," his death held to be the result of his failure to obey the order to withdraw the picket. But if Fisher had *really* believed him killed, why had he put in such a report? On the face of it, he could have been motivated by malice, but . . . *had* malice been his motive? Would not Drummer Smith have told him that Te Heata's raiding party had made no attempt to kill him? That they had, instead, seized and pinioned him, before letting the boy go free?

It was puzzling, and there appeared to be no logical explanation of Fisher's conduct. Although—

Doran broke into his thoughts. "Cheer up, lad," the old sergeant urged. "This is a celebration, not a bloody Irish wake!" He gestured to the door of a low wooden hut, which bore the legend SERGEANTS' MESS in chalk on a paper tacked to it. "You're home, Shannon me son—home with your own folk! An' there'll not be a man in there who won't be proud ter stand you a pint! Includin' meself!"

He pushed Adam through the door in front of him and shouted, in a stentorian voice, "Look who's here, boys! Adam Shannon's back from the dead!"

There were gasps of astonishment, and then the other sergeants crowded round him, wringing his hand, calling his name, slapping him on the back and thrusting drinks into his hand, as they pleaded for explanations and demanded to be told where he had been.

Once again, the story had to be told; but with a glass in his hand and beaming faces surrounding him, it came easier this time.

Doran was right, he thought, able at last to relax. He was, for however short a while, at home with his own folk, and the faces of Te Mata Atia, Te Heata, Keri, and the others, started to fade from his memory as if they had never been. . . .

* * *

Emily Carmichael rummaged through her sewing box and found the yellowed newspaper cutting she kept hidden at the bottom. She was alone in the sitting room; her mother was upstairs, not feeling very well today, and her father had not yet returned from court. Emily knew it was pointless to keep reading and rereading the miserable little scrap of paper—she ought long since to have thrown it away—but she could not bear to discard this final link with one of the finest persons she had ever known.

It was an old casualty list—six months old, from the *Sydney Morning Herald.* Her father had endeavored to conceal it from her, and she still remembered the look on his face, when he had come home from court that day. Something had upset him, and he had been trying not to let it show. He had been especially hearty and convivial in her presence, but Emily knew her father well, and knew that something terrible had happened. Later she had gone through the newspaper he always brought home with him, searching for news of the war in New Zealand, and found a page missing, and understood immediately that it had something to do with her —something he did not wish her to see. Her father always tried to hide the accounts of the worst battles from her—the battles in which Adam Shannon might have taken part.

But it was a pointless little deception; the servants shared their own copy of the *Herald,* which they passed down the ranks and finally discarded, and Emily retrieved it the next day from the dustbin.

Now, in the empty sitting room, she swiftly scanned the old casualty list until her eye came to the place where it always stopped—the entry that would not go away no matter how often she looked at it.

Shannon, Sergeant Adam. Missing, believed killed.

There was nothing more, no hint of what might have happened to him, and . . . A tear dripped slowly down Emily's nose, and, hearing her father's footsteps in the foyer, she hastily buried the newspaper cutting in her sewing box and wiped away the tear.

"Emily, I—" Judge Carmichael came into the sitting room, his folded newspaper in his hand, and stopped as he saw her. "Is something wrong, my dear?"

"No, nothing, Papa," she responded, attempting a smile.

He was bursting with news of some kind, she saw. He pulled up a small chair and sat opposite her, his face showing the effort of framing what he was about to say.

"Emily, my dear . . . perhaps it isn't wise to tell you this, but it's an extraordinary piece of news, and it will be on everyone's lips tomorrow, and—oh, blast, I think it will make you happy!"

Puzzled, Emily waited for further disclosure. After a moment, her father worked himself up to continue. "Emily, I did not tell you at the time, but some months ago, Adam Shannon, of whom, I know, you are fond, was reported as missing in action. . . ."

"Yes, Papa, I know," she said quietly.

"You *know?*" he exclaimed, his face falling. An expression of deep concern came over his wrinkled features, and he took both of her hands in his. "You've known all along, haven't you? Oh, my poor darling."

Emily said nothing. Oh, why had those words slipped out, she thought miserably. Now she had given her father pain, he who was the kindest man in the world, and whose intentions had been the best—as if her own pain were not enough.

But he was smiling now. "Well, I have good news, my dear. Adam's been found, and he's all right. It's an amazing story—he was a prisoner of the Maoris, living among them all this time, and he escaped. Bearing vital military information, I might add. Those are the bare bones of the story—Adam's been very reticent as far as the journalists are concerned—but it's splendid news, and I thought you'd want to know."

Emily sat there, stunned. Then she flung her arms around her father's neck and sobbed.

"It's all right, my child, it's all right," he comforted her.

When she had collected herself, her father said hesitantly, "Emily, my dear, I know that Mr. Shannon cares for you, but he is a honorable man, and he sees no future for himself and you, and—"

"I know, Papa," she said, smiling through the released tears. "Adam does not wish to encourage me, and I understand that. It is enough to know that he is alive."

Auckland was full of troops: imperial regiments, still in the immaculate scarlet that denoted new arrivals; old hands and the various volunteer and militia units in sober dark blue; seamen and royal marines from the frigates in the harbor—all were much in evidence, and everywhere the talk was of war.

Caroline hated it. She had suffered agonies of seasickness during a rough passage and had taken a strong dislike to most of her fellow passengers—in particular to Lady Kitty Broome, who had displayed little sympathy with her suffering and who, it seemed, was a privileged passenger, on Christian-name terms with the *Dolphin*'s owner and captain, Claus Van Buren.

And Lady Kitty's husband, tall and bearded and in militia uniform, had met the ship and borne her off in style, after being entertained in the captain's cabin; while Leonard had sent one of his sergeants, with a note, pleading a staff meeting to explain his absence, and a soldier with a handcart had been detailed to take her baggage from the quay to her quarters.

Caroline sighed in exasperation. That had taken hours, the baggage being sent ashore by oared boat, and the sergeant had vanished, with soldier and handcart, as soon as he had delivered her to the small, drab house in which, apparently, Leonard expected her to live.

There was Milly, of course; thank heaven she had insisted on retaining Milly's services! The girl was stupid, and she spoiled little Jon appallingly, but at all events she was devoted to both children and could be relied on to keep them quiet and out of the way.

Leonard had engaged a married couple as cook and manservant. Would-be settlers, deprived of their expected land grant, they had been driven to offer themselves as domestic servants, in order to keep a roof over their heads. . . . Caroline sighed again. Both were completely unversed in their duties—young, bucolic, and willing enough, but clumsy and possessed of even less intelligence than Milly. The woman, who called herself Eliza, was quite a good, plain cook, but she had not the faintest idea of how to serve meals or even to prepare a tea tray, and her husband was dirty and as heavily bearded as John Broome. He had wanted to volunteer for military service, but a pronounced limp and, he had told her sullenly, bad eyesight had caused the recruiting sergeant to reject him as unsuitable.

And as for the house . . . Caroline looked about her with despairing eyes. They had had such a lovely house in Sydney, with a large, rambling garden and a beautiful view; but this dark, decaying hovel—there was no other word for it—standing in a street of similar dwellings was—oh, it was impossible! The furniture was old-fashioned and strictly utilitarian, battered and ill cared for, even dirty. Leonard had purchased it lock, stock, and barrel from the previous tenant, who apparently hailed from the Scottish Highlands and had fathered a dozen destructive and uncontrolled children.

Feeling the tears well up, Caroline rose from her chair—the only comfortable chair in the whole house—and, dabbing at her eyes, crossed to the window, which, like everything else, was smeared and filthy from months, if not years, of neglect.

Outside it was raining in a steady downpour, leaving a succession of puddles on the front path and reducing the road to squelching mud, crisscrossed by the tracks of the innumerable wagons, carriages, and handcarts that came up in an endless procession from the docks. A new regiment had arrived, the uncouth Tom Minter had told her, but Caroline had not bothered to ascertain which or even to ask whence it had come.

Auckland was an awful place, she thought miserably, for all the beauty of its surroundings, and she wished that she had never left Sydney. True, she had not liked Sydney initially and had found its inhabitants a trifle proletarian; but it had grown on her, and she had enjoyed mingling with the Government House set and dining with Their Excellencies. And . . . She stared out unhappily at the teeming rain. She had improved the house, done wonders with the garden—even Leonard agreed that she had—and, although with difficulty, she had contrived to train their Australian servants into some semblance of efficiency.

Now she would have to begin all over again, with the whole of Auckland obsessed with the imminent prospect of war, and Leonard, back with his regiment, no longer holding a privileged government appointment and, indeed, almost cetainly to be ordered into action in some area of the country they called the Waikato.

There was no entertaining to speak of here; the governor had no wife, and in any case he appeared to spend the bulk of his time on peace missions or with the troops in the field. She had been here for over three weeks now, Caroline reflected moodily, and she had received only three invitations, two of these to female tea parties. And she had never met the governor or, come to that, General Cameron, who was also completely taken up by the impending hostilities.

Why, oh, why had Leonard insisted that she must accompany him? And with the children, too! Why had she given in to him? Why had she listened? He would go away to the war, and she would be left alone in Auckland, knowing no one, in this awful little house. Perhaps it had been a mistake not to have tried to make friends with Lady Kitty Broome during the passage, but . . . oh, heavens, she had been too ill, too weak to make the effort, and Lady Kitty had offered little encouragement to her, on the few occasions when she had felt well enough to dine in the saloon.

But she would know people; she had lived here before and would have a wide circle of acquaintances—civilians, no doubt, government officials and politicians, who would not be required to do battle with the Maoris. She—

There was a stir outside, the hall door opened, and Leonard came in, followed by the bucolic Tom, who was trying ineptly to relieve him of his rain-sodden cloak.

Stamping his booted feet to rid them of moisture, her husband said, "I've only twenty minutes, Caroline. Is lunch ready?"

She had no idea, Caroline realized with annoyance. He was early; usually they lunched at one or one-thirty, and although she had given precise instructions to Eliza, she could not be certain that the woman had done all she had asked.

"I'll go and see," she answered, hiding her irritation. "But you are early, Leonard. Why not have a word with Jon, whilst you are waiting?"

Her husband went in search of Jon—but with his pocket watch in his hand—and Caroline hurried to the kitchen. To her pleased surprise, Eliza had started to dish up the meal; the table was laid, after a fashion, and it needed no more than a few swift adjustments before she was able to call out that luncheon was served.

Leonard brought Jon down with him, the boy, as usual, noisily proclaiming his delight and begging his stepfather to stay and play with him after they had eaten.

"I'm sorry, Jon, but I cannot. The army needs me more than you do this afternoon, boy." He sounded genuinely sorry, Caroline thought, and observing that Jon was about to burst into tears, she bustled him off, sharply bidding him to find Milly and take his luncheon with her.

"You needn't be so abrupt with the little fellow, Caroline," Leonard protested. "He's surely old enough now to take his luncheon with us, and I think he should. He needs to learn proper table manners."

But, to Caroline's relief, he did not insist. Time was evidently pressing; he kept the watch on the table in front of him and ate quickly, scarcely noticing what he was eating.

"We're launching an offensive against the Waikato tribes at last," Leonard said, his mouth full. "You won't understand the tactics, my dear, so I will not go into the finer points. But we've sent a force across the Mangatawhiri and another across the Waikato River itself at Tuakau, where they're to build a redoubt on high cliffs dominating the river. I shall be leaving with the main column tomorrow, under the general's command, so you need not expect to see me for a while. Headquarters will be at the Queen's Redoubt, beyond Drury, but—" As Caroline stared uncomprehendingly, he moved saltcellars and cutlery into positions on the table, endeavoring to indicate the objectives, all the while reeling off outlandish names that meant nothing to her.

The Koheroa Hills, along the Waikato River to Whagamarino, a rebel *pa* at Mere Mere . . . she listened, taking little of it in, but not interrupting, and trying to smile encouragement.

Finally her husband drained his coffee cup and rose, pocketing his watch.

"My kit is packed—I'll send a man to pick it up during the afternoon. Take care of yourself, my dear, and bid Jon good-bye for me, will you? I don't want to upset him. Now I must go—we've a staff conference in twenty minutes." He dropped a light kiss on her cheek, and then he was gone, calling to the servant Tom to bring his cape.

Feeling curiously drained of emotion, Caroline went to the door to see him off, tearless but frightened. She had known it was coming, had known that Leonard would have to go, but . . . it had come so suddenly. Or perhaps she had let the warning signs pass by unnoticed.

It was still raining, not quite as heavily as it had been earlier, and she stood back in the open doorway to keep from getting wet as she watched her husband stride away, his cape swinging behind him. He was almost out of sight when she heard Milly frantically calling from the kitchen, and Jon dashed past her, head down and arms clenched at his sides, sobbing his heart out.

"Papa—Papa's gone to war, an' he never said good-bye to me!" the little boy flung at her, eluding Caroline's attempts to stop him. He was out on the muddy road before she had regained her scattered wits sufficiently to go in pursuit of him, but gathering up her skirts in both hands, she ran after him. For his age, Jon could show a fair turn of speed over a short distance, and he would have escaped had not an officer emerged from a house farther down the road and, hearing her shouts, stepped ahead of the fugitive and deftly caught him up in his arms.

"Yours, ma'am?" he asked pleasantly when Caroline drew level with him. He was a slender, nattily tailored young man, not much taller than Caroline herself, with ginger side-whiskers and a rather overcultivated cavalry mustache.

In some confusion, she thanked him, but he made no move to return little Jon to her. He was staring, deliberately it seemed, at her bosom in a way she would have found offensive had she not been flustered and at a disadvantage. His eyes found her face and rested there insolently, and, to her exasperation, she knew that she was reddening.

Jon, overawed by the presence of a stranger, had ceased crying. "There, little chap," the officer said with perfect self-possession, "go to your mama." He raised his hand to his cap in negligent salute and with a little, half-mocking bow, said, "Captain Marcus Fisher of the Fortieth, at your service."

Through the discomfiture he had inspired, Caroline felt a not unpleasant warmth. "He . . . wanted to bid his papa farewell," she managed. "I . . . Colonel Forsyth of the Seventeeth." She had gained control of herself and the situation, she thought, and would soon put this upstart captain in his place.

"Ah, yes, quite. The Seventieth are moving out to the Waikato on the offensive tomorrow morning. And your husband with them, Mrs. Forsyth—that's so, is it not?"

Caroline returned his gaze calmly; he was not at all unsettled at being confronted with a colonel's wife. She recognized the type, she thought: poodle-fakers, Leonard called them—the sort of unattached young officer who hovered about other men's wives like flies around sugar water, waiting their chance. They were always available to escort a post's grass widows to teas, tennis, and theatricals when their husbands were called away on duty, offering a nominally respectable form of distraction, though women who were seen too much in their company were frowned upon. Of course, one could always be discreet. . . .

She looked at Captain Fisher with new interest. He had not actually done or said anything incorrect. It was perfectly proper to respond in kind. "Yes," she said, "he is. Will you be joining the offensive, Captain Fisher?"

"I'm afraid not." He laughed. "I have a scandalously cushy little staff job that will keep me here in Auckland for the foreseeable future. That is the way of the army, isn't it, Mrs. Forsyth—to send married officers off for weeks or months at a time, leaving lonely wives to pine for them, while unattached officers like myself, who are free as birds, are left behind. It is an arrangement that makes no sense at all, don't you agree?"

Her pulses quickened. It would be a little, innocent flirtation, she decided. Auckland was so dreary, and she would be lonely in the days to come without Leonard, without friends. A mild dalliance, stopping short of anything serious, would add piquancy to her life.

It could do no harm, if she were prudent. Of course, there were the servants to consider, and the children—Jon was old enough to talk—and that tedious little Mrs. Macandrew, the adjutant's wife, who persisted in calling almost every other day, ostensibly to offer help, but who, Caroline was sure, carried gossip back to her dismal circle of other officers' wives. There was the case of that major's wife, whose reputation had been irrevocably ruined by idle talk . . . Caroline bit her lip, a trifle nervously. But such catastrophes were the result of stupidity and carelessness; nothing of the sort could happen to *her!*

Fisher sensed the swing in her mood and pressed his advantage. "You live in this road, I take it?" He did not wait for her answer. "But of course you do—it's that house on the corner. I saw you standing by the door."

"Yes," she confirmed, feigning reluctance. Jon tugged at her hand, urging her back to the house now that he had had his little adventure. Caroline tried to frame the words that would admonish Fisher to caution.

But warnings were unnecessary. "I'll walk you back to the house, shall I?" he said. "And . . . tomorrow evening, when the troops have gone, I trust you will be at home if I call on you?"

Caroline took the proffered arm. She could send Tom and Eliza out, she thought—they would be glad enough to go. And she would put the children to bed early.

"I shall be at home, Captain Fisher," she answered softly.

Johnny Broome lay with his wife in his arms, her head resting on his shoulder, and as he listened to her regular breathing and looked down at her sleeping face, he thought that he had never experienced so much happiness as he had during the past few hours.

They had had Patrick and two other officers—both, like Kitty's brother, so-called military settlers—to dinner. Big, cheerful men, they had been recruited from the Australian gold diggings, and it had been evident that Patrick was on the best of terms with them. One was Irish—Nick O'Hagan—and he and Patrick had regaled them with crazy Irish stories, told in exaggerated brogue and with much laughter, and Kitty had loved every minute of it, Johnny recalled, gently teasing him and the other military settler—a Scot —for their failure to appreciate Irish humor.

They were all under orders to move out next day, his squadron of Volunteer Horse given the unenviable task, Johnny thought wryly, of wet-nursing the military settlers, who as yet had no experience of bush fighting, wherever else they had done battle. True, they had trained hard since their arrival in Auckland; they had listened attentively to lectures on the terrain and Maori fighting tactics, and had been shown models of the enemy's ingeniously constructed *pas,* but . . . He smothered a sigh.

They still had a lot to learn, and Johnny found himself praying that Patrick would survive his first lesson. Her twin brother meant so much to Kitty. In Patrick's company, she was a different person —gay, lighthearted, and warmly affectionate. Since her return to Auckland, she had been affectionate to him, and he had gloried in it, more in love with her than he had ever been. She had shared his bed; they had made love joyously, and he had begun to feel that, for all his doubts and fears, their marriage was now on a firm basis, not easily to be broken or thrust into the background of Kitty's thoughts.

She had not asked about Sean O'Hara, but instead had encouraged him to talk of *his* doings during the months of separation, and not only when Pat was there, but also when they were alone together. And she had seemed both interested and concerned in how he had acquitted himself, how he had felt when he had gone into action.

Feeling her move, Johnny let his arm go slack, not wanting to waken her.

They had had Red and some of his officers to dine and had, in turn, dined on board his strange-looking command, the *Mercia,* which was preparing to take troops up the Waikato River, in support of General Cameron's main body. A naval brigade had been formed, with seamen and marines from the four frigates now in port; and in addition to the *Mercia,* two other light-draft steamers, *Avon* and *Pioneer,* had arrived and taken on naval crews. *Mercia* and *Pioneer* were protected by armor, and between them they could transport six hundred troops in almost complete safety, so far as fire from the riverbanks was concerned.

It would be war in earnest, Johnny thought. The governor had the imperial regiments and the naval vessels he had begged for, and men were flocking to join the militia and volunteer units, anxious to make an end to the Maoris' murderous raids on the farms—

Once again Kitty stirred, coming closer to him in her sleep, and with her movement his own desire was awakened. She could rouse him as no other woman ever had, and his hand went out, to caress her breasts and then to move gently but insistently about her thighs. He sought for her lips with his own, murmuring her name as he kissed her with swiftly kindled passion, forgetting his earlier determination not to disturb her sleep.

She was so beautiful, so pliant, and . . . she was his wife, and he loved her. And he was going to war in a few short hours.

"Kit," he whispered. "Darling Kit! God forgive me, but I want you so!"

Kitty wakened and pulled away, regarding him with sleep-filled, reproachful eyes.

"Johnny, please . . . I'm tired. We had such a late night. I—I want to sleep."

Johnny released her instantly, all desire fading as if it had never been.

"All right, darling," he said gruffly, and turned his back toward her, hiding his chagrin. Silence fell between them, and then Kitty sat up, propping herself on her elbows and looking down at him.

"Johnny," she pleaded. "Johnny, you will bring Pat safely back, won't you? He—he should never have joined the military settlers, and he must have told a host of tall stories to persuade them to accept him . . . and to give him a commission, too! He doesn't know the first thing about the army. He . . . Oh, Johnny, promise me you'll look after him. If you love me, Johnny, please!"

There was a coldness about Johnny's heart as he saw and recognized the truth. Kit was his wife, but it was her brother Patrick she loved; it always had been, and, he supposed dully, it probably always would be.

He did not turn round, did not look at her as he answered flatly, "Don't worry your head about Pat, darling. I'll look after him if it's the last thing I ever do. I'll see he comes safely back to you."

Kitty was satisfied. She snuggled down into the pillows, and a

moment or two later she slept. In the faint light seeping in through
the uncurtained window, her lovely face was, Johnny saw, serene
and untroubled.

He did not touch her again, and for what remained of the night,
sleep eluded him.

Chapter XVIII

By MID-NOVEMBER 1863, Adam had seen more fighting in the five months since he had left Auckland than in the whole of his naval career. It had been savage, hand-to-hand fighting, with no quarter given or asked, with days of marching through trackless bush country and many nights spent on the bare ground, often without food or even the comfort of a campfire.

He had learned a great deal from the men of the Forest Rangers, all of them skilled bushmen, and he had conceived a warm liking, as well as a profound respect, for their commander.

Gustavus von Tempsky was a Prussian aristocrat by birth but an adventurer from personal choice, and he had a fund of fascinating tales to tell of his experiences in Mexico and the California goldfields. He was tall and handsome, with his flowing dark hair and small chin-beard, seemingly without fear and yet a devoted family man, with a pretty wife and three small children living in Auckland. He was a talented painter, author of a book on his South American travels, and an expert linguist, but his proudest boast was that as a young man he had held a commission in a famous regiment of Prussian hussars.

Adam recalled, with gratitude as well as some surprise, how von Tempsky, happening to be present when he had made his report to members of General Cameron's staff, had gone at once to the general himself to request his transfer to the Forest Rangers.

"This is the type of man I want, sir," he had told Colonel De Lancey, the general's chief of staff. "He is wasted as a sergeant in your Fortieth Foot. I shall ask the general to give him a commission, and he can then aid me in training my company for the service you require of them."

The general had made no demur, and, again to his surprise, Adam had found himself commissioned as a lieutenant in the newly formed Rangers and engaged in a training program devised by von Tempsky, calculated to produce an auxiliary force that specialized in deep patrolling and scouting and which, well armed with carbines, revolvers, and bowie knives, was capable of living frugally in rebel-infested forest, without even the glimmer of a campfire to betray its presence.

The main body, under Cameron's personal command, had soon been in action. A spirited battle, with the general in the forefront, armed only with a cane, had driven a large force of Waikato Maoris from their entrenched position on the heights of the Koheroa Hills, and they had pushed on, across the range, to erect a stockade in sight of a strong *pa* at Mere Mere, overlooking the river. The transport of guns and supplies had caused some delay after that, since there were no roads in the undeveloped terrain of the King country, and both the imperial troops and the Rangers had been constantly engaged, fighting off attacks, ambushes, and raids and going to the aid of units that had found themselves cut off.

In September, at a place called Pukekohe, Adam's own detachment had had to fight for their lives when an overwhelming number of fanatical Kingites had discovered and attacked them. But their stubborn defense and the arrival of a company of the 70th commanded by Major George Ryan had saved the day, and—Adam smiled thinly. Von Tempsky had lost his temper and bawled them out and then, in ludicrous contrast, had embraced each one of them and called them heroes.

At the beginning of October, the steamers *Mercia, Avon,* and the gunboat *Pioneer,* towing armored barges, had made their appearance, bringing supplies and reinforcements, with Commodore Wiseman and—to Adam's somewhat disconcerted surprise—Captain Red Broome in command. The general had reconnoitered in the *Pioneer,* and three weeks later an assault force had embarked in the steamers and sailed up to Mere Mere, to find the great *pa* abandoned by its garrison, which had vanished southward into inaccessible, rain-drenched country.

Now, with Mere Mere fortified by means of a strong redoubt and the raiders driven at last from the Hunua forest, and a line of blockhouses set up between the Thames and Waikato rivers to protect his supply lines, General Cameron was preparing to advance, his objective the King's capital at Ngaruawahia. Blocking his advance, however, was another formidable *pa* at Rangiriri—a name, in the Maori language, meaning "angry heavens"—twelve miles upriver and sited across an isthmus that ran from the river to Lake Waikare.

Adam, accompanied by an ex-seaman named George Hill now serving as a trooper in the Rangers, had spent all day and the previous night concealed in the swamp, observing the movements of the Maori defenders and endeavoring to assess the strength of the *pa*.

It was a formidable work, consisting of a long line of high parapets with a double ditch, the outermost twelve feet wide and at least eighteen feet deep. The center of the line was strengthened by a square redoubt, of which little could be seen either from the river or the ground in front. Adam had studied it with his glass for as long and as closely as he dared, but beyond registering that it was very expertly constructed and loopholed for musket fire, he could ascertain no more. A line of rifle pits, set at right angles to the main line, faced the river; and some five hundred yards behind the front position, the summit of a high ridge was also fortified with rifle pits.

George Hill had attempted to make sketches, but an almost continuous downpour had smudged his efforts, and finally he had desisted, cursing freely. With the need for silent vigilance, they had conversed little during their long, damp stay, but now, with the coming of night, they were on their way back to the British lines, and Hill observed suddenly, "By God, I know who you are! Bin worryin' me, it has, 'cos I couldn't place you—yet I knew I'd seen you afore."

"And where," Adam answered discouragingly, "do you imagine you saw me before?" He was cold and wet and not in the best of tempers, and the ex-seaman's unexpected claim added to his annoyance. Hill was a nice enough man, but his own past history was somewhat obscure, and there were those who suspected that he had deserted from the Royal Navy and volunteered for the Rangers in search of action and excitement.

Captain von Tempsky had apparently been satisfied, however, Adam recalled. "The only time Hill took French leave was in the Mediterranean, three years ago," von Tempsky had informed him. "He enlisted with several others in Garibaldi's army of liberation, fought with them until he was wounded, and then went back to his ship, where his desertion was overlooked—because British sympathies were wholeheartedly with Garibaldi. He'll do for us."

And perhaps he would, Adam thought a trifle sourly, as he repeated his question.

George Hill chuckled, in no way put out. "Her gracious Majesty's frigate *Shannon*, that's where, sir. I should have guessed, seein' that's the name you go by now. You was a mate, promoted acting lieutenant in the naval brigade when we relieved Lucknow durin' the Sepoy Mutiny. You was mentioned in the late Captain Peel's dispatches, and 'e recommended you for a promotion." He paused, glancing at Adam quizzically in the semidarkness. "Vincent—that's your real name, ain't it?"

What was the point in denying it? Adam shrugged. "I don't want that talked about, Hill. There are . . . well, there are reasons."

"Don't you fear, sir," Hill said reassuringly. "I'm not one to talk out o' turn. I remember you in the naval brigade and on the passage out—Singapore first, wasn't it? Then Hong Kong an' then Calcutta. I wasn't in your watch—I was a gunner. But I remember you. You was a good officer, as officers go. An' they gave you a Victoria Cross for service in the Crimea—it was presented to you and one to Mr. Daniels at our camp, after Captain Peel died. Gyah, middle of July 'fifty-eight, sir . . . I'm not wrong, am I, Mr. Vincent?"

"No," Adam conceded shortly. "You're not wrong."

Hill halted, shifting the weight of his sodden haversack from one shoulder to the other. In an unexpectedly sympathetic voice, he asked, "What happened, sir? You ain't in Her Majesty's Navy now, an' you don't wear even the medals I've got, still less the V.C. The lads—well, you know how they talk. They reckon you come to us from being a footslogger, a sergeant in the Fortieth Regiment."

"That's right, I was." Still Adam hesitated, and finally, repeating his shrug, he added bitterly, "I lost my ship, Hill, and most of her company. I was tried by court-martial and cashiered. They deemed the medals forfeited, so . . . I can't wear them. Does that satisfy you?"

"I wouldn't go so far as say I was satisfied, sir," Hill answered gruffly. "No, I couldn't. A man's awarded a medal for an act considered worthy of it, and—hell, it's *his*. No one got a right to take it away from him—not in justice, have they?"

Perhaps they hadn't, Adam thought; in any event, it was a right they had taken. He said no more, and Hill, too, lapsed into silence as they made their way back through the trees to their own camp. A change of clothing and a hasty meal followed, and then von Tempsky went with them to report their observations to the general's staff. Duncan Cameron came in person, to study Hill's smudged sketches and question them both, in minute detail, concerning what they had seen and heard.

There were others there, too, and more officers came in as the morning advanced and the plan of assault was discussed and finally agreed upon. The naval commodore, Wiseman, and his second-in-command, Red Broome, were among the first to arrive, followed shortly afterward by the infantry commanders—who included Adam's old C.O., Colonel Arthur Leslie—and then Captain Henry Mercer of the Royal Artillery, Commander Augustus Phillimore of the *Curaçao,* and Commander John Mayne of the *Eclipse,* who was to lead a naval force of ninety men. Adam was relieved when Red Broome, catching his eye across the room, merely nodded in recognition but made no attempt to approach or speak to him.

"Much will depend on your steamers bringing up Colonel Leslie's force, Commodore," the general was saying, "and landing them here"—his finger jabbed the map spread out in front of them —"in the rear of the enemy position, simultaneously with our main attack from the front. There will be a preliminary bombardment by your Armstrongs, Captain Mercer, and the naval vessels from the river." He went into precise detail, several times turning to Adam with a brusque request to refresh his memory as to the position of the Maori rifle pits. "The main body of the naval brigade—your force, Commander Phillimore—will land with the Fortieth from the steamers and armored barges. I need hardly stress again that timing is all important, gentlemen. As Mr. Shannon's observations have amply confirmed, together with mine from the river, the *pa* is a formidable obstacle. But it must be taken; and when it is, God willing, our way to the so-called Kingite capital of Ngaruawahia will be open. When we have taken that, I confidently believe that the rebellion in this area will be all but over."

He invited questions, answered a number himself, and then left Colonel De Lancey to deal with any remaining details.

"Tomorrow morning, gentlemen," the general said on leaving. "And may God preserve you all!"

Most of the officers stayed behind, to put more questions to Adam and to examine Hill's sketches; then the conference began breaking up. As the officers filed outside—Red Broome among them—Colonel Leslie laid a friendly hand on Adam's arm.

"Well done, Shannon," he offered. "You seem to have found the right *milieu* for your undoubted talents. Von Tempsky speaks highly of you." He smiled. "Feel free to pay a call on your old comrades whenever you wish. They will, I know, be pleased to see you." He nodded pleasantly and strode off.

Commodore Wiseman was one of the last to leave, and Adam heard him say to his companions, "May God give us a clear passage upriver, gentlemen, with no adverse wind and a slow current. Granted these, we shall be able to observe the general's timing."

That afternoon, Adam asked for and was granted permission to visit his old comrades of the 40th, whom he found in good heart, preparing to evacuate their bivouac and board the armored steamers in readiness for the next day's assault. Doran gave him an impeccable salute and addressed him as "sir" and "Mr. Shannon," only a fugitive grin betraying his pleasure in the reversal of their roles. Alone together and sharing his beer ration, however, the old sergeant unbent.

"That bastard Fisher's been sent back to us," he announced, wiping the froth from his mustache with the back of his hand and his smile fading. "Pity—we were doing pretty well without him."

"When did he come back?" Adam asked.

"Couple o' days ago. And he was actin' like the cat that swallowed the cream—been having it off with some lonely grass widow woman in Auckland, I shouldn't wonder." Doran drained his beer mug and bent forward to replenish it. "They should've kept the swine there. As it is, he's been appointed to my company, and he's been throwing his blasted weight about, like he always does." In a fair imitation of Fisher's exaggerated drawl, he went on, "And what, may I ask, is *this* meant to be, Sergeant Doran? A man's kit, you say? God Almighty, it looks uncommonly like the proverbial pig's breakfast! Put him on a charge."

Adam laughed. "You have him to a tee, Doran. Thanks be I've managed to avoid him so far."

"Give the bastard a wide berth tomorrow," Doran warned. "You know what he's like when there's fighting to be done. Luckily for us, we've the colonel in command of our lot in the *Pioneer*. And a half-colonel of the Seventieth, a staff wallah named Forsyth, as second-in-command. A good bloke, they tell me. D'you know him?"

Adam shook his head. Gratefully, he accepted another beer, which Doran had somehow managed to cool.

"The only Seventieth officer I've met recently is a major named Ryan, who is now on General Cameron's staff. He is a splendid fellow—he saved our lives when some of us were cut off at a place called Pukekohe. He told me that he had spent nearly two years in Otago, in South Island, keeping the pace between rival gold diggers. Odd to think that all they bother about is digging for gold and running sheep, whilst here we're engaged in a full-scale war. Ryan said that the population of Otago and Dunedin doubled within a year, and some of the people there resent having to pay taxes to finance our war. Before he left, they were even demanding secession!"

Doran grunted his disapproval. "They ain't got the number o' Maoris we've got here—that's the long an' short of it, Shannon. And most o' the diggers are from Australia, anyway, ain't they? A bunch of lawless rogues, in my opinion, and few of 'em native-born. Well—" He set down his mug and rose reluctantly to his feet. "I'll need to go to me lads now, *Mr.* Shannon, just in case that bastard Fisher's on the prowl." He held out a gnarled hand. "Glad I seen you. We'll have a few more beers after we take that *pa,* eh? God go with you, son."

"And with you, Sergeant Doran." Adam wrung the old man's hand. "Watch yourself tomorrow. That *pa* is going to be a tough nut to crack."

He was on his way out of the 40th's bivouac when a man's voice hailed him by name and he turned to recognize Captain Broome. After the general's lengthy conference, Red Broome had made no attempt to contact him, and Adam had been grateful, both for the man's restraint and the brief smile he had given him.

Now there was a tall, red-bearded officer with him, whom Adam remembered as the commander of one of the squadrons of Volunteer Horse that had patrolled the new South Road, and . . . Yes, of course, he must be Red Broome's brother, since there was a strong likeness between them. The *Mercia's* captain confirmed his supposition.

"My brother John Broome—recently promoted to a captaincy in the Volunteer Horse. Adam Shannon of the Forest Rangers. How are you, Adam?" He held out his hand. "It's good to see you again."

"And you, sir," Adam acknowledged. He bowed to John

Broome, who, to his surprise, produced a crumpled envelope, which he passed to Adam, his bearded lips parted in an amused smile.

"A letter from a young lady in Sydney, Shannon, entrusted to my wife for delivery to you, and then given to me because the Fortieth told her you had left the regiment and transferred to the Forest Rangers."

"Thank you very much, sir," Adam said. He glanced at the writing on the envelope, realized that it was Emily Carmichael's, and, pleased to think that she had remembered him, thrust the letter into his breast pocket. "Your wife's here, is she, sir?"

"In Auckland," John Broome confirmed. He hesitated, glancing at his brother, but Red waved him to continue, and he said, his smile vanishing, "I wasn't at this morning's conference—too high-powered for the likes of me—but I gather from Red that you were the one who did the reconnaissance of this infernal *pa*, and you appeared to think it's liable to be a tough one?"

"I'm afraid it is, yes." With the toe of his boot, Adam traced the outline of the Rangiriri *pa* in the sandy ground, pointing out its rifle pits and ditches. "They've designed it very well, and it's evident that they intend to defend it in strength. But this central redoubt is what worries me, Captain Broome. I could not obtain a proper view of it, either from the river or the ground in front—and I tried, believe me." He gave an account of what he had observed and again saw the brothers exchange glances. Both asked questions, to which he replied as well as he could, and John Broome said resignedly, "It looks as if much is going to depend on your steamers getting into position early on, Red."

"We'll be there, if the current lets us," Red returned crisply. "The *Pioneer*'s taking three hundred men of the Fortieth, and I've two companies of the Sixty-fifth . . . damme, Johnny, I *know* how much depends on us! But the preliminary bombardment ought to soften their defenses considerably. Well—" He smiled from one to the other of them, put an arm briefly round his brother's shoulders, and then, pleading work to be done, took his leave.

John Broome, walking back to the Rangers' bivouac at Adam's side, talked of the war generally and, halting suddenly, slapped his thigh with a big hand, as if remembering something.

"Lord!" he exclaimed. "I know who you are! It's been chasing round in my head, because I knew I'd heard of you." Adam opened his mouth to speak, dismayed, and then closed it again when Broome went on, with a dry chuckle, "Of course—you are the fellow the Maoris captured at the Queen's Redoubt. Sergeant Shannon of Her Majesty's Fortieth, who lived to tell the tale, after being given up for dead! That's right, isn't it—it was you?"

"Yes," Adam admitted. "It was, sir. But I—"

John Broome put in quickly, "Look, Shannon—I used to be a journalist, and I still file pieces for my old paper. I think your story is worth telling. I'll make a bargain with you. If we both come through tomorrow's attack, tell me about it, will you, and let me write it?"

He would not understand, Adam thought, but . . . he had to refuse. He did not want his name in the newspapers, did not want to be singled out. All too easily it could get back to England, to his father, to the rest of his family, and . . .

"Think about it, man," Broome urged, evidently sensing his reluctance. "I'd let you see what I'd written before sending it in, naturally."

"I'm sorry, sir," Adam said awkwardly. "I have to say no. I . . ." He remembered Red Broome, and the tension drained out of him. "Ask your brother, if you will. He'll tell you about me, in confidence, if you ask him. I do have a very good reason for my refusal, sir, I promise you."

George Hill knew his real name, Adam reflected despondently; so did Marcus Fisher, and heaven knew who else besides. It had been a mistake to call himself Shannon, but he had made the choice hurriedly, without thinking, giving the first name that came into his head.

John Broome was looking at him oddly, but shrugged and said, without rancor, "Obviously you know best, Shannon. I'll have a word with my brother." He nodded, affably enough, and continued on his way.

It was nightfall when Adam found time to read his letter. It was disappointingly short and impersonal, and evidently had been written before his capture.

Dear Adam,

I have given this letter to Lady Kitty Broome, who is leaving for Auckland in a few days on board a ship called the *Dolphin*. She said she would try to ensure that it is delivered to you, wherever you are.

Also taking passage in the *Dolphin* are Mrs. Forsyth, with

her children—the dear little boy I told you about, called Jon, and a baby girl, with their nursemaid.

Lady Kitty's husband, Mr. John Broome, is serving in the New Zealand Volunteers, and his brother, who is a naval captain everybody calls Red, is going out in command of a strange-looking paddle steamer, the *Mercia*. I have watched them set sail from Sydney this afternoon, with some Australian volunteers, including Lady Kitty's brother and Colonel Forsyth of the 70th Regiment, who, as I told you in a letter you may not have received, is Caroline Forsyth's husband.

I thought you would wish to know of her impending arrival.

Wishing you well, as always.

The signature was simply "Emily."

A warning, Adam reflected wryly—poor child, Emily had felt that she must give him warning of Caroline's coming! He had not spared Caroline a thought for—good Lord, for a very long time—months, in fact. And . . . Adam closed his eyes, trying to remember her face, her smile; but his memory was blank, and he could recall only the harsh mockery in her voice on the last occasion they had met. That had been at a Portsmouth inn, and he had broken arrest in order to go to her. Broken arrest and been charged with having done so . . .

"Shannon—I want to see your Mr. Shannon, man! Take me to him."

It was impossible to mistake that imperious, drawling voice for any other, and returning Emily's letter to his pocket, Adam reluctantly stood up. His jacket unbuttoned, he went to the door of the hut he shared with two other Rangers officers, to see Marcus Fisher striding impatiently toward him, accompanied by a soldier with a storm lantern.

"I'm here, Captain Fisher," he said, with noticeable lack of enthusiasm. "How can I serve you?"

Fisher came in. Looking about him curiously, he observed, "Lord, but you do yourselves proud, you bloody Volunteers! This is a palace. I'm in a damned leaking tent with four others, and the infernal thing's pitched on the side of a hill!"

"We built it ourselves," Adam pointed out mildly. He gestured to one of the unoccupied bed spaces. "Sit down, if you wish, sir. My companions are on duty."

"No, thanks." Fisher remained standing, continuing to study the interior of the hut with narrowed eyes. "Split logs and, damme, a shingle roof! Better than the sergeants' mess, eh, Shannon?"

Recalling what Sergeant Doran had said concerning Fisher's probable doings in Auckland, Adam suppressed a smile. *Having it off with some lonely grass widow woman in Auckland,* Doran had suggested. Well, perhaps he had been doing just that. Certainly Marcus Fisher had put on weight, and . . . yes, there was something oddly smug about him, a gleam in the slate-blue eyes that Adam did not remember seeing there in the past.

"How can I serve you, Captain Fisher?" he repeated. "Presumably you have a reason for seeking me out?"

"Oh, yes," Fisher confirmed. "Tomorrow's an imperial show, as you'll have gathered. You militia boys will just have to mop up. But there's been a change in orders. My company is to support the main body's assault and the ladder party, instead of embarking with the colonel in one of the steamers." He paused, eyes again narrowed. "I obtained the colonel's permission for you to accompany us—that's if you wish to, of course. But damme, a firebrand like you, I imagine you'll jump at it, won't you? Incidentally, Sergeant—I mean *Mr.* Shannon—your C.O., von Tempsky, raised no objection when I asked if we might borrow you."

He had been placed in a position from which there was no retreat, Adam realized, and as he accepted the offer, he found himself wondering why Fisher had troubled to make it.

"Good," the other said, with almost fulsome approval. "You'll be useful as a guide, if nothing else. I gathered from Colonel Forsyth that you know the ground and the—er—general layout of the *pa*. That's so, isn't it?"

"I made the recce," Adam admitted. "But—" He broke off. Fisher had mentioned the name Forsyth—Colonel Forsyth—and he was—good God, of course, he was Caroline's husband! Was *that* the point? Surely it could not be, for how could Marcus Fisher know anything about Caroline? Unless . . . He recalled what Emily had said in her letter concerning Caroline's arrival in Auckland, and then, suddenly sickened, he remembered Doran's words.

"I've seen a fair bit of Mrs. Forsyth whilst I've been in Auckland," Fisher interrupted his thoughts. "*Caroline* Forsyth," he added, with heavy emphasis. "She has been most kind. Indeed, she has entertained me with immense generosity. I was vexed at having to leave her. You do know, of course, to whom I'm referring, don't you, Shannon? She was John Omerod's widow—the poor fellow you managed to drown, with, I believe, over a hundred others. Oh, yes, I know the whole miserable story now—Caroline told me. And I know who you are." He was openly scornful, delighted with what he clearly saw as his personal triumph. "And, *Mr.* Vincent, Caroline does not ever wish to set eyes on you again. She charged me to tell you so."

Adam, unable to find words to answer him, curbed his burning desire to strike him and managed to say, very stiffly, "Sir!"

It was evidently not the response Marcus Fisher had expected. He hesitated, looking disappointed, and then, recovering himself, he said sharply, "That's all, then—so long as you understand. See you in the morning. We're parading at first light."

"Sir," Adam responded woodenly. "Very good, sir."

The new day dawned damp and chill, and at first light, as the assault force ate a meager breakfast and prepared to go into action, the artillery bombardment began. Captain Mercer's two twelve-pounder Armstrong guns, well served and admirably sited, poured a withering fire into the Maori *pa*, evoking little response from the defenders and doing little visible damage to the strong timbers of the palisade.

It was difficult to see clearly through the smoke and the pouring rain, but after a while Adam realized that Commodore Wiseman's prayer had not been answered—the two steamers and the barges they were towing were being delayed by wind and current from reaching the position the general had selected, to the rear of the *pa*. Both ships opened fire at a distance, and the naval six-pounder on shore did the same, but the range was overlong and the fire largely ineffective. Nevertheless, the assault force, led by a storming party of the 65th, advanced along the right bank of the Waikato River, the ladder party on their heels, the detachments of the 12th and 14th Regiments to the left, and the two companies of the 40th and 65th coming up in support.

A tall officer, with lieutenant colonel's insignia on his tunic, who had been surveying the scene through a field glass, came to squat down at Adam's side.

"Forsyth, Seventieth," he announced, speaking loudly over the roar of gunfire. "You're Shannon, I take it?"

"Yes, sir," Adam confirmed, liking the officer's brisk, professional manner and then, his thoughts wavering for a moment, wondering how Caroline could have married such a man. Forsyth would not yield to her every whim, as poor John Omerod had done. Yet he was handsome, in a stern, masculine way, and judging by the spate of relevant questions he asked, he was also an experienced soldier, well on top of the job he was doing.

"Those bloody steamers must have reached their objective at last," Forsyth said. "Or else—" He gestured to a galloper spurring past. "Or else the general's decided not to wait for them. At least they're joining in the bombardment, which should help. But with the best will in the world, Captain Mercer's twelve-pounders aren't going to breach palisades like those, I fear. And you say the ditch is eighteen feet deep?"

"From the crest of the parapet, sir, as nearly as I could judge," Adam told him.

The colonel grunted. "Then our ladders will be too short, dammit! Ah—" The men in front were starting to move, and he jumped to his feet. "This is it, then. Come on, Shannon."

It was three in the afternoon, and, Adam learned afterward, Colonel Leslie had managed to land his force to the rear of the *pa* and, at the head of the first company, had seized and occupied the dominating ridge overlooking the main enemy redoubt.

Ahead of him, Adam could just make out the first wave of stormers of the 65th Regiment crossing the intervening six hundred yards under heavy fire and scaling the Maoris' earthen entrenchment on the left. They went on, gallantly charging up the hill, to carry the second line of rifle pits, with the 12th and 14th close behind them. Then his own detachment came under fire, and Adam attempted to direct them away from the center, but only Fisher and some half dozen of the men heard and obeyed his shouted advice. The rest went on, following Colonel Forsyth, and Adam stayed with them, finding himself unexpectedly beside Sergeant Doran, who was yelling encouragement at the top of his lungs.

The outer lines were overrun by the assault force, but now, as Adam had feared, the central redoubt held them in check. A murderous fire was inflicting heavy casualties, and every attempt by the British troops to gain a lodgment ended in failure. Again and again the men rallied and were scythed down. They jumped headlong into the ditch, but their ladders proved too short; and those who clawed their way up to the parapet were almost instantly shot down. Adam himself attempted it, with Doran and two others, and they were fortunate in that their ladder broke before they were halfway up the steep incline.

Men were falling everywhere. Adam saw Tom Burnaby clutch his leg and crash down. Sergeant Doran was wounded in the head, blood coursing down his face, but he went on loading and firing, seemingly indestructible. A party of gunners, led by their commander, Captain Mercer, and armed only with revolvers, made a brave but useless attempt to enter the redoubt, to retire with Mercer shot through the jaw and half their number killed or wounded.

Commander Mayne's party of seamen were the next to leap into the ditch and seek to scale the parapet. A handful of them reached the top and went in with cutlasses; the others, repulsed, carried out their wounded, who included Mayne, shot through the hip and moaning softly.

Adam helped them, carrying several badly injured men back to the young naval surgeon's makeshift hospital, and later, seeing a gap in the side of the redoubt, he helped lead a second naval party under Commander Phillimore to it, and for a while they lobbed grenades into the work, with little effect. The commander withdrew them, cursing horribly.

Of Fisher there was no sign, until, with dusk falling, Adam found him, crouched down out of the line of fire and sobbing with pain from an arm wound. Without a word, he jerked him to his feet, and leading him across to where most of the casualties were lying, left him, ignoring his plea for water.

It was then that he witnessed an extraordinary act of compassion by one of the Maori chiefs. The chief, whose name he learned later was Te Oriori, jumped down from the top of the parapet and, although under fire from several of the soldiers, ran across to where an officer of the 65th was lying, badly wounded, and, picking him up, carried him back across the ditch to shelter. There, kneeling beside the wounded officer, he gave him water, and, to the vengeful comrades who surrounded him, he said simply, "He is my friend. *Hickety-Pip* Regiment . . . long time do battle."

With touching gentleness, he raised the dying man so that he could see the last glow of the setting sun, and held him thus until he died. Not a man attempted to lay hands on him.

But now the bugles were sounding, and as darkness fell, the weary, dispirited assault force was ordered to lie down on the rain-soaked ground, with their arms beside them, maintaining the positions they had won at so high a cost. Adam spent most of the night assisting with the care and evacuation of the wounded and taking water to those too badly injured to be moved. Fisher had gone—presumably, since he was able to walk, he had presented no problem—but, toward dawn, when he encountered Colonel Forsyth, Adam found the 70th's officer sunk in despair.

"You were damned well right about that infernal redoubt in the center of the *pa,* Shannon," he observed with a bitterness he did not try to conceal. "That was our undoing, and it cost us most of our casualties. The C.O. of the Fourteenth, Austen, is dying, and so is poor brave Henry Mercer, I'm told. Why in God's name they sent him in with his gunners I simply cannot imagine—it was an appalling waste of men we can't replace. As nearly as I can gather, we've lost about a hundred and fifty in killed and wounded, and the damned place still defies us. I just hope that tomorrow—no, devil take it, it's today—I hope that today won't be a repetition of yesterday."

"It won't be, Colonel," Adam said, his voice suddenly unsteady. "Look, sir—they're running up a white flag! They're surrendering!"

"By heaven, so they are!" Forsyth exclaimed in astonishment. "Well, it's victory, but a bloody one. And . . . good Lord, look at our fellows! Some of them are shaking hands with the Maoris, and —damme, I think I could do the same! They put up a good fight, and they're a gallant enemy, no doubt of that. But what has caused them to surrender? Didn't they realize they had beaten us?"

"I imagine they ran out of water, sir," Adam said. "Or ammunition. Or both."

It had been a costly victory, he thought, but it was a victory. And as General Cameron had said, taking the Rangiriri *pa* opened the way to the Maori King's capital.

He went with Forsyth and Doran and many others to shake the hands of the warriors who had fought so bravely.

It was impossible to assess accurately the Maori casualties, since most of their wounded had been spirited away during the night, but over a hundred and eighty prisoners were taken, including the chivalrous chief, Te Oriori, and two hundred stands of arms.

General Cameron made a rousing speech, praising the valor of his troops and of the enemy, and when he announced that he was asking the New Zealand government to treat the prisoners well, the weary men somehow found it in them to cheer him.

*   *   *

Leaving a garrison to hold Mere Mere and the newly captured
pa, the force marched on along the banks of the Waikato River,
passing through deserted native villages and abandoned fields of
corn and sweet potato, and meeting with no opposition.

On December 9, the Union Jack was flying from King
Tawhiao's crude palace in Ngaruawahia. The troops pitched camp
in a potato field, and General Cameron soon learned that the
Kingites had withdrawn up the Waipa River, to build new *pas* and
carry on with their rebellion.

Adam spent Christmas with a party of Rangers under von
Tempsky's command, reconnoitering the country ahead, as reinforcements arrived under Colonel Sir Henry Havelock of Indian
Mutiny fame, and two more regiments landed in Auckland—the
43rd Light Infantry and the 68th a month later.

Toasting the New Year of 1864 in, Colonel Forsyth remarked
gravely, "The war goes on, Adam. I hope to God it's worth the
cost in men's lives."

Colonel De Lancey, standing just behind them, raised his glass
and observed with a hint of cynicism, "My dear fellow, of course it
is—to the settlers. Their land is being bought in blood." Unsmilingly, he added, "I know—I was once one of them. Not anymore,
though. When this war's over, I am going back to Sydney, where I
belong. And with a clear conscience."

He set down his glass, smiled briefly, and turned away. Adam
was surprised to see the glint of tears in his eyes.

Chapter XIX

MARCUS FISHER CONTRIVED, by a mixture of bluff and the exaggeration of his suffering, to obtain a transfer to the hospital in Auckland.

He was transported there with the most seriously wounded and in considerable discomfort in bullock and horse-drawn wagons, having, for the last part of his journey, the company of Captain Henry Mercer's heartbroken widow, who, heavily veiled and weeping silently, had been placed beside him.

In other circumstances, Marcus would have deemed her a charming companion, but having listened at least half a dozen times to her account of her husband's end, he would have given a great deal to have been able to share his equipage with virtually anyone else.

"Poor, darling Henry," she had sobbed. "He was shot through the jaw, you see, and he could not speak. They sent me to the Queen's Redoubt to be with him till the last, and I—oh, I was grateful, of course. And yet to witness his terrible agony was—oh, God, it will never be erased from my memory for as long as I live! When he was . . . was sinking, he was given a pencil and paper with which to write his last words. And he wrote, 'Do not grieve for me. I die contented and resigned to God's will.' Imagine it, Captain Fisher! The poor brave soul was dying, and that was what he wrote. To *me*—his thought, for all his pain, was for me. He did not want me to grieve for him, but how can I not grieve? He was so brave."

Her sad, stumbling words haunted him. Was there, Marcus asked himself, any woman in the world—save, perhaps, his mother

—who would grieve for him, as Henry Mercer's widow was grieving for her dead husband? Would Caroline?

It was true that, before he had been ordered to leave Auckland, they had given themselves to each other without reservation, he and Caroline, had made love with passionate abandon, oblivious of what Auckland society might think of them, deaf to the gossip and the malicious rumors their association inspired, and . . . he had been happy. Deliriously happy, and—yes, wildly in love.

But was Caroline? Did she feel the same as he did? She had said she did, but . . . could he, dared he believe her? Caroline was a woman of strong emotion, impulsive, infinitely exciting, but she was easily swayed and changeable. In her husband's absence, she had had no hesitation in responding to his overtures, but Marcus had seen something of Colonel Forsyth, had seen him in action and knew him for the man he was, and he knew also that Caroline went in awe of her husband. She would be wax in Forsyth's hands when the war ended and he returned to her. She might not love him, but she was certainly afraid of him, and Forsyth was not the type to tolerate infidelity, were he to find out about it or take the gossip seriously.

Marcus Fisher sighed deeply, thinking again of Henry Mercer. Why had Mercer been killed in the ghastly battle for the Rangiriri *pa,* while Leonard Forsyth had not sustained even a scratch? Vincent—Shannon or whatever the fellow called himself—was no longer a rival and could safely be discounted, but Colonel Leonard Forsyth was a very different matter. And Caroline was married to him.

An orderly brought him a luncheon tray, and he regarded it sourly. Greasy soup, already cooling; some unrecognizable stew, the meat in large, unappetizing lumps and the potatoes overcooked; a bowl of local fruit. What a meal to serve to a wounded officer, with only one hand that he could use! Scowling ill-temperedly, Marcus ate the fruit and quaffed the glass of lukewarm ale for which he himself had paid, finding no pleasure in either.

He had sent a note to Caroline the previous evening, on his arrival in the hospital. God grant she had received it and would answer it soon! What with the poor food and the still poorer ministrations of the old pensioners who acted as orderlies, he did not want to stay here for a moment longer than he had to. He pushed his tray to the foot of the bed, his shout to the orderly eliciting no response. Devil take the fellow! Why couldn't he do his job?

He lay back, fuming, and closed his eyes, praying fervently that Caroline would come. Another imperial regiment—the 43rd Light Infantry—had recently disembarked and marched out to the Otahuhu camp, one of the orderlies had told him, and the 68th was said to be on the way. It was to be hoped that Caroline knew none of the officers, and—damn it to hell, why did she not reply to his note? She—

"Well, now—Captain Fisher, I believe?" The voice was polite but faintly derisive, and Marcus Fisher opened his eyes to find a small, bewhiskered surgeon in a long white coat looking down at him. The coat was heavily stained and crumpled, and a number of threaded surgical needles of different sizes were pinned seemingly at random into the front of it. The old orderly, galvanized into a show of activity, offered a sheaf of papers to him, with an obsequious "The reports, Major, sir."

The little surgeon took them, gestured to the tray with a sharp "Take that away at once!" and then read one of the reports, clipping pince-nez glasses onto the end of his nose to enable him to do so.

"A musket ball in the left arm, removed at the field hospital six days ago," he observed. "And healing nicely, according to the colleague who examined you on admission, Captain Fisher. And yet . . ." He paused, frowning over the top of the glasses, as if puzzled. "You were sent down from Otahuhu with the seriously wounded. A mistake, surely?"

Marcus Fisher sat up. Reddening in embarrassment, he denied that any mistake had been made.

"Ah, then, perhaps amputation was considered," the major suggested, his expression relaxing.

"No, certainly not, sir," Fisher protested indignantly. "I assure you, nothing of the kind was ever mentioned. Indeed—"

"I had better take a look for myself," the little surgeon said, cutting him short. "Remove the dressings," he bade the orderly. The man did so clumsily. "Always pays to see for oneself, my dear young man."

His examination was thorough, and, still apparently puzzled, he gestured to the orderly to replace the dressing.

"Exactly as my colleague reported," he confirmed. "You should never have been sent here, Captain Fisher—this arm will be as right as rain in a week, which I'm sure you will be pleased to know. Missing your chance of glory, I fear, but—well, I'll give you ten days sick leave, and then you can return to your regiment." He looked round the crowded ward and gave vent to a weary sigh. "But we cannot keep you here. As you can see, we've all the badly wounded men we can cope with, and I understand that more are on the way. Have you friends here, people who can give you a bed?"

"Yes, sir," Marcus Fisher asserted eagerly. Caroline, he thought . . . Lord, even if she had not responded to his note, she could hardly refuse him a bed! "That will not be a problem, sir."

"Good," the major approved. He scribbled on the report with a stub of pencil. "Ten days sick leave, and I'm discharging you right away." He nodded to the orderly. "Give this officer his clothes and provide him with a sling. Good day, Captain Fisher."

Dressed and with his arm in a grubby sling, Marcus thankfully left the ward. To his intense relief, he met Caroline in the cluttered reception area. She was engaged in argument with one of the new female nurses, and seeing him, she started toward him, calling his name.

"Oh, Marcus . . . poor, poor Marcus, there you are! That stupid woman tried to tell me she'd never heard of you and you weren't in the hospital! Oh, my dear, why are you walking about? Surely if you were badly wounded, you should be in bed?"

"I'm on ten days sick leave," Marcus told her. "I've just been discharged, with nothing but the clothes I'm standing up in. I . . . that is, I'm hoping that you will take pity on me, Caroline." He urged her toward the door, conscious of the interest they were creating. "Let's talk outside."

Outside, the sun was shining, and he drew deep breaths of the cool, invigorating air into his lungs before launching into his explanation. His spirits lifted even further when he saw that Caroline was smiling, her eyes bright with pleasure.

"Yes, of course—dear Marcus, of course I can give you a bed! How lovely that you've come back, even if it is only for ten days. But I—" She started to laugh, a musical, happy sound. "My dear, I'm afraid you will have to share a room with two others. The wretched little house is full to bursting. I had to send the children with Milly to board with a Mrs. Hudson, and—"

His heart sank. Two others? The house full to bursting? "Caroline—my love, what do you mean? Why is the house full?"

Caroline went on laughing. "I didn't know you were coming back, Marcus. So I—well, when there was an appeal for residents to give accommodation to new arrivals and convalescents, I responded. What else could I do? With all these new regiments coming here, there simply aren't enough quarters for them in this little town." She linked her arm in his uninjured one and skipped beside him like a carefree little girl, glad, at least, of his return, Marcus realized, a trifle mollified. They would be in the same house, and the gossips could make little of that, however hard they tried. . . .

"With whom," he asked, "do I have to share a room, Caroline?"

"Oh," she responded lightly, "just two young ensigns of the Sixty-eighth—part of the advance guard, I suppose you'd call them, darling. They're boys, Marcus, sweet little boys, and they will be going to the war as soon as the main body of their regiment arrives. And two militia officers. I . . ." She turned to look at him, with wide-eyed innocence, pleading for his understanding. "I was so lonely, after you had gone. And I truly *didn't* know that you would be coming back so soon. If I had . . ." She left the sentence unfinished, her fingers twining with his.

Against his better judgment, Marcus believed her.

"I love you, Caroline," he said tensely. "My God, I love you, darling!"

"And I love you," Caroline echoed. "Dearest Marcus, it's going to be wonderful to have you back!"

Again, he believed her. She had not asked about her husband, he realized, which augured well. And the two ensigns—what had she called them? The two sweet little boys would know better than to question him concerning his absence from their shared bedroom.

He quickened his pace, his heart racing, eager to enfold her slim, beautiful body in his arms and make her his own again.

If only he could marry her, Marcus thought—if only she were free of that damned martinet of a husband of hers, whom she could not possibly love. He would quit the army, sell his commission, and find something to do here—enter the political arena, perhaps, since that was where power and influence lay, and he had neither the desire nor the money to go on the land.

"Dearest Caroline," he said, his voice harsh with strain, "I want you so! Darling, will you let me come to you tonight?"

She did not answer, but he felt her fingers tighten about his hand and was content.

Sean O'Hara sat in Kitty Broome's drawing room, awkwardly balancing a teacup and a plate in his two big hands and cursing the impulse that had led him to call on her when she was giving a tea party. The other guests were all military—imperial and militia officers and their dowdy, gossiping wives, with whom he had nothing in common. And one of the militia ladies—a big-bosomed woman in a ludicrously unbecoming flowered hat—had been persistently questioning him, in a loud and carrying voice, as to why he was still a civilian. The fact that he was an elected member of the Assembly failed to impress her, and he heard her say scornfully, "My husband was farming in the Waikato country—for over ten years, Mr. O'Hara—and the wretched Maori rebels stole our livestock, burnt our house and buildings, and murdered our workers! Ambrose was a magistrate, too," she added indignantly. "We lost everything, but he still saw it as his duty to enlist in the Volunteer Horse and go and fight them!"

"Wholly admirable of him, ma'am," Sean said, trying to sound approving. "But someone has to administer the country, and since I was elected to do so, I cannot enlist." He glanced pleadingly at Kitty, wishing that she would rescue him from his tormentress, but she only smiled back, apparently amused by his discomfort, and went on talking to one of the newly arrived 68th Regiment's captains . . . about the war, of course.

"General Cameron has been honored with a knighthood," he heard her say. "He is Sir Duncan Cameron now, after his splendid victory at Rangiriri. And they say he will go on and capture the so-called King's capital at Ngaruawahia, if he's not done so already."

"Is your husband with the troops?" the captain asked, and Sean saw her smile widen.

"Indeed he is, Captain Casement. With the Volunteer Horse. And my brother is one of the military settlers."

She spoke proudly, Sean noticed, conscious of resentment. Casement wore the Indian Mutiny ribbon on his tunic and looked a competent, professional soldier—eager for action, too, judging by the nature of the questions he was asking and the steely brightness of his eyes as he listened to Kitty's answers. She was well informed; no doubt her husband and the brother she so clearly adored wrote to her regularly and managed somehow to have their letters delivered . . . certainly she had every detail of the attack on the *pa* at Rangiriri ready to trip off her tongue. And fancy the British government's giving old Cameron a knighthood, simply for doing what they had sent him out here to do!

"My brother Patrick says that conditions are improving," he

heard Kitty add. "Supplies are being sent up by the steamers now, and some of the friendly Maoris are supplying fresh meat and vegetables, so they are able to eat well. But he told me that since the rain has stopped, the whole place is covered in dust, which blows up in blinding storms, and they cannot see a hand in front of them. But"—she took pity on Sean at last—"he says that the horses Mr. O'Hara provided are worth their weight in gold."

"Do you breed horses, Mr. O'Hara?" the stout lady asked. She was regarding him with a contempt she made not the smallest effort to hide, as if horse breeding were, in her view, an occupation strictly not for gentlefolk, and Sean, in spite of himself, flushed scarlet at the slight.

"Yes, ma'am, I do," he returned icily. "Bloodstock of the highest quality. But I've none for sale, if you were wanting a mount for yourself. The government's taken all I had broken."

His neighbor did not deign to reply, but she, too, flushed, then turned away to address one of the other guests—it being evident, Sean thought, enjoying his small triumph, that she had scarcely the figure for horseback riding. He grinned and received a reproachful look from his hostess.

At last the party broke up, and the guests started to take their leave, save for two young Volunteer officers—both apparently recovering from wounds—who were being accommodated in the house. But they, too, excused themselves and went out with Captain Casement, and Sean was left alone with Kitty.

"You were cruel to Mrs. Allsop," Kitty accused. "Very cruel, Sean." But there was the ghost of a smile playing about her lips, and he echoed it, his sour mood instantly forgotten.

"Ach, the old bag was cruel to me," he retorted, putting on a heavy Irish accent. "Why amn't I serving in de forces, she kept askin'—bein' a member av de government counts for nothin' in her eyes. And as for breedin' horses, why God love ye, dat's an occupation for de lowest av de low!"

"Even so, she was a guest in my house."

"More's de pity, den. You shouldn't have invited her."

"To tell you the truth, I didn't invite her," Kitty admitted, smiling openly now. "She happened to call—as you did."

"Touché!" Sean was unabashed. He leaned closer, seeking to capture her hand, very conscious of the attraction she had for him. She was so lovely; a truly beautiful young lady, with her slim figure and those deep-set eyes, meeting his gaze with a challenge in them

that he found irresistible. "Ah, Kitty, it's been an age since I saw
you! All those months you spent in Sydney, and then coming back
here with that brother of yours—and your husband. I was going
out of my mind, missing you so, and fearing to call, lest I was
unwelcome."

"You are never unwelcome, Sean," Kitty assured him. "You
surely know that. But with Pat and Johnny fighting the Maoris,
and then those two poor wounded boys, I—well, I've been run off
my feet, truly I have. At one time I had six convalescents here, and
they took some looking after—Pat's lads, they were, who were
wounded at Pukekohe."

The war, Sean thought with bitterness. No one in Auckland
could talk of anything except the infernal war—not even Kitty. He
changed the subject.

"What I told the old—that is, what I told Mrs. Allsop was not
strictly true. I've not parted with all my broken horses. I kept one
back, a beautiful filly, the same sire as Gold Dust. Rising three she
is, and I call her Ringdove. She's a dark bay, like her dam, and
made for you, Kitty. I was hoping I could persuade you to come
out and try her."

"I don't have time for riding now," Kitty began. A tinge of
embarrassed color crept into her cheeks. "And remember what
happened the last time I came out to try one of your horses, Sean.
A broken collarbone and . . . almost a broken marriage."

"That won't happen again, I swear it will not." Sean kept her
hand in his, but he did not make the mistake of raising it to his lips,
for all he wanted to do so, aware that Kitty Broome would fight
shy of him if he attempted any intimacy she had not invited.
"Auckland is safe now, and sure those Maoris were simply a wandering band, who had no reason to be where they were. And as to
your marriage—well, that is your business, Kitty."

"Yes," she agreed, avoiding his gaze. "It is my business, Sean."

"And I'll not say a word about it," Sean countered, greatly daring. "Save that if *I* were your husband, my lovely lady, I'd not go
off to the war as John Broome has seen fit to do, leaving you for
months on your own."

"John had his—his reasons."

"Then they must have been powerful good reasons."

"I . . . suppose they were," Kitty said.

But she sounded uncertain, and, wisely, Sean did not pursue the
subject. Instead he urged, with beguiling charm, "Trust me, Kitty.

Sure I'm head over ears in love with you, but what man is not? And all I want to do is give you a filly. Only you would have to choose which one suits you—I've a couple of others, apart from Ringdove, and a chestnut mare you might fancy." He expanded on the animals' breeding, and then rose to take his leave, sensing that it would be unwise to press her too strongly. "I must be on my way, the better for having seen you. And . . . I'll be going out to the stud on Sunday, leaving at about eight o'clock. Come with me, Kitty. I can pick you up. We can take our lunch there, ride in the afternoon, and I'd have you back in town before dark, on my honor. *Please!*"

Kitty wavered for a long moment, then threw back her shapely head with a warm smile. "All right—thank you, I will come. It will be good to mount a horse again, it's been so long. Eight o'clock, you said?"

"Eight o'clock," Sean confirmed, his heart leaping at the prospect of having her to himself for a whole day. "And don't be worrying your head about propriety. I've the same couple looking after the farm as I had before, so you will be properly chaperoned. *Au revoir,* Kitty, and thank you for the tea party." He made a mockingly grave face. "And for Mrs. Allsop! I'll be looking forward to Sunday."

"And so shall I, Sean," Kitty told him. She went with him to the door and, as a parting quip, bade him "Go off and govern the country," adding, with more feeling than perhaps she had intended to display, "And put an end to the war if you can, God helping you. It is time that it should end."

Not so far as he was concerned, Sean reflected. If the war ended, Johnny Broome would be back, and then . . . He grinned and echoed, "Aye, God willing!" and went on his way.

Throughout January, when General Cameron brought up troops, guns, and supplies to the old Kingite capital, and February and March, there were several small battles and numerous Maori ambuscades.

Adam, with Hill and once with von Tempsky himself, made observations of two strong Maori *pas* at Peterangi and Piko-Piko, and on the strength of their reports, Sir Duncan Cameron decided to bypass both strongholds, while leaving a small force of detachments to hold them in check.

A bathing party of men of the 40th and 50th at the Mangapoko

Creek were attacked, and Adam was with the rescue force, commanded by Colonel Sir Henry Havelock, that went to their aid. In a savage hand-to-hand fight, the Maoris were driven off, after inflicting thirteen casualties and losing some thirty of their own number.

It was a time of uncertainty and hard work, with guns and supply wagons, drawn by bullocks, having to negotiate mere tracks through bush country, preyed on by wandering war parties and constantly in danger from the nature of the roads they had to travel. In mid-February, there was an unfortunate affair in a defended village called Rangiaowhia, in which a colonel of the Defense Force Cavalry was killed by a sniper's bullet and his men took terrible revenge by putting the village to the torch.

The next day, a scout of the Forest Rangers reported that the *pas* at Peterangi and Piko-Piko had been abandoned. The erstwhile defenders were digging in on a ridge beyond Rangiaowhia, and General Cameron made the decision to attack at once, before the Maoris had had time to consolidate their position.

It was an inspired decision. Two companies of the 70th, commanded by Colonel Forsyth, drove in the enemy skirmishers; then the 50th, supported by the 65th and the remainder of the 70th, took the ridge at bayonet point. Their advance was made down a narrow track, hidden by high fern and *manuka* scrub, from which they emerged only a hundred yards from the Maoris' forward rifle pits, and in a gallant charge they overran the entrenchments, killed some forty of the defenders, and put the rest to flight. Casualties were light, prisoners were taken, and the general, in a brief speech, gave the gallant 50th high praise.

On March 22, sensing that rebel morale was low, Cameron moved his headquarters and the main part of his field force from Te Awamutu eastward to the Upper Waikato, leaving behind, under Brigadier General Carey, the 40th and the 65th—Adam's Ranger company—and the Waikato militia and two six-pounder Armstrong guns.

Six miles away, in the pastoral setting of Orakau, amid fruit orchards and fields of wheat ripening in the sun, sweet potato, melon, and pumpkin gardens, the famed warrior Rewi Maniapoto built a *pa* and made ready for his last stand.

Once again, Adam and Hill, taking their lives in their hands, went forward under cover of darkness to assess the defenses of the *pa.* They returned to describe these as formidable and to confirm Rewi's presence.

"He's directing them, sir," Adam reported to General Carey. "I saw him at least three times—or I'm pretty sure it's him, judging by the respect the warriors were according him." He was also reasonably sure that he had seen Chief Te Mata Atia of the Ngatihaua tribe among those clustering about Te Rewi, but he did not say so, aware that the name would have no significance for the general. Instead, he described the layout of the *pa,* with its outwork of double rifle pits and the strong redoubt constructed to the rear, reinforced with great bundles of fern and flax, intended to protect the defenders from cannon fire.

He answered questions from the general's staff and the commanding officers of the two regiments and heard Carey say decisively, "Dawn tomorrow, gentlemen, we'll attack. I want the Armstrongs in position tonight."

Adam spent the evening with Sergeant Doran and some of his old friends in the regiment, and was absurdly pleased when, returning to his own billet, he found little Wiremu Tata there, eagerly awaiting him.

"I am transferred," the boy told him proudly, "to First Waikato Militia, Mr. Shannon. Now I am Bugler Tata. Tomorrow I go with you into battle."

He displayed his gleaming brass bugle, grinning delightedly as he claimed, "Bugler is much better than drummer, is it not, sir? I tell Dickie Smith so, and he punch my nose!"

"You have to stay with your own company, Wiremu," Adam said, with mock severity; but moved by the young Maori's obvious distress, he permitted him to pass the night at his side.

At dawn the next day, the Armstrong guns opened fire, but they made little impression on Orakau's well-planned palisade, and two assaults were driven back by the concerted barrage from the cleverly sited rifle pits. Two hundred men, including a company of the 70th under Colonel Forsyth's command, arrived next day to reinforce the attackers; so, too, did a rebel force of Waikato and Ngatiraukawa, to dance a defiant *haka* behind the great timber walls of the *pa,* their voices sounding a strangely eerie note across the intervening darkness.

On the following morning, dense fog enveloped the battlefield, and a sortie from the *pa* was met and beaten back by the 65th and the Rangers. Brigadier General Carey fell back on the old tech-

nique of sapping. It was hot, exhausting work, but by the morning
of the third day the head of the sap had advanced within range of
the outer trenches, and grenades, lobbed over with skill and accu-
racy, began to take effect, and the Armstrongs opened two
breaches in the *pa* palisading.

General Cameron arrived on horseback, with members of his
staff, and assessing the situation, he ordered the cease-fire call to be
sounded.

"They are brave fellows, George," Adam heard him say, "but
they are beaten. Let us give them the chance to surrender."

He sent one of his interpreters, a man named William Mair, to
the head of the sap under a flag of truce to speak to Te Rewi and
his warriors.

Adam, crouching nearby, felt a touch on his arm and recognized
Colonel Forsyth lying beside him.

"You speak the lingo, don't you, Shannon? Tell me what is said,
like a good fellow."

"If I can, sir," Adam agreed. He listened tensely. "Mair said,
'Friends, hear me! This is the word of the general. Great is his
admiration for your bravery. Stop—let the fighting end. Come out
to us, that you may be saved!' "

"The right note," Forsyth approved. "Let's hope they will heed
it."

From where he lay, Adam could see the Maori chiefs inclining
their heads together in consultation. They looked exhausted, their
dark faces caked with dust, and some of them were wounded. Once
again he recognized Te Mata Atia—this time beyond all possibility
of doubt—with Te Heata standing at his back, and, recalling the
brief comradeship he had enjoyed with them during his captivity,
Adam prayed silently that, as Forsyth had said, they would heed
the interpreter's words. They were surrounded, cut off from their
supply of water, and heavily outnumbered, with the sap reaching
the ditch of their last entrenchment. To fight on would be to die.

It was Te Rewi who answered. He was a tall, dignified figure,
standing alone, the dark face proud and unyielding as his voice
rang out in rejection:

"Heoi ana! Ka whawhai tonu, ake, ake, ake!"

"Chief Rewi says 'Enough! We will fight on, for ever and ever
and ever!' " Adam translated.

Mair answered, and again, a trifle haltingly, Adam repeated
what he had said: " 'That is well for men. It is not right that

women and children should die. Let them come out.' A chief asks, 'How did you know there were women here?' And Mair says, 'I heard lamentations for the dead in the night.' "

Colonel Forsyth drew in his breath sharply but said nothing, as the chiefs talked to each other in low voices. Then Te Rewi gave answer.

"Ki te mate nga tane, me mate ano nga wahine me te kupu!"

"The chief says, 'If the men die, the women and children will die with them.' " Adam felt sick at heart. "They will not surrender, God forgive them!"

"As you observe, God forgive them," Forsyth said. He rose. "Thank you, Shannon."

For an instant, the colonel's professionalism deserted him. He was so moved that, as William Mair dropped back into the head of the sap, he stood up to offer the interpreter a hand, and a Maori warrior on the top of the redoubt took aim at him and fired. The range was short, and the bullet just tipped Mair's right shoulder before striking Forsyth in the chest. The 70th's colonel reeled and, as Adam attempted unsuccessfully to break his fall, collapsed with a low, half-strangled cry. Both Adam and Mair bent over him, but he was dead.

"Shot through the heart," Mair exclaimed bitterly. "By a bullet that was meant for me! God rest his soul! It was that traitor Wereta who fired—he had me covered the whole time I was speaking with the chiefs, the miserable swine."

A soldier of the 70th, crouching nearby, picked up a grenade and, taking careful aim, hurled it at the man who had fired. It exploded, and Wereta and two others near him paid the price of his treachery.

Feeling coldly angry, Adam was sent with a warning to the 40th, a company of which was spread out in a thin cordon at the rear of the *pa,* under Marcus Fisher's command. Before he could deliver his warning, however, the entire Maori garrison, with dramatic suddenness, came out of the entrenchment into the open in a silent and compact body, walking without haste and apparently without fear. With their women and children and their principal chiefs held protectively in their center, they advanced toward the thin line of soldiers, their weapons slung, not one of them making an attempt to fire or to offer the smallest provocation.

Fisher, as startled as his men, gave no order, and the soldiers, gazing pityingly on the gaunt, weary faces of the warriors who had defied them for three days and nights, made no move to dispute their passage. The Maoris passed through the first line and were almost through the second when Fisher, recovering from his astonishment, yelled at his troops to fire.

Scarcely half a dozen men obeyed him, but then the Defense Force Cavalry came galloping up. They had their colonel to avenge, and they charged into the flanks of the Maori warriors with sabers flailing, cutting them down. The whole body broke and ran, though still shielding those in their center, making for the bush and the swamp and offering no resistance as they sought to escape. But von Tempsky's ranger company was covering the swamp, and Adam saw warriors fall under volley after volley of coordinated rifle fire. Some of the women were hit, and the silence they had so stoically maintained was broken by their pitiful cries as, clutching children in their arms, they stumbled blindly on.

To his horror, he saw Keri—or imagined it was she—and ran forward, shouting at the soldiers to cease fire and hoping to reach her before she was hit. But she went down when he was only yards away, and, weeping unashamedly, Adam knelt beside her, fumbling for his water bottle. He saw her smile, and then, as he raised her head and said her name, the smile vanished, and he knew that she—like Leonard Forsyth before her—was dead.

The pursuit went on, but Adam took no part in it, yielding up Keri's poor, small body to a warrior he did not know.

Later Sergeant Doran caught him up. The old sergeant had been wounded and had his right arm in a filthy, blood-soaked bandage, but he made light of it, grinning defiantly.

"You don't kill an old campaigner like me as easy as all that, Mr. Shannon. Come on, laddie—I have some beer stashed away, and you look to me as if you need it. Take my rifle, if you really want to help." The grin widened. "I've young Wiremu standin' guard on the beer, so the chances are it'll still be there."

Miraculously, it was, and Wiremu, dust-stained but cheerful, yielded it up to its owner with a happy smile.

"You will drink to great victory?" the boy suggested innocently. "Defeat of Chief Te Rewi Maniapoto by brave soldiers of Queenie Wiktoria?"

His small, brown face puckered in puzzled distress when Adam turned on him in fury and said in a stifled voice, "No! Before heaven, that is the last thing I'll do!"

Chapter XX

THERE WAS A memorial service for Colonel Leonard Forsyth, arranged by his widow, at which the aging but indefatigable Bishop Selwyn preached.

Red Broome, who had returned to Auckland in the *Mercia* with wounded men from the recent battles against the Waikato tribes, found William De Lancey in town before him, and they attended the service together. Each had been called separately into consultation with the governor, Sir George Grey, but beyond agreeing that His Excellency's relations with his military commander in chief left something to be desired, the two friends had not discussed their meetings or, indeed, had an opportunity to talk in private before the service.

The church was nearly full, but Red found seats in the row behind Kitty Broome, and she turned to smile and wave a greeting when they came in. She was not alone. Red did not recognize the tall, good-looking civilian who sat beside her, but William, better informed, identified him as Sean O'Hara.

"Member of the General Assembly," he whispered. "Breeds bloodstock at a place he calls Killaloe, six or seven miles from town. Good animals—he supplies the militia. Politically he's an opponent of the governor."

Which scarcely made him the ideal companion for his brother's wife, Red thought; but if Johnny persisted in leaving her alone, there was nothing that could be done.

Forsyth's widow came in, to take her place in the front row of seats. Caroline Forsyth was in unrelieved black, a veil hiding her face, and she was leaning on the arm of a young officer of the 40th Regiment. A fair-haired, bright little boy followed her into the pew, clinging to the hand of his nursemaid and looking frightened and overawed.

"Leonard's stepson," William supplied. "The poor fellow worshiped him!"

Red bit back a sigh, wondering how long it would be before he was able to see his wife and children again. Rumor had it that the Royal Navy frigates now on station were to be reduced in number, but the governor had made no mention of this; and although Red had virtually relinquished command of the *Mercia* to his first lieutenant, Their Lordships of the Admiralty had as yet dispatched no orders concerning a new command or a change of station.

Thinking of this and then, regretfully, of the loss of Leonard Forsyth, Red did not pay a great deal of attention to the service. He had not known Forsyth well, but those who had—including Will de Lancey—spoke of him with admiration as a splendid soldier, and with affection as a man. Hearing his widow's subdued sobs as the service progressed, Red found himself wondering whether Caroline Forsyth was as heartbroken as she sounded. She must have been considerably younger than the colonel, and—yes, of course, if the little boy had been his stepson, then Caroline must have been married before.

Caroline . . . Caroline *Omerod!* It came back suddenly, as he recalled the gossip one of the members of the court-martial of Adam Vincent had tried to pass on to him. Could it be the same person? It was a long shot; plenty of women were given the name Caroline. It was a fashionable name.

"What is the little boy's surname, do you know?" he asked William softly as they rose to sing a hymn.

William confirmed his guess. "Omerod, I believe," he answered. "His father was in the navy—drowned at sea."

So this was the woman for whom young Vincent had sacrificed his promising career! It was on her account that a fine young officer —and a holder of the Victoria Cross, by heaven—had enlisted in the ranks of the 40th Regiment and was now, on merit, serving in commissioned rank in von Tempsky's Forest Rangers!

Shocked by this realization, Red took in little of the bishop's address, save to register that it was unlikely to please Governor Grey. But at least H.E. was not present; he was spared that much —although, of course, the gist of the bishop's outspoken tirade would, in due course, be reported to him. Selwyn was a wholly admirable prelate and a good Christian, but his sympathies, unlike

Grey's, were with the dispossessed farmers and would-be settlers, whereas Grey's were with the Maoris.

The service over, the congregation filed out, pausing to offer condolences or bow to Caroline Forsyth as they passed her at the church door. Outside and out of earshot, Red suggested a drink on board the *Mercia,* and William accepted readily.

"A good idea if we exchange notes, Red. But . . . don't you want a word with your sister-in-law, the lovely Lady Kitty, before we go?"

"No." Red's refusal was, he realized, a trifle brusque, and he saw that William was regarding him in some surprise, so he added quickly, "I'm not keen on the local politicians, Will, and if you are right about O'Hara's sympathies, I'm still less keen. The politicians are giving the governor a hard time, and he is, after all, the governor. They should toe the line."

"That's just what they will *not* do," William demurred. "They're determined to fight Grey to a standstill and devil take the hindmost! Do you know that Frederick Whitaker refused special treatment for the prisoners we took at Orakau and Rangiriri—even the compassionate Chief Te Oriori, who saved the life of one of the Sixty-fifth officers! *He,* if Whitaker has his way, is to be tried by court-martial!"

"Good God!" Red exclaimed in disgust. "H.E. did not tell me that. But—" They had come in sight of the anchorage, and he broke off and pointed, his earlier ill humor instantly vanishing. "Look, Will—the *Dolphin*'s just come in. What a happy coincidence, with both of us here. News from home and mail, if we're lucky. I'll send Claus Van Buren an invitation to dine on board. You'll stay, won't you?"

"With such an inducement?" William laughed and clapped a hand on his shoulder. "I most certainly will, Red—thanks."

The signal was made as soon as they boarded the *Mercia,* and a few minutes after they had settled down in Red's day cabin, the midshipman of the watch delivered an affirmative reply from the *Dolphin*'s master.

They talked during the time of waiting, catching up with each other's news, and both of them concerned about the governor and the change in him that the last six months had brought about.

"He looked damned ill to me," Red confessed. "And he admitted that he has become overwrought and that, at times, his judgment has been clouded and he has failed to act resolutely or consistently. But he assured me that rather than permit Whitaker and others like him to deal unjustly with the Waikato Maoris, he is prepared to dissolve the ministry. Whitaker wants the land recently taken to be confiscated and given to the military settlers, but Sir George won't hear of it. He told me that to do so would needlessly prolong the war—and I feel sure he is right. He spoke of impending trouble in the Tauranga, Bay of Plenty area, too. Do you know about that?"

William nodded. He sipped reflectively from his glass. "Colonel Henry Greer, who is commanding the Sixty-eighth at the Te Papa mission there, was under orders from General Cameron to remain on the defensive. Greer's a fiery old Irishman, who rules his regiment with a rod of iron, but his men love him, and . . . well, the general doesn't entirely trust him, if he's provoked. Which"—William smiled faintly—"he was! You see, the tribe of a chief named Te Rawiri Puhirake had been fighting in the Waikato, and after our victories there, they started to return to their own lands, near Tauranga. This Te Rawiri sent a letter to Colonel Greer, inviting him to come out and fight, and even including a code of conduct for the proposed engagement! The code was remarkably fair, not to say farsighted. It called for civilians not to be molested, prisoners to be treated kindly, and the dead respected . . . and the chief added that, for the convenience of the soldiers, he was constructing an eight-mile-long track, leading directly to his *pa!*"

Red roared with laughter. "What a man! Good Lord—what effect did it have on Greer?"

"He was beside himself with rage. You don't know him, do you? Well, he's a very hirsute gentleman, with huge, fuzzy whiskers and pendulous mustache, and one of his officers told me that he was quivering with annoyance at the insult." William shrugged, still amused. "But he could not disobey his orders—he had to stay on the defensive—and when Te Rawiri received no reply and there was no attack, he wrote again. Still very courteously, I would have you know. He said that as he had apparently taken up a position too far away from the soldiers, he would build one much nearer. And that's what they've been doing—watched by Greer and his men and, on one occasion, by myself. And it's a massive place."

On the back of an envelope, he sketched a plan of the *pa* and its surroundings.

"This is the Te Papa mission, founded in 1838 by Archdeacon Brown, who still preaches and entertains the troops there—a fine old man. It stands on the tip of a narrow tongue of land about three miles long, formed by the muddy saltwater estuaries there. The boundary between the mission and the Maori land runs across the peninsula at its narrowest point—here—and it is marked for all its length, about five hundred yards, by a ditch. Where it is crossed by the raised track leading south from the mission there is a strong timber gate. We call it Gate *Pa,* and the Maoris know it as Pukehinahina. Te Rawiri has, since the beginning of April, been constructing an oblong *pa* here, see? It is strongly palisaded and holds a redoubt, with the usual fire trenches and shelters, situated behind the boundary ditch, which they have deepened and reinforced. Greer and his fellows have watched it being built, powerless to interfere, as I told you."

"Until he's sent more troops, presumably?" Red suggested, studying the roughly drawn plan with interest.

"Precisely," William agreed. "And he'll get them, as soon as I've made my report to the general. The Arawas are staying loyal to us, but Te Rawiri's people are *not,* and Cameron's not going to like the present situation one little bit. Indeed"—he smiled at Red—"I don't doubt that you'll be under orders to move troops from here to Tauranga within—well, the next couple of weeks, at a guess. And Cameron will ask for a naval brigade—I'm pretty sure of that. Unlike some of his brother officers, he has a healthy respect for your jacks."

"Well, most of our captains will be eager to go," Red offered. "Especially Hamilton of the *Esk* and Hay of the *Harrier.* And Mayne of *Eclipse,* who was at Rangiriri with the naval brigade. You would think he'd had enough, wouldn't you? But he says he can't wait to have at 'em again!"

There was a discreet tap at the door, and the midshipman of the watch came in.

"Boat from the *Dolphin* approaching, sir," he announced. "Officer of the watch said to tell you."

"Right, thank you, Mr. Mercer. I'll come on deck."

Red excused himself and returned, a quarter of an hour later, escorting Claus Van Buren. The *Dolphin*'s owner looked tanned and well, and he was in excellent spirits. Settled with a drink, he took letters from the breast pocket of his blue reefer jacket and, beaming, handed them over.

"Here you are—mail from Sydney, and all the latest news! From your devoted and lovely wife, Red . . . 'twill take you half the night to read it, I'll be bound. And your boys, Will, with a note from the judge and your mama, and one from Francis. And I'm charged to give you both greetings and good wishes from about half the inhabitants of New South Wales, including those at Pengallon."

He filled his pipe from Red's tobacco jar, lit it, and drew contentedly on the smoke. Both Red and William plied him with questions, which he answered as fully as he could, interposing a few of his own concerning the progress of the war.

"I've come from Rangirata," he explained, "where, thanks be to God, all is back to what it used to be. The chief, Te Anga, joined the Waikato tribes in the recent rebellion. His tribal overlord is the great Te Rewi Maniapoto, and so, when called upon to go to his support, he had no option. But after you people defeated Te Rewi at Orakau, Te Anga took his warriors back to Rangirata, and having sent a message to me, asking me to return, he occupied the time of waiting by rebuilding my wharf and warehouses." Claus laughed. "It was amazing! I took the *Dolphin* in, and, in very truth, I thought the clock had been put back! Everything was as it used to be, with cargo ready to be loaded and Te Anga's daughter, whom he had reclaimed, awaiting her husband's return in their newly built house—with, would you believe, a small son called Robbie!"

"Good Lord!" Red exclaimed. "How extraordinary, Claus! I gather you weren't expecting such a welcome?"

"No, indeed I was not," Claus assured him. "The peace terms rigorously observed, and by Te Anga, of all people. I returned his son, Korriko—much improved, if I may be forgiven for boasting—but the other young man has elected to stay with me, for which I'm glad. He's shaped up very well as a seaman and is as happy as a king with his new A.B. rate. Which, I may tell you, he has deserved."

"So it has all worked out very well?" William suggested.

"Better than I ever dared to hope, yes."

"Will you cut down on your government contracts?" Red asked.

Claus shook his head. "Not immediately—I cannot. I took as many as my ships can handle, not anticipating Te Anga's change of heart. I'll cut down gradually, but it will take a year, at least—unless the war ends earlier than anyone expects it will. You mentioned trouble in Tauranga, Will. Is it serious?"

"It could well be." William repeated briefly what he had told Red. "I'm due to report to General Cameron at Camp Te

Awamutu, and as I told Red, I can confidently predict what his reaction will be. Reinforcements and an attack on Gate *Pa.*"

Dinner was served, and over the meal they continued to talk, Claus contributing news in detail from Australia. He spoke at length and with guarded approval of the new governor, Sir John Young, and concluded, with characteristic modesty, "But I've met him only at a couple of official receptions, so you can take my opinion or reject it, as you see fit."

The other two laughed, and William said, "You are a shrewd observer, Claus—I'd take your opinion against any other. But tell us about your family. You haven't mentioned them yet."

Claus grinned. "Thus encouraged, I will, Colonel De Lancey! They are in good health, although Mercy now plagues me to let her accompany me on my voyages, and our two elder boys give me no peace, for the same reason. We now have two daughters, as well as the twins. The boys are idle scholars, I fear—unlike your adopted lad Andrew, Will. Now, there is a scholar! He tops his class in almost every subject—or so Nathan and Joseph tell me, without envy. They have just started at the Grammar School, incidentally, and Andy is their hero. But—" He broke off, his grin fading.

"But what?" William prompted.

"It will be in his letter—I know it is, because he read me part of it. Open it, Will, and you will see."

Over coffee, William opened his letter and skimmed through it, his brow furrowed. "There's nothing new in this, Claus," he objected. "Andy wants me to permit him to join the army and come out here—to fight the Maoris with me, as he calls it. He's said the same thing ever since I sent him to Sydney, with little Harry, and I've said no, just as consistently. He's just a boy."

"He will be sixteen on his next birthday, Will," Claus pointed out.

"Good God, will he? Time passes so fast—I hadn't realized."

"I'm afraid he will." Claus looked across at Red and shrugged his broad shoulders. "Your two have grown so much you'll scarcely know them, Red. Jessie is a beauty and no mistake, and young Rufus is coming on by leaps and bounds." He turned back to William and went on, almost apologetically, "Andy's been trying to persuade me to sign him on for one voyage—to see you, he says. I've refused, believing you would not want him to do anything of the kind, but—well, not to put too fine a point on it, Will, if I don't take him, someone else might. He's well grown for his age

—looks older, in fact—and he can be mighty persuasive. Why don't you get him a commission in a regiment stationed in England or Ireland, since he wants it so badly?"

William sighed. "He would not take a commission in a home-based regiment." He tapped his letter. "He says so here, for about the hundredth time."

"Cannot Magdalen influence him?" Red put in.

"She tries, Red," Claus answered. "The boy adores her, and he does listen to her, I think. But he's set his heart on coming back here. And, to be honest with you, Will, I fancy he'll come, with or without your consent, when he's sixteen."

William hesitated and then said resignedly, "Very well. If that's how it is, then . . . sign him on, Claus. I know you'll look after him."

"Are you sure, Will?" Claus sounded uncertain. "I'll bring him as a passenger, if you like. That might be better for him."

"No." William, it was evident, had made up his mind. "Sign him on. Let him learn what it's like to be a seaman. One voyage only, though—he must agree to that." He rose, setting down his cup. "I'm afraid I'll have to go, Red—early start in the morning. Thank you for your kind hospitality, which I've greatly enjoyed. And if I might trouble you for a boat, I—"

"I'll take you in mine, Will." Claus, too, got to his feet, offering his thanks in turn to their host. "It's been a great pleasure to see you both. Thanks for arranging it, Red, my dear friend." He shook Red's hand. "Now you will be able to read your letter. If there is a reply, have it sent to the *Dolphin*. I expect to be here for five or six days."

Red escorted them on deck and stood by the rail, watching them out of sight, filled with an odd sense of sadness and wondering when—and where—the three of them would meet and talk together again. In Sydney, perhaps? He hoped it would be in Sydney.

After a word with the officer of the watch, he returned to his cabin and, divesting himself of boots and jacket, settled down to read his wife's letter.

It was, as Claus had said, a long letter, written almost in the form of a diary, informing him of what she had done, whom she had seen, and giving him news of their children and the two boys, Andy and Harry. It included school gossip, personal impressions, descriptions of a Government House reception and of a picnic given by people he did not know.

The fact that he did not know Magdalen's picnic hosts was inconsequential, yet it added to Red's sense of sadness and nostalgia. It had been too long, he thought, and the infernal war went on, so that he could see little prospect of a speedy end to it or, come to that, of his own return to Sydney. Little Jessica—Jessie—was attending school and, her mother proudly claimed, was reading very well, and Rufus—Lord, how the name stuck!—was not far behind her. As to the boys . . . He read on.

They are both doing so well at the Grammar School, particularly Andy. Harry tries, but he is, of course, younger, and lacks the grounding Andy had. They have both made friends, but Andy, I fear, is restless. He will soon be sixteen, Red dear, and he talks of nothing but enlisting so that he may join you and Will in New Zealand. He reads everything about the war that appears in our newspapers and, I truly believe, knows where you are most of the time.

Claus Van Buren tells me that Andy has approached him, with a request that he be signed on as a member of the *Dolphin*'s crew. So far, I have refused and said he must obtain *your* permission, and I gather he has written both to Will and to you about it. I think, however, that to allow him to serve under Claus might be the best thing, in the circumstances. If he is forbidden, he just might run away and enlist, and at sixteen he would be old enough.

So he would, Red reflected glumly. And the boy was spirited—he would be capable of it. But it was up to Will rather than to himself to give any sort of permission, and Will, it seemed, had done so. He had asked Claus to sign Andy on for one voyage, as a seaman—poor lad, that might come as a rude awakening. His letter was enclosed. It was short, well written and persuasive, and in it Andy laid stress on the fact that Harry had made friends of his own age and would, in consequence, need him less . . . which was probably true.

Red returned to Magdalen's letter. She wrote of Johnny and Kitty but only a trifle guardedly, contenting herself with asking him to convey her best wishes to them both, if he saw them. Of Caroline Forsyth, she wrote a trifle more explicitly:

We heard, very sadly, of Colonel Forsyth's death in action, his name being on the list of casualties published here. I wonder very much how his widow has taken the loss. Caroline Forsyth is not a woman I would have chosen as a friend, I am afraid, but I am genuinely distressed for her and should be grateful if you would offer her my deepest sympathy at the first opportunity. Most folk here believe that she will return to Sydney now, but I am not so sure. Strictly between our two selves, Red, I feel that her marriage was not entirely happy and that, perhaps, she may find consolation for her loss with some much younger officer currently serving in New Zealand. But I could, of course, be wrong.

Red frowned, reminded of the young captain of the 40th Regiment who had been Caroline's escort at the memorial service. He had not taken much notice of the fellow, having been too shocked at the realization that Caroline's previous marriage had been to the late John Omerod, but—yes, the fellow *had* been very solicitous to the sobbing widow; and he was not in Forsyth's regiment, which was the 70th.

Red sighed, coming at last to the end of Magdalen's letter. He folded the pages and, rising, placed them carefully in a folder, ready to be read and reread. Then he helped himself to a nightcap and, after a short turn on deck, went below again and retired for the night.

A week later a signal from Commodore Wiseman ordered him to prepare to embark troops for Tauranga, with the frigate *Falcon*. Only hours after he received his orders, the clipper *Dolphin* sailed for Sydney, and, not for the first time, Red wished that he were aboard. Had the time come, he asked himself, to end his naval service and retire to the life of a family man?

Certainly he had lost much of his zest, but . . . it was too soon. He was not yet ready to quit the sea, and there was, it seemed, another battle to be fought.

"Boat from the *Falcon* putting off, sir," the officer of the watch warned, peering through his glass. "Captain on board, sir." He hesitated. "And—yes, I think he has Captain Hamilton of the *Esk* with him."

"Muster the side party," Red bade him, "if you please."

Two war enthusiasts, he thought resignedly. And before long the troops would start to embark, and they would be in the war once again. He sighed deeply as he prepared to receive his fellow commanders. He was naval adviser to His Excellency the governor, second-in-command to the commodore, and—devil take it, he would be only forty-nine on his next birthday! He must cease wishing he were on his way back to Sydney on board the *Dolphin*. . . .

The boat came alongside, the bo'sun's mate's pipe twittered as the side party came to attention, and Red was smiling as he strode forward to bid his visitors welcome.

Chapter XXI

CAROLINE FORSYTH LAY in her lover's arms and closed her eyes, glorying in her happiness. Marcus Fisher had his faults, admittedly, as a man, but he was well versed in what was required to give pleasure to a woman. He had proved himself an eager, passionate lover, and, freed at last of her houseguests, she had slept with him every night, careless of what the servants might think or gossip about.

She was free; her husband had died in battle, and while Marcus's leave lasted, she was content to share her bed and her waking hours with him. Only little Jon was upset—he was jealous, of course, and he missed Leonard greatly. Also, for no reason that she had been able to understand, the boy did not like Marcus and went into his shell whenever they were thrown together.

Caroline sighed. Now she avoided that, whenever she could; both Jon and the baby spent virtually all the time with Milly, and Milly, wise girl that she was, kept a still tongue in her head and offered no criticism of her employer's conduct . . . or, come to that, of anyone she chose to entertain. And the other two servants were too stupid. Granted, their work was improving under her tutelage, but they were still without the brains or the acumen to understand what she was doing or what she really felt about Marcus.

She moved into a more comfortable position and looked down, for a long moment, into her lover's sleeping face. It was not a particularly good-looking face, but . . . tanned by New Zealand's summer sun, it was personable enough.

Marcus was young—the same age, in fact, as she—but he had a rich and indulgent father, thanks to whose generosity he held the rank of captain in a good infantry regiment, and at an age when most men had not advanced beyond subaltern rank. True, he was constantly begging her to wed him, even promising that, if she did so, he would sell his commission and quit the army . . . and the hateful, never-ending war. He had been arguing with her this evening, over dinner, assuring her that he could find a chaplain who would perform the marriage service and then keep quiet about it, but . . . Caroline repeated her sigh.

The prospect of becoming Marcus's wife had a strong appeal, only it was too soon after Leonard's death to be . . . well, to be practical. Her period of mourning was not over; and there would be talk—malicious talk—if she agreed to his proposal. On the other hand, Leonard had left her very little. He had had his pay and a small private allowance, both of which would stop with his death, and although they had told her she would be granted a pension, she had no idea when or even how much it would be. And the regimental adjutant had twice suggested delicately that she might wish to return to Sydney—or even to England—instead of staying on out here.

"Go back to your parents, my dear Mrs. Forsyth," he had advised her. "We can arrange a passage for you and the children—from Sydney or Hobart, if not from here—and I feel that's what the colonel would have wanted."

It almost certainly *was* what Leonard, had he been alive, would have wanted, Caroline reflected rebelliously. He was dead, therefore there was no reason for her to remain in Auckland, and . . . there had been hints concerning her continued occupation of this house, which the adjutant called "the colonel's quarters" and which, with the buildup of imperial troops, would be eagerly snapped up if she vacated it.

Marcus stirred restlessly, and even though he was only half awake, his arms tightened about her, and she heard him whisper her name.

"Hush, Marcus," she chided him. "Lie still, I—I'm thinking."

But he, too, was now awake, roused as he always was by her proximity, pressing his body against hers, his lips seeking her breast, a hand moving possessively about her thigh. As always, she responded, unable to resist him, conscious of the strong attraction he had for her and of the excitement his lovemaking induced.

"I love you," he told her, mouth on hers. "God, Caroline my darling, sweetest of women, *how* I love you!"

Leonard had never made love to her like this, Caroline thought ecstatically. He had never worried about her response, and John—oh, poor John! He had tried but had lacked Marcus's passion. And Adam . . . But she must not think of Adam. He was in the past, he— Marcus's hands moved purposefully, and Caroline cried out, willing him to take her, her heart pounding in her breast, all inhibitions gone.

"What were you thinking of?" he demanded, suddenly still.

"I—I don't know. Marcus, please, I—"

He held her close, so tightly that she could not move. "Were you thinking of us, my darling? Of our marriage? Were you thinking of that?"

"I—yes, I—I was. But—"

"Were you thinking that I have to go back to the infernal war? In two days time, Caroline!"

"Yes, I—I suppose I was. But truly, Marcus—"

"I'm not giving in, my love." His voice was hard, demanding, his arms like steel bands about her. "Marry me—tomorrow, Caroline. I can find a padre, bring him here. Nobody need know, except your servants. *He* won't talk, and I won't. But I'll quit the army. If you become my wife, I swear to you I'll quit. Darling, please, promise me you'll wed me. If you won't, then I—"

She was never to hear his threat. "Yes," she managed, her voice a sob in her throat. "Yes, Marcus, all right—I will. I *promise* you I will."

Satisfied, Marcus let out his breath in a long-drawn sigh. Then roughly, almost brutally, he took her, and Caroline was weeping in his arms. . . .

He brought the parson next afternoon; an old man, with a tired, pinched face, and the smell of drink about his person. He stumbled a little over the marriage service, as if it had been a while since he had performed a wedding, but he wed them, signed a certificate, and the servants witnessed it, and then he took himself off, thanking Marcus for the privilege and Caroline for her hospitality.

When he was gone, Marcus said, with new authority, "Come, wife, we will dine out, in celebration." He offered her his arm and then, suddenly relaxing, took her into his embrace and whispered proudly, "I love you, Mrs. Fisher!"

"And I—I love you, Captain Fisher," Caroline answered, believing it with all her heart.

* * *

It was on her third visit to Sean O'Hara's property, Killaloe, that with almost no warning Kitty was caught in a heavy thunderstorm. Riding the bay filly Ringdove, to which she had taken a great fancy, she followed Sean back to the house at a brisk canter. They were both soaked to the skin but laughing and joking cheerfully, for they had enjoyed an exhilarating ride, and the storm had not dimmed their spirits.

Regretfully, Kitty wondered why she and her husband could not share such lighthearted moments; but Johnny took everything so seriously, particularly if she were involved. He would not have laughed had he been with her when the storm struck. He—she smothered a sigh—he would have been concerned lest she catch a cold. He would have worried about her, as if she were a weaker vessel than he, insisting that she take a hot bath, and—yes, of course!—that she retire to bed.

Whereas Sean . . . She looked at him, smiling when she realized what his cure was. A large glass of rum, spiced and with hot water added . . . effective, to say the least. Bridie Riordan, buxom and helpful as always, brought a big brass kettle of hot water for the drink and added, as she left the room, "I'll have water for de baths ready in twenty minutes, my lady. An' you can give me your clothes then so's I can get dem dried."

No fuss, no obvious concern, Kitty thought thankfully, but all that was necessary organized and about to be ready. Sean echoed her smile as he joined her in front of the huge, roaring wood fire Bridie had prepared as soon as the thunder had echoed across the valley. He was in his shirtsleeves, and the water steamed from his sodden breeches, but he cared not at all.

"Sure and doesn't it rain worse than this at home?" he quipped, raising his glass to her. "To you, my most beautiful young lady— my eternal devotion! Drink yours down, now. 'Twill do you a power of good, so it will, and there's plenty more where it came from."

Kitty obediently drained her glass, and Sean refilled it, brushing aside her protests.

"Ah, now, you're surely not wanting the pneumonia, are you? That is a sore complaint, and don't I speak from experience, by heaven?"

"I must be sober for the drive back to town, Sean," she reminded him.

"You cannot go back to town tonight, Kitty!" Sean exclaimed, the jocular manner vanishing abruptly. "For the Lord's sake, it's fairly flinging it down! It would be murder in an open gig."

"Yes, but—"

"Ah, now," he pleaded, "what's the harm in your staying here overnight? Who's to know, in any case? You have no husband waiting, have you? And this is a fine, respectable household, with Bridie Riordan to give it added respectability. Besides, you know what a fine cook she is. She will put on a dinner you'll enjoy. Stay, Kitty, please. We don't want both of us being half drowned, do we?"

She did not, Kitty reflected. Of course she did not, and . . . Johnny was not waiting for her this time. He and Pat were fighting the miserable war, God preserve them both. And besides . . . She looked down at her dripping riding skirt and from it to the beautiful, blazing fire and relented.

"Oh, very well, Sean, I will stay. But you—"

"But I," he mocked, cutting her short. "Oh, I'll behave, difficult though you make it for me. I'll not do anything you don't want, Kitty. But I love you, my darling—God, how I love you!" He sighed and, very gently, took off her jacket. "Look at this! You cannot go anywhere in it; sure it's soaked right through and would be the death of you if you tried. Swallow that drink down and then go and take one of Bridie's hot tubs. She'll lend you something to wear for dinner."

"All right," Kitty agreed. She obediently drained her second glass of punch, conscious of the warmth it induced and of a slight haziness in her vision. He had made the rum strong, or perhaps she had taken the second glass too soon after the first, but . . . the hot tub would restore her to complete sobriety. And, as Sean had reminded her, she had no husband waiting, no brother even, and . . . Overhead the thunder rumbled, and a shaft of lightning lit the room to momentary brilliance. Certainly it was no night to drive six miles or more in an open gig; surely even Johnny would not expect it of her?

Sean reached for her hand. He took the empty glass, set it down, and then bore her hand to his lips. Conscious of a little thrill, Kitty drew away, the color leaping to her cheeks.

"Sean, you promised," she began. "You—"

"I said I'd not do anything you don't want, Kit, my darling. But you want me to kiss you, don't you?"

His arms were about her, and she felt his hard, strong body pressed close to hers, his lips first on her neck, then finding her mouth, kissing her with a yearning passion to which, for all her resolution, she found it impossible not to respond. They clung together, lost to the outside world, Kitty heartbreakingly conscious of how faint was her resolution now. But she *had* to resist him, she told herself; for Johnny's sake, she—

A loud knock on the door and Bridie's voice, calling out that their tubs were ready, broke the spell, and Sean released her.

"Go and have your tub, Kitty," he said, in a flat voice. "We can talk at dinner."

The tub was blissful, and Kitty stayed in it for as long as she could, soaking up the warmth, thinking of anything but Sean O'Hara. Yet he intruded into her thoughts, and she wished that the storm would pass over, enabling her—even at the last minute—to change her mind about staying overnight at Killaloe.

But it did not pass over. There was a brief lull in the crashing thunder, but the rain continued to fall, and by the time she had dried herself and donned a shapeless garment of Bridie Riordan's, the thunder returned, seemingly centered above the house.

The dinner, as Sean had promised it would be, was a true revelation of Bridie's culinary art. They started with soup, as only an Irishwoman could make it, and then progressed through a magnificent pie and a succulent lamb roast, with half a dozen vegetables, to a fruit duff topped with cream, and delicious little pastry cookies, accompanied by coffee. Sean served the wines, pressing her to taste one of his own bottling, and then producing, from some secret hiding place, a fine French red and finally a brandy, which he poured with reverence, urging Kitty to sip it slowly.

They talked of the horses during the meal, of the Assembly, the governor, and of the prospects for New Zealand, once peace had been gained. But they did not talk of war, and almost in gratitude for this, Kitty finally promised to accept Sean's gift of the filly Ringdove.

"I'll bring her into town for you," he promised. "As we planned for poor Gold Dust, Kit. I will have the livery stable look after her for you. But I'm not yet quite satisfied with her training. If she's to be yours, she must be perfect, and she has one or two points to iron out before I can say she is right for you. You can come out here and ride her, though, whenever you wish."

He was, she knew, planning for her to repeat her visit to Killaloe and wanted also to resume their old relationship in town, when he escorted her to dinner parties and such other social functions as there were in Auckland these days; and as she had accepted the filly, she did not demur, knowing that it would be pleasant to be in his company again.

Sean dismissed Bridie and her husband, who had waited on them, offering warm congratulations for the meal and giving Bridie one of the bottles of French red, to drink at her leisure.

"You've earned it," he said, and added pointedly, "We'll not be early in the morning."

When the servants had gone, he came to sit at Kitty's feet in front of the fire, and although she knew to what all this was leading, she made no attempt to escape from him, offered no excuses, and, when his dark head leaned against her knee, she bent down and kissed his forehead and heard him whisper that he loved her.

They lingered over their coffee, as if they were both conscious that this day would stand out in their minds as one to remember for as long as they lived, and Kitty thought of Johnny at last, faintly shocked to discover that she could not visualize his face or even, in memory, hear his voice.

Sean got to his feet and held out both hands to her. Kitty took them, and he drew her into his arms.

"You know I love you," he said, "and that I'll love you till the day I die. You know that, don't you, Kit?"

"Yes," she answered. "Yes, I know that, Sean. And I—God help me, I love you."

He kissed her long and tenderly, and then, hand in hand, they went together to her room. Sean helped her into the great, curtained bed, pulled the coverings over her, and said, "It will be us now, won't it? Kitty and Sean—whatever the gossips care to make of it."

"Yes," she whispered, suddenly happy and free of doubts and fears. "Yes, Sean, that is how it will be."

"No John Broome?" he persisted. "No husband but me, darling?"

"Only you," Kitty managed. "But I—"

Sean put a hand to her mouth. "Darling Kit, I've waited a long time for you." He held her close and then released her. "You know where the bathroom is—at the end of the corridor. I'll be back in—ten minutes? Twenty?"

"Ten minutes," she decided. "Ten minutes, Sean."

He was back in precisely ten minutes, wrapped in a loose robe, and Kitty held out her arms to him as he flung it off and got into bed beside her.

"Oh, Kit," he whispered softly. "Darling, sweetest Kit, I love you so!"

Their union was swift and passionate, infinitely satisfying, and Kitty knew, as at last they lay still side by side, that she loved him as, in all her life, she had loved no other man. And Johnny's face continued to elude her.

Magdalen returned home at afternoon teatime, from a busy half day with a Government House hospital charity committee, making up dressings and rolling bandages for New Zealand's wounded, to learn that Claus Van Buren had called in her absence.

"The captain said he would call again, ma'am," her new maid, Hannah Lucas, told her. "He is just back from Auckland, and he left letters for you." The woman's homely face was lit with a smile, as if anticipating her mistress's pleasure, as she handed over the letters. Hannah was a treasure, Magdalen thought. Widowed, tragically, on the passage out, and with no children, the poor woman had been compelled to seek employment, and, in very truth, Magdalen had been fortunate to engage her. Hannah was wonderful with the boys and Jessie, which left Biddy free to help with Rufus and assist her with the work of the house.

One of the letters was from Red, she saw, and when, unbidden, Hannah brought her a tea tray, she settled down in an armchair in the warm evening sunshine, poured herself a cup, and started to open her husband's letter with eager anticipation.

"The lads are not back yet, ma'am," Hannah informed her. "But when they come, I will give them their tea and leave you undisturbed, until you are ready to see them."

Magdalen thanked her and opened her husband's letter.

Like all Red's missives—and, indeed, like hers to him—this contained details of his day-to-day doings, which she loved to hear. He told her of Colonel Forsyth's unfortunate death in action and of the memorial service, which, it seemed, he had attended with Will De Lancey:

. . . His widow was there, dressed in deep mourning and weeping copiously, as was to be expected. She was being squired by an officer of H.M.'s 40th—Marcus Fisher, I have since discovered, whose name you may recall as the supposed hero of the *Pomona* wreck. And Kitty was there, escorted by a politician cum bloodstock breeder, an Irishman, Sean O'Hara. We greeted each other, Kitty and I, but that was all—no invitation to call on her, either to Will or myself, and little warmth, I'm sorry to say. My esteemed brother Johnny is making a terrible mistake, leaving her so much alone.

There was no other criticism. Red mentioned his meeting with Johnny at the end of the Waikato operations, described his encounter with Adam Shannon—the ex-naval officer whom the little Carmichael girl had praised so highly—and added with evident pleasure that the young man had been commissioned into a militia unit called the Forest Rangers.

The letter went on with a description of the dinner on board the *Mercia* with Will and Claus Van Buren, the last-named having given them all the news from Sydney, much to their pleasure.

We talked at some length of the two boys, Andy and Harry. Claus went to some pains to explain how eager Andy is to come out here to join Will in the war, and Will told him that the boy is too young and that he had refused to apply for a commission for him in one of H.M.'s regiments serving out here.

However, as you will see from the enclosed note from Will —who has also written to both lads—he *has* given his consent to Andy to sign on for one New Zealand passage on board the *Dolphin,* on the condition that he promises to return with the ship to Sydney.

Whether Andy will be able to see Will is uncertain, since we are ordered to Tauranga, in the Bay of Plenty, where there is fresh trouble. I expect to embark troops and leave within the next few days, and the general is likely to bring his force there to join us.

He gave details, which caused Magdalen to worry a little on his behalf, but added that they would have some sixteen hundred men, with artillery, and including a naval brigade and a number of ships, and he sounded so confident that her anxiety faded.

Red did not mention Johnny again, except to say in passing that he too would probably accompany the general's force to Tauranga, and that he thought, but could not be sure, that his brother had transferred to the militia unit in which Kitty's brother Patrick was serving. "At Kitty's behest, one imagines," he wrote, "rather than his own choice."

The letter ended with a rumor that a redoubt, named Fort Colville, at Maketu, fifteen miles down the coast from Tauranga Harbor, was under attack. "However, I understand that relief is being sent, by sea and land, and that the garrison is holding out."

With good wishes to family and friends, Red had concluded his account.

The letter from William was quite brief. He had written at some length to Andy, he said, and this note was only to confirm his permission to the boy to sign on with Claus Van Buren's *Dolphin* for one voyage to Auckland and back.

"Red will undoubtedly have given you all our news, so suffice it to offer you my best wishes and my thanks."

A businesslike, almost cold note, Magdalen decided, but . . . probably it was expressive of William's feelings in the matter. Clearly he did not want Andy to follow him to New Zealand, and most certainly he did not want the boy to join one of the armed forces and take part in the war with the Maoris. Probably he had extracted a promise from Claus that Andy would not be permitted to enlist, even though he was now sixteen.

But he would be one more to worry about, until his return, Magdalen thought resignedly, and . . . She picked up Red's letter again. Red had not mentioned the possibility of his own return to Sydney or Hobart or, indeed, anywhere in Australia. It was all about what he called "fresh trouble" in some place or some area known as Tauranga, in which, of course, he was due to take part. Still, it was good to have heard from him at such length, to know of his doings and to have news of Will De Lancey, Kitty, and the widowed Caroline Forsyth. And no doubt, when she saw Claus, he would be able to tell her more. He— The sound of raised voices broke into her thoughts. Magdalen stiffened, recognizing Harry's shrill young treble and Hannah's deeper voice, raised, it seemed, in reproach.

She waited, folding her letters and putting those for the boys to one side, ready to give to them. Andy, apparently, was not yet at home, since she could not hear his voice. But he was often later than Harry these days, since, as a prefect at school, he had duties

that kept him back. Prefect or . . . monitor. She could never remember which term the boys used, but—

"Mrs. Broome, ma'am!" Hannah came in, marshaling Harry
before her, both hands on his shoulders and her expression anxious. "Master Andy's not come home," she announced. "And
Harry says he won't be coming, but he refuses to say where he's
gone or why. Maybe you can talk to him."

Maybe she could, Magdalen thought; but aware of Harry's fierce
loyalty and the admiration he felt for Andy, she doubted her ability to extract the truth from him, however hard she tried. Hannah
had tried threats, without success, so she would have to make a
different approach.

"Harry dear," she began gently as the little boy stood defiantly
in front of her, "I am responsible for your and Andy's safety, you
know. I'm responsible to your uncle Will, so I must know where
Andy is and what he's doing. Please tell me, won't you?"

"I—I can't, Aunt Magdalen," Harry replied.

"Whyever not, Harry?"

"Because I gave my word. You said yourself that one must not
break one's word."

And so she had, Magdalen recognized; she had long preached
the principle to both boys, and she could not go back on all her
teaching now. Harry was very red in the face, very unhappy, but it
was obvious from his expression that he had no intention of breaking his word.

"Did you give your word, your promise, to Andy?" she asked.

He nodded. "Yes, ma'am, I did."

"I see. Well—" Magdalen gestured to Hannah to leave them,
and when the door closed behind her, she poured a second cup of
tea and passed it to the boy. "I expect you are ready for this. And
there's cake—lovely fruitcake, the kind you like. Sit down, Harry,
and I'll cut you a slice."

Clearly her reaction surprised him; he had expected anger, the
threat of punishment—not to be given tea and regaled on cake.

"Thank you, Aunt Magdalen," he stammered uncertainly, accepting the cake and obediently taking the chair she had indicated.
He crammed his mouth full, hoping to avoid giving any answers,
and wisely Magdalen left him alone, cutting him another slice of
cake and pouring herself a cup of tea, which she did not want. She
sipped it, studying his face but saying nothing. Andy, she thought,
must have run away, after swearing poor little Harry to secrecy,

and she could only hope that he had not attempted to enlist. Well grown though he was, the boy could not pass for much more than his sixteen years, and the regiment had been warned about him. Which left the possibility that he might have signed on as ship's crew. Sydney Harbor was always full of trading vessels, and most of them were short of hands.

Harry crammed the last piece of cake into his mouth. Magdalen let him chew it, but before he could ask to be excused, she asked sternly, "Harry, at what hour will you be free to tell me the truth? At sundown, perhaps?"

Taken by surprise, the boy nodded.

"Yes, ma'am. At sundown."

"Then it's a ship? Andy has signed on with a ship? Is that right, Harry?"

Taken aback, Harry stared at her in dismay. "How did you—how did you know, Aunt Magdalen?"

"It wasn't difficult to guess," Magdalen answered, hiding her own dismay. Andy could not have signed on with Claus's *Dolphin,* she reasoned, since the ship had only just come into port and would still have cargo to land, port dues to satisfy, and, in any event, Claus would have told her or sent word to warn her of the boy's action. It had to be a vessel whose destination was New Zealand; but with the war there and the need for men and supplies, there must be a number of traders bound for Auckland. From the window behind her, it was possible to see ships in the harbor, but . . . She braced herself, aware that sundown was less than an hour away. And William *had* given his permission for Andy to sign on with Claus. . . .

For over half an hour, at intervals of rising and going to the window overlooking the harbor, Magdalen tried to persuade Harry to divulge what he knew, but the boy was tearfully adamant. He had given his promise; he could not break it. Finally, in despair, she was about to resort to threats when Harry joined her at the window. He peered out, his expression very tense as he blinked his tears away, but then, suddenly, the tension left and he raised an odd little smile.

"Might I see Uncle Will's letter, please?" he asked. "You did say there was one for me, didn't you?"

Reluctantly Magdalen gave him his letter. He read it and then turned to her in glad relief.

"Aunt Magdalen, Andy *has* permission from Uncle Will—he says so here! He says that Andy may be allowed to sign on with—"

"With Captain Van Buren's *Dolphin,*" she reminded him, a trifle coldly. "Not just any ship, Harry."

"He could not wait for the *Dolphin,* Aunt Magdalen."

"Yes, but—"

Harry came and put his thin young arms endearingly around her neck. "Please don't be angry with him," he begged. "Or with me, Aunt Magdalen. Andy *had* to go, you see." He hugged her and then, holding her hand, led her to the window again. "That's his ship," he told her, pointing to a ramshackle old steamer, flying a pennant Magdalen did not recognize and heading down the great harbor with a cloud of black smoke rising from her single funnel. "That's the *Lady Fawcett.* She's bound for Auckland. And Andy signed on as cabin boy."

Magdalen's heart sank. But at least, she reflected, the *Lady Fawcett* was a trader, not a naval vessel, and was bound only for Auckland; perhaps there was no harm done. She would have to try to send a letter to William, warning him, but . . . She looked into Harry's glowing face, unable to be angry with him.

"I'm not angry with you, Harry," she managed, in a shaken voice. "But I wish Andy had waited and gone on board Captain Van Buren's *Dolphin.* I just wish so much that he had."

"Yes, Aunt Magdalen," Harry answered. He hugged her again. "I'll try to make up to you for Andy's not being here. I will try, Aunt Magdalen."

They clung together, watching Andy's ship out of sight.

Chapter XXII

ADAM WAS THE first to encounter Andy Melgund. The boy Wiremu brought him, wet and cold and clad in what appeared to be a Maori uniform, to Adam's billet. He said simply, "If you please, Mr. Shannon, this is Andy. He's a volunteer."

It was evident, even in the fading light of dusk, that Andy was not a Maori. His skin was tanned but unmistakably white, his eyes anything but dark, and the uniform he wore was too small. He also seemed to be badly frightened, and Adam, although he was equally wet and cold and tired into the bargain, had not the heart to deal with the lad unkindly. He extracted his full name, which meant nothing to him, and Andy admitted, shamefacedly, that he had deserted from his ship, a trader plying under the name of the *Lady Fawcett.*

"I had to, Mr. Shannon, sir—desert, I mean. The ship was leaving, you see, and I've come here to—to fight the rebel Maoris, sir."

"You're a mite young, aren't you?" Adam suggested.

"I'm sixteen, sir."

Adam studied him, guessing that, in the matter of his age, the boy had probably told the truth.

"Why?" he demanded. "Why have you come to fight? You're from Sydney, aren't you?"

Andy inclined his head. "From Sydney, yes, sir. And I've come to fight because—oh, because the rebel Maoris killed my folk. My father and mother, my brothers and sisters—all of them, sir. In the Taranaki four years ago. I—I promised my uncle, you see. He's here, on General Cameron's staff."

The boy's averted eyes made Adam skeptical. "Is he, now? And what is his name, Andy?"

"I—I cannot tell you that, sir." The boy's tone was obstinate. He was shivering and still frightened, but he made it plain that he would offer no more explanation of his presence. Adam took pity on him. One of the men was brewing coffee, and he sent Wiremu to beg three beakerfuls from him.

"You could do with a hot drink, couldn't you, Andy? You look a mite cold."

"I am, sir," Andy confessed. He hesitated. "I swam ashore, you see. But I didn't take my pay. I thought I—well, that I wasn't entitled to it, seeing I intended to run. But I couldn't have stayed with the *Lady Fawcett,* sir. They—the whole crew, I mean—they were a bunch of rogues. And the master—why, he was the worst of them." He shivered again, his small, earnest face pale under its tan, and once again Adam took pity on him.

"Take off that uniform," he advised gruffly, "and wrap yourself up in this blanket. I'll root around and find you something better to wear."

"Oh, thank you, sir!" The boy did as he had been bidden, and, wrapped in the blanket and sipping the hot coffee, he regained his lost color and, with it, his confidence. From odd remarks, it did not take Adam long to identify his uncle as Colonel De Lancey, but he kept his conclusions to himself. He would see De Lancey later that evening, when he went to report to the general and his staff the observations he and Hill had made of the formidable Gate *Pa* . . . although, he reflected wryly, since Colonel Greer of the 68th and his men had watched its construction, there was really not much he could add that the general did not know already.

This proved to be the case when, leaving both boys sleeping by the fire, he made his report, accompanied by Hill.

Sir Duncan Cameron had his plan of attack ready, and with the aid of a sketch map, the general illustrated what he wished done.

"We have a total of sixteen hundred troops, including the naval brigade, gentlemen, and five Armstrong guns, eight mortars, and, I believe, two howitzers," he announced. "Tomorrow morning, the guns and mortars will be brought up, aided by the commodore's seamen and marines. These should be positioned thus. . . ." Again the map was referred to, as the positions were indicated. "At dusk, Colonel Greer, I want you to move to the rear of the *pa.* We will launch a feint attack, to cover your movement, and you will have Mr. Purvis, a local settler, and a policeman named Tu as your guides." He went into brief details, and Greer's heavily bearded face expressed his pleasure, for he had waited a long time for this attack. He asked two or three questions, and then Cameron went on, "At seven a.m., gentlemen, the artillery will open up on the *pa*." Once again he gave details, as the men about him made their notes, occasionally putting questions. "The storming column will consist of a hundred and fifty men of the Forty-third, under Colonel Booth, with support provided by the seamen and marines of Her Majesty's ship *Harrier*, under the charge of Commander Hay. The signal for the assault will be given by rocket . . . and by me. Colonel Greer's force will be deployed in a wide semicircle here, on this spur running behind Gate *Pa*, where, if God blesses our arms, they will cut off any retreat by the enemy. Now, if you have any further questions, be so good as to put them."

There were a number, and as he listened, Adam realized that this was to be an assault by the imperial regiments and the Royal Navy, with the colonial force left only as the backup, should they be required. Backup, he thought disappointedly, and rescue parties, should casualties prove heavy. The general stood down, and various staff officers said what they had to say and answered questions. They included Colonel De Lancey, who, as always, was brief and very clear.

The briefing over at last, Adam stood at the end of a small queue, waiting to speak to De Lancey. Captain Red Broome and his brother were ahead of him; he exchanged smiles with them and listened to their questions and De Lancey's replies, and then, when they both moved away, he drew himself up and saluted.

"Colonel De Lancey—if I may have a word, sir."

De Lancey recognized him at once. "Ah, Mr. Shannon of the Forest Rangers. Certainly—what can I do for you?"

"I have your nephew in my billet, sir—Andrew, Andy . . . but he refuses to tell me his surname or, indeed, to admit that he is your nephew." Adam quickly repeated the story the boy had told him. "I worked out his relationship to you, sir, from some of the things he told me. He didn't intend, of course, to reveal the truth, and he doesn't know I've come to you. But I—well, I thought I'd better." He saw the older man's expression harden and added quickly, "He deserted from an old freighter, the *Lady Fawcett*, and swam ashore, sir. He was cold and wet when my Maori bugler brought him to me, but I can assure you he's quite all right."

"Good God!" De Lancey sounded dismayed. "He swam ashore, you said?"

"Yes, sir, that's right."

De Lancey shook his head. "I saw the *Lady Fawcett* this morning, and it's no wonder he ran from that old wreck. But . . . oh, Lord, Shannon, I've a night's work ahead of me!" The colonel gestured to the pile of maps and papers on the table in front of him. "Can you keep the boy with you, until after we've launched our assault on the *pa?* Andrew Melgund, his name is, actually, and his family were killed in India, during the Mutiny, not out here. He told you the story of his friend . . . not that it matters. He was there when it happened, and he identifies himself with the tragedy, poor little fellow."

"Yes, sir, I can keep him with me," Adam agreed readily. "We're not to be actively engaged in the attack."

"No—it's to be an imperial show. But I don't want Andy joining in, Shannon, in any capacity." De Lancey hesitated. "Perhaps I *had* better see him. Tomorrow morning, after we've broken our fast and the bombardment has started. But put the fear of God into him, won't you? He's jumped the gun, the young rascal—I'd given him permission to sign on with Captain Van Buren's *Dolphin,* not that ghastly old tub the *Lady Fawcett.*"

"Right, Colonel, I'll do my best. But he *is* pretty badly scared already." Adam smiled. "From the little he said, I fancy he had quite a shaking up on passage, sir. He said the crew were a bunch of rogues and the master the worst of the lot!"

"Good," De Lancey echoed heartlessly. "Perhaps that will teach him to do as he's told."

Perhaps it would, Adam thought, although he doubted it. He returned to his billet, to find Andy Melgund fast asleep, with Wiremu beside him, both curled up warmly beneath the blanket. They had eaten, he was told, and given no trouble to anyone. He scared up some clothing, left it beside the boys, and, after drinking some more coffee and consuming a plate of leftover stew, sought his own rest.

Next morning, with Greer and his men fully deployed in a semicircle seven hundred yards from the rear of the *pa,* the bombardment commenced. It continued throughout the day, as Colonel Booth's storming column and the naval brigade awaited the order to make their attack. Rain poured down, virtually without cease, but in spite of this, one of the six-pounder guns was dragged across the swamp to high ground, from where it successfully enfiladed the *pa.* Under the assault of the British artillery, a breach was blown in the center of the palisade, and as the light was beginning to fade, General Cameron ordered the rocket signal to be ignited.

At four o'clock, cheering their heads off, the first wave of stormers went in, led by Booth and Commander Hay. Watching, as well as he could, Adam saw them gain the breach with little loss and pour into the *pa,* still cheering. But then a terrible fire, at almost point-blank range, met them from defenders occupying trenches and dugouts in the depths of the *pa.* Adam could not see through the haze of gunsmoke, but he guessed, from the shouts and screams, that the officers in the van of the attack must have been shot down.

A second wave of stormers had gone in and joined in the hand-to-hand fighting with the Maori defenders when, without warning, the attack, blunted and lacking leadership, became a rout.

Shouts of "They're coming in their thousands! Retire! Retire!" reached the watchers faintly above the crackle of musketry as the stormers struggled to escape from the *pa.*

"Dear God!" an officer who was watching beside Adam exclaimed in dismay. "Te Rawiri and his people must have been trying to escape from the rear, but they ran into Colonel Greer's fellows, who drove 'em back into the *pa!*"

And if the officers who had led the storming party had been killed or wounded, Adam thought, what could be expected, save panic on the part of their men when they found themselves facing what appeared to be Maori reinforcements, rushing forward to meet and do battle with them?

He let out his breath, feeling sick at heart. The attack on the Gate *Pa* had, as William De Lancey had reminded him, been undertaken solely by the imperial forces, the men chosen to take part in it selected by General Cameron, and the militia and volunteer units ordered to hold their fire. But with men dead and dying now inside the *pa,* it was up to anyone able to walk to go in and succor the wounded . . . himself included. He had left Andy and Wiremu in the care of a reliable old corporal of the Rangers, with instructions not to let them out of sight, and, satisfied that both lads were safe enough, he got to his feet, glancing questioningly at the staff officer who had shared his vigil.

"I'm going in, to see if I can help," Adam said. "Are you coming?"

Dazed, the officer looked up at him and then slowly shook his head. "No point in committing suicide, is there?" he responded thickly. "The C.O. will be dead, God rest his soul . . . and Hay, and the Lord alone knows how many more. I—I *can't* go in."

He was weeping, Adam saw, and seemingly paralyzed into inaction. Acutely sorry for him, he laid a hand briefly on the man's shoulder in wordless sympathy, then set off for the *pa* at a dogged run, trying in vain to rally the men he encountered fleeing back to their own lines. Only two took heed and turned to follow him—a grizzled seaman, armed with a cutlass and bleeding from a head wound, and a young soldier of the 43rd, who was sobbing as he ran.

Inside the *pa,* all was smoke and wild confusion, the dead and wounded lying where they had fallen. A small naval party, with Surgeon Manley, a Crimean veteran, in charge, carried out the dying Commander Hay. Manley called out, as they passed, "I'm coming back, as soon as we have the commander settled. Bring any severely wounded men here."

"Right," Adam acknowledged, and pressed on, through sporadic fire, with his two battered volunteers at his heels. They found the commander of the *Miranda,* Captain Jenkins, covered with blood, as he fought to free himself from one of the trenches, so packed with Maori defenders that they were unable to use their tomahawks or reload their firearms. Jenkins had somehow held them off with his telescope, but he was nearing exhaustion when Adam and his party, now augmented to seven, helped drag him out. Two of the naval officers assisted him back to the field dressing station, and two petty officers joined Adam in their place. They worked on grimly, bringing wounded men to Surgeon Manley or, if the wounded were too badly injured to move, giving them water.

The rain continued to pour down, but with the first gray light of dawn, Adam realized that the firing had ceased or virtually so, and that the Maori defenders had evacuated their *pa,* taking most of their wounded with them and even some of their dead. In the dim light, he saw two small forms, carrying water to wounded men— European and Maori alike—and, coming across William De Lancey, seated at the side of a dying soldier of the 43rd, he gestured to the two lads and said, "Our boys, sir—doing good work. Though how they contrived to escape Corporal Davies I'll never know."

"Low cunning," Colonel De Lancey suggested. His face was black from the smoke of battle, his voice oddly faint, but Adam thought nothing of it until the older man added, "Leave them to their work of mercy, Shannon. Perhaps if they see at firsthand the aftermath of war, they will be less anxious to take part in it. And now, if you would be so kind, I'd appreciate your aid. I've been shot in the thigh, unfortunately."

Adam gave him the help he had requested, and the two boys, responding to his call, came over to assist him. As they made their slow way to the field dressing station, Colonel Booth, evidently very seriously wounded, was being carried out by two of his officers just ahead of them. General Cameron, recognizing him, stepped up to offer his condolences.

"My poor dear fellow," he began, "you are grievously hurt. You—"

But the gallant Booth would have none of it. Somehow he managed a salute and, the tears streaming down his ravaged face, apologized for failing to carry out the orders he had been given.

"My fault, sir," he exclaimed hoarsely. "Not my men's. They did all . . . I asked of them. And—and more."

His name headed the list of killed and wounded, which numbered more than a hundred and sixty-eight, of whom forty-six officers and men lost their lives.

During the next two weeks, General Cameron had redoubts constructed on the site of the Gate *Pa,* and with the position again to be left under Colonel Greer's command, most of the naval vessels and the troops were ordered to return to Auckland.

On a visit to Colonel De Lancey, recovering in the field hospital, Adam met Captain Red Broome, and from him and the colonel learned, for the first time, of a religious movement known as the Hauhau, which was causing fresh trouble in the New Plymouth and Taranaki area.

"The Kingites are virtually defeated," De Lancey said. "True, Te Rawiri won a moral victory at Gate *Pa,* but one more assault on his part here will finish him. And he'll make it, never fear. But Colonel Greer is a most competent commander, and he'll have his own regiment, with some excellent officers, and a reputation to retrieve. No, I'm not worried about matters here—but the infernal Hauhau are another story altogether." He glanced at Captain Broome. "You know more about them than I do, Red, I think."

Red Broome shrugged. "My brother John is in New Plymouth, with his Volunteers, and he was at the successful attack on Kaitake. I know only what he told me in a letter. He was full of praise for the Fifty-seventh and for Captain Atkinson's company of Rangers, Shannon, as well as Mace's Mounted Volunteers." He described the battle very briefly and smiled as he added, "Kaitake was one of the strongest of the rebels' positions, but now it's in our hands, and the erstwhile defenders have made off into the bush. But—the Hauhau are still a force to be reckoned with."

"What exactly *are* they, sir?" Adam ventured. "Some sort of religious order?"

"Well, you could call them that, I suppose." Red Broome's smile faded. "As far as I can make out, a self-styled prophet by the name of Te Ua Haumene, of one of the Taranaki tribes in the Cape Egmont region, began preaching a new religion—*Pai-Marire,* the Maoris call it, meaning "the good and the peaceful" in their tongue. Te Ua was a former slave, my brother told me, who was brought up by a missionary, John Whiteley. His new religion is a mixture of the old pagan beliefs, Christianity, and Judaism, with the Bible and the Book of Revelations, in particular, as its basis. The central emblem is a flagstaff—the *niu*—about which the converts march, chanting and emitting the chorus of *hau hau,* which —according to my brother—sounds like the barking of a dog."

"It doesn't sound very menacing, sir," Adam suggested, a trifle disappointed by the description he had been given.

"There's more to them than perhaps I've suggested, Shannon," Red Broome answered, with sudden gravity. "And they *are* gathering adherents, particularly among the villages in this area and in the Taranaki, who have lost so many young warriors in the recent fighting. Te Ua offers *utu*—revenge—and he has apparently told his followers that the Angel Gabriel will give immunity in battle to all true believers."

"A trifle dangerous, surely?" Colonel De Lancey put in.

"Not really, Will. If a man is killed, it's simply said that he lacked faith—the angelic immunity is conferred only on the truly faithful."

"Is there not some tale about a head—one of our officer's heads?" De Lancey pursued.

Red Broome frowned. "Well, Johnny told me there was, but he hasn't seen it. The head is said to be that of a captain of the Fifty-seventh—Lloyd, I believe his name was. He was caught in an ambush outside Kaitake. There was quite a battle, in which Lloyd and a number of his men were killed and decapitated. Poor Lloyd's head has been carried round among the worshipers, precipitating

scenes of fury and—well, savagery, I suppose you would call it."
He grimaced in distaste. "The heads, I gather, have been preserved
by some process Johnny called *moko-mokai.*"

"Praise be to God," William De Lancey said, when Red fell
silent, "that I shall not have to go into action against the
Hauhaus." He gestured toward his leg, which was suspended from
a sling attached to the ceiling. "I don't know what sort of ball hit
me, but the surgeons here say they cannot remove it."

Adam stared at him in astonishment. "You mean you are—or
you expect to be invalided, sir? Is that what young Andy was on
about? I confess I couldn't understand him."

William De Lancey's smile was wry. "Let's say I expect to be,
Shannon. And frankly I shall not be sorry. I'll take both lads back
to Sydney with me—in your ship, Red, if I'm lucky. But not the
Mercia, I gather."

"Not the *Mercia,* Will," Red assured him. "I'm commanding the
Esk at the moment. But I'm on standby for Sydney." He smiled.
"For which, as you say, praise be to God! I've had enough of this
war."

They both looked at Adam, and De Lancey said quietly, "So we
shall have to leave the Hauhaus to the likes of you, Lieutenant
Shannon. In due course, that is. I hope you are ready for it."

"I hope so, too, sir, truly I do," Adam responded. "But these so-
called Hauhaus . . . well, I don't know. They sound like an odd
bunch. At least, sir, one could *respect* Chief Te Rawiri. He adhered
to his code of conduct, and he and his warriors fought well at Gate
Pa. I saw for myself how they aided the wounded of both sides. But
taking heads and using them as—as a means of recruiting followers
is—damn it, sir, it's reverting to the primitive, is it not?"

"That," De Lancey assured him, "is expressing precisely my
feelings concerning them, Shannon. And I wish you well in the
forthcoming battle against this Te Ua fellow. I trust you will have
no objection to my taking Wiremu from you? He wants to come,
he tells me."

"No objection, sir," Adam answered. "I'm glad for his sake,
poor little devil."

Wiremu had been a good soldier, he reflected, despite his tender
years. He had confessed to the act of treachery that had led to
Adam's capture but had tried, ever since, to make up for what he
had done, and he *had* made up for it, ten times over. It was good
that he was to go to Sydney with Colonel De Lancey and young

Andy Melgund—good and not undeserved. In Australia, he would have friends and—yes, a family.

As Colonel De Lancey had forecast, Chief Te Rawiri did make one last attempt to follow up his victory at the Gate *Pa,* but Colonel Greer was waiting for him, and, at Te Ranga in June, in a bloody and savage affray, Te Rawiri was among more than a hundred Maoris killed and interred. On July 25, his people—a hundred and thirty of them, including chiefs—came to Tauranga to make their submission to Greer. Only King Tawhiao, Te Rewi, and a few others withdrew into the bush, refusing to surrender.

The end of the Waikato campaign and the coming of winter entailed redeployment of several regiments. The British naval frigates remained on duty in the colony through October, when Governor Sir George Grey requested Frederick Weld, the minister for native affairs, to form a ministry. Weld agreed to do so, on condition that his "self-reliant" policy was followed, and for the first time the home government was asked to take away all the imperial regiments and the naval frigates, leaving the defense of New Zealand in the hands of militia and volunteers.

Adam had done little fighting, but to his surprise, on reaching Auckland at the end of the year, he was sent for by his late commanding officer.

"I am not taking you away from the Rangers, Shannon," the colonel said. "You seem to have done well with them. But, as you may or may not know, Captain Marcus Fisher is leaving us. He has sold his commission, and with the casualties we have unhappily suffered, there are a number of vacancies. I propose to give you a commission in your present rank and—" With a stiffly raised hand, he cut short Adam's embarrassed attempt to thank him. "Say nothing, my dear young man—in my view, you have earned the rank. I am proud to have you as one of my officers." He smiled and offered his hand. "Captain Fisher has married," he added, his smile fading abruptly. "The widow of the late Colonel Forsyth of the Seventieth, whom I believe you knew . . . ah, Mrs. Caroline Forsyth."

"Yes, sir," Adam admitted, startled by this item of news but anxious not to show it. Caroline, he thought, *Caroline* married to the unspeakable Fisher? He felt no pain, no sense of loss, but for all that was unable to think of any reason why she had chosen Fisher.

"I knew them both, sir. Captain Fisher commanded my draft on board the *Pomona.*"

"Ah, yes, the *Pomona.* Lost at sea, wasn't she? And Captain Fisher was the hero of that affair, according to some report I read of it . . . in the *Sydney Morning Herald,* I think." The colonel frowned, making a tired effort to remember, then giving up. "One cannot always go by newspaper reports." He chuckled softly. "There was one in a local paper here, the *New Zealander,* which accused the men of the naval brigade—and, in particular, those of the *Esk*—of deserting their wounded officers at the Gate *Pa.* Did you hear about that?"

"No, sir," Adam denied. "I was there, at Gate *Pa,* but—"

"Were you, now?" the colonel said. "Well, anyway, Shannon, two hundred of the *Esk*'s men landed at Winyard Pier and invaded the newspaper office in Shortland Street. They threatened to pull down the shack in which the reporters were working, unless a denial was published. Needless to tell you, a denial *was* published in the next edition." He laughed aloud. "Showed a good spirit, did it not? I take it they didn't desert their officers, eh?"

Carried back in memory to the chaos at Gate *Pa,* Adam murmured his assent. Poor devils, he thought, they had had little choice, and . . . they had gone back afterward, with the surgeon, Manley.

Outside in the street, a little later, he was still thinking of the Gate *Pa* battle when, to his astonishment, he saw and recognized Caroline Forsyth—Caroline *Fisher*—walking past, on the arm of her new husband. He kept his head averted and was too far away to hear what they were saying, but . . . undoubtedly they were quarreling, and Caroline sounded very angry indeed.

I wish you joy, Marcus Fisher, Adam thought. My God, I wish you joy!

And for no reason that he could have explained, he found himself remembering Emily Carmichael. There had been no letters from her after that one, long ago, in which she had naively warned him of Caroline's coming to New Zealand. He ought to have been glad of that, and yet . . . against all reason, he continued to harbor the hope that one day he might hear from her again.

The impulse to write to Emily was, for an irrational moment, very strong, but he mastered it and, with a sinking heart, strode on down the street.

Chapter XXIII

IN THE WHARE of Te Ngara, the leaders of the new converts of his tribe, to whom he had administered the Hauhau rites less than ten days ago, had gathered for the purpose of agreeing to their future strategy. Because those present came of two different *hapus* of the same tribe, agreement was by no means certain, and Te Ngara had to argue long and loud before he had the majority in favor of the action he had put forward.

"This *pakeha*, Sean O'Hara, breeds horses," he told the assembled leaders. "He has fifteen, maybe more, broken and ready to be sold to the Volunteers. The Volunteers lack horses, but so do we, my friends. Imagine with what pleasure and relief the great Te Ua will receive them! And we can take this place of O'Hara's easily."

"How do you know we can, Te Ngara?" one of the older chiefs, Te Wangi, demanded.

"Because I have had the place watched. I have myself watched it. And"—Te Ngara's plump face split into a grin—"because I have one of O'Hara's servants reporting to me. He—"

"Is this man reliable?" another asked.

"Certainly he is. Topia Tiki is my cousin. He knows well what he is about. There are barely half a dozen men in O'Hara's employ."

"Yes, yes, Te Ngara," Te Wangi exclaimed impatiently. But will this *pakeha* permit us to take his horses without firing a shot? How can you say that we shall meet with no resistance?"

"Because he gives a party tomorrow night," Te Ngara repeated. "As I told you, all his servants will be in the house or the kitchens. Believe me, I have planned everything most carefully. The *pakeha* O'Hara has stolen the wife of a friend of his who is in the fighting.

A man named Broome. His wife is a lady, very beautiful. Her name is Kitty Broome. She lives in Auckland, but she comes to ride O'Hara's horses." He gave chapter and verse of the lady's visits, and, impressed at last, the Hauhau recruits murmured their assent. Patiently they listened to Te Ngara's plan for the attack, and Te Wangi finally permitted himself a smile, which was echoed by the others as they listened.

"This will please Te Ua. Yes, it is good. You have done well, Te Ngara. We will ride to join Te Ua with O'Hara's horses, and he will know that we are with him, heart and soul. And if we should have to kill any of the men—why, his head shall be placed on our *niu* pole!

Johnny Broome sat in the empty living room of his house in Auckland, his brow furrowed as he sipped the tea the maid had brought him and reread the brief note from his wife.

He was very tired and was, in fact, on sick leave, after a strenuous campaign in the area between New Plymouth and Wanganui. Serving on the governor's staff, he had accompanied the volunteer force under the command of Major Rookes, with Patrick much in evidence in the Yeomanry Cavalry, and they had made an arduous march through the bush in heavy rain, to come up to the rear of the Hauhau stronghold of the Weraroa *pa*. This was the *pa* that General Sir Duncan Cameron had claimed he must have two thousand regular troops to capture. . . . Johnny's expression relaxed as he remembered how the Hauhaus had deserted it, when they had found themselves surrounded. Brigadier General Waddy, not sure whether he was supposed to obey his general's orders or those of the governor, had obeyed the latter, and his imperial troops, making a show of force in front of the *pa*, had been brilliantly successful in perpetrating Sir George Grey's plan.

It had finished General Cameron, of course. He hung on, writing bitter dispatches to the British War Office, but he had left New Zealand four months later, to take up the post of governor of the Royal Military College, Sandhurst.

In the meantime, Pipiriki, on the upper reaches of the Wanganui River, had had three redoubts manned by only two hundred Volunteers, and by mid-July the Hauhaus had put them under siege. The commander, Major Willoughby Brassey, anxious when his supplies of food and medicine had started to fall short, had sent off messages in Latin and French, sealing these in bottles and throwing them into the river. Finally, when no reply had come, he had sent off by canoe two volunteers, who, to their joy, had encountered the relief force next day. Commanded by the splendid Rookes, they had included two companies of von Tempsky's Rangers, the Volunteer Cavalry, and some two hundred of the Maori friendlies.

Resistance had gradually faded; the Volunteers at Pipiriki had been relieved by the 57th's two companies and moved to the West Coast. He had not been able to go with them, Johnny thought, with sudden bitterness. Patrick had been wounded—severely, but not fatally—and, before taking his own sick leave, Johnny had managed to pay a visit to him in the hospital at New Plymouth.

Johnny moodily poured himself out a second cup of tea. His brother-in-law had been badly shot up; one wound, in his right leg, had incapacitated him, and he could barely walk, even with the aid of a crutch. He was a man of action, Patrick, and he hated to be laid up and out of the war. While the governor, in September, had issued a proclamation declaring that the war was now officially at an end and that there would be no more confiscations of land, Patrick had stated grimly that the proclamation was a "mere paper tiger."

"Do you suppose the blasted Hauhaus will take a blind bit of notice of it, Johnny? I'm damned if I do! Why, it is holding the government up to ridicule and worse! You know the way they have of putting the treated heads of enemies they've killed on their *niu* poles? D'you know whose head the Hauhaus under Te Kereopa have on their pole? That of a *German* Lutheran, the Reverend Carl Volkner!"

He had had to confess that he did not know, Johnny recalled, and . . . Patrick had told him the whole awful story from beginning to end, with anger and hatred in his voice.

"Poor Volkner, with the Reverend Thomas Grace, ignored warnings and returned to the Bay of Plenty in a small schooner, the *Enterprise.* The fellow Kereopa—a bloodthirsty warrior who had fought in the Waikato—whipped up the population into an hysterical Hauhau mob, boarded the *Enterprise,* looted her, and took the two missionaries prisoner. Grace and the captain of the schooner were spared because they were Jewish and thus, heaven knows why, regarded as co-religionists. But Volkner was taken to his old church, tried by Kereopa, and most barbarously hanged." Patrick had given shocking details of the killing and of the use of the unfortunate missionary's decapitated head to decorate a *niu* pole.

"I've conceived the greatest respect for von Tempsky's Forest Rangers," Patrick had gone on, and had given at least half a dozen reasons for his opinion, to which Johnny had listened without comment. "They are all seasoned bushmen, Johnny, and one of the best is, I think, a friend of yours—a chap named Shannon. Adam Shannon, holding a commission in H.M.'s Fortieth, but seconded to the Rangers. You do know him, don't you?"

"Yes, indeed I do," Johnny had replied, and had once again listened to Patrick's account of how, with Captain Mace of the Taranaki Mounted Volunteers and three others, he had been ambushed by a party of seventy or eighty Hauhaus and been wounded.

"It's thanks to Mace and Shannon that I'm here at all," he had asserted, and then, when asked whether he had informed his sister Kitty of where he was, he denied it, with red-faced indignation.

"Good Lord, no—I told her nothing! Time enough to tell Kitty if and when I'm transferred to the main hospital in Auckland. She can come and visit me then. I'll be walking by that time, God willing."

Johnny stifled a sigh. His visit had been two—no, damn it, *three* —weeks ago, but here he was, back in Auckland at last, and it was evident that no word of Patrick's wounding had been received by Kitty. Her odd little message had made no mention of it; it was a cold, unfeeling note, addressed to him as if he were a stranger, rather than her husband, merely to inform him of—how had she put it?—"of a change in their relationship," which . . . well, he told himself bitterly, which was calculated to upset him. And it most certainly had.

Scowling, he glanced at the note again. Kitty had acknowledged receiving his letter. She had known he was coming to Auckland on leave, but there was no warmth in her welcome, no eager greeting. Just "please use the house as you wish. If you want to get in touch with me, you will find me at Killaloe, where I am the guest of Mr. Sean O'Hara."

No apology, no . . . devil take it, no sense of shame! Just a plain statement, saying where she was and where she proposed to remain, until he, Johnny thought angrily, finished his leave and returned to his military duty. There was even a brief mention of Patrick, with no hint at all that he had been wounded, simply the statement that "he seems to be enjoying his military experience"—and, yes, "I hope to see him again soon—it has been such a long time since I did."

Finally, as a postscript to her letter, Kitty had mentioned the new housekeeper she now employed, giving her name as Mrs. Martha Montrose.

"Martha lost her husband last year at the Gate *Pa*," the note said. "I took her on, as housekeeper, and think the world of her. She will look after you, in my absence."

Still no apology, Johnny registered. Still no explanation, beyond that bald statement that Kitty was "the guest of Mr. Sean O'Hara" at Killaloe. She—

There was a knock on the door, and Martha Montrose came in. She picked up the tea tray and said, in a quiet, businesslike voice, "I expect you must be ready for a meal, sir, after your journey. It will be ready for you in ten minutes, in the dining room." She listed what she had prepared, and Johnny studied her as she did so, seeing a neatly dressed woman of perhaps fifty or so, with a pale, lined face and a pair of wide-set blue eyes. Conscious of his gaze on her, Mrs. Montrose met his stare unsmilingly and asked, "Will that be all, sir?"

He assured her that it would. "You've chosen pork, which is my favorite meat, Mrs. Montrose. I don't know how you knew that, but—"

"Mrs. Broome told me what to order for you, sir," the housekeeper answered. She moved toward the door. "In ten minutes, if you please, sir," she bade him, and the door closed behind her.

The meal was excellent. Mrs. Montrose waited on him, but for all his efforts, Johnny's questions were stalled or brushed aside, his compliments accepted, and his attempts to draw the woman out adroitly disregarded. Only once, when she brought his coffee, did something he said—a comment about the Gate *Pa*—appear, for a moment, to get through to her. She said, avoiding his gaze, her tone flat, "Gate *Pa* was a defeat, Captain Broome, wasn't it? Unusual for General Sir Duncan Cameron. But there—it happens, doesn't it, even to the best of generals? I'll bid you good night, sir, and trust you will sleep well."

Tired and well fed, Johnny slept in his old bed until, next day, Martha Montrose brought him his breakfast in bed.

"I let you sleep, Captain Broome," the woman told him, setting his tray on the bedside table and, for the first time, smiling when he sniffed the contents of the plate she uncovered.

"What's this? By heaven, Mrs. Montrose, steak, I do declare! And eggs with it! I could ask for no more, indeed I could not! Thank you."

"I know how men eat, after months in the war, sir," she admitted. "I'll let the day in." She crossed to the window and drew back the drapes with something of a flourish, revealing a sun-bright day outside. "It's afternoon, sir, as you may see. I'd have left you longer to sleep, but—Mrs. Broome sent a note for you. I hesitated, and then . . . well, the man who delivered it, Mr. Riordan, who works at Killaloe, sir, said that Mrs. Broome wanted you to have it straightaway. He—Mr. Riordan, that is—is waiting for a reply from you, sir."

Johnny's appetite, stimulated by the smell of the steak, threatened to vanish. He looked at the note Mrs. Montrose laid on the bed beside him, and, as if guessing his thoughts, she picked it up and carried it across to the dressing table. Smiling briefly again, she added, with unexpected tartness, "Eat your breakfast now, Captain Broome. I'll give Mr. Riordan a little something, just to keep him quiet. Call me when you are ready with your reply, sir."

What was the rush, Johnny asked himself; if Kitty had written another cold little note, like the one he had read yesterday, he could wait until he had eaten before reading it. . . . For God's sake, who did she think he was?

Contrary to his expectations, he enjoyed his breakfast—Mrs. Montrose was, indeed, a very good cook. But . . . the damned letter on the dressing table had to be read. Annoyed with himself, even so, as he crossed the room, he looked out at the street and finally picked up the envelope. He carried it back to his bed, fingers tearing at its fastenings as he did so, impatience driving him beyond the bounds of prudence. He read it quickly.

Johnny,

Riordan tells us you are back in Auckland. Sean O'Hara is hosting a small party this evening at Killaloe, and we both thought that, in the circumstances, you would wish to be present.

As you will obviously not know, Sean has had a most generous offer from the Auckland Militia, for his horses in training and the farm—land and buildings—which he is tempted to accept. This will cover his retirement and would amply pay for a visit to Ireland by us both. . . .

Johnny's heart was suddenly in his mouth, as he visualized Auckland without his wife.

Kitty might be engaged in having—what the devil did they call it these days?—a love affair, he supposed dully, with the blasted fellow from the land of her birth . . . although she must have kept pretty quiet about it, since no one had said a word to him since his return. Although the injured husband was often the last to be informed, and he had not been back for very long, so that perhaps . . . Smothering his sense of outrage, he picked up the note again and read on.

Sean has asked me to go with him, but you are still my husband, Johnny, and I feel very strongly that I cannot accept this invitation without first, at least, discussing its implications with you, and obtaining your consent to my accepting it.

If you cannot come out to Killaloe this evening, please say so in your reply to me, and if possible, will you be so kind as to tell me when you could come out to Killaloe. The matter is urgent, as I feel sure you will understand.

She signed it simply "Kitty," and Johnny fought down his anger as he reread the note. The matter *was* urgent; he understood this, and—oh, the devil fly away with the woman! She had known he would have no engagements, so that he might as well accept the invitation for this evening, and—damn it, get it over with, once and for all!

Mrs. Montrose, anticipating the fact that he had to pen a reply, had left writing materials on the dressing table. Johnny picked up pen and paper and wrote, with restraint, that he would present himself at Killaloe that evening. . . . "after your party has eaten," he added. "I will dine here and call about nine-thirty."

He gave his note to Riordan, explaining that he would be at Killaloe by nine-thirty, and the man said, politely, that he would arrange for a horse to await him at the livery stable. "Unless, sir, you have your own animal—"

Johnny shook his head. "No, I came by ship. A horse will be very convenient, thank you."

Riordan gave him directions and prepared to return with his

note, and Johnny, faced with a day in Auckland, made first for the headquarters of the new general, Trevor Chute. He found the staff considerably changed, but a number of officers he had fought with were there, and he learned, greatly to his disappointment, that Colonel De Lancey had been invalided some five weeks earlier, and that Captain Red Broome had left for Sydney only ten days ago.

"The river steamers have been left behind," a major of the 50th told him, "including the *Mercia,* now crewed by and commanded by the Auckland Naval Volunteers. Captain Broome though, is being promoted. He will take over as commandant after a spot of leave, which I'm sure will please him. Pity you missed his farewell dinner, Johnny—it was *quite* an occasion, I can tell you!" He had added, smiling, "But he'll be glad enough to go back to Australia, I'll venture."

Other officers came in, including Adam Shannon, who greeted Johnny warmly, and over an early dinner in the mess, more news was exchanged, Adam giving a wryly humorous description of his march under the new general, Chute, in January.

"There were only forty-five of us Rangers," he had ended his account, "and the orders we mostly heard were 'Fifty-seventh, advance! Rangers, clear the bush!' Or 'Go in, Die-hards!' And, by heaven, the Fifty-seventh went in, but you should have heard their grumbles, once it was over. They suffered heavy casualties, but— the general wasn't satisfied. He's an India Mutiny veteran, and he became annoyed because the gibes of the colonial society hinted that his imperial troops were fitted only for the open field. So he decided to show 'em the fallacy of such an allegation." Adam chuckled. "He led an imperial column along an ancient war-track, opened up twenty years since by the New Zealand Company as a bridle path and badly overgrown, leading to the distant Waitara block . . . *behind* Mount Egmont!"

"But you made it, didn't you, Shannon?" one of the staff officers suggested, a hint of envy in his tone.

"Yes, we made it," Adam agreed. "Three companies of the Fourteenth, von Tempsky's company of Rangers, and about eighty picked warriors of the Native Contingent. *We* were given the pioneering duties, and the blasted rain never ceased!" He shook his head ruefully. "Now, of course, it's all talk of sending the imperial regiments home." He glanced across at Johnny. "How do you feel about it, John?"

"Me?" Johnny had not really given the matter much thought,

but . . . well, Kitty's notes—in particular the one this morning—had left him without feelings. Almost dead, as if . . . as if nothing mattered any longer. "I'm not sure, Adam. Like every one else, I suppose. We ought to be able to cope now, with the militia and the Volunteers."

Adam, he saw, was frowning; one of the other officers, a major, listed the regiments that had gone. The 65th had been the first, after nineteen years in the colony; then the 70th, the 68th, and the 43rd had all sailed for England between January and March, and the 40th—Adam's old regiment—had sailed in May, for Portsmouth. Now, according to the major, the 14th and the 50th were ready to sail for Australia, which left—good God, Johnny thought, as the major said so—only the 12th, the 14th, and the 50th, with the last two preparing for departure!

"And I'm going soon," the older officer announced, with relief. "Taking passage on board the *Brisk*. You should have gone in May, with your regiment, Adam. Why didn't you?"

"I transferred, sir," Adam answered flatly. "To the Fiftieth. But—" Again he was looking at Johnny. "Did you not say you were going out to Killaloe, John?"

Johnny glanced at the mess clock and saw, with a sense of shock, that it was time he left. There was the horse to pick up, from the livery stable, and he would have close on an hour's ride, if he were to reach Killaloe by nine-thirty. He rose at once, made his excuses, and left the mess, with Adam Shannon accompanying him.

"My company of Rangers is at Mere," Adam told him, "about four miles out of town. We could ride part of the way together, John, if you are willing."

He would have preferred to ride alone, but . . . Johnny inclined his head. "I have to collect a horse at the livery stable. If you don't mind waiting, then fine—we can ride out together. Only you—"

"I'm in no hurry," Adam assured him. "It will be company. It's a dull ride."

In a tactful manner, as they rode out of town together, Adam endeavored to find out whether Johnny knew of his wife's affair with Sean O'Hara. Initially he hinted, but as Johnny replied in seeming doubt, he was driven at last to ask in straight terms.

"Your lady has been very careful, Johnny," he said, "but I'm afraid the gossips have seen through her care. I mean you—well,

CAROLINE WAS TIRED to death of hearing about the war, which was supposed to have been over, and she breathed a sigh of relief when the women, taking their cue from Lady Kitty Broome, rose from the table and started down the hallway to the withdrawing room, leaving the men to their port and cigars.

She had been reluctant to accompany Marcus to the dinner party at Killaloe in the first place, but he had insisted on going, claiming that it was, despite its distinctly Irish cast, the best society that the country around Auckland had to offer. And as if to confirm her doubts on the matter, all during the meal the conversation had kept returning relentlessly to the recent Hauhau attacks near Poverty Bay and the rumors that some native chief or other—Te Ngara, the name had sounded like—had constructed a new fortified *pa* in the bush not too far east of Auckland itself.

With increasingly strained patience Caroline had listened to her husband argue with a dashing young captain of the 50th about the advisability of withdrawing the Queen's regiments from the colony, and she had hardly been surprised when Marcus, while reminding his listener that the governor had declared the war over, had been rudely interrupted by one of O'Hara's settler friends—a sun-browned bush farmer called Wherry.

"Over, is it?" the man had cut in angrily. "It's too soon for the imperial regiments to be pullin' out, too soon by a damn sight—beggin' your pardon, ladies. It's nothing but a bald-faced attempt by the War Office to put the expense of the war on the shoulders of the colonists!"

Another of the red-faced settlers—a man in ill-fitting evening dress by the name of Dobson—had supported him, and even insisted on describing, in lurid detail, how the lower half of a constable had been found not two weeks earlier near Rangiriri. The rest of the body, he had said, had been dragged off by the Hauhaus for use in their heathen rites—although Caroline had no idea what those could be, and did not wish to know. Some of the ladies from Auckland had turned quite green, and Sean O'Hara, for once to his credit, had reproved the man gently and changed the subject.

Still . . . As she seated herself in the withdrawing room and the maid poured her a cup of coffee, Caroline was uncertain if she would not rather hear talk of the war than have to listen to *Mrs.* Dobson expound on the glowing prospects of the colony, as if it were the Promised Land itself.

"Oh, yes, I've written to both my sisters, and Charles has written to his brother in Warwickshire to advise them to come out," the woman announced from the sofa in her thick Cornish accent. "Why starve at home, I says, when there is plenty of work for your husbands at double the wages and the living just as reasonable as in England, and the government will assist you in getting land. The captain was perfectly right when he told Mr. Fisher that there are opportunities here!"

Caroline chafed with annoyance at the recitation. How *dare* that tiresome woman speak of Marcus as if he were on the same plane as her vulgar husband and her flock of relations in England! What made it worse was that Lady Kitty Broome—presumably their hostess—showed every evidence of listening attentively, an encouraging smile on her face, as if she actually took the creature seriously. And the Auckland ladies, taking their cue from her, sat with correct postures and unreadable expressions, murmuring polite responses.

Caroline set down her coffee cup with a force that threatened to chip the delicate Staffordshire saucer, and O'Hara's Irish servant was instantly at her elbow with a silver pot, offering to refill her cup. The pot was the last straw; Caroline herself had had to make do with a coffee service of Sheffield plate, Marcus having told her that he could not afford solid silver at colonial prices.

"Thank you, no," she said icily, and the Irishwoman, blithely unaware of the rebuff, smiled at her and moved on to pour coffee for one of the Auckland ladies.

Another of the bush farmers' wives, a mousy little woman in an old-fashioned shawl and cameo brooch, carried on Mrs. Dobson's refrain: "Be sure to tell them to bring as little luggage as possible, because the new ones always imagine they can get nothing in New Zealand. But they *should* take twelve shifts and at least ten pairs of stockings to save washing during the voyage, and not their best because the salt water spoils them. And baking powder—three or four shilling-tins, or they'll have nothing to eat but ship's biscuits. I'm sure I wish someone had told *me* that. And above all, warn them not to answer any letters that may be written to them by sailors, for as they are not allowed to speak, they write."

Oh, it was not to be endured! Caroline felt like screaming. Only Lady Kitty's example, as she sat smiling and sipping her coffee, kept her from leaping to her feet and venting her exasperation. She wondered how Marcus was faring with their boorish husbands back in the dining room. . . . Why, oh, *why* had he accepted the invitation?

"O'Hara's the cock of this particular dungheap, whatever you may think of him," he had told her. "There are one or two people he can introduce me to. Somehow—God knows how he does it— he gets the *petite noblesse,* such as they are of this backwater, down to that horse farm of his to rub shoulders with the bucolic inhabitants of his district. And he keeps a good wine cellar. You may find it amusing, but his hostess evidently is to be Kitty Broome, née Lady Kitty Cadogan—who, gossip has it, is planning to leave her Australian clod of a husband and go back to Ireland with O'Hara."

One of the Auckland ladies had beckoned the Irish servant to her and, getting her to lean over, had whispered, with a delicate blush, into her ear. The Irishwoman, with an utter lack of discretion, led her to the door and pointed the way, too obviously, to the rear of the house. Over the next quarter hour, four more ladies, paired for company, followed her example, but only when Lady Kitty rose to her feet in her unaffected manner and started for the door did Caroline—to forestall anyone else from attaching herself to the ranking lady—get up as well. In any case, she thought, it would be good to get away, even briefly, from the lot of them, and alone with Lady Kitty she might have the chance to strike up the closer acquaintance that she had stupidly failed to claim on the ship from Australia. Lady Kitty looked at her with surprise—she evidently hadn't expected anyone to accompany her—and then with a minute shrug led the way.

Caroline tried to engage her in conversation. "What dreary company you must endure here," she offered. "That frowsy woman with all the relations back in England queening it over the others! I wonder what *she* was, back home. Someone's scullery maid, I dare-say."

"Mrs. Dobson, do you mean?" Kitty replied evenly. "Her hus-band started out twenty years ago as a cockatoo, as the cottage farmers are called hereabouts, with twenty acres and a lean-to. Now he has ten thousand acres of freehold and employs forty men, some of whom now own their own farms. He was a great help to Sean when Sean was trying to establish Killaloe—lent his laborers and gave him all sorts of good advice."

Their destination, to Caroline's dismay, turned out to be a primi-tive place built out from an outer wall, with a slatted wooden floor and a drain to let out water. It was the function of one lady, her hostess informed her with cool amusement, to stand guard for the other and keep a lookout for snakes. Caroline was sure that Lady Kitty, with her misplaced Irish humor, had said it to rattle her, but, joke or no, when it was her turn in the chamber she was tense with anxiety and was sure she heard all sorts of rustling sounds and whispering movements from beyond the outer wall. The green carpet of turf that surrounded the farmhouse notwithstanding, there was the wild bush beyond, and anything could be out there.

As they started back to the withdrawing room, Lady Kitty eluded her attempts to renew the conversation, and Caroline found herself trailing behind, trying to keep up with her hostess's man-nish strides.

They had just passed the door to the dining room when an un-holy howling came from outside, followed by shouts and screams. Lady Kitty stopped in her tracks and grasped Caroline painfully by the arm. "Wait!" she commanded.

No sooner had she spoken than a footman, blood streaming down his forehead, came stumbling through the central foyer, wav-ing his arms and shouting, "Back, for God's sake! Get back!" With a wild look in his eyes, he rushed past them and into the dining room.

Lady Kitty hesitated only an instant. "This way," she ex-claimed, dragging Caroline with her into the room. The men were rising to their feet and scrambling around, looking for weapons. The wounded footman—there was a hideous gash in his skull and face, Caroline realized—was leaning against the table. "The Hauhaus are attacking!" he managed to blurt out. "God help us, they've got the place surrounded. The—the windows at the end of the house where the ladies are—" He collapsed in a heap on the wine-colored carpet.

As if to punctuate his words, shots were heard from outside, the heavy blast of ancient muzzle-loaders, and then, chillingly, screams issued from the withdrawing room, muffled by the intervening walls.

O'Hara was passing out weapons—a brace of pistols from a mahogany box in the sideboard and shotguns from the gun case—to those gentlemen who, unlike the army officers and bush farmers, had not thought to bring their own. Turning around, he caught sight of Kitty and Caroline.

"Good God," he blurted, "what are you doing here, Kit? . . . and Mrs. Fisher. You can't—"

An explosion interrupted him as the young captain from the 50th fired his pistol at the tattooed face of a Maori that had appeared at the end window. The face was hurriedly withdrawn, and the captain strode to the window and fired twice at something outside. "Crawling away over the grass!" he announced. "Two more of them. They won't soon be trying to gain entrance to *this* room from outside, now that they know it to be defended!"

"The ladies!" Dobson blurted. "God help us, the ladies! We must get to them at once!"

Wherry, gathering cutlery from the sideboard to supplement the firearms, waved a carving knife at the window through which the captain had discharged his pistol. "We've taught them caution," he said gruffly. "We must help the lads outside."

O'Hara took command. "Two of you—you, Mr. Bluett, and you, Mr. Green—go to the withdrawing room and look after the ladies. Get them to lie down on the floor, in the center of the room —and keep a sharp lookout at the windows." He had chosen the oldest and the fattest of the Aucklanders for the job, and they promptly obeyed him. "Captain, can you take a few men and slip out through the scullery entrance and set up a field of fire across the lawn to discourage the fellows from sneaking up on our rear? The shrubbery will afford you some concealment—not much, I'm afraid."

The captain swiftly rounded up several of the military men, avoiding a puffing major who looked as if he were about to open his mouth. "Mr. Fisher—" O'Hara turned toward Caroline. "You've had your share of battle against the native johnnies, I expect. Do you have a weapon, sir?"

Caroline suddenly realized that Marcus was standing behind her. White-faced and looking as if he were moving in a dream, he produced a cavalry pistol that he had concealed on his person. He stood rooted to the spot, looking about at the windows.

"Marcus, don't leave me," Caroline pleaded, grasping his arm.

Marcus found his voice. "Someone should stay with the ladies," he ventured.

Ignoring him, Kitty addressed Sean across the room. "You gentlemen need not worry about us—we shall find our way to the drawing room with the other ladies. Go, and don't delay on our account." Again she had taken Caroline's arm, but as she began to pull her away from Marcus and toward the door, the loud thud of a blunderbuss was followed instantly by a tinkle of broken glass from the hall outside as one of the foyer windows shattered.

O'Hara swore under his breath. "No, damme, you can't go back that way!" He strode over to Kitty and said urgently, "Listen, Kit my love, Killaloe was built one wing at a time, and you'll recall my showing you where they were joined badly and the mistake covered over to hide it—near the back of the scullery, remember? There's a space of about eighteen inches between the wall and what was once the outer wall of the original wing, but . . ." He paused reflectively. "The gap's covered by a heavy cupboard. Someone would have to move the cupboard back over it afterward."

The rest of the men were milling about impatiently at the door, brandishing their weapons. "Come on, man," Dobson urged him.

Marcus, his face deathly pale, interjected, "I'll see to it—to the cupboard . . . then join the rest of you in a moment."

"Thank you, Fisher," O'Hara said gratefully, then turned and stormed out the door with the crowd of armed men at his heels.

Caroline flung her arms around Marcus's neck, but he thrust her brusquely aside, saying, "There's no time to lose!" Lady Kitty was already ahead of them, and Caroline was left to scramble after the other two as shots rang out and more windows were broken.

As they burst through into the scullery, they made a horrible discovery. The body of one of the soldiers who had followed the captain—the last one out, evidently—was sprawled near the doorway, a bullet through his skull. Caroline felt herself losing control, becoming lightheaded.

"They're mad," Marcus whispered, beads of sweat breaking out on his forehead. "Mad to think they can hold off those savages.

They'll be slaughtered, every one of them. No one can get out any of the doors alive now."

Giving the lie to his words, the crack of a rifle sounded outside, as one of the captain's men, hidden in the shrubbery, took aim at some Maori foe. From the front of the house a hullabaloo could be heard, Sean O'Hara and his small party apparently having encountered a mob of Maoris storming the entrance. Caroline heard the bloodcurdling screams *"Kokiri, kokiri!"* and *"Ka horo, ka horo! Hapa hau!"* and the bark of Enfields and revolvers at close range.

Marcus cocked his head toward the cupboard, then strode over to it and quickly pulled it aside. In the wall behind, as O'Hara had promised, was a gaping hole where laths and plaster had been removed and never replaced. Marcus stuck his head inside and looked around. "The gap goes all the way down to the foundations," he announced. "I can see the bare earth between the stones." He withdrew his head as a cry outside indicated that one of the defenders hidden in the shrubbery had been hit.

"In you go," Lady Kitty ordered, grabbing Caroline by both arms and propelling her inside. It was a long step down to the ground. Caroline whimpered at the darkness and the damp, but a moment later Kitty was pressed in against her, causing the compressed crinoline to dig into her legs—and then, incredibly, Marcus was squeezing inside with them.

"Mr. Fisher, what are you doing?" Kitty demanded.

His voice shook as he said, "It's death to go outside. They'll be breaking into the house at any moment. I'll . . . I'll stay to protect you ladies." He was clawing at the underside of the cupboard, trying to draw it inward to conceal the gap in the wall. Caroline could not believe what was happening, and in the confined space she felt paralyzed, her panic growing.

"Mr. O'Hara and the others need your help, sir!" Kitty exclaimed in tones of shocked disbelief.

"They'll soon be dead—or worse," Marcus muttered through gritted teeth. "Haven't you heard what the Hauhaus do to their captives? Be quiet, you foolish woman, or you'll draw them to us. Caroline, talk some sense into her."

Kitty, a sob in her voice, cried, "Sean will *not* die! He will survive this night's work, and when I see him I shall tell him of your craven behavior!" Quickly regaining her calm, she pointed out, "In any event, your cowardice will do you no good, sir. If the cupboard cannot be pushed against the crack from outside, the Hauhaus will discover our hiding place very quickly."

Indeed, although Kitty blocked her view somewhat, Caroline could see that Marcus was having trouble finding a handhold sufficient to allow him to drag the heavy cabinet backward. He ceased his grunting efforts and said, reluctantly, "You're right." Instead of stepping back out into the scullery, however, as Caroline had expected him to do, he crouched to examine the foundations. "There are large gaps between the stones down here. I wonder . . ." His head disappeared from sight, then popped into view again. "I can see light down at the other end—lamplight shining through cracks in the floorboards. One could crawl between the floor joists all the way to the outside sills, and with luck find a gap in the stones that would let one out into the shrubbery without being seen. I noticed a gully leading down to the river . . . I could get away, bring back help. . . ."

"You'd never get across the lawn alive," Kitty said vindictively. "And you've not the courage to try. You'd rather hide in your rathole until they find us."

"You—" His retort choked in his throat. He looked past her to Caroline and said in a curiously remote tone, "Don't worry, Caroline my love, I shall bring help . . . at whatever risk to myself."

Then he was on his belly in the dirt, wriggling like a snake through the narrow spaces. "Don't leave me alone, Marcus," Caroline pleaded, but there was only a faint muffled reply and the diminishing sound of his scuttling through the crawl space. She began to sob, but Kitty snapped, "There's no time for that. Here, give me a hand."

On her knees in the workmen's leftover rubble, and heedless of her taffeta dress and the encumbering taped steels of her crinoline, Kitty managed to insert her slender forearms all the way under the cupboard and hook her fingers around the front. Straining like a navvy, she heaved the heavy piece of furniture back a quarter inch at a time. "For heaven's sake," she gasped, "take me around the waist and pull when I do."

Caroline did as she was instructed. It seemed to take forever, but at last one edge of the cupboard thudded solidly against the wall, and Kitty levered the other side around until some irregularity in the floor frustrated her efforts. "It's almost flush," she announced, straightening painfully up. "Perhaps they won't notice."

With the opening blocked, the hiding space was totally dark.

Caroline could only listen, terrified, to the sounds of the battle at the main door and the frugal, single shots of the defenders at the rear. It was soon over. The awful howls and doglike barks of the attackers were very close, indicating a final turmoil of hand-to-hand combat, punctuated by pistol shots, shouts, and the hair-raising screams of the horses who were trapped between the shafts of the carriages outside. There were cries of *"Patua, patua!"* and then Caroline heard a man's voice say clearly, in English, "Oh, God, no—" The words suddenly cut off and were followed by a bloodcurdling cry of triumph. Excited voices drew nearer, laughing, calling back and forth, and in the midst of it Caroline could make out something like *"Kei au a Tu, kei au a Tu,"* answered by a barking chorus that sounded like *"Hau hau, hau hau!"*

"What are they doing?" she asked in a whisper.

After a long hesitation, Kitty replied. "They're taking the heads and hearts, from what my husband told me. Be still, and don't make a sound."

The Maori voices moved around the side of the house, babbling with pleasure and high spirits, for all the world like an unruly crowd leaving a sporting match. Then they suddenly stopped, as some surviving defender in the captain's small party fired off two shots from the shrubbery. The voices paused to have a conference, during which there appeared to be some argument as to who was to have the honor of dealing with the situation, and then there was a chanted incantation of some sort, and a final rush of yelling men. The lone soldier got off one more shot—perhaps his last—and there was a scuffle, sounds of effort, and a drawn-out scream of agony ending abruptly in silence.

The two women huddled, mute and rigid, while the scullery filled with the sound of congratulatory voices, the scuffing of many bare feet, and the high-spirited smashing of crockery. Kitty clutched Caroline's arm with fingers like claws, but she had been right about the cupboard she had moved; none of the invaders appeared to have noticed the tiny gap where one edge stood out a half inch or so from the wall.

The voices quieted down as someone else entered the scullery, and the newcomer was clearly angry about something. *"Topia Tiki, teihana!"* he rumbled. *"Whakarongo mai!"* Somebody was being reprimanded severely, and the miscreant responded with sullen mumbles. And then, to multiply horrors, in the midst of the tirade, the person asserting his authority distinctly pronounced Kitty's name: *"Ka waere, whai Kitti-broom?"*

Caroline felt Kitty stiffen. The attack, it was now evident, had been no random raid on an isolated homestead, but had been planned by someone who knew the inhabitants by name, and who would now be searching for their missing victim.

The sullen one was full of excuses, but his questioner's patience stretched thin and snapped. He loosed a new diatribe, this time culminating in Sean O'Hara's name: *". . . korero Ohara, Kitti-broom wahine Te Ohara . . ."* The scullery emptied quickly to the patter of many bare feet, and then from the hallway came groans and the sound of something heavy being dragged over the floor and deposited there.

"What d'ye want with me, you devils?" a gasping voice said. "Why didn't you kill me and butcher me like the rest?" The voice was weak, shot through with pain, but it unmistakably belonged to Sean O'Hara.

Kitty went limp and gave a little moan. "It's Sean," she whispered. "Dear God, he's still alive." Caroline tensed with alarm, but luckily there was no one left in the scullery to hear them, and Kitty, remembering where she was, fell silent again.

"Many warriors are dead, O'Hara," the heavy, authoritative voice said in fair English. "We did not think so many would be killed. The stupid Topia Tiki did not tell me so many *pakehas* would be here tonight. Now we must make a great *tangihanga* to mourn our dead. We will eat the flesh of our enemies and place a head specially pleasing to the god *Tu* on our *niu* pole."

The voice that had been identified as that of Topia Tiki broke in to protest. "Listen to me, Te Ngara. I did not know that O'Hara would invite so many *pakehas* here tonight, or that there would be *pakeha* soldiers among them. Would I betray you? Am I not your cousin?"

O'Hara overcame a coughing spell to say, "You gave me poor return for my wages, didn't you, Topia Tiki, damn your soul!"

"You are a brave man, O'Hara," the chief returned, "but this day I shall eat your courage. *Tenei te mea kei te mou ki toku ringa.* Your flesh will be cooked and offered in *Whangai-hau.*"

O'Hara laughed weakly. "So you're the famous Te Ngara? You're going to eat me, are you, you old devil? I warn you, you'll find me tough."

There was a murmur of admiration from the Hauhaus, who

must have been surrounding O'Hara's crumpled body. Te Ngara cut in with a barked command: "You have hidden the woman you stole, Kitty Broome, O'Hara. Topia Tiki says she is not among the others. She is a great lady, is she not? Where have you hidden her?"

"You'll not have my Kit," O'Hara said defiantly. "Do your worst, you painted scoundrel, and the devil take you!"

Caroline, shivering uncontrollably with fear in her dark hiding place, could not help feeling a stab of resentment. The savages were not aware of *her* presence at the farmhouse; and if it had not been for Lady Kitty, she would be safe now from further search. She—

Her thoughts were suddenly cut off by a dreadful crunching sound, and O'Hara let out an animal cry of pain. Over her pounding heartbeat, Caroline could hear stertorous breathing, and Kitty said in agony, "What are they doing to him?" Caroline clutched at her as a signal to be quiet, and then they heard O'Hara's hoarse voice croak, "Damn you to hell!" The Maoris babbled at one another, and again there was the noise of a terrible crack and thud. O'Hara howled in torment, and Kitty swayed so that Caroline had to hold her upright.

"I'm going out there," Kitty wept.

"No, no, you mustn't," Caroline whispered, and held her fast.

"Where you hide Kitty Broome?" the chief demanded, and O'Hara cursed weakly at him. The other Hauhaus buzzed like bees, and the chief angrily cried, *"Tangata kuware!* You *pakeha* fool!"

Twice more the terrible sound was heard, but O'Hara screamed only once, and then was silent. "Enough!" the chief ordered. "He can speak no more."

Kitty's body was wracked with silent sobs, and Caroline clung to her in fear that she would carry out her previously expressed intention to make her presence known. The sounds indicated that some of the Maoris were leaving, but then there was a commotion outside the scullery door, accompanied by shouts, and to judge by the thud of bare feet on the wooden planks, some of the Hauhaus who had been leaving came hurrying back. The chief's deep-throated roar was heard, and the eager replies of the warriors who had come in through the rear, and then, stunned with disbelief, Caroline heard the terror-stricken voice of her husband. "No, no, don't kill me! You are honorable men who keep your word! For God's sake, I'll show you where Lady Kitty is hiding!"

The bare feet tramped closer, and the heavy cupboard scraped against the floorboards as many willing hands shoved at it. The two women cringed away from the aperture as the cupboard toppled over.

And then the opening was filled with the grinning, tattooed faces of Maori warriors, beyond whom could be seen an ashen-visaged Marcus Fisher, held fast in the grip of two enormous savages whose weapons and half-naked bodies were smeared with blood.

Lights were blazing at Killaloe when Johnny came in sight of the house, and he was at first puzzled and then alarmed when, for all the lights, no one came to meet or challenge him. No servants, no night watchman, only silence; and yet . . . He drew the pistol he was carrying and urged his horse forward, his heart sinking.

Then, as he came nearer, he saw a number of carriages lying in ruins about a hundred and fifty yards from the main door. There were no horses in evidence, and what remained of the traces trailed on the ground. The carriage servants lay where they had fallen. Some of their employers were nearby, shot down as they had come out of the house, but—Johnny gagged as he saw the state they were in and, fighting down his nausea, pulled his horse up to have a closer look.

Some of the bodies were headless—and worse. The odd arm or leg had been hacked off and carried away, and in one case, only the lower half of the body, from the waist down, was left. Other bodies had been split open, spread apart like butchers' carcasses, and in the pale light of the moon Johnny could see the glistening organs within. There was a smell of cooked meat in the air, and he leaned over in the saddle to spy, lying on the turf, a singed gobbet of flesh the size of his fist. The bile rising in his throat, he identified it as a human heart.

Kitty was uppermost in his mind, but he did not dare to call out her name as he rode his horse up to the front door, dismounted, and tied its reins to one of the pillars supporting the veranda. Another headless body was sprawled in the entrance, and overcoming his queasiness, he stepped around it.

At the end of the hallway to his right he saw a bright billow of fabric, which after a moment his reeling mind identified as a woman's gown and its butchered contents. With a cry, he hurried to it. The head had been smashed to pulp by what likely had been one of the flat stone Maori clubs that were swung with tremendous force by a thong, but Johnny could see enough to tell that it was not Kitty.

More heaps of crumpled fabric lay outside a doorway, where two more women had been slain, either having been dragged from the room by their attackers or having tried to flee. Steeling his nerve, Johnny satisfied himself that neither body was Kitty's before he entered the room beyond.

A scene of carnage met his horrified eyes. Eight or nine women had been clubbed to death in these confines, and some of the bodies had been mutilated. Two male bodies lay nearby—one of them, its head still intact, was that of an old man who had been shot to death, and the other was a fat, headless corpse. The room dimmed and swung around Johnny's head, and he feared he might collapse, but after a moment he recovered sufficiently to be able to look at the women's bodies and assure himself, again, that Kitty was not among them. He left the scene of slaughter and, feeling himself close to madness, staggered down the long hall, calling out Kitty's name, then O'Hara's, in a voice so shaken and altered that he could not recognize it as his own. A sense of relief mingled with apprehension broke through his numbed senses when a groan answered his call and someone croaked weakly, "Here, man, this way."

He hurried to the source of the sound and found a man in the tatters of evening clothes lying near a threshold that was littered with broken glass. He knelt beside the sprawled form and exclaimed, "Is it you, O'Hara? What in God's name happened here? Was it the Hauhaus?"

With an effort, O'Hara raised his head, keeping the rest of his body curiously motionless, and managed a painful smile. "So you came after all, did you, John Broome? 'Twas lucky for you that you refused my invitation to dinner."

"Don't pass out, O'Hara. Where's Kitty?" He tried to lift the older man, but O'Hara screamed.

"For heaven's sake, man, don't try to move me," O'Hara begged. "They broke both my legs and my two arms as well. And they took my horses, all of them. They aren't men, they—oh, God, they're devils! And they took heads. For their bloody *niu* poles, they took them, just as they pleased." His voice dropped to a whisper, sounding mad. "And hearts. I saw them take a man's heart while they held me, and singe it over a flame till it sizzled and smoked, while they mouthed a heathen prayer over it. Ah, no, man, don't try to move me, please do not."

"Why didn't they kill you, O'Hara?" Johnny whispered.

"They were saving me for last," O'Hara informed him. "As the lord o' the manor, don't y'see? They were going to take me back to their *pa* for their murderous pagan rituals, but . . . then they told me that I was *tina-toa,* a true warrior, and that I had earned their respect. *Te raiana,* the chief called me—the lion. I wouldn't tell them where Kitty was hidden, you see. The chief told them that I was henceforth *tapu,* and that no man could harm me." He coughed, and blood appeared between his lips.

"Kitty, hidden?" Johnny responded, hope suddenly stabbing his heart. "For God's sake, O'Hara, where?"

O'Hara shook his head, and the effort caused him a grunt of pain. "They found her somehow . . . I don't know how. I passed out for a while. But I saw them take her with them—her and another woman, Mrs. Fisher."

"Caroline Fisher?" Johnny said, having heard of Colonel Forsyth's recently remarried widow.

"Yes. Her poor devil of a husband must be dead with the others, God rest his soul, and it's sorry I am for what I said about him—"

"Never mind that, O'Hara. How many of them were there—which way did they go?"

But O'Hara had started to ramble, and after a few more attempts, Johnny decided that further questioning was useless. Working with infinite care, he contrived to settle the injured man a bit more comfortably, using his belt and pieces torn from a dead man's shirt to secure the broken limbs. Then, ignoring O'Hara's agonized pleas to leave him alone, he managed to set him up with his head resting against the wall.

"You can't . . . follow her, Broome," O'Hara gasped when he was able to talk again. "They said she would be killed if we—if we tried to send men after them. And no one could track them through the bush . . . not without alerting their scouts."

"There's one man who might," Johnny said grimly, thinking of Adam Shannon. "Someone who lived among the Maori himself, as a prisoner, and knows their ways."

His mind went racing ahead. Adam's company of Rangers was at Mere, only three or four miles away. If he could get there without being seen—

"Get me some drink, Broome, and leave it with me," O'Hara

gritted, "and do what you want for Kitty. She's your wife, isn't she?"

And so she was, Johnny decided. He went through the house, looking for drink. The scullery was a wreck of smashed glass and breached casks, and he went on to the dining room, which had been left as it was when the men had risen from the table to run out to meet the Hauhau attack. The cigars had burnt themselves out in the ashtrays, and someone's glass of port had overturned to leave red stains on the long white tablecloth, which had been pulled slightly awry where it trailed to the carpet. He picked up a decanter of port and, spying a large decanter of brandy on the sideboard, was making his way toward it when he heard a sound from under the table.

Johnny froze and, setting the decanter carefully down, drew his pistol. "Come out from there, whoever you are," he ordered brusquely.

The folds of the tablecloth parted, and a ginger-whiskered face peered out. "Don't shoot," its trembling owner pleaded. "I'm a white man—Captain Marcus Fisher, late of Her Majesty's Fortieth Regiment."

"Get to your feet, Fisher," Johnny said. "What were you doing under there?" Still keeping the pistol trained, he reached out cautiously and whipped the tablecloth aside, to make sure that no armed Maori was, somehow, under there. Satisfied, he holstered the pistol and turned to face Fisher, who, having dusted himself off, was trying to regain his dignity.

"I . . . I heard you moving about, and thought you were one of the savages, coming back," Fisher stammered, and then, looking about and seeing that he was in no evident danger, attempted to assert his command of the situation. His own dinner clothes were smudged with dirt down the front and a little worse for wear, but he stared disdainfully at the sober dark blue affected by the volunteer forces. "You're not a proper military man in Her Majesty's forces, are you? You have a commission in one of those ragtag colonial units."

"I'm Captain John Broome of the Volunteer Horse, on the governor's staff, at your service, sir," Johnny returned stiffly.

Fisher's eyes glittered, coming to life. "Ah, I thought you looked familiar. You're the fellow who married Lady Kitty Cadogan, aren't you? I've seen you hereabouts, but you've not been much in evidence in Auckland, have you? You've been . . . away . . . a good deal."

"I am that John Broome, sir," Johnny said, reddening at the implied insult. "And I have been absent serving in the campaign against the Weraroa *pa*, which, as you may recall, was the stronghold that General Cameron declined to attack, but which five hundred Volunteers, with two hundred regulars obligingly lent to them, occupied bloodlessly." Johnny forced himself to keep his temper. "In case you don't know, my wife is missing, sir, and so is yours, from what Mr. O'Hara told me."

That jarred Fisher's composure. "O'Hara is alive?" he questioned, visibly disconcerted.

"Did you not know, sir?" Johnny frowned.

"No, I did not," Fisher snapped.

"He is grievously wounded, *Captain* Fisher," Johnny said, the distaste evident in his voice. "He has been lying in pain and in sore need, only a few feet from here. I would have thought you would have searched the house instead of—" He bit off his words.

Fisher drew himself up. "I was one of the outside defenders, sir," he declared. "Holding off hordes of howling natives from the rear of the house. All of my companions are dead, and I'm lucky to be alive myself. I must have been grazed. Lord knows how long I lay unconscious. I made my way back to the house as soon as I could. I'm sure I would have found O'Hara in a very few minutes had you not found him first."

Johnny looked him over. Fisher didn't appear to have been hurt, and for all the dirt stains smeared down his front, even his clothes were in no particular disarray. Perhaps, however, he had been lying prone in order to fire from concealment, and Johnny decided to give him the benefit of the doubt. "Be that as it may," he said evenly, "my wife is gone, and yours too, and we've got to do something about getting them back. The devil take it, Fisher, you don't seem overly concerned about it!"

"There's—there's nothing we can do about it. They're probably dead by now." He added piously, "God knows, they'd be better off dead. Make up your mind to it, man. There's not a thing we can do to save them."

"Oh, yes, there is," Johnny disagreed. "But first, let's see to poor O'Hara. Pick up that decanter of brandy, will you, and follow me."

Back in the hall, Johnny knelt beside the injured man and helped him to swallow a generous portion of brandy, while Fisher hovered at a distance. O'Hara gulped the fiery spirit greedily, choking on it when Johnny went too fast. At last he said, "Ah, that will do for now, Broome. Sure and the drink's a mercy."

"What will you do when I'm gone, O'Hara?"

"Put the drink on the chair by me, at the level of my head, and I'll manage somehow. Don't worry about me. Go after your wife."

Johnny explained his plan to Fisher, but he might as well have been talking to himself.

"It's death out there in the dark, man," Fisher protested. "The savages are all around in the forest. We'd never get through alive. Best wait till daylight. Somebody will come by eventually, and we can send for help."

Johnny could scarcely believe his ears. "Time is of the essence, Fisher. We've *got* to intercept the Hauhau raiding party before they reach their *pa*. Once the women disappear behind that stockade, we'll have lost whatever slim hope we have of getting them back alive."

Fisher shook his head stubbornly. "*You* go, if you're fool enough. If one man can't get through, two can't. It would only be an extra target. I'll . . ." His gaze fell on O'Hara. "Someone has to stay here to look after him."

Johnny gave up on the man. It was almost as if Fisher didn't *want* his wife and Kitty found. Cowardice he could understand, but Fisher had actually tried to discourage *him* from going. Clearly the man was an unpleasant sort, but his own wife was at risk, and what reason could he possibly have for wanting to prevent the recovery of the two women?

After putting the bottle on a chair as O'Hara had requested, Johnny promised the almost unconscious Irishman that he would send help from Auckland as soon as he could, then hurried through the house to where his horse waited.

He climbed up into the gray's saddle, spun the animal around, and set off for Mere.

Two miles farther on, where the road to Mere narrowed to little more than a forest track, hung over by underbrush, Johnny had to slow his horse to get through a litter of branches that lay across the path, almost as if someone had cut them and put them there.

Before a warning alarm had time to ring in his brain, two armed Maoris stepped into the path from either side, blocking his way. They were stripped for war, wearing only flax mats round their waists, and they had on war paint—red smears on their cheeks and red lines traced above their brows. They both were strapped round with cartridge boxes made of tattooed human skin, and both carried guns—one a double-barreled shotgun and the other a long Enfield rifle. Johnny cursed under his breath. They would be Hauhau pickets, posted here to watch for troops coming from the direction of Auckland.

"Here, you *pakeha!*" one of them shouted, leveling his weapon at Johnny. "Get down off horse! I kill you suppose you not get down!"

There was no time to fumble for his revolver. With a cavalry yell, Johnny spurred the gray, and the startled animal lunged forward. The two Hauhaus leaped aside, and Johnny crouched low over the horse, hanging on for dear life. He had just cleared the barrier of underbrush when the twin explosions of the shotgun and the Enfield came from behind at close range. The impact knocked him forward against the horse's neck, and his blind fingers tangled themselves in the mane, as the gray, whinnying with terror, followed the road to Mere at a gallop.

Chapter XXV

ADAM, STRETCHING HIS legs before turning in for the night, strolled around the encampment with the scout Tu-Mahuki at his side, while puffing contentedly on the short Maori pipe that Tu-Mahuki's wife, Takiora, had prepared for him.

"Too many campfires, Tu-Mahuki," he said with a smile as he looked across the field of conical tents gleaming whitely in the moonlight. "The Splitter-of-Canoes would not be pleased."

An appreciative grin stretched the scrolled tattoos on the scout's face. "Splitter-of-Canoes," or *Wawahi-waka,* was one of the many admiring names that had been given to Major von Tempsky by his Maori foes because of his exploits in the war. Von Tempsky, who had learned his style of guerrilla fighting in Mexico and Central America, was stern with his men about things like campfires, but the major was away now, looking into reports of Hauhau activity near Hawke's Bay.

"Maybe *Wawahi-waka* not mind so much," the scout responded. "Here in *pakeha* country, fires not betray us to enemy." Tu-Mahuki, a friendly Maori of the Whanganui tribe who had served on the British side throughout the war, was a tall, well-muscled man with a bushy head of hair and, giving a final garnish to his tattooed face, a British-style cavalry mustache. Under his feather stole he wore a fringed and ornamented flaxen kilt woven and charmed by his wife, and girded round his waist were a short hatchet, a prized revolver, and a British cartridge case. A thoroughly picturesque fellow, he had been painted in watercolor by the many-faceted von Tempsky, who in addition to his other accomplishments was a talented artist.

"I wish I could be as sure as you are that we are not in enemy country," Adam demurred. "There's every evidence that Te Ngara's operating somewhere between here and the Rangiriri area. And that's less than a day's march away."

"Sometime we find his *pa,*" the Maori said confidently. "And then the Splitter-of-Canoes will go in after him."

They took a final turn around the encampment, Adam nodding pleasantly at the men who were still outside their tents to enjoy a late pipe or to boil a bedtime cup of tea. He was about to call it a night when a sound of drumming hoofbeats came from the road and he heard the sentry unsuccessfully challenge the rider: "Who's there? . . . Stop, I say!"

And then the horse was in among them, acting riderless despite the slumped form leaning across its neck, and heading in Adam's direction. He sprang forward to intercept it and, somehow managing to grab the dangling reins, ran alongside, tugging to turn the beast and make it slow down. At last it stopped, blowing and foaming, and the man in the saddle, losing his death-grip on the mane, slid down. Adam and Tu-Mahuki caught him and lowered him gently to the ground.

"Good God, it's John Broome!" Adam exclaimed. "I left him not two hours ago!" His hands, where he had handled Johnny, were sticky with blood, but he could detect breathing, and then he saw the eyes open, and there was a flicker of awareness in them. "What happened at O'Hara's, Johnny? For God's sake, man, try to speak!"

"Hauhau attack . . ." Johnny gasped. "Everybody killed except O'Hara . . . broke his limbs . . . and one guest . . . Marcus Fisher. The raiders took Kitty, Adam . . . took her with them . . . and Fisher's wife. You've got to find them, get them back before it's too late!"

The import of the disjointed words finally sank in. "Caroline? At Killaloe?"

Johnny clutched at Adam's shirt. "They'll . . . they'll keep the women alive until they reach their *pa* . . . but once they're inside, not even the Rangers could get them out alive."

"How long ago, Johnny?" Adam demanded urgently. "How long ago was the attack? Was that how you got wounded?"

"No," Johnny managed. "Shot at road ambush, two miles from here. But attack at Killaloe not long ago . . . you can catch them if you hurry. The heart was still smoking, do you see?"

Adam could make no sense out of the last words, but the rest of what Johnny had said was clear enough. He looked up at the circle of men who had come running to see what was happening. "One of you fetch the surgeon," he said, "You, corporal, move smartly!"

"Yes, sir!" the corporal answered, and went trotting off. By the time he returned with the surgeon, Johnny had drifted off into unconsciousness.

"Bad," Tu-Mahuki said dolefully. "Him shot bad, maybe die."

The company surgeon confirmed the scout's opinion. "I'll try to save him," he said. "I'll do what I can to patch him up here, Mr. Shannon, and we'll get him to Auckland at first light. Here—some of you men give me a hand and get him to my tent. And one of you go into town and see if you can borrow a wagon—one with good springs."

Adam, losing no more time, strode off to saddle his horse, with Tu-Mahuki and a small but growing knot of men following him. The corporal, a squat, powerful Australian named Hanes, said, "Beggin' your pardon, sir, but what is it ye're intendin' to do?"

Adam turned to address him and the others. "Someone's got to get to Killaloe immediately to see what has happened. There's at least one wounded man there. Tu-Mahuki and I will attempt to track the raiding party. We'll need a large armed force to follow, in case there's fighting to be done."

"The captain's spending the night in Auckland," the corporal volunteered, referring to the company commander. "We could send someone into town to fetch him, if you don't mind my saying so, but he won't be likely to move the men out till daylight."

Adam nodded in approval. "See to it, will you, Hanes? Here, has anyone got a scrap of paper and a pencil? I'll write a note."

When the note had been scribbled—Adam using the willing back of a Ranger as a writing desk—the corporal took it and handed it to a courier he had chosen from the men, then turned to Adam again. "Pardon me for askin', sir, but ye're not planning to track that gang of murderers in the dark?"

"There's no other way, Corporal," Adam said.

"You can't go to Killaloe alone, that's for sure," Hanes declared. "How about it, lads?"

A throaty roar of agreement went up from the surrounding men. Adam was deeply affected. He looked around at their faces, reassured at what he saw; they were the toughened veterans of dozens of skirmishes and campaigns, sent in where the fighting was thickest, and little thanked for it by the British regulars, who did not understand von Tempsky's tactics. They were trained to hardship, and each was armed with carbine, five-shot revolver, and bowie knife; von Tempsky had learned the use of the knife in Mexico and had seen to it that his men were taught to throw it and use it for close-in fighting.

"I can't order you to follow me," Adam told them. "The captain might not approve."

"We'll explain it to the captain when we see 'im," a rough voice roared from the throng, and a hearty chorus affirmed the words. By the time Adam had saddled up, some twenty men had turned out to accompany him, and as he rode out of camp with his contingent, several more were making ready to follow and catch up.

The ride to Killaloe was without incident; no attackers were in evidence at the scene of Johnny Broome's ambush—the Hauhau pickets having surmised correctly that an armed force would shortly be coming back this way—and it took Adam's men only a few minutes to clear away the cut underbrush blocking the track. When they reached Killaloe, even von Tempsky's hardened veterans were appalled at the carnage they found there. "They took their own dead back with them, Mr. Shannon," Hanes said. "That will slow them down on the trail." He turned away from the sight of the headless carcasses and spat into the bloodstained grass. "And they may stop to smoke-dry the heads on the way, as well. That will hold them up a few hours."

Adam left Tu-Mahuki to sniff out a trail and posted most of the men outside the house, before going inside with Hanes and a medical aide. He found O'Hara lying unattended in a hallway. The young assistant surgeon quickly examined him and, looking up, announced, "He's dead drunk, sir. And that's a blessing, seeing the condition he's in. Corporal, can you find me some chair legs or slats, and tear up some linen? I'll try to make some rough splints so he can be moved. We'll get him to Auckland when it's daylight."

Hanes hurried off on his errand, and Adam bent over O'Hara's sprawled and twisted form. "Mr. O'Hara, I'm Adam Shannon of the Forest Rangers," he said loudly. "You're all right, sir. The Hauhaus are gone, and we'll have you in a hospital in Auckland as soon as it's light."

O'Hara made an inarticulate response, his head lolling. Adam noted the smashed decanter of port that lay on the floor at the foot of the chair someone had placed near O'Hara. Unable to use his arms, O'Hara must have knocked it there while trying to get at the neck of the bottle with his mouth. A decanter of brandy, lying on its side on the chair seat, showed that the manuever had been more successful with the harder spirit. A good measure of the liquor was still retained in the decanter's square depths, Adam noted, and O'Hara must have been able to tilt it for his tipples, though a good deal of brandy must have been spilt over him.

Adam tried again. "Mr. O'Hara, one of your guests is supposed to be still alive—Marcus Fisher. Do you know where he is, sir? Why isn't he here taking care of you?"

O'Hara opened one bleary eye. "Fisher . . . don't know. Went away. Didn't he go with Broome to fetch help?"

"He's not badly wounded, then?" Adam urged, but his effort was fruitless. O'Hara nodded and dropped off again.

"Just as well, sir," the young surgeon offered. He looked up as Hanes returned with an armful of bed slats and some torn-up sheets. "I'll need a good strong man to help with the splints, Corporal."

"That's me, then," Hanes said cheerfully as he took a position next to O'Hara.

Just then there was a commotion from the entrance, and Adam heard a familiar, overbearing voice giving orders. "Take your hands off me! Where's your commanding officer? Show me to him at once!"

A moment later, Marcus Fisher stormed in, followed by two very unhappy-looking privates. Adam felt the old, well-remembered tightening in his guts, and he straightened up to meet the onslaught. Fisher was in reasonably intact evening dress, considering his ordeal, save for a broad smear of dirt down his front.

"We found him hiding in an outbuilding, sir," one of the privates tried to explain, "and—"

Fisher, not yet recognizing Adam in the dark hallway, whirled on the private in a fury. "*Hiding?* Damn your insolence! I'll have you on report! Give me your name, you blockhead! I was keeping a lookout—from a post that commanded a view down the river—in case the raiding party returned." He spied Hanes, who was getting a grip on one of O'Hara's limbs while the surgeon stretched it. "You there, Corporal," he barked, "leave off what you're doing and take down this man's name!"

Adam stepped between them, and Fisher, catching sight of the officer's tunic, shifted his attack. "It took you long enough," he snarled. "Wanted to make sure they'd gone before you set out, did you?" He broke off as he finally recognized Adam. "Oh, it's you, is it? I might have known you'd find soft duty near Auckland, Mr. . . . Shannon, or whatever name you're going by these days!"

Controlling his temper, Adam said tautly, "We came as soon as we could, Mr. Fisher. Mr. Broome was seriously wounded, riding to us to give the alarm. He may not survive."

"*Captain* Fisher to you, Shannon!" Fisher snapped, and then, as he took in what Adam had said, his tone suddenly changed. "Broome—hurt, you say? And not expected to live?"

"No. He had been shot in the back at close range. It was an ambush about halfway to Killaloe. He was able to tell us that there had been a Hauhau attack here, and that Car—Mrs. Fisher and Lady Kitty had been kidnapped, but that was all."

"Then he was not able to give you an account of events here?"

"No," Adam conceded. "I'm depending on you for that. How in God's name did you and O'Hara manage to keep your lives?"

A hood seemed to come down over Fisher's eyes. "These Maori savages have a sort of code of honor of their own, Shannon. They respect the valor of their opponents. They . . . they had me in their hands, and some of them were preparing to practice their ritual butchery on me. But then their chief called me . . . lion, I guess the word means. . . ."

"Yes, *te raiana,*" Adam supplied, somewhat skeptical.

Fisher went on in a rush. "So they . . . they promised me that I would not be killed, and I was able to . . . to strike a bargain with them for O'Hara's life, since he had been badly injured and didn't matter much to them anymore." He added belligerently, "And that's how it happened, no matter what O'Hara might have told you."

"He hasn't told us anything," Adam said. "I doubt he'll be able to talk for a while. Certainly not till after we've moved him to the hospital in Auckland and they've done what they can for him, poor devil."

"I see," Fisher said, sounding curiously relieved.

"He *did* seem to be under the impression that you had gone with John Broome to fetch help," Adam continued. He remembered the smashed decanter of port that poor O'Hara had tried, unsuccessfully, to reach, and his voice hardened as he asked, "As you did not go for help, why did you not remain with Mr. O'Hara and see to him?"

"There was nothing I could do for him," Fisher said sullenly. "It was more important that I keep an eye out for the savages, in case they decided to come back." He looked indifferently over to where the assistant surgeon was splinting one of O'Hara's shattered legs. "At any rate, you're here now, and your man seems to have it well in hand."

"We shan't be here long," Adam asserted. "I'll leave the surgeon behind to look after Mr. O'Hara, and a man to carry a message back to our main company when it's light, but I'm taking the rest of the men with me to follow the Hauhau."

"But *why*, for God's sake?" Fisher protested. "You can't follow them in the dark, and if you bumble about, you'll only endanger the hostages. It's more important for your soldiers to remain here and guard Killaloe. There has been a massacre here, Mr. Shannon, in case you have forgotten!"

"I have not forgotten," Adam said grimly. "There is nothing more we can do for the victims. And it is not likely that the raiders will return. They have done their deed, and they will not be eager to walk into the arms of our troops. In any case, the main force of Rangers from Mere will be here in the morning. But we *can* attempt to rescue the hostages. My God, man, one of them is your wife! Don't you care? I'd have thought you'd be urging us on to make all speed in going after her!"

"Yes, *my* wife, Shannon, and don't you forget that!" Fisher blazed. "What I care about her, and what is between us, is none of your business! You may have cuckolded John Omerod, before you sank his ship and killed him, but you won't cuckold me! Caroline despises you, and . . . and I'm raising your bastard out of the goodness of my heart!" He regained control of himself and stood panting, glaring at Adam.

Adam, trembling with disgust and anger, managed to reply in a steady voice: "It is of no concern to me how Caroline—Mrs. Fisher —feels about me. I'm duty bound to try to save her, if I can. Her and Mrs. Broome."

He turned to go, but Fisher, in a final effort to detain him, scrambled round to stand in his path. "Your soldiers are needed to guard the house, Mr. Shannon!" he said shrilly. "You don't have the authority to remove them in the present situation. Your commanding officer would not approve, and, when it comes to that, this von Tempsky of yours . . . this . . . this Polish adventurer is under the orders of Colonel McDonnell, no matter what fanciful airs he may give himself." He added pointedly, "May I remind you that you are merely on loan from Her Majesty's Fortieth, *Sergeant!*"

Adam faced out the tirade stolidly, then responded, "Major von Tempsky is a gentleman and an aristocrat, and it is my honor to serve under him. I earned my commission on merit in the Rangers, and, as you doubtless are not aware, I have been granted a dual commission in the same rank in the Fortieth. May I remind *you*, Mr. Fisher, that you are a civilian, having sold your commission—as you bought it—and that you have no authority over me."

He strode past the fuming Fisher and found Tu-Mahuki waiting outside for him on the veranda. "I find Hauhau trail," the Maori scout said, grinning. "They have horses with them, so easy to follow. They try leave false trail where they come out across river, but I find this."

He held out a scrap of fabric for Adam's inspection. "Calico, looks like," Adam said, frowning. "From a woman's crinoline." The bright piece of under-material had been tied into a tight knot around the stem of a fern, which was still entangled in it where Tu-Mahuki had broken it off.

"I find three in row," the scout informed him, "in straight line to show direction."

"One of the women," Adam asserted. "Damned clever of her. It must have taken a lot of pluck to do that under the eyes of her captors."

Tu-Mahuki pointed a powerfully muscled arm across the river in a southerly direction. "They come out *te wai* there with a few horses; rest horses wait in river. They go small way, leave horse droppings, *punga* broken under foot, then lead horses backward into *te wai*, come out again down there." He swept his arm toward the southeast. "They clean horse droppings, sweep trail, but I find." He grinned his pleasure and waited for Adam's reaction.

"Good man," Adam approved. "Let's be on our way."

Marcus Fisher had emerged from the house and come up behind Adam, and now he said peevishly, "Your blackfellow's got it backward, Shannon. They came out of the river *there*, and went in *that* direction."

"What are you saying, man?" Adam questioned. "Are you sure? Did you observe them long enough to be certain that they didn't backtrack?"

"I was out here long enough to see what I saw," Fisher said defensively. "At the risk of my life, I might add."

"No, cannot be," Tu-Mahuki protested. "Trail end in place of *punga*, I see. I look again more past there, be sure they not take up again to fool. Other trail hide first, not end past long way. This is trail where point cloth from lady's *piu-piu.*"

Adam peered across the river again. "It seems unlikely they'd head due south," he mused. "That would take them into Waikato and Ngatimaniapoto country. It seems far more probable that they'd have their *pa* in Ngaiterangi territory."

"Whose word are you going to take, Shannon?" Fisher scowled. "The word of an Englishman or that of a bushy-headed native who'd as soon stab you in the back as look at you?"

Adam turned to Corporal Hanes, who had come out onto the veranda and was awaiting orders with visible impatience. "Get the men ready to travel, Hanes," he directed. "And be as quick as possible. Tu-Mahuki will lead the way."

Fisher exploded. "I shall make a formal complaint to Governor Grey about your incompetence! I demand that you dispose the men about the surrounding terrain, in case those Hauhau scoundrels attempt to sneak up on us again!"

Adam was too exasperated to argue further. "We shall be ready to ride shortly. Are you coming with us, Fisher?"

"My wife is dead," Fisher said venomously. "And if she isn't, your foolhardy actions will condemn her to death—and Lady Kitty as well. You'll answer for this! I'll see to that!"

Adam gritted his teeth. "Are you coming with us?" he repeated. "I can use every available man."

"Someone must act in a responsible manner," Fisher retorted. "I shall remain here with the surgeon to guard O'Hara. Now see here, Shannon! I demand that you leave a detachment of armed men behind with me!"

Without a further word, Adam turned on his heel and stalked away, Tu-Mahuki at his side.

Huddled in her shawl against the night damp, Kitty rested as well as she could under the watchful eyes of her Hauhau guards, with her back against a gnarled old *mahoe* tree at the edge of the forest clearing. Her dress was bedraggled and muddy from the streams she had been forced to ford, and her skin was scratched by brambles and bitten by night insects. Her captors had offered her food—cold corn and potatoes, and the flesh of a snared parrot, almost raw—but she had been unable to eat it, her mind preoccu-

pied with the horrid preparations going on around the fire. Beside
her crouched Caroline Fisher, on the edge of hysteria.

"They're . . . they're going to kill us now, aren't they?" Caroline whimpered. "And first, they're going to . . . to do awful
things to us!"

"No, I don't think so," Kitty soothed her. "I expect they plan to
save us until they get to wherever they're going. That's the object
of this, isn't it? I don't think that fire's meant for us."

"Oh, if only Marcus were here. . . ." Caroline sobbed, then
stopped as she remembered.

"Your Marcus sold us to them," Kitty reminded her dryly. "To
save his own skin. I don't think he'll want *that* tale told."

"Do . . . do you think someone will come after us?"

"I don't know," Kitty admitted. "If someone does, we must be
prepared to do whatever we can to save ourselves. To run away
into the underbrush, perhaps." She stopped and gazed at Caroline
with mounting exasperation. The silly woman was still wearing the
hoops of her crinoline, though one of them hung awkwardly askew
where the tape had torn loose on one side. Kitty herself had long
since removed her steels, and her billowing dress now hung in
straight folds. "Listen to me, Mrs. Fisher. When we leave this
clearing and it's apparent in which direction we'll be traveling, I
want you to make a fuss about your crinoline. You've got to get rid
of those steels anyway, or you'll be a danger to both of us. The
Maoris are used to the reticence of Englishwomen, and they're
gentlemen in their own way. They'll allow you a measure of privacy." Quickly, she sketched what she wanted Caroline to do.
"I've already left signals three times, where a turning was in doubt,
and they may be getting suspicious of me."

"Oh, no, I couldn't!" Caroline exclaimed, her fingers flying to
her throat. "These . . . these beasts have us in their power, and it
would be stupid to call attention to ourselves any more than we
have to."

"Mrs. Fisher," Kitty patiently explained, "if you don't, then I
shall have to."

"Oh, don't!" Caroline begged. "Don't do anything to make them
angry at us!" She collapsed into a paroxysm of sobbing that made
the Maori guards cast curious glances at her and exchange questioning looks among themselves.

Kitty gave up for the moment. At the fire, the *tohunga,* the
stringy old priest who accompanied the war party, dumped an-

other load of *mahoe* branches on the flames. He stirred things up until he got a fine bed of glowing embers, then heaped up earth to fashion an impromptu oven. The Hauhau warriors lined up and, one by one, handed him the severed heads they had been carrying in the flaxen kit bags they wore on their shoulders. Kitty stared with fascinated revulsion. The brains had been previously removed, during an earlier stop, and the eyes stuffed up. Now the heads were arranged over the open top of the oven to smoke. The old man, with the practiced fingers of an artist, began to smooth down the skin of the faces to prevent it from wrinkling while they were being smoke-dried. Caroline's sobs turned to wails, and she jumped up and blundered off into the ferns to be sick. The Hauhau guards made no attempt to follow or to interfere with her, though they kept their eyes on the patch of giant leaves to make sure that she did not attempt to wander off too far. The crowns of foliage shook with Caroline's movements for some time.

When Caroline returned, Kitty demanded of her, "Did you do anything useful while you were in there?"

Caroline, looking miserable and sick, moaned, "No. Oh, leave me alone, will you? I don't want to die, can't you see? I don't want to die!"

"Then it's up to me," Kitty said grimly. "I shall require your assistance, Mrs. Fisher. I shall want you to distract them—keep their attention on you to the extent possible."

"No, no, I won't!" Caroline cried, sounding like a child having a tantrum. "Leave me alone! Leave me alone!"

Alarmed, Kitty risked a glance at the Maori guards and saw that they were staring at Caroline with frank interest. She said no more but did what she could to calm the woman down. Caroline, however, was beyond reason, trembling and moaning, her eyes fixed on the old medicine man and his ghastly oven.

The head-smoking went on another hour, and then the priest scattered the dull embers and handed the revolting trophies back to their owners. The Hauhaus moved about, preparing to break camp. Some of the men, leading the stolen horses, trampled a path a short way into the forest, then returned, grinning. The direction in which the party was actually going to leave the clearing was soon made evident by the way they were pushing foliage aside to watch how it sprang back into place to conceal the narrow track.

Kitty stood up, smoothed down her skirts, and, as casually as she could manage, walked over to the patch of giant ferns. The

William Stuart Long*

pursuers—if any, and if they had been intelligent enough to draw the correct conclusions from the first clue she had left—would, with any luck, stop to examine patches like this at forest crossroads where the trails branched out. The Hauhau guards watched her progress with no signs of unusual interest, but . . . Caroline, to Kitty's growing alarm, was staring straight at her in fright, her eyes round as saucers, her face drained of color. One Hauhau nudged his companion and spoke to him. Kitty unhurriedly crouched down in the fanlike undergrowth with the top of her head showing and, working under the cover of her skirts, tore a strip of calico from her petticoat and knotted it deftly around a stem. She had just finished tying her second flag when a pair of bare feet planted themselves in front of her and a Hauhau warrior grasped her by the hair and hauled her upright, while a second warrior bent to retrieve the scrap of calico and hold it aloft for the others to see. Then, all at once, she was surrounded by angry men, waving their hatchets and shouting at her.

Chapter XXVI

TU-MAHUKI KNELT TO examine the ashes of the fire and the earth-work surrounding the pit. He poked around with a stick to his own satisfaction, then, rising, announced, "Not long they here. They stop maybe *tu, tiri* hour, smoke heads, then clear out."

At Adam's elbow, Hanes said eagerly, "They can't be too far ahead of us, then, sir. We're catching up."

Tu-Mahuki signified agreement with a grunt. "They lead horses, not ride them. Prisoners slow them down, too."

"If they keep the prisoners alive," Adam said worriedly. "But if they decided the women are too much trouble . . ." He left the sentence unfinished. So far they had found three sets of the calico markers, which had kept them from making wrong turns and get-ting delayed. The women were taking a great risk in leaving the clues, whatever the circumstances, and Adam could only hope that their stratagem would not be detected by the Hauhau.

"I'll feel better if we find something in the vicinity of this clear-ing," he said. "It's the sort of place where we ought to expect a sign, particularly since they stopped here for some time."

"The men are searching all the patches of new *punga* growth," the corporal replied. "That's the pattern we've found so far. One of the ladies—"

He broke off as a ranger who was rooting about in the under-growth hailed him. "Over here, corporal! You'd better have a look!"

Adam and Hanes hurried over. The trooper held up a broken stalk that still had a wisp of fabric attached to it. "Looks like it was pulled up and thrown away," he observed. "Look—there's another over there."

Adam despaired as he saw a second calico pennant lying on the ground where it had been dropped. "The Hauhau discovered them," he agreed. "We won't be finding any more of these tokens."

"We won't need them, Mr. Shannon," Hanes assured him. "The other signs are fresher as we get closer, and Tu-Mahuki here won't have any trouble sniffing them out." He clapped the Maori scout on the back. "Isn't that so, Tu-Mahuki? As for taking our bearings from this clearing, the broken stalks will give us a straight line!"

A search of a few minutes, on hands and knees by all three of them, confirmed the truth of what he had said. Adam got to his feet and began to issue orders. "Tu-Mahuki and I will go on ahead from here, without our horses," he said crisply. "Have someone take charge of them, will you, Corporal? I want the men to dismount and lead their horses, and follow at a distance. At this point, we can't risk alarming the Hauhau. When we need you to close in, one of us will backtrack and let you know." He gazed back with a troubled expression along the route they had taken. "We're a few hours into daylight now. The captain should have reached Killaloe from Mere with the main force and, if he has read things correctly, started out after us. Send a messenger back along the trail to meet them, Corporal. The captain should be apprised of what we're doing and urged to make all speed to catch up. But on all accounts he must hang back from Tu-Mahuki and myself, until we are able to assess the situation."

"Yes, sir," Hanes said, and turned to carry out Adam's instructions.

For the next few hours, Adam and his Maori companion glided silently through the forest, following the increasingly warm trail. Adam was urgently aware of the need for speed at this point, if he were to intercept the Hauhau raiding party before they reached the security of their *pa*. It was, therefore, with a sense of frustration and disappointment that he broke out at last into a cleared stretch of fernland and saw, past a forested gorge that made an effective moat, the tall stockade that marked a strategically situated *pa*.

"They're inside," he said bitterly to Tu-Mahuki. "They're already inside with their prisoners. It can't have been above an hour ago." With building resentment, Adam thought about the precious minutes he had wasted arguing with Marcus Fisher. The man had even tried to steer them onto the wrong trail, devil take him!

"Maybe hour, maybe less," the scout agreed. "No time yet to put head on top *niu* pole."

Adam followed his companion's gaze to the sacred flagstaff, set in the middle of the village and visible high above the stockade. It displayed two of the banners, bearing mystical Hauhau devices, that had been sent round at the beginning of the war by the mad prophet Te Ua to rouse the villages. One was a red half-moon on a white calico ground, and the other was a five-pointed star representing Venus. Perhaps Tu-Mahuki was right, Adam thought, and the Hauhaus simply had not gotten around yet to choosing from the collection of smoked heads brought by their warriors. Or perhaps . . . His blood chilled at the thought. Perhaps the top of the pole was reserved for some special head, to be hoisted after the appropriate ceremonies.

From the cover of the underbrush, Adam studied the fortifications with a professional eye. The outer stockade, the *pekerangi,* as the Maoris called it, looked flimsy. It was about eight feet tall and, except for the main supporting fenceposts, was made principally of light saplings that did not quite reach the ground. Its seeming flimsiness, Adam knew from experience, was a trap. The only access was through a tall, narrow gateway surmounted by the intricate Maori carved faces, and just beyond, the entrance would be blocked by a blind fence, so that an enemy would be exposed to withering fire from loopholes in the stout inner palisade, the *tuwatawata.* And the open spaces at the bottom of the outer barrier were for defenders, protected by a trench dug between the two stockades. The Maori, Adam reflected with grudging admiration, were superb strategists.

"Take many soldiers, many lives, to get inside this *pa,*" Tu-Mahuki said at his side. "By that time, *pakeha* women dead."

"It can't be taken by frontal assault," Adam agreed. "Our only course is stealth and deception."

"What you do?" the scout queried.

"I'll be a deserter," Adam answered promptly. "One with a grudge against authority and the British in general, forsaking the *pakeha* world and come to live among the Maori. There are such. The Hauhau are flattered by them—they say the gods have sent them—and they don't mind having a tame white man, a *pakeha mokai,* about as a bond servant. I ought to know. I've been a prisoner myself, offered a wife and implored to stay of my free will."

"How you get *pakeha* women out?" Tu-Mahuki asked doubtfully. "They watch you close, maybe they decide to put *your* head top of *niu* pole."

"I don't know," Adam admitted. "I don't know what I'll find inside, or how I'll be received. I'll simply have to take my chances and await an opportunity." He stripped off his tunic, with its insignia, and handed his revolver, belt, and cartridge case to Tu-Mahuki. The bowie knife he retained, thrusting it into the top of a boot. "Go back to Corporal Hanes and tell him what I'm up to. He's to wait where he is until after dark. If the main force of Rangers arrives, they're to hold back too. Then they're to take up positions around the *pa* and wait for a signal. Here, I'll write notes for Hanes and for the captain. I'll want a diversion." He looked across the cleared land, with its cultivated squares of maize and potatoes, toward the carved gateway of the *pa*, and his expression hardened. "Of course, if they see my head atop the *niu* pole, or those of the women, they're free to attack immediately."

Tu-Mahuki nodded understanding, and when Adam handed him the hastily penciled notes, the scout bade him good luck and wriggled off through the underbrush.

Adam set about to make himself comfortable for an hour or two. It would not do to rush into the *pa* in the wake of the excitement that must follow the return of the raiding party with their prisoners and their trophies of *pakeha* heads and flesh. Best to give them a little time to settle down and become pleased with themselves. Adam used the interval to tear and soil his shirt and breeches artfully, and generally to put himself in the disarray to be expected of one who had spent days or weeks wandering through the wilderness.

When the afternoon sun began to sink, he picked himself up and boldly walked to the front gate, in full view of the sentry on the lookout platform. "Hey, you, *hoa,* up there!" he shouted. "Let me in, friend!"

The sentry gaped at Adam in astonishment. "What you want, you *pakeha* fool?" he shouted back harshly. "Go 'way from this place, *tangata kuware!* Don't you know *t'e Hauhau* kill you?"

"I want to join you," Adam persisted. *"Whakarongo mai,* listen to me! I am *pakeha* Maori, for sure. I run away from *Angore* soldiers. Let me in, I say."

More heads popped up above the inner parapet to stare at Adam —openmouthed warriors and curious children. *"He pakeha, he pakeha!"* the children shrieked, rousing the village. Warriors armed with hatchets and guns poured through the narrow archway, to seize Adam and drag him inside the fortification. Adam looked about with seeming normal inquisitiveness, but actually memorizing the layout of the defensive trenches and firing pits.

With the screaming children tagging along at their heels, Adam's captors hustled him across the *marae,* the village square or parade ground, from whose center rose the tall *niu* pole with its crosstrees and flag halyards. Women emerged from the thatch-roofed *whares* on either side of the square to stand in their doorways and stare at him. Adam was not encouraged to see the pile of human heads stacked at the foot of the *niu* pole, or the bodies of the slain Hauhau warriors that were laid out in the square. A tattooed crone who was busy stacking wood on what, evidently, was to be the funeral pyre, paused in her labors to give him a hate-filled look and to curse at him. *"Ka taona koe ki te umu!* Soon you'll be cooked in the oven!"

They took him directly to a large *whare* whose carved embellishments—corner posts of grotesque figures with their tongues thrust out and a guardian *teko-teko* at the peak of the roof—proclaimed it to be the dwelling of an important personage. Waiting there for him, splendid in a feather cloak and bearing a plumed staff, was an imperious figure who could be none other than Te Ngara, the chief.

Te Ngara questioned him at length and, impressed by his command of the Maori language and his evident knowledge of Maori ways, said finally, "Why do you run away from the *pakeha* soldiers and come here?"

Adam launched into a long tale of floggings and abuse. He removed his shirt and showed the marks of the flogging he had received aboard the *Pomona* at the direction of Marcus Fisher. "They do not trust me anymore because I lived so long among the Ngatihaua," he finished, "and my life is harder than before."

Te Ngara examined him shrewdly. "You run away from Maori once. How do I know you not run away again?"

"I was a prisoner then," Adam replied readily. "I was honor bound to run away. I come here of my own free will."

A heated discussion began among the attending warriors. Te Ngara had a shouting match with one old man, whom Adam took to be the priest, and who kept waving a greenstone hatchet around. At last Te Ngara turned to Adam and demanded, "Will you ever leave the Hauhau and go back to the *pakehas?*"

"No," Adam replied promptly. "I want to live with the Hauhau forever."

"That is good," said Te Ngara grudgingly. "If you had not said at once that you would never return to your people, I would have killed you with this sacred spear in my hand."

He turned to quiet the arguments that broke out among the other men present, then faced Adam again. "We will decide," he said. "If I permit you to become my *pakeha mokai,* then we give you a Maori name and a wife." He barked orders, and an escort of warriors closed around Adam. "Many, many brave *toa* die just now in war raid. People my *hapu* very, very angry at *pakehas,* want to kill you, eat you to make war god Tu happy again. We see, by and by." He barked more orders, and the escort relieved Adam of his bowie knife and led him away.

They took him to a small, windowless *raupo*-reed hut, thrust him inside, and fastened the door behind him. A small, unvented fire in the middle of the hut had been allowed to go out, and at first all Adam could see was a dull cluster of red embers in the darkness. Then he heard a rustle of movement and a smothered cry of alarm. "Who's here?" he said sharply.

"It's an English voice, thank God!" a woman gasped.

"Mrs. Broome?" Adam questioned. "Mrs. Fisher?"

He felt around the dirt floor with his hands and found some twigs and scraps of vegetation. He laid them over the coals and blew on them until they caught. In the dim, flickering light, he could see the huddled forms of two women against the far wall. One, the small, trim figure with the mass of dark curling hair, was Kitty Broome; it seemed a thousand years since he had warned poor Johnny that he was losing her to Sean O'Hara and had offered to ride out to Killaloe with him to give him moral support. The other—Adam's heart leaped like a wild thing in his breast, despite himself—was Caroline.

"Lieutenant Shannon?" Kitty said before Adam could identify himself. "I was never so glad to see a human face in my life— though I'm sorry for your sake."

"Adam?" Caroline quavered. "Is it really you? This is like a dream. Have you come to rescue us?"

Adam almost thought it was someone else speaking at first. He had never heard Caroline sound like this; she had always been brittle, hard, self-assured—even at her most passionate.

"I fear, madam," he said with an impersonality he found hard to maintain, "that for the moment I am a prisoner myself."

"Adam . . ." Her voice was small and high, like that of a little girl. "I . . . I was wrong. Marcus—"

"I left Mr. Fisher well and in good health," Adam said, biting off the words. "He is quite unhurt."

"And Sean?" Kitty interjected anxiously. "Is he . . ."

"Mr. O'Hara is alive," he told her with some restraint, having expected her to ask about her husband. "Though he was badly injured. He's been taken to a hospital in Auckland, and there is every reason to believe that he will recover. But—"

"Johnny!" Kitty said quickly. "Johnny was coming to Killaloe to . . . to speak to me—after dinner, his note said. What do you know of Johnny, Lieutenant Shannon?"

Briefly, Adam told her of how Johnny had been wounded while riding to Mere to fetch von Tempsky's Rangers. "I'm afraid it's quite serious, Mrs. Broome," he said. "He received a shotgun blast in the back—and possibly a bullet as well. He was being looked after when I left him, and there were plans to get him to Auckland in the morning." He did not tell her that the surgeon had not expected Johnny to live.

"Thank you," she said simply, her eyes downcast. "Thank you for doing what you could for Johnny. He would not have been at Killaloe that night had I not asked him to come."

"Johnny is a brave man," Adam said. "He rode alone, at night, through country that he knew to be infested with hostile Hauhau. His one thought was to try to rescue you . . . and Mrs. Fisher, of course." He refrained from adding what he was thinking—that there had been no reason for Johnny to have been alone; that Marcus Fisher ought to have been with him.

"And how do you come to be a prisoner, Lieutenant?" Kitty inquired.

Adam hesitated, and then in the sparest possible terms he told her—he did not once glance at Caroline—about tracking the raiding party with Tu-Mahuki, about the contingent of Rangers he had left hidden in the forest, about the balance of von Tempsky's company, which he hoped was coming up to reinforce them, and about the ruse he had employed to get inside the *pa*.

Kitty sat up straight in the semidarkness. "Then there's a chance we might be rescued?"

"More likely a chance of getting killed in a rescue attempt,"

Adam said honestly. "Unless we can manage to find a way out ourselves and signal for a diversion."

"Never mind, Mr. Shannon," Kitty said with a catch in her voice. "The important thing is that Johnny tried to send help after us, at the risk of his life." She glanced over at Caroline Fisher, with something like pity. Adam could only guess at what she was thinking, but surely the two women must have an inkling of Fisher's behavior at the farmhouse. Kitty turned to Adam and went on with a rush of warmth, "And you, Mr. Shannon! You are a brave man as well, to put yourself into the jaws of the lion this way."

"It may be to little purpose," Adam said, reddening. "I'm of no use to you while I'm locked up like this. But if they decide to accept me into the tribe, and I'm free to move about within the *pa* . . ."

From outside, the sound of chanting increased in intensity. Out on the parade ground, flames must have been leaping higher, because even within the windowless hut a flickering red light showed through the spaces between the reeds.

"What is that?" Caroline exclaimed in sudden fright.

Adam addressed them equally. "They've lit the funeral pyre," he said. "Now they will have a great *tangihanga*—a wailing over the dead—and then they will share the flesh of their enemies. The ceremonies will take some hours. And then they will decide what to do about me—about all of us."

Kitty raised her chin and, with a steadiness that compelled Adam's admiration, said, "It will be a very long night, Mr. Shannon."

The chanting and wailing went on for hours, while Adam and the two women waited, helpless, in the darkened interior of the hut. Adam worried about Caroline, who was cowering, deathly pale with terror, in the corner farthest from the door. She seemed almost paralyzed, and if by some miracle a chance for escape presented itself and decisive action were called for, he feared she might prove a dangerous hindrance. Kitty Broome, on the other hand, looked alert and ready for anything, listening with creditable self-control to the sounds outside, as if they had nothing to do with her.

"What is that they're singing now, Mr. Shannon?" she asked.

"It's a *tangi,* a dirge for the fallen." He cocked his head. *"Ko tai ko ki . . .* in the fullness of life they fell. *Haere ake ra te ihi o nga toa . . .* farewell, spirits of the brave."

"They can't be very fond of us, then," Kitty said with a tired smile.

"No," he said shortly.

The chants reached a peak, followed by cries and wails, and then the sounds outside took on a new tenor, a rising litany with rhythmic responses. Adam listened intently. *"Rewa, piki rewa, rongo rewa,"* he heard. *"Tone, piki tone, rongo tone! Rori, piki rori, rongo rori!"*

"What are they saying now?" Kitty questioned him.

"They're affirming their own immortality," he informed her. "It's a kind of magical incantation taught to them by their mad prophet, Te Ua. There are all sorts of charms—one of them is supposed to make you immune to bullets. That's why they're so reckless in battle. They believe they can't be shot if their faith is strong enough."

"What do the words mean?"

"They're just nonsense, really, a mixture of Maori and pidgin English that Te Ua claims came to him through the Angel Gabriel in a vision. 'River, big river, long river.' 'Road, big road, long road.' 'Bush, big bush, long bush.' Things like that. But it's supposed to have a mystic meaning."

Outside, the invocations and responses worked up to a hoarse frenzy and came to a sudden halt:

"Hai!"

"Kamu te ti!"

"Oro te mene!"

"Rauna te niu!"

Kitty shivered. "And what was that all about?"

"Didn't you recognize it?" Adam said with a wry smile. "It's more or less in imitation of us British. 'Hi! Come to tea! All the men, round the *niu!*' "

"It would almost be amusing if . . . if one didn't know what was in store," she retorted wanly.

"Try not to think about it, Mrs. Broome."

Kitty's reserve cracked. "It's hard *not* to think about it, isn't it, when one has seen the cooking ovens being stoked in honor of our arrival, and seen small children smile at one in the friendliest possible way whilst rubbing their bellies."

From her corner, Caroline gasped in fear. "Please don't say things like that!" she begged. "Why must you be so horrid?"

Kitty frowned in resignation, and Adam, looking at his former lover as she crouched against the wall, felt pity for her, but nothing more. How could he ever have been in love with this woman, he wondered . . . been so blinded by desire that he had thrown away his naval career—thrown away his name and his very honor? His thoughts went in a rush to Emily Carmichael in Sydney—poor Emily, who, in the letter she had entrusted Kitty Broome to deliver to him—how long ago?—had sought to warn him of Caroline's arrival in New Zealand. Poor Emily indeed! She could not have understood why he had been so reserved with her; surely she must have assumed that he was still in love with Caroline Omerod, with whom he had once had a ruinous affair—

"And you, Adam Vincent!" Caroline, between sobs, was suddenly railing at him, as if she could read his thoughts. "Why did you bother to come here if you could not help? You've only made matters worse—stirred them up against us, endangered our lives! I never wanted to see your face again, and it . . . it was cruel of you to give us hope!"

"Mrs. Fisher, I—" Adam began, and then the door to the hut was flung wide. Adam's fingers curled impotently, weaponless. He had felt all around the floor of the hut in the darkness for something he might use as a club or cane, but he had found nothing stouter than a twig.

"Haere atu, haere atu!" the Maori warriors summoned him with rough voices. There were two of them—big, powerfully thewed fellows armed with spatulate greenstone war clubs whose sharp edges could cleave through a man's skull as if it were an eggshell.

Adam sprang to his feet with alacrity. It would be fatal, he knew, to show the least hesitation. He managed to whisper to Kitty, "Hold yourself in readiness, Mrs. Broome."

"Good luck, Mr. Shannon," she returned.

Adam's heart sank when, hemmed in between the two hulking warriors, he was led out to the *marae*. The whole Hauhau nation, it seemed, was gathered there to await him. A ring of stakes had been prepared, and in the center of it a roaring fire sent sparks up into the night sky. Adam was taken within the ring and told to kneel. He complied, feeling his belly crawl; he had been ordered to the positon most convenient for execution. A circle of half-naked Hauhaus surrounded him. He raised his eyes and saw the chief, Te Ngara, and the old priest who had wanted to club him forthwith.

The priest waved the flat stone club at him. "You see the *ahi tapu*, the sacred fire?" he demanded.

"I see," Adam replied.

"Now I ask, will you ever return to the *pakehas?*"

"No, I want to stay with the Maoris always and to become one with them."

The old priest grunted. He lowered the club and said, "It is well. If you had not given your promise, you would have been thrown into the fire."

Te Ngara stepped forward and, pulling Adam to his feet, shook hands with him English fashion. "You are Maori now," he said jovially. "Now I give you Maori name. Because your hair is fair, you are called Urukehu."

At that, the circle of warriors pressed in on Adam to pump his hand and clap him on the back and call him by his new name. It was exactly like being welcomed into officers' mess. All animosity toward him seemed to have been put aside. They insisted that he divest himself of his European clothes, and someone handed him Maori garb: a knee-length flaxen kilt and a dyed cloak. His shirt, breeches, and boots disappeared into the crowd to find new owners. Adam noticed that he was given no weapon; trust went only so far, evidently. A grinning warrior told him, in high good spirits, that undoubtedly he would be given the ugliest and most misshapen of maidens for his wife, and that he must not refuse her or he would be killed on the spot. Adam smiled to show that he appreciated the joke.

For the next hour or two he mingled with the celebrants on the *marae,* and after a while most of them ceased to take particular notice of him. He roamed restlessly among the *whares* and along the margins of the stockade to get the others used to his moving about, and although he attracted the stares of people he came near —and at one point a shotgun-toting warrior barred his way when he approached too close to the entrance—he established the fact that no one had been assigned to follow him and keep an eye on him. The celebration went on through the small hours, with singing, some desultory marching round the *niu* pole, on which some dried heads had now been hung, and speechmaking, to which fewer and fewer people listened. Rum was being passed around, Adam noticed—as well as bottles of what must have been O'Hara's wine—and as the night wore on, the participants in the protracted *korero* became blearier. Adam was in no better shape, for he had had even less sleep than they.

He had one bad moment when the women came in a procession

from behind the *whares,* where the cook ovens had been going through the night with their dreadful smell of roasting meat. Several of them carried little round steaming baskets, which they laid before the warriors. Adam refused the basket that one of them, with a giggle, tried to present to him, and by doing so he aroused the ire of a great big fellow who was armed to the teeth with club, ax, and liver-cutter and who had a handkerchief with feathers bound round his head. "Eat!" he commanded in a fury. "You must eat! *Kainga, kainga!* This is the food of Tu! If you do not eat, I will kill you, and you yourself will be cooked in the ovens!"

"Yes, eat, *pakeha!*" jeered another warrior. "It is only pork!"

Te Ngara came storming up and demanded, "What is this? You must not tell my *pakeha* to eat his own people. This flesh is *tapu* to him. I have said so. Go, Urukehu. The women will give you pork and potatoes."

Gratefully, Adam slipped away. He kept out of sight as the *korero* wound down and people sought out their sleeping mats. A gray dawn was approaching. This was the hour of dread for the Maori, and the watchman on the lookout platform periodically called out an all's well to reassure light sleepers that no enemy was creeping up on the *pa.*

It was now or never.

Adam looked quickly around to make sure that no one was eyeing him, then edged along the back of a row of *whares* until he came to the one in which he had been held prisoner. A single Hauhau guard was posted outside, scowling at the dying fires on the *marae* and the stragglers who still fought sleep there. By one of the cook ovens Adam found a piece of firewood—a light, hard stave about two feet long. He crept along the side of the hut under the shelter of the low eaves and rounded the corner, swinging. The guard's back was to him. The club bounced off bone, and the man went down without a sound. Quickly Adam undid the fastening on the door and dragged the body inside. Caroline screamed, but with great good sense and swifter responses, Kitty Broome stifled her cry with the palm of her hand.

"He's dead," Adam announced after examining the limp form. "Now there is no choice. We're in for it when he's discovered. We must move very quickly."

Caroline immediately began to berate him for putting their lives in danger, but Kitty silenced her with a few well-chosen words and said to Adam, "What is it that we must do, Mr. Shannon?"

"First I must give the Rangers a sign that they are free to attack
—now, before first light, to provide a distraction—and pray that
someone with sharp eyes is watching the stockade." He reddened
slightly. "And for that, I shall need a woman's petticoat."

He turned expectantly to Caroline; they had once been lovers,
after all, and this was no time for false modesty. Lady Kitty, he
had been pleased to note, had taken his scanty Maori costume in
stride. But Caroline averted her eyes from his half-naked body, as
if she had never seen it before, and his request was ignored.

"Oh, for heaven's sake," Kitty said in exasperation. "Mr. Shannon, turn your back," she ordered, and a moment later handed
him a small bundle of calico. "It's a bit torn," she said, "but I hope
it will serve the purpose."

He thanked her and, after rubbing soot from the remains of the
fire into his blond hair to blacken it, turned to leave. Caroline burst
out shrilly, "Where are you going? You're not going to leave us
here, alone and unprotected?" She gave a distraught glance toward
the dead body near the door and seemed on the verge of becoming
hysterical again. "I refuse to remain here with *that!*"

"Keep your voice down," Kitty hissed at her, and Caroline subsided. Adam paused to plunder the dead body of its weapons and
slipped outside, fastening the door behind him.

No one challenged him as he crossed the *marae,* and he hoped
that in the milky obscurity of the predawn mists he would pass for
a Maori with his soot-blackened hair. The fires of the *korero* had
died down, and there were only a few shadowy figures about.
Adam hoped that as the first rays of the sun warmed the ground,
the mists would clear enough for any outside watchers to see his
signal; but for now the fog was a friend. An owl hooted, and he
heard the lone sentinel give his *"Whakaara-pa"*—the all's well.

He climbed the inner parapet like any honest Hauhau warrior
having a look-round, then swiftly extracted the bundle of calico
from underneath his cloak and hung it outside the fence. The
watchman was occupied looking out across the approaches to the
pa, not paying attention to what was going on within the stockade,
and only two small corners of fabric, impaled on the sharpened
saplings, would be visible from inside the walls. His errand accomplished, Adam hurried back to the prisoners' hut.

The primitive latch was still undisturbed, and no one was about
to notice him let himself inside. There was a gasp from the women,
which subsided as they recognized Adam. In a low voice he told

them what they were going to do, then finished by saying, "But for
now we must wait quietly. Soon there'll be a lot of confusion out
there, and that's when we must move."

He stripped the dead man of his cloak, but Caroline shrank from
him when he approached her with it. "Give it to me, Mr. Shannon," Kitty interposed, and bundled herself up in it, covering her
head. "One cannot have scruples at a time like this." Adam removed his own cloak, and together they coaxed Caroline to drape
it over her head and shoulders.

"Here, take this, Mrs. Broome," Adam said after a moment's
thought, offering Kitty the dead warrior's war club. "It will add to
the deception, and with any luck everyone will be too occupied to
scrutinize us closely."

Not more than a half hour could have passed, though the waiting seemed interminable, and then there was a cry and a warning
shot from the sentry outside. The alarm was answered instantly by
a fusillade from beyond the stockade that sent flocks of screaming
parrots fluttering into the air and filling the predawn darkness with
their raucous cries. Adam opened the door of the hut a crack and
saw Maori warriors pouring out of the other huts with their weapons. The women tumbled out after them with shouts of *"Kia maia,
kia maia! Be brave!"* and began to gather on the *marae*. Adam
snatched up the dead man's long Enfield rifle and thrust the two
women out the door ahead of him. Caroline balked, protesting.
"No, no, I won't go! We'll die!" but he grabbed her by the upper
arm and dragged her along, while Kitty, carrying the heavy club,
crowded in at the rear. The Hauhaus were all around them, hurrying to their various posts, and now the parapet and the trenches
between the two palisades were alive with gunfire.

Adam quickly found the entrance to the covered ditch he had
previously noted. Fortunately it was not too far from the reed hut
in which they had been held captive, and the three of them
squeezed through under the camouflaged roof of timber and reeds.
A last look behind him revealed that a number of the Hauhaus
firing from the parapets had fallen, despite the magic charm of
"Hapa! Pai marire!" and the upheld palm that was supposed to
turn away bullets. Some of von Tempsky's men had crept close
enough to the stockade to lob hand grenades, and it must have
seemed to the defending Hauhaus that the *pakeha* troopers had
launched a suicidal frontal assault.

Adam rounded a bend in the trench and, to his consternation, saw a Hauhau sharpshooter wriggling on ahead of him. "I am here," the warrior said without turning around. "Go find another firing post!" Regretting what he must do, Adam clubbed the man at the base of the skull with the butt of the Enfield, and together he and Kitty managed to haul a frozen Caroline past the body. Hearing the sound of firing all around them, they crawled through the tunnel made by the roofed trench and came out in a hollowed *pukatea* tree, well outside the stockade, that had been fitted out with small loopholes so that Hauhau riflemen could fire from behind on unsuspecting attackers who succeeded in reaching the outer walls of the *pa*. Fortunately the position was unoccupied, though the tree trunk was large enough to accommodate two Hauhaus. Adam and the women squeezed inside.

Cautiously, Adam peered through a loophole. Von Tempsky's raiders were retiring, firing as they went. Adam could see the dispersed muzzle-flashes from concealing vegetation, and the occasional blue uniform wriggling through the ferns; but the Rangers were putting on a good show. Now, he realized, came the tricky part; he and the two women had to reach the Rangers' lines without getting shot by their own people. All at once he was painfully conscious of his Maori costume.

He bade Kitty and Caroline to shed their borrowed cloaks and, at the first lull in the shooting, pushed aside the camouflage joining the tunnel and tree and told the women to run for it while he brought up the rear. Caroline froze again, and he and Kitty had each to take her by an arm and run with her between them. Adam kept the thick bole of the *pukatea* tree between them and the *pa* at the start, and by the time it no longer afforded them protection, they were among the tree trunks of the forest, zigzagging from cover to cover as much as possible.

His lungs were on fire, and Caroline was gasping for breath, forcing him and Kitty to half support her as they dragged her along. Ahead he saw a cluster of blue uniforms; an officer waving a sword was exhorting his men, not taking any cover himself. Adam recognized the long, curved sword, which could belong to only one man, and the raffish, drooping mustache and shoulder-length black hair under a carelessly tilted forage cap. It was Major von Tempsky himself; he must have returned from Hawke's Bay in time to take charge of the relief force, Adam surmised. But there was no time for speculation; rifles were swinging round in his direction, and Adam found the breath to shout, "Don't shoot, don't shoot, we're English!" He was close enough to see the pop-eyed faces, and realized what an apparition the three of them must have appeared —the disheveled women in the ruins of their party dresses, in the company of a bare-chested, soot-streaked Hauhau—then heard a flabbergasted ranger calling him by name. He found himself laughing with relief and joy as he stumbled into their midst, and then there were many willing hands to catch Caroline as she fell.

Squatting on his heels in the clearing, Adam waited in respectful silence as von Tempsky scratched diagrams in the ground with the point of a knife, working out whatever problem of strategy or tactics he was currently engaged in. All around, rangers sat under makeshift cover, taking advantage of this interval of respite to clean their rifles, stuff some cold rations into themselves, attend to their equipment. They hadn't been allowed to light their pipes; there were no campfires here, and no tents had been pitched. There were tents—but no fires—at the base camp von Tempsky had set up a couple of miles farther back, and Caroline and Lady Kitty had been taken there, to relative safety, until an escort could take them back to Auckland. It had been proposed to leave them at Drury, the closest settlement, but Caroline had raised such a fuss that von Tempsky had decided he could spare the men.

At last von Tempsky finished, and turned his swarthy visage in Adam's direction. "Well, Lieutenant, you've had quite an outing for yourself," he stated dryly.

Adam knew better than to interrupt. Von Tempsky's expression was unreadable as he went on: "You took a fourth of our force at Mere out of camp—on a wild-goose chase, at that—without authorization and, I must say, against my standing orders. Well, what have you to say for yourself?"

"They were volunteers, sir," Adam defended, conscious of the inanity of his words, "and . . . and I did not feel it wise to wait."

"And then," von Tempsky pursued, his eyes narrowing to slits, "you risked the lives of two hostages in a harebrained scheme to let *yourself* be taken captive, with no clear plan in mind, while committing an inadequate force—you could not know at the time whether I would arrive or not—to risk annihilation in a foolish and ill-conceived feint on a fortified *pa* . . . a feint that could serve no useful military purpose except to inform a superior enemy of the presence of our troops. If you had engaged in such insubordinate folly while assigned to the imperial regulars instead of to our . . .

rather more *dégagé* outfit, you would most probably by now have found yourself under arrest and on the way to a court-martial. Are you aware of that?"

"Yes, sir," Adam said miserably.

"And," von Tempsky rumbled on relentlessly, "as I am technically under the command of Colonel McDonnell, you have therefore misappropriated *his* troops. Colonel McDonnell could very well, if he is so disposed, still decide to have you court-martialed, and I would not be in the least surprised."

Adam, all too conscious of the unmilitary appearance he must present with his bare torso and Hauhau kilt, lowered his gaze.

"But, of course," von Tempsky continued with a sudden, brigand's grin, "Colonel McDonnell may wish to court-martial *me* for exceeding *my* instructions and going in to take Te Ngara's *pa* with the Rangers, without waiting for his orders and without recourse to his regulars."

Adam found his voice after a stunned moment. "You . . . you intend to storm the *pa*, Major? But I thought—"

"You thought that, having gotten the women out, I would retire, and leave the taking of the *pa* to Her Majesty's regulars, with us as auxiliaries so that they could use us to do the dirty work and have the glory for themselves? But Adam, it would take weeks—months —for them to make up their minds and then to march here with full equipment and supply wagons and display themselves in proper military array. On the other hand, we are here *now,* we have them rattled, and we know their strategic position and numbers as of this moment—before they have a chance to seek reinforcements from neighboring tribes. Is that not so?"

"Well . . . yes, it is, sir. I can give you a plan of the fortifications . . . the trenches, the firing pits, and the weak spots . . . and they have two hidden exits at the rear of the *pa*."

"Excellent, excellent!" Von Tempsky beamed. "You will draw me a map, my dear fellow, and then we shall find a proper uniform for you so that you may lead a contingent without getting shot by your own men. We shall move the main body of Rangers here from the base camp and mount the assault without further delay."

Adam stood up, his fatigue melting away at the prospect of action. "If you can lend me writing materials, sir, I'll make a detailed sketch." He glanced a bit sheepishly at his superior. "But Mrs. Broome and Mrs. Fisher—we ought to be sure they're well out of the way before—"

"They'll be on their way within the hour," von Tempsky assured him brusquely. "I've loaned Tu-Mahuki to their escort. Mrs. Broome is very anxious to get started. She wants to rejoin her husband without delay." He shook his head sadly. "Poor fellow. I had a word with the surgeon before I left Mere. I fear that Mrs. Broome may reach her husband only in time to be at his side when he dies."

Adam was sorry to hear von Tempsky's estimate, although it was as much as he had expected. Still, it was ironic, he thought, that Kitty was racing to be at Johnny's side rather than at Sean O'Hara's; the reconciliation had come a little too late for Johnny.

Von Tempsky was on his feet, his restless mind already racing ahead to the problems and details of the impending assault. He checked his impatience long enough to say to Adam, "Mrs. Fisher, on the other hand, does not seem all that eager to rejoin her husband in Auckland." He looked curiously at Adam. "She wishes to see you before she departs. She was most insistent about it, in fact. I can spare you for an hour or so if you want to return to the base camp while I am getting things ready here."

"No," Adam said. "I have no wish to see her."

A curtain had been erected around Johnny's bed so that Kitty could attend him away from the eyes of the other patients in the ward. He was not expected to last through the night, the resident surgeon, a young Scot named MacGregor, had told her.

"I'm afraid the carriage ride undid the work of the Rangers' surgeon," he had said when she arrived at the Provincial Hospital, breathless and in a hastily donned dress that had been provided by Martha Montrose. "Your husband lost a good deal of blood, Mrs. Broome, and indeed we were reluctant to attempt an operation. It was the rifle bullet that did most of the damage—though fortunately it missed the vital organs—and some of the shot had penetrated quite deeply too. The operation itself went entirely well, but of course now the danger is secondary hemorrhage and septicemia. Healing of wounds of such severity in these cases is unusual, and I fear that, given your husband's condition, he could not resist post-operative fever."

The curtain parted, and the night nurse came inside, a fresh-faced young girl recently out from England, whose name was Daisy Hudd. "Would you like a cup of tea, my lady?" she inquired with a blush.

"Thank you, Daisy, no," Kitty responded.

With a murmured apology, the girl pushed past Kitty to inspect Johnny's dressings. Biting her lip at what she saw, she peeled away plaster and removed a pad of bloody linen, to replace it with a wad of linen soaked in fluid from a corked bottle.

"What is that?" Kitty inquired.

"It is a solution of Condy's fluid," the nurse informed her. "It is believed to retard suppuration. Doctor insists on absolute cleanliness." She lowered her voice confidentially. "He follows the recommendations of Miss Nightingale to the Sanitary Commission."

"And are you a devotee of Miss Nightingale, Daisy?"

"Oh, yes," the girl said worshipfully. "I'm a certificated nurse of her training school at Saint Thomas's Hospital—the training takes a whole year. And I've read her *Notes on Nursing* from cover to cover I don't know how many times."

"Will all that make a difference, do you think?" Kitty asked wearily, gesturing at the bottle of fluid and at the square of metal foil that Daisy was now affixing to the saturated dressing.

The nurse bit her lip again. "We mustn't give up hope, I always say, my lady. Dr. MacGregor's saved many a one that would have been buried, times past."

Kitty was not so sure. She watched as the girl gathered up her materials and left—a new kind of nurse, true enough, rosy-cheeked and crisp in her starched apron and cap. The Provincial Hospital itself was a far cry from what would have been found in England; it had the advantage of starting fresh in a new place, with new ideas. It was clean, spacious, sunlit, and the staff was earnest and efficient —proud of their work. She turned back to Johnny and examined his pale face in the lamplight. He had been barely able to speak when she arrived—only a few disconnected words, but he had recognized her. "Kit," he had murmured, "you've come. Went to O'Hara's . . . to fight for you. My fault . . . should never have left you alone . . . Adam told me I was . . . fool. Stay with me, Kit." But after that he had lapsed into a restless unconsciousness. He had felt hot and feverish, and there had been no words, not even the babble of delirium.

She left his bedside once, for about five minutes, to look in on Sean O'Hara. He was cheerful and unruly—having failed in his attempt to convince the doctors of the benefits of alcohol in relieving pain, but having found someone to smuggle in whiskey anyway —and despite the clumsy boards to which his limbs were bound, he

418   *William Stuart Long*

looked, Kitty was relieved to see, much his own self, and not the
broken creature of whom she had had a horrified glimpse as the
Hauhaus dragged her out of the house.

"Whatever happens, Sean, it's over between us," she had told
him.

He had replied with forced gaiety that had brought her close to
tears. "And sure, didn't I know that, Kit, when I saw you sailing
past here on your way to your husband? At Killaloe, I knew it
would all be up if he came to see you, and I prayed he would stay
away—though praise all the saints he did not, for I never thought I
would be so glad to see a rival. And how is the man?"

At that, her self-control had given way, and she had burst into
sobs. He had tried to comfort her, clumsy in his stiff wrappings.
"The doctors here are grand, Kit, and if anyone can work miracles,
they can. For didn't I expect to lose me leg—the splintered one,
with the bones showing through. The gangrene, that's what does it
—there's always the gangrene in a case like that. But they put in
their little wet pads with their tweezers, and the wounds do not
run; they do not! I'll be a bit stiff, Kit, and I'll walk with a limp,
but by God I'll be able to sit a horse again! With a little luck,
they'll do the same for your husband."

She sat with Johnny through the night, and toward dawn he
began to mumble in his sleep. Day broke through the tall windows
at the end of the ward, and the scrubwoman came in to mop the
stone floor. Johnny's eyelashes flickered, and he looked straight at
her. "Kit, you're here," he said thickly. "I thought it was a
dream." He tried to sit up, but he was too weak. "Lord, I think I'm
hungry," he announced.

Dr. MacGregor came then, with a train of nurses, and when he
examined Johnny, his dour face lit up with pleasure. "The fever's
gone down," he told Kitty. "He's going to be all right now."

She squeezed Johnny's hand, the tears trickling down her face,
and their gazes locked. She could not say anything with the doctor
there, but Johnny's eyes told her he knew what she was thinking. *I
won't leave you, Johnny*, she promised silently. *We can try again.
And this time I shall try to be a wife to you.*

Beside her, Dr. MacGregor, removing one of the dressings and
dropping it into a tray, said, "You . . . ah . . . were involved in
that action at the Hauhau *pa* south of here, were you not, Mrs.
Broome?"

She nodded. The doctor knew very well she had been. News had been spread in Auckland very quickly by the Forest Rangers who had escorted her and Caroline Fisher, and MacGregor had been at pains to keep parades of nurses and staff from coming by to gawk at the woman who had been at the center of the incredible tale of rescue and heroism.

"You'll be pleased to know, then, that von Tempsky's Forest Rangers have taken the *pa*. And with very little loss of life. The news came in less than an hour ago. There is . . . ah . . . much jubilation in the streets and, I'm afraid I must say, in the hospital too, to the detriment of efficiency. The hero of the action was a Lieutenant Shannon, with whom . . . ah . . . I believe you are acquainted. He was able to lead the Rangers in through the network of defenses, and when the rascals found that their magic charm against bullets was no proof against the Rangers' shooting, they quickly lost heart. Those who did not surrender made their escape into the forest through the rear exit, which von Tempsky was wise enough to leave unimpeded. Lieutenant Shannon's name is on everybody's lips, and I believe Governor Grey has some sort of commendation in mind for him." The bony Scots face gave a wry smile. "I'm afraid . . . ah . . . there is rather less jubilation on the part of Colonel McDonnell and General Chute, however, as von Tempsky achieved his marvelous victory on his own initiative, and without recourse to Her Majesty's regiments."

Kitty felt Johnny squeeze her hand. "Good old Adam," he whispered. "I wish I were well enough to write the story—if he'd let me. Did I ever tell you, Kit, about the time he refused to allow me to write the account of his capture and escape at the Queen's Redoubt? The fellow avoids the limelight like the plague—doesn't want his past dug up, I assume. A pity. He's covered himself with glory this time; perhaps he'll be clever enough now to realize he's not unworthy of that young lady in Sydney he's been avoiding."

He sank back on the pillow, exhausted with the effort of talking.

"That's enough for now," Dr. MacGregor admonished him. "Keep him quiet, Mrs. Broome." He looked at her questioningly. "Ah . . . if you intend to stay, this is."

"Yes," she affirmed. "I'll stay."

Governor Grey rose at once from his desk and came around to shake Adam's hand. "Ah, Captain Shannon, I see you've managed to find your way to Government House. What do you think of our new quarters?"

"Very impressive, sir," Adam offered. He looked through the tall windows at the striking view of Wellington Harbor and the Parliament buildings that were perched overlooking the busy port. True, the vicinity of the governor's residence itself was still mostly a primitive landscape, with the undergrowth held at bay by a rickety picket fence, but there was a fine broad drive leading up to the door and a decently tended expanse of lawn.

"Yes, the Centralists have had their way," the governor agreed, "and it *will* be more convenient to have the seat of government here, rather than in Auckland. We have two islands to administer, after all, not one, and we can no longer leave everything to the provincial councils, can we? A very large future is opening out for New Zealand, Captain Shannon, very large indeed." His deep-set blue eyes looked penetratingly at Adam. "But you're not wearing your new badges, Captain," he observed.

"I haven't got around to it yet, sir," Adam confessed. "We don't go in much for that sort of thing in the Forest Rangers. Even Major von Tempsky doesn't bother about insignia half the time— just goes about in that open-necked gray flannel shirt of his, with his forage cap and long boots." Indeed, Adam reflected, von Tempsky had been casual about the field promotion. He had summoned Adam to his tent and said, simply, "You are a captain now, Adam. In the Rangers, anyway. I'm writing a strong letter of recommendation for promotion in kind in the Fiftieth as well, which, under the circumstances, they are bound to accept. No, don't thank me— you deserve it. But I shall be sorry to lose you. The Rangers need good men like you. There's still a lot of fighting to do—the East Coast still needs cleaning up. But I won't stand in your way. Good luck." And that had been the first Adam had learned of his impending separation from the Rangers.

Governor Grey smiled at Adam's accurate portrait of the Polish soldier of fortune. "But you've been breveted captain in the Fiftieth as well, I understand," he persisted. "You'll have to do something about acquiring proper insignia when you report to Her Majesty's regiment, or run the risk of being out of uniform."

"I shall, sir," Adam allowed, with an answering smile.

Adam forgave the governor for what he said next, for obviously it was well intentioned. "You're wearing your V.C., at least," Sir George Grey observed, eyeing the small bronze cross hanging from its short length of dull crimson ribbon on Adam's chest. "Good show. It's not every day one is awarded the Victoria Cross, is it?"

Again the image rose unbidden, as it had when General Chute had pinned the medal on him in front of the troops at dress parade and the onlooking civilians . . . the image of his first Victoria Cross, the one that had been stripped from him by anonymous hands at his court-martial, when he had forfeited his decorations. No, he thought bitterly, it was not every day one was awarded the V.C.; but he had won it twice—once under his true name and once under this sham identity, this Lieutenant—no, Captain—Shannon.

"What are your plans now?" the governor went on, oblivious of the hurt he had caused. "Your old regiment is back in England by now, but I don't doubt that you'd be allowed to retransfer if you had a mind to."

"I plan to stay in the colonies, sir," Adam stated flatly. "I shall sail to Australia with the Fiftieth." He had no wish to see England again, the England that had broken him; or, for that matter, the father who had disowned him.

"I can't persuade you to remain in New Zealand, I suppose?" the governor pressed him. "We need men of your stripe here, Shannon. Special consideration will be given to those who served in the militia and the Forest Rangers, and I don't doubt that you could secure a land grant on very advantageous terms."

Adam shook his head. The land given to the military settlers, he knew, was likely to be that confiscated from the Maoris, and he had no wish to work a farm for years while keeping his weapons handy. Besides, he had no one here to share it with, whereas in Australia . . . He broke off that line of thought. Emily Carmichael was in Australia, but he had no right to ask her to share with him what he had salvaged of his life—not while the shadow of dishonor still hung over Adam Vincent, as it appeared it always would. Still . . . the memory of her sweet face in its frame of fair ringlets would not go away.

"Thank you, sir," he said, "but such small ties as I have are in New South Wales."

Governor Grey chuckled understandingly. "What draws you back, Captain Shannon?" he asked, his tone forgiving. "Some young woman, I suppose?"

Adam swallowed his bitterness. "No, sir," he said. "There is no one."

Chapter XXVII

ALICE CARMICHAEL LIFTED her head at the sound of the front door closing and observed to her daughter, "Your father is home early. I wonder if anything has happened at court. I'm sure he said he had a full day. Emily, dear, do try to be a little more cheerful for him; it will distress him to see you looking so unhappy. I don't understand you at all. You've hardly said a word all afternoon."

"I'm sorry, Mama," Emily apologized with a quick attempt at a smile. "I didn't mean to seem gloomy. It's too fine a day to be sad. Of course I'll cheer up for Papa."

She turned away, as if for a view of the sunny park outside the window, while she attempted to compose herself. It *had* been a fine day, until she had gone out on a morning errand to Elizabeth Street and encountered Adam Shannon; the meeting had dredged up anew emotions that she thought she had succeeded in repressing.

She had seen him at first from a distance, and her heart had turned into a heavy, cold lump, because he had been talking to Caroline Fisher. True, their postures suggested that she had discovered them only in a chance, momentary encounter: Adam, a stiff figure in his red tunic, had inclined his head in the briefest and most perfunctory of nods before walking on; but the beautiful Mrs. Fisher had seemed to have more she wanted to say, and Adam's departure had left her openmouthed. Then Marcus Fisher had come out of a shop to rejoin his wife, and that, to Emily, had explained things; Adam had not been at all anxious for an encounter with the odious man who had once had him flogged—still less so in view of the fact that he had once loved the man's wife and asked her to run away with him, as Caroline—then Mrs. Caroline Forsyth—had spitefully taken pains to let her know.

And then, Emily remembered with a pang, Adam had caught sight of her, and as it was too late to avoid an encounter, he had continued walking in her direction. "Good morning, Miss Carmichael," he had said in formal greeting, and they had exchanged a few impersonal words on the weather, on Emily's family, and Adam's assignment with the regiment. He had seemed uncomfortable, and Emily had been sure he was on the verge of breaking through the cool reserve that had grown between them; but in the end they had parted as stiffly as they had met.

It had been like all their encounters—unavoidable in Sydney's restricted society—since Adam's return from New Zealand some five months earlier. He had twice refused invitations by Emily's parents, and accepted a third time only because it would have been rude not to do so. It had been a large gathering, and the conversation had been general, and he had avoided being alone with her. The tears brimmed in Emily's eyes as she thought about it. How could Adam behave that way toward her unless he was still in love with Caroline Fisher? He had saved Caroline from rampaging Maoris who had held her prisoner—the story had appeared in all the newspapers and been on everyone's lips—though Marcus Fisher also had emerged as a hero of the incident, having single-handedly, it appeared, defended the besieged farmhouse after all the others were dead or disabled. Certainly the bond between Caroline and Adam must still exist. How, Emily thought in despair, could she hope to compete with the beauteous, twice-widowed woman of the world for whom Adam, admittedly, had once thrown away his naval career? The Fishers, gossip had it, were about to strike out for Victoria, where Marcus was planning some new enterprise, but Emily knew that she could never feel comfortable as long as Caroline was in the same city as Adam.

The tear that had been welling in her eye finally ran down her cheek, and Emily wiped it angrily away and faced her father with a brave, determined smile.

"Hello, Papa," she said, rising. She gave him a kiss on the cheek. "Shall I tell them in the kitchen that you wish to dine early?"

"Wait a bit," he said, leading her back to her chair. "Time enough for that later."

"We didn't expect you at this hour, Gerald," Alice Carmichael remarked with concern. "Is something wrong?"

"There's nothing wrong, my dear—quite the contrary," he replied with a twinkle. He beamed at both of them. "Do you think you might be up to a small dinner party in—oh, say two days time?"

"Of course," her mother agreed. "Who—"

"You needn't put yourself out, Alice my love. It will be a small affair. Captain Broome and his wife, and his journalist brother, John, ought to be there, with Lady Kitty, of course. And I suppose Will De Lancey ought to be invited—he and those orphan boys of his are guests of Red and Magdalen at Elizabeth Bay while they're awaiting passage back to New Zealand." He paused for effect, then added, with a warning glance at his wife, "And of course we shall want to invite Adam Shannon."

Emily's hand flew to her throat, and the color drained from her face. After a moment she found her voice and protested, "He won't come, Papa. He'll refuse, as he has refused your previous invitations."

"Emily is right, Gerald," Alice Carmichael agreed, coming to her daughter's rescue. "The young man has an aversion to being lionized. All of Sydney society is after him, but he goes nowhere unless he cannot avoid it."

"Particularly he does not come here!" Emily burst out, then instantly regretted it.

"He won't refuse this time," the judge said confidently. "Captain Broome will prevail on him. And"—he addressed Emily gently—"as the invitation will be for the Elizabeth Bay house, Adam will not know that we are to be there as guests." He went on briskly. "And he can't want to avoid Johnny Broome anymore, now that the damage has been done by other journalists. Besides, Lady Kitty owes him her life, and it would be churlish of him to seem to offer her a snub. Adam may be unsociable, for reasons of his own, but he is not churlish."

Alice Carmichael said in confusion, "The invitation is to be from Captain and Mrs. Broome? But I thought—"

"Oh, Red doesn't know yet that he and Magdalen are giving a dinner party," Judge Carmichael chuckled. "I'll send a note round to him to come see me tomorrow in chambers so I can explain."

"Explain what?" Mrs. Carmichael said in exasperation. "Gerald, why are you being so mysterious?"

But her husband was enjoying himself too much to reply. "All in good time, my dear," he smiled. "All in good time."

* * *

Red Broome scanned the note once again with a baffled expression. "What on earth can it all be about?" he appealed to Magdalen. "Judge Carmichael wants to see me this morning in chambers, but there's not a hint why. He says only that it's urgent, and that it concerns me."

Magdalen disentangled little Rufus from her skirts and, with a small pat, sent him off to join his sister, Jessica. "Well, then, you'd better go see him, Red. He and your father were the warmest of friends. In fact, I'm a little ashamed of the fact that I haven't asked the Carmichaels here since his death. Perhaps . . . it has something to do with your father?"

Red shook his head. "No, if that were the case, he wouldn't have waited this long. I get the impression that it involves the Carmichael family's business, not ours. Mrs. Carmichael? Emily? But what have I to do with them?"

"I think," Magdalen observed sagely, "that Judge Carmichael is about to ask you for a favor, and that as you have nothing better to do this morning except play with the children, you had better find out what it is."

And so it was that Red, an hour later, found himself in Judge Carmichael's chambers in the somber building off Phillip Street that housed the High Court. The judge greeted Red effusively and bade him sit down and, after the briefest of inquiries into the health of Magdalen and the children, sailed at once into the matter at hand. "It concerns our mutual friend Adam Shannon, Red—or perhaps I should say Adam Vincent."

"Yes, poor fellow," Red retorted. "After being at such pains to keep his past a secret, he is now the subject of every sort of speculation and gossip. It's common knowledge that his real name is not Shannon—though as yet only a few of us know the full story, and, thanks be to God, his commanding officer has chosen not to inquire further, in view of the glory the young man has brought to the regiment. And as the further price of his bravery, the journalists will *not* leave him alone—" He added hastily, "—though my brother Johnny has been scrupulous in respecting his wishes."

"Word of his prowess has also reached the Admiralty," Judge Carmichael plowed on, "not without a little help from my friends in England—and for that, Red, I sincerely apologize, even though I am only a minor instrument in your impending separation from Magdalen and the children . . . for there are irresistible forces at work in this matter. And that is what I wanted to see you about. I'm afraid you must be prepared for a trip to England. It will not be too onerous, I hope, in this marvelous new age of steam, when passage may be accomplished in ten weeks time or less."

"What is this all about, Judge?" Red asked in bewilderment.

"Adam Vincent's court-martial has been reconvened," the judge announced. "I learned of it privately from a friend at Whitehall . . . the news arrived yesterday by fast packet. You'll not learn of it officially for a few days."

Thunderstruck, Red exclaimed, "But how did this come about?"

The judge settled back to explain. "You'll remember my saying, after our confidential talk some time ago, that I was acquainted with Adam's father, General Lord Cheviot, and with Sir David Murchison, the Queen's counsel, and that after what you told me I would make some inquiries on behalf of the boy?"

"Yes, I do, sir. Very well."

"Sir David, though he was not allowed by young Vincent to do his best for the lad, nevertheless has a brilliant mind and was not able to leave the case alone. For his own satisfaction, he took a glass to the charges and, as an abstract exercise, dismantled them. There were four of them. Do you remember what they were?"

Red squinted, going back in memory to the great cabin of the battleship *Copenhagen* and the semicircle of officers, of whom he was one, sitting around the table to decide the fate of Adam Vincent.

"Yes, sir, I do," he said finally. "First, that he was drunk. Second, that he failed to shorten sail in time. Third, that when the fire broke out, he gave the order to abandon ship prematurely, thus dooming the ship and costing the lives of the men in the boats. And fourth, that he absented himself from quarters for several hours while under arrest."

"Let us deal first with the most serious of those charges—that he ordered the ship abandoned prematurely," Judge Carmichael elaborated, his hands folded comfortably over his abdomen. "The third lieutenant, Amos Cantwell, testified that he did not know who gave the order to abandon ship—that he only heard it repeated. But he also testified that the order was suddenly—and disastrously—given only *after* Captain Omerod appeared on deck. In the absence of direct evidence to the contrary, the supposition would have to be that the captain was responsible for the order. And yet Vincent declined to cross-examine the witness to bring out this point, though Cantwell was obviously eager to help him."

"True, sir," Red allowed. "And what was worse, he refused to help himself even when I asked him point-blank who gave the order to abandon ship—himself or Captain Omerod. He would not implicate the captain and, when pressed, damned himself once and for all by saying that the command was his own responsibility."

The judge nodded soberly. "And then there's the matter of shortening the sail. We have Cantwell's testimony that the captain refused permission to take in sail, according to Adam, but that Adam gave the order after the captain was taken ill. And that it was Adam himself who went aloft first. The captain's refusal is hearsay in that instance, but it is corroborated by the testimony of that scoundrel of a royal marine, Lane, who admitted that he heard Adam arguing with the captain that the ship was carrying too much canvas, and the captain telling him to be damned. As for the charge of Adam being drunk, Sir David obtained a deposition from Lane, and when the right questions were asked—as they were not asked during the court-martial—a very different picture emerges. For instance, Lane admits that Adam's 'staggering' could have been caused by the pitching of the ship. As for Adam supposedly reeking of brandy—in a deposition from the escorting officer, Lieutenant Fleming, it appears that Adam told him that Omerod threw a decanter of brandy at him, and that it was Omerod who was drunk. Lieutenant Fleming was quite willing to break his word to Adam to keep silent when Sir David convinced him that it was the more honorable course to tell the truth and help a brave and decent man in spite of himself. He also revealed that the captain's steward, Symons, had to lock Omerod in his cabin, and let him out when the fire started, which makes it pretty certain that it was Omerod who started the fire. When Sir David confronted the marine, Lane, with *that* piece of information, Lane confessed—as he had *not* done at the trial, damn him!—that he had seen Symons standing guard outside the cabin door and spoken with him about it. And that, my salty friend, constitutes the necessary 'new evidence'—though not the only new evidence that Sir David unearthed—that made it legally possible for the Admiralty to reopen the trial!"

"Sir David has been taking depositions?" Red said, startled.

"Oh, yes, from everyone involved. Cantwell, Loomis the cook, the injured man, Bowman—everyone. And it's amazing what a little proper cross-examination can accomplish. Red, I tell you, Adam would never have been found guilty if he hadn't been such a stiff-necked young ass."

"But Judge," Red protested, "surely this goes far beyond an 'abstract exercise' for Sir David's own satisfaction, as you put it?"

"Yes." Judge Carmichael looked smug. "I failed to mention that I was able to prevail on my good friend the Earl of Cheviot to reengage Sir David on his son's behalf, after I apprised him of Adam's exploits in New Zealand, and presented him with . . . a clinching piece of evidence that makes the outcome certain. Lord Cheviot, you may appreciate, is also anxious to redeem the family name and restore the reputation of his youngest son."

Red pondered what he had been told. "That still leaves the charge of absenting himself from quarters while under arrest."

The judge positively beamed at him. "And that, Red, is precisely where I myself was instrumental in procuring new evidence—evidence that opens up the entire case and, moreover, throws light on Adam's behavior during the trial and shows him to be principled to the point of self-destruction, as I hope the court will agree. My agents in London were able to interview Caroline Omerod's father, Major Clive Mason, formerly of the East India Company. Major Mason, it seems, had such regard for Adam Vincent as to pay a man in his regiment—a fellow named Tom Burnaby—to keep an eye on Adam and report on his welfare. He did not, I may add, have a similar high regard for his own daughter, and in fact was rather shocked by her treatment of Adam. She extracted a promise from the lad, it appears, to say nothing at his court-martial that would discredit Captain Omerod and cause her to lose his pension."

Red whistled softly. "Well, I'll be damned! It had to be something like that, of course."

"It was while making the promise that Adam was absent from his quarters for those few hours. Major Mason is fully aware of the circumstances—in fact was a part of the sorry bargain—and is willing to testify to that effect at a new trial. He's feeling rather guilty, you see."

"I don't wonder!" Red exclaimed indignantly.

"Tom Burnaby, as it turns out, kept Major Mason informed of Adam's many acts of heroism—from his part in rescuing the survivors of the *Pomona*—for which I myself am forever in Adam's debt—to his exploits at Rangiriri and the Gate *Pa.* And my own agents were able to bring the major up-to-date with newspaper cuttings from the press here, with those extravagant stories of his feats at the Hauhau *pa*, when he saved the lives of Kitty Broome and Major Mason's daughter, and went on to lead von Tempsky's Forest Rangers through the Hauhau defenses."

"Well, damme, Judge, you've been busy."

Judge Carmichael looked pleased with himself. "Major Mason, oddly enough, had offered, directly after the court-martial, to make over land deeds in New Zealand to Adam and assist him in his passage there—an offer Adam refused, of course. You may take the offer as payment for Adam's silence, or as compensation for an injustice, or as a means of getting Adam out of England, as you choose, Red."

"I know how I take it!" Red growled indignantly.

"Be that as it may, Major Mason now wishes to make amends. He is no longer tender of his daughter's feelings, or disposed to indulge her wishes at the expense of a man he admires—and in fact I believe he finds her behavior even more despicable in view of the fact that Adam saved her life at the Hauhau *pa*. He considers that she owes Adam a fresh debt, and if she is not willing to pay it, he will take it upon himself to do so on her behalf. As for the matter of the pension, it is moot now, two marriages later."

"As is any question of having the reputation of Captain Omerod hung round her neck and the necks of her children."

"Yes, their name is Fisher now, in any case. Major Mason does not like what he has heard about Marcus Fisher, and likes still less the gossip attached to his daughter's impulsive marriage when she had scarcely time enough to mourn Colonel Forsyth; but at least Fisher has given his name to the children."

"So what remains, Judge, is the reputation of a dead man as opposed to that of a live one. And the man of the hour, at that. The journalists will be watching closely to see an injustice corrected, and, quite frankly, it wouldn't surprise me if questions were raised in the House of Commons." He lifted a hand. "No, don't tell me, Judge—you have friends on the *Times*, as well."

The judge's face was wreathed in a smile. "Adam's acquittal would seem certain—particularly with you on the court, Red, to contribute what you know of his conduct here. I think we may take it that the Admiralty will not be at all eager to punish the hero of the Hauhau wars."

Conscious of treading on delicate ground, Red ventured, "Have you said anything to Emily?"

"Not yet," Judge Carmichael said with a frown. "It all depends upon Adam's willingness to undergo retrial . . . and to allow the evidence he suppressed to come to light. It will all come to nothing if Adam doesn't testify in his own behalf."

"True, it's a house of cards without Adam's cooperation," Red agreed.

"He *shall* cooperate, Red, if not for his own sake, then for Emily's!" the judge declared passionately. "And that is where you and I come in. We *must* persuade him . . . convince him that his pledge to Caroline Omerod no longer applies to Caroline Fisher; that even her father—and yes, the grandfather of Adam's child—wishes this farce of injustice to end!" He mopped his brow and went on more calmly, "The boy is proud, stiff-necked. He must be made to see the hurt he is causing. He has earned back his honor—tenfold. Did you know, Red, that I long ago offered to buy him out of his regiment and help him establish himself here in Sydney?"

"No, I did not know that," Red replied, surprised at the revelation and at Judge Carmichael's outburst. Even the most even-tempered of men, he reflected, will fight for the happiness of those they love.

"He avoids me like the plague," the judge admitted ruefully, "and he goes out of his way not to impose himself on Emily—so we shall have to trick him. The young rascal has manners enough to submit with grace when trapped. Can you persuade your charming wife to arrange a small dinner party at Elizabeth Bay?"

"Have no fear, Judge," Red assured him. "Magdalen will be more than willing. I can speak for her now, since only this morning she expressed the wish"—he grinned at the judge—"to have the Carmichaels to dinner."

"Pat always said that he was never cut out to run sheep," Kitty Broome addressed the table with a wry smile, "and the fates must have thought so too, because he's discovered gold on his property and now may run his sheep as a rich man's hobby—with Luke Murphy to relieve him of the tedious job of actually managing the station. He's made Luke a full partner, you know, and now is free to spend his time in the society of Collins Street and the Melbourne Club—when he's not flitting about Ballarat and Bendigo."

"As a matter of fact," Johnny Broome elaborated, "Patrick is trying mightily to persuade us to join him in the district. The Victoria government is eager to encourage pastoral settlers, not gold seekers, and land can still be gotten on the old system at a pound an acre. I have already spoken to the *Herald* about becoming their correspondent there, so I would not even have to give up journalism."

Kitty declared fondly, "We shall turn you into a gentleman farmer, Johnny. Pat swears that the Melbourne racecourse is the finest in the world, so you will have to oblige me by mixing horses with your sheep."

Red, engaged in carving Magdalen's excellent roast, was pleased to note that Kitty and Johnny seemed to be thoroughly reconciled. At least the old tension between them was gone. Sean O'Hara had long since departed for Ireland without a word, having gracefully accepted defeat. And Johnny, apparently, had come to terms with the special place that Patrick, as Kitty's twin, would always have in her affections; indeed, he was genuinely fond of his brother-in-law.

Red's eyes roved down the length of the table to where Adam Vincent sat next to Emily Carmichael, in the place that Magdalen had less than artfully assigned to him. But that seemed to be going well too, he was thankful to see. Adam had given in gracefully once he had gotten over his first surprise at Judge Carmichael's benign deception, and, warming to Emily's presence, he was making every effort to be a charming dinner companion. Red exchanged glances with the judge, who he could tell was thinking, as he himself was, that Adam's reawakened longing for Emily would make the job of persuading him to fight for himself that much easier.

Will De Lancey, recovering from his wound and looking fit, remarked, "Yes, Melbourne is a bustling place these days, I'm told. But you'll be rather remote from it, won't you?"

"Not at all," Johnny declared. "There are now rail lines to the principal goldfields, and Ballarat is only a hundred miles by rail, via Geelong—and there's even talk of a direct line. From there, there's a daily Cobb's coach. Travel is quite easy."

"Yes, it's only a day's journey to Bundilly, so we shall be rubbing elbows with Johnny's uncle Will and aunt Dodie," Kitty supplied. She frowned, and her animation momentarily left her. "Of course the nearest town of any consequence is Urquhart Falls. It's run practically as a fief by a dreadful man named Brownlow—through whom, I'm sorry to say, Pat is forced to convey his gold." She brightened with an effort. "Still, Mr. Brownlow has provided the district with a bank, a ferryboat, and a hotel, so the place is gradually becoming civilized."

Red noticed Kitty's reluctance to speak of Urquhart Falls, and he was reminded that the place held tragic memories for her. It was there that, several years ago, her brother Michael—known throughout the territory as "Big Michael" Wexford, an escaped political prisoner and the leader of the Lawless Gang—had been shot and killed in an attempt to rob Brownlow's bank. Michael's royal pardon had come too late, as had his title as Lord Kilclare, which had gone to Patrick on his death. Red was moved at Kitty's quick recovery; his brother's wife had spirit. Johnny had confided to him that Kitty had extracted the promise that their firstborn, if a boy, would be named Michael.

"The only drawback," Kitty went on with her usual vivacity, "will be the presence of Marcus Fisher. I understand that he has allied himself with Mr. Brownlow in some sort of dummying scheme, by which he may acquire cheap land from those unfortunate selectors who are in debt to Mr. Brownlow's bank. They will make a pretty pair—likes attract! Mr. Fisher, Pat tells me, plans to enter politics in Victoria once he has transplanted himself there—and is actually representing *himself* as the hero of Killaloe, when we all know that it was Captain Shannon who saved the day." Her tone became indignant. "The man is insufferable. His actions at Killaloe were those of a scoundrel and a coward . . . he betrayed his own wife to the marauders to save himself, and why she remains with him I cannot understand, except that she is a silly fool. It is intolerable to see him swagger so, but too many people know him in Sydney, and that is why he is seeking a new stage for himself."

"I could not agree more heartily with Kitty's estimate of Fisher's character," Johnny confirmed. "When I arrived at Killaloe—too late, I'm afraid—I found him hiding under a table like the poltroon that he is."

Red noted that Adam had grown uncomfortable at the mention of Caroline Fisher. Judge Carmichael noted it too, and intervened smoothly with a mild witticism.

"Perhaps Fisher was not hiding, Johnny," he suggested facetiously. "Perhaps, like Captain Bligh, who was discovered under a bed when the Rum Corps rose to depose him as governor, he was attempting to conceal confidential papers."

There was general laughter, and to Red's relief, the conversation shifted to Will De Lancey's renewed plans to settle in New Zealand. Although Will was by no means eager to again leave New South Wales—as he had confided to Red more than once—New Zealand, he had decided, would be the best place for the boys, who all wanted to return there.

"I shall never amass land as the squatters did in Victoria before the Grant Act," he allowed, "and furthermore"—he smiled at Johnny—"I shan't have a rich brother-in-law next door to assist me in getting established. But I have the next best thing. As a military settler, I'm eligible for a land grant on the most advantageous terms. And I shall have the further advantage of a Maori foster son to help me stay on the right side of my newly pacified neighbors."

"Wiremu is a fine young man," Magdalen put in with a warm smile. "We shall be sorry to see him leave us."

"And Andy and young Harry," Red hastened to add. "But then, New Zealand is home to Harry, isn't it?"

"And to Andy, too," William asserted. "Before the uprising drove us off our little farm, he had gone a long way toward taking root there, and putting the tragic loss of his family in India well behind him. And now that he is grown up, he is proving a second father to Harry; indeed, he has more in common with Harry than I do."

The words were spoken bravely and without self-pity, but Red could not help remembering, with a catch in his throat, that Will De Lancey also had suffered a loss in India during the Sepoy Mutiny—lovely, brave Jenny, whose memory would always bind him and Johnny to Will as brothers-in-law. Will and his adopted boys, with gallantry and grace, had turned themselves into a close-knit family that was seemingly self-sufficient, but Red hoped that one day a strong and loving woman would be added to the group—if not a new wife for Will, who seemed determined to mourn Jenny forever, then the right sort of girl for young Andy Melgund, who, with his growth complete, was proving a lad of fine mettle.

"Will you be returning to the old place?" Johnny inquired.

"No—I can set my sights a bit higher now, thanks to the generosity of a grateful government," William replied. "And the farm was hardly stocked before the Maoris burned us out. Best start from scratch in the newly opened lands. The old district has too many disturbing memories for Harry anyway."

Johnny nodded in understanding. "Let us hope that the government is grateful enough to provide roads and bridges for you new pioneers. But as they are anxious to develop the northern provinces, I imagine those will come soon enough."

De Lancey turned to include Adam in the exchange. "If a broken-down veteran of the Volunteer Cavalry like myself can get prime land under the new dispensations, then Captain Shannon here ought to have his pick. What are your plans, Adam? Will you be taking advantage of the government's inducements?"

Adam seemed reluctant to reply. "No, sir," he said, shaking his head. "Governor Grey was kindness itself when he attempted to sway me to remain in New Zealand. But at the moment farming holds no attraction for me. I shall remain in Australia with the regiment for the time being and see what turns up."

Red, alert for Emily Carmichael's reaction, saw the girl's color rise when Adam announced his intention of remaining in Australia. The look of longing that crossed her face, though fleeting, did not escape the attention of her father, either. Red saw the sudden firming of Judge Carmichael's lips in unspoken resolve before the man reached for his napkin and his expression was hidden.

Magdalen took the hint and, catching the eyes of the other women, rose to lead the way to the drawing room for coffee. Red passed down the port decanter and handed round cigars, then, before his guests settled down, got to his feet and said to Will De Lancey and Johnny, "The judge and I have a little business to discuss, if you'll excuse us for a few minutes. Can you entertain each other while we go to the library? Adam, would you mind coming with us? This concerns you."

"Me?" Adam looked puzzled, but he got out of his chair and, taking his port with him, followed Red and the judge.

No sooner had Red closed the library door behind them than Judge Carmichael extracted a folded sheet of stiff, coroneted notepaper from his pocket and, handing it to Adam, said without preamble, "Their Lordships of the Admiralty have seen fit to reconstitute your court-martial, Adam. You'll be receiving official notification in due course, but I thought it best to give you a chance to prepare yourself."

Adam turned pale. He unfolded the letter and read it swiftly, then handed it back. "You take much on yourself, sir," he said in a voice trembling with anger.

Judge Carmichael was unperturbed. "I confess to being in communication with your father and with the lady's father—for my own interests as a father are involved, and I make no apologies for that."

That took some of the wind out of Adam's sails. He protested woodenly, "I did not give my consent to have Sir David Murchison reopen the case."

"Sir David is in the employ of your father, who is interested in ascertaining the basis for a new trial, but the decision to employ him in your defense is yours to make," the judge parried. He added softly, "And I hope you *will* decide to do so, Adam—for your own sake, and Emily's, and your father's and Major Mason's, and all the others whom this miserable affair has touched. Yours are not the only interests that are involved."

Adam, still shaken, retorted feebly, "It is a presumption on your part nevertheless to intrude into my affairs, I am bound to say, sir."

"Come, come, Adam," Judge Carmichael said kindly. "I have told Red that powerful forces are at work here—the Admiralty is determined to reopen the case before the penny press reopen it for them; and your father, who has every right to wish to see the family name restored, will not be denied. There will be a retrial in any case. We have intervened to see that it comes out right this time."

Red spoke out firmly. "And it *will* come out right this time, Adam. You need have no fear of that. The outcome is certain . . . provided that you cooperate."

Adam's face was as white as a sheet. "I will not hear anything said against Mrs. Omerod—Mrs. Fisher," he floundered.

"Nothing need be said," Judge Carmichael assured him quickly. "The decision to protect Captain Omerod's reputation was yours, and there is no need to go too deeply into your motives. In any event, you gave your promise to Major Mason, did you not, and he is willing to carry the testimony on that point. That will suffice for Their Lordships. No one is interested in sullying the former Mrs. Omerod's name. But justice must not only be done, it must be *seen* to have been done, and the Admiralty—in the interests of its own reputation—is not eager to punish a brave and honorable man for his misguided attempt at gallantry toward . . . a widow and her child. Indeed, Adam, you must reconcile yourself to the fact that things have gone too far to be stopped. You would only make mischief for the Admiralty if you tried."

"It's for the good of the service," Red interjected persuasively. "You were an officer of the Royal Navy once—and can be again, if you wish."

"You are a man of conscience, Adam," the judge said gently, "but you must respect the consciences of Major Mason and those who will be judging you. You must not force them into an injustice. Your continued sacrifice can only do harm now. Harm to them, and to your father . . . and to Emily. But you must defend yourself this time. The thing cannot be done without your cooperation. Will you do it?"

Adam's face contorted; he was clearly a man in torment, Red saw with pity.

"Will you?" the judge pressed him.

Adam sat down and buried his face in his hands. Red and the judge waited without speaking. Finally, Adam looked up.

"I will do it," he said.

Red exhaled; he had not realized that he had been holding his breath. "Let's go and rejoin the others," he said.

Emily Carmichael found no difficulty in contriving to be alone with Adam before he departed for his barracks; indeed, it seemed that everyone present was conspiring to help her do so. The moment Adam had risen to take his leave, Captain Broome had bent to whisper into his wife's ear, and Mrs. Broome had fixed her with a brilliant smile and said, "Miss Carmichael, perhaps you would be kind enough to see Captain Shannon to the door? Do forgive my rudeness, Captain Shannon, but"—her eyes sparkled mischievously—"I do seem to be enmeshed at the moment in my duties as a hostess." In fact, Emily couldn't see that Mrs. Broome had anything requiring her immediate attention—the last cup of coffee had long since been poured, and the last cordial refused—but everyone was looking at *her* expectantly, and her father gave her an encouraging smile, and so she had smoothed her skirts and accompanied Adam to the entrance hall.

Something important had happened tonight—the thing her father had been unable to keep himself from hinting at all day—of that she was certain. It had something to do with Adam. When the men had come from the dining room to join the ladies, Adam had looked dazed and preoccupied, as if he had had some kind of dreadful shock; but then he had seemed to recover a forced sociability, and when, briefly, he had been thrown together with her in conversation after Mrs. Broome had insisted on her singing one of her Mozart pieces, he had kept glancing about, as if impatiently awaiting an opportunity to tell her something in private. Captain Broome, in the meantime, had gone about looking like the cat that had swallowed the canary, and Colonel De Lancey and John Broome had acquired that stuffy, important look that men got when they were in on something together. Her father, at one point, had whispered in a corner with her mother, and they had both turned to look at her, then looked away when they were caught at it. Everyone, in fact, seemed to know a secret that was being kept from her. . . .

When she could bear it no longer, Emily had managed to get her father aside for a moment, and he had said, "There has been a change in Captain Shannon's fortunes, my dear. He may wish to speak of it to you."

"Is it something bad, Papa?" she had asked in trepidation, immediately thinking of Caroline Fisher, and he had looked startled and replied, "No, on the contrary, my dear." But that did not mean anything, because her father, though he was the kindest man in the world and had even offered to buy Adam out of his regiment, might have thought it all for the best for Adam, with no suitable prospects before him because of that hideous court-martial, to remove himself decisively from her sphere and for her to forget him.

Now, alone with Adam in the entrance hall, Emily looked up at him with her heart beating wildly in her breast and waited for him to speak.

"I am going to England, Emily," he said so grimly that she felt as if a knife had twisted in her heart. So that was it; she would never see him again.

But no, he was smiling—a cautious smile, as though he feared to commit himself to happiness. And he had called her "Emily"—not "Miss Carmichael" or "Miss Emily."

"Your father has been working behind the scenes on my behalf . . . as have many other people, it seems," he went on. "The Admiralty has decided to reopen my case."

"But . . ." The words escaped her before she had time to think. "What more can they do to you, Adam?"

He took her hand in his. "I have nothing to fear from this court-martial, your father has taken pains to assure me," he told her. "Their Lordships are determined to see me acquitted, and—" He allowed his smile to broaden. "I shall have Red Broome as one of my judges."

"Will . . . will you remain in England?" she ventured timidly.

His hand tightened round hers with fervent pressure. "Emily . . . my dear . . . I told you once, long ago, that I would be at your side when I could come to you with honor. Adam Shannon might have done that even now, but there would always be the shadow of Adam Vincent hovering over his shoulder. No—" He halted her attempt to interrupt. "It is time to speak of these things. They have remained unvoiced long enough. And in the meantime the world speculates on my past. When I return to Australia, it will not be Adam Vincent's shadow I bring back with me, but himself!"

Emily's head was swimming. It was too much to take in all at once. It was enough—her mind clung to the fact—that he had said he would come back to her. "Then . . . then you have not decided to go away with Mrs. Fisher?" she said haltingly.

"Good God, no!" Adam exploded. "I never want to see her again!"

Her happiness was too much to bear when he swept her into his strong arms and kissed her—a measured kiss, her senses registered —and then he was gently prying loose the arms that her instincts had flung around him, and putting her from him.

"But the shadow is not yet dispelled," he said regretfully, "and until it is, my darling Emily, I have no right to ask you to be my wife."

"It doesn't matter," she cried, fearful of losing him. "None of it ever mattered to me."

"I shall be gone six months or more," he warned her soberly. "England could not be farther away. The *Stornoway* has accomplished the passage lately in sixty-four days with sail alone, but even with steam to help, you must not count on my setting new records."

"However long it takes," she promised, "I shall wait for you, Adam."

Adam sat alone in the small cabin on the gun deck during the adjournment, his stomach a tight knot, while he waited for the dull thunderclap of the court-martial gun that would summon him to his fate. Rob Fleming, his escort again, had offered to wait with him, but Adam had felt that he could not bear company during this interval in his private limbo.

"I understand, Adam," Fleming, with his good-natured disposition, had assented. "The door will be unlocked, and I'll be nearby in the passageway, so if you need anything just stick your head outside and call."

His father, Adam reflected, was no doubt at this moment enjoying a fine luncheon with Sir David Murchison in the admiral's cabin, and his eldest brother, Newton, who would someday be the tenth Earl of Cheviot, would be with them, having obtained leave to show his support. Adam had begged off seeing them until the ordeal was over, and indeed, if all this had been a horrible miscalculation and the verdict went against him, he would make his departure without seeing them at all. Sir David had not been in the least affronted; he had done all he could—had done magnificently —and Adam was sure that he would much rather be enjoying a chop and a fine vintage than having to linger in a stuffy cabin with a nervous client.

As Judge Carmichael had predicted, the members of the *Lancer*'s crew had done their utmost to corroborate Adam's testimony once they had been given the opportunity to do so. Before, the prosecutor had badgered them to admit that they could not swear that Adam had been sober. Now they were badgered by Sir David to testify that they could not swear that he had *not* been sober. The reek of brandy, finally, was explained by Adam's direct testimony that John Omerod had thrown a decanter of brandy at him, and there was nothing to contradict this. Even the recalcitrant royal marine lieutenant, Lane, was forced to concede that Adam's "staggering," which he had previously testified to, could have been caused by the violent pitching of the ship. "And were you yourself 'staggering,' Lieutenant Lane?" Sir David had thundered at the unfortunate man, whereupon Lane had replied, "Yes, sir, I fell down several times before I could get to my cabin, and could not keep my feet, and that was why I decided to stay in my bunk"— and that, to the accompaniment of the muffled titters of the spectators and the smiles of the court, had disposed of *that*. Then Lane, seeing that the temper of the court had changed, fell all over himself to please, volunteering for the first time that, in the quarrel he had overheard, he had clearly heard John Omerod utter the words "Do you think I care if this blasted ship goes down? I've nothing to

live for anymore, and I hope to God you go down with her!"—
followed by a crash of glass that could have been the shattered
bottle of brandy. And when similar tactics by Sir David established
the fact that no one could testify that Adam had given the order to
abandon ship, and Adam testified positively that he had *not* given
the order, the issue seemed no longer to be in doubt.

But, as Sir David had taken pains to point out to Adam before
the recess, nothing can ever be said to be certain, and Adam was
acutely aware that in his new testimony, in an effort to be utterly
fair to the memory of John Omerod, he had admitted that he had
hit the captain on the jaw and locked him in the cabin. He had
taken command in extreme circumstances to save the ship, Sir
David had forced him to amplify, and that was provided for in the
Articles, but still, if the court decided to take a severe view, it
constituted an act of mutiny. And the penalty for mutiny, as Adam
was miserably aware, was not merely being cashiered; it was death.

Footsteps pounded on the deck planks overhead as the journalists and other spectators scrambled to reclaim their places in the
great cabin before the proceedings resumed, and Adam heard, a
minute or two later, the piping of the royal marines. Then, after a
heart-stopping interval, came the deep thud of the cannon. The
latch of the cabin door clicked, and Rob Fleming entered with a
sober face and said, formally, "They're ready for you now."

Adam rose to his feet, straightened his tunic, and automatically
felt for the sword that wasn't there—the sword that either would
be returned to him, hilt first, to show his innocence, or would be
lying on the table with its blade pointing at him, to damn him—
double-damn him—forever.

"Courage, Adam," Rob Fleming whispered to him as he ducked
his head to get out the door. "It's only a few steps to go." But the
few steps to the great cabin were the longest walk Adam had ever
had to take. The marines stood aside, and as he entered his eyes
found his father, white-haired and dignified, sitting in the front
ranks of spectators with Newton, his heir, stiff as a ramrod in the
dress uniform of the Scots Guards. He searched their faces, but
their expressions told him nothing.

He walked toward the curved table, his chin held high to meet
the gaze of his judges squarely. Red Broome was among them, a
stranger in his blue uniform with its gold trim, his face stony and
unreadable.

He came to a halt and, for the first time, let his eyes drop to the surface of the baize-covered table. His sword was lying there, in front of the president, and its hilt was presented toward Adam.

Lying beside the hilt were the medals that he had forfeited, that now were to be returned to him—the campaign medals and the dull bronze glint of his first Victoria Cross.

He stood there numbly, hardly hearing the little speech of congratulation from the president or the growing murmur from the spectators that ended, finally, in cheers. And then somebody was buckling the sword around his waist, and someone else was shaking his hand, and his father was at his side, and Newton was clapping him on the back, and Red Broome, with a broad smile, was pinning the V.C. back on his tunic.

"It's all over, Adam," Red said softly, in a voice that was meant for Adam's ears alone. "We can go home now."

Epilogue

CLAUS VAN BUREN puffed contentedly on his pipe while his wife, Mercy, bustled about the great cabin removing pictures from the walls and gathering up vases, glass candlesticks, and other breakables that would have to be stowed away before the *Dolphin* cast off. Bright sunlight streamed through the ports, and over the water the sound of church bells carried from the city of Sydney beyond. It was a fine day for a wedding, he thought, and an even finer day for putting to sea, though he had lost the land breeze by waiting so late in the morning.

"It is good to have you aboard again, Mercy," he admitted, his tone affectionate. "It has been lonely at sea without you and the children. All during that misbegotten war with the Maoris the *Dolphin* was only a ship. Now it is a home again."

Mercy stopped by his side to lay a hand fondly on his cheek. "It has been a difficult time for me, too, Claus," she returned. "The boys missed their life at sea, and the girls were growing up hardly knowing their father."

"Where *are* the girls?" he inquired with quick concern, removing the stem of his pipe from his mouth. "They know, do they not, that they are not to go beyond the foremast?"

"Hori Kaka is keeping an eye on them," she reassured him. "They are playing at jacks on deck."

Claus relaxed. There was no one he would have trusted with his own life or the safety of his family more than Hori Kaka—and it was a tribute to the Maori sense of honor that he could feel that way about a man who had once been responsible for seizing his ship, killing two seamen, and kidnapping Mercy and the twins. But Hori Kaka had long since expiated those acts of violence—warfare, to him—and was one of Claus's most trusted sailors, with an A.B. rating and the ambition to go further. Perhaps, Claus mused, it was a sign that the two races, so recently enmeshed in bloodshed, could go forward together and build a peaceful and prosperous New Zealand.

"But I wish you wouldn't send Joseph and Nathan aloft," Mercy added. "They're still such babies."

"They're old enough to take their turn with everyone else," he disagreed, "and they would be ashamed in front of the crew if I made them exempt. In the Royal Navy, they would start as young." He broke into a broad smile. "At any rate, Mercy, you may be thankful that the *Dolphin* is schooner-rigged, and that I shall not be using the tops'ls and topgallants to get under way. The boys shall only have to help work the halyards this morning."

"When *will* we weigh anchor, my dear?" Mercy inquired, turning back to the job of packing away her display china. "Won't we lose the tide if we delay much longer?"

Claus returned his attention to his pipe. "We must wait until our passengers come aboard," he replied calmly. "Their baggage is already loaded, and we shall be off the instant they set foot on deck." He took out his watch and looked at it. "It will be a close thing, but I have told them when the tide turns and warned them that the *Dolphin* will sail without them if they are late."

"Oh, Claus, you would not!" she chided him.

"They will be on time," he promised. He lifted his head to listen to the sonorous pealing of the bells from across the harbor and smiled at her. "They may have to leave the wedding in a hurry, my dear Mercy, but *you* would not have them miss it, I am certain."

Mercy's lovely face softened, and Claus knew that she was thinking about their own wedding and the happiness it had brought them, and the kindness of other people, so long ago, that had made it possible. "Indeed, Claus," she agreed, "not for all the world."

"Adam Colpoys, wilt thou have this woman to thy wedded wife, to live together after God's ordinance in the holy state of matrimony?" intoned the rector of Saint Philip's. "Wilt thou love her, comfort her, honor and keep her in sickness and in health and, forsaking all other, keep thee only unto her, so long as ye both shall live?"

The bridegroom's voice rang out firmly, reaching every corner of the timeworn church that sat between the parade ground and Sydney Cove. "I will."

"Emily Margaret," the old clergyman went on, "wilt thou have this man to thy wedded husband, to live together after God's ordinance in the holy estate of matrimony? Wilt thou obey him and serve him, love, honor and keep him in sickness and in health and, forsaking all other, keep thee only unto him, so long as ye both shall live?"

"I will," Emily Carmichael responded in a small, clear voice.

In their pew on the groom's side, Red and Magdalen Broome exchanged a proprietary glance. It had all worked out as hoped, Red thought with satisfaction, and he was not displeased at being one of the authors of today's happy event. Strictly speaking, he and Magdalen ought to have been sitting on the bride's side, considering their friendship with the Carmichael family, but . . . Red's gaze returned to the groom. Adam and he had been through so much together, including the ordeal of the court-martial, and then had been thrown so closely together during the long voyage home, that he felt almost like Adam's godparent. "Of course the bride's party shall regretfully relinquish you and fair Magdalen," Judge Carmichael had acquiesced genially. "The Carmichael clan has friends aplenty to fill up our pews, and Adam deserves a fine show of support from—no, don't deny it, Red—the pillars of Sydney's society." Adam had asked Red to be his best man, and Red, though not declining the honor, had pointed out that Will De Lancey's feelings would be hurt if he were not asked, since Will and Adam were fellow officers in Her Majesty's forces and had been fellow volunteers in the New Zealand fighting. He refrained from pointing out that he himself was now Adam's fellow officer as well, in the Royal Navy—a fact that Adam, in the awkward position of holding double commissions, would soon have to do something about—and to his relief, Adam had given way on the point.

His eyes strayed to Will De Lancey, standing to one side with the ring, then searched out the three boys—no, proper young men now—sitting together in a pew, all freshly scrubbed and looking uncomfortable in their stiff new suits. He saw Andy Melgund flash an admonitory glance at young Harry Ryan to stop his fidgeting, while Wiremu, his tattooed face rising in odd contrast above the tight white shirt-collar, was regarding the ceremony with strained respect.

Will and his three wards would have no time to spare after the

service if they were to get to the Sydney Cove anchorage before the
tide turned, Red thought. Fortunately, it was not far; they could go
on foot along George Street and cut across to the foreshore opposite the *Dolphin*'s mooring . . . and, if it came to that, Claus was
sailor enough to kedge out against the tide into the fairway until he
could catch a breeze.

Red could not help but admire his brother-in-law. William had
refused to quit after losing his arm at Balaclava during the charge
of the Light Brigade, refused to quit after losing his beloved Jenny
in India during the Sepoy Mutiny, but instead had given over his
life to raising Andy, who had lost his own family in the dreadful
events at Cawnpore, and who had been beside Jenny up until the
very end. And, as if that were not enough, Will had assumed a
similar responsibility for poor Harry, whose parents had been
among the first victims of the Maori war, and then had taken
Wiremu under his wing as well. But if Will had saved the boys,
they had saved him, too, and given him purpose in life. They made
an oddly assorted family, but they were a family nevertheless, and
Red wished them well in their new life as pioneer farmers in New
Zealand.

He twisted his head round to locate his brother Johnny, sitting
with the exquisite, willful Kitty, the wife he had lost and won back,
and—from all appearances—managed to hang on to since. They,
too, would be pioneers, in the booming land that Victoria had
become since the gold strikes, but Red found it hard to think of
them as farmers. Kitty, of course, would be caught up with the
horses that she was determined to raise, and Johnny, with the
printer's ink in his veins, would never cease being a journalist,
whatever else he might play at.

His was not the only head turned in Kitty's direction, Red was
amused to see. As much of Sydney's society as the church would
hold had turned out to see the dashing hero of the Hauhau conflict
get married, and necks had not ceased craning for a glimpse of the
titled lady he had saved from the cannibal ovens. People were
standing in the street outside, too, waiting for the married couple
to emerge. . . . Red glanced back toward the solid phalanx of red
coats occupying their own section of the church; *they* were not idle
strangers, it was certain, but the officers of Adam's regiment, come
to do him honor.

Only one figure was conspicuous by her absence, Red reflected—
Caroline Fisher, the other woman whom Adam had rescued from

the Hauhaus. The milling crowd outside would probably not understand why she was not here; certainly they had every reason to expect her to be present, if only in simple civility toward Adam. Yet it was just as well, Red decided, that they had no inkling of the truth. Thankfully, the Omerod scandal, whose airing Adam had feared, had remained under the lid of its Pandora's box during the court-martial and had not filtered back to Australia, to sully Emily's life with Adam. And Caroline Omerod—Caroline *Fisher*—would be leaving Sydney, if she hadn't done so already, in the company of the one man she seemingly deserved. Indeed—

Magdalen's nudge brought Red's attention back to the service. A bit guiltily, he rose to his feet with the rest of the congregation to sing the final hymn, and then the bride and groom were repairing to the vestry to sign the register, with Will De Lancey following. Andy, Harry, and Wiremu began edging unobtrusively out of their pew so as not to be caught in the crush when the church emptied; they had arranged, Red knew, to meet Will by the side entrance. Will had confided to him the night before, at the going-away party Magdalen had given for him and the boys, that Adam intended to sign the register as Shannon, not Vincent. It was as Adam Shannon that he had met Emily, and as Adam Shannon that he had made a life and a reputation for himself these last years. "I've earned the name," he had declared to Will, "and, by God, I'm going to keep it! Emily and the Carmichaels think it's a fine idea. All I did to earn the name of Adam Vincent was to be born the fourth son of the ninth Earl of Cheviot, and now that *that* Vincent has had the name restored to him untarnished, the poor fellow can be put to rest."

Red had understood Adam's feelings perfectly. "He wishes to start fresh—as an Australian," he had told Will. "On his merits."

Will had nodded in agreement and added, "He will go far in this colony, Red, whatever he decides to do with his new life. Whether as soldier, sailor, or as the private citizen and man of substance that Judge Carmichael is determined to make of him. We shall hear more from that young man, I promise you."

At least being an Australian, Red reflected, was no longer a hindrance to advancing in the Queen's service—his own example had proved that. And in the past years he had managed to have his career *and* make his home on the Australian station—though long absences, as he had ruefully told Magdalen many times, were a sailor's lot. He hoped that Adam would take him up on his offer of a post under his command.

"What are you thinking so fiercely about?" Magdalen teased him as they emerged from the church with the crowd that was pouring down the stone steps. The press of people grew thicker as those in the street surged forward to mingle with the exodus.

"I was thinking of new lives and new beginnings . . . and of our good fortune, my love," he responded, taking her arm and steering her through the throng. In the distance, he saw, just turning the corner of George Street, with the bright morning sunshine on their backs, were the hurrying figures of Will De Lancey and his little flock.

Magdalen's eyes, moist with emotion, moved in the direction of the crowd's attention to watch Adam Shannon, tall and handsome in his scarlet coat, help his bride into the waiting carriage. "Yes," she breathed tremulously, "I hope that good fortune will be theirs as well, Red."